D1475142

The Collected Stories of John William Corrington

Books by John William Corrington

Poetry

Where We Are
Mr. Clean and Other Poems
The Anatomy of Love
Lines to the South

Fiction

And Wait for the Night
The Upper Hand
The Lonesome Traveler and Other Stories
The Bombardier
The Actes and Monuments
The Southern Reporter
Shad Sentell
All My Trials

With Joyce Corrington

So Small A Carnival
A Project Named Desire
A Civil Death
The White Zone

Edited with Miller Williams

Southern Writing in the Sixties: Fiction
Southern Writing in the Sixties: Poetry

The
Collected Stories of
John William Corrington

Edited by Joyce Corrington
Introduction by William Mills

UNIVERSITY OF MISSOURI PRESS
COLUMBIA AND LONDON

5   4   3   2   1   94   93   92   91   90

Library of Congress Cataloging-in-Publication Data

Corrington, John William.
    The collected stories of John William Corrington / edited by
Joyce Corrington ; introduction by William Mills.
        p.   cm.
    ISBN 0-8262-0753-7 (alk. paper)
    I. Corrington, Joyce H.   II. Title.
PS3553.07A6   1990
813'.54—dc20   90-40655
                                                                     CIP

∞™ This paper meets the minimum requirements of
the American National Standard for Permanence of Paper
for Printed Library Materials, Z39.48, 1984.

The Collected Stories of John William Corrington is composed of *The
Lonesome Traveler* (G.P. Putnam's Sons, 1968), *The Actes and Monu-
ments* (University of Illinois Press, 1978), *The Southern Reporter*
(Louisiana State University Press, 1981), and "Heroic Measures/
Vital Signs" (*Southern Review,* vol. 22, no. 4, Fall 1986).

Designer: Kristie Lee
Typesetter: Connell-Zeko Type & Graphics
Printer: Thomson-Shore, Inc.
Binder: Thomson-Shore, Inc.
Typeface: Palatino

A.M.D.G.
and for our children
and their children
and generations yet to come

CONTENTS

The Collected Stories of John William Corrington

INTRODUCTION

Risking the Bait
by William Mills

In Bill Corrington's novella "Decoration Day" (*All My Trials* [1987]), a character who appears frequently in his fiction, Judge Albert Sidney Johnston Finch, watches a distant fisherman cast his bait for bass late one afternoon. Judge Finch has recently retired from the bench after the death of his wife but is slowly being drawn back into the turbulent affairs of others. As he reflects on several troubled lives and watches the unknown fisherman, he suddenly whispers to himself, "He's not doing it right. Damn it, you've got to get in close, you have to brush the shore, risk the bait. You can't just stand off and throw." From the time that I first met Bill in 1953 at Centenary College in Shreveport, he was always ready to "risk the bait." He was after the large, deep-down things of the world, and writing was not something for throwing towards them as if it were a pointless exercise or something to be done halfway.

By the time I met him as a student, he was already well-read for someone our age. He had attended a Jesuit high school, then called St. John's, and was able to quote from Augustine and Aquinas easily, let alone some of the early Church Fathers and Aristotle. All this was very impressive at a Methodist college. He had a very good memory for what he read. St. John's threw him out before he could graduate, which he loved to tell about, for "having the wrong attitude." Since the Jesuits were not successful in what I guess today would be called "attitude adjustment," he finished at Byrd High School. (He was to do combat with the Jesuits once again when he, Miller Williams, Tommy Blouin, and I went to teach at Loyola in 1966.) Still, all his books contained the epigraph, "A.M.D.G.," motto of the Society of Jesus—*ad maiorem Dei gloriam*.

Besides girls and the Korean War, the constant and high talk of

---

This essay appeared in slightly altered form in *The Southern Review* (Summer 1989).

our student years was of theology, philosophy, and literature. We had philosophy with Bryant Davidson, German and anthropology with Bruno Strauss (who was head of the public schools in Berlin before he was run out by the Nazis), and of course English and American literature with John R. Willingham, Edward M. Clark, and Lee Morgan. Before graduation I shipped out to Japan and the army; after graduation Bill moved to Rice, where he took an M.A. in English, and would have completed a Ph.D. there (instead of at the University of Sussex) but once again was accused by a professor of having the wrong attitude and was made to understand that he would only graduate from Rice over the professor's dead body.

By this time he had married Joyce Hooper, who had finished in chemical engineering, and the two of them started a family in Houston, then moved to Baton Rouge, Joyce to engineer and Bill to teach English at LSU. This was in 1960. Including the births of four children, the decade of the sixties was to be a very productive one. Bill published four books of poetry: *Where We Are* (1962), which won the Charioteer Award; *The Anatomy of Love* (1964); *Mr. Clean* (1964); and *Lines to the South* (1965). *Where We Are* begins with an epigraph by Auden, and I think it is fair to say that Bill's poetry was significantly influenced by Auden—and at least in its topography by e. e. cummings. He admired the work of Charles Bukowski and Lawrence Ferlinghetti. Many of the themes that were to occupy him throughout his life make their earliest appearance in the poems. He was fascinated with violence, during and outside declared war. He was an avid student of the Civil War and the two world wars (his father had fought at Chateau Thierry in World War I and his novel *The Bombardiers* [1970] takes place during and after World War II). As his work is studied more deeply in the future, the brilliant imagery of war and violence will surely hold the critics' interest. One of the best early essays on Bill's poetry is Richard Whittington's introduction to *The Anatomy of Love*. Whittington characterizes the poet's attitude as rebellious and challenging, his rhythms phrasal, and his language colloquial and epigrammatic. He further notes that at the center of the work "lies the nugget of faith, without which both the intellect and emotions become the instruments of caprice." One of the three long poems in the volume, "Prayers for a Mass in the Vernacular," is a manifestation of this faith that serves as a substrate for the various dramas that take place in the poem and, at the same time, is a criticism of the vernacular mass initiated by Vatican II, with the unfortunate associations that may be accidentally introduced by the vernacular, as opposed to the Logos of the Latin Mass.

In the fall of 1961 I moved to the French Quarter and began teaching at LSU-NO; on Bill's visits we would walk down to see Jon Edgar Webb and his wife Gypsy Lou, who were putting out the first issue of *The Outsider* magazine. It was a powerful issue, with such folks as Corso, Snyder, Ginsberg, Ferlinghetti, Bukowski, plus some of Henry Miller's letters to Walter Lowenfels. Bill's offering was a poem called "Hard Man." All these, plus our former poet laureate, Howard Nemerov, were in the second issue. In the third, Bill had a striking essay on *The Outsider* "Man of the Year," Bukowski. *The Outsider* was one of the best little magazines of those days. It was a labor of love for the Webbs and a constant financial struggle. Done on a C. & P. handpress with handset type, it took the editors 4,500 hours to prepare the first issue.

Besides writing all the poetry and teaching full-time, Bill published two novels and a book of short stories in this same decade. In the early part of the sixties he was consumed with reading on the Civil War, and his first novel, *And Wait for the Night*, came out in 1964. It was set principally during the Battle of Vicksburg and during the postwar occupation of Shreveport. This north Louisiana town was to play a central role in much of Corrington's fiction; he raised it to mythic proportions in much the way Faulkner did his own region with Yoknapatawpha County. It was a Shreveport that reached back at least to the Civil War, and he understood himself in terms of that past. Like many other Southerners, he did not believe he had invented himself. His absorption with history grew out of his desire to transfigure the past in such a way as to resist historicism and especially a secularism devoid of purpose. Memory was not a place to escape to in sentimental nostalgia, although the journey was always open to that danger. The horrors of the Civil War and two world wars were too graphically evoked for anyone to maintain that about his work. This part of his aesthetic was what Lewis Simpson, talking about other writers, has called the "aesthetic of memory." Further, he was assertively a Southern writer. He told one interviewer, "If someone said, 'Are you an American writer or a Southern writer?' I'd say very clearly, 'I'm a Southern writer.' I have no desire to represent or even fiddle around with New York and California or the rest of it. They appear in my work simply because I've been there and I've had encounters there and the experience is useful. But I would maintain I am a Southern writer, and if nobody else wants to be, that's fine; then we would have only one: me."

His next novel, *The Upper Hand* (1967), begins in modern Shreveport, but a quarter of the way through moves to New Orleans. (These two cities are also the settings for his final novel, *Shad Sentell* [1984].) It borders on allegory, with characters like Christopher Nieman ("nobody") who is a lapsed priest, a Jewish ex-Nazi abortionist named Dr. Aorta (whom it pleased Bill to put in an apartment above mine on Royal Street), and a Negro dope addict named Mr. Christian Blackman. One finds in this novel the ironic technique that was used in the poem "Prayers for a Mass in the Vernacular," with the terrible divergence from the traditional role of a priest to a priest who has stopped in the middle of Mass, forgotten the Host, and bolted out of church, ultimately to become a truck driver in New Orleans for the Staff-of-Life Bakeries. The bread truck, driven now by Mr. Christian Blackman, ends up crashing through the doors of St. Louis Cathedral. Secular life becomes a gross parody.

Several of the threads that have appeared so far in the poetry and the two novels persist in the skein of Corrington's work. The "nugget of faith" that Whittington observed radiates throughout the corpus. Principally, this has been Christian (specifically Roman Catholic), but as we shall see in a couple of later stories, the scope of this faith and belief seems to expand to become more ecumenical as a result of Bill's readings in Buddhist and Vedic materials. A second thread is Southern existence, an existence suffused, pregnant with its history. A third thread, enlarging from the Southern experience, reveals a broad interest in war, its horrors certainly, but also the courage of men and women who believe in something deeply enough to risk their lives.

The Lonesome Traveler (1968), a collection of nine stories, closes the decade, but begins what will become three collections of stories—all of which will be woven from these threads, and others as well. Without attempting to diminish the achievement of the novels and the poetry, I suspect that the surest bet for that which will endure in Bill's work, and I am speaking of the level of achievement of our finest writers, will be his stories. These stories, collectively, can match anything that has been written by his generation. Ignoring perhaps the futility of measuring him by other writers (and what reader, what critic, does not have a palimpsest before him that includes such benchmarks?), I don't feel uneasy in suggesting that the best of Corrington's work can compare to that of Flannery O'Connor, Faulkner, and Hemingway.

The first story of this first collection, "If Time Were Not / A Moving Thing," is told from the point of view of a Creole woman named

Marie Bouvier shortly after the end of the Civil War, and alternately from the point of view of Mr. Posey, a railroad engineer who lived a hundred years after Marie's story. Marie is convent-raised, deeply devout. She marries a wealthy New Orleans Creole and is a dutiful wife, yet she feels herself to be the lover of Christ in a more profound way. Corrington's evocation of her passion is entirely believable. She has her sights on that which is outside of time. "Time," she says, "is surely the fool of love." Yet she is in time, and as the new life of her sons stirs within her, Christ seems to be displaced. He is not there.

A century later, Mr. Posey is also concerned about time. Both Posey and Marie Bouvier share a sense of the world as a single fabric, but as I read the story, Posey's understanding of it is in ironic contrast to Bouvier's. Unlike Bouvier, Posey is no longer a believer. Although he has been raised a "foot-washing Baptist," he hasn't been in a church for thirty years. Instead of listening to the "Gospel," or Good News of the church, he listens to evening TV news and tries to make sense of that version of the world, its rapes and muggings, murders, riots, and wars. He thinks to himself that he

> could not make out what, taken together, they meant. Surely not some kind of religious or spiritual truth hidden amid the day's miseries and confusions. No, Mr. Posey had come to see it in other terms. Scientifically. He had come to believe that every happening had, of necessity, to be linked with every other happening. There were no discontinuities in the world, and whacking a fly on a porch in Jackson, Tennessee, might determine the outcome of a family dispute in Jonesboro, Arkansas.

Yet for all the connectedness, a connectedness many physicists could agree with, Mr. Posey has no peace and sees no purpose.

Maria, in the passage of time, loses her husband to war and her twin boys to the fever. Yet her own sense of the world, her sense of the presence of God, sustains her. She thinks of time as a "medium in which, like sea creatures, we swim" and "that each of us sustains the world as it moves within us, all to the rhythm of time." Even though her husband and sons are dead, she is able to feel that ultimately nothing is lost. She comes to "feel that perhaps, like one of Heraclitus's endless transformations, I had become the center of a star." Her consolation derives from a sense of being a part of Being, which is unlike the connectedness of things that Mr. Posey considers to exist. For him the things one has to do and suffer mostly "get shoved in front of you like a plate of cold fried eggs."

Between the two visions of Maria and Mr. Posey lies the sharp difference between one with a sense of transcendence and one without. Mircea Eliade has remarked that it is by analyzing a man's attitude toward time that we can understand his mythological behavior: "We must never forget that one of the essential functions of the myth is its provision of an opening into the Great Time, a periodic re-entry into Time primordial." Mr. Posey is a modern man, a secular man. His is not a traditional society wherein labor and love are sacraments and man may break out from profane time into primordial time; Mr. Posey rides in his engineer's cab feeling isolated, like an "observer rather, someone who must watch the feast." Driving a train is just driving a train. What seems to heighten Mr. Posey's experience, charge it with some mysterious, distorted meaning, is the TV news. Eliade's remarks about one of the functions of reading can be applied to watching TV, I think, and help to elucidate Mr. Posey's behavior: "It provides a modification of experience at little cost: for the modern man it is the supreme 'distraction,' yielding him the illusion of a *mastery of time* which, we may well suspect, gratifies a secret desire to withdraw from the implacable becoming that leads toward death."

Following Bill's time in law school and his brief legal practice, the stories often reflect his interest in law and justice, and the difference between the two. Eight or nine of them have these and collateral themes. In the title story from his second collection, *The Actes and Monuments* (1978), A New York Jewish lawyer comes to live in Vicksburg in a kind of semi-retirement and takes up defending blacks and those who cannot pay. He becomes friends with W. C. Grierson, an older attorney who is, after a fashion, a prototype for old and wise attorney-judge figures in Bill's later fiction. It falls to the two of them to defend a young man named Rand McNally, who initially had been arrested by deputy sheriffs on two counts of "reviling." He had called them pigs. After he is in jail it is discovered that he has raped and murdered an old woman. He had been whitewashing a fence for her and came indoors to get his two dollars. When she told him he would have to do another coat before she would pay him the two dollars, he stabbed her with one of her kitchen knives and discovered that he had become sexually aroused. That the killing had been linked to something remotely like love had greatly disturbed him. He knew he needed to die. The two lawyers were going to plead insanity, when Rand McNally waived extradition, saying "it was a goddamned piss-poor legal system that gave all these rights to a . . . fucking pervert." Even so he was sent to the

state mental hospital, whereupon he hanged himself. The story resonates mysteriously with Flannery O'Connor's "A Good Man Is Hard
To Find." Both stories are theological, and in both instances the
"misfits" have an unrelenting understanding of truth and evil, an
understanding that would not have permitted the concealment of the
Incarnation beneath church bingo games and Easter parades. It was
this bizarre epiphany that permitted Rand McNally (the "world") to
break out of history, to break out through divine grace. Mr. Grierson
remarks, "Something else I remember from Luther: certain it is that
man must completely despair of himself in order to become fit to
receive the grace of Christ." Throughout the fiction and especially the
stories that are overtly about law and human courts, there is a
pervasive recognition of the difference between man's law and justice. One does not have to be an accomplished accountant to con-
clude that a serial murderer-rapist like Ted Bundy or an Adolf Eich-
mann has not received justice, for how many times can you execute a
man? All that can be administered is law, with all its limitations.

In "The Actes and Monuments," and elsewhere, there is an eerie
premonition of the way Bill was to die, which was of a heart attack.
The New York lawyer says, "After the coronary, I quit [my established practice]. I could have slowed down, let things go easier,
taken some of the jobs where little more than appearance was
required. But I didn't do that." Neither did Bill. A year earlier he had
had a "minor" heart attack. He told me ruefully, "I didn't have any
kind of out-of-body sensation, nothing like it." Later in the year he
had back surgery. Yet he kept on working in television and writing
movie scripts with Joyce, a collaboration that had lasted thirty
years. As early as *The Upper Hand*, there are musings by a character
(Christopher Nieman's mother) about dying from a heart attack.
"Like an uncertain wild bird thrashing in a cage, [the heart's] tempo
has increased until, even in the velvet Louisiana summer evening,
she has sweated and felt her body's chill liquor drench the sheets
below and above. She is dying and she knows it, and she knows
that she cannot know when the water's source will cease forever,
when the bird will fly."

Mostly one does not get to choose where he will die, but Bill
would surely have appreciated the irony of his dying in Malibu. In
the long story "Nothing Succeeds" (from his third collection, *The
Southern Reporter* [1981]), he has an old attorney, René Landry, go
out to California to bring back a wayward heir who has gone off the
deep end. Mr. Landry gets caught in a drug raid and while he lies on
the floor to escape the gunfire, he "closed his eyes, thinking this

was God's will, he would go on here in California. Why not? Why shouldn't a man die in a foreign place? He was surely justified, being in this artificial hell by way of doing his duty, wasn't he? Afterward, someone would surely send him home." And send him home someone did. As Andrew Lytle remarked, "Tell me where you bury and I'll tell you where you're from." Bill's family and friends buried him in the same cemetery in Shreveport that had appeared in his fiction. In the story, a young colleague has witnessed the death of a woman he loved, and amidst the gunfire and chaos Mr. Landry manages to cough out, "I know. Everything. It . . . it's all right. . . ." These words echo those of one of Bill's idols, Stonewall Jackson, after he was wounded and told to prepare for his death— "Very good, very good; it is all right." As Bill's sons and wife Joyce frantically raced with him to the hospital, he saw and felt their anguish and sense of helplessness. His last words were, "It's all right."

The last time I saw Bill was at a Liberty Fund symposium in New Orleans on the work of Eric Voegelin. From the time Bill began reading Voegelin, I believe in the early seventies, that work had a profound influence on him. The extraordinary breadth and depth of Voegelin's history of ideas, the history of order, helped Bill to draw together for himself his own reading and experience, giving it a unity that it probably did not have before. As the twelve people at the symposium sat around the table, there came a moment when, tears welling in his eyes, Bill spoke movingly of how Voegelin had changed his life.

As Voegelin's thought developed and shifted directions, Bill followed it with him. After the appearance of *The Ecumenic Age* (the fourth volume of Voegelin's *Order and History*), he wrote a brilliant essay describing Voegelin's expansion of analysis, which now included spiritual movements in India and the Far East. This broadening of Voegelin's subject matter was accompanied by a corresponding one in Bill's. "Heroic Measures/Vital Signs," the fourth of his stories to come out in the *Southern Review* (Autumn 1986), is what Bill called his Buddhist story. Harry Rawls is a Shreveport used-car salesman whose daughter is lying comatose in the hospital after a terrible automobile accident. The doctor, Harry's former wife, and her guru (amusingly named Sri Lingananda), who is the Spiritual Director of the Dammapuka ashrama, all want the daughter declared brain dead. But Harry seems to know that she is not yet dead, no matter what the machines and medical materialism have to say. The story employs language throughout that resembles, sometimes parodies, that of Zen masters and Zen Buddhism. "If you asked him if he believed in an afterlife, he would have smiled and said nothing. If you had asked him if he did not believe, he would have said nothing. If you asked him if he did and did not believe, he would have maintained that smile which might signify wisdom or foolery. And said nothing." What he is able to see through clairvoyance, or a different kind of consciousness, is a figure in a white cloak struggling to ascend a mountain and then melting, merging with the undifferentiated white of the snow.

"The Risi's Wife" Bill called his Hindu, or Vedic, story. This novella, concluding *All My Trials,* is told from the point of view of the lawyer we encountered at the beginning of this essay, Albert Sidney Johnston Finch. Another lawyer tells Finch a story about Charlie Babin and his wife Leslie. Charlie had been sent to India flying the "Hump" during World War II. He fell under the instruction of a Risi, or teacher, and came to know "the pathway out of multiplicity." The Risi says to him, "Where you come from, all they know how to use is the will. You treat things as if they were different from you. Here you are, there they are. The Great Illusion. You act as if you were the only truly living one in the universe, and your own life is . . . only a side effect. It's all alive, all one." The story is too complex to unfold here, but I think the Vedic materials had begun to shape Bill. In the last letter he wrote to a friend before he died, he said, "I see you haven't lost your faith in God, or your love of His Word. Neither have I. I've spent all the time since I saw you watching for His utterances in trees and Sanskrit books, the faces of other people and the dark waters of Louisiana swamps. I can't say for certain, but it seems as I get older, I begin to see Him everywhere. I am persuaded that the Vedantists and the masters of Kabbalah are right. He did not create the world—He expressed the world within Himself."

It seems unnaturally early to be writing eulogies or memorials about friends, and friends who were writers, when "our generation" is only in its fifties. Rereading and reviewing Bill's works as a "corpus" has been quite different from reading it as he wrote and published all the stories, the novels, the poems. Partly it's the difference in living a present with someone, and living it in memory. The view from here, I think, is much like the assessment Mr. Landry made, that of Stonewall Jackson, and the one Bill made at the end: "It's all right." It certainly is.

The University of Missouri Press is performing a genuine service by publishing *The Collected Stories of John William Corrington.* Not only are many out of print, but these stories make clear the magnitude of the achievement of one of our best contemporary short story writers.

The Lonesome Traveler
(1968)

If Time Were Not / A Moving Thing
New Orleans: 1868–1968

When I felt them stir within me, I could tell that He had gone away. Not he *or* her: them. *I knew as if a window had opened in the sky and clouds of golden sungrains fallen like tiny hail tumbling through all space seeking my body. And when I knew, I thought first not of them (though I wrote that single word "them" on a slip of paper, dated it, sealed it with wax, and placed it in Emile's desk for later) but of Him who had been so long with me when I was alone in the convent and then given place to Emile when I pleaded but had stayed nonetheless. Now my heart was crowded, and I could not find Him in the clutter. They were coming, and I had to prepare. Not simply a nursery but a place within myself, beyond myself. And as I looked there, searched the space within, I felt Him fade, dwindle, vanish. I said, —He is gone. It was as if He had never been more present than the memory of a memory, something told of an old place under a different sun, a green sky where stars moved in solemn dance under the Maker's eye. I said, —Perhaps He was the fairy prince who does till dreaming is over and one's claims on the world begin to be honored. I was sorry, and I whispered, —Come* back. *Come back because they will only be flesh and the world at its best is stone and gold and shell and horn. They will need you. Come back and love them as I already do. But I whispered softly,* pro forma, *as one might call faintly after a friend who has done great good but stayed long in the doing.*

—Think of Him as a lover, Sister St. Claud had told us in the convent. —He will be true, treasure you, desire you, fulfill you. You need no other ever. He will not take from you that precious jewel. . . . Behind her back many of the girls giggled at Sister St. Claud's tense desperate appeal, her manner of a wife ignored in certain ways, yet still loyal, still loving. But I did not laugh at her. Beyond her tired and petulant intensity lay His truth. It was not the world that was real, I thought. But something else. One dealt in the world's fantasy, ate, slept, danced, studied because it was His will that we do so, pretend to care for things in the world and do our duty in the world despite our ignorance of His purposes. But He was that something else: a flavor I had dreamed but never tasted, a perfume imagined but never smelled, a triumph. He was the indescribable dimension of each experience from which among the world's poor representations we drew some pulse of exultation, a hint at eternity.

In my heart's less private reaches, Emile Bouvier was my Joseph, and I cared for him well enough as partner in the world's game, gave him the pleasure, the respect that was his according to the world—gave him all of myself that was subject to the world and yet as he made love to me, embraced me, took what he supposed to be my love, I was elsewhere, a little distant, watching it all not with disgust since there is nothing disgusting about the body doing the body's things. Rather with amusement because it mattered so to him. I thought, I cannot love flesh. It is not enough. It belongs to the world, and there is an end of it. Love must be long to be true. I must play the whore to a good man, be a wife of flesh, and speak my heart only from my prie-dieu. *It was not difficult. Men in their vanity and celebration of hands and bodies, minds and acts, demand so little. It is a poor forger among women who cannot convince a man that he has touched her most sacred inward privacy and transformed it. It is the simplest of masquerades and one for which the knowledge is sewn into our bodies.*

On our wedding night, when my jewel had been bartered, handed over with the lightest of hearts and no concern at all, when Emile slept full of his happiness, I rose and knelt before Him crucified and whispered that my own Calvary had begun: that long time of pretense dividing me soul from body. I could not take my eyes from His tortured face in which was captured the anguish of all time past, present and yet to come, all places, all men. I promised to share His pain as happily as I had shared His ecstasy. My tears matched His as I cried not over New Orleans or the minor losses of my own life, but over the limitations, the hungers of flesh, the dumb yearning of the world. I counted over the sorrowful mysteries, thinking on the Virgin whose heart was a target, who had brought salvation to Israel out of her body only to see it torn asunder on the cross, had watched it, a Power gathering to it all worldly evil, all divine anger, so that, as in a crucible, all things might be purified and made whole once more.

By morning He had heard my promises and sent to me a sleep as free of trouble as a child's, as Emile's. So that, waking in early afternoon, I smiled at Emile, embraced him and sent him on his business. I knew whose bride I was, whose mistress I would have to be. And yet

I

knew

that

Mr. Posey

almost

never

missed the six o'clock news on television. He would come stumbling into the hotel room he had occupied for the past nine years, strip off his greasy overalls, and stand naked except for his socks and brogans, staring out the dirty window down into heat-cramped traffic that never ceased to flow late or early along Terpsicore Street. He would stand and scratch himself with both work-stained hands, eyes moving back and forth across lounging Negroes in front of Locofoco's Liquors and the boys, black and white, pitching pennies at street cracks beside Tamburino's Groceries & Notions. He would scratch until the dull unbearable itching that had troubled him all the way down from Vicksburg turned by degrees, by stages to bright raw identifiable pain. Then, when he was done scratching, he would walk down the hall in a towel bathrobe beginning to unravel along the hem, take a quick shower, and, stripped naked once more, sit down and turn on the news.

It was funny about Mr. Posey and the TV news. He could hardly stand to watch it, and yet when once in a while he was thrown off schedule and missed it, despite the fact that he would be pulling down triple time on the railroad, he felt as if he were bereaved, as if he had lost beyond recall an entire day and its events. A newspaper was no good. You couldn't trust a newspaper. A newspaper could say anything. On the television, you actually saw it. You knew it had happened, whatever it might be, because it had happened right before your eyes.

And yet beneath that certainty, the TV news brought with it a kind of creeping and unspecified horror to Mr. Posey that made him feel in some small recess of his mind a vague relief when he missed it. As if, when he had finished his run for the Illinois Central, it were his duty to watch the day's anguish and stupidity, blasphemy and brutality, unfolded at six o'clock and that only fate, the intervention of some superior, or at least overruling duty could free him from that responsibility. The whole thing had gotten out of perspective, Mr. Posey thought, but what could he do? Sometimes he wondered if this mixed fear and compulsion had something to do with the fact that, raised a foot-washing Baptist in South Georgia, he had not entered a church since his wedding day thirty years before. He wondered and immediately wondered why he wondered if going to church on a Sunday and adding Wednesday night prayer meetings somewhere here in the city might take the place of the news. Maybe a preacher howling the great thundering good news of the Gospel from a rickety pulpit would free him from the TV news. By any measure the threat of hell and even a detailed accounting of the crimes of mankind could never equal in ferocity that list of atrocities quietly recited every evening by a well-dressed young man who cleared his throat and said it was Channel Six before he began to tell what the world and its people had done today.

But Mr. Posey let the church idea go. Something in him stronger than an urge but weaker than a voice said that he could not put off the news by fooling around with religion. If religion had anything in it, there wouldn't *be* any six o'clock news. If Jesus weren't a joke, the six o'clock news would be about conversion and whole tribes and peoples turning to religion. And maybe if it weren't a joke, Mr. Posey wouldn't be fifty-eight, a widower, with six years more to go before, as a certified senior citizen, he could move to the cottage he had bought on Grand Isle the year after Mrs. Posey died. Where he could fish until Judgment Day.

But you don't pick what you do in this world, Mr. Posey had come to see. You get picked to do things, or the things you have to do get shoved in front of you like a plate of cold fried eggs, and something in the universe says, —*Do it.* And the six o'clock news on TV had picked, been shoved in front of, Mr. Posey somehow. Without any real mystery to it, Mr. Posey was called to endure every violent death, every rape, extortion, accident, election, assassination, strike, state funeral, rebellion, war that the world could spawn. Quarrels between white men and yellow men, Jews and Arabs, and every other kind of foreigner were the staple, spiced with riots and muggings, embezzlements, and robberies with violence. All of them as they unfolded on the screen seemed to be secret messages aimed squarely at Mr. Posey's heart. Or rather they didn't. They should have, but Mr. Posey could not make out what, taken together, they meant. Surely not some kind of religious or spiritual truth hidden amid the day's miseries and confusions. No, Mr. Posey had come to see it in other terms. Scientifically. He had come to believe that every happening had, of necessity, to be linked to every other happening. There were no discontinuities in the world, and whacking a fly on a porch in Jackson, Tennessee, might determine the outcome of a family dispute in Jonesboro, Arkansas.

So he would sit, mouth open, fleshy face rapt, one hand gently massaging his raw groin, and slowly absorb the day's quotient of the unspeakable, trying to see how the flaming crash of a Grand Prix car in Germany might be tied to twenty men trapped beyond hope in a West Virginia coal mine. Putting aside his rationalism, Mr. Posey would whisper almost below the threshold of sound as burning race car was followed by grimy men dragging wrapped bundles from a mineshaft elevator: *Oh, Christ. Oh, Sweet Jesus. Oh, I didn't have nothing to do with that. Never saw such. I never had no hand in nothing like that.*

And it was true. In the nearly six decades of his life, Mr. Posey had done nothing like the things he saw on the six o'clock news. Once his locomotive had run into a car at a grade crossing, demolishing it utterly. But the Negroes inside had been uninjured. And, as it turned out, had been drunk and parked on the track with some uncertain gin-revved notion of collecting insurance on the car. And amid their planning had gone to sleep, forgetting or unable to get out before Mr. Posey's train arrived. He could not forget the car appearing far down the shimmering path of the rails, first as a tiny jot which might have been no more than a possum tranced by the huge revolving lamp on the engine's front, then growing, beginning to take on form and mass and finally even color. He had hit the brake so that the whole train, seventy loaded freight cars, began sliding down the rails as if on oiled glass. But there was nothing he could do more except lean on the whistle so that its roaring, ear-shattering flatulence blew apart the soundless delta summer night. That, and watch each line, each part of the car grow into terrifying clarity as the turning light made it seem to leap and swell in that last single instant before collision. Mr. Posey had been more shaken than the Negroes, and for weeks he had dreamed of great and terrifying holocausts in which his engine smashed through buildings, crushing people, causing fires, destroying whole cities, bringing down societies, burying pasts, gutting futures. It had taken him months to put himself back together, and even now as he watched the six o'clock news, he could not believe his own half-whispered denials of responsibility for what had happened that day, what he was forced to witness—as if only through his observation could each incident sink bloody and memorable, absurd and unforgettable into its place amid the swirling wash of what would one day be called history. He had done none of it, and yet it belonged to him as if by some means of travel faster than light itself, he had dropped explosive into the mine and managed to get to Germany in time to loosen a steering knuckle in a certain car before the race began.

Because what is responsibility? Mr. Posey wanted to know. Why, it is being involved, admitting that your every action is part of every other action. Who lives and breathes in all this shrinking and decaying world and is not involved in its happenings? Nobody, that's who. Mr. Posey could bring to mind the shade of his dead wife, who had been the daughter of a Baptist minister, the very one who had baptized him. And she, for so being, hated Jesus and all His works and pomps. Hated the notion of sin, which she had always claimed was no more than mess. Hated the idea of redemption, which she said was no more than getting a load off your mind. Hated the communion of the saints, which was no more than living people leaning on dead ones and downright morbid. And humbug. When Mr. Posey thought of her, an ugly dwarf of a smile would slouch across his face, but there was no humor in it. Rather it was the fading replica of the expression he had used so long ago to fend her off, something between placation and an ironic shrug.

Mrs. Posey had lived uninvolved, without responsibility or at least the acknowledgment of it. Had insisted they have no children. Because if you have children, you must see to them and they are just mess, and it could never come out well, and only a fool took on what was bound to go badly. A child, Mrs. Posey always said, is a target pinned on your heart. A child is a way to lose. A child will drain your heart and thwart you, is what a child will do. A child will never treasure you, fulfill you. But you can't lose or be hurt by what you never had.

While she lived, Mr. Posey had been stymied by such arguments. He had not given up religion and put away having children. He had simply never found the flaw in her logic while Mrs. Posey was alive to buttress her opinions with her presence, her red mottled face, hennaed hair, and thick-veined hands. But she had been gone almost ten years now, and Mr. Posey had come to see the depth of her trickery. Of course, you can lose what you have never had. Never having what you ought to have is losing. The worst kind of losing. Because in it there is no way back at all—not even the warm, hopeless, comforting shadow of remembering. All of which had been the sum of Mr. Posey's thinking on the long clattering twice-weekly voyage between New Orleans and Memphis, Memphis and New Orleans, day after week after month after year.

He would sit in the isolation of his cab, not wanting to pass time with the fireman, feeling the warm or chill, always moist air of South Louisiana and the Mississippi Delta, the swamps and long flat fields, blowing in his face. He would smell the deep fecund odors of the land and its endless spiral of life and death, its million creations and destructions, births and deaths, triumphs and defeats, and feel himself a witness—no; not a witness, that was a church word, and it spelled an end to loss, the very summation of responsibility. Felt himself an observer rather, someone who must watch the feast and the execution unpleasured by the one, unmoved by the other. It was an odd kind of pain he felt. Without the fine edge of physical hurt or even the specific definition of some personal catastrophe. Sometimes he thought that his pain was to have no pain; to stand or sit or kneel in the midst of life's elements without being able to experience any of them truly.

Mr. Posey had seen movies that moved him to tears. One about the Alamo when Crockett and Bowie and Travis went down beneath a storm of Mexican bullets and bayonets knowing somehow that their dying was a birth, their destruction a new creation. Mr. Posey wished he had been there. To die. So that he might have lived. Might have felt the soaring exultation of losing something worth having had. After that particular movie, which Mr. Posey recognized as a hopelessly melodramatic thing, a perversion of fact perhaps, he had gone back to his room in the hotel on Terpsicore Street and wept beside his bed because he could not kneel, having nothing to do there in the shabby familiar darkness

on

his

knees

for

two

years

our life went on like a quiet movement in a symphony, without depth, without height. The season began on Twelfth Night in those days, the 1850s, and the better people began their time of play in January and continued until Carnival. There were balls, suppers, levees in the homes along Rue Royale, Rue Bienville—throughout the old town—and we attended almost all of them. There were parades and public dancing in the streets for servants, people of color, tradesmen. There were feasts, I have heard, and unspeakable orgies in the shambles along the river. Emile would release the house servants except for a cook and a maid during the week before Shrove Tuesday, as the Americans call it, upon their promise solemnly given that they would return on Ash Wednesday to take the sacrament with the family. I would watch him attend to this ritual each year, watch his eyes glisten as he followed the young blacks, living in his imagination through each liaison, each brief brutal fight, every stolen pleasure. He could not go to those places, do those things. But he could send his own devils, feel within himself the tremors and turnings storming through that flesh he owned and commanded and dispatched one week each year on a demon's holiday.

I did not hate him for it. I did not care. For if I gave love to Emile according to the world, I did not, could not, love him enough to experience that peculiar pique of jealousy at second remove that women feel when they know their man would like to be somewhere other than with them. For myself, I had learned a shift, to balance the hallucination of the season. As I dined, danced, smiled at Emile's friends, suffered the endless nonsense of women presumed my friends, I would keep some portion of my consciousness aloof, and within that place, I would speak to Him. I devised a strange game, a way to come closer to Him. At suppers I would look down the length of a long table covered with plate and candelabra, fresh camillias and azaleas. I would imagine that there was no such thing as time, that duration or an end of it lay within my hands. I would pretend that this certain supper had begun from all eternity and would go on to everlasting. If I willed it. It became then a matter of self-control, of supposing that He had some reason for my being, for my being here and now a part of this social farce. I might withdraw if I wished. But was it not His will that I should seek rather than my own? The weakness of the world, its insufficiency, is such that every creature suffers alike. The poor may suffer abuse or hunger or degradation. Those who possess more of the world's goods must bear, with frustration, the certainty of limitation. One who is poor or a slave has at least his station in life to blame for life's unutterable crabbedness. But the wealthy, the powerful, come to understand that nothing one does in the world, no matter how pleasurable, long escapes ennui. Boredom is the cross of the fortunate as poverty is of the unlucky. But in the end, the world is a place of suffering, for it is a place where we search for Him and cannot see.

Then I would see the table and its burden, those feeding from it, come to a stop as if between the smallest subdivision of an instant and the next, time itself had ceased to be. In that warm rosy candlelight stasis where full forks were frozen on the way to chattering mouths, a voice paused between syllables of a word that did not matter, an eyebrow about to be raised stopped in its ironic punishing course, I would see as if in the sharp intensity of a magic lantern the crude joints of the world, the vulgarity of those who lived for it. A tiny fleck of food dependent from a well-groomed mustache, stains upon serviettes that bleach and slaves' labor had failed to remove, a mist of hair above the lip rouge of a celebrated Vieux Carré *beauty, an almost invisible film of dust on the mirror across from me, where the death of movement, the end of sound, the cease of time itself were reflected over and over again.*

And in such moments He would come to me there and tell me of a place without death, dustless, where food and drink were the flesh and blood of divinity and all things were perfect in His sight. He would touch me with His grace and sweep me up into the chill night sky, where even the earth itself and the stars had ceased to move and turn, show me the tiny huddle of lights caught in a twist of the river, New Orleans, a sliver of community almost lost in the gloom of an empty continent. He would show me the depths of the sea and the distant peaks of high mountains, all the poor humdrum wonders of the shuddering creation which had denied Him for so long. Then His love would close about me; His heart, His precious blood, His matchless passion would fill my soul and drive from it any last lingering care for the world's good. I would promise Him again that I would yield to time and to flesh its demands and no more—that all my most inward being and desire belonged to Him alone. And He would answer with the wind's voice and be satisfied.

There were times amid my passion when Sister St. Claud and the other nuns who had taught me would come to mind. I would smile recalling their ugly habits, their dried, pinched faces, aged before age came to them. Sister St. Claud was small and homely, wore her black veil with a touch of hopelessness as if, virginal and unwed, unbedded for so long, she had realized at last that He would never come. That all her sacrifice and prayer, hopes and vows, were of no use. That her best gifts were nothing to Him. That she had had no better luck with a heavenly spouse than she might have had with an earthly one. Because at last she had come to the Prince of Creation like a peasant woman with red hands and a dull, potato-fattened face, bearing her dowry on her back tied in a black kerchief. There is a way to approach power, and those nuns had not learned it. All the pretended mystery of their ritual marriage had come to nothing, and the proof of it was in their lust for discipline, for plainness among the girls trusted to their keeping, their loud voices at mealtimes, their growing vulgarity and carelessness as time and age grew upon them and the magnitude of their loss was manifest.

Perhaps of them all, nuns and girls alike, I was the only one to discover what lay beneath the midden of commandments and sacraments, the heap of useless trivia reared up by two millennia over His love and its simplicity. Grace comes to discover grace; love is drawn by love. That is the secret of the divine affair, the ultimate conquest. As the sweetness of that revelation swept through my soul, I would nod, and the table, the room, time and the world's operations would break from the stasis I had imposed and begin again. Time, I would smile to myself, is surely the fool of love.

One evening at the Duplessis engagement party, while Emile smoked with some of his friends in the legislature, his brother came and sat beside me.

—Charles Bouvier, I said to him with a smile reserved for men of the family. —What have you been up to?

I did not care for Charles. He was young, dark, almost embarrassingly so, and thought of as quite handsome by the girls in our circle. But he was not gallant, empty, shy, coarse, contemptuous—any of the customary charac-

*ters I knew and understood in men. He watched a great deal, held his liquor
with remarkable éclat, ignored most of his contemporaries, rode a black
stallion with four white stockings that had been purchased in Tangier at all
hours of the night, pushing, urging the beast forward into utter darkness as
if he and the horse possessed either individually or in concert some second
sight, were preserved against their own logical and inexorable destruction
by some force that made straight the way for them there in the night. And
he was adamantine in his passions, his determinations. I could not remember when he had set himself a task and not achieved it. He was utterly of the
world and master of it. I thought,* The children of this world are wise
unto their generation. Charles Bouvier knows what I know and has
taken it into account.

—*I behave very well, Marie Ducote, he answered, crossing his legs. —And
you? He smiled questioningly.*

—*Never a care. Life runs like a river.*

—*There are currents and deep places in a river. Rapids now and again, he
said, still smiling.*

*He moved along my figure of speech, that polite insufferable grin of his
touching and pointing it here and there. I had watched him do it before,
turning the most innocent phrase into what appeared a veiled confession.*

—*You're punctilious, he said softly, abstractedly. —I've noticed that. A
very smooth stream. A bayou deep and unexplored, I think. He was stating
and asking simultaneously, as he did so often. A man without passion or
rancor. A man walking up and down in the world and to and fro in it. Satan
in Bienville's town. Why not?*

—*You want to ask me something, I think.*

*He shook his head. —No, I wouldn't ask you anything. Is there some-
thing you want to tell me?*

—*When I feel compelled to tell something, I go to Emile. I returned his
smile with the least feeling of unease.*

—*Do you really? Charles asked, his tone suggesting to anyone who
might have overheard in passing a certain wonder, a conversational polity of
impeccable warmth and politeness, an invitation for me to enlarge on the
depth of Emile's and my relationship. But it was much more. It was a
rejection of what I had said, an almost brusque slighting of my professed
loyalty to his brother couched in the smooth manner common to all Bou-
viers, improved upon—no, perfected—by Charles.*

*He bent close to me and reached for my champagne glass. —I think you
do something else. I think Emile knows you no better than I do. Except in a
way that does not matter. He smiled once more and went off to fetch more
wine.*

I wondered what he meant. There was nothing he could know. There had never been so much as a hint of scandal about me, and yet he spoke as if I were light and he knew each time and place, each occasion of his brother's betrayal, the name and character of the man I was seeing. I was not angry or concerned. There was nothing in the world to be angry or concerned about. But beyond the world? I was fascinated. I wanted to know if Charles had guessed anything of my inner life. I wondered if, in a most literal sense, he might be Satan's man. Someone who lived his life in a way almost identical to mine, his love and strength dedicated to that other prince, his instruments all the dark paraphernalia of magic, voodoo and the rest. If he knew anything—even if he had an intuition of my life's deepest course—he must have been told, and by no human agency. If he knew my lover, it was from my lover's enemy. I wondered if Charles and I were in some way mirror images of each other, pitched against each other to test powers beyond the world within the tissue of the world. Why not ask? Nothing could come of it here in the Duplessis library.

He returned with brandies. —Something more substantial than champagne, he said. —For weighty topics.

—I thought perhaps lightness was more to your concern. Do you suppose I have a lover, Charles? I asked him, my eyes fixed on his. He did not blush or smile or turn away. My question had not disconcerted him at all. It was as if he had expected it.

—Oh, yes, he answered most seriously. —Of course. I never doubted it. I knew from the day we first met, when Emile brought you home to meet the family. Long before you married. It's been no secret between us. We're something of the same sort, you know.

I was amazed. What could I ask, say now? That would not destroy what raveled veiling still stood about our conversation. —And it doesn't matter to you?

—No, he said coolly. —Why should it? We have our primordial loyalties. We can only give others what we have to give. If they can't be satisfied with that, so much the worse for them. We are what we are, and they must leave us alone. Mustn't they?

—No one is left alone, I said.

—Oh, yes, they are, Charles disputed me. —I'm surprised you haven't discovered that yet. Probably too young. Or perhaps women aren't ever really alone, none of them. Perhaps that's so.

—You've been alone? I asked archly. Charles was only two years older than I.

—Yes, he said, ignoring my irony, turning to me as if about to declare his love. —Yes, I've been alone. And I've had a look at the future. It's been nothing yet. We'll all be alone a lot. Even those who have no practice at it. We're living at the edge of an abyss of loneliness.

—I think I won't be, I said, and wished at once that I had left that theme buried in Charles's own sudden melancholy.

—No, he said slowly, almost grudgingly. —Probably not. You're an exception to almost everything. And

then

of

course

Mr.

Posey's

mouth

snapped shut and the lines in his forehead converged for a moment as the newscaster went on with something about a private-plane crash near Los Angeles. Now that, Mr. Posey considered, is a thought. If all things are of a piece, why, even an old man without sons could plunge into the flood and bring new things to pass. All there was to it was not to lie passive, letting the current of linked events wash you along with it. You had to *do* something. Could you change the destiny of a nation? Of course not. Could you stop disaster in its tracks? Not a chance. But what you *could* do, what a man could do, was to hold it at bay. No way to avoid loss, that was sure. Late or soon every soul born has to lose. The loss cannot be gainsaid, and you have to bow to it. But what about the agony between knowing it is on the way, but still hoping to avoid it, and the moment it arrives and cannot be ignored or pushed aside or sloughed off any longer? Maybe that was the weak place in the world's otherwise perfect construction as an infernal machine. A man couldn't do it for himself, but that is as it should be: he *could* do it for others. Say a man was to lose his whole savings in the market but somebody called and said it was a mistake, that his money was all right. Such a call could give a man hours of peace of mind before the world fell in on him. If it all happened on a Friday afternoon, he'd be all right until Monday. For two days, he would live outside time, beyond reality. He would have the loss all right, but he would have had those days, Saturday and Sunday, free. They would be a gift someone had sent you. It would be as if time itself had a switch on it, a button that, once found, could be pushed to bring it to a stop for a little while. And when time began again, the loss would be no worse than it would have been anyhow. Something like that could be done. If anybody cared. If those who only observed would get involved and look for that switch on time and hit it and give the gift of time robbed out of time to someone about to lose.

Just then the announcer broke Mr. Posey's reverie. It seemed there had been a kidnapping in Jefferson Parish. A little boy was missing. There was great concern because his family had no money to speak of. There was thought that his abduction might be some awful attempt at revenge. No ransom note. No call. And something about a disappointed lover of the child's mother who had sworn to be square with her one time or another: a deranged shipfitter named Cecil Serge who had had a bad name in East Baton Rouge Parish anyhow, who had only a month before finished serving concurrent terms at Angola for aggravated assault, extortion, and contributing to the delinquency of a minor. Be on the lookout for a man who looks like this police artist's sketch. The mother is searching her old scrapbooks, and it is expected a photo will be available momently. If you have information, call this number in New Orleans. Do not attempt to apprehend the suspect. He may be armed and should be considered dangerous.

Mr. Posey shuddered as the relentless screen, pitching its myriad dots of gray together, showed the mother's face. Her eyes were large and dark in a sallow, unintelligent, vaguely pretty face, and her anguish heightened, underscored, some latent strain of character, strength never called on before. It made her seem almost beautiful, awesome. The camera closed on her like a hungry animal that thrived on pain while the reporter asked about her missing child in a conversational tone laced with what he must have thought sounded like genuine personal concern.

—Ah went to feed . . . no, it was when he never cried and Ah woken up and said why, my, it's time he, and then Ah went in to where and, Oh, Jesus . . .

She covered her face with her hands, revealing bitten nails and a thin wedding band. The camera lingered a moment too long before shifting away, back to the reporter, as Mr. Posey had known it would. He cringed. As if the pain were his own. As if by what he knew of the interlacing of creation, he was bound to take on himself some portion of her suffering. As if her fear and uncertainty, her almost delirious transition into reality from whatever trailer-court or shopping-cart world she had inhabited before being moved like a current through the tube's cool medium that engulfed Mr. Posey in its callous intimacy, had entered into him, invaded him. He could feel tears on his beefy cheeks, and they were not tears of sentiment or empathy but of loss. That anonymous child was his—the boy he might have had if things . . . His own.

The TV played on behind him while amid a blur of feeling he had never experienced before, Mr. Posey found himself calling the number given by the announcer. His blood flared as if a night wind were rising in his veins, as if he had become a force instead of an aging man. As if the train of his life had found some new and dangerous track and had switched onto it thoughtlessly, valorously.

—Hello, Mr. Posey was saying in a gruff, slightly hysterical voice that was not his. —Hello, I'm the fella you got a picture of on the news. That Cecil Serge. Yes, I'm one bad sonofabitch, but the little boy is okay. You tell his momma that. I can't forget what she done to me, but I won't hurt that little child. You tell her I'll let him go day after tomorrow.

On the television, a rock-and-roll group with long hair and electric guitars was playing something loud and singing with foreign accents:

. . . what a drag it is to get up. . . .

—I got to go now. Got other scores to settle, Mr. Posey snarled. —And I got to get this little child something to eat.

Before he hung up, he could hear muffled sounds in the background, and the man on the phone, obviously stalling for time, had begun to tell him what you

feed a

small

boy

in

December

1860

late in the afternoon it happened . . . When I turned from giving Elodie in-
structions for dinner and sat down for a moment in the solarium with Him
before Emile should come home. I opened that portal in my soul to discover
Him, to laugh and share a little time outside time among the joyful
mysteries, His and mine.

But He was not there. Then, at that instant, there was some tiny shift,
some small movement within me, and where He had been always, they had
come and occupied me as silent troops steal into a citadel at night, raise
their flag unseen so that the sun's first light reveals them and the mark of
their triumph. They had taken His place, and the quietude I had always
entered myself to find was replaced with a simmering cheerful jangle of
feelings as if a pair of chipmunks had come to play in His tenantless place. I
could not imagine why, why He had not stayed, had fled as if they were His
mortal foes. And as I sat bereft and filled anew, Emile entered, his face dark
and distracted. He dropped a broadside printed on cheap paper on the divan
beside me. Across the top it said the Charleston Mercury, *and below I*
read: THE UNION IS DISSOLVED.

—My God, I said aloud, thinking of Him and the strange new rest-lessness stirring within me. —What does it mean?

—War, Emile said, sitting down opposite me. His eyes were rimmed with red and his hand shook as he lit a cigar. —It will mean war. South Carolina seceded four days ago. The whole South will follow, then . . .

I had ceased listening. It was politics, and I had more than politics to concern me. THE UNION IS DISSOLVED. Was it His annunciation to me? I remembered suddenly that it was Christmas Eve. Tomorrow was the anniversary of His birth, and He had done with me. Now in His place they moved and grew. Somehow I could hear them as they touched one another, in touch constantly. They would arrive out of me, use my body and blood until they were done with it. And come into the world. I wondered if I should tell Emile. They would be his, too. That was unavoidable. But he had already left the house without supper, Elodie told me, as if he did not know where he was going. Or where he was.

All during the season, talk was of politics. Some of my acquaintances who had barely presence of mind enough to see their food and linen shelves properly stocked were to be found in discussion about what it all meant, what would come of it. At a supper for Blaise Marmot's sister, I saw Charles. He was dressed in a showy blue uniform with epaulets, brass buttons, sash and sword.

—Good heavens, Charles. Did you misread your invitation? It's not costume, you know. That will be later.

He kissed my cheek and whirled me around. —I knew you'd say something like that. I counted on your being here. I'll be by to see you both before I leave, but . . .

—But where are you going? Really, what is the uniform for? You can't have joined the American Army. Your father would . . .

Charles shook his head in disbelief. —It's the Washington Artillery, my dear, and it's not American anymore. It's Louisianian now. We haven't been American for four days. Didn't Emile—no, of course. You two don't discuss that sort of thing.

—You mean this isn't the United States anymore?

Charles shook his head again. —We're a republic now. Allied to South Carolina, Mississippi, Georgia, Texas. How do you like that?

I shrugged. —I don't know, really. It sounds nice. No more United States. That sounds rather fine. But Emile says there'll be trouble.

—I told you last year we'd all be alone soon. Now we are. Marie, Charles went on, touching my hand, —there's going to be a great deal of trouble.

—Well, I said, —it will come and be gone.

—No, he said. —I don't think so. I think we've stepped through a breach in time. I can't explain it. But nothing will ever be the same again. If your secret still holds, keep it fast, my sweet. You may need it.

I felt a chill as he spoke, and the constant chirping that almost always continued within me, them at play, went silent. Because my secret was no more and was made new. I almost told him, almost returned the touch of his brown hand to tell him what I had not told Emile, what no doctor could yet affirm. But I told him nothing. And a week later, in the coldest part of the new year, he was gone beyond telling to those places where the trouble would be. Emile followed him less than a month later. And when he was gone, when the farewell party and the last leave-taking was done, I realized that I had not told him, either.

They were born that September following. With their father and uncle and almost every man able to walk in either Tennessee or Virginia. An old Negro midwife saw to me along with Elodie, since the women in my circle, though they had the best of intentions and were around constantly, did not have the faintest idea how to see a baby into the world.

Emile and Charles, I named them, and they were fine. I would sit with them for hours, playing, admiring their tiny limbs, the smooth, even olive of their skin. I was bemused at the exactitude of my own knowledge, and now that they were here, that gift of prophecy frightened me. I would sit with Elodie as she fed them, dried their tears, and I would think how they had grown from seed so small that no eye, no instrument, could have detected it. And still I had known. I wondered if He had sent them, resided within them waiting for me to discover Him. As I lifted them from their beds in the morning, I could see that they were no changelings. They were themselves. My gift to the world, given without volition, but given no less. They were my deepest life, that which I had shared with Him, given flesh and bone, and as I watched them playing, I thought that to bear children, to see what has been within you move and struggle to express itself is like sending one's soul outward on its own way. Whatever I had been at center was there before me now, not taking direction from me, its course divided in twain—my blood flowing beyond me as if I had been never more than an envelope, a fleshy container for these tiny futures probing their new world as I smiled, ebbing, aging nearby.

And I thought then that I was truly alone. I wondered if all my life, the vision filling me had been nothing other than this possibility of children. Perhaps life is like those small Chinese boxes one can buy in which a smaller box is concealed in each larger one. It is the idea which amuses us—and the intricacy which makes us go on, opening each box, saying no, this is the last. They could not make one smaller. Even if they could, why? Why should anyone take time and trouble over such nonsense? I thought that life *may be His Chinese box—for which there is no reason but His will, His whim.*

Then I began to understand that we are indeed children of unreason, and that time must be the medium in which, like sea creatures, we swim. We are lonely because we are ourselves and not some other thing which needs, wishes, nothing but itself. I might lie for hours listening to spring rain, plunging into myself as deeply as I could, seeking some smallest hint of a presence, a resonance. But I was alone with nothing but memories to examine over and over again: pleasures and days, summer evenings and musicales. Riding in the park, a visit to Highland Plantation. I remembered Charles with a peculiar clarity. Far better than Emile who had become no more than a calm and imprecise place of rest among the tides and characters in which my life was written. But I recalled my conversations with Charles, his strange knowledge, his notion that we had stepped outside time, all of us, that twentieth of December in 1860. What an idea. How could it be? If time were not

what
was
Mr.
Posey

fell down on his bed and scratched himself. He realized of a sudden that he was sweating, shivering. Like the time his locomotive had hit the carful of Negroes. It was as if for a moment he had *been* the mad, hateful disappointed lover with the child right there in his hotel room. *I didn't make the snatch,* he thought, all the old gangster movies he had seen on television spinning through his head in series and in parallel. But he could not convince himself that he had not somehow had a part in it. Maybe he had once seen the man who had done it, said good morning to him. In a store or the café where he had chop suey on Wednesdays. In Natchez? How about Memphis? There were desperate people everywhere. How could anyone say he was not responsible for anything? The chain of events in the world had a million million links, and if you look hard enough for long enough, you find out that every word and gesture fits somehow into every other. Mr. Posey sat up and wiped his beef-red face with his hand. When you thought of it, there was no end to guilt, to loss. God knows how many people might die because he had not laid down the law to Mrs. Posey and had a son who might have been a great scientist or surgeon or statesman. The murder of Julius Caesar had caused the *Hindenburg* to fall. Garibaldi and King Zog had been accessories to the killing of Huey Long.

Once Mr. Posey had known a brakeman out of the Nonconnah yards in Memphis who was also by way of being an itinerant preacher on Sundays and during his vacation. He claimed that this world is hell, all the hell there is or need be, and that its occupants are being punished for their innumerable and contemptible outrages against deity in other worlds. We are like fish thrown up on the bank, our gills flaring, our fish minds seared with pain as we try desperately to draw in an alien medium. The brakeman had preached as well that not a thing in this world is real—that is, of the slightest eternal meaning. Except pain, and that pain, in its reality, is the only thing of value that befalls us, and we should treasure it.

Mr. Posey grinned weakly beneath his glistening coat of perspiration. If that brakeman were right, it could be that by his phone call Mr. Posey was meddling with the process of salvation. He had heard a lot crazier ideas than those of the brakeman, heard them every day on the six o'clock news, and for all he knew, they might every one be true. He had small truck with religion, but there was no way to be sure.

Which was just fine. He felt better that it was unsure. A real man didn't spend his days looking for sure things. Jim Bowie and Davy Crockett knew the Alamo was a thin edge, but they never backed off. A lot of Mr. Posey's grandfolks had been in the Confederate War under famous generals whose names he could not bring to mind, and they had never figured for a sure thing. It didn't matter. Because he had to do what seemed right, and right was to cheat loss, to put off pain that could not at last be avoided, to weaken the iron chain of circumstance wherever he could strike at its links. If they found the little boy, his poor mother would have passed the worst time on the strength of that phone call that had said her baby was alive and not dead. If the child *were* dead, it could be no worse for the false hope he had sent her. Mr. Posey closed his eyes and saw against the stageless murks of his lowered lids a great schematic of the world's operations in all their bewildering complexity, each incident the product of millions before it, its own implications fanning out like the numberless ripples in a pool. Then he was asleep, and the world's tortured body relaxed into a long-vanished summer evening in South Georgia thirty years ago with Cape jasmine and gardenia everywhere and someplace, just beyond his seeing, a young girl in a cheap print dress with soft hair and warm lips, her body full and firm, walking through the cooled dust to meet him. A girl who would never be Mrs. Posey, who would

not

see

the

war

engulfing

us left New Orleans in the hands of the Federals, and news from outside,
real news, was difficult to come by. In those latter days I had managed to
isolate myself even from the hope of learning what had happened to Emile
and Charles or any of our friends. I paid no mind to anything outside the
round of my own life. Our courtyard, bursting in almost every season with
new life, was the limit of the world. It was enough to see the varieties of
flower and shrub and tree bloom and spread new leaves and fruit, to watch
the boys grow and learn to walk, begin to talk. The year they were born,
Elodie and I had planted a pair of mimosas outside the parlor windows.
Now, in the summer of 1864, they flowered, and the boys ran back and forth
across the flagstones, laughing, chasing downy seeds floating up and down
on stray currents of warm breeze.

They were three that summer, and only Elodie and I could tell them apart
with certainty. Even we distinguished between them by intuition because
there were no marks, no slight differences in personality, by which we could
determine which was which. They were identical and beginning to find
names for all the world. —What's this? Charles would ask, and just
afterward Emile would point at the same thing. —What's this? Once both
of them found my breviary, and pointing to a picture of Him revealing His
Sacred Heart, Charles wanted to know, —What's this? —An old friend, I
told him. —An old lover I had before my boys came. —An old lovie, Charles
told Emile most seriously, almost covering the picture with his hand.
—Lovely? Emile asked, frowning in concentration. And I smiled, considering how little thought I had given Him since my sons had begun to grow.
Amid bad times, the city's churches were frequently filled even at weekday
masses. But we paid only the minimum of protocol visits needed to allay
questions. But He was not present in my mind always as once He had been.
I had found ways to live outside myself. Charles had been right. The war
had only made our loneliness manifest. Being alone was nothing to dread. It
was our nature, and we could be said to mature only as we accepted that
isolation. I hoped Charles and Emile had learned as much.

I knew all this and I believed it, and yet in that circuitous part of me
which ignored head-on truth, sneered at reality—the place where He had
reigned—something exulted and whispered, —It is true for the rest of them,
but you have the boys. You're not alone. Not really alone.

But then I would feel a certain coldness, as if a wind blowing from the river had found its way into my room, bringing with it the stench of death and dissolution, that peculiar odor associated with every large body of water. The opposite of that sweet living scent which comes with spring and summer showers. As if, once more, I were about to prophesy. Then I would shake my head, close my eyes and concentrate on where I might be able to find eggs for the children, worry about M. Bouvier's failing health, wonder where Charles and Emile might be. Anything to put time aside. If it had claims on me—us—then it would have to assert them, force them on us. In this new world racked with war and confusion, what could there be that one would wish to forsee? I had no desire

to

know

that

the

next

day

Mr. Posey took an early run to Baton Rouge, trying hard to keep his mind on the signals and the country crossings, which had always raised hair on the back of his neck since that night when, too late, he had seen the car parked across his tracks. He was unusually tired when he got back to New Orleans and so broke his routine. He decided to buy a beer at Modrian's Bar on North Peters Street, where he would neither be caught in the roaring silence of his hotel room or troubled with the expense of spirit brought on by the loud accents of tourists from Nebraska and the Bronx, who honked to their overdressed wives in incomprehensible patois and dragged their camera-laden lengths along Bourbon Street and past St. Louis Cathedral day after wearying day.

It was cool and overcast and the garish, unreal green of Jackson Square was muted, almost dingy, as he walked through, past the proud bronze fiction of a general who had won a bloody battle after the war was over. Mr. Posey squinted at the few people sitting in the square as if, in their tired, disinterested faces, he might find some clue to their loss or their involvement in the world. But when anybody noticed Mr. Posey looking at him, he would turn away or lift his *Times-Picayune* or simply return Mr. Posey's gaze with the stark, detached, unembarrassed glare of a caged animal. It was as if each person existed within his own invisibly bounded territory with a supply of air and moisture exclusively meant for him alone, as if he had no dependency on the world beyond his own purlieus and all the rest of creation were no more than objects of curiosity drifting aimlessly by, in and out of view.

The tavern was dark with only a bored barkeep leaning half-asleep against the sagging backbar and two men huddled over beers in front. Above them in the gloom, a globe, blue and green and girdled with a wide lettered band, floated like a projection in a planetarium. On the band it said SCHLITZ. One of the men wore overalls with a rusty hammer caught in the tool strap at his side. Under the overalls he wore a short-sleeved T-shirt, and his hairy arms were gauded with flecks of white and azure and terra-cotta house paint. Mr. Posey wondered if he had been decorating some kind of Catholic church. The other man wore black slacks and a tight-fitting black golf shirt with a tiny alligator embroidered over the left breast. He had slick black hair and was absently swinging a key chain with a tiny telescope at the end of it. He was overweight, and his paunch sagged against the synthetic fabric of his shirt.

Both men and the barkeep, whenever his eyes fell open, were watching a small-screen television that peeped from the dun-colored wall. Out of it, someone was telling about volcanoes, how Herculaneum and Pompeii had been buried by one called Vesuvius. And another one, Krakatoa, had killed thirty thousand people, filling the air with dust for years, sending a destructive tidal wave around the whole world. What happens with a volcano is that great pressures build deep in the earth and find weak places in the crust through which to erupt. Don't think that the processes of geology, the rearing up and tearing down of the world, have stopped just because you don't see them in action every day, the narrator told them portentously.

—I don't, Mr. Posey said aloud, paying for his beer, eyes glued to the wavering gray screen. —I don't forget it at all.

—Ain't it the shits? the man in the overalls muttered. His face was lined deeply as if lava had run down the uncertain ravines from forehead to neck, and his hair was a peculiar off-white almost matching some of the blots of paint on his arms. —The whole goddamned world is like a time bomb fixing to go off. We could all go off in two seconds.

—I'll give you eight to five on that and start anytime you say, the alligator shirt sniffed. —Hell, I'll give you thirty minutes. At twelve to five.

The barkeep had fallen back into his place after drawing Mr.

Posey's beer. —Who cares? he said. —Wouldn't kill nothin' but sonsabitches if it was to go up right now. Nothin' lost.

—I ain't no sonofabitch, the overalls snapped, half rising off his worn plastic-covered seat. —I don't appreciate that.

—Nothin' personal, the barkeep groaned, his fatigue removing any reasonable motive for offense.

—If people thought about time, about other people, Mr. Posey ventured.

—Thirty to one on that, and no time limit at all, alligator shirt coughed, pulling long and reflectively on his beer.

Behind them all, the Schlitz globe turned slowly, its broadly etched continents bathed in the dim red glare of the bar light, occasionally brightened by lightning flashes as the television picture flared and faded in intensity.

—Geologically speaking, nothing in the world is fixed. Our time, our whole history, are but jots too small to discover in the enormous aeons since the creation of the solar system and its planets and sun. All around us in the universe, the law is change. The earth is a moving thing and we, mankind, only tiny parasites occupying for an instant its outer crust. . . .

—What'd I tell you? the barkeep sighed.

—Jee-sus, the overalls muttered. —Parasites. I be just as happy if he called us sonsabitches.

—We got to realize about each other, other people, Mr. Posey began again as the program on volcanoes ended and the screen filled suddenly and overwhelmingly with a lovely girl's armpit.

—That's more like it, alligator shirt whistled, lifting a pair of sunshades from the bar and slipping them on. —Volcano up your ass.

But the girl put something in her armpit and smiled and went away. It was time for the six o'clock news and

it

was

in

the

spring

in 1865, I remember, and the afternoon had been long and soft, filled with high fluffy clouds and the faintest of cool breezes. Toward dusk I began to feel drowsy and only the hum of mosquitoes kept me awake. There had been little supper because we depended now chiefly on fish and vegetables caught and grown by neighbors on the levee or Negroes sympathetic to us, to our family.

As twilight deepened and I drifted toward sleep there in the courtyard, I remember wondering how death might be. Not because I wanted to die, but because as I swam onward through the shadowy uncertain reaches of time, I had begun to tire of it. Except for the boys, it was a bore. Because even those matters of greatest moment, an end at last to the war, the fate of Emile and Charles, the shape of my future life, seemed to matter very little. A handful of stars had begun to show then, and I tried to keep my eyelids from falling shut so that I could watch them, wondering whether the fate of a star or the destiny of a person was the more important. Or if either really mattered in the least. I had read one of Emile's dusty books the night before when sleep would not come: a collection of writings by the most ancient philosophers who could not agree among themselves whether the universe was a shower of particles, falling from nowhere to no place, purposeless and isolate, or earth, air, fire, and water locked in eternal roiling confusion, each striving for mastery. Or simply an endless flux, a kaleidoscope of form and color changing without reason from one array to another, each pattern bright and lovely and various as the last, as the next, and none mattering at all.

I watched the stars wheeling above, the moon rising over a pair of mimosas at the far end of the courtyard, and, slapping a mosquito, seeing it vanish in a tiny blot of red, disagreed with all the philosophers. I believed that the world was a presence within and that I was the world's reality as it was mine. I wondered why so many wise men had not realized, one of them at least, that each of us sustains the world as it moves within us, all to the rhythm of time. Then I thought, After all they were nothing but men.

—Madame, Elodie whispered, interrupting my reverie, almost awakening me by a certain urgency in her soft voice. I felt for a moment how much I loved her, how kind she had always been to us all and I tried to gather my wits, to understand what she was telling me.

—Madame, the children. . . . Master Charles is feverish. Master Emile . . .

But it was no use, and I felt my head loll and fill with warm strengthless dreams, becoming warmer and warmer still until I came to feel that perhaps, like one of Heraclitus's endless transformations, I had become the

center
of a
star
announcer
who
began

the news as he always did with a pitch for the warmth and humanity of the telephone company. —They care, he said, staring into the camera and on out through the screen into Mr. Posey's heart. —*They* care.

Then there was news of battles in some godforsaken Asian place with a three-word name, serious erosion of the pound, the franc, the dollar. Somebody, presumably *in extremis,* had been implanted with sheep's kidneys. In Salt Lake City they had auctioned off the chair in which Joe Hill had been executed fifty years ago. Then the announcer cleared his throat for the local and regional news.

—The body of four-year-old Mike Stones was found today only hours after authorities had . . .

He went on to tell that police felt the Stones boy may have wandered from his home and fallen into the open drainage ditch where he was found, facedown, almost buried in mud and water. Or maybe not. The possibility of foul play had not been entirely ruled out. The story told by the Stones woman was not consistent in certain details. There had been a family quarrel over the child.

The television camera was panning all the while from shots of police carrying a small wrapped bundle up to a waiting ambulance, to an empty ditch, to a slab-faced man in a dairy delivery uniform. The man, his large hands working, twisting within each other, was the Stones child's father, who had very little to say except that his wife was insane and capable of anything.

Then the camera snapped back to the studio where the announcer, clearing his throat again, went on.

—An ugly sidelight to the Stones tragedy was revealed by police today when it was pointed out that they had been misguided by a phone call from someone who claimed to be Cecil Serge, the Stones woman's former boyfriend. The call served to shift police attention to the kidnapping possibility rather than to continue to search the neighborhood for the child. It could be that the mindless call of an unidentified crank was the margin between life and death for little Mike Stones.

—Now ain't *that* the shits? the man in overalls said, pulling a baseball cap out of his pocket and fixing it on his off-white head. It said MEMPHIS CHICKS across the front. —Some fool getting a child killed for a joke.

—No joke, Mr. Posey choked, trying to get free of the barstool that seemed to have captured his legs. —No joke.

—Five to one. Alligator shirt laughed shortly. —On that dumb cunt killing the kid herself.

The television announcer claimed their attention once more. —A final note on the Stones case. Police said this afternoon that rapid tracing had revealed the whereabouts of Cecil Serge, suspected of possible kidnapping of the Stones child earlier. In a dramatic change of role, the former ruffian was found at a Franciscan monastery in

Kentucky, where he is applying for lay brother status. When reached by reporters, Serge was unwilling to be interviewed. His only remark was: "The death of a little kid is a terrible thing in the sight of the Lord, and I wouldn't touch it with a ten-foot barge pole."

Mr. Posey's eyes widened, and he knocked over his empty beer glass as he leaned down the bar toward the sport in the alligator shirt. —You reckon that poor crazed woman . . .

—Why not? Alligator shirt shrugged. —Trying to get to her husband because he pissed her off about something. It ain't a new thing. But the joke's on her. He don't care. What the hell, a kid. Who needs a kid? They'll catch her. The cops got time working for them. They got

nothing
but
time
began
again
and

I opened my eyes to see someone nodding in a chair next to my bed. At first I thought it must be a doctor, some stranger, perhaps a Northern man, one of those who had come in with the Federal Army. I studied him for a long minute. His face was terribly scarred, one side of it apparently paralyzed so that his left eye did not close. The left corner of his mouth was twisted upward into a permanent ironic sneer, and his arm, swathed in black, lay useless in his lap. My eyes moved back to that warped involuntary smile. I recognized him even as his head rose and he looked at me with tenderness, love.

—Oh, Charles, I said, trying to rise, holding out my arms to him.

He rose clumsily and came to me. —Marie Ducote, I never expected to see anything as beautiful as you again. Not in this world.

—I fell asleep in the courtyard, I told him, coming to myself. —I'll whip that Elodie for letting you find me this way, for not waking me.

Charles's ravaged face darkened. —No, Marie, he said slowly. —You've been ill. The fever . . .

He pressed me back into the pillows. It was not a night I had lost. It was almost three weeks. Charles had come back a week before and alternated with Elodie sitting beside me, waiting for me to recover. Or not.

—Emile, I began.

—At Five Forks, he said, as if it were a name from ancient history he was reciting. —He was with Lee almost to the end. An officer from Mississippi brought me his watch and some papers. At the end, they didn't keep records. The Mississippi man couldn't say where they laid him.

I was silent. Neither of us was prepared for theatrics, false emotion. I shook my head and wiped my eyes on the counterpane—not for a lost love but for a good man gone out of the world.

—Marie, are you strong?

That made me smile. What is strength but the ability to bear what we cannot avoid bearing? I nodded.

Charles lowered his eyes. —I would wait, but it's impossible. I can't wait. I can't spare you anything.

But he was able to spare himself after all. Because even as he stumbled toward revelation, seeking words for what cannot be said, I knew what he had to say. Knew because I realized suddenly that the world had changed, that the sweet quietude of that last evening I remembered, its warmth and its resignation were gone. And so was my emptiness.

—Was it the fever? I asked him, and saw that his poor ruined face was dissolved in tears, that awful twisted corner of his mouth wrenched into a false smile too awful to bear, too heartbreaking to see. For he had lost them, too, lost them having never seen them, and with them the last trace of a brave brother.

It had been the fever. And they had been taking the children away when Charles rode up in front on a borrowed horse. He had seen to it that they were secretly taken to an icehouse on Iberville Street in hope that I might survive and see them laid to rest. Or be buried with them. The cost had been great because keeping the dead more than a day or so was against the law and there were Federals to see that no rebel family broke the least important law.

So with Charles and Elodie to support me, I stood under an umbrella and watched them place all our futures in St. Louis cemetery. It was raining, and the single grave was filled with water. I closed my eyes as they bored holes in the two small coffins so that they would settle and could be covered with clods of wet clay. The gravediggers stood on each coffin until it vanished into the muddy water. It seemed strange that of all the family and friends gathered there, I alone kept my composure. It was attributed to my recent illness, to shock. But it was neither the one nor the other.

It was something else.

Later, when the others had left us, Charles and I drank a great deal of tea and talked while the rain went on falling outside. I wanted to tell him what I felt now.

—You remember our long talk? About my lover? About being alone?

—Yes, Charles answered, staring out the window into the courtyard where harsh windblown rain worried the mimosas. —It seems we had that conversation in another country. Somewhere outside time.

—When I got the children, my lover went away.

—*Lovers are like that, Charles said abstractedly.*

—*He left when I realized they . . .*

—*He? Charles turned toward me. —My God, you mean . . .*

—*He had been with me always. But they . . .*

—*You meant—you really meant someone?*

I could not understand his surprise. —What did you think I meant?

—*Your . . . own personality, he said wonderingly. —I meant that perfect self-centeredness of yours. You were never alone because . . . you were always alone. With yourself.*

—*Of course, I said, and lay back in my chair, closing my eyes and opening myself completely for the first time perhaps. I felt His presence within me, sure now and certain, bringing with Him all the world's beauty, all its long rhythm of sadness. I did not know whether to greet Him as one unknown or as my dear one returned again.*

—*Of course, I said again, touching Charles's scarred cheek with my fingertips, my hand, and wondering if I should tell him, if he would understand that nothing is lost,*

that

time

is

a

grinning

man

with dentures was eating an apple on the television, and then it was the weather as Mr. Posey walked the length of the bar, losing and regaining his balance like a drunken man. The painter in overalls had vanished into the gloom ahead of him, and Mr. Posey, staring back over his shoulder as if he were loath to follow, to go out into that night that had grown darker than the bar, took one last look at the slowly spinning miniature of the world turning, turning, each tiny continent green and of a piece, outlined against the everlasting blue of seven seas. Mr. Posey felt giddy watching it and after another moment stepped out into the evening as some Confederate secret agents began a plot against Grant which would end disastrously in exactly fifty-eight minutes.

First Blood
Atlanta: 1864

Near Atlanta: 27–28 July, 1864

That summer the sky was no good and the trees were dusted the color of old clothes. From early morning till long after midnight the guns coughed and stammered in the opposed lines outside the city. Along the roads, squadrons of anonymous horsemen ran a gamut of shellfire from both sides and staccato hooves beat the thin surfacing into a boil of dust. In the afternoon when one side or the other tried an assault or when a few growling cannon managed to bring on a full-scale artillery duel, the dust would merge with thick bluish smoke, would rise and mingle, a single impenetrable pall in which the sun was only another shell bursting with pale brilliance and fading slowly back into dense and vaporless fog.

I

The old man had been trying to get to the well since dawn. Ordinarily, he and the boy hardly used a bucket of water a day. But the heat inside the shell-blasted house was standing now above a hundred degrees, and the wounded men called for water constantly.

He inched out into the yard on his hands and knees, a pair of outsize cavalry canteens slung across his shoulders. As he passed the edge of the house that hid him from sight of the Union lines, a scattering of riflefire chirped distantly and scallops of colorless dust sprang up near his hands.

—Watch yerself, old man, a voice called cheerily from inside the ruined house.

Butchers, the old man thought. *Sittin' up on that ridge with all the food in the country. Squattin' with them telescoped rifles, shootin' people outa windows, killin' hogs a mile away just to keep meat outa folks' mouths. Stinkin' butcherin' sonsabitches.*

—Old man, the voice from inside called again. —You didn't let 'em put one in you? This time the voice had no fun in it.

—Shut your damned mouth, the old man called back without rancor. —You'll get your water.

The well stood less than twenty feet from him. Once there, he could lie behind the stone wellhead, lift one hand to tilt the bucket over, and then crank it up without exposing himself much. If he could get there.

—Longer you lay there, harder it gets, another voice from the shattered house called.

—Don't tell me nothin', the old man shouted over his shoulder. —I don't need you tellin' me nothin'.

The palms of his hands felt as if they were full of hot grease. He noticed suddenly that the sun on his neck was as sharp and absolute as a knife blade. He hunched his shoulders and coiled his legs beneath him. The well seemed to dance and curtsy as he watched it, and his eyes went wet with the squinting. Then, without willing it, without even submitting to the necessity of it, he was up and running, falling and sliding behind the well's stone safety. As the shadow of the well came between him and the distant Federal earthworks, a cascade of balls chipped at the stone and chewed into the dust on either side. One ball, passing over the well, struck within inches of his shoe, and he drew his foot in quickly.

Knees pressed against his chest like those of an improbably dusty and wrinkled fetus, he thought of the boy. *Never voted, never knew him a woman, and they got him in the lines. Ain't never had a razor on his face, and they got him fightin' like a man full-growed.*

Facing the stone of the well, the old man cursed quietly, almost impassively. Thinking of the boy and of his wife dead and buried almost within the Union earthworks, he found his fingers digging into the loose powdery earth at the well's base. *They don't leave you nothin'*, he thought. *They don't leave nothin' at all.*

—You got there, old man, the second voice called from the house. —All you got to do now is come on back—if they let you get that water.

—Shut up, the old man shouted back. —I'll get it. I'll get all I want. It's my well, ain't it?

—It's all yours, the first voice chuckled across the dangerous dusty yard. —Tell them miniés about it. Show 'em your deed, Grampaw.

As he raised his hand to tilt the bucket into the well, a stab of pain shivered up his arm. A ball had glanced off the brass strapping that held the oak staves in place.

Maybe this is the place, he thought. *Maybe I'm fixin' to die out here tryin' to get water outa my own well. The woman, the boy, the house . . .*

II

They had been in the house the better part of four days. John Henry Milburne, the old man, had watched the broken Confederate division retreating back across his fields only minutes ahead of Federal cavalry and skirmishers. First, the Southern ambulances and supply wagons had rolled and yawed down the long slope from his north ridge heading east for the main road beyond Peachtree Creek. Then, before the last of the wagons had clattered through the yard, a few Confederate horsemen reined up, filled their canteens and doused their heads from the well, mounted again, and rode back over the ridge. He had seen no one at all for a time—except distant tiny squadrons of cavalrymen in gray or butternut and blue who might skirt the long rise of ground five or six hundred yards up the field, then wheel in summer dust and disappear.

Then came the artillery. A dozen guns had jammed into the yard, four or five of them turned north toward the ridge and firing rapidly for a while at nothing the old man could see. On caissons and slumped in commandeered surreys and carriages lay dozens of wounded Confederate soldiers, none of them more than twenty-five or so. As the surgeons began to work on them, handfuls of infantry, no more than ten or twelve in each group, began topping the ridge and waving wildly at the flaring cannons. The artillerymen would hold their fire until the covey of footsoldiers cleared the heights and then, even as they ran down the long dusty slope, would open fire again over their bobbing heads. A captain of artillery, coatless and hobbling back and forth behind the guns on a bandaged foot, held a large gold watch in his hand and glanced from it toward the ridge, then back at the watch again.

Milburne had watched it all from his porch. Neither the noise nor the occasional impact of enemy shells beyond the house moved him greatly. He watched the surgeons take off a man's arm near the shoulder with no better anesthetic than bad whiskey and heard his shrieks above the mounting rattle of musketry coming from across the ridge and the muted rumble of retreating wagons. In the midst of it, he had stared fascinated at the branches of a persimmon tree across the yard. As he watched, the tree's leaves began to shed as steadily as if it were instant winter in July. The artillery captain, pausing in his walk for a drink, followed the old man's gaze.

—Minié balls, old-timer. And carbine projectiles. They're lying along the ridge up there and cutting your persimmon to pieces.

Finally, late in the afternoon, the pressure had become too much.

No Federal artillery had yet managed to bring its angle of fire on the farmyard itself, but the shells were no longer falling into distant fields, and the cavalrymen they saw now were all blue-coated. The captain, grimacing and glancing one final time at his watch, shut the case, sent a corporal over to the surgeons who had not stopped working even for water, and ordered the artillery limbered.

—You'd better come with us, old man, he told Milburne.

—I'll be stayin', Milburne answered with bravado.

—It's going to be hotter than the floor of hell around here in an hour or so.

—It's hot now.

—That's so, the captain said reflectively. —All right, then we'll give you a job to do.

—I'll do it, Milburne said, still sitting on the porch, his feet hanging off the side.

—We've got four more wounded than we have places. We can't take them and we won't desert them. All you have to do is turn them over to the Federals when they come in.

—*If* they come in, Milburne answered coolly.

The captain mounted, pulled his horse around to the east, toward Atlanta. —They'll come, he said. —They'll come.

III

But they didn't come. Not that evening after Milburne had the four battered Confederates comfortable in the house. They didn't come the next morning. Instead, an hour or so after sunrise, one of the soldiers spotted the Federals digging trenches and placing artillery along the crest of the ridge.

—Marlo, the infantryman said to the one-armed man in the bed, —them sonsabitches are puttin' the box on us.

The one-armed man said nothing. His face was turned to the wall, his eyes open and unblinking while the stump of his gone arm twitched rhythmically in the rising morning heat.

—Old man, the infantryman said, turning toward the table where Milburne was patching harness, —them Yanks ain't comin' down here.

Milburne looked up from his work. —Well?

—So goddamnit we got to get movin'.

Milburne picked up a piece of stitched leather and jerked it, testing the spliced place. It held, and he put it down on the table. —If they don't come, there's nothin' to be excited about. If they do come, we can't do a thing about it. That captain of youall's took my wagon and mules. You want to walk thirteen miles into Atlanta?

The infantryman, holding his bandaged abdomen tightly, eased himself onto the bed next to the one-armed man. He stared at Milburne in exasperation.

—Old man, he said with careful patience, —the reason them bluebellies ain't comin' down's 'cause they figure we've got a bushwhack rigged for 'em. They don't know but what we've got a regiment scattered around this house and back into the fields. And just to be safe, they're fixin' to shell us for a day or so afore they send anybody down here. Does that mean anything to you?

Milburne shrugged, and pushed the harness and knife away from him. —Youall are soldiers.

The third man, a cavalry sergeant lacking both legs, with a tracery of old scars across his face, tried to sit up in the small bed.

—But we ain't ducks in a barrel, old man, he said. —If we don't get out of here, they'll blow us all to hell. We didn't go to sojerin' to get blowed up layin' on a pallet.

Milburne did not look at him. —You just as well lay back down and take the weight off them stumps. I can't move none of you, and none of you can move yourselves.

—Goddamn old man, the infantryman coughed to no one. —He ain't got no stake in this except his scaly hide, and he don't care a thing about that.

—I got a stake, Milburne told him. —I got a boy in the trenches around the city. He's in there with the militia.

The fourth of the wounded men giggled weakly. —I was milish, he croaked. —They said I wouldn't have to do nothin' but hold a gun and look scary at them Yanks.

—You damn well look scary. The infantryman laughed. The militiaman touched a blood-soaked handkerchief that covered a red vacancy where his nose had been.

—Looks like a damn highwayman, the cavalry sergeant said.

—Looks like a highwayman who don't know his work.

Touching his bandaged side, the infantryman turned back to Milburne. —You got a cellar, old man?

—There's a storm cellar.

The sergeant groaned. —Why don't we kinda crawl on down there before the Yankees save us the trip?

—You don't want to go down there yet, Milburne told him. —It's hot down there. You want to wait as long as you can. There's time.

But not much time. Because the Unions, field glasses scanning the farmyard, cavalry patrols feeling out the surrounding country, had found things too quiet. Had convinced themselves, the officers at least, that the barn, the house, the sheds and outbuildings concealed at least a battalion of infantry waiting to ambush the first elements the Federals sent down. To be safe, they began shelling.

The first bursts puffed white like enormous seedpods several hundred yards from the huddle of buildings around the farmhouse. Skillets rattled on the walls, and the infantryman cursed shortly, viciously.

—Here it comes, the cavalry sergeant groaned. —Open that damned trapdoor, old man, and give me a hand down.

Milburne rose to his feet heavily and walked out onto the porch. He squinted up the sloping field and watched shells bloom in the dusty earth like quick ephemeral flowers, each blossom closer to the house. As he watched, a tool shed disappeared in a shower of smoke and splinters.

—All right, old man, the infantryman yelled, —you seen enough?

As he went back inside to raise the trapdoor, Milburne was thinking of the boy.

IV

So the shelling went on for four days. Twice during the siege, they saw Confederate horse artillery supported by perhaps a brigade of infantry. Each time, the shelling, which had by then begun to taper off, increased to an uninterrupted cascade of explosive. On the first day, almost before they had got the legless cavalryman and the one-armed catatonic down into the cellar, a shell struck the edge of the house, sending needles of wood and metal snarling through the paneless windows, and a portion of the wall fell inward.

Pulling the trapdoor shut after him, the infantryman almost fell from the rough wood ladder. His face twisted with strain, he leaned over Milburne. —How's Marlo?

—He's quiet, the old man told him. —He just lays there with that stump quiverin' and his eyes open and empty and his lips blowed out.

—He wasn't none too good 'fore he got hit, the infantryman said heavily. —Some tromp around under all that lead without no more care than a baby. But every time Marlo heard somebody spit he'd like to climb a tree. It wasn't that piece of shell that sprung his head for him. It was too much damned noise all at the wrong time.

—Man like that, the cavalry sergeant said, —man like that dies ten or fifteen times a day. Probably thought the one that got him was another false alarm till he took a look at where that arm used to be.

The shelling went on for the rest of the day, slacking off or building up in intensity with no pattern, no purpose. But no more struck the house.

—It ain't just us, the sergeant mused. —They're bombardin' all up and down that ridge up there. They must of met some of Cochran's boys over to the right of us.

The infantryman chewed on a sliver of straw. —Reckon somebody told 'em to keep it goin' and then forgot to call 'em off?

—It happens, the sergeant told him. —They been hurt back up in the hills and Forrest kicked hell out of 'em 'fore they ever took notion to come into Georgia. They're shy.

The infantryman stretched out on the cool earth floor and closed his eyes, grinning. —Forrest'd sure as hell shy me, he said.

It went on like that for three more days. During the early hours they would climb out of the cellar quietly and take the fresh morning breeze while the Union artillerymen broke off for breakfast. They would eat dried fruit, and Milburne would cook a little salt pork and corn pone, using dry pieces of timber from the collapsed wall that would not cause smoke enough to call attention to them. At night, when the firing stopped for long periods, the old man would take canteens out to the well and fill them for the next day. It was safe enough to walk out at night, the old man reasoned: If the Unions didn't have the guts to come looking for Confederates in broad daylight before they began wasting their metal, it didn't seem likely they'd screw up enough courage to come poking around at night.

—That's good thinkin', the infantryman told him. —It's just what I'd'a thought two years ago. But I found out better. Just 'cause they're yella don't mean you can count on 'em. The time you start trustin' to that yella streak, believing they'll run if you leave 'em runnin' room, then's when they'll turn on you, get 'em a spine from somewheres, and stand off the best you got. Youall ever hear of Missionary Ridge?

So, when he went for water, the old man carried the sergeant's pistol with him. On the third night, he moved through the darkness deftly, needing no light in his own yard. Up the north field, he could see the glow of Union campfires across the ridge. The whole sky pulsed red.

As he lowered the bucket, something less than a thought, more than an image, something that had been nagging at him for hours snapped into focus. It was the mules. *My head knew they were gone, but my nerves kept wantin' to feed and water 'em,* he thought. *Like the boy. For three months I been tryin' not to call to him when I come up out of the fields, but I still got to cut it off, stop it down in my throat like brakin' a runaway wagon. Hands and muscles teach themselves after so long a time. Man could do without a head if he never cared to do a new thing.*

The bucket's splashing almost covered the other sound. But Milburne, tense and edgy after the infantryman's warning, heard muffled scuttling near the barn behind him. Turning, he saw nothing but the dark bulk of the empty barn and, beyond it, stars burning cold and solitary above the dull crimson of the encircling Union camps. He turned back and began raising the bucket. A scrap of breeze blew chill and sudden across his hunched shoulders, and he heard the scuttling again—this time from beyond the barn, nearer to the chicken roost that hungry soldiers had emptied a month before.

This time he did not turn. He lifted the bucket slowly and balanced it on the stone of the wellhead. The wind was cold on his neck, and it brought the sound to him again, clear and unmistakable. He turned his head slightly, easing the pistol out of his breeches top. As he did so, there was a flurry of movement on the near side of the roost. Something was trying to get out of his line of sight. Whatever it was moved low to the ground: either a large animal or a man running stooped over to keep from standing out against the glaring sky.

—I'm sayin' it once, Milburne called out. —Stop and come on over here. If you take another step, I'll drop you.

For a static instant, Milburne and the edgeless dark smudge across the yard seemed to study each other. *If it moves and I shoot one of my own mules come home, or maybe a big hound, them Johnnies in there'll laugh theirselves to death,* the old man thought. Suddenly, the patch of deeper black near the roost burst into frantic movement. As it tried to cut between him and the house, Milburne cocked and fired, cocked and fired again, knowing instinctively that his target was no mule, no hound.

He pushed the pistol back into his breeches, wincing at the touch of the hot barrel against his belly, and started back to the house. The infantryman was standing on the porch.

—Heard you barkin' out here. The infantryman grinned. —Thought somethin' had gotten you, old man.

—Somethin' got itself gotten, the old man said without interest. —Over to the side of the house.

The infantryman was still holding a handful of discolored rags against the long wound across his lower ribs. He shifted the dirty bundle slightly, his eyes tightening at the corners when dried blood pulled flesh with it. —You done killed a hog, he told Milburne.

—No, the old man said. —It wasn't no hog. Ain't been no loose hogs in this county since youall come backing over Peachtree Creek. Not even the ghost of a hog.

—Well, the infantryman said, rising carefully, still pressing the unclean rags against his side, —gimme that pistol. If you ain't got no curiosity, I do.

Milburne started into the blasted house with the water. The infantryman called after him: —You better get some of that water to boilin', old man.

—What?

—Got to steep this hog of yours.

But it was no hog. As Milburne stood looking at the shattered rear of his house, at the broken joists and splintered planking scattered over the floor and lying in the yard beyond the jagged hole, he heard the infantryman call out: —Old man.

Milburne paid no attention. He was thinking of the work it would take to put the place back together. He couldn't use jokes.

—Old man, goddamnit, I need a hand out here.

Milburne was thinking of the timber in the north corner of his land, just over the brow of the bridge. There was a heavy stand of pine there, some of it virgin, most of it tall and straight. If he could get it to Pratt's mill and back, if any—even one—of the mules were returned, or escaped and managed to find its way home, he could put things in shape. Then he thought of the Federals camped across his bridge. *There won't be a stick left,* he thought. *Not a branch.* He remembered how the Confederates, despite orders, despite their officers' sharp eyes, had broken up fencing, torn down outhouses, and stripped woodpiles for firewood and to build little sheds topped with tenting to keep off the sun, the dew and the short torrential bursts of summer rain. *If this bunch don't chew it up,* he thought, *the next ones is sure to. Or the ones after them.*

—Old man.

Milburne walked back across the porch and around the house to join the infantryman.

—I don't reckon we'll have to scald this'un, the infantryman said. They stood looking down at the Union trooper lying sprawled on his face in the dark shadow of the house. The infantryman knelt beside him and held his burning pine knot close while Milburne turned him over.

He was possibly eighteen, and his yellow hair was long and matted with dirt.

—Hell, ain't a mark on him 'cept for that hole in his leg. Sure is brittle for sojerin'.

Milburne tore away the dark blue pants leg. The ball had struck just below the hip and ranged forward and outward a few inches below the crotch. The bleeding was slow and undramatic. —Like to caught an artery, Milburne mused. —No wonder it put his lights out. Boy can't take what a full-grown man can take.

The infantryman spat into the dust and took one leg of the boy, while Milburne caught him under the arms and started carrying him around to the porch.

—They damn near blew my ribs loose from my chestbone, the infantryman complained. —I never went out for a blink.

They lay the boy down near the trapdoor. —I seen men hurt worse than you doin' a full day's march or plowin' from can't see to can't see. You got a deep scratch. This here boy's got his legbone broke all to pieces, and he's been bleedin' like that hog you thought he was.

—I didn't shoot him, the infantryman said sullenly.

—Don't I know that? the old man snapped at him. —Don't I know that?

V

In the cellar, the militiaman was wide awake, his small bright eyes reflecting the uneven rays of the pine knot torch.

—Heard all that ruckus, he whispered hoarsely, —an' I thought they was here.

—Shut up, the cavalry sergeant said without heat. —What'd youall bring us?

—Leave it alone, the infantryman cautioned him, grinning. —You can't eat it.

Marlo, the one-armed speechless one, still lay where he had been placed, his bandaged stump directing some invisible orchestra. The militiaman crawled past him to look at what Milburne and the infantryman had brought.

—Union?

—It ain't a sack of turnips, the infantryman told him.

—Why'd youall have to bring him down here? Ain't the air bad enough without youall got to bring in a Union?

—Shut up, the legless sergeant told him again. —Was he by hisself?

—He's all there was.

—I never knowed the Yanks to use no children before, the sergeant mused.

Milburne was tightening an old shirt hem high on the boy's leg.
—When you get caught short, you use what you got. What they got is this.

—Bounty jumpin' and bummers kinda cut down them odds of theirs, the infantryman noted wryly.

—Reckon he come to save the Union? the militiaman asked.

—He come because he heard it was brave and there was a lot of flags and bugles. Because a trooper don't have to slog through the mud, the sergeant said sadly.

—More like he heard you could burn and kill and get paid for it, the militiaman sneered.

—That'd be a powerful draw for a boy. The infantryman laughed.
—Seems like they ought to of told him we'd shoot back.

—Easy to see you ain't no recruiter, the militiaman wheezed good-humoredly.

At dawn the Federal artillery began in earnest again. This time, instead of the light and unconcentrated fire that had swept the fields, the woods, and the farmyard impartially, the shells began to close in on the house itself. The near hits forced clouds of dust up off the cellar floor, and Marlo's stump thrummed rapidly in time to the endless thunder of the guns. The others sat or lay against the cool dirt walls, eyes white and large in the rounds of their dark faces.

—They put one in your barn, old man, the sergeant called to Milburne above the roar outside.

—That's what your Union brought with him, the militiaman grumbled. —Him not comin' back brought us all this misery.

—If he'd gone back, it'd be infantry instead of shells, the sergeant said. —Why don't you shut up?

—But it's all right, the militiaman went on, —we ain't gonna be hurt. I ain't gonna get a scratch. I got it on the word of a Confederate officer and gentl . . .

Before he could finish, the dirt walls of the cellar seemed to collapse inward as if they were made of dusty rubber. Jars and gourds and some old cracked plates spiraled off the long plank shelves, some breaking, but most simply bouncing off the dirt floor and rolling into corners. The concussion laid Milburne and the rest on their faces, and chunks of earth fell from the shuddering walls. As the walls settled back into place, and the cloud of dust and particles of damper dirt fell away, a shard of bright sunlight sliced down into the cellar and lay across the face of the unconscious Union soldier. They raised their heads slowly, the drop and rumble of smashed timbers still echoing and dying in their ears.

—Well, the sergeant said in the sudden quiet, —they finally got around to it. They done blown your house all to hell.

—Figger that floorin' is gonna hold? the militiaman asked.

—It's inch and three-quarters milled pine, Milburne said. —It'll hold.

—That chink the sun found don't look like holdin', the infantry-man said without concern.

—Just knocked the dirt out of it, Milburne told him. —Them planks never was flush. My boy helped me put in that floor when he was five or six. He left a couple places wide.

Milburne touched the Union soldier's forehead. —Let me have a cup of that water, he said to the infantryman.

The infantryman tilted the last of the canteens and poured what was left into a tin cup. —That's it, he told Milburne. —All that shootin' last night, and you come back with two empties and one three-quarters full.

—Ain't even enough to pour over my stumps, the sergeant said in a hurt voice.

—Marlo's gonna need some, the infantryman mused.

Milburne blushed beneath his white scattering of whiskers. —I thought I had 'em full 'fore he ever showed up.

The infantryman shrugged and smiled. —Man not used to all this is bound to lose hisself some. I knew a feller up around Slaughter Creek who fought all afternoon the first day he was in the line. Thought he'd shot him twenty or thirty Yankees, and then he found out he hadn't fired a shot. Had paper cartridges jammed into his rifle all the way up to the muzzle. Kept loadin' and pullin' the trigger without puttin' no cap on.

Milburne was still red. He finished bathing the boy's forehead. —I'll go get some water, he said, without looking at them.

—With them sonsabitches flingin' shells all over creation? the militiaman asked.

Milburne eased his arm under the boy's head, raised him a little and offered him the rest of the water. The Federal took it without opening his eyes. —They ain't likely to make too much of one man goin' for water.

The infantryman shrugged again without smiling and glanced at the sergeant. —Why don't you tell him?

The sergeant shifted his partial legs uncomfortably, still looking at the empty canteens. —Old man, he said, —they'll let go a battery at you sure as hell has an iron floor. They might take you for a scout or a courier, or maybe they're just bored or sore 'cause this place has been holdin' 'em up for three days. But any way you cut it, you ain't gonna prance out there and get water and wave at 'em and come on back in. You can count on it.

Milburne was inspecting the bandage on the boy's leg.

—Well, he said. —Maybe I better not try.

—Well, the sergeant echoed him, his voice trailing off into silence.

—I need that water, old man, the militiaman said petulantly, his voice rising. —Marlo needs it real bad. You done give the last we had to that Union sonofabitch. Least you can . . .

—Shut your mouth, the infantryman said shortly, —and keep it shut. Onliest thing you're good for is to toss outa here and draw fire. Gimme them canteens, old man. I'll run 'em on out there and see what kinda well you got.

—Stay put, Milburne told him. —I ain't that old. Anyhow, them Unions' fingers ain't no quicker than my legs.

—Lord God, old man, the sergeant put in, —you don't need no fast finger when you're firin' twenty-pound shell or canister.

—We'll see, Milburne said, letting the Union soldier down gently and reaching for the empty canteens.

VI

He saw. He was seeing now as he lay behind the stone barrier of the well and rubbed his arm and hand still throbbing from the ricochet that had glanced off the brass band of the bucket.

—I might as well of taken that one through the hand, he said to himself. —Feels like the fingers are gone.

He raised his uninjured hand cautiously and pushed the bucket over into the well. The rope played out rapidly. The ungreased wooden spindle squealed. From the ridge, two or three more shots sounded, as balls puffed in the dust and skittered past him into the dry lifeless grass beyond the yard.

—They ain't thought of them damned siege guns yet, the infantryman called out cheerfully. —Wait'll they drop one of them big'uns right down the well next to you.

As his voice stopped, another rifleball smashed into the spindle of the well, scattering slivers of wood over the old man's bare head. As instinct flattened him out, he smelled the hot bland odor of his own earth beneath him. There was no strength or promise in the smell of the dust. *On my own place,* he thought. *They've made the whole country a slaughterhouse, and now they're gonna kill me in my own yard for tryin' to draw water out of my own well.*

—You ain't hit, old man, the militiaman croaked. —They're just playin' with you. Get us that water an' quit layin' around.

Milburne sat up slowly and exposed himself just enough to catch hold of the well rope. There was no way to use the crank without being shot, and anyhow the spindle was probably broken and jammed. But he could pull on the rope itself and, tilting the bucket, spilling some of the water, manage to drag it over the wellhead into the safety of his stone shield.

As he began tugging on the rope, twisting each coil around his forearm between elbow and hand in order to keep it taut, he thought he heard something behind: horse's hooves at a distance—or a man running close by. But by then the bucket was at the top of the well, and he had left the pistol inside anyhow. He put the sound out of his mind and rose carefully to his knees in order to pull the bucket out of the well.

But even as he rose, the firing began again, began fiercely and determinedly, as if the Yankee riflemen, devils for certain, had some preknowledge of the exact instant of his rising. A crackling hoard of bullets pounded against the stone of the well's far side and chewed through the wooden uprights that supported the spindle. Milburne fell backward, bucket in his arms and the water in it splashing over him and turning the dust beneath him into mud. And even as he fell, fell helpless, sodden and caught in the uncontrolled coils of rope, even as the relief of feeling no bullets in his flesh met the counterpoise of fear that his fall had carried him beyond the protection of the wellhead, he realized that hands on his shoulders were pushing him back toward the well.

—Yankee, he howled. —Dirty butcherin' . . . shoot . . . you . . . in the house . . . shoot . . .

But the hands were doing him no harm, and no shot came from the blasted house. Still cowering, he heard a voice close beside him, above the fading distant prattle of riflefire. —Pa . . . Pa . . . don't be scared . . . Pa. . . .

The old man's shoulders went round, and the starchy power of fear flooded out of him. —When we get in out of this, he coughed, —I'm gonna whup you into puddin'.

—Pa, the boy was saying. He lay outstretched beside his father, his clothing neither blue nor gray nor colored at all, but the neutral shade of dust itself, and his teeth white against a fringe of skimpy beard. —Pa, I didn't mean to get 'em goin'. I didn't even know they was . . .

—Never you mind, his father told him, still trying to steady himself, —just stay down. I still got water to draw.

When they finally made a clumsy dash for the house, canteens swinging and bouncing about their hips, only a shot or two came from the Union lines. Inside, the infantryman and the militiaman squatted in the ruins of the kitchen, safe from stray shots because of the collapsed roof.

—Told you the old bastard'd make it. The infantryman grinned. —Gimme that five dollars.

The militiaman offered him a torn, stained note. —It's a Georgia fiver, he apologized. —But when youall get mad and run Sherman to hell back on Tennessee, it'll be good as gold.

Milburne and the boy slid down beside them, next to the open trapdoor. The militiaman grabbed one of the canteens and began to drink, part of the water cresting over his chin and running down his neck, cutting white channels through thick dirt there. The infantryman glanced at the boy. —Army or corn pone sojer?

Milburne's son narrowed his eyes and studied the other's dirty bandage. —I been in Johnston's army—I mean Hood's—thirteen weeks yesterday, and I don't need no lip from you, neither.

The infantryman smiled kindly and turned to Milburne. —This your boy?

—What's left of him. Looks like they given up feedin' the army.

—Never did feed, the militiaman put in. —Didn't feed the earliest day I even seen 'em. Don't pay, neither.

The boy's mouth whitened beneath his scrap of beard. —Maybe you oughta go see if you can't get a better deal outa them bummers over the ridge. I'd be proud to see you run on up there.

—Was he as mean as all that when you turned him loose, old man? the infantryman drawled.

—Son knows his rights, Milburne said grimly. —If he's old enough to get shot, he's old enough to get respect.

The infantryman looked at the sullen boy whose face, beard or not, was still pale and youthful beneath the dirt. —That he is, he said. —That he is.

They went below, and Milburne and the infantryman passed water around. They talked about the shelling and what it would take to put the house and field to rights again. Milburne mentioned the trees beyond the ridge.

—I wouldn't count none on 'em, the sergeant told him. —If youall find branches enough to fire a pot of coffee, you'll be lucky.

The boy laughed harshly. —I reckon that's so. I seen officers hit men with the flats of their swords for it, and I even seen one captain swear to Almighty God he'd kill the next man he saw at them fences. But the next morning there wasn't a snip of fence left and that captain had done swore hisself to a lie.

The sun stood high above the house, and they brought the sergeant and Marlo upstairs out of the heat. While Milburne's son and the militiaman boiled beans and some fatback the boy had brought with him, the old man and the infantryman brought up the Federal, still unconscious, and laid him near Marlo, under the canted broken roof. There was no rifle or artillery fire at all now, and the lack of it was spooking the infantryman.

—They may be gettin' up their nerve, he whispered to the old man. —Keep an eye on that ridge and you're gonna see you a handful of skirmishers in a little while.

—It was bad, the boy was telling the sergeant and the militiaman. —They kept pushin' and pushin', and every time they come on, we'd kill us a hundred or so, but it wasn't no stoppin' 'em. Couple of days ago, they got it in their heads they was comin' right on through and across the Peachtree whether we moved out or not. And it was awful bad. When they wasn't suicidin' their infantry, they had them damned big guns goin' way off behind 'em. You couldn't talk; you couldn't sleep. You couldn't hardly die for the noise and the smoke. Then, that night, somebody back in town said we'd got to pull on back 'cause they had us ten to one. Only we never heard in my company. We was way up ahead in some holes and gullies. One minute we'd be goin' after 'em and the next minute we'd be fallin' back. We never knowed whether we was winnin' or losin'.

—You was losin', the infantryman put in. —Ain't no doubt when you're winnin'. When you got 'em on the hip, the damned cavalry comes up so's to take the credit, and then you know.

The boy paid no attention to him. He was no longer talking to any of them, was talking rather past them, beyond them as if he were trying to deliver a report to some infinite superior who would be able to understand not only the action and the dispositions, but his own feelings: his fear, his anger, and the rightness of what he had done.

—So me and this fella named Lonnie out of Delhi, Louisiana, we had us this hole one of them big guns had dug. There was plenty other ones there toward four o'clock, but most of 'em was back maybe forty or fifty yards in this long gully where it catches water in the winter and spring but stays dry all the late summer. And it got dark, and them orders for pullin' back come up as far as the gully, and they started on back without a sonofabitch there either thinkin' or carin' about us up to the front of 'em.

—And so we never heard or never knew they was movin' back. Maybe eight or ten of us up in them craters. Till it was plumb dark, and we started hearin' a whole lot of rumblin', and pretty soon here come the whole damn Yankee army with artillery and wagons and a few cavalry and no skirmishers at all. They started into that field and on across like there wasn't a Confederate within eighty miles.

—And Lonnie was edgy already, and he'd draw a bead on some fella ridin' a caisson or whippin' a team, or he'd hunch down in the hole and mumble to hisself about the Lord God of Hosts.

—Then about ten fellas on real fine horses come ridin' past the artillery and wagons. One great big heavyset fella was out ahead of the others and he was talkin' loud and givin' orders and sayin' how the Rebs was headed for the Atlantic and they'd be lucky to swim for the Indies. And when he was about twenty or thirty yards off, ole Lonnie made up his mind. He drew down on this big fella and put a ball right through his head. It was dark, but there was a moon risin', and you could see it all like it was on a stage. And that bigmouthed one howled out somethin' and fell off his horse like he'd been hit with an ax.

—Then they come after us. What cavalry they had, and some infantry, and even some of them artillery with trace chains and pistols. It wasn't no use. We used our guns and knives, and we bit and kicked, but they got me and Lonnie and most of the other fellas who was caught up in it 'cause they didn't know how to pull out. So they trussed us up like fryin' hens and carted us back to where the officers was hangin' out.

—So this Yankee captain starts telling us it's a court-martial trial and we're gorillas outa uniform and we done bushwhacked his men and killed a United States brigadier general. And ole Lonnie whistled and says, "I figured that loudmouthed sonofabitch was somethin' big. Youall dead sure it wasn't Uncle Abe?" And this Yankee says, "Don't worry, you're gonna pay for it." And Lonnie said, "We ain't no gorillas or whatever. We're Confederate sojers, Hood's army, Clifford's brigade." And the Yankee says, "Talk's cheap, but ain't one of youall got on a uniform. A sojer wears a uniform, and youall ain't got no uniforms, so you ain't sojers. That makes youall gorillas, and gorillas hang."

The boy paused and licked his lips. The others, except for Marlo and the unconscious Federal, sat listening silently. His eyes snapped back into focus, and the boy looked at his father.

—And, Poppa, they started in to hang the whole lot of us. They got the rest of 'em up on ammunition crates, and they was workin' on me and Lonnie when a whole troop of our cavalry come ridin' into the clearin', and they was shootin' at everythin' that moved. And Lonnie and me kicked loose from the fellas holdin' us and started runnin', but my hands was tied and I stumbled into some bushes. And I heard the Yankee captain yell, "Kick them crates over. Hang them bastards 'fore the Rebs cuts 'em down."

—And they did. They swung every damn one except me and Lonnie, and one of 'em drew down on Lonnie and shot him in the back just 'fore a Confederate trooper cut his head off for him.

—So it was over. And the Yankees had pulled out and took their dead brigadier with 'em, and the cavalry boys was tryin' to help Lonnie, and one of 'em found me and cut me loose, and some others was cuttin' down them poor fellas who got hung. And I rubbed my face where it was all scratched and went over to see Lonnie.

—He was done for. The Yankee had put one right where his suspenders cross. His lungs was gone, and he took hold of my hand. He looked up at that Virginia cavalry lootenant. "Boys," he said, "it was a good ride an' youall done your best." Then he turned to me. He says, "Hoss, you remember this. Don't you ever forget none of it. Don't never forget it. Tell your childrun. Innocent . . . men."

—And he died.

—And I sat down on the ground and cried. Because it was over and I could still feel the air in my body, because I knew it wasn't over and that tomorrow I'd be back in it again. Because, maybe because I couldn't even remember a time when I wasn't in it. I don't know. But while I was gettin' it out and splashin' it all over the ground, one of them cavalry troopers come up behind me.

—I got something for you, he said. And when I turned around, he had that Yankee captain with his uniform all mussed, and his face scratched worse than mine, and his eyes the size of ripe persimmons and near the same color.

—They know we ain't got no uniforms, the sergeant said abstractedly. —Where'd we get any uniforms?

—What'd you do? the militiaman asked the boy breathlessly.

The boy shook his head, trying to stifle a grin. —Never mind what I did. You just better know he ain't gonna hang you.

Milburne looked up. —You killed him?

The boy was still talking. —So they rode me back to Atlanta, and I figured I had me some time comin', so I come on out here.

—Boy, Milburne rasped. —I asked you a question.

—Pa?

—Did you kill that man? Did you kill him when they brung him back a prisoner?

His son flushed, and the grin broke through. —I reckon I killed hell out of him, Pa.

The old man stood up slowly, as if the effort cost him pain. He threaded his way through fallen lumber to the porch and sat on the edge of it farthest from the ridge. *They done blown the house down around my ears, and now they got the boy killin' like it was all he ever knew. Maybe there ain't nothin' left to build up again.* As he sat looking out into the dusty yard, a ball tore into the post next to him, and another skipped across the yard nearby. He fell backward, trying to determine where the fire had come from. *Not from the ridge. They've started down,* he thought. *Maybe it won't never stop. Maybe they'll camp up there in my pasture forever and the boy will go out and catch one and tie him up and shoot him every morning and they'll bushwhack him every night. And I'll build the house back on a Monday and they'll blow it to hell again every Saturday.*

He began crawling back along the porch and on into the house. As he pushed fallen timbers aside on his way back to the sheltered kitchen, he could hear the boy's voice loud and angry, filled with bitterness: —Where'd he come from's what I want to know.

—Come sneakin' around while your old man was gettin' water.

—Well, why didn't youall finish him off? the boy asked accusingly.

The militiaman shrugged his shoulders and started down the ladder into the cellar. —I'm just a butcher, he said. —I ain't even got no business in all this.

—*You* knew what to do, the boy barked at the infantryman.

—No, boy, the infantryman answered lazily, —I ain't no butcher. I didn't know a thing in the world to do.

The boy's face was blood-red and warped into the ugly curve of a tragic mask, its empty eyes awash in tears. —You ought to have put your pistol right down against the head and pulled the trigger a coupla times—just like he'd of done us.

The infantryman broke a splinter off a shattered wallboard and probed between his teeth with it. —Boy, I leave that kinda thing with the folks over to Andersonville.

—Don't you care about them friends of mine?

—I never heard you say they was friends except for the one. I heard you say they was just fellas that got left.

—Lonnie was my friend, the boy almost shouted.

—And all they did was shoot him when he run. Boy, we all been shootin' people when they was runnin'.

The boy looked from the infantryman to the sergeant. —Ain't neither one of youall gonna do for this Yankee sonofabitch?

Milburne came into the kitchen in time to see the boy standing over the unconscious Federal. The Union soldier's face, misted with a light beard, tinctured with the high color of fever, looked like that of a healthy child in the shadow of the broken roof. Above him, the boy stood in his colorless rags pointing angrily at the others.

—Boy, why don't you sit down 'fore I crawl over there and knock you down? the legless cavalry sergeant said resignedly.

The old man, coming up behind, caught hold of his son's shoulder. —I never raised you to . . .

Without turning to face his father, the boy jerked free, knelt quickly, and pulled the sergeant's pistol from its holster slung across the leg of an upended table.

—You didn't raise me to nurse no snake, he spat at his father. —I swore to God I'd kill 'em as long as I lived, and I ain't gonna break that swear.

The cavalry sergeant threw himself forward, grabbing clumsily for the boy's legs. Milburne and the infantryman moved together, but even as they caught hold of him, the boy was firing into the unmoving body of the Union soldier, firing once unhindered, cocking the piece in a flare of motion and firing again as the combined weight of his father and the infantryman dragged him down.

As the sound of the shots boomed and scattered across the long rise of dusty pasture up to the ridge, Milburne and the others heard a few answering shots pop weakly, distantly, from the Union lines. The cavalry sergeant scuttled over to the side of the Yankee trooper as Milburne and the infantryman dragged the boy away from him.

—Well, the sergeant said tonelessly, —he got himself a Federal.

—Dead? the infantryman asked almost casually.

—Dead as two in the heart can make you, the sergeant told him.

The militiaman's head had popped up through the trapdoor as they struggled with the boy. He giggled. —No harm done. He was eat up with fever anyhow and we ain't got no medicine. Anyhow, he'd as soon of shot us down as looked at us. Ain't no harm done.

—Shut up, the sergeant said, —before I stretch you out beside him. That really wouldn't be no harm done.

He pulled himself painfully back toward the thin pallet of blankets Milburne had prepared for him. As he moved, he left a dribble of dark stains behind him on the uneven wood floor.

—Your stumps leakin' again? the infantryman asked him.

—No, the sergeant told him. —It's off the Federal.

The infantryman, still holding Milburne's son by the soiled collar of his shirt, slipped the pistol back into its holster. Then he jerked the boy into sitting position. —I ought to break the barrel of that damned pistol across your nose, he said without passion. —I ought to tie you to that dead Union and then let the both of you lie out back till he comes apart, meat from bones.

Milburne's son looked past the infantryman, sullen and unashamed. —I reckon you never killed one of 'em, he sneered. —I reckon maybe you just can't stand blood. Killin' 'em awake or asleep, out cold or runnin', it don't make me no difference at all. I ain't scared of killin' 'em, and I'll kill you . . .

This time, the report of the pistol broke the afternoon to pieces. Before, as they had struggled with the boy, the shots had been expected, had been somehow inevitable even from the moment of his coming. But this shot sent the militiaman tumbling backward down into the cellar, brought the sergeant up, his face white and drawn in the growing shadows of afternoon, turned the infantryman toward Milburne as the boy under his hands jerked like a puppet badly handled.

—You . . . The infantryman's eyes were wide with disbelief. —This ain't no way . . .

And Milburne's son sprawled against the overturned table, his eyes losing focus, a growing stream of bright blood coursing down his chin, sopping into his shirt, spattering on the floor near the dead trooper's boot. —Poppa.

The old man leaned across his son to replace the pistol in its holster once more. He did not look at the boy, did not allow—or force—himself to look at the smoldering powder-burned hole in the boy's back.

The infantryman was standing now, looking down at both of them, watching the rivulet of blood at the boy's mouth crest, ebb, and finally stop altogether.

—Po . . . p . . . pa.

—Why? the infantryman heard himself saying. —You can't bring nothin' back.

—Nor keep nothin' neither, Milburne whispered slowly, his hands, almost free agents, reaching toward the slumped body of his son.

—What the hell was . . . ? the militiaman asked as his head rose from below again.

—Shut up, the sergeant said wearily, without bothering to look at him.

—Marlo's comin' around. I reckon he's comin' out of it, the militiaman said, taking it all in, staring at the others, staring at the second body.

The old man stood up uncertainly, his legs trembling under him with the outsize grotesque motions of a clown seeking laughter. He moved beyond the shadow, heedless of the lines on the ridge, out into the still bright, still merciless sun.

—Let me . . . the infantryman began.

—Nothin', the old man said, waving him away. —I want to sit down. I need to sit down. I never killed a man before.

That autumn, rain began early and fell for days on end with the terrible regularity of a mourner's tears. It fell on blackened fields where there had been no harvest; it gathered in shivering pools along the ruts and sloughs of deserted roads. It boiled down long grassless slopes and into raw ditches filled with dissolving rifles and shattered cannon. It leached indifferently into shallow unmarked graves strewn across the land like sites of awful treasure, ran finally into sluggish streams that crept through stripped forests and empty towns and lost themselves in rivers flowing nowhere. Overhead, the sky was relentless gray strung across unleafed branches of scarred trees. Where there had been farms, only charred brick chimneys stood above rusting stoves, twisted skeletal bedsteads, and acres of cold ash. Where the armies had battered one another, the vacant land, tortured into union, stretched like a rotten blanket over a forgotten corpse. It would be that way for a long, long time.

Reunion

Gettysburg: 1913

I

All the way up from Milledgeville it had rained off and on. It was early July, and when the rain stopped and the sun came out, you could see steam rising from the rutted roads in southern Virginia. But by the time the train crossed into Pennsylvania, there was little sun, water stood in the roads, and there was no steam.

There were just three of us: Grandfather, my brother Bedford who was nine, and me. I was almost fifteen. It was the first trip out of Georgia for Bedford and me, and the first time out of the South for anybody in the family in a long time. Grandfather had been North one time before, but it had not been on a train, and he had been only a few years older than me then.

—I don't see how he sleeps like that, Bedford whispered to me.

—When you get old, you sleep more, I told him. —It doesn't matter where you are. You could sleep for fifty years, I guess.

Bedford looked out the coach window and squirmed in his seat. He had wanted to come but he had wanted to stay home, too. It was something to take a train trip all the way to Pennsylvania, but at home the fishing was reaching its peak, the woods were full of birds, and the sun had warmed the water until it felt like part of your skin when you were swimming in it.

—How much longer? Bedford asked.

—Not long, my grandfather said from the seat opposite. He did not open his eyes or push his hat back from his face.

—Thought you was still asleep, Grampaw, Bedford said.

—I been some. It comes and goes. You sleep more at my age, he said without smiling.

He was sixty-five years old that summer, and his face was brown and spotted with little discolorations, each one smaller than a dime. His eyebrows were thick and still black, and they made his wrinkled face seem fierce and somehow young under a scattering of pure-white hair that was beginning to show some pink scalp through it. The backs of his hands were brown as his face and neck, and tendons showed through the skin almost as if he held a powerful light cupped in each palm.

Under his shirt there were three dead-white depressions in his chest. Each one was the size of a quarter, and they were clustered together along his ribs on the right side. In back there were two white puckered gatherings of flesh, and now we were going back to see the place where he had got the marks on his chest and back.

—See those rises, my grandfather said, pointing out the train window. He had opened his eyes. They were large and still bright blue like my father's. —Over there. Those humps.

—Sure, Bedford said. —If it snowed, you could use a sled on 'em.

—No, Grandfather said. —They're too rocky for that. They're called the Round Tops. Little Round Top and Big Round Top.

—They look like they'd be fun to climb, I said. Then I remembered and bit my lip. But my grandfather smiled.

—They might be. If it was a cool day and nobody minded you climbing.

Then we saw the station up ahead at the end of a long curve of track. All around the edges of the station there was red, white, and blue bunting and a United States flag above the station. There was a painted sign that read WELCOME VETERANS with roughly drawn cannon and canteens and bayoneted rifles around the border of it. Underneath the eaves of the station on our side, there was a little wooden plaque hanging down. It said GETTYSBURG.

II

They registered Grandfather and gave him a kind of medal to wear that said he was a veteran who had fought there and what his rank and regiment had been.

—I expect I'll be a rarity, he said.

—What do you mean, Grampaw? Bedford asked him.

—A private soldier. You can't hardly find a private any more. Seems only officers survived.

—That doesn't make any sense, I said. —The officers would have been older to start with.

But he was right. There were all kinds of captains and majors and even a few brigadier generals. My grandfather said the promoting hadn't ended yet, either.

The people in town were nice, mostly. Their voices were funny and harsh, and they moved fast as if they were all after something about to get away from them, and they seemed to be real careful not to say anything that would slight the Southern soldiers. With the Union veterans it was different. They acted as if everybody had been in the same army, fighting for the same thing. We met a man who had been with Sickles's staff.

—It's cooler now, he said to Grandfather. —It's a lot cooler.

—The sun's older, Grandfather said. —We can use all the warmth we can get.

The Union man laughed. —I thought we'd given each other enough heat those three days to last out the rest of all our lives.

—I expect we feel warmer than the ones who paid to stay home or hid under the chicken house when the conscription officer came by.

—That's so, the Union man said. —That's so. Who are these fine boys?

—These are my grandsons. Meet Captain McCleoud. Robert and Bedford.

—I expect the Robert is Robert Edward, the captain said, smiling.

—Yes, sir, I said.

—There wasn't a better name on either side. If I had a grandson, I just might have risked it and named him the same.

Bedford kept looking at the captain with an expression on his face like the one you see on a whiteface calf when you come up on it suddenly.

—You're an honest-to-God Yankee?

—Bedford, Grandfather said mildly, —watch what you say to the gentleman.

—I take that title as an honor, Captain McCleoud said, still smiling.

—I expect so, Grandfather said. —It's just that I'm not sure the boy intended it that way.

During all that, Bedford was still staring at the captain's rusty blue uniform with its gold shoulder bars and the wide-brimmed black hat. One side of the brim was turned up against the crown and pinned there.

—I never seen a Yankee before, Bedford said. —Grammaw said the last ones was run out of Georgia a long time ago after the Drunkard was gone from the White House. Grammaw said . . .

—Hush, boy, Grandfather told Bedford. His smile was gone, and I could see the cords in his neck tightening. —Just hush.

Grandfather never raised his voice to either of us, and Bedford was beginning to snuffle because of the tone of voice Grandfather had used.

—I'm sorry for that, he said to the Union captain. —My missus never took to the outcome of the war or what followed it. In her latter days, she talked a lot to the boys. She's over it now, I reckon.

The captain didn't say anything. He ruffled Bedford's hair, bowed to me, and shook hands with Grandfather. —I know. I suppose it will be a while yet.

—I expect, Grandfather said.

After signing up at the encampment office and drinking lemonade, we walked around some. It was hot with the sun standing high above us, and on all sides, as far as we could see, were long rows of army tents set up in orderly streets. In one corner of the tent city, we found the place reserved for us. It had four cots in it, and Bedford and I put the pallets we had brought to sleep on under one of the cots.

—I expected they'd be here, Grandfather said. —They said the second of July for sure.

—Grampaw, Bedford said, —how come you didn't wear no uniform up here like that Yankee captain? How come you ain't ever showed us your uniform?

—I had a uniform in 1862, he said smiling softly. —It was blue. Almost as blue as the captain's.

—Lord, Grampaw, you weren't a Yankee.

—No. It was a militia uniform. It was all we had, and when they mustered us into the regular army, we went on wearing it until it wore out. Then we wore whatever we could get hold of.

—I wouldn't have fought if they didn't give me a uniform, Bedford said.

—Yes, you would, Grandfather said. —If you had to fight, it wouldn't matter what you had to wear.

—Who are we waiting for? I asked him.

—A couple of old friends. They were in Armistead's brigade with me. They were here before.

That afternoon and evening there were speeches welcoming everybody, and a mayor or governor said that the war had been like a great burning sword that had cauterized the soul of America, and from much wrong, much good had come, and that now, North and South, we were united under one flag.

—Huh, Bedford said afterward as we walked in the dark down the torchlit tent city streets. —That's all he knows. I reckon Grammaw could tell him something.

—Your grandmother is dead, Grandfather said evenly. —She remembered too much. Sometimes a good memory does you no service.

—How can you help remembering? I asked him. —You've got holes in you to help if you were to start forgetting.

—Holes, Grandfather said. —Maybe I fell onto your great-grand-father's picket fence when I was courting your grandmother.

—Maybe not, too, Bedford said darkly. —Maybe it was some of these bastards . . .

—All right, Grandfather said shortly. —Watch your tongue, boy. I remember what your mother told you about coarse talk.

—I don't give a hoot in hell for their flag, Bedford said defiantly.

—Grammaw used to say the red in it was Southern blood. That the Union got fat eating its own people when they tried to be free.

We reached our tent and went inside. Bedford lighted a kerosene lantern and hung it on the main pole.

—Your grandmother said a lot, Grandfather said wearily. —But her text was always the same.

—But . . . I began.

—Do you want to carry the graves home from here with you? Do you want to carry the graves inside the house and set them up there?

—What're you talking about, Grampaw? Bedford asked him.

—This is just a celebration, he said, sitting down heavily on his cot. —It's something for a lot of old men who want to remember that they were once young and brave and maybe held the fate of their nation in their hands. They want to remember that they fought well and did all they could, whether they did or not. The other people just want to look at them like they'd read a history book or look at a painting of Waterloo. It doesn't mean anything anymore.

—If it doesn't mean anything anymore, why'd you come back up here? Bedford asked cagily.

Grandfather pulled off his trousers and carefully swung his legs up onto the cot. —If it meant anything, he said, —I don't reckon I could have stood to come. It's like a picture in my mind, like pho-tographs in one of those little books Charlie Stokes has—the kind you riffle through and it looks like the pictures move. I see men and horses and cannon, and I see bursts of dark smoke in the air and on the field, and I see men falling. But I can't feel the sun on my back or feel the fear in my belly when we started out. I know my mouth was dry. It was so dry I couldn't move my tongue. And my feet were cut and blistered and wrapped up in pieces of tent cloth.

Grandfather touched the slanting side of the tent with his fingers. —But I can't feel the pain of the grass stubble underfoot. All I can feel is sorry for that boy. I feel sorry he had to get himself hurt and had to hurt in his turn. I guess I feel sorry for all of them, but it doesn't mean anything anymore. I can't get hold of the heat and the sweat. I can't hope for the Confederacy; I can't hate and respect that goat-whiskered terrible proud Jeff Davis anymore. All of it seems like a picture I saw once. How much can you care about a picture?

—Grammaw cared, Bedford said accusingly.

Grandfather's eyes were closed, and the soft buttery light of the kerosene lantern played across his face in profile. You could see how the flesh of the jaw and around the chin had melted away and left the sharp outline of the bone. The creases around his eyes and on his forehead and cheeks stood out like elevation markings on a map.

—Your grandmother wasn't here, Bedford. Her imagination wasn't limited by having been subjected to the facts. I expect she was making up for not having been here. I think she believed had she been here, it might have been different. She had to keep it going until she felt she'd done her duty. But death caught her short.

I almost blushed and I was glad he had his eyes shut. Bedford looked at me, not understanding. But I understood. Because I had felt the way he said Grandmother must have felt. I could remember, even when I was younger than Bedford, how I had felt when Grandfather took off his shirt to chop firewood or for a bath. I would see how thin and flat his chest was, and the three milky depressions through his ribs and the ugly drawn-up little mouths in his back, and I would feel a funny cold thing move from my tailbone up into my scalp. I knew when he said it that what I had felt was shame just as if I had been alive then, in the brigade, and had run, or been a cook or a staff officer and had stayed behind.

—All I remember, my grandfather was saying, —is a boy just a little older than Robert running across that road filled with fear and thirst and barely aware of his feet being opened again by the stubble. And the smoke and uproar, the artillery and riflefire, and then him being hit and falling, but still holding onto his rifle and crawling on until the smoke closed all around him. But even that doesn't mean much because when I remember, it seems he was a boy cut out of paper like a doll, and the minié balls only punched through his paper guts, and the paper boy lay down near a lot of other cutouts under a sun painted on a piece of blue canvas sky with the blue maybe overdone some. How can you care about something like that?

—You were that boy, I said as the fatigue of the long day came over me.

—I expect so, he said, his voice blurring, trailing off. —I expect so. Then, after a minute: —Youall hang up your clothes, turn down the lantern, and sleep on those cots. They won't be in before morning now. Good night, boys.

III

Before the sun was up, I heard voices just outside the tent. Then I heard somebody fooling with the flap.

—All right, I heard Grandfather say without any sign of sleep in his voice. —All right, come on in.

I couldn't get my eyes open right away, but I heard Grandfather move toward the lantern and heard someone else come into the tent.

—I thought maybe he'd caught up with both of you, I heard Grandfather say.

—He ain't none too far off, a strange voice answered.

—Specially in the early morning, a third voice said. —Twilight and first light I feel like one of them Greek heroes on the Happy Isles. Like my body was gone, and nothing left but what I look and think with.

—How is it up here?

—All right, I guess, my grandfather said over the sounds of his dressing. —We got here yesterday and they had already started the speeches full tilt. I think today is the big day.

—I reckon so. Today was the big day.

I managed to get up finally and open my eyes. The two of them were sitting on either side of Grandfather. The one who had been talking about Greek heroes was short and fleshy without really being fat. His face was red and blotchy, and it showed no feeling at all. He had on a gray uniform with gold braid on the sleeves. The other old man was just under Grandfather's six feet in height. His voice was reedy and pleasant. He was narrow all over. From his long head to his narrow hips he looked as if he had spent all his years standing up in a close room, or as if someone had tied him between horses at intervals in order to force his growth.

—Hello, boy, the smaller one said bluffly when he saw I was awake.

—This is Michael Clinton, Grandfather said. —We were here together.

—This would be Robert Edward Lee, Michael Clinton said, nodding toward me.

—That's him, Grandfather said with only a slight smile. —Over there's Nathan Bedford asleep.

—Fine, Michael Clinton said. —Robert, this is John Edgar Turner.

—Sorry, Grandfather said. —I was fixing to do the rest of the honors.

—All right, John Edgar Turner said in that soft breathless voice that sounded like a clarinet or a flute. —I been looking him over.

—He's all right, Michael Clinton said. —He's just fine.

I was getting embarrassed, but about then we went outside and found the cook tent where there were a lot of old men, most of them Union veterans, standing in line for coffee and rolls. Up where the food and coffee were, I saw a young man with a fur-collared overcoat on. He was talking to one of the army officers who was trying to make sure everybody was happy and getting to the speeches and fireworks and whatever was going on. The man with the fur collar was gesturing toward the men in line, and the officer, his face set and showing nothing, was listening without seeming to agree or disagree. The young man's face was red, and I thought it was the early morning chill until we got close enough to see all the pimples and scars of old pimples on it. He had a high celluloid collar and kept talking about spectators and the angle, but the officer looked away, and when another officer came by, he excused himself and walked off as if he had something important to do. The young man with the pimples didn't look insulted. He pulled a notebook from his pocket and read something and then started in the direction opposite from that the officer had taken.

Later we were walking on the east side of the big Pennsylvania memorial. All around us, people looked at tablets and statues and little pillars with bronze plates. Bedford was with us, and we were waiting for the time when President Wilson would speak.

—None of us ever got this far before, John Edgar Turner was saying. —I guess we stopped over there a couple hundred yards.

—That's right, my grandfather said. —If you stand on one of these tablets, you can see the wall.

—Do you want to walk over there? John Edgar Turner asked quietly.

—How about some lemonade? Michael Clinton asked us. —Would youall like some lemonade?

—Where did you get your uniform, Mr. Clinton? Bedford asked. —Did you wear it here before?

—Lord, no. John Edgar Turner laughed. —We didn't any of us have uniforms.

—My sister . . . Michael Clinton started to say. He was looking gray, and his hard-lipped expressionless face was covered with moisture.

—His sister in Danville had it made for him. We didn't any of us have uniforms that last time.

—I wouldn't have done no fighting if they hadn't given me a uniform. What's the good of joining an army if they don't give you a uniform? Bedford asked.

—I reckon they gave us a kind of uniform, Grandfather said. —They gave us one that day.

—That's so, John Edgar Turner said.

Bedford shrugged, and Michael Clinton still looked sick. John Edgar Turner looked at him and frowned.

—Don't be silly, he said to Michael Clinton. —Come on. We'll take a look at the angle. We'll take a look at Cemetery Ridge right after we hear the President talk.

—Maybe the boys would . . .

—Like to see where their country died, John Edgar Turner finished. His long narrow face looked hard and naked in the bright sunlight.

Michael Clinton shrugged and looked as if he had shrunk some. He followed a few steps behind us.

—You'd think . . . John Edgar Turner began.

My grandfather cut him off. —Hush, John. Maybe it doesn't seem so long to Mike. I expect he's got something to remember.

—It was the worst way to be hurt. I remember he screamed all the way down through Maryland. I remember . . .

—All right, mind the boys.

—Oh, John Edgar Turner said. —I wasn't going to say anything.

IV

All the President had to say was about how close we all were and how the Boys in Blue and the Boys in Gray were all heroes and brought glory and unity to the country after all.

—*Whose* country? Bedford snorted right while the President was talking, and some of the old men with Grand Army of the Republic badges stared and frowned at him. My grandfather hushed Bedford hard, but then he stared back at the other men without blushing any at all.

While the President was getting the good old U.S.A. off his chest, Michael Clinton still looked pasty and sick, and after it was over, we started back to see the angle and the fence which we had been headed for when it was time to go hear the President.

We went past the little monument they call the High Water Mark, and there right ahead of us was this little square of field, a few trees, and a broken-down snake rail fence running along one side of it. What was left of a broken-down stone wall maybe three and a half or four feet high straggled out perpendicular to the fence. Beyond was a long wide field knee-deep in drying summer grass, and down the slope a few hundred yards was a road. That was all there was.

But Grandfather and John Edgar Turner and Michael Clinton all walked slowly, as if the place were full of cannon or big statues. Michael Clinton stopped under a tree and mopped his head with a checkered handkerchief.

—Right out there, he said, —I gave 'em my life.

—Sure, John Edgar Turner said, looking over at us kind of nervously. —You gave it all.

—I gave it all, Michael Clinton said after him. —I was only twenty-two. They got as much from me as if I was buried out there. Do youall know what it's like going through life without . . .

—The boys, Grandfather cautioned him sternly.

Michael Clinton leaned against the tree. His eyes were damp, but he still had no expression. Just that strange bluff red face with a tortured voice coming out of it, and nothing in the face to match the voice. Like one of those wooden puppets they use in shows.

—Reckon I made it about three-quarters of the way, Grandfather said to John Edgar Turner. —I never saw it from this point of view. They say we covered the whole field there as far as you could see.

—I expect we looked like judgment on the way from up here, John Edgar Turner said in his reedy voice.

—I don't see anything, Bedford said. —It's just a pasture. I don't see nothing but a pasture.

—Shut up, I said. —They'll hear you.

—All the way up here to see a pasture and a fence with a couple of trees and a dinky road running through it.

—You want to go back, I said. —I'm going to kick you all the way back to the tent if you don't shut up.

But then a man came walking up and started talking to Grandfather and the others. It was the man with the pimples and the celluloid collar. At first I couldn't make out what he wanted.

—In an hour or so. The Pennsylvanian veterans are scheduled to present the Pickett's Division Association folks with an American flag right here.

My grandfather was nodding courteously, and John Edgar Turner was craning his long neck first to one side and then the other like a tall puzzled bird looking down on a hedgehog for the first time.

Michael Clinton was still leaning up against the tree and looking out over the field.

—Lots of folks from all over, the young man was saying earnestly. —From South and North. Lots of good people to celebrate with you, and we thought . . .

Michael Clinton had stopped rubbing his face with the outsize checkered handkerchief. He stepped over to where the others were talking as if he were drawn by a magnet. His eyes widened as the pimple-faced man went on, but he kept listening as if he couldn't help it and couldn't believe what he was hearing either.

—If you fellas would get together and go on down by the Emmitsburg road there, and then kind of run back up toward this wall here, and maybe give us the old Rebel yell . . . you know . . .

My grandfather remained placid and showed nothing of what he was thinking. John Edgar Turner's long gentle face was like rubber, passing from a kind of embarrassed horrified smile to a frown, and back again, like the face of someone confronted with a preposterous and unexpected situation that might turn out funny or dangerous or both.

—Lord, John Edgar Turner said slowly, softly.

—What're they going on about? Bedford whined irritably. —I want to go back. I want to go back. I'm tired.

But now it was coming through to Michael Clinton. —Oh Jesus Christ, he moaned, looking away from the young man who had not stopped talking even then, but continued to tell how much the good folks would enjoy it and how much it would add to the celebration.

—Oh, Jesus Christ in heaven, Michael Clinton crooned, and now his rough scarlet face was no longer bland, no longer even a face but a collapsing unsorted collection of wide eyes, a twisted mouth, and fresh streams of sweat flowing into both like the catch of a violent spring rain. —Do you know what they . . .

But the pimple-faced young man only stared at Michael Clinton curiously and drew breath to begin his persuasion again.

—Pickett's charge all over again, he said. —This time the Pennsylvania boys will meet you with open arms. Think of how proud . . .

By then John Edgar Turner and Grandfather had turned away from him. They were watching Michael Clinton, who had begun staggering back in the direction of the tents. He had gone only a little way when he fell heavily against one of the trees. He held himself up long enough to get turned around. Then he sagged into a sitting position facing us, his back against the tree, his eyes wide and staring past us into that wide grassy field beyond. There was no expression on his face at all.

I started toward him but Grandfather caught my arm.

—No. You take Bedford and go back. If you see one of those boy scouts or army people, send them down here with a stretcher. Tell them to hurry.

As I pulled Bedford along, I could hear the young man with the pimples and high celluloid collar saying to Grandfather, —After you get the old gentleman taken care of, maybe we could go over it with the others . . .

By that time we were too far away to make out words, but I heard my grandfather say something in a short vicious tone, and his voice was as strong and deep as a young man's. Then I heard nothing more.

V

We had some late lunch, and Bedford fell asleep in the hot stuffy tent afterward. I sat on a campstool outside for a long time, but Grandfather didn't come. Elderly men in blue suits and gray suits moved past, quietly talking or, once in a while, laughing in that high womanish shrill of the very old. The sun began slanting downward, and when suppertime was near, I began to worry. Bedford woke up covered with sweat. He was sullen and uncomfortable and kept saying he wished he was home, and how all of this didn't mean anything.

—It ain't like all the stories, he said. —All it is, is a lot of old men and ground with the grass all cut and some big places built of marble with iron horses on top. It's not anything.

I sent him on to supper and went to look for Grandfather.

I found him my first try. He was sitting on the low stone wall at the place we had been, the place they called the Bloody Angle. All around the green well-trimmed acre or two, there were pieces of paper scattered, some bread crusts, and what looked like a jam jar. My grandfather was facing west, looking at the long deserted slope that flowed downward to the Emmitsburg road, and then up again to the bulky shadow of Seminary Ridge, where the sun stood low and red like a swollen wound.

—I got worried about you, I said as I climbed up on the stone wall beside him.

He turned and looked at me. It seemed at first he didn't recognize me.

—I'm sorry, he said after a moment. —After we left the hospital, I meant to come back to the tent. . . .

—How's Mr. Clinton?

—Mr. Clinton is dead, my grandfather said. —Too much heat. Too much excitement.

—No, it wasn't. . . . Did you tell them about that man . . .

—I didn't tell them anything. They told us Michael Clinton was dead. There wasn't anything to tell them. So I came here to take another look before time to go.

He stood up and stretched, and when he yawned, with his head thrown back, it seemed all the wrinkles in his cheeks dissolved. It may have been some trick of light in the early summer evening, but he looked for a moment, squinting toward the darkening sun, his mouth open as if to cheer invisible friends forward, no older than myself, and just as strong.

—We should have gone right on, he said quietly. —We never should have stopped.

VI

It was twilight. Then it was dark, and we had put our things in the cardboard suitcase and said good-bye to John Edgar Turner, who held my hand and Grandfather's for a long minute and who embarrassed Bedford by leaning down and kissing him in front of some old men who were shuffling past on their way to a regimental reunion.

—Good-bye, John Edgar Turner called after us. —God bless youall.

—I'll be seeing you, Grandfather said, waving. —We'll see you again.

—Sure enough, we heard John Edgar Turner call in his soft reedy voice. —Sure enough.

On the train we split two hot dogs among us, and got the porter to sell us two bags of salted peanuts for a nickel instead of just one. By the time we finished eating, Bedford was beginning to be contrite. He was sorry for letting it show that he wished he had stayed home.

—He was a mighty nice old man, Bedford said. —I'm sorry about it.

—I expect he was ready, Grandfather said. —It comes to be that time, and then you get set for it.

He rolled his coat into a ball and set it in the corner of the seat next to the window.

—It's beginning to rain, I said.

—Yes, my grandfather said. —It would.

Outside we could see the raindrops striking our coach window and shattering into long shivering beads that tracked down and across the glass and then spun off into the night again. There were blurred yellow lights in town windows and on farm porches as we passed. Once there was an empty crossroads with lamps above it on poles. The roadway was slick and shiny with rain and light, and the lamps had halos of swirling mist around them.

My grandfather had pulled his hat down over his eyes, and his arms were folded across his chest.

We rode for a long time in silence, looking out at the rain. I could feel myself going slack inside. It would be easy to sleep in a little while. Bedford took his Ingraham watch out and looked at it.

—It's almost one o'clock. It's the fourth of July.

—Shut up, I said. —He's trying to sleep.

Bedford leaned over and tried to look up under Grandfather's hat.

—You asleep, Grampaw? he whispered.

We could see his mouth twist into a smile under the battered hat.

—Sure now, he said softly. —I reckon I could sleep for fifty years.

A Time to Embrace
Shreveport: 1929

There is no remembrance of former things, neither shall there be any remembrance of things that are to come with those that shall come after.

—*Ecclesiastes*

In those days Shreveport was not a whole lot bigger than it had been at the end of the Confederate War, and you could walk or ride fifteen minutes in any direction and find fishing places or hunting space. When summer came, my cousin Bobby Lee Lindsey and I would head for the Red River and spend weeks sometimes fishing for channel cat or running foxes with Mr. Sentell's hounds.

Mr. Sentell lived just across the river. He was not especially old as years went, but there was a fine and indescribable quality about him that led all of us, even the adults, to ascribe wisdom and prudence and great understanding to him. We would cross the river in a small boat, Bobby Lee blowing my father's deer horn, and Mr. Sentell would step onto his porch, wave to us, and have the poles ready before we landed. He would not often go with us. Usually he would sit on his porch with Enoch, an ancient Negro who rarely spoke, and then only to Mr. Sentell. They would sit together, smoking and watching us, impassive as a pair of Cherokees, until we had brought in a mess worth cooking. Then we were done, and it was Enoch's turn. He would fry the cats and add a few pieces of slow-cooked venison dried and saved from the previous fall, a fresh rabbit or a couple of squirrels, a salad with tomatoes and peppers, and collard tops, and okra stewed and cooled. And always a huge platter of hush puppies fried along with the fish. We would take his place on the porch, and while he cooked, we would share Mr. Sentell's Indian composure and listen to stories about old times, hunting down around Alexandria and into Mississippi, or about the great day of the steamboats before the century turned. He told us about Dick Taylor's boys at the Battle of Mansfield, where Banks's Yankees were turned back, and about the days when Shreveport was a railhead and gathered most of the West's cattle to be shipped north before the war.

Then there would be the food, and we would eat until we could hardly paddle back to the Caddo Parish side of the river. Behind us, in the gathering dark, Mr. Sentell and Enoch would be sitting on the porch again, Mr. Sentell waving, Enoch pulling on his pipe, watching the dogs finish off whatever we had left. Ahead of us, set out against the fading shadows, would be the town, that other world which even then was beginning to gather speed, rushing into a new age in which there was little time for fishing and cooking and almost no time for old stories at all.

We came home late from fishing and eating at Mr. Sentell's that night. Bobby Lee, who was my second cousin on my mother's side and cursed with the unquenchable volubility of the Lindseys, had been speculating all the way home. Bobby Lee knew a man in Minden who claimed Mr. Sentell had had no father, that he was a bastard. And that the old colored man he lived with was Sentell's blood brother. I had heard from an old man in the Benton sheriff's office that Mr. Sentell's father had been a Confederate officer, who had given him (Sentell) his name and died in a duel or, more probably, a plain out-and-out gunfight before he could work things around to marriage with Mr. Sentell's mother.

Bobby Lee was talking to me on the porch when my father came out with his pipe.

—So he could be a bastard of mighty good blood, if that old man up in Benton ain't just rattlin' on. But whatever story you take, or even if you take bits and pieces of all the stories goin', he comes out a bastard. You reckon everybody's lyin'?

I did not realize it then, but that was our first brush with rumor. The first tale we had heard worth carrying at an age where we were old enough to be prone to keep it going. Later we would understand the dynamics of it. But this was our maiden voyage.

I was interested, too, and about to say something I imagined was humorous, when my father loomed over us in the rushing twilight.

—Bobby Lee, he said, not angrily, but as near to anger as he usually got with his own kin, —I don't want to hear you talking that way here. If you've set your mind to scandalmongering, you'll have to practice your calling somewhere else. We don't do it here. I'm surprised you'd eat a man's food and then come away to pass scandal on him.

—Sir?

—I thought Mr. Sentell was a friend of youall's.

—Well, he is. That don't change the stories, the truth.

—Stories? Truth? Do you reckon the word "story" and the word "truth" are interchangeable?

—No, sir.

My father sat down in a cane chair just behind us, just out of our sight. My sister had come onto the porch with a new kitten.

—Go along, honey, he told her. —I need to talk to the boys.

Bobby Lee started to his feet.

—Sit down, sir, my father said, as if he were talking to a man, and not only to a man, but to a stranger whose appearance was not satisfactory, or whose accent made him draw from the arsenal of his personality the cold and formal manner he and every one of his friends almost never used, but always had ready to discipline young boys and Negroes or keep strangers at a proper distance for business or unpleasantness.

Bobby Lee fell backward as if my father had slapped him. His face was dark with embarrassment. He was almost five months older than I, and had always made something of my youth.

—Neither one of you has the least right to speculate about your elders, he began. —And most especially one of your elders who is known and well received by your fathers and kinsmen. But since you seem old enough to peddle every loafer's tale that comes floating across the parish line, you must be old enough to know what we know. Old enough to take on a grown man's knowledge and handle that burden the way a man handles whatever comes his way, whether he has sought it or not.

We were still seated there on the steps, riveted by my father's voice which encircled us from behind, still cool and formal and distant, as if he were speaking not to us, but to the stand of pine, the pair of young magnolias growing halfway across the yard, almost on the street.

—What a man knows, however he comes by it, he is responsible for. Remember that. Not simply because I am correcting both of you (as much you, Jeff, who listened as Bobby Lee who spoke), but because it has to do with the truth of all this. Mr. Sentell's truth.

—And what a man—or woman, for that matter—does, whether he understands at the time of doing all that will come of his (or her) act, he is responsible for. Words, even thoughts sometimes, are acts. A man is judged not simply by what he does or says—or thinks—initially, but by how he lives with the results, the outgrowth of his (or her) acts or words. Or thoughts.

—Because what is ill begun, what flowers in the heart or mouth or hand of a young person who cannot or will not think, can be righted even if it is irreversible. Can be rectified by simply living with the results of the evil. What you cannot change, at least you can endure. What you outlive, you have conquered. Do you understand?

—No, sir, I said, honestly. Bobby Lee was still sulking.

—Mr. Sentell is old, my father said. —He was a grown man when I was a boy. I remember fishing with him. Old Enoch, the colored man, would cook for us. We would sit there in the evening and drink home-churned buttermilk and he would talk. He always seemed to enjoy having boys to talk to. He would tell what he had heard about the war, about the old days. I think what he was really telling us was who we are, what we come from. I think I came closer to growing up, thinking like a man, by listening to him than by hearing all the bilge they handed us in military school, all the pious chatter that oozed out of the pulpit.

—Which is not, my father went on quickly, —to denigrate the military or the clergy. It is only to say that some of us understood Mr. Sentell better than either. It is a matter of understanding. Do youall understand?

Bobby Lee was calmed down now. —I guess so, he said. —I reckon.

—And once, late at night, when none of us dared go home because we had been frog-gigging till almost two o'clock, Mr. Sentell told us about his mother. Not meaning, probably, to go quite so far with a story that any young man was likely to understand awry at best or not understand at all. But he started with her appearance, the sound of her voice, the way she would walk like some ancient priestess despite the town and what it said and thought. And that broke the dam. I think now Mr. Sentell had been wanting to tell it all, tell the truth about it, most of his life. But then, on that night, with us, he found at last the audience he required. Not one of our parents who knew much, but whose very knowledge, tainted with opinion and hearsay, was worse than no knowledge at all. No, it was us he needed. Who knew nothing—had been shielded from any fragment of it—and could, at least possibly, understand. Boys called upon to do men's work because all the available men believed that the work of understanding those hearts long dead and gone was already done, and done, if not well, at least sufficiently.

—So it was us. And later, as you'll see, it was us who published the news in Askelon and Gath, who managed without even realizing it, to alter, transform, completely remake the record of those dead whose whole posthumous existence had flickered in Sentell's heart and was passed to us. Not under a pledge of secrecy or even with an unspoken vow of silence. Told us without any instructions at all. Again as if we were men, and men wise and honorable enough to know what should be done with his story, and to see that it was done and done rightly. Which is why I say I grew up in Mr. Sentell's cabin.

My father's voice softened and paused. Bobby Lee and I stared into the growing darkness, mesmerized by the silence as we had been transfixed by his speaking.

—My God, he said unsteadily. —I'm still only beginning to see, to understand. After so long. After so long. . . .

The moon was low and flat behind the trees down near the road. It was rich and creamy yellow and enormous. Inside the house my sister was playing the phonograph. It was a novelty record about the Ford automobile: "Henry's Made a Lady out of Lizzie." Even in the darkness, I could picture the contemptuous, almost despairing expression on my father's face. He loathed the world. "Modernity" and "cheapness" *were* interchangeable words to him. There was neither form nor substance in it. He admired a new poem which read:

> Shape without form, shade without color,
> Paralyzed force, gesture without motion;

—I cannot do the woman justice, he began again, setting his pipe aside, still staring out into the darkness. —Barring appeal to lust, no woman can be adequately described except by a man who loves her. To another man who feels the same. But I do love her. As much as I can love anyone I never knew, but of whom I hear nothing but good reports. We love Lee, don't we? And Jackson and Davis?

—So I will try. Some of this came from Mr. Sentell himself that night. But not all. Some of it from my father who wanted to love her, honor her, I suspect, but had to give way to form in the end because form and substance were so nearly one in the majority of his generation. Some from your mother's father, and some God knows from where. So it is a composite, and suffers and triumphs in proportion to its various sources.

She was called Cissie when she was young. Daughter of a merchant here whose store is still open, owned by a cousin or some connection with a different name. He was not much of a man, by all reports. Chose not to go to the war, but to serve at home. His son, Edward Norton, Jr., lived through the war to die with a lot of wild hopeless young men resisting the Yankee troops here in town afterward. She, Cecilia, saw her brother's body brought into the parlor covered with mud, trussed into a canvas tent half like a butchered hog, half his head carried away by a shotgun. There is no detailing all she saw. But standing next to her brother's bier, she swore (and this she once told Sentell) that no man would ever claim her until she had good reason to believe him at least as much a man as her brother and the young men who preceded and accompanied him into death. "I will not be mated to dregs left by the Yankees," she said, and every able-bodied man her age or a little older was suspect for simply being alive.

—She could not stay under her father's roof. She took what money her mother could give her—money saved originally for her brother, for Edward's portion—and found a small house on Common Street. She taught in the grammar school. Then she was barely eighteen, you see, and young ladies of such years and even the pretense of gentility did not set up their own establishments. Form demanded otherwise. So the first low tide of opinion began, even then, to erode the foundation of her good name.

—Because she did not discuss her reasons, did not say that her brother's brave wasted corpse lay like an iron gate between her and her father. Because, you see, she did not want to harm her father's currency in Shreveport. That would have been senseless. What she wanted of him he could not give and she could not take. She wanted him dead at Vicksburg, or at least sharing the dull red mud of that farmyard where his son had died. So there was nothing whatever between them. Not even enmity. One can die today for one's child, or commit suicide tomorrow. But there is no way to die yesterday, and Ed Norton, Sr., whatever his faults, understood this and perhaps even honored his daughter for it, and did both of them the considerable favor of never addressing her again till the day of his death. When, to some folks' surprise, Cecilia went into her home again and knelt beside his body (she a full-fledged scarlet woman by then, beyond erosion or even the claims of wholesale flood) and cried like the child she still was in her heart's landscape. Which only made the townspeople harden their hearts more, and say "She has killed her old father and now she cries at his tomb, tasting the bitterness of her selfishness, her wrongheadness." Which was ultimately bizarre, since, in fact, even her mother knew that she (Cecilia) was crying because he had taken so long to die, had at last died of some disorder of the heart in his own bed without a blot of mud to lend him dignity. Crying, too, because he had stepped timidly and unwillingly into the darkness, into Hades, where his own son had dived headlong like a desperate young god. And crying for the loins that had made her and her brother and had ended a small dry goods vendor unworthy of his children. Possibly she was crying (and this is only my own belief) for his soul staggering unattended out there, cut off forever from those who had gone before, shattered, mangled, with the last full measure of devotion blasted from their bodies. And their souls.

—But this is a little wrong. I mean the emphasis. She was not bloody-minded. From the night of her brother's death, blood was a horror to her. But she weighed that horror against others. There are worse things than killing, worse things than dying. The worst is to have lived badly, and to have never found anything worth blood— dying—killing for (and this is, of course, mine, not hers. God knows no man can read a woman's heart, and everything I am telling you has been roughened, has lost its patina that was particularly hers, adulterated by passing through so many masculine brains and hearts). What she was looking for was substance. She had had enough of forms. They had brought her brother's form in one night with its substance oozing all over the parlor rug. It taught her a lesson the rest of us learn in the classroom: that a form robbed of its substance cannot live. Sometimes we forget our metaphysics, but Cecilia Norton never forgot. Almost every night, she told Sentell, her dreams reminded her.

My father paused. Even as his voice stopped, I realized that my legs, my back, hurt fiercely. Bobby Lee was shifting in discomfort.

—All right, my father said. —Come find a chair. Call your sister and ask her to bring us the last of the coffee. This will be a long night. You've only heard the prologue. You have to hear all of it now. That will be your penance. And my pleasure.

—And so we have her almost twenty-two now. The better part of five years away from home. It is 1872, and the superficial scars of the Confederate War are over. The dead are phantoms, beloved but already distant, like titanic figures seen through a telescope reversed, moving backward in that narrow corridor we call history, carrying with them all the immediacy, the instantaneousness of their lives and deaths, leaving only the brittle, oversimplified carapace of their meaning behind. That and the lush, well-cared-for graves, and a generation of older men who will laugh immoderately in four years' time when they hear that Sitting Bull has done for Custer what Longstreet neglected to do. It is 1872, and the blue-clad soldiers in our—their—streets are a common sight neither worth a glance or a sneer. They are present, a distasteful potential like storms up from the Gulf or a tornado coming down from Arkansas or the Indian Territory. The country, if you can call it a country, is insane for money, for business, for profit. Except here. Not that the South was above chasing a greenback. There simply were few of them, and only the most potent hunters—too many former Confederate officers—even got a swing at them. The less adroit existed in a state of enforced virtue—except for a handful of men from that old army who were in fact what legend attributes to them all: incorruptible. Two of these, former captains, lived in Caddo Parish.

—And Cecilia is lonely. Strange about women and loneliness. Some women are ravaged by it. A lonely woman of twenty-nine can look like a crone of sixty. Some women lose the juices that freshen them if some presence, some love, some involvement, does not churn, circulate those secret fluids.

—Nuns, Bobby Lee put in thoughtfully. —Like nuns.

—Yes, my father said, not even pausing. —Sad, but fair enough. Although even among nuns you see the exception. That woman who, no matter what her age, reaches out and touches the chords of our maleness and makes us think, despite our piety, *What a shame, what a woman!*

—And that was Cecilia Norton. She was mature before the war was well over, before the last Rebel soldier found his way home. Perhaps because of what happened that July, the Negro trooper, the boy, Ripinski's son.

—I know, I said. —They said about the rape. Some girl up on Texas Street . . .

—Not a rape, my father cut in. —And not some girl. A special girl, Cissie Norton, carrying lunch to her father and brother. Who was dragged into an empty store a child and came out a woman. But untouched. That is gospel. Even the most inveterate scandalmongering liar living down on the river in the shambles knew that, would vouch for that until later, when her rape by a Negro trooper fitted too well into their stories to pass it by. But Ripinski's boy made liars of them. Another child who had gone into the vacant store to see that Cissie was not touched, to act the part of a man, and who died as well as any man and managed the job he had started, too.

—I'm glad you remember the story, the Jew storekeeper's son. Because the boy was part of the weight, the burden, she carried. I had never thought of it that way. But she had seen that corpse, too. Screaming, hysterical, she had seen Nathan Ripinski's body lying in the rain, his head battered by that poor mindless Negro's pistol, and even hysterical, considering it was Cecilia, she would have realized why he was dead. And *then* Ed Junior. Then her brother, and the same reasoning, the same terrible knowledge that, right or wrong, another life was destroyed to keep her safe, inviolate, to hold together at least some shards of the world she had been raised to grace.

I was ahead of my father. I thought of his poetry. —These fragments I have shored against my ruins.

Bobby Lee frowned, puzzled. But my father smiled.

—Why, then I'll fit you, he laughed. —Yes. And the price of these fragments. How many lives touched by a brace of deaths. Time moving and yet frozen while an hour's destiny is worked out in a hundred years. Only men can remember. And women.

—But she is lovely and unfaded and her loneliness standing against her beauty is remarkable. She spends her Sunday mornings in church, her afternoons at the cemetery where her brother sleeps. And no one said, because stories move for them in straight lines, but she visited, certainly, the tiny plot of land reserved for Israel's children among whom she had a champion, too. Until one Sunday afternoon Captain John Pepper comes to see an old derelict named Barney something-or-other buried in a decent grave. This Barney was half an idiot, half a hero at Sharpsburg, and the town forgave him the first for the latter and saw to it he had a shack and a living. Major Edward Sentell employed him, and it was that Sentell and Captain Pepper, who, with a few townsmen, carried his coffin and told the Negroes to stand aside, that they would dig his grave, that he had been a soldier.

—Captain Pepper had been a soldier, too. He carried his Yankee metal where it was plainly visible. His face was pocked like the surface of the moon. His neck, his breast, was mottled and scored dull angry red, an almost iridescent purple. The only life in that face so like a side of fresh-killed pork was in the eyes. If the face was too scarred to smile, the eyes could sparkle, could generate kindness, understanding, compassion. They say that Captain John Pepper was a favorite with everyone. He was more often sent for by the sick and dying than was the preacher. They knew he had looked into death's open jaws and laughed—at least smiled—at what he saw there. And they knew he was no fool.

—He was not much for convention. Forms were absurd to him. A man with a blasted face and a quick mind behind it is bound to come to that, he said. Only the substance of an act mattered to him. And the poor, the halt, the blind, and, as I have said, the dying—all of them flew to him like moths to a sweet flame.

—And what did Captain Pepper do? Why, he trained himself in the law with Major Edward Sentell, who had taken a degree in the civil code after the war. Then, already a lawyer, he began working in his spare time, his time outside the courtroom, with old Dr. Ewing, who had been Zachary Taylor's physician in Washington, and who spent his last years on the Texas-Louisiana border. And when he was done with that, he began to read theology. So that, finally, he thought himself prepared. Soldier, lawyer, physician, scholar—all but a minister. My God, they still talk out in the country as if he had been the reincarnation. No man ever came to him, they said, who went away unsatisfied. And still he was lonely, incomplete. Himself unsatisfied.

—So that Sunday, when the burial was done and Captain Pepper was walking out of the cemetery, he chanced to see Cecilia, who had come to spend an hour with her brother. He paused and passed the time of day, knelt down beside her and asked about her brother, how he came there.

—It is strange how, even in a small town, lives can be so close and yet totally apart. Like parallel translations of the Bible. Lived within sight of each other, and yet without communication. That was how theirs had been. Pepper had come from Natchitoches before the war and had not even gotten to Shreveport until 1867. He had served time after the war in a Federal prison for some infraction of Yankee rule as he passed through western Tennessee. He had met Cecilia, they had spoken a score of times at musicales, in the home of mutual friends, and so on. But he had been working superhumanly hard, you remember, and now, only lately, could he call even an hour on a Sunday afternoon free to do with as he wished.

—They talked. What about, besides that grave's contents, not even Mr. Sentell could guess. What had the newspaper reported that Saturday? The weather? How our land seems meant for flowers, how it exaggerates growth and sends up a tree where you are lucky to get a weed in Ohio or Maine? No one knows. Only at some time before he rose and left her, she noticed that there was red loamy mud on his hands from digging and filling in the grave, Barney's grave. And a smear of it on his torn irreparable cheek. And he was saying something—probably, "I wonder if I might call on you, Miss Norton," hoping that her eyes widening, her hand rising from the rounded earth was not a sign that suddenly she realized how scarred, how ugly, he was, hoping that his own eyes, his voice, what she knew of him was enough, and then her hand touched his cheek. At first he thought simply a gesture, to brush away the trace of earth on it. But her fingers moved along the scarred patches of his forehead, the tough pale ridges of flesh where youall and I have eyebrows. And finally reached the bit of mud, flicking away only a bit of it, enough to rub between her fingers. And her eyes still wide, as if recalling something she had forgotten, and looking then toward the grave and back at him, beginning to smile, to let him share in an instant's transfiguration of her beauty. She said, "This will do, Captain. It will do for a beginning." And he stood up, legs shaking under him, looking down at her hair, at its brown length falling around her shoulders, over the yellow and white dress like a cataract.

—Walking out of the graveyard, his legs at last steady, he remembered that she had said, too, that he might call, that she would be pleased to see him. And he reached up then and touched the tiny trace of loam still clinging to his cheek, as if it were a talisman, a piece of bloodstained lace, or a bit of rose petal fallen from a vine on Flodden Field.

My father stretched his legs. —I believe we have whiskey inside, he said. —Are you gentlemen old enough to share a glass with me?

—I know where it is, I said. But Bobby Lee was already up and walking into the house. My father rose and walked up and down the porch. —I expect this is a man's work. These are a man's hours, God knows. I hope Bobby Lee's folks won't object to the hours or the stimulant.

—We've . . . I began, and then fell silent.

—I'm sure you have, my father said. —But not under my aegis.

—We'll be fine. We'll be just fine, I said pointlessly.

—I know. My father smiled, looking upward where the moon rode high, like a silver chariot, a handful of clouds racing across its face. Far away, I heard low thunder.

—We could use a night shower or two, my father said. —It's been dry.

—It'll drive the fish down. They won't feed if the water's troubled.

—The big ones will, he said as Bobby Lee reappeared with whiskey, glasses and a pitcher of ice water. —The big ones will bite anytime. You fish still waters to fill the frying pan. Fish troubled waters for sport.

We sat and drank. The evening was turning cool, and a sullen pulse of lightning showed through distant clouds.

—That takes care of one captain, my father said. —But Captain Draper remains to be accounted for. Which is not especially difficult, but pretty unsatisfactory.

—Why is that? I asked.

My father shrugged. —I suppose it's the buried storyteller in me. I want symmetry. And that may mean I'm not even a good story-teller, because symmetry is usually false.

—Anyhow, there was nothing soft, gentle about their first encounter, Draper's and Cecilia's. Softness, gentleness, had been shot out of him. Almost every breath, every step, was painful to him. People said the pain would have been less had he consented to limp, to favor his legs. But he walked perfectly, and paid the price for walking well on shattered legs. He had, studded here and there in his legs and trunk, Yankee shrapnel collected at Beaver Dam Creek, at Chancellorsville and Sharpsburg, at Franklin, Tennessee, and finally at Five Forks. His hair was white before his twentieth birthday, and it is said of him that he spent the whole war considering the Jesuit priesthood when he had finished his duty and saw the Confederate States established and free. I have heard it said that he promised Almighty God he would enter the novitiate down in New Orleans the day a treaty of peace was signed between the Confederate States and the United States. That day never came. There were no Confederate States. And no Jesuit priest. Seven years later there was a man of thirty-three with snow-white hair, impeccable manners, a piece of Bossier Parish land, and a heart drained of God, despising the carcass of a country whose soul had perished along with his own in that ghoul's war, and having no more traffic with the people around him—even his kinsmen on this side of the Red River—than he had with Yankee appointees and the local Judases who pretended to authority. It is said, too, that if you could approach Captain Draper, you would marvel at his smooth unlined face. And at his fixed terrible eyes which had the look and even the cold brilliant glaze of a dead man's.

—He came to the school one morning (whether before or after that Sunday in the cemetery, I cannot say) with a request. Or a demand, since his manner, the tone of his voice was not calibrated to supplication. He had a nephew in the school, one of his kinsmen on this side of the river, and he wished to remove the boy from school for a time. To teach him.

—Cecilia was slow to answer. The boy was bright, a happy child. Perhaps more than simply bright. But she was not sure what his uncle had in mind. "Why should you take him?" she asked. "What can he learn from you?"

—"He can learn anger. He can learn never to forget what cannot be forgiven. He can become a historian. We all must become historians. We cannot waste any of it, for fear of damnation."

—She understood. His white hair, his white face, his cold doomed eyes that were fixed forever on the death agonies of thousands. She knew that he communicated with no one, that he had been locked inside himself for seven years and that now the dam was beginning to crack, that the boy was instrumental. *It will not hurt him,* she thought. *He is young and strong and even a little wise. He will listen and part of it he will remember, and the rest forget. He is old enough to choose what he can use.*

—And so she let Draper take him. On the condition that she might visit once a week to see what progress he was making. As much, I expect, to see what progress Draper was making.

My father leaned back in his chair and drained his whiskey. —There you have it. A stock situation. Every element of a stage romance, wouldn't you say? A beautiful woman marked by the past, by the undertow of a catastrophe; two men, each one scarred by the same agony. Each of them lonely, each trapped in the bitter preservative of past hatred and present purposelessness. And one thing more: time passing. Not the time of golden girls and boys. More nearly that of chimney sweeps. Time flooding past, over them, and each day carrying them closer to the grave. This no one told me, but these three people were human, and that is what human beings feel: their lives ebbing away as they sit or stand or pace through anticlimactic years. I have to add this, you see, this touch of honorable desperation. Because the stock situation fell apart, and the three of them shifted from melodrama to something almost epic. The desperation does not explain or justify or even render credible. It only serves to stay our doubt that any of this actually happened.

Rain had begun to fall. At first a drop or two; then a rising wind blew soft unhurried sheets of it, soft as mist, across us. None of us moved. My father poured more whiskey, cutting it with the well water and ice.

—Because of rain, my father said, his voice soft, almost incantatory. —It was rain that kept her at Draper's place through the afternoon of her first scheduled visit, on past supper, till her charge was in bed and asleep, and she and the captain sitting on his porch, his colored man inside playing a guitar and singing old songs (drinking, I suspect, the captain's good whiskey, knowing he would not be called down at all then, and not even later unless the evening went badly).

—And the captain starting to talk about the war. "Never mind the war," she said, or something like it. "I'm sick of that war. Sometimes I think it was fought only so that youall would have something besides dogs and hunting and politics to talk about in your old age."

—And the captain surely taking courtly but clear exception to this, knowing of her brother and amazed that she does not fall into the half-weeping, half-sighing recital of past glories and present anguish that is common—no, proper—to her sex and her breeding. "What else is there to talk of, madam?" he answers.

—"The next war, perhaps," she replies, with an edge that even a self-centered, ego-nursing recluse can recognize. And so he knows that his honorable obsession will not serve. That he will have to invent, create, for the lady. It has been seven years since that was necessary—even possible. And now he tries again. To make light conversation, to see, God's wonder, if he can make her laugh. The grim soldier trying to become a parlor clown. But, of course, as a man sinks into love (Falls in love? Only one figure, and not the best: some of us creep into love, plunge into love. Only the clumsy fall.), he becomes less the soldier, more the clown.

—It is a small miracle, you see, that he is breached, and the fluids of his loneliness boiling out, shaping themselves into graceful fountains, brooks, cascades, for her pleasure. It is a miracle that it should happen at all, but if it were going to happen, anyone could see that it would happen quickly. And before the most casual notion of decorum shrieks that he must take her home, he has asked her not to allow him to pay court, but to marry him. Now. I mean then. That night. As absurd as any sheik with his flapper of two hours' acquaintance.

Bobby Lee grinned and reached for the whiskey. —I guess maybe young people are always going to hell in a handcart.

—Ah, my father said, as if he had been primed for just that speech. —But some of them do. In every generation. There is one great difference in your sheik and your captain. The latter knows, even amid passion, the approximate price of things. A soldier has a vision of hell. And when Draper asked Cecilia Norton to marry him, he was ready to accept the implications of her answer—even those he could not foresee. What we spoke of at first: the responsibility of knowledge. Your captain was becoming, in a limited, conscious way, love's clown. But your sheik, unless I do him wrong, begins as a clown, and every word, every gesture, he utters has scrawled across it the proviso: *unless I should change my mind; unless it should be too hard.*

Bobby Lee did not answer, but held his whiskey out in the mounting rain, letting the pure water dilute it.

—Of course, she said no, my father went on. —Not, "Never sir," only no. As if the hour or the rain or some certain mood had as much to do with her refusal as anything else. And so when he handed her down from the carriage and they both ran onto the porch, the rain cooling at least his flesh, he was not resigned, not halfway back into the corroded armor of his own past, or even trapped like a hermit crab, half in, half out. He was free of it. At least in relation to her. (He would never be free of it much beyond her. Mr. Sentell remembers him to this day as kind, very considerate, sincerely affectionate, but formal, with a veneer of icy punctilio that neither time nor fortune nor friendship nor less could melt or reduce or chip away.) I can imagine his exhilaration: it is never pleasant to live in a charnel house, even if the corpses are your family and dearest connections. And in those days the bones were not yet white, not free of moldering flesh, much less the alabaster and marble they are today. But now he has a stake in this world. He can leave the gateway to Valhalla or the Elysian fields or wherever Pickett's men and Hill's men and Stonewall's squadrons attack forever the ghostly lines and works that they will never take, and we will never let them leave off assaulting. Now he has touched unbroken flesh. He has caught the odor of a perfume never created on Cemetery Ridge. It is life and tomorrow, and the rain is sweet and romantic, and he is a living man again, and not just a man but one who knows prices and values, who cannot be surprised or hurt beyond his ability to endure hurt, a better man than most. And the new battle will be as tender as a tumble in fresh-cut hay, and he can win it. It is not stacked against him from the start. And the victory proposes only winners: no losers to suffer as he has—as he can now barely remember he has.

—And so riding back, permitting that horse his own pace, almost too excited to stay in the rig, don't you reckon something of the soldier came back through the fresh greasepaint? Not the wounded soldier, but that other one who could laugh and wish for combat and say with Lee that it is well war is so terrible, lest we grow too fond of it? Certainly enough of that young invincible soldier to be glad that she had said no, that there would be blood-rousing charges and spirited defense, and no one wounded, if God permitted. And from this battle's womb life would spring rather than death. I envy him that ride back, those two inimitable hours in the rain. Life is very long. That was a rare time, and Draper, newly free, must have understood it.

—But that very tomorrow changed things. Because, riding into town on some errand ill defined even to himself, simply hoping for a sight of her, a word, at best the precious moments of a chance meeting on Texas Street, he found her walking with Captain Pepper. Going toward the hospital, or to the home of some luckless Negro—but, wherever, she was walking with another man, and her hand was on his arm, and his face, ruined, barren of beauty as the fields of Petersburg, was transfigured by her nearness. He was with her, close to her, moving beside her in the measureless rhythm of an hour's walking. And you know that Captain Draper almost froze. I expect he had never, in the wildest psychotic nightmare of his life, waking or sleeping, hated a man as he hated Pepper. Because if a man kills and burns and humiliates you, there remains in both you and him (at least in those days) a kind of formality of feeling, and we give it the formal name of war or duel or feud. But this is another thing. It is visceral, and while we call it jealousy, it is void and without form, and can make even a soldier-turned-clown into an animal.

—But we can drop this. Both of you are male enough to feel all you need to feel. You can be Captain Pepper, walking in paradise, and Captain Draper staring in, saying, "Oh, hell, what doth mine eyes behold?" The rest of this part is simple reporting. There came to be bad blood between them. No one can remember where it first surfaced or how, or what her initial response was. The aftermath made it irrelevant. But one of the Mitchell boys—Albert Neiman's cousins—told me he recalled a story of the first run-in. Recalled it because, in a way, it almost ruined both Pepper's and Draper's currency in the town. Because, you see, neither of them was personally involved.

I almost jumped to my feet. —I know, I said. —I've heard. It was the niggers. Their niggers.

—Sure enough, Bobby Lee said. —The nigger duel on Travis Street. There's still a hole in the bricks over Barnwell's garage. Somebody said it was a forty-four bullet one of those damned fools . . .

—All right, my father said. —I don't know about the bullet hole. And I don't know whether there were any damned fools involved. I know it wasn't funny. Except to the Federals who broke it up and the mangy loafers and barflies who hold every feeling, every life as meat for belly laughs. Except their own.

—There were the two of them: John Paul Jones, who had been born in New York and suffered family reverses, married to a negress who produced children and meanness with equal vigor, and who took the unusual step of fleeing South. He managed to establish himself as a free Negro in New Orleans, and came to the war with Captain Pepper. He pulled Pepper's shattered carcass off so many fields with so much danger to himself that he was damned near decorated. He came back to Shreveport with the captain. Not a slave, not even a body servant, really. Almost an associate. He had, they say, one peculiarity: after the war, he would not answer or even give the slightest heed to anyone who called him by less than his full name. If you wanted John Paul Jones, you called out, "John Paul Jones, come here." Anything less was a waste of breath—even for Captain Pepper. You could call it a kind of self-bestowed decoration.

—The other was just Enoch. Born somewhere in western Tennessee and sold cheap as dirt when he was twelve or thirteen. Because he was something close to a hunchback, had a bad leg, and all the way around was a dead loss to any slave dealer. Too misshapen to work the fields; too ugly to serve in the house. So Draper's father bought him. Because then, in the early 1850s, Draper's father was a man in motion over in Bossier Parish. Half a farmer, half a planter. He owned nine hundred acres and was mortgaging crops two years ahead to buy more land. He managed to get even, to buy his son a man—if a defective one—and to die, all in the year John Brown's body began a'moldering and his soul to marching on.

—But Enoch was worthy of his hire. No pyrotechnic displays: his master was wiser or luckier, and only caught Yankee metal twice. At which time Enoch dutifully packed him onto a mule and brought him to a surgeon. But Enoch's long suit was tenacity. He outlasted others. He outlived the man who bought him, and all the rest, Draper, Pepper, Cecilia. Even John Paul Jones. I lost a dollar bill when he lived through last year. I expect he'll outlive Mr. Sentell.

—I know Enoch as well as anyone. Surly, unsmiling, incredibly old, and a cook to thank God on. Fish, duck, venison, rabbit, Creole food—dirty rice, crawfish. Anything he touches is transformed. Half the women in Shreveport cook Enoch's biscuits, and call them such. Even in the bad times that were to come, when no decent woman, so called, and no timid man would be seen talking to Draper or Pepper, much less Cecilia, there were women who would try to find some transparent excuse to worm a recipe out of Enoch. Which says something about forms of morality. Or women. Or both.

—But the run-in, what the drunks and loafers still called the Great Duel even when I was young. It fell out that both Pepper and Draper began spending little time downtown. Only necessity brought them in. For the most part, they let their men handle errands. Three evenings a week, each of them came to call on Cecilia Norton. No one knows how that was worked out, but Mondays, Wednesdays, and Fridays belonged to Draper, and the others to Pepper. They alternated Sundays taking her to church, and you could be sure when it was Pepper's Sunday, Draper would pray at home. And vice versa. Because Pepper could no more stand the sight of him white-haired, fair of face, than Draper could bear Pepper's visible wounds. Pepper had found her standing talking to Draper one morning (I like to suppose it was the day after Draper's vision of an easy uncontested siege was destroyed), had seen him touch her arm or take her hand in his—some mark of familiarity, and so the feeling between them was equal. Each man shattered a little, each fearing that she would find in his rival a wholeness that he lacked. And so hating that rival even more than the common enemy who had maimed them both.

—What about Sunday afternoons? Sunday nights? Bobby Lee asked, shivering a little in the rising mist-filled wind.

—Sunday?

—Who got her then?

—And the duel? I asked. —What happened between the niggers? Did Enoch kill John Paul Jones? Who . . .

—Wait up. Hold on, my father said. The whiskey was softening his voice, mellowing it. I could hardly hear him above the rain. —The Sundays after church, he mused. —They still belonged to her brother, to Ed Norton, Jr. And the evenings? Those she kept for herself. Probably considering in advance what she would say, how she would answer when it became necessary, imperative, to answer one way or the other. Even though when she did answer, it wasn't one way or the other, but a third way, something out of another dimension. And as it fell out, that answering time came sooner than she thought. Only a day or so after Pepper, a quiet deliberate man, finally got around to asking for her hand not because he was ready to do it, but because he could hear that silver-haired Draper's chariot hurrying nearer with every passing day. And, of course, from her, that "no" again.

—The duel, I said. —What about . . .

—All right. The duel. That was it. The Negroes brought it to a head, set the answering time up a lot sooner than any woman with two good men after her (even a sweet charitable honest woman like Cecilia Norton) would wish. It may even have had something to do with what she decided. Maybe if she had had world enough and time, she would have done something else. But there is not so very much world, and hardly any time at all. It was the Negroes' encounter that set it off, though.

—It was early in the morning when John Paul Jones and Enoch got to town. They tied up their mules almost next to each other, and I have heard that words passed then. Which may or may not be so. But later, this time with people in the streets, they crossed paths in front of Ramsey's saloon, and one of them—my money is on John Paul—made a remark. Something to the effect that Draper was a dandy, a buffoon, who had brought home no scars from the war. A man, in other words, unfit to vie for the favors of a Southern white lady of good station. God only knows how he said it. And then Enoch gave him the like: "Yo' boss look like he been drug over a rocky hillside a'hint a pair of mules. Dat's what dey did to rustlers. How many head did ole Pepper come away wif fo' dey caught up to him?"

"Watch yo' mouf, nigger. Cap'n hear his name in de street, he whip yo' ass and send you scufflin'."

"Whip *my* ass? I don' know he could even whip *yo'* ass. Dat sorry white man ought to buy him a feed sack an' cover his ugly face. Fo' de ladies. 'Specially fo' Miss Norton. I reckon she too kind to run him off."

"I done tole you to leave off de cap'n. If you wants trouble, jus' keep yo' mouf goin'."

"You gone send fo' him? I don't see him much in town nowadays. Reckon he afraid he might cross wif Cap'n Draper?"

"He might be afraid he'd have to kill him. Ole Draper done made hisself scarce, too. Maybe he don' want his clothes mussed. Ole fancy Dan."

—And so on. Which is only speculative dialogue built out of bits and pieces. But the idea is there, because Enoch told Sentell. Old and aimless and past ready to die, he still remembers, and gets angry, even though John Paul died his friend and he almost grieved himself into the grave over him then.

—But one of them pushed the other, and before anyone could step in, both of them came up with army pistols and opened fire.

—It was close on to noon now, and the streets were full. Mostly men, since the women were at home fixing dinner. But the first shot cleared the street. Your grandfather, Bobby Lee, was a young man then and he told it. He said those were tense times, and Louisiana politics were bad, and the Federals still remembered the summer of 1865, and all things taken together, your grandfather said he was in a horse trough—not behind it, *in* it—before he heard the second shot. Then the shots came like an infantry regiment assaulting. Those Negroes couldn't have been more than ten or fifteen yards apart by any account, and they fired twelve shots, emptied both

pistols with people ducking into doorways, and people falling off
horses, and a regular traffic jam in front of Ramsey's saloon with the
ones inside trying to get out to see, and the ones outside trying to
get in to live.

—And finally, after the holocaust, when the thunder faded and a
few people dared raise their heads to see how many dead there were
besides the Negroes, there stood John Paul Jones and Enoch, shoulders hunched, arms akimbo, empty pistols hanging down. And
neither of them scratched. Down toward the city hall, a mule lay in
the street kicking and twitching, with a Yankee soldier lying caught
beneath him howling rebellion and murder—and not hurt either.
But the U.S. mule quivered one final time and some of the loafers
went over to pull the soldier out from under him.

—Meanwhile, Enoch was staring at the dirt, and John Paul Jones
was looking at his feet. Finally, one of them (this time my money is
on Enoch) tossed his gun down, said, "Shit," softly, despairingly,
and slouched off to his own mule. John Paul never made it. Enoch
had had his back to the mule, so the marshal let him ride away. But
the soldiers caught John Paul and took him down to the city hall for
destruction of government property, assaulting a United States
trooper in performance of duty (which meant, he, the soldier, was
neither asleep, drunk, in Rosa Gruber's honey hut, or absent without leave, and too many niggers had been causing the commandant
of the garrison trouble of one kind or another lately), disorderly
conduct, and disturbing the peace.

—But that evening, the word was all over town. One oaf at
Ramsey's said it was the first time in Louisiana history when the
seconds met before either of the principals had given or accepted a
challenge. And some other fool claimed that as a matter of fact, the
seconds had not even shown up, and that the principals, Enoch and
John Paul, had done tolerably well, considering their supporters
had backed out on them at the last moment.

—And, of course, the laughter flowed. Not only over Pepper and
Draper, but Cecilia, too. She had been at least the secondary cause
of that abortive affair of honor, and so the three of them were
lumped together in ridicule. It was embarrassing for the men. But it
was more than that for Cecilia Norton. She had left her home, and
that had set a few tongues wagging. Then she had begun to receive
not one but two men on alternative evenings. Now she had been,
willy-nilly, party to a farce with two Negroes shooting on the town's
main street. Even the most reticent tongues were going by that
evening.

—Which was a Thursday, as I remember. Not that it matters. And so, by protocol, it was Pepper's night. But protocol—and almost everything else, as it turned out—was by the board. Captain Pepper had barely taken off his hat when Draper showed up on the porch.

—I don't know what passed between them. That part is a blank. What do you say to a former comrade-in-arms when you have hated him for the sake of a woman, and then found yourself and him—and the woman—mutual shareholders in a fund of humiliation? I can't even invent something to fit. But they ended up inside, sitting across tea and biscuits from Cecilia, and one of them began. Probably Pepper, since, after all, it was his night anyhow.

—He told her that he was sorry—that both of them apologized for their Negroes. That today's scene had been absurd, but the next time might be tragic, and there well could be a next time because he—both of them were men of strong passions and so forth. This part always bothered me because I couldn't believe it even though it is true. You just have to remember that people are not always the same—at least not in how they express themselves, how they act.

—I'd have just shot Draper and had done with it, Bobby Lee said. —If I really loved her.

—No, you wouldn't. You couldn't. I can't explain to you how it was to be a Confederate officer in those days. If you had good character at all, you were the soul of the people: all they had left to sustain them, all they could show for four terrible years of war. You had to think of that.

—But Cecilia heard him out. Hands folded, skirt arranged above her ankles, gray eyes fixed on both their faces. I see her sitting there like Lee at the midnight campfire near Chancellorsville with Jackson proposing a mad solution to an insoluble problem and that great old lion knowing he will have to break every rule, even the most elementary rules of horse sense to mend the situation, and saying finally, "Very well, what will you leave me, General?" And Cecilia, probably already having solved the dilemma within, is listening to see if he, Pepper, or Draper either will say anything to render her solution void or inoperable or irrelevant even before she states it. But, no, he doesn't. And Draper is silent, no longer a free agent, a conquerer-in-embryo, but only a suppliant awaiting the queen's doom. Perhaps it had gone too far too fast. Or maybe he was still embarrassed for his Negro's part in it: remember, even then he was not without some feeling for form. The Jesuits had given it to him; the Southern society had reinforced it. But like any good Jesuit—or good constitutionalist, for that matter—it was the meaning beneath form that moved him. The accidents clothed the substance, and without form, everything was void. So it says in a book of note. Ignatius and Calhoun were at one on that point. So the mock duel, this parceling out of evenings between him and Pepper—all of it was hard on Captain Draper. But beyond his love of order, he was a man, and Cecilia moved him like a sacrament. There are things in the universe that dictate our acceptance whether we grasp their formal order or not: gravity, honor, the love of a woman.

—And so Pepper is done, saying, "Choose, for the love of God and the peace of our souls. And even for the good order of this town." Or something of the sort. And Cecilia sat silent for a moment before she started.

—"I cannot—will not—choose between you. Because neither of you is complete, and each of you is too precious. I love you both, and so I will have neither of you to the exclusion of the other."

—Which, of course, felled them both. They assumed she meant she would give them both up. And I think that is exactly what she meant, almost had to mean, even though it seemed otherwise afterward. So Draper rose and bowed and left. But not Pepper. Remember, forms meant nothing to him. And words are only forms. He stayed. And even having gone so far, having invented and patched and pulled together the recollections of a score of people now dead, I know when to draw up short. What he said, what he did, I have no idea. Unless, of course, it began that night. It could have, but I don't think so. Don't ask me why. I'm too tired for surmise.

The rain had slowed to a steady downpour, and the distant streetlamp seemed veiled, as if it lay behind a scrim of muslin, a soft corona around it like an autumn moon. The whiskey was gone, and Bobby Lee had brought out a bottle of brandy. I learned that night how much one's mood has to do with drunkenness. I have never become drunk unless, one way or another, I wanted to. My father held his brandy under a steady stream of water dripping off the roof. —That's a good idea, he told Bobby Lee.

—So there was a lull after that night. For what seemed a long time. At least a week or so. Until some old woman, or old woman of a man, or Negro maid or wagon driver saw Draper coming out of Cecilia Norton's little house about five-thirty one morning.

—Pepper, Bobby Lee said, lying back in his chair, eyes closed.

—You mean Pepper.

My father paused for a moment. —I mean Draper.

Bobby Lee's eyes opened. —You mean Pepper talked her into . . . Draper?

My father laughed and drank some brandy. —Good God, you've been reading Miles Standish. Or Walter Scott or something. Hell, no. These were two men, and either one would have run a bayonet through the other on ten seconds' notice. Except, being men and not boys, they realized that that was no solution. That one, the survivor, would lose her, whether he escaped jail or not, and that Ed Norton, Jr., would have to do with a little less time on a Sunday.

—No, Draper was there at her invitation. I see what happened— Mr. Sentell saw it. Maybe no one else did.

—You mean she gave herself to Pepper, I began.

—Yes. Probably. Almost certainly. Never mind how. I mean what form the seduction took with a man who cared nothing for forms. But the night of their talk, or Pepper's next night—or some night before Draper was seen coming out of her house.

—And she sent . . .

—For Draper.

—Goddamn, Bobby Lee muttered. —I don't believe it.

—That's all right, my father said. —You don't have to. But the alternative is that what Pepper managed, Draper also managed independently. That's not Draper.

—But nobody saw Pepper coming out. The first one they saw was Draper. So why Pepper first, and then her sending for Draper . . . ?

—Because of Draper. The Jesuit, the formalist, the gentleman, I said. —Anybody but Draper.

—Fair enough, my father said. —And anyhow, it could have gone on quietly for months except for the old woman or the Negro or whoever saw Draper. It may not even have been Draper's first early morning exit. Except, knowing Draper . . .

—You'd bet it was, I finished.

—Yes, my father laughed. —The compromised captain. If it had been Pepper, he would have come out with his medical kit, thrown a dollar to the Negro, or told the old woman Cecilia was taken seriously ill. But Draper had no shifts. What decorum or violence couldn't manage went unhandled.

—But anyhow, in a sense, nothing changed. Three nights a week it was Draper; the other three Pepper. Except sometimes Cecilia would go to Draper's place, sometimes to Pepper's. When she pulled the stops, she pulled them all.

—And her name, her reputation . . . I began.

—She had none. None at all. I don't mean it was bad. Or heaven knows, good. She had no reputation at all. Because no matter what she did, no one was about to talk about it, use her name for laughs in Ramsey's or Cleburne's store. The Negroes were one thing: you could talk about that and neither Pepper or Draper was likely to call you out for it. But Cecilia was something else. No one had to be warned. They knew. Just a word, even the casual hint that they had bad-mouthed her, and the whole Yankee army wouldn't have saved them. You'd have not only Pepper and Draper after you, but those crazy Negroes, too. And you couldn't count on them to miss again. One morning the school principal where Cecilia taught sent her a note saying they would have to do without her services. By that afternoon, before school was out, he had a note from Captain Draper requesting an interview. He sent Cecilia a long letter asking her— no, petitioning her—to stay. Some woman dragooned her husband into pulling their child out of school, the woman saying she wouldn't have the boy educated by a Jezebel. The same evening her husband got his notice from the sawmill north of town, and the next day they had a wagon packed, and Captain Pepper, who owned a piece of the sawmill, stood on the sidewalk watching them leave. And after that, it was quiet. Never indifferent, only quiet. The townspeople had gotten used to being silent about what they didn't like. The Unions had taught them that.

—It was wrong, Bobby Lee said. —You shouldn't shut people up that way.

My father shrugged. —I don't know. I used to think not. But when you say that, you go to the heart of the system—the only thing we held or even hold in common with the Yankee: the idea that a man can do as he wishes with what he holds. And if you have the power to shut a man up, and you want him shut up—well, I expect you'll use it. Especially when it has to do with someone you love.

—Cecilia Norton was using what power she had to get what she wanted, Bobby Lee put in. —Against the whole town, religion, everything. Maybe it was catching.

My father grinned ruefully. —Leave it to you to reduce things to manageable terms. I don't know what she wanted. I could never tell for sure. That would be the center of the story. Only it's blurred.

—Does a woman want to be counted a common whore, even if no one dares say it? Does she want no home, no security—nothing but the love and erratic companionship of two men, both caught in a closed system of permanent and public cuckolding, each of the other? I think she wanted something else. Something without a label, that even she couldn't have given a name. I think she wanted to hold as much of the past in her arms as she could: those fragments, human bits and pieces left after the war and the Yankee robbed her of the dances and the servants, of her brother and the little boy, one generation out of Warsaw, who died like a Southern gentleman for her. I think she was bone-tired of the little pretensions to gentility of those bourgeoisie who had managed one way or another to survive. She wanted as much of what was left real as she could gather to herself. To shore against her ruins.

—Better be a good man's whore than die the wife of a pretentious pig, I said.

—You're learning to turn a phrase, my father said, standing up and pacing, watching the rain. —Best not turn that one in front of your mother and sister.

—Anyhow, my father went on, —it continued. All the elements of a public scandal. Except for the tongues to give it flight. There may have been deaths from apoplexy in this town among those who had to talk about it and didn't dare. Hardly dared turn over in bed and whisper it to the husband, the wife. What if a servant heard? A man scything the yard? He might know John Paul or Enoch. What one Negro knew today, everyone in town would know tomorrow. And Captain Pepper was loved. He still doctored the poor, defended them in court. And Draper knew judges and some people in Baton Rouge and New Orleans. And something else: the children loved Cecilia. The poor, the Negroes, the children loved Cecilia. The poor, the Negroes, the children. How do you like that phalanx? Not a vote or a dollar among them, but they could talk. And so no one else did. Until Pepper's and Draper's and Cecilia's peculiar institution became a fact, a facet, of Shreveport's life. Part of the mosaic, a kind of bar sinister in the town's arms. Not the only one, or even the worst—after all, Don Juan Cleburne still lived in town, despite the general knowledge that he had been part and parcel of selling Ed Norton, Jr., and his friends to the Yankees. There was another man just out of town who had had four children by his widowed daughter. So the town humped and stood for it. Which is what any town does when there is nothing else to do.

—And the page comes in from the wings with a sign reading: TIME PASSES. Indeed it does. Long, full, peaceful years. A few things change in the passing. She decides to divide her time by weeks instead of days. A week with Draper, a week with Pepper. Sometimes she goes to New Orleans. As Mrs. Draper. Or to Memphis as Mrs. Pepper. And amid these years, she gives birth to a child. Whose nativity is as mysterious, if less portentous, as that other boy's whose fathering was perpetually in doubt. This is a special time. It is the first meeting between Draper and Pepper since that night. It must have been five or six years later. They meet at the baptism. Which is Catholic, not at anyone's insistence, but simply because the priest, who has a small flock in Shreveport at best, since North Louisiana is Protestant to the core, has no objection to the charge. Parentage is no problem to him. There is a child, *ergo* a human soul. I suspect Catholicism in this country has never thought of itself as a pillar of the community, and hence owes no debt to the powers that be. Especially in a town where Baptist, Methodist, and Presbyterian ministers hold sway. The priest is not much concerned with parentage, or bastardy, or whatever. These are problems in manners, and only the powers care about manners. Do you suppose a Negro minister would ask for a marriage license before he pours the water? When you live at the level of reality, you leave manners and preferences for those well off enough to indulge them.

—So the child is baptized John Thomas. Two good saints' names. But no last name. The Catholic ritual never mentions the surname. Which is either wise or kind or cynical, but convenient. And so John Thomas. Surname later. Both Draper and Pepper holding the boy, each seeing himself in the child, each secretly sure he has planted a bit of immortality for himself. And each corroded by the possibility that he is holding the other's immortality in his arms.

—But habit, if you can establish it, conquers almost everything. Which explains how, one day, the lion will lie down with the lamb. A question of recovering the mode of conduct they acquired in Eden. The lamb seems willing enough, but lions—all kinds of lions— have gotten out of the habit.

—Finally, the boy became old enough to begin questioning. Children outdo all of us when it comes to forms. They can sense anything out of the ordinary even before you expect them to grasp what is ordinary, and so they suffer. But Cecilia was wise. She knew he could never be schooled in Shreveport, and that sooner or later he would tire of the daily undivided attention of Uncle John and Uncle Thomas, and even John Paul (and John Paul's children, an illegitimate brood—no, I don't know if normal desire or emulation moved him) and Enoch, and want playmates. Hunting, fishing, riding— camping for a week sometimes with Uncle Thomas Draper (while Mother and Uncle John were in Memphis) in the East Texas woods. The boy is already, at five or six, the equal and probably the superior of most boys twice his age. He can shoot, mend a dog's leg or a bird's wing, has heard the law—and, of course, the war—discussed. But even so, he headed north to Nashville to school without much sadness. It was a good life, but he had been missing something. Something useless by adult standards: I spy and pet snakes, and running and yelling and hiding and seeking in old barns, and secret societies and pacts signed in blood—playfellows. Someone to set oneself against—and beside. All childish rubbish, but needed. And he had to go to Nashville to get anything like it.

—And he had to have a surname for the trip, Bobby Lee said.

—Yes. And he got as good a one as Caddo Parish could give him: Sentell.

—How . . .

—I don't know the mechanics. Neither does he. Except Major Edward Malcolm Sentell sponsored him as a young nephew, whose father had died, and he kept the name. It wasn't the first time Sentell had stood against the town. I suppose it had gotten to be a habit with him. Remind me sometimes—the next rainy night—to tell you about him in the war and just afterward.

Bobby Lee poured the last of the brandy. The rain was beginning to slacken, and through gaps in the drifting cloud, we could see the moon again.

—And more time going by. Under the same moon, with rain and drought alternating, the good and the evil sharing both indifferently. The boy growing, realizing that his home is, to say the least, not like other homes. But gifted with blood wise enough to know that "different" is not a pejorative word, whatever society thinks about it. The woman still lovely, still like Diana, seeming only to become more desirable, more radiant, more a center from which life—as opposed to organized, socialized, commercialized existence—sprang. By then there were even those in the town who cared more for her, for what she seemed to radiate, than for their cleavage to custom and opinion. Frequently people would call. The Sentells, the major and his wife, Vera (who had always called, even in the worst times), and Wesley Grimes, who had taken over the remains of Norton's old store and owed Draper a deep debt and a lot of money, who came not for debt's or money's sake—it had been a straight business deal—but mainly because he liked Draper. And Cecilia. And because, though he did not discuss it, he respected Pepper, too. He once told Mr. Sentell years later that he went because he wanted to go. Because there was kindness and courage and much love in the atmosphere. I understand he dropped a local girl because she—her family probably—refused an invitation to Cecilia Norton's, given through him. There were others, former students whose moral characters had mostly survived the ghastly ravages of having for a teacher the town's most prominent hussy. And people who had met her when she made the rounds with Captain Pepper. Those years were full. And then they were over.

—She died. Alone, without a day's sickness. Without, a few local ladies of quality pointed out most quietly, time enough to gather her sins up, much less time to wash them in the Lamb's dear blood. My God, the stories. They were still circulating when I was old enough to hear. She had died by her own hand, guided by the same demon who had driven her to make her stewy bed with three places in it. Or better: they had murdered her, one of them. Out of final desperation, sudden passion. Invent your own motive; it will be as likely as any given at the time. However it was, she was dead, and the town seemed suddenly dark. No one could explain it. It was as if some band under tension had snapped at last, as if a slave's bonds had parted, and the end of tension, the sudden freedom, was ashes and debris. There were no sermons using her as an example of the fruits of perdition. There was only silence. And a good portion of the town showed up at the Catholic church where the same priest who had baptized her child said a requiem mass for her. Which I understand was highly irregular, even uncanonical, but the priest was still a freewheeler who told Mr. Sentell (he was fourteen then, and came home to stay when they sent for him, with Major Sentell, his third uncle) that the mass might work some spiritual good for his mother, and could not possibly put God out of sorts, who has, after all, a monopoly of understanding where the depths of the human heart are concerned.

—They buried her next to Ed Norton, Jr., of course, with the two captains bearing her coffin alone and between them, and carrying on the same tradition by digging her grave themselves. It was not claimed that she had been a soldier, and I expect no one considered her a victim of the war then twenty-five years past. But they might have. That war shaped all our destinies—theirs more than ours, but the years only diminish the influence; they do not erase it.

—I was there. I remember a graveyard filled with people crying. Mostly poor, many black. Students who had not asked permission, and former students there with their own children. People who had not the time or money—or possibly the mischievous blood—to judge those few who chose to do them a kindness. And the captains, side by side, at attention, beginning, both of them to slump a little; Pepper as white-haired as Draper; Draper's face almost as ravaged by time as Pepper's by artillery silent a quarter of a century before. The priest telling them that time is an illusion and that time's wrongs are righted in eternity, time's losses made good in the arms of Almighty God. "So be it," Captain Draper said. "Amen," from Captain Pepper. And when the grave was filled, they exchanged one long searching look between them as if they had never seen each other before. Or as if each were going on a long journey and wished to remember the face of the other.

—Suicide, I put in. —They both killed themselves. At least one.

—No, my father said. —You're paying more attention to the story than the men. Keep your eye where it belongs. There were no suicides. I wonder if those movies are getting to affect your judgment.

—No, there were no dramatics then. Each of them turned away, turned their backs on the grave as if someone had given the order "About face." Captain Draper shook young Sentell's hand, held his arm with the other and tried to speak. But it was no use. Then Captain Pepper came up. "Boy," he said, "I reckon you know what we've lost." "I know," Mr. Sentell told him. "I know well enough." "My God," Captain Pepper said, looking around as if he had just come to, had just realized himself. "My God."

—And they made their own way out of the graveyard. Draper in one direction, Pepper in the other, each with his Negro beside him, all weeping in their own way, too. Leaving Sentell standing over the grave of an uncle who died in a blast of Yankee gunfire before he was even born, and that of a mother he loved but could never hope to understand. Watching his father walk out of the cemetery in two directions, his head turning first one way, and then the other. Until Major Sentell, the man whose name he bore, came up, made the sign of the cross, and took him away as twilight came on.

—And nothing changed, I put in, almost as if I had already heard my father say it.

—All right, he said. —Maybe your judgment hasn't quite gone to seed. You're right. Nobody, even Mr. Sentell, knows how they agreed, whether the Negroes met and decided it, or maybe no one met and decided anything, because there was no need. But they went back to the old arrangement. Cecilia Norton was buried on Sunday, and Monday morning Captain Draper and Enoch turned up early and began to plant flowers around her grave. On Tuesday it was Pepper and John Paul and his wife. With shrubs to put around the whole plot. And so on.

—And Mr. Sentell on Sundays, I said.

—Boy, you want to tell this story. My father smiled. —That's right, too. Sunday was still family day. You understand Mr. Sentell told me all this. I'm not guessing, improvising, from here on. He spent his Sunday afternoons alone out there. With a book, a pair of sandwiches. Sometimes he would fall asleep against Ed Norton's headstone. He told me it was strange how much life there was out there. Rabbits, a garter snake or two, squirrels. Once he saw a doe in the woods just beyond the fence. He liked it, and the duty, the inner demand that he present himself there amid that silence each Sunday, became what it had been for his mother, what it assuredly was for Draper and Pepper: a pleasure, something to look forward to, a few hours completely withdrawn from the rust and scratches of society, of living. To be spent with those who had already passed what Aeschylus called the goal of life, and were done with it, complete. As complete as any of earth's creatures can ever be. He told me once that it may be the cemetery kept him from marrying. Not only because his going there every week served to remind those who might have forgotten or at least put out of mind his antecedents when and if he began paying court to their daughters, but because the place made him yearn for completeness, too. He came to want to be automatic: self-moved. Which in turn brought him to pity Draper and Pepper both. If you see what I mean. And something else Mr. Sentell never said. Maybe hasn't even thought.

—Sure, Bobby Lee said, —one day at his mother's grave . . . like her at Ed Norton, Jr.'s.

—Youall amaze me, my father said. —Sure enough. That's my guess. I thought I was done with guessing from Cecilia's burying on since I had good dependable firsthand account. But . . .

—His account is no good, I said. —I mean, he can't help what he does to it.

—Like the stories we heard about Mr. Sentell himself, Bobby Lee cut in. —Ain't nobody around here wants to hurt him. It's just they tell what they know.

—And they don't know anything, I finished.

—So he said, or didn't say, but had to feel at least, if he were going to draw on that buried treasure of self-sufficieny, of completeness, that there would have to be another woman as good as his mother, my father said.

—You want to muddy it up real good? Bobby Lee asked suddenly, his voice excited.

—What?

—Maybe the other grave, too. Maybe he was waiting to find enough of Ed Norton, Jr., in himself, at least enough of what Ed was supposed to have been, to avoid ending up a Draper or a Pepper. A half-man with his mainspring knocked out and buried, running from habit in the end.

—No, my father said. —That's too far. Because I'm not done with them, not just yet.

—Aw, Bobby Lee grimaced. —Where do you go from there?

My father shook his head almost wearily. —It's funny, he said. —Youall do fine with the guessing, with the hard part, the variables and imponderables. But you keep losing track of the givens.

—How's that? I asked.

—Character, goddamn it. You seem to keep believing we've spent the night dredging up the phantoms of a pair of Shreveport businessmen slouching around town here in 1923, playing the Victrola, driving new Fords and talking about expansion. They never get perfect or fall apart completely. But they do change. They get better. Or they get worse.

—They changed, Bobby Lee said in an awed voice. —Honest to God. You're going to tell us . . .

—What Sentell told me. About the first anniversary of her death. Which fell on one of Pepper's days. And while he was watering some plants, he looked up and it was Draper. Who was already talking, already saying something in a soft urgent tone, in a voice hardly his own, and Pepper's hard scarred face upturned to his was beginning to change, and both of them, old men now, purely and simply old men with their black clothes and their pasts and their years hanging loose and heavy on them, each leaning toward the other, closer over that quiet sunken flower-covered grave where their manhood and youth and the balm of their hurts lay, until Pepper stood up, his hand thrust out to Draper. Who looked at it as if it contained a mystery or a judgment, and then took it, drawing Pepper close to him, his other arm around his rival's neck. Then both of them embracing, talking, laughing, still holding onto each other, while Sentell, standing in shadow over by the tree line watched, his eyes full to overflowing, having to bite his lip to keep from crying out something, anything. And then both of them walking slowly away together, and Sentell seeing his father leave the cemetery without having to turn his head, and walking over to the grave and falling beside it, his hands thrust toward the green ravenous earth, and laughing, too, full, complete, satisfied. And, God's sweet wonder, alive.

The rain was gone now, only a slow and rhythmic dripping from the eaves left behind it. To the east, the sky was already gray and turning pink, almost the rich flush of new and healthy blood.

—What else is there? my father said. —You know. You know how they lived together. How they went together to visit her and Ed Junior together. How they sat on the porch of Pepper's house in town or at Draper's during the summer when they went there to get out of the heat. How you would walk past and see them sitting for hours, heads together, talking, gesticulating, sharing every moment they had spent with her until each one had lived that half a life denied him, until they had become, for all intents and purposes, one old man telling himself how much there had been, how rich it was, how there had been life enough for two. And Sentell coming from his law practice or his plantation (something from Pepper, something from Draper, and a remembrance in Major Sentell's will, too) to add what he could and share what they chose to give him—which was probably not all, but more than enough, seeing that he would be heir to everything preservable, portable from one—I mean two, no, three— human souls to another. Until they had all gotten it done, completed.

The sun was up by then, almost blinding, and our eyes hurt from it, from the long night. Bobby Lee and my father squinted at me, grinning, and I back at them. Our boots were wet from dew and the night's rain, and the grass and bushes and trees sparkled with it, catching the sun, breaking it to bits and hurling the shards abroad.

—A new world, my father said, his voice soft and awed and a little jocular all at once. —The ghosts sleeping again, and another day. I guess this one belongs to us, if any of us can stay awake to use it.

I put my arm around my father's shoulders and followed his gaze down the long slope of quiet untenanted yards, down the cinder-covered street toward the bayou, where brown water glinted and rolled slowly, like a serpent rousing with the bright summer sun.

—You reckon any of us could use it better than them? I mean even if we'd got our sleep? Bobby Lee asked him.

—Ah, my father said, smiling, squinting up into the sun above our trees, —that's not it. Not better. Just as well. That's the trick. Can we come near to using it as well?

And from behind us, my mother's voice calling, something about coffee, and biscuits not baked yet, and work to be done, all in the mystified and sleep-strewn voice of one waking from long and dreamless rest.

The Retrievers
Shreveport: 1933

When you come into Shreveport from the southeast, you might end up driving along Fairfield Avenue, which is a long shaded street of big white frame houses and thick with old moss-covered oaks, magnolias, gum trees, and a scattering here and there of tall pines. All the houses were built in the decades just before and just after the Confederate War, and in the days I lived there—all through the late thirties and early forties—the houses themselves had begun to decay a little. One might be needing paint; another would lack some shutters or have a column beginning to sag with the combined weight of long years and close money. Even so, though, it was still a beautiful street, still impressive.

When my father brought us down from Memphis, we used to drive out along Fairfield Avenue on a Sunday afternoon in the Ford. My young brother, Nathan Bedford, my sister, Malissa, and my mother and I would just look. We had lived in a pretty nice house on Poplar in Memphis before my father's business, cotton factoring, had gone to pieces, and we couldn't get used to living in a little three-bedroom place my father had bought in a suburb of town. It was like a sardine tin, and when my mother's father heard we were living in a one-story house, he had taken my father aside during a last visit to Memphis and asked him if this was the way he meant to provide for his family.

So I guess my father was yearning some, too. He'd see a big fine house and point it out to mother. —Looks like our old house, he'd say. —Don't you think?

It really wouldn't, much. At least no more than any big boxy white frame house with a lot of trees and bushes around it looks like any other. But my mother would frown in concentration and then smile. —Yes, she'd answer. —Yes, I believe it does.

Whereupon my father would get glum and forget to stop by the ice cream shop on his way home.

The houses were no mansions. Just great big square places with wide porches and galleries and high ceilings and sometimes some of that ornate cutout wood my mother called gingerbread. They were just comfortable, exuding a kind of lasting hard-won quietude and tranquillity. But they seemed like castles to us. Much later I saw Blenheim and Hampton Court in England, and neither seemed quite so fine as that long procession of houses sitting serene and certain in the shade of Fairfield Avenue.

After we had lived in Shreveport awhile, we came to know something about the people who lived on Fairfield. Some of the houses were owned variously by old families whose eldest male might be called Captain or Major or Colonel—either because he had earned that title in person or because he had received it from a father or grandfather as part of his patrimony and managed to keep the family reputation at least intact enough not to forfeit the title granted by the town and as easily withdrawn by simply letting it lapse. Some of the houses, though, were owned by small merchants who had scrambled for years and managed to get hold of a mortgage or buy it up when the last of a family died off. They would move in and be models of austerity, hoping that enough time would finally pass to give people the impression that they had always lived on Fairfield Avenue. A few of them, anxious to hasten the process, even tried to parlay a captaincy or majority in some world war regiment into a title:—captains of crockery, majors of merchandising, brigadiers of banking. My father would laugh.

Because we didn't much care about being big shots. We just wanted a place on a quiet shady street we could rattle around in without stomping on one another's toes. The only titles we had were three privates and a corporal, my father's great uncles, who had ridden with General Forrest in western Tennessee. My father said our family had been too busy fishing and cutting bait both in the war and after it ever to get hold of a rank. Anyhow, everybody knows that a corporal in Forrest's cavalry was worth any two majors kicking around in a trans-Mississippi commissary company.

But what I want to tell about is how we came to live on Fairfield Avenue without opening a plumbing shop or finding that we were the lost heirs of General Kirby-Smith. We came to be thought of as part of the old folks, one of the families to be consulted, and we got that way overnight. No waiting period. We just overshot the whole gaggle of Heathertons, Priors, Richleys, and Gaineses who had bought in and were busily trying to live down the buying.

It all happened because of my young brother and sister, Nathan and Malissa. They became, you might say, the true founders of the Shreveport branch of the Tennessee Armisteads. It was quite a trick, starting as an embarrassment and ending with a big legal thing complete to U.S. Internal Revenue sneaking around and every trimmer in the parish grinding his teeth and trying to figure a way to cash in on our good luck.

Which is getting ahead. Because it started in the summer of 1933, when we were living out off Highway 20 in a new and nameless suburb a little closer in than Dixie Gardens. There were twenty or thirty houses in the development, and all of them rested on small lots taken from one big tract of land that had once constituted the old Sentell place. I asked a boy I knew at Byrd High School about how it used to be.

—Belonged to the Indians, Joe Hobbs told me. —Then somebody nobody even remembers. Then a man named Sentell who fought in some war. Then his son got it, and that was a shame. 'Cause he went yellow in the war against the Yanks. Come home and stopped fighting, and afterward the Yanks took his place anyhow. Which was good enough for him. Then some colored guy had it till they run him out. And old Cleburne, the storekeeper, got hold of it. Bought up all thousand and five hundred acres. Kept the house and the land that runs where youall live. Broke up the rest and sold it piece by piece. Some Eyetalian truck farmers got 'em a little of it. Where the Cashios live now, and the Firinas. Then Dixie Gardens took up a lot along the river. Then Cleburne died. The rest went for taxes. Till some contractor in Alexandria bought it and parceled it out in lots a few years ago. Which is what youall live in now.

Joe Hobbs's family lived one street behind Fairfield Avenue. His grandfather was still alive, and had seen the soldiers pull down the last Confederate flag. He had watched with a bullet through both legs picked up near Rome, Georgia, while the Yankees marched in. What Joe didn't know wasn't worth knowing. Not because he cared about it, not because he was much interested in family or history or anything, but because he couldn't help himself. It just drifted in. What are you going to do when you live in the middle of a place where things have happened slowly but surely, like a glacier moving, for a century? Joe picked up the pieces, the tags and ends, names and dates as if he were part of the glacier. The only thing he didn't know was when his people had got to Caddo Parish. —I bet we was there to see the Caddo Indians movin' in, Joe Hobbs would say. But it meant nothing to him.

Sometimes Joe would come over to the house and we'd talk. All I had to do was ask the questions. He was like a memory machine. He could tell you *where* and *when* and *how*. Except, being a natural-born engineer (like his older brother at Centenary College), he could not only not tell you *why*, but could not quite understand what you meant when you asked him *why*.

—After Vicksburg, he told me, going on about the Sentells, Major Edward Malcolm Sentell, who had not gone back to fight. —Summer, late summer of 1863. Come home riding and walking all the way across Louisiana with a Yank parole in his pocket.

—How come? I asked. —Was he really yellow?

—Reckon. If you won't fight, you must be yellow.

—Did he fight at Vicksburg?

—Lord, I reckon. They told about this mine he helped plant, and the fighting all along the works. Fought like a tiger. Most of 'em did.

—So why did he stop? You don't fight and then just stop for no reason.

Joe Hobbs shrugged. —He did. And he lost his place. Good enough for him. Lived on right here in town till he died. Folks mostly couldn't stand him. Died just before I was born.

—People said he was yellow?

—Naw. Just said he wouldn't go back.

—Maybe he got religion.

—Naw. They never said nothing except he wouldn't go back.

So he was like some kind of unbelievable parrot, an enchanted one who could tell you everything except what you wanted to know. It made me mad as hell. But I kept pumping him. It was as if I had hold of a human Rosetta stone, and just needed to ask the right question to get a free trip back to the Shreveport that had been almost a hundred years before. I don't know why I wanted to. Maybe it had something to do with the big houses on Fairfield where those old families had lived. Maybe I wanted to know how you managed to get into one of them the right way, what kind of people had lived in them to begin with.

While we talked, Nathan and Malissa would fool around on the porch in their bathing suits. Nathan was building a paper-and-stick model of the *Spirit of St. Louis* with Malissa commenting on every drop of glue he squeezed out.

—Why don't you get your own? he would say finally. —They got a real nice Curtiss Jenny down at Wiseman's shop. I'll even give you fifteen cents toward it.

—No, she'd tell him. —It's a waste of time.

—Then why don't you leave me alone?

—You need help. You can't do anything by yourself.

—I'm going to bust your . . .

—Nathan, my mother would call from the kitchen. —Watch that.

—Yessum.

But neither of them paid any attention to me and my attempts to get something out of Joe Hobbs. Which was a break. Malissa could help you out of your mind.

—They say old Cleburne left a potful of money somewhere, Joe Hobbs said without my even asking. —Say he saved up maybe a million dollars. But nobody ever found a thing. He owned land all over the north part of the parish. Sold a lot of it, but they never found the money. Somebody said he had him a whole bunch of mulatto kids and passed out the money. But most people thought he'd buried it.

—Wow, Nathan put in suddenly, letting the LePage's glue run all over the plans for the *Spirit of St. Louis.* —You mean there's money somewhere around here? Just waiting for somebody to pick up?

—Never said that, Joe Hobbs answered, his voice as smooth as molasses. —Folks say it. Folks say a lot.

I was still interested in Sentell. This buried treasure thing is something you get over after *Treasure Island.* Unless you're a case of arrested development. Spanish galleons. Pieces of eight. Cutlasses. Blood in the scuppers. Wow. But Sentell. And not only him but the Old South. The place we were now in space, but another time. I was kind of hung on it. So I started asking Hobbs what kind of man Sentell was, what did he do.

—Rode good. Shot a pistol like it grew in his hand. Killed a man in Bossier Parish one time.

—Before he went to Vicksburg?

—Naw. Years afterward. Man over to Benton called his wife white trash. Said she wasn't no better than her father. In 1873. Said she was no better than old Murray Taggert, who was sure enough white trash. Said everybody reckoned she'd blowed her old man's head off. Somebody had, back in the summer of 1865. So Sentell called him on it, and this other fella drew down on Sentell, and shot him once in the leg and another time in the side. And Sentell come up with a one-shot derringer and put his shot right between the fella's eyes. They say he walked a mile and a half to a doctor and then stayed outside to get bandaged up so he wouldn't track blood all over the doctor's parlor.

—He did that after the war? And you say he was yellow?

—Must of been. Wouldn't go back after Vicksburg.

I just shook my head, and Nathan started in on the treasure again. So I went and got some iced tea that mother kept already sugared in a big crock out in the kitchen. Then I walked out on the porch again and tried to tune them and their lost million dollars out while I thought of that strange shadowy major, whose face I couldn't make out, but whose heart I would have given that imaginary million just to see into.

The next day it was pretty quiet around the house. I came in so tired from playing ball in ninety-six-degree heat that I just spread out in the bathtub and kind of stared in a trance at the little gas heater which stuck out of the wall like a dormant volcano waiting for winter to start up again. It was fine. The water was only tepid, but cooler than the air, and I lay in it for over an hour before it came to me that I hadn't heard or seen anything of the kids since I woke that morning. No Malissa to yell that she wanted her second bath of the day. No Nathan to barge in and sit on the closed lid of the commode and point out to me in agonizing detail what new struts and spars had been added to the grisly skeleton of the *Spirit of St. Louis* since the last time I had seen it. Nothing but silence. A rustle and an almost indiscernible hum where my mother was weeding a stand of hopeless zinnias out in back. But not another sound. I wondered about that, and then got to thinking about Sentell again. I reckoned I might go up to the public library and see if I could get hold of some old newspapers. Or maybe there were others like Joe Hobbs around. With something going for them besides total recall. There had to be some way to get back there. Nothing that has happened is ever really gone. Nothing can move and have being in time without leaving its traces, going on and spreading, getting fainter and fainter like the ripples that move from the point of a stone's impact in some quiet pool.

I dried off and dressed in a T-shirt. Mother was just coming in with some flowers. —Where are the kids? I asked her. —"Down by the riverside," she sang, smiling. —Searching the terrain. They caught a huge soft-shell turtle this morning. I expect them to come back with a good-sized leviathan and a pair of small behemoths by suppertime.

I didn't blame them. In the summer, with school out, things got pretty dull. All you could do was swim or stand around in front of Weber's Seabreeze root beer parlor or play baseball like a lunatic seeking sunstroke in one of the parks. All of which I did. With Joe Hobbs and Lafayette Gruber and Punch Perkins and some others. Then, in the afternoon, if we could still function after the baseball, we would fish some in Bayou Pierre or down off the river bluffs, half-asleep under a cottonwood tree, waiting for every scrap of breeze that blew up off the water. It was hotter than I can describe, and the heat starting before nine in the morning would go on as late as four or five in the afternoon.

But over the next couple of days, whether I was fishing or swimming, so long as Joe and Lafayette and I were near the river, we kept seeing Malissa and Nathan. They would show up in the sandy stretch back from the river that was choked with second-growth trees and brush and Bermuda grass. We could see them for a moment and then they'd vanish like a pair of foxes or rabbits trying to get across a clearing. I kept wondering if they were just fooling around and not paying any attention to us. Or if they were staying clear of us on purpose. Considering it was the second, I wondered what the purpose might be.

They kept showing up in the vicinity of the old Sentell house. Lafayette or I would wave to them, but Malissa would just look up like a doe and go diving back into the brush or behind the house. Nathan wouldn't even bother looking up. He'd just vanish. Looking back, I can remember that I didn't really pay much attention to this once I got used to not having the carcass of the *Spirit of St. Louis* jammed under my nose every hour and to the quiet around the house without Malissa's loud vocal help stirring up the sweltering afternoon.

Finally, one afternoon, Joe Hobbs and Lafayette Gruber and I were stretched out on the porch like a pack of hounds. We were drinking some of my mother's sugared iced tea, trying to recover from a thirteen-inning game and a bout of seining for river shrimp. Joe and Lafayette were arguing about Sentell. Not because they were interested, but because I had started them off with one of my questions.

—I think you and your grampaw are both missing some marbles, Lafayette was saying. —Major Sentell was a fine man. You better watch your mouth, too. His family is still around. If one of the Sentell boys heard you say his grandfather was yellow or a Yankee-lover, he'd deck you for keeps. Them people have family feeling.

—How come he wouldn't fight after Vicksburg?

—He signed one of them papers. Promised not to. Give his word.

—To the Yanks.

—You figure two years in a prison camp somewhere was better? Listen, I never heard of anybody comin' back from one of them camps.

It went on like that till my father came home. Then, while mother was fixing sandwiches, we all got into it. My father told about the time Nathan Bedford Forrest rode his horse into the Gayoso Hotel in Memphis looking for a Yankee general. Who managed to sneak out a window, but had to leave his pants behind. We were laughing and just joshing around when Malissa and Nathan turned up running into the yard from across the street and over the rise that led down to the Sentell place.

—Hey, Malissa called to me. —Look.

She handed me a piece of old and faded paper with some pencil markings on it, while Nathan squatted smirking at everyone on the edge of the porch. —Just look, he echoed.

—It's real. Malissa grinned like an idiot.

—Sure it's real, I said. —Real paper. What are all these squiggly circles?

—Trees, Nathan put in quickly. —In scouts, they showed us how cartographers . . .

—Whats? Lafayette asked.

—Mapmakers, Malissa translated.

—Show trees like . . .

I shrugged and tried to signal Joe and Lafayette not to laugh. The kids were asking for it, but you don't have to give people everything they ask for.

—Reckon some pirate captain left it laying around? Lafayette laughed. —Must of been a boy scout. Reckon even a eagle scout pirate captain with fifty merit badges, huh?

Malissa jerked the paper out of my hand and she and Nathan went on into the house. They stayed in there sulking till mother brought out sandwiches and they heard us all laughing and talking. Then they couldn't hold it anymore. They had to come out and tell us how they had been swimming down the river and almost caught a gar bare-handed, and how after that they had gone up to the old house to eat lunch. It was while they were looking for a shady place where the noon sun didn't come through the shattered roof that Nathan stepped on a board which came loose and cracked him in the shin, which knocked him into the wall.

—And he went through the wallpaper, and it was so brittle it just fell all to pieces. And his head knocked out another board in the wall and jarred one of the joists loose and . . .

—My God, my father whistled, interrupting Malissa. —He sounds like a portable wrecking crew. Is there anything left of the house?

Which only brought on another long reign of silence until after mother brought out some homemade peach ice cream. Then Nathan had to let go again. —And behind that joist, next to the clapboards that covered the outside there was this kind of canvas envelope. And inside we found this here map.

Father looked at it. It was a kind of gray-brown like butcher paper or a paper bag. It looked pretty old, but not all that old. Stuck in a wall out at the Sentell house with the weather coming in on it, a month would age it as much as a hundred years.

—It wasn't canvas, Malissa said.

—What? I asked.

—The thing we found it in. It was kind of like oilcloth. Like somebody had tore up a tablecloth and sewed up a little sack of what was left.

—Looks old, my father said. —What are these little irregular circles?

—Trees, I said. —It's a plan for a formal garden somebody forgot to plant.

—Shut up, Malissa said. —It's trees all right. And here's a road. And this is the house.

Everybody was down on the porch floor now. Joe Hobbs, with his eyebrows raised, taking it all in for later recital to whoever asked him. Lafayette, almost strangling to keep from laughing out loud. My father and I caught between curiosity and something in the neighborhood of what Lafayette had called family feeling. Maybe the kids were a little nuts. All kids fourteen and sixteen are a little nuts. Two years before, I had been sixteen and probably a little nuts myself.

—Can't be the old Sentell house, my father said.

Malissa and Nathan turned on him. —Why not? they said together.

—Because this place on the map is at least a quarter of a mile from the water, if the scale means anything. The Sentell place is maybe two hundred yards from the river. And where's this road? There's not even a calf track that looks like this around that old house.

—Maybe the pirate had him a place in the Bahamas. Lafayette sniggered. —Maybe that thing is the right map in the wrong country.

That took care of the rest of the evening as far as Malissa and Nathan were concerned. In fact, it took care of the next couple of days. They just sat around the house and moped. On Saturday Nathan finished the *Spirit of St. Louis*. That afternoon he and Malissa took it up on the garage, set fire to it, and let it fly off in flames over toward Bayou Pierre. Then they sat on the garage till suppertime. The next day was Sunday, and when my father asked if they wanted to take a ride out Fairfield Avenue, Malissa burst into tears and Nathan said something filthy.

So that Sunday evening, it was a pretty gloomy dump when Joe

Hobbs showed up. I poured him a dipper of sugared iced tea and we went out on the porch to watch the moon and slap mosquitoes. He looked worried, and that surprised me. Because Joe Hobbs never looked any way at all. His great-grandfather had been a blacksmith, his grandfather owned an automobile garage, and his father had the biggest hardware and feed-seed store in the parish. And not one of them, so far as I could tell, had ever registered any expression at all. The most dramatic thing that ever happened to a Hobbs face was when a rill of sweat ran down it.

But Joe was troubled, and I thought I'd leave him alone about Sentell and wait to see what he had to say. He finished his tea and kind of picked at his shoe.

—That map . . . he started.

—Forget it. The kids will be over their sulks in another day or two.

—Naw, that map . . .

—Some guy stuck it in there. Probably meant to sell it to some fool later on and forgot it.

—Naw, Joe said as if I had not even interrupted him, as if he were trying to get it clear in his own head. —I got to talking to my grampaw. He said the river's changed maybe twice along about here in the last fifty years or so. Said it keeps cutting back and forth, but the Corps of Engineers never would come up and . . .

I felt as if a December wind had just snuck onto the porch and let me have it in the back. Really, as he said it, I could see the whole past laughing at me. What if? Just what if that map?

—The road . . . I said weakly.

—Used to run up along there till they cut it out when they run Highway 20 back in the 1910s. They just straightened it out on account of the only place that got slighted by the new route was the Sentell place, and there wasn't anybody owned a big enough piece of it to complain. It was there, all right.

So there had been a road. And the river in another place. And I was so hung up in all the history and my circles in a pool that I forgot things do change. That you can concrete or dig up or cover over or build on anything a lot in eighty years. —That doesn't prove the map means anything, I said weakly.

—Naw, Joe said. —It just proves whoever was funning around knew the place he was joking about.

By the next morning, when I woke up and talked to my father about it, I knew that Malissa and Nathan had either heard us or talked to Joe or something. Because they were gone, too. The garage was always a mess, with maybe three or even four hundred old bottles and plenty of newspaper all over. But when one of us really needed money, needed it so bad we were even willing to do something to get it, the garage was always in the way of getting cleaned.

—They woke up before daybreak, my father told me at breakfast.
—And took the bottles down to the Youree Drive drugstore and got a dollar and a quarter for cleaning it up. They even took the newspapers to sell.

That afternoon they came tramping in, covered with dust, Malissa's swimming suit wet with sweat, and Nathan almost ready to drop. Nathan got me out in the backyard as if he had murdered somebody and wanted me to help dig the grave.

—That Joe Hobbs is a friend of yours, ain't he?
—Sure.
—He's got a brother out at Centenary College, huh?
—Yep.
—I need a transit.
—You need a kick in the fanny.
—Listen, don't fool with me. You tell him to get me a transit to borrow, and I'll pay him for the loan. I'll pay him so good he won't believe it.
—Sure.

But that misplaced river and that ghost road had made me a little skittish of just shoving Nathan over on the grass and letting it go. So I talked to Joe. Who talked to his big flat-faced identical brother. Who for no reason I could imagine brought a transit over to the house (which was my first chance actually to look through one and get to know what it was really for). He told Nathan that it was borrowed from the college, only nobody knew it had been borrowed since they didn't need it during the summer, and that if anything happened to it, he, Buddy Hobbs, would ravel Nathan's spine for him. I asked Joe about it after his brother had left and Nathan and Malissa hit out for their daily rounds.

—Well, I told him about that map.
—So what? It's a joke.
—He said Nathan was old enough to use it.
—But why?
—That map, Joe said, narrowing his eyes, trying to explain. But it wasn't clear in his memory and he couldn't say it. If it had been anybody but Joe, I would have called it a hunch.

—That map, me and Buddy looked at it with Nathan. Looked like somebody knew every tree. Buddy used to hunt squirrel over there in the fall. Said there used to be one old out-of-place cypress which ain't anything but a stump now, and so buried you can't even hardly see the stump. But it was on the map. Just like another tree. Even said "Cipres" next to it on there.

Which was the end of that. We talked about Sentell. He told me about a boy Major Sentell and his wife had taken in. Who had lived across the river until a year or so ago when he died. Just talk. The major and his life were fading again. Maybe that goofy map had broken the spell. Some things cancel other things. As if everything were all hooked together in crazy combinations. As if a Chinaman could pull up a rice stalk in his paddy field and make a tree vanish on the Caddo Parish courthouse square.

It was almost time for supper when I saw Nathan and Malissa running through the open fields across from us and up into the yard. Malissa held out her hand.

—Spider bit me, she said. —Probably a black widow.

—Probably a giant tarantula, I said.

Nathan set up his transit out on the curb. He aimed it toward the house and beckoned to Malissa. I just sat on the porch and watched them. It was like watching somebody making a movie. Or the way I guessed it would be.

—Thirty-five yards, Nathan said. —Dead that way.

—Through the front door? Malissa asked a little quizzically.

—You want to see that map?

—Okay, she said. —Gimme the tape-line.

Then I saw where their bottle and paper and garage-cleaning money had gone. It was the biggest, shiniest tape measure I ever saw. It must have been a hundred yards long. Malissa took the end of it in her unbitten hand and skipped into the house with it.

—You must be surveying for a railroad, I told him.

—Boy, you're funny, he answered, squinting through the transit. That was the first time my little brother had ever given me the brush-off. But not the last. So I went on inside and washed up. When I came back out of the bathroom, they were in the kitchen. My mother was standing in the breakfast room.

—Look, Nathan was telling Malissa, —you can go all the way back to the last tree if you want. Were we right up to there? I mean, from the house, from that last porch post on out to the tree?

—I reckon.

—Okay. Were we right from there to the curb, even if that road is changed?

—I believe.

—Then we're right now. It's here. Maybe a foot or so off one way or the other. But it's in here. I bet it's right under the stove.

—Will youall . . . my mother began. But she wasn't in touch with them.

—We've got to get an ax and a couple of shovels, Nathan said. —I forgot that. You reckon we could swap this tape-line for an ax and some shovels?

This time my mother came through a little stronger. —Youall clear out. You've had too much sun. Didn't I tell you they were getting too much sun? she asked me.

—I believe you did, I said.

—And something else. Youall forget that ax and things. You just put it out of mind. If you even look like you mean to go fooling around this kitchen . . .

—Maybe they could widen it some, I said. —Everybody is always complaining how little it is.

My mother looked at me for a few seconds. —You're funny, she said, and walked out to meet my father who was just putting his car in our clean garage. That did it for me. I guess I sulked until after supper. I guess I sulked longer than that. Because when I went to bed, I never even realized that the kids had been out and were back again and had gone to bed before me. All I remember is hearing my father tell them that the kitchen better stay the way it was, map or no map. If they wanted to stay the way they were.

But it's hard to put the fear of God into a sixteen-year-old, much less into a fourteen-year-old. And I guess it's impossible to hold down a kid of any age who's got a headful of buried treasure. Anyhow, I went to sleep kind of feeling sorry for them. I guess I halfway wanted to see whether there really was anything to that map. But I could see my father's position, too. Who tears up kitchens on a hunch?

About three-thirty or four in the morning, I found out who. It seems I was dreaming of this girl I had seen at Centenary College one day when I went over with Joe Hobbs. She was tall and tanned dark as walnut, and we were sitting in the student union, and she was looking at me. And somebody was tunneling under our table. Or something.

Then I was awake, and I could still hear it. Like a giant armadillo scratching and scuffling in the dirt. I got up, amazed to find I was as alert as if I had never closed my eyes. Maybe in a way I hadn't. Maybe I knew, not just suspected, but really knew what was going to happen. I passed the door to my parents' room. It was closed. Of course. Then the hall door. Also closed. Of course. So was the door into the dining room. But the door into the kitchen wasn't closed. Just as I reached it, feeling my way in the darkness, I fell into a pile of dirt as tall as I was. I couldn't see anything of the kitchen at all. Except a kind of soft glow coming from up over the dirt as if somebody were using a flashlight with some paper Scotch-taped across it. Which they were.

I managed to scramble up to the top of the pile, and since I'd been asleep, I could see pretty well. The floor in the middle of the kitchen was gone. Just gone. At the back door was a pile of stovewood which I reckoned had once been it. One leg of the stove had fallen into the hole, which was already six or six and a half feet deep. And when the stove leg went in, it had pulled the gas connection loose from the wall. They had plugged the fractured pipe with a carrot, though, and the odor of escaping gas wasn't really too bad. Down in the hole, there they were, Nathan and Malissa, in underwear, digging like a pair of matched badgers. I was spread out on the rampart of dirt above them, and it was cool beneath me. They had started throwing dirt into the breakfast room, so I didn't even have to worry about a shovelful in the face. I just watched for a while.

—You got maybe an hour to . . . I began finally.

—Find it, Malissa cut in without even looking up at me. Nathan glanced at me and kept digging.

—Hit oil, I finished. —And it better not be any ten-barrel a day squeaker, either.

—Listen, we'll have . . .

—Better be a gusher. Even a water gusher would do. That way you can swear you never got out of your bed when it happened, and that the earth's natural forces pushed a waterspout right through the kitchen. Then you could set off the gas and blow the whole kitchen away. Which would probably obscure the evidence. Or if you don't like that, there's a bus for Texarkana leaving every hour, and I'll give you a day's head start before I tell 'em which way you went.

—Don't even talk to him, Malissa told Nathan. —There's no sense in it, Nathan Bedford. He wouldn't believe it if the Lord was to come down and . . .

—In about an hour that's just what it will take, I told them.

—What? Nathan asked.

—The Lord. And his angels and his saints. And you better pray he still knows how to carpenter and brings about a hundred and fifty feet of prime floorboard. But they were both digging again, and so I just slid back down the pile and walked out onto the front porch. I could feel a cynical, kind of superior smile plastered all over my face, and I tried to let it fade. Because they were going to catch nine kinds of particular hell, and it wasn't really their fault. It wasn't even the fault of whoever had stuck that nutty map in the wall of the Sentell place. It was just something in all of us that came out especially strong in them. I stared toward the long low rise of field and sparse trees that rolled down to the Sentell house on the far side, and I thought how all of us are retrievers one way or another. We all want to recapture the past. I had been hung on finding out about a man who was dead before I was born, who had lived and died in a world eighty years and six hundred miles from where I was born. And the kids were caught by it, too. It wasn't just money they were after, not even money for a house. It was the past. They were looking for special money from a special place, and if they missed Cleburne's treasure and found a million dollars worth of nice fresh bills in a bank bag, it would be as much of a letdown in some ways as if they found nothing at all. So over behind the rise the Sentell place was vacant and empty, moldering in the first sickly gray light before dawn. This same kind of summer morning eighty years ago, the Negroes would have been up, listening to Sentell or somebody ringing a bell or a wheel band for breakfast. This time of year there would still have been plenty of cotton to chop, and the sun would have been rising at the same moment over Sentell or Cleburne or the anonymous Negro soldier who had owned the land, and they would have been readying themselves for another long burning day, blowing out the coal-oil lamp, finishing a handful of cold corn bread. Ready to throw the dice another time with this land, to see if they could wrench a dollar's worth of cotton out of five dollars' worth of sweat. Somehow that was what I had been trying to touch, to conjure up again. Nathan and Malissa, too. But it was all past, and there are no maps to it at all.

Then, as the sun rose, a great pale-yellow disk in the east, over the distant rise I heard Malissa call. —Hey, come help, will you? Come on.

The cynical smile was gone, and I felt better. Those kids. Those goofy kids. The past dissolved as I turned back into the house, and I found myself wondering if I could hold back the firing squad that would be waking up in a few minutes, not even knowing it had a job of execution to do. Or at least provide some bandage of affection before the first volley went off. I never loved those kids so much. I thought, *They never needed it so much.* Which makes for a good conjunction.

—Okay, I called back to what had once been the kitchen. —You got about ten minutes. Any last words?

—Just one, I heard Malissa say in a muffled tone, as if she were a long way off.

We were just climbing out of the hole when I heard my father coming. He hit the pile of dirt and cursed in a sleepy unexcited voice for a moment. Then it was quiet over there. You could tell when he got his eyes open and oriented and realized what he was up against.

—My God, he whispered in awe. —Youall . . . I'm going to . . .

He was scrambling up that rampart of loose dirt then, and I could feel Nathan shivering up against me as he came over the top. But about then the sun came sliding through the breakfast room windows, and my father could see what Malissa was spreading out on the table.

—I get a hundred and twenty-one thousand dollars, Malissa was saying dryly, still arranging gold coins in the bright morning sunlight, stack after stack after stack. —Not counting those bundles of Confederate bills. Or the silver. And I haven't started on that old carpetbag full of greenbacks yet.

We were all in the dining room a little later. We were eating some doughnuts from down at the Dixie-Maid, and drinking coffee borrowed out of the next-door neighbor's pot. Mother was still looking at all of us as if she had awakened to find her family turned into werewolves during the night.

—Two hundred and one thousand dollars, my father said when the counting was done. He was shaking his head, looking from one of us to the next as if he needed sympathy. —We'd better get this to the bank.

—Bank? Malissa asked, her eyebrows going up. —What for?

—Bank, Nathan repeated. —You mean we got to telephone London for a numismatist.

—Never mind that, I said, —Dad can take care of the taxes.

It was Malissa's turn to look around for sympathy. It is a sad thing for a pretty young girl to have an idiot brother. —A numismatist, she said quietly, —deals in old coins.

'Specially like this one, Nathan said, handing me a kind of worn old silver dollar. —It's an 1804 silver dollar.

—That's nice, I said.

Even my father stared at me then. —1804? That would be worth . . .

—Maybe seventy-five thousand by itself, Malissa said evenly. —And we'd lose at least thirty percent trading all this in at the bank.

Even the banknotes are worth more than face value. But we need a numismatist.

—Oh, sure, my father said. He and mother seemed to have all the starch taken out of them.

Nathan sat frowning, looking at the burdened table. —And maybe you could call a carpenter, too. And whatever you call a man who fills holes.

I choked a little and set twelve thousand dollars in gold certificates down next to my cold coffee.

—I'd do it myself except I have to take Buddy Hobbs's transit back to him.

My father fumbled in his robe and found a match. He tamped his pipe and shrugged at Mother. Just as he was about to strike the match, I remembered. —I wouldn't do that, I said. —There's only a carrot between us and glory if you do.

—Say, Malissa put in brightly. —Maybe you could stay home from work today. And we could all get dressed and . . .

—Yes, my father said.

—We could go drive out on Fairfield Avenue.

Which is what we did. And that's how we came to live here after the lawsuits and the Internal Revenue and the coin dealers and all were over with. And the nice part is that we never felt like we were outsiders. Because we really belonged on Fairfield Avenue, somebody told my father. After all, we weren't what you'd call new rich, Malissa said. Our money had been in Caddo Parish almost eighty years.

The Lonesome Traveler
Mississippi: 1935

I

The state editor put him on the train. He bought the ticket, and he bought Robert Pleasance a copy of *Time* magazine with a picture of Jean Harlow on the cover, and told him, —You read this on the way, boy. You read the news and see if you can learn to write this way.

And the boy, who was two weeks out of Princeton College then, and less than a week out of Philadelphia, and three days in the newsroom of the *Press-Scimitar*, and who was the only available man for a trip out of town, listened to the state editor tell him, —You could wait ten years for a break like this. You're not going to where a lynching has been. You're going to see one making. By tomorrow night there'll be a nigger hanging off the courthouse balcony or roasted or floating facedown in a creek somewhere near Wildwood or I'll give you my autographed picture of Bilbo descending from the cross. Now what you want to do is keep your mouth shut and stay out of the way and make sure they don't know where you're from.

—You mean the paper? the boy asked quickly, trying to put the question before the state editor got his breath.

—Sure, I mean the paper, the state editor said.

Then he paused. —Oh, Christ, he gasped, —I never thought. If those plow polishers spot your accent . . .

—Maybe I could fake a Southern accent, the boy said obligingly.

—That's okay, the state editor told him. —Just don't miss any of it. Maybe there's a tree near the jail.

They stood on the platform now, and the brake boxes poured steam around them. Negroes pushing baggage carts and hauling ice vans moved past in the haze. The engine coughed heavily, and the state editor shouted, —What?

—I said, shouldn't I have a camera? the boy called back.

—Jesus, the editor moaned. —Not unless you want to eat it or have it shoved in your ear. You got a rubber camera?

—If somebody asks me what I'm doing there, what'll I tell them? the boy asked him.

—You tell 'em you're from the Singer Sewing Machine Company or a drummer for Nabisco or maybe that you're out from Gayoso Street shopping for fresh talent. Tell 'em what it looks like they'll believe. Unless they ask you to help. Hey, maybe that would be an angle.

The state editor's eyes gleamed, and he licked his index finger, scratching bold headlines in the steam:

—"I was part of a mad dog mob" . . . by . . . what's your name, boy?

—Robert Pleasance.

—"By Robert Pleasance. I was caught up in the subhuman pulse of a murder machine. I was a single cell in a combination of judge, jury, and executioner. All around me raw throats and gaping animal mouths spewed hate and determination. . . ."

The state editor stopped.

—No, he said ruefully. It would be great. It would make the wire and run all around the country, but I guess you better play it coy. Jesus, I wish I was on beat again. . . . I could . . . But if you were to slip up, we wouldn't have anything, would we?

—I guess not, the boy said doubtfully.

—You remember, the state editor told him. —"All the news that'll fit in the print." If it looks safe afterward, get details. If this sheriff goes out for sandwiches, you find out whether they're cheese or bologna. Try to get interviews with the local heroes. Talk to 'em like you're an admiring citizen. Maybe you could get a wild slant on it. Maybe you could get one of the educated ones to say Hitler has the right idea. See if you can get Hitler into it.

—How can you be so sure . . . the boy tried to ask him.

But the train brakes were releasing now, and the quick spumes of wet steam circled them as the state editor pushed him up into the coach entry. The baggage Negroes were moving back from the train, and the single stooped conductor waved his boxy cap, whining, —All aboard . . . board.

Robert was on the bottom step of the coach now, and he had to shout: —What's on Gayoso Street?

—What?

—Gayoso Street . . .

The state editor's face was screwed into an impossible expression with his effort to hear. —Oh, he yelled back, —nothing now.

Then what . . .

—Never mind, the state editor shouted hoarsely. —Just keep your eyes on that jail.

—How do you know for sure they'll lynch that . . .

—Oh God, the state editor howled above the rising clatter of the coach wheels. —He's a nigger who raped a white woman and then showed his ass to half of Wildwood, Mississippi, running away from her house, and who doesn't even deny . . . he . . . maybe you . . . they'll get him a psychiatrist . . . have a prayer meeting . . . maybe you . . .

But the state editor had stopped trotting alongside the moving train by then, and stood arms akimbo, as if he were pleading with Robert, or as if he had a heavy satchel in either hand. His lips still moved in voiceless reply, his face still pumping forth words Robert could not hear. And as the train gathered speed, Robert watched the state editor's face diminish from melon to baseball size, and finally to an indistinguishable smear of white framed by columns supporting the platform roof, a shapeless jot lost in the blur of steam and station lights strung out over the vacant silver rails that struck cold and shining backward from the coach's rear, backward through darkness toward the tiny glimmering island of the platform's end.

II

The sheriff was watching a shred of peaked moon switch quickly through a raft of low-hanging cloud. In the southeast, thunder coughed, and the clouds were packing dense and solid along a line five or six miles below the Haggard place. Outside, the air was hot and stiff and motionless, and even the insect sounds were muted, tentative as the air.

A tall round-shouldered Negro man stepped up onto the board-walk and placed a paper bag and a Dixie Cup on the plank beside the sheriff.

—Ike, Sheriff Wilson said, —I want you to go on home now.

—It could be a lot of trouble for one man.

—There won't be any trouble, the sheriff told him, opening the sack and spreading the two sandwiches and the slice of pickle out on it. —Did you bring me sugar?

—Already in the coffee, Ike said. —One spoon and a little more.

—That's right, the sheriff said.

—I reckon I could stay awhile.

—No, the sheriff said, pulling a shard of wilted lettuce off the first sandwich and closing it again. —I want you home.

—Seems like you ought to have somebody here.

—Ike, the sheriff said, —there's not a white man in Mississippi I could show my back to with Lemmy in that cell.

The old Negro sat down a step lower than the sheriff and pursed his lips. He drew three lines in the dust of the street, and his eyes, dull with the subtle scum of age, marked the course of his fingers.

—You know how old Lemmy Fuller is?

—I know, the sheriff said.

—Seems like they could take it out on an old man, Ike said.

—Who'd you rape? the sheriff asked him. —Are you volunteerin'?

—Ain't hardly grown, anyway.

—I reckon he was old enough to pull that old lady down.

—That what she say.

—Well, they'll try Lemmy.

—Will if he still around in a couple weeks.

—He'll be around, the sheriff said. —Now go on home, and if it looks quiet, I'll send for you tomorrow or the next day.

—I'll go home, Ike told him, —but if they's trouble, I'm goin' to sneak back up here.

—Don't do that, the sheriff said shortly. —If there's trouble, I'll be shootin' at anything that shows. And anyway I can't take care of all the niggers in Wildwood unless I shove 'em in with Lemmy. Let me take care of one at a time.

—Anyway, Ike said, —you send for me.

—I'll do it, the sheriff told him. —Now move. Look down south. You're goin' to get wet through before you make it home.

—No, Ike said, —I'll just get out on the road and run a piece.

—No, the sheriff said, —you take the wetting. I wouldn't do any running tonight.

III

The train was moving faster than it seemed. Robert could feel almost no motion, but trees and wide fields snapped past in the deepening twilight. The coach lights were not yet on, and he stared out at the tranced landscape: tiny crossroads stopping places—a gas station, a general store, a house or two. Farther on, a town with one narrow string of streetlights running through its center like a line of fire cutting it in two. As he watched, the darkness became complete, a porter turned on the warm weak overhead lights, and a man laden with carrying cases almost fell into the seat opposite him.

Robert watched him set cases under the seat, over the seat—two on the seat. He wondered incuriously what was in them. Then he found himself studying the man. He tried to turn his eyes away, to look out the window, down the aisle. He understood vaguely that Southerners, particularly country men, did not like to be stared at, that they took it as a form of discourtesy and sometimes reacted violently. He had seen a cripple on Beale Street knock a Negro down with his cane for no more obvious staring than Robert was doing now. But he couldn't help it.

It was as if the man had stepped into the train out of another century. He wore a bright yellow and black houndstooth suit with a matching vest, a pocket watch on a chain, a light brown bowler, a striped tan shirt with a black tie worked in a design of something like lemons. Robert did not look down. He felt almost certain that the shoes would be high-topped, and a tan so light it could be called yellow.

—Hot and sticky, the man said softly. —Sometimes it seems like the whole world is simmerin'.

Robert smiled without answering. The remark gave him at least a shade of excuse for studying the man's face.

It was classic. Classic Southern red-neck, Robert thought. Cheeks like slabs of overcooked ham, hair thin and colorless strewn across a pink scalp. Below the hair, above the bright cheeks a pair of small eyes seemed to have been shot into place from an air gun. Deeply seated, they were of no discernible shade between gray and green— something the color of slate with a peculiar quality of depthlessness as if they were bogus eyes cleverly painted upon expensive porcelain, surface only, without nerves or ichor or sight behind. Yet overall the face bore an expression of amused and indifferent benevolence.

—I always say this last heat makes a man feel like a walkin' sore, the man said. —Job in the refuse.

—Is it always like this? Robert asked. He wanted to talk, to feel the man out as a kind of prelude to Wildwood. He tried to soften his accent.

—Like this? Always like this? Great Jesus, no. It gets worse, and it gets better. I've seen it in the nineties in November. And I've seen it zero. I've seen the time you could freeze to death in Mississippi.

—You live in Mississippi?

The man smiled. His teeth were even and white—like those of a matinee idol in the face of a country storekeeper.

—Naw, he said. —I don't live anywhere. I'm a travelin' man. I go one way and then another. I walk to and fro in the earth, and up and down in it. Just a son of God tryin' to make his way.

—You're from the South, aren't you?

—The man showed his amazing teeth again. —That's funny you should ask. I must be the only man in the world who honest-to-God don't know where he was born. I don't even know who I was when I was a young fella.

Robert frowned. He had heard that people here had a peculiar, broad and unpredictable sense of humor. There was almost no formality in them. An outlander, listening seriously to a fantastic story, might find himself on the butt end of a bizarre joke.

—How's that? Robert said cautiously, trying an idiom that did not fit his tongue.

The man shrugged. —I came to myself in some woods over around Athens, Georgia, one day, he said. —I was half-naked, and a nigger man was shaking my shoulder and asking me my name. When I got to sittin' up, I found out I didn't have a name. Anyway, I couldn't think of one that sounded right. I had all kinds of names in my head, from alpha to omega, but they was just Tom and Joe and Smith and Jones. None of 'em meant anything. I couldn't remember a damned thing before I woke up with that nigger poking me. This here is all I had on me outside of a pair of pants and a dirty undershirt.

The man extended the fob end of his watch chain so Robert could see a small metal key with a crest of some kind on it.

—It come from the University of Edinburgh, the man said. —In Scotland. I don't know how I came by it. I looked it up in a book. Maybe I went to school there. I seem to remember a good deal of things to be a poor boy. Like the Bible. I found out that very night in Athens that I knew the Bible like I'd wrote it. Picked up a Gideons in the hotel and started to read; pretty soon I was reciting whole chapters without a word missed. Reciting at the top of my lungs, so the hotel man, who already had a fishy eye for me on account of the words we'd had when I registered, come up and threatened to throw me out.

—When you registered?

—Yeah, my name. I still didn't have one when that nigger got me into town. So I had to . . .

The porter was passing through the car, striking his melodious three-toned gong. —This is the first call fo' dinner. First call.

—How about that? the man asked Robert. —Why don't we just follow that darkie to where he's got the eats?

They were picking up fried chicken with their fingers. Robert still found his eyes stopping each time they lighted on the man opposite him. There was some indescribable quality about him—some aura generated perhaps by the clothes (which no longer seemed quite so wild, so outlandish), the eyes, the pink scalp beneath the colorless hair. Maybe it was the story, still unfinished, unresolved—left in escrow with an anonymous clerk in a nameless hotel two states over upset and threatening because of some unspecified happening: something about a name. The chicken was fine. There were biscuits and honey with it.

—So I had to come up with some kind of name. And the clerk didn't like it. I don't think he even believed it.

—What . . .

—Lord, I ain't even introduced myself. I'm Gone. Abel Gone.

—Gone?

—Sure. If I'd had more time, or if I'd had any sense at all comin' in with that bighearted nigger, I could of come up with somethin' better. Or at least somethin' not purely calculated to raise the back hair of a room clerk or make a deputy sheriff start thumbin' through old posters. But you got to keep in mind that I woke up just a little this side of a child. My growin' up took place on that wagon between the woods and Athens. The first sign we passed, I couldn't seem to read. By the time we got into town, I could even read the Atlanta papers. And later that Gideons Bible. That ain't bad.

—But Gone?

—I don't know. Afterward I tried to figure how Abel Gone came out when that register was in front of me. I reckon it was because everything in the past was gone for me. And I felt like the original man—the first man who ever yawned and came awake. But I had to be the second, didn't I? 'Cause there was that nigger pokin' me when I come to myself. So he was Adam. Or God. And even havin' to think fast for that register, I'd be damned if I was gonna put down Cain.

Mr. Gone buttered a biscuit delicately. Robert almost unconsciously waited for the twist, the punch line that would reveal that it had all been a joke, a monstrously long shaggy dog of a yarn to pass time for them both. But Gone only smiled and swallowed his biscuit.

—So now I'm a drummer, he said.

—Drummer? The term meant something to Robert. But it was alien. He could not determine whether its strangeness was a matter of region or archaism.

—I travel in Bibles, Mr. Gone said. —I cover the Old Confederacy selling the Holy Word. You can have both Testaments and the Apocrypha for twenty-five dollars or fifty cents. One reads the same as the other. King James only. No Douay-Rheims or Revised. Just the old Word. For the Old Confederacy. But I throw in Missouri and Kentucky, takin' good intention into account.

Abel Gone came into focus suddenly for Robert. —You know the South, then? You really understand it?

—As well as a panther knows panthers, Mr. Gone said, reaching for a chicken wing. —As well as a man can know anythin' he's always movin' through and never stoppin' in.

—How well is that?

—Fine and poorly. All the top and none of the bottom. I know the streets of Nashville and the alleys of Biloxi. I know a hundred men in Memphis and a little teeny old lady in Milledgeville. I know a veteran in Petersburg who looked on the livin' face of Robert E. Lee and a boy in New Orleans who called John Bell Hood father.

—What else is there?

Abel Gone showed his teeth again as he signaled the waiter for coffee.

—Ah, he said. —Not one of those hundred in Memphis is a true man, and the little old lady forgets things. That man who saw Lee threw down his gun at Five Forks and never marched to Appomattox. Hood's son curses his father's name because the old general died a crippled pauper with nothin' but pride in his pocket. And those streets and alleys are dark and empty, and a man can't see the reflection of his own face in a puddle of rainwater there.

They walked back to the day coach. Robert swayed, almost off-balance, as they crossed between cars. The night had turned cool, and there was no moon. They were silent for a moment, watching tiny patches of light rise and vanish as the train pounded southward. Mr. Gone produced a book from somewhere. He drew a pair of gold-rimmed spectacles from a vest pocket. He began to read slowly.

—"But the South signifies those who are within the church, namely, those who are in light as to cognitions; in like manner it signifies the light itself."

—What's that? Robert asked.

—"The North signifies those who are outside the church, namely, who are in darkness as to the varieties of faith. It also signifies the darkness with man."

—Did you write that? Robert asked, knowing somehow the question was absurd.

—Me? Good Jesus, no. That's Swedenborg. Some man who had a

vision. But it's in Holy Writ, too: "Out of the South cometh the whirlwind, and cold out of the North."

Robert frowned. —What does it mean? What do you think it means?

Mr. Gone smiled gently. —Why, I ain't a preacher. I just deal in the Book. It's words. A lot of words. What do words mean?

—I deal in words, Robert said without meaning to. —I write for a paper.

—Well, Mr. Gone said, —you ought to be able to make out the Word and old Swedenborg better than I can. I'm just a naked babe compared to you. I'm only four years out of Athens. You can't expect too much.

—Do you believe in all that—about cold and darkness from the north? About the light in the south?

—If cold don't come from the north, my almanac and the weather bureau have been lying for a couple hundred years. And I understand it's dark all winter way up in the north. I never been to see. It gives me gooseflesh. I like the sun. And where's the sun hottest and strongest?

—That's all in the natural order, Robert said, as if he were being cornered.

—Sure enough, Mr. Gone said. —That's just what Preacher Swedenborg seems to say.

Robert felt warm, overheated—as if he had been fighting or arguing against odds.

—I wish I could understand this place, he said irrelevantly. —I keep feeling I need to know something I can't even guess at. Tell me about the South, Robert said. —Everything you know.

—It is a terrible land, Mr. Gone said slowly, in rich unstressed accents, turning toward the window, staring out at the seamless night.

IV

It was dawn when the conductor nudged Robert awake and told him Wildwood was next. He sat up suddenly and stared for a moment without comprehension into the monkey face beneath a box cap studded with a tarnished Southern Railroad insignia.

—I say Wildwood comin' up.

—Oh, Robert said.

It took him whole seconds to place himself, and by the time he had the triangulation worked out, the old man had slouched down the coach toward the Negro section punching tickets and stirring other sleepers.

—Thanks, Robert called after him, and began straightening his tie and looking for his cigarettes.

He glanced across at the seat where Abel Gone had been. It was empty. The sample cases were gone, and the seat looked as if no one had ever occupied it. For a moment Robert wondered if Gone had been something spawned by his imagination. In the light of dawn, the whole encounter seemed unlikely. But then so was this assignment. So was this inscrutable place.

When he stepped off the train, the sun was still down, but morning's pallor had begun to fade the darkness. Tight ranks of pine and sweet gum, the toy depot, the sign-encrusted junction of two dirt roads were stark and ugly, and somehow portentous as if the last troops of a defeated army had passed through only minutes before and the dust from their boots and caissons and horses barely settled in the angular roadway that speared off northwest and southeast, northeast and south.

One unshaded bulb spread itself thin behind a dirty station window, and the strengthless light played out against the gray of morning made the window shine with a vague flush of passing fever. Robert looked inside and saw that the ticket office and waiting rooms were empty. The single pendant bulb swung in a minor arc, almost imperceptibly moved by the fading vibrations of the train that was already far down the lusterless tracks, picking up speed and heading south. The inside of the station was as desolate and untenanted as if its occupants had gathered their belongings swiftly, and had departed suddenly a century before, leaving yellowed obsolete schedules for trains that no longer ran and gumless ticket envelopes and flyspecked baggage checks; had left behind all the matter of their calling in one last static moment before confusion had undone them.

He walked down the length of the creaking platform and out into the silent asphalt street that, as far as he could see, was the town's only paved way. Down toward the end of it, down where it turned and disappeared in a jumble of trees and shadowy buildings, he saw one blur of weak spectral light that, even as he watched it, seemed to fade and join the rising glow of morning. Then, in the distant bulb's slight area of shine, he saw a white board sign: INEZ'S LUNCH. He picked up his bag and walked across the dusty junction, where a speckled mongrel sat staring down the southeastern extension of the road as if it heard an approaching wagon or perhaps was still listening to the last faint subaural rumblings of one passed long enough ago for the dust to have settled behind it, its passage known only to the mottled cur that did not even turn its head as Robert stepped past.

As he cut diagonally across the street, Robert passed a warped curl of oak which made a shadowy pool of darker gray against the quickened morning that was moving through the quiet streets from east to west now. The higher branches of the tree pulsed fitfully in a breeze he could not feel; its leaves drummed softly, softly sounded against one another, caught in that morning breath that had not dipped to touch the street, had not yet shaken the faded board signs hanging out over the street beyond shabby whitewashed store-fronts.

Robert stopped short of the rough uneven boardwalk ahead and stared down the empty street. There was nothing. Nothing except a mute expanse of shops and stores lining each side of the street; nothing except the pastel glow of the street's asphalt shimmering under untracked dust. Nothing but an unquenched mumble of insects in the grass and in the trees rising visible behind the scant double file of stores.

Robert stepped up onto a moaning length of pine planking that served for sidewalk and entered the café.

He dropped his bag near the door and sat uncertainly on a scarred creaking stool at the counter. A withered slattern moved opposite him behind the counter, stopped, said nothing. Waited.

—Coffee, Robert said, and wondered if he should have added "please" when his voice, the first he had heard in half an hour, sounded out brusque and brittle from the massive silence.

—Coffee, the woman repeated toward the rear of the place. And from behind two incredibly greasy and hand-smeared swinging doors came an answering rattle, and the sound of shifting crockery—cup against cup, metal against wood.

He felt the stringy muscles of his shoulders and upper back relax as if some imminent and terrible danger had just passed him by, as if by acceptance of the order, the hag had validated his right to be in the town. The moisture that coated the palms of his hands went chill now that he had stopped walking, and the imponderable silence of the café, the street—the whole town—seemed to move in upon him as surely as if it were some recognizable pattern of sound.

Where could they find violence in this place? he wondered. Where would they get it? It's like an embalmed village. Like Pompeii or Herculaneum. As if some unsubstantial volcano spews misty lava over these streets every night and nothing moves or changes, decays or grows until the sun clears away the darkness. And every day is a hundred years after the last, so what kind of violence can you find in a town where no issue reaching farther than the end of the street has been argued since those men cut their mules loose from ruined cannon and empty supply wagons and rode home a hundred years ago? Maybe I'll write a feature about a ghost town two hundred miles from Memphis.

Some movement across the counter brought his eyes up from the scarred and crusty varnish of its top. As he raised his eyes, a thick white cup slid across the opaque surface toward him. A circlet of steam stirred lazily above the flat dark liquid inside and drifted almost intact toward his face. There was no cream beside it; the sugar bowl contained the only spoon he saw. The woman had moved back down the counter toward the swinging doors; was standing arms folded, hips propped against the low wooden sideboard that stretched from one end of the counter to the other below a chipped and lusterless mirror, and staring absently at a silent jukebox huddled between a file of empty booths that lined the far wall.

—It's a quiet town you have here, Robert said, his voice sounding high and hollow and alien in the empty reaches of the place.

And she, still staring sightless at the squat unlighted phonograph, said, —Mostly.

—It must be nice to live where it's quiet and where there aren't traffic problems and factory smells . . . all these woods.

The woman had not looked at him since putting the coffee down. As far as he knew, she had not even looked at him then. Still her voice was easy; if there was no friendliness in it, there was no animosity either.

—I reckon all places are nice in their way. Some like city; some like country. I reckon there's a place for everybody.

And now her eyes left the jukebox, passed upward across the dirt-flecked mottled skylight, moved back down through the cool air that hung like fresh-laundered work clothes in the place, and settled casually on him.

—You a drummer?

—A what?

—Drummer. You sellin' something?

—Well, Robert said, —yes.

—What're you sellin'? she asked him.

—I sell . . . sewing machines.

—What kind?

—Singer.

—Funny, she said. —They got a store here sellin' 'em now.

—I just service the account. I bring in new models and so forth.

—What you got new this time?

And Robert wondered just what he did have new. What technical improvement he could manufacture quickly enough to move out of the impasse. And in another second, he didn't need it.

Because the springless screen door of the café rattled open and clattered shut behind a huge overalled man who dropped a feed sack at the end of the counter and lumbered over to the stool nearest that same end. He tossed a shapeless soiled felt hat over onto the feed sack, and Robert saw his belly and shoulders settle slowly as he hunched forward over the counter.

He was not an ugly man. There was no particular feature distorted, no limb missing or made askew. No sullen or brutal cast to his expression. And yet there was an ugliness about him. Something beyond the gracelessness and the sag and the hunch. *He looks like Unreason or Force or some abstraction in a morality,* Robert thought. *He looks shiftless, but I'll bet he's not. He looks run to fat, but I'll bet he's stronger than five of me. It's the look of all these people. In Philly I learned to read the look of the people. But here I can't tell size and strength apart. He might be the town drunk or the mayor up early to do chores. They all look tough and none of them have expressions. Only faces.*

—Coffee, the man said without inflection, with no more volume than was needed to carry his voice down the counter to the woman who had not moved, was still standing hips pressed against the near counter and eyes bright and noncommittal upon Robert, who turned his eyes from the man and studied the nicked rim of his cup.

—Coffee, the woman said in monotonous relay.

And behind the enigmatic doors at the rear, Robert heard again the identical sounds that had followed his own order: metal, wood, crockery in indistinguishable order. And this time a Negro woman came through the doors, handed the waitress a steaming cup and propped the doors open with a sliver of wood while she carried a wire rack of glasses from the rear, hefted it onto the back counter, and began stacking the thick tumblers in rows beneath the mirror.

—What about it? the woman said, and Robert's head jerked in a half-circle from the rear of the place to where the waitress was setting coffee down in front of the overalled man.

—Nothin' yet, the man said. And his voice was still innocent of inflection, as clear and inhumanly precise as some mechanical speaker operated by bellows and a metallic diaphragm.

—What're you goin' to do? the woman asked him.

—Wait, he said, and raised the cup to his lips.

—Wait?

—He ain't goin' nowhere, the man said. —He's just sittin' there wondering if it was worth it. Or maybe he's past wonderin' about that. Maybe he's wonderin' how long he's got.

—You talked to Tom Wilson?

The big man wiped his mouth with the back of one hand. His mouth was hidden in a thicket of dark beard, whiskers that covered chin, cheeks, and ranged upward to meet an uncut swatch of hair that drooped down in front of his ear. If he possessed any expression at all, it had nothing to do with his eyes, and if it centered on his lips, it was invisible, lost in the wilderness of unkempt hair that covered his face below the thick nose.

—No, he answered the woman, pushing the empty cup across the counter toward her and heaving himself up off the stool. —There ain't no use talkin' to him till I got somethin' to say. There ain't nothin' to say till we know what we want to do.

He walked stiff-legged toward the door, saying nothing else, gathering hat and tow sack up in one sudden anomalous graceful movement, pushing through the noisy screen to stop on the board-walk in front of the place. Robert's eyes followed him and saw the expressionless indecipherable face go bright as a first shard of morning sun glinted off it; saw the single eye of the overalled man that was in his line of vision shimmer like a tiny golden medal in the sun, or like the scales of a dead serpent turned belly up, obscene, uncompromisingly dreadful in the shrill light of morning.

An old Negro was fumbling with the shades in the sheriff's office when Robert finally crossed the street a few minutes later. Robert watched him through the dirty glass of the unbarred window. At first the old man could not get the shades raised. Then, one after another, they clattered and flapped to their uppermost limits, and the old man, cursing quietly, without anger or even impatience, stood back surveying them as if they might come down again as quickly and unpredictably as they had fluttered upward beyond his grasp. The shade pull was an inch or two higher than he could reach. It dangled and arched from side to side like a tiny impotent noose. Robert stepped into the office.

—Every mornin', the old Negro was saying. —Seems like one mornin' or another I could get 'em to do right.

He turned to face Robert. —You from Memphis, ain't you?

Robert stared at him. —Yes. I came in this morning.

—Wif de paper. You come down on account of that useless sonofa-bitch Lemmy Fuller. You come to see 'em take him out.

Robert's mouth was dry. He tried to figure how even a Negro handyman had already found him out. Found out not merely that he was an outlander (which anyone in the town could have told with a single glance), but just what kind of outlander he was, and what he was up to. And found out all of it before he had even opened his mouth in the town. Except to buy a cup of coffee. He remembered what Mr. Gone had said. A terrible land. The whirlwind breeds in the South. And what else? Magic? Second sight? Or more probably some idiotic mistake that had run before him mutely announcing everything he wanted to keep hidden. He wondered for a moment if the Negro Fuller felt this way: naked. Condemned without trial or even indictment. He was guilty. What he was, what he was there for were known. There was nothing to discuss, nothing to deny. When the town had decided what to do about him, it would act. Or not act. He felt more lonely than if he had been marooned in the wild dark reaches of Alaska.

—Sheriff be along. You want a look at that nigger?

—What? Robert said. —What nigger?

He had said it, had for the first time in his life elided and buried the final vowel of that formal noun as a Southerner would, had followed the old man's tongue. He felt the rising sun reflecting against the back of his neck and shoulders.

—The one you here to see about. The one what laid hands on Miz Calhoun, de widow. Sheriff don't mind if you has a look.

—What would I want to see him for?

The old man arched his gray eyebrows and studied Robert as if he were another refractory window shade. —I reckon if you gonna write about somefin', you gonna want a look at it. How can you write about somefin' you ain't even seen?

Robert stared at him. He could think of nothing to say at first. Then, weakly, almost apologetically, —What kind of man is he? Why did he do it—if he did do it?

There was disgust in the old man's eyes. —He just a common ordinary nigger what work out of Mr. Biff Moles's cotton mill, and he done it 'cause he was born half a fool and whiskey took care of the other half. And he done it. 'Cause if he hadn't done it, he wouldn't be back there playin' two-handed blackjack by hisself wif my cards.

—How does anybody know he did it? What kind of proof is there?

The old man shrugged. Robert had ceased to interest him. Robert was either a dolt or some kind of foreigner who could not quite grasp even the simplest, most elementary information. But there remained courtesy. And he was not especially in a hurry to pull the shade down again.

—The sheriff know on account of he talked to Miz Calhoun and then asked around to the neighbors and then got to askin' the colored folks. Preacher Slim Torrant of the African Congregation asked, too, and they found out it was Lemmy. Wasn't no hard thing to find out. I don't know nothin' about no proof. He didn't steal nothin' you could see, so they couldn't find it on him. It don't make no difference. Everybody knows.

—Isn't a man innocent until he's proved guilty around here? Robert asked.

—I ain't no lawyer. I reckon a man is innocent till he's done wrong. After that, as best I can tell, he be guilty.

It was a standoff. The old man and Robert had had enough of each other. Robert stood in the doorway as if he were awaiting an invitation to come all the way in. The old Negro dragged a chair to the window. Robert, turning to watch him, caught a glint of sunlight off metal out of the corner of his eye. He turned and looked at the featureless windows of the upper story across the street. As he looked, a gun barrel was drawn back inside, and a dun curtain with a lighter patch on it fluttered across the dark opening. Robert looked back at the old man. He had hold of the shade pull and was drawing it down slowly as if it were alive and might try to escape.

—There's somebody across the street in that window. Somebody with a gun.

—Sho, the Negro said, stepping down from the battered chair with the careful heaviness of age. —Sho.

—What can we . . .

—Nothin'. That's the law. That's Sheriff Wilson. He been sleepin' over there since he brung Lemmy in. In case somebody was to go for him. He got a ten-gauge over there. He kin clean off this whole street if he please.

—What if they came when he was asleep?

—That gun stick out the window all night long. They can't tell when he's sleepin'. What if they picks the wrong time, an' he's awake? An' anyhow, he sleep in a chair. An' he sleep light as a cat. That nigger Lemmy ain't worth a wad of number three shot in the back. Most folks see it that way.

Across the way, a man stepped through one of the unpainted

doors. The lower story had a shoe shop and a feed store. Upstairs, only vacant windows with fading badly painted signs for a lawyer, doctor, and dentist, all dead now or gone away. And that single open window with its dust-colored patched curtain swinging and jerking in the morning breeze.

The man carried a shotgun cradled in his arm. For an instant, Robert thought there was something theatrical, self-conscious, in the way he walked, the way he carried the gun. It was almost a relief to think so, to believe that someone else, black or white, in this miserable crossroads of a town was no more self-possessed than he was.

But the man stepped through the office door, his stride clean and unbroken until he reached a worn gunrack on the far side of the room next to the door into the block of four cells.

—Ge'man down out of Memphis, the old Negro announced almost formally.

—Tom Wilson, the sheriff said, putting out his hand without looking at Robert.

His eyes were still on the street, as if its dust were the guts of fowls, and he schooled to read tomorrow there. The sheriff stood over six feet, his body so carefully made that it appeared almost slender, his legs almost spindly. But Robert knew better. It was the body of an athlete: probably untrained, but balanced and kept in a kind of kinetic tension like the coil of a crossbow. For all his slender seeming, the sheriff weighed over two hundred pounds.

—Mr. Pleasance, he said, his voice soft as a boy's, apparently without fortissimo range, without the false or at least forced heartiness of most big men. —I'm afraid you wasted a trip down here. Unless you like to look over rural landscape.

Sheriff Wilson took his hand as if it were an egg he feared breaking.

—You've got a problem, don't you? Robert asked, his tone of voice not quite at ease, almost assuming that synthetic heartiness he loathed.

The sheriff smiled. —You mean Lemmy? I reckon your could call him a problem. A problem in timin', mostly.

—What do you mean?

—Well, it ain't any problem what's goin' to happen to him. The problem is makin' sure it happens when it ought to.

—You sound as if he were already tried and convicted.

—No, that's the problem. To keep him alive long enough to get tried and convicted. People here tend to get their sequence all messed up.

—Can you manage it? Robert asked. —Can you keep him alive?

The sheriff shrugged. —I can try. It don't seem like Lemmy was much interested in stayin' alive. He kinda put me on the spot.

—Does what he did—what people say he did—make any difference?

Wilson's eyebrows raised. He glanced over at the old Negro. —Well, I reckon it makes a difference to the lady he raped. And it makes a difference to most of the white men around here who feel real bad about a nigger man rapin' a white woman. And it makes some kind of difference to all the colored people who've got to lie low and lose time on the job or sweat it out in a dark shack till this business gets sorted through.

—I mean to your taking care of him.

Wilson sat down behind a cheap, scarred, badly varnished oak desk. —Nobody ever took a prisoner away from me, he said. —Nobody ever took anything away from me.

Robert noticed his eyes for the first time. He almost started back. They were the same peculiar eyes he had seen before: somewhere between gray and green, cold as polar stars—generally aimed behind or to one side of the one spoken to. Then suddenly snapping into focus like tiny traps, or the barrels of a shotgun brought to bear on an unsuspecting target.

—Say, the sheriff said, starting to smile. —Since you're so interested in Lemmy, I reckon you ought to meet him. Ike.

The old man shuffled to the cellblock door. He opened it with an ordinary house key.

—Anybody could get in there, Robert said, surprised.

—If they got this far, Wilson said.

The old man stood aside. Robert could see down the corridor into the four cells. At the end, there were fresh two by fours nailed across what must have been a window. In the last cell, Robert saw the Negro.

—Lemmy, the sheriff called out in his remarkably soft voice. —Man from Memphis come down to see you.

—Huh, came from the last cell.

—Man wants to see you're gettin' taken care of.

—Huh?

The old man walked down the dark corridor, beckoning Robert to follow him. —What you want fo' breakfast?

—Reckon some mo' ham 'n' eggs, a sleepy voice mumbled.

The Negro in the last cell had hunched up on his cot. His dark close-cropped head hung between his raised knees. His feet, misshapen and calloused, were on the uncovered mattress, pressed back crosswide against lean buttocks. Ropy muscles ran down his long arms, and his fingers twined beneath his thighs. From a distance, he looked like an old man.

—Lemmy, Sheriff Wilson called, still seated in the outer office.

—Yessah, the bundle of intertwined arms and legs called, its head still swaying limply between its knees.

—Tell this gentleman how come you're in here.

—On account of what I done.

—Done what?

—Done wrong to Miz Calhoun.

—Did you do like they said?

—I reckon.

Wilson was standing at the door. —Yes or no.

—Yessah.

Wilson stared at the dark huddle in the last cell. His face was impassive; his voice soft, almost compassionate. —Lemmy, what are they goin' to do to you?

As Robert watched, the bundle on the cot became animate. Its head came up. The face was that of a boy, eyes wide and bloodshot, mouth uncertain, quivering.

—They gone kill me, he said. His expression was composed, but tears were coursing down his cheeks.

—He's just a boy, Robert said.

—He was old enough to rape Miz Calhoun, Wilson said. —And just old enough to die for it.

—Sheriff, Lemmy said.

—All right.

—They gone come fo' me.

—No, Lemmy. You got a trial comin'.

—They gone come fo' me.

—If they come, they'll go away without you. They can wait.

—Is there anything you want? Robert asked, feeling impotent, even less self-possessed than before.

The boy looked up at him, mute, still trapped in the uncertain horror of his own imagination, in what the sheriff had made him say. —Can I have them ham an' eggs now?

—All right, the sheriff said. —Ike, go on down to the café. If Inez asks you anything, tell her it's for me. She might not want to accommodate Lemmy.

They walked back into the outer office, the old Negro walking on into the bright street.

—Well, the sheriff said, his eyes following the old man as he shambled down the boardwalk.

Robert said nothing. It was as if he had stepped into some other universe almost like his own, but different enough to be terrifying: a universe in which the ritual of justice, the plausible fictions of innocence and guilt, truth or falsehood were all transposed or annihilated altogether.

The sheriff stretched out in his ancient swivel chair, wincing as it squealed under him. He wore no pistol belt, and his uniform was khaki shirt and pants and a medium-brimmed Stetson. He watched Robert now, his eyes curious, almost friendly.

—You could of sat right there under the fan in the press room and wrote this story, couldn't you?

Robert shrugged. —I guess so, he admitted. —I don't know what I expected. I'm not even sure what I've seen.

—You ain't seen much, Wilson told him. —Because I mean for there not to be anythin' to see. No news is good news. Or maybe you could say good news ain't no news. If it goes the way I mean for it to, you ain't gonna have enough to fill the space under a cross-word puzzle above the classified.

Robert smiled. —I hope it works out that way. I don't want anything to write about.

—You go along now, Wilson said. —You tell Sam Moseley to give you that room that looks out over the street. You can see the river if you kind of stretch your neck.

—You don't expect any trouble this afternoon?

—I don't expect any then or later. Anyhow, whoever heard of a lynch mob in the daylight?

—Maybe there won't be but one or two.

The sheriff smiled. —I don't reckon one or two would come. You go along. I'll see you about suppertime.

Robert started for the door. He had almost reached it when a man in overalls pushed past him, heading for the sheriff's desk. Robert almost fell moving out of his way.

—You sent that nigger Ike down to Inez's place for food, the man said. His voice was cold, level.

Wilson smiled up at him, his hands folded on the desk.

—That's what a café is for, Wilson said.

—We don't feed nigger rapists, the man answered, his words covering Wilson's. —If you want that black sonofabitch fed, you can cook for him.

—Rupert, the sheriff told him, —watch your mouth. I ordered a plate of ham and eggs. I didn't rape nobody. And you best remember I ain't a nigger.

Robert watched the man's face. It looked like a slab of tan marble with whiskers unaccountably sprouting from the bottom of it. But the eyes were those same predictable agates without expression or warmth. Like Wilson's, like the man's on the train. Even the color was the same. Then Robert recognized him. It was the man in the café. The man who had come in for coffee.

For a moment the office was silent. Robert could hear two men talking as they passed in the street.

—Did you hear?

—Sure I heard. My wife called old man Fowler whenever she heard. That goddamned Wally Post.

—If the sonofabitch didn't know how to fly, they ought not to of let him.

—Jesus, don't you know it was cold and lonesome up there?

—Terrible place to die.

—Alone.

The big man in overalls shifted his weight as if he were considering vaulting over the sheriff's desk. —It might be a good idea for you to come down to the café for a sandwich and a piece of pie tonight. On the house.

Wilson's smile was brittle. —That's nice of you. Did you have some entertainment in mind?

—What?

—Maybe a floor show featurin' the Gayoso Girls, Earl Lively and his Country Cousins, and a nigger soaked in kerosene and lit up on the courthouse lawn for a grand finale.

The man hitched his overalls. —That nigger is gonna die, he said, his voice still controlled, matter-of-fact.

—In my time, Wilson said. —Not yours.

—We'll see about whose time.

—Rupert Dee, the sheriff said, —you got maybe twenty or thirty years of livin' to get through, with any luck. You got a sawmill, and you got Inez and that café. You hunt when it pleases you. You drink when it don't. You scratch or lay still all accordin' to how you feel. You done grabbed the brass ring, boy. Ain't all that a hell of a trade for one worthless nigger who's got a rope around his neck already?

—That rope's two days and some hours late.

—That ain't for you to say. It takes you and eleven others.

—I can get thirty over here inside ten minutes.

—You can get ten of 'em killed thirty seconds later.

The big man shrugged. —Think about that sandwich. Inez has got some good home-baked pie. About ten-thirty. Folks would respect you.

Wilson was rising, moving toward the window from which he could see the old Negro, Ike, returning slowly, empty-handed.

—And not a goddamned order of ham and eggs in the house, huh?

The big man stepped to the door, staring at Robert as he passed, his eyes revealing nothing.

—Folks would appreciate it, he told Wilson as he stepped into the street.

The sheriff grinned at Robert. —Didn't I tell you to get over to the hotel? Your eyes look like a couple of holes pissed in a snowbank. Go along now.

V

When he awoke, the sun was just down, and his room was bathed in soft beige light falling through tattered shades. He felt strangely rested, filled with new strength, almost optimistic. As if the shards of death and foreboding in Wilson's office had vanished with the sun. Robert stretched on the brass-framed bed. He felt the power in his legs and arms. It was luxurious to extend his muscles and sinews. He was hungry suddenly, and realized he had eaten nothing since the night before on the train.

Downstairs he passed the indifferent clerk hunched over his cigars and tobacco, yesterday's Memphis and Jackson papers, and last month's *Collier's* and *Liberty*. The clerk was talking to a middle-aged woman with steel-rimmed spectacles, her hair done up in a bun, almost a conscious parody of an old maid schoolteacher. The woman was talking softly in a listless defeated monotone as if she were telling the clerk of her own death sentence.

—They always come in threes. Did you ever see it fail?

—No, ma'am, the clerk nodded, his own spectacles nodding in time with hers, his lank gray hair pushed forward in a hopeless and oily pompadour. —No, ma'am. I never did.

—First Miz Calhoun and that nigra savage, and now this. We'll be in a war before the week's out. Unless somebody takes a hand.

—Unless God takes a hand, the clerk mumbled as if he had small hope of it.

—I never missed him on the radio, the woman said.

—I missed Major Bowes sometime, the clerk told her, —but I never did miss him.

—To have all them jokes and that laughter gone.

—Dead cold and alone without a soul to help, the clerk intoned.

Robert reached the long narrow porch of the hotel and stared down the street. Most of the shops and stores were closed. Only one wagon and a battered car or two were still parked in the street. A bread truck from out of town, the kind that delivered from Jackson or Meridian to the outlying towns, was parked and empty near the porch.

—A day in this place is as ten thousand years, Robert heard someone say. —Ain't that the solemn truth?

He knew the voice as if it were his own or that of a friend. For no reason he could imagine, cold sweat came suddenly to his forehead, his shoulders, at the small of his back. Not fear, or even a return of that earlier foreboding so much as some kind of stark, almost sensuous anticipation.

—They already got you jumpy, and it ain't a shot been fired or a voice raised, Mr. Gone said, almost at Robert's elbow.

Mr. Gone's chair was tilted back against the clapboard side of the hotel. His yellow and black houndstooth jacket was open. His belly pushed his vest outward, and a gold watch chain lay across the expanse. He held a paperboard fan with a reed handle, waving it to and fro, stirring the heavy air. On one side was a four-color lithographed picture of Jesus suffering the little children. The other side had an advertisement for the Mills and Marchant Funeral Home of Vicksburg.

—The heat's broke now. In an hour or two, it'll be fit to live hereabouts, Mr. Gone said easily.

Robert stared at him. —What are you doing here? You were gone when I woke up this morning on the train. How did you . . .

Mr. Gone smiled broadly. In the diminishing light, his eyes were the color of a tiger's. They held Robert's almost hypnotically.

—I'm gone in the mornin', gone at night. He laughed. —I'm just a lonesome traveler.

He sang a few bars of the old tune softly. —"I travel in the mountains, and in the valleys. . . ."

Robert pulled up a chair and sat beside Mr. Gone. After a moment, he put his feet upon the porch railing, a bit self-consciously.

—"I travel cold, then I travel hungry," Mr. Gone sang into the dusk.

—The sheriff . . . Robert began, but Mr. Gone cut him off.

—I got by to see him this afternoon. It wearies me to see a good man sweatin'.

—That Negro . . .

—Is a dead man. And knows it. And already give up prayin' for life. He's in there now singin' real low about the riverside and askin' his crucified Saviour to make it quick and easy and not to let it be hurtful and drawed out. He just wants a sweet chariot.

—Do you think the sheriff . . .

—I know Tom Wilson real good, Mr. Gone said. —If that nigger is meant to have a trial, Tom'll see him through it.

—Meant to?

—Man proposes, Mr. Gone sighed.

—A man came in while I was there. He told the sheriff to take a walk tonight.

Mr. Gone smiled. —Waste of time. Like fartin' into a whirlwind. Sheriff walks his own way, and if a man crosses him, he better give his soul to God. 'Cause his ass is Tom Wilson's.

—You think the sheriff will hold things together? Robert asked, pulling his feet down, edging to the front of his chair.

Mr. Gone scratched his armpit and pulled a cigar from some hidden pocket. It was a stogie, and when he had bitten and lit it, his profile looked more like that of a Wall Street broker than a back-woods peddler of Bibles.

—I met Tom's grandfather one time, Mr. Gone told him. —Old fella was broke down with the years. Terrible decrepit. But under all that white hair and eyebrows, behind that old woman's voice, there was the leftovers of some godawful fine man. He was with Forrest all through western Tennessee. He ended up at Vicksburg and got hit real bad there. One leg with two old fifty-caliber balls in it. The day of the surrender he drug himself to a Yankee medical post and asked for help, but some Union colonel told him to haul his rebel ass, that they were takin' care of Northern soldiers and Southern niggers, and he wasn't either one.

Mr. Gone pulled on his cigar. The darkness was almost full now, and a few lights were blinking on up and down the street.

—Which was the biggest mistake that Yankee colonel ever made. Or at least a bigger one than it turned out he could afford. Because later some doctor had to take Slim Wilson's leg off and he told Slim that leg would of been all right if he'd got it treated soon enough. So three years later to the day he stood out in front of some restaurant in a fine part of Boston on a homemade wooden leg with a Remington army pistol in his hand till he saw this fella, this prominent banker, come walkin' out on two good legs. What for? To walk up and call out his name—Slim's—to tell that Boston banker what it was for, and then to empty that cap-and-ball revolver into the banker's belly before he could hit the pavement. All that happened on July fourth, the third anniversary of Vicksburg's fall.

—But why?

Mr. Gone grimaced. —You're a fine boy, but dull. That banker with six balls in his belly had been a colonel three years earlier at Vicksburg. It was just squarin' up accounts. Though I'll admit six in the belly is kind of overpayment for two in the leg, even if the leg was gone. But old Slim said no sonofabitch livin' could claim to of took anythin' away from him. None livin'.

—Good God, Robert said. —Right out of your Old Testament.

Mr. Gone's eyebrows arched. —It may not be the fashion like Mr. Darwin, but that old Book holds the heart. Men know themselves in it. It ain't but only God's Word.

Robert shook his head. —That old man . . .

—He's dead now, Mr. Gone said shortly, —and that murder is seventy years behind us. But you asked if Tom Wilson will hold things together here. I don't know. But he's Slim's blood. If he don't keep things together, I reckon he'll punish the pieces. How about a little supper?

They walked down the quiet street. The heat had dissipated as Mr. Gone predicted, and a light breeze like that of the morning fanned across them. They stopped in front of the café.

—It ain't like eatin' food, but it's about all they got around here, Mr. Gone said.

—But the man at the sheriff's office. His wife owns this place.

—Well, come on in and mix, Mr. Gone said. —If it comes to you writin' about these folks, you ought to at least have a good look at 'em.

Robert hesitated, but there was no place else. They went in and found one of the two booths empty. There were perhaps a dozen people at tables and along the counter. Robert could hear a man with small pointed ears talking to another, who wolfed down chili with a tablespoon.

—Sonofabitch Wally Post.

—*Uugnh,* the chili eater mumbled, reaching for free crackers.

—Man's got a right to kill his own ass.

—*Ughff.*

—Ain't got no right carryin' innocent people down to hell with him. That cold, that ice.

—Yeah, the chili man muttered.

—They say it's dark all night and day up there.

There were no more crackers. The chili bowl was empty.

—You can't turn nowhere but what you see the truth of it: "Sufficient unto the day is the evil thereof."

Mr. Gone had taken off his coat and rolled up his shirtsleeves. He tucked the napkin into his vest. He had ordered ham and eggs and grits for Robert and himself.

—That man whose wife owns this place, Robert began. —He looks mean. He looks like he'd do anything.

—Sure, Mr. Gone said. —Anythin' he could get by with. That's always the big question. What can you put past other folks? What will they sit still for? What can you get 'em to go along with?

—Like lynching?

—Or buildin' Standard Oil, Mr. Gone said. —Or stealin' the Panama Canal, or playin' funny games with the stock market.

—Lynching is different, Robert protested.

—Sure, Mr. Gone said. —It's like a big ugly boil. You can tell the blood's bad right off. Then there's syphilis. Lots of times you can't tell a woman's got it till you've got it, too. You're right about old Rupert, though. He's a bad actor. His old man and his grandfather both ended up gettin' shot. Seems as if none of 'em like blood inside a man where it belongs.

Robert shivered as a waitress set their orders on the table. The woman he had seen that morning was not in the place.

—That nigger, Mr. Gone breathed, as if he bore a wearisome burden. —That goddamned crazy nigger.

—What do you mean? Robert said around a mouthful of unfamiliar grits.

Mr. Gone chewed his ham and shook his head. —For five minutes with a poor broke-down widow lady who probably thought for sure she'd suffered that particular indignity for the last time, old Lemmy has set his foot on the way of the cross. And it's God's own best guess whether he's gonna get crucified in the prescribed manner or in some fancy irregular way. And even whether he's goin' by himself or get somebody else nailed up, too. It don't make a lick of sense.

—No, Robert said eagerly, dropping his fork. —It doesn't. Why can't these people see that?

Mr. Gone wiped his plate with a slice of toast. —I don't know you and I mean the same thing. I ain't especially worried about Lemmy's hide. I don't see I got to worry more about any hide than the man inside it does. I'm thinkin' of the botheration.

—Justice . . . Robert began.

—Sorry, Mr. Gone cut him off. —It ain't my field. Human justice is folly in the sight of the Lord. Your righteousness and mine are filthy rags. Between corruption and what passes for virtue among men is a distance too small to measure.

—That's not so. Justice is everything, Robert shot back.

—Hume didn't think so. Remember what he said? If you went out resolved to give a beatin' to the wicked and a good meal to the virtuous, you'd find nobody worth the cost of either. And Meredith: expediency is man's wisdom. Doin' right is God's.

Robert stared at him bewildered. —But, he began, —we've gone beyond that. We know what's right. We . . .

—You mean Yankees, I expect, Mr. Gone said dryly. —You all are big for progress.

—Yes, Robert said defensively. —Yes. We're not in the caves anymore. We don't believe that colored people . . .

—"Progress is the hypocrisy which refines the vices," Mr. Gone quoted, staring at a ceiling fan as it turned futilely, slashing the unresisting air. —I forgot who said that. He must have spent a vacation in New York.

—That's not . . .

—Your progress and your knowledge and your civilization are vanity, Mr. Gone said kindly, as if Robert were a dull child. —What you believe or don't believe about caves and colored people don't make any difference. You're sittin' fifty yards from a poor nigger who done wrong and has to pay one way or the other. And not ten feet from some of the folks who may be decidin' which it'll be. Or who may have already decided. Which is to say nothin' but what any fool with eyes and a care for his own hide knows right from the cradle: every last one of us is a victim. Condemned. And guilty, too. There ain't but one hope.

Robert looked across at him. —Mercy of the court, Mr. Gone said. —If God decides, he just might commute ten years of cancer to an airplane crash.

Robert shook his head. Not in negation or even in qualified disagreement, but in weary confusion. —I don't know, Robert said. —It's like trying to go through college in two days. None of this means anything to me. I never came across anything like this before. I just don't understand.

—That's right, Mr. Gone said kindly, —You don't. Like me wakin' up in them Georgia woods with nothin' but an old nigger to show me my way. But you're on your way. Beginnin' of wisdom is to feel the lack of it. Now just keep your eyes open.

They paid the waitress, who studied their clothes and faces casually. Outside, in the street, it was beginning to turn cool, almost chill. Mr. Gone put his coat on, watching an old car or two that drifted by coughing exhaust fumes as they moved down the street. Mr. Gone called Robert's attention to them.

—Five and six men in each car, he said slowly. —And all of 'em starin' straight ahead like kids in school who threw spitballs. Tryin' to look on their good behavior. Tom Wilson's got him some trouble. I was hopin' he might just bull through. Fond hope.

As Mr. Gone talked, a stooped Negro moved from the street and stopped beside him. Robert jerked about, his nerves like puppet wires again. It was Ike, and he had materialized out of the darkness as if he were part of it, as if the color of his skin were some occult endorsement that permitted him instantaneous passage through the medium of night and shadow.

—Mr. Abel Gone, he said, as if the name were part of a minor incantation. Mr. Gone did not look at him, but fumbled in his coat pocket for a cigar. Still staring into the ill-lighted street, he scratched a match across the sole of his shoe and drew deeply on the cigar.

—That's right, he said. —I reckoned Tom would have you wrapped up tonight, Ike.

—Can't wrop me up, the old man said, standing clear of the soft yellow light that fell like mist through the café's screen door. —This business gone too far. It ain't no way to cover nobody up.

—Poor naked wretches, Mr. Gone sighed, pulling on his cigar again.

—Who naked? Ike asked quickly, as if the phrase offended him.

—All of us, Mr. Gone told him, touching his shoulder. —Every one of us. The whole shebang. I expect Tom will be wantin' to see us.

—If you ain't got no better way to spend the evenin', Ike said. —That was what he told me to say.

—Not a way in the world, huh, boy? Mr. Gone said, turning to Robert.

—No. Yes, that's right, Robert said, distracted by a passing car full of men. It was one of the same cars that had passed a few moments before.

—That's right, Mr. Gone repeated, following his eyes. —They're patrollin' the street. God knows what they expect.

—Youall comin'? Ike asked, moving off the sidewalk, vanishing again into the darkness.

Sheriff Wilson opened the door for them. He took Mr. Gone's hand. —You got a Testament with you? He grinned.

—Old and New, Mr. Gone said. —You know the text. For they shall be satisfied.

Wilson shook hands with Robert and locked the door behind Ike. —I don't know, he told Mr. Gone. —Justice is a mouthful of air. I'll settle for peace.

Mr. Gone studied him without smiling, but his gray-green eyes were bright and certain.

—In that case, he said, —you can send Ike out to flag down one of them cars that keep passin'. And go on over to Inez's place for a sandwich.

Robert looked quickly at Wilson. Some instinct told him that if he had said those words to the sheriff, he would be stretched on the floor now, his jaw bent or broken.

But Wilson was smiling. Ruefully and without humor, but smiling nonetheless, and regarding Abel Gone with what, for him, passed as an expression of understanding, of fondness.

—Just a manner of speakin', he said finally. —You know just when to poke, don't you?

—A gift, Mr. Gone smiled, his arm circling Wilson's shoulders. —And now what do you reckon to do with that poor dead nigger in back?

—Save him for the ceremony, the sheriff said. —Get him over to Meridian or some town with a jail you can't break with a sardine key. It ain't no good waitin' here. I thought I could bull 'em, but that's gone sour. Did Ike tell you?

—Tell what?

—Mrs. Calhoun went plain out of her head this afternoon. Her son-in-law had to carry her over to the hospital.

—Too much time to think on it, Mr. Gone said sadly. —Nothin' to take her mind off it. Where do we go first?

—I need a car, the sheriff said. —Mine wouldn't make the corner.

—Can you borrow?

—Wouldn't dare try. Who can you borrow a car from to carry a nigger rapist out of harm's way?

—Wouldn't be much of a list, I guess.

Robert stepped close to the desk. —We could steal one. There was a truck down by the hotel. A bread truck, a panel truck with some bread company's name on it.

—Bread truck. Mr. Gone laughed. —Sure, Tom. You want it?

—I guess. We ain't got time to sit around swappin' ideas.

—Being a commercial truck ought to help, Robert put in.

—Maybe, Mr. Gone said. —It could go half a dozen ways, and

there ain't a pair of eyes on God's earth can see what's best from here. Come on.

Wilson unlocked the door. Ike started out after Robert and Mr. Gone. The sheriff caught him by his shirt collar. —You hold up. I've been tellin' you to go home for two days. This time I goddamn well mean it. You reckon those sonsabitches are gonna care which or how many niggers they get once it starts rolling?

Ike stared at him. —You reckon I care what that white trash is up to? Ain't we got a job to do?

—*I* got a job, Wilson told him roughly. —Sometimes you forget you're a nigger, old man. I want you home and out of the way. I'll see you tomorrow. On time for a change.

Ike's shoulders sagged. As he stepped off the walk and into an alley close by, he did not turn to see Wilson's expression.

—That's hard, Mr. Gone said quietly. —That's the hardest thing so far.

—Shut up, and get that truck, the sheriff barked at him, slamming the door of the office and locking it.

—Want to talk about justice on the way? Mr. Gone asked Robert slyly.

—No, Robert said, his belly churning, feeling an unutterable sadness flow over him like dark water. —No, I just want that truck.

VI

Mr. Gone and Robert were in the cab of the truck. The café and the hotel porch were empty now, and they had hunched down in the seat when one of the ubiquitous quiet cars had gone by, its occupants squinting up and down the street.

Mr. Gone twisted the steering wheel sharply. Robert had not seen him move so rapidly and surely before. He heard a metallic crack.

—Broke the steerin' lock first time out. That's good luck. Now. He plucked a fifty-cent piece out of his pocket and frowned at it. —Got a quarter? he asked Robert.

Robert fumbled in his trousers and handed him one. —Good, Mr. Gone said. —Half's too big. I got to touch two of these points. If I get the third, it'll shock hell out of me.

He placed the coin below the dashboard and carefully positioned it with his fingers. Then he stepped on the starter. The engine coughed alive, and Mr. Gone gunned it softly.

—Put your hand under here. Right over mine. See you don't let that coin shift.

As Robert took it, Mr. Gone put the truck in gear and moved off, making a fast shallow U-turn and heading for the sheriff's office.

—So far, so good, he breathed. There was no tension or nervousness in his voice. His face still bore that inalterable expression of cool and disinterested intelligence that Robert had seen on the train. His hands rested lightly on the steering wheel.

—We'll get us a piece of friction tape in the office. You don't want to hold that quarter all the way to Meridian. Especially if we get to goin' fast and makin' corners.

—I will if I have to, Robert said, and immediately wished he had said nothing.

—Sure, Mr. Gone said, —we all got to do our bit.

Wilson was waiting in his office. He had Lemmy out of the cell and handcuffed. The boy sat next to his desk, slumped over, head still between his knees as if he had been transported instantaneously from the cot in his cell. Wilson was loading a .45 automatic.

—Can't carry my shotgun. I might blow us all to hell tryin' to swing it out the window. I hate a pistol. I'd just as soon use a broken bottle.

—You should of told us to bring a carton of Nehi when we went for the truck. Mr. Gone grinned, taking a roll of tape out of the desk and stepping outside quickly. —We got to hurry before one of them cars comes by.

Wilson had Lemmy on his feet. He was tall, Robert noticed, and slender to the point of emaciation. His eyes were bloodshot, still filled with moisture. There was no expression in his face, unless total and unrelieved terror which spread from him like an odor is expression. He watched Wilson finish with the pistol and jam it into his belt. '

—Now, Lemmy, I'm takin' you to Meridian. They got a big new jail there, and it'll be all right till you get your trial. You understand?

—Yessah.

Wilson took the boy's arm and started him toward the door as Mr. Gone came in.

—And I don't want any trouble out of you, boy. I want you to sit still and behave. I got enough trouble already for four or five men.

—Nosuh.

—I'm mad with you for doin' wrong to that old lady, and I don't want you actin' silly and tryin' to get loose. You hear?

—Mr. Wilson, I ain't gonna try nothin', Lemmy said. —I'm studyin' on what I done. I know you mean right.

—I can maybe get you a week or a month if you behave.

—Yessah.

—It's all fixed, Mr. Gone said. —We're ready to travel.

—Not you, the sheriff said. —I want you to stay here. Move around, make some noise. If they come in, you were just waitin' for me. It might give us ten minutes.

Mr. Gone studied Wilson's face. —Who'll drive?

—This boy, the sheriff said, pointing to Robert. —Give him somethin' special to write up.

—I'll do it, Robert said quickly.

Mr. Gone paused, his eyes focused past Wilson's shoulder as if on the far wall there was writing in some indecipherable script. As he looked back at the sheriff, Robert thought he shivered. But the breeze that came in through the partly open door was warm and pleasant. —All right, Mr. Gone said, almost in a whisper, seating himself heavily in the chair Lemmy had vacated. —The Lord make his face to shine on you.

—An' gimme peace, Lemmy said automatically.

Outside, the street was deserted. There was one weak light on the porch of the hotel, and a few in Inez's café. Wilson pushed Lemmy into the truck. —You'll be in the middle. Sit still.

Robert got behind the wheel. —If you want to kill the engine, let out the clutch in gear and hit the brake, he heard Mr. Gone call softly as they pulled away.

Robert remembered afterward thinking, as the bread truck moved off, that perhaps the heat had broken a little, that the drive to Meridian would be cool, and that he would be able to relax, to put into some kind of perspective what he had learned in a single day. The air that streamed through the window, smoothing his face, was scented with the odor of late summer flowers. They grew in the large quiet shaded yards, along fences—even in the weed-strewn vacant lots. He did not know their names or even what they looked like. He thought: *Tomorrow, when we get back, I'll come and find them, see if they smell as wonderful in the light of day.*

They made it almost to the end of the street, almost to the crossroads where the depot lay in shadow, where roads vanished in the darkness bearing northwest and southeast, northeast and south. But as they reached the junction, an old Ford auto cut in front of them, and another car pulled just behind it to form a vee in which the truck was trapped. Robert's eyes followed the truck headlights, locked on the springing chrome figure of a greyhound on the hood of the Ford. He heard voices loud and angry, saw at the edge of his vision smears of color and motion and light. Saw then, as his eyes broke away from the static leaping figure on the car's hood, Wilson's .45 large enough to fill the whole truck, moving upward from his belt and then, seemingly in slow motion downward to the open window. Robert heard a shout and then its report. Not once or twice but over and over again, a terrible hammer blasting away all the tense hours past and the gaudy abstractions that had filled them. Over and over the automatic crashed, and at last Robert saw the blurs of motion and color eddy and organize themselves into men in work shirts and straw hats and one enormous figure in faded blue overalls whose filthy shirt was already bright with blood, but who neither fell nor even slowed up in his dash for the truck, who rather ran across the patch of dusty street, firing his own pistol with both hands, becoming even larger, moving closer in that same inexorable and incomprehensible slow motion, clumsy and uncoordinated. Behind him more men came, one or perhaps two falling backward, jerked off their feet by the thunderous and continual clap of Wilson's pistol, the rest closing on the truck at some insane velocity between the speed of light and total stasis, while Robert tried without volition or success to grasp, to place a high-pitched sound that pierced his head like the keening of a plane in irreversible nose-dive.

Then the man in overalls, his face a paste of blood and sweat and dust, reached the truck and fired one final shot before he fell against the door with as much force as if he had been another vehicle, some kind of machine himself, rather than flesh and blood.

Wilson was battered backward against Lemmy, and Robert saw the windshield shatter into a bright web of reflections as the bullet ricocheted through the sheriff's body.

—Goddamn it, Wilson said conversationally, without heat or excitement as he tried to sit upright.

Lemmy's manacled hands were on his shirt. Wilson shrugged him off. —Goddamn it, he said, trying to aim the pistol out the window again, —ain't I told you to behave, Lemmy?

By then others were almost at the truck. One held a kerosene can in one hand, a lighted torch of pine wrapped with rag in one hand. Behind him another held a coil of barbed wire and one of the long jagged knives used to scale and gut fish.

—Black sonofabitch, one was screaming as he ran, seemingly oblivious of Wilson's unsteady gun.

—Goddamn it, the sheriff said one last time.

But now Lemmy had seen the men and what they were carrying. —Aw, Christ Jesus, Mr. Wilson, he cried. —Aw, Christ Jesus.

Wilson's head turned slowly, his own eyes bright and moist as

Lemmy's but bereft of any fear at all. He looked into the boy's face, touched his shackled clutching hands with his own free one.

—Yes, Wilson said with immeasurable care. —All right, Lemmy, all right.

And as Robert watched, watched Wilson's face and that of the Negro boy whose thin taut body was pressed against his own, the sheriff turned his pistol from the window and brought it around in that same parody of motion that Robert would always believe took so long that it must have been, had to have been, somehow outside time while the men in work shirts with their ugly implements were frozen into immobility.

Even as the pistol found its new focus, as Wilson's forehead creased with effort, with concentration, Robert saw his eyes meet Lemmy's, saw without belief or even detachable, separate emotion, the Negro boy's eyes close with those of the sheriff, his hands rest on Wilson's chest, his head move closer still. Until in that last portion of an instant, still outside, beyond time, Robert saw pass between them not the look of a victim and an executioner, but that of a son claiming his father's protection. Then the pistol thundered one more time.

Even then, and for a moment longer, Robert felt that strange inchoate separateness, detachment, that held him together. But Lemmy's body, pushed violently against him by the force of the shot, turned slowly, and the boy's ruined face seemed to dip inch by inch until it rested, wet and gleaming, against his shoulder. Wilson was lying slumped on his side of the seat. His eyes were still open, his face shining. Only the slackness of his lips, the loose uncontrolled attitude of his pistol hand from which the automatic had slipped, was different.

By then they were wrenching open the truck's doors. By then those still standing were trying to drag Wilson's body out of the car to get to Lemmy; dragging Robert from behind the wheel despite that continuing high-pitched sound that Robert recognized finally and without interest as his own voice raised not in terror, but in the sudden total and immitigable knowledge of what spiritual pain, bereavement really mean.

As they pulled him out, Robert's foot released the clutch, and the truck bounded forward, smashing into the Ford automobile. Robert felt hands fall away as he landed rolling in the dusty street.

—Dead, he heard someone howl. —Both of 'em. The nigger's dead.

—Gimme some light, another voice shrilled. —I lost hold of that Yankee. . . .

But a third voice was screaming in agony, and another was crying for help. —Goddamned truck pinned Tobin. For Jesus' sake gimme light over here. More light . . .

And Robert had rolled until he felt the raised edge of the board sidewalk under his hands. Then he was on his feet running. Not toward the sheriff's office or the depot, but away from the tangled cars where men still howled like animals, and sudden flames had begun to crease the darkness from a can of spilled kerosene.

He was thinking nothing, and feeling only the warm humid night air flowing past his running body—still somehow without fear (except that animal withdrawal of the body that the mind and brain and soul can only partially contain, and that only sometimes), without concern. Only the drumming sound of his feet on the heat-softened pavement reached that part of him still unshorted, still capable of any feeling at all. He ran on toward, into, the darkness as if it were light.

Until, hundreds of yards beyond the sight of the work-shirted men, almost beyond the sound of their voices, he tripped, sprawled headlong, and fell again. This time into cool dew-moistened grass. He realized quizzically that his mouth was involuntarily agape, that he was gasping like a catfish tossed carelessly on the bank. He was almost amused by the hollow rasping sigh of his breath, by the ponderous and growing ache in his head. His hands moved in the grass, and he remembered afterward thinking that this patch of grass and this long dismembered night was as good a place, as favorable a time to die as any he was likely ever to find. Then a hand touched his heaving shoulder.

—Not yet, Mr. Gone was saying softly, —not yet.

Robert rolled onto his back, fists doubled, ready to permit the body whatever absurd defense it might make against barbed wire, gut knives, kerosene.

—They ain't sorted themselves out yet, Mr. Gone went on as Robert's hands fell to the grass again. —We got five or ten minutes to get travelin'.

They walked for what seemed like hours. Mr. Gone's pace was hard. He seemed to move as well in darkness as in light, and he walked with a smooth rolling gait that kept Robert breathing shallow and fast. They moved through fields, Robert stumbling across planted rows. There were low hills and steep-sided gullies that Mr. Gone skirted or moved down and across effortlessly. They paused at last. Robert tried to tell him, tried to gather wind enough to tell him.

—Wilson. He shot . . .

—We'll hit Howard's Junction in another thirty minutes if we stomp down on it.

—When they got to us, he turned around and shot . . .

—The train goes about a mile to the west. We can flag down that one fifty-five out of Jackson. I know the boys in the cab. One of 'em is a Gideons. We done business together. You'll eat breakfast in Memphis. That is, if you mean to stop in Memphis long enough for breakfast.

—He shot the boy. He knew what those lunatics were up to, and he took the boy with . . .

Mr. Gone smiled in the gloom. Robert could see his white teeth, the dark shadowed caverns of his eyes.

—Now you're comin' at all of it from the other way, Mr. Gone said patiently.

—He cared what happened. He did everything he knew to do, and then there was that one more thing. . . .

Mr. Gone chuckled. The sound was low and almost obscene, Robert thought. It was the understated overcontrolled laughter of a man who recalls an unspeakably filthy story and laughs before the telling of it in anticipation, savoring in advance its effect upon hearers.

—There ain't no learnin' you, Mr. Gone said. —When you come here, you wondered if Wilson would end up strollin' down for a cup of coffee when it looked like those boys meant business. Now you talk like he was Christ Jesus risin' up off the mount with that poor fuddled little nigger Lemmy Fuller under one arm. Eyes that see not; ears that hear not.

—What . . . Robert began.

—I know what happened. I knew Tom Wilson, and I knew there wasn't fifty men in Mississippi could take a mustard seed away from him, much less a bound-over nigger.

—It wasn't that, Robert said. —He . . .

Mr. Gone shrugged and got to his feet. In the darkness Robert could not make out his face. —It wasn't anything you or I can say, can spit out on a table and take a look at. Maybe he felt sorry for that boy. Surely he was mad about it all goin' wrong on account of that sonofabitch who drove the bread truck findin' it missin' and sendin' word to the others. But for a fact, Tom Wilson never let go of nothin'. He come from a family that never learned to let go, and never forgot how to hold. It come with farmin' thin soil and squeezin' dimes for a hundred years and buildin' with cast-off lumber and bricks from chimneys left after the Yankees got done burnin'. What do you say, maybe he was just holdin' on in the only way left?

—No, Robert almost shouted. —No, that's a lie. I saw him. I know . . .

Mr. Gone helped him to his feet. —*Know,* he said loudly, as if he were addressing a jury, a congregation. —We don't either of us *know* anything. God's wisdom is to do right, remember? And remember what ours is?

—I know, Robert said again, less strongly, a note almost of pleading, desperation in his voice.

—Or maybe after all it was justice, Mr. Gone said. —Maybe Wilson knowin' the verdict as well as you or I, was afraid that boy would cut and run and somehow or other make it. Maybe you witnessed a law officer performin' his painful duty under tryin' circumstances.

They were walking again, and Robert had no breath to answer. He shook his head, his eyes still on the ground.

—But for the love of God, Mr. Gone was saying, as if to himself, his voice moderated now. —Is that likely? In 1935? In Wildwood, Mississippi?

The railroad track ran like an enormous glistening snail path through the untenanted pinewoods. They stood silent, watching, as from an immeasurable distance the firefly lamp of the train closed with them. Mr. Gone took out his watch and struck a match. —Seven minutes behind. We got more luck than mortal men deserve.

—Ain't that so? he said, looking at Robert.

The train had stopped and Mr. Gone had spoken to the whey-faced fireman, who passed his words to the engineer.

—He can pay his fare to the conductor, the fireman called down.
—But for Jesus' sake hurry up. We got ten minutes to make up.

At the coach, Robert had started up the hastily lowered steps before he realized Mr. Gone was not following him.

—Aren't you . . .

—I got my sample cases back there and a territory to cover. Mr. Gone smiled.

—But those men . . . You . . .

—Is a panther safe in the jungle?

—If . . . if I was still going to be a newspaperman after this, if I could write it all down . . .

—Publish it not in the streets of Askelon, Mr. Gone said. —It ain't a new story anyway. The world is full of it, whatever you take it to mean.

—But what, Robert asked him, —how should I . . .

—Nothin', Mr. Gone called, stepping back from the train, which even then was beginning almost imperceptibly to move. —Most likely nothin'. A killin'. Two killin's. Something for a tired coronor and some farmers and shopkeepers to sort out. Two graves in different cemeteries—not countin' those others Wilson carried along.

The train was picking up speed, and Mr. Gone walked slowly along the right-of-way at first. —It didn't mean anything. You'll see that later. It didn't mean a thing.

—I'll see that later, Robert repeated, as if he were hypnotized.

—You'll see, Mr. Gone called as the train's motion outpaced him. —You'll see.

And something more which Robert could not hear for the high and distant moaning of the train's whistle as it found its speed and headed toward Memphis while Robert stared backward, his cheek pressed against the chill metal side of the car, watching Mr. Gone rapidly grow smaller, more shadowy, waving what looked like a red bandana or handerchief, withering, diminishing, until he and the dark woods behind him were one indistinguishable blur in the humid night.

VII

The newsroom was chaos, and Robert pushed between close-ranked desks to the hollow circle in which the state editor sat, tossing copy to head writers and rewrite men. He looked up as Robert neared him.

—Got back okay, he said. —Come on, I got enough to keep you busy for a week. We got a special page to lay out.

He turned to one of his men. —Anything hot?

—They figure to bring 'em out tomorrow, AP says.

—Okay. Box it on page one.

—Listen, Robert broke in, —let me have one of the rewrite men. I want to tell him . . .

The state editor stared up at him uncomprehendingly. —Tell him what?

—What happened in Wildwood, what you sent me down to Mississippi about. You never heard . . .

—For Christ's sake forget it, the state editor said. —We've got more copy than we can use. Don't they have radios down there? Didn't you hear?

—Hear, Robert repeated woodenly.

The state editor reached for fresh copy in his basket. —Yesterday, he said, —Will Rogers was killed in Alaska. The whole country is crying.

The Dark Corner
Shreveport: 1946

And what yet was left we burnt in branches freshly cut,
and heaped a high raised grave from out his native soil.

—Antigone

I

It had been in the back of my mind all the way from Shreveport, but
it was Paris before I realized it, became conscious of it. I thought:
None of them understood, had not needed to understand, and so what could
they tell Billy or me? What could they tell Sarah even if she had sat still or
kept quiet long enough to be told anything? If I had been old enough, or
even being young had been smart enough, Grammère or Grampoppa could
have either explained it or put it far enough past explaining so that I could
have stopped thinking about it, and stopped caring whether Billy or Sarah
understood or not.

—M'sieur, the cabby was saying, —rue de Rome. Hotel Gallion.

I handed him some of the brightly colored bills that would never
seem money to me and took my luggage inside. I was finished
registering and waiting for my passport and a room key when the
American officer came up beside me. —Mr. Turner. Edward Lee
Turner?

—All right, I said, looking at the bright brass metalwork on his
collar and the innocuous row of ribbons across his jacket.

—I'm Lieutenant Murphy. With Graves Registration Section, he
went on after a pause.

He was clean-shaven, and his voice was clear and honest. It had
the snarl of Boston about it, but he had worked to hold its edge to
decent proportions. I always appreciate men who manage to clamber past natural infirmities.

—I was going to look you people up tomorrow, I said. —I didn't
expect . . .

—I would have been at the airport, but these cabs . . .

—I wouldn't want to be in a hurry when I use one, I said.

The clerk gave back my passport and handed my key to a boy. The lieutenant and I headed for a tiny cagelike elevator. As we started up, we could look out of the openwork sides and see the lobby retreating below us.

—No, Murphy was saying, —we didn't want you to have to look us up. Your brother. He paused. —Your brother was something special.

—Special?

Murphy's innocent eyes widened. I realized he had never been in combat, had only just come over. —The decoration, he said.

—Oh, yes, I said. —That medal. We got the medal out at the air base in Shreveport. They gave it to my mother.

—So we want to make this as easy as we can, he went on with controlled eagerness.

In the room I took off my coat and tossed the envelope with the airline ticket stubs into a wastebasket.

—Did you get the Italian medal? Murphy asked.

—I don't think so. —No, the Italians didn't give us anything.

—When you get to Anzio, you might ask the American chargé. He could tell you where—anyhow, you'll need him to find the place, the cemetery. Then he could take you to the Italian . . .

—Sure, I said. I'll remember that.

After Murphy left, I stretched out in a plush chair near a balcony window. Outside there was a gentle drizzle: something between heavy fog and light rain. I wanted to walk down to the Place de l'Opéra, and then possibly on to the Champs Élysées. I wanted to walk up to Boulevard Hoche past the little park they locked at ten o'clock. Where Billy and Sarah and I had climbed the wall that night in 1931, while the folks were at the convention banquet, while we were supposed to be asleep.

Because, I thought, watching the rain, *nothing changes here: it is all down there in the street. The patisserie, the old woman with carnations. The bridges over the neat brick-lined concrete-contained river.* (—God Almighty, Bill had said. —The Mississippi, even the Red, could take all the water in this little old piss-ant river and never rise a foot. —It's a civilized river, Sarah had sniffed. —Sure now, Billy laughed. —And all you catch in a civilized river is maybe a boot or some-body's brassiere.) *The slick reflection of a dozen lights in the paving stones of the street. Go on down and see them; see yourself racing through the streets still young enough to think: this is Paris and this is France, and Louisiana is five thousand miles away and Shreveport High School is not even a smudge on anybody's map, and all of this is for you to use up, and when it is over, you'll go up in smoke, the mist of pure overpowering happiness, and all they'll find is a cap or a hair ribbon caught on a branch in the Luxembourg Gardens.*

But I did not go down there. Because it was a Saturday evening and the streets would be crowded with locals and provincials far into the morning, and besides, the thought that any of us had ever been that young—least of all I (who am the eldest in a family that by tradition and necessity put great stress on being eldest) made my face grow warm. And finally, the plane for Rome would be leaving early, and I had to fly south to find my brother's grave.

II

—This here, Uncle Ellender told us, —was George Robert Winston. He would be your great-great-grandfather's mother's father.

—Good Lord, Billy sighed. He leaned against the flaking wrought-iron fence and stared out into the woods.

—He was, near as anybody could tell, some kind of off-brand religion, Uncle Ellender went on. —But he was a good farmer.

—A Catholic? Sarah asked.

—Good Lord, Billy breathed again.

—Naw, Uncle Ellender smiled. —I heard tell from my great-aunt Charlotte Sentell that George Robert was a Holiness or something. Anyhow he come all the way to New Orleans, and then up to Natchitoches, which was then maybe five houses and a store, and then that wasn't enough, so he kept northwest till he got here.

—What was it about Caddo Parish made him stop? Sarah asked.

—Lord. Uncle Ellender smiled. —It wasn't any Caddo Parish. It wasn't even the state of Louisiana for another twenty years. It was a piece of France, but what was special about the parish—which wasn't the parish yet—was that there wasn't any Frenchmen up here to bother him. Only a few Englishmen, some Indians, and maybe a Spaniard or two.

—And niggers, Billy put in. —You forgot the niggers.

—No niggers. Not yet. It was George Robert and some of his friends who grew indigo or whatever they grew, and took some skins and went downriver to buy slaves. To come back and build a church.

—A Holiness church? I asked.

—Not exactly, Uncle Ellender said. —I reckon from what they tell, it must have been a kind of Nazarene church.

—With all that yelling and stomping. Billy frowned.

—Just a guess, Uncle Ellender apologized. —But I expect they did go on some. Anyhow, a man was killed during one of their meetings. And later, they accidentally killed a nigger man.

—When? Sarah asked, her large gray eyes fixed on the weathered indecipherable gravestone.

—Seventeen eighty-nine. Or ninety, Uncle Ellender said simply. —It was just their way. They made more out of religion than we do. It was important to them.

—I think I'll go get me a rabbit, Billy said abruptly. He vaulted over the fence and started back across the plowed field.

—What changed people? I asked.

—They got something besides religion, I reckon, Uncle Ellender said.

—What do you get besides religion? I mean, to calm you down on it?

—This, I guess, Uncle Ellender said, waving his hand to include the woods, the fields, and the wide fenced plot in which we stood.

—This?

—The land. A man, or even a family, that goes to loving land doesn't have time to go to meeting every night. He has work, or he's too tired. Sweat of his brow.

—We don't have any land, Sarah said, —and we don't go to church much either. What do we have?

—I don't know, Uncle Ellender said. —This over here was Charles Winston Turner. At Port Hudson he lost a leg, but he went on to the north, and they did for him at a crossroads dive called Yellow Tavern. And your grandfather swore to God and the archangel Michael that if he had had that leg, C.W. would have come back on a horse instead of in that cedar box, and don't ask me how I know it was cedar because I don't even remember.

III

The flight was, you might say, satisfactory. Even the ride down from Rome was all right. We stopped for something to eat at a village called Cassino at the foot of a mountain, and then went on into Anzio. The Italian driver let me off at a barracks and said he would be back in a few hours. He would not be back for eight or ten hours, but there was no rush, and I suspected he had a girl in the town. His price for the drive had been almost reasonable.

Inside the little office building, an American sergeant sat at a desk drawn away from those of the Italian clerks. I handed him the papers they had sent us from Washington, and he stood up and walked with me over to one of the Italians.

—Who's blowin' bubbles? the seargeant asked.

—Whattaya need? one of the Italians said. It was a New Jersey accent. His face was heavy and pockmarked. He might have been drinking.

—You know that little annex up in the hills? Where they put those guys?

—The place near the chapel, the Italian said without interest. —The place where they put the officers and the heroes. . . .

—That's it, the sergeant said quickly. —This is Mr. Turner. His brother is up there.

—Okay, the Italian said. —Gimme your handle. I got to use your jeep. And gimme some cigarettes. It's a long trip.

—Jesus, the sergeant said. —Ten miles.

—It seems long. The Italian grinned. Then to me: —You wanna come on this way? It'll be dark in two hours.

IV

—I don't give a damn, Billy had said. —They can put Poppa wherever youall say. But that place gives me the creeps. Nobody out there but Uncle Ellender whenever he takes off a day to ride over. Nothing. No flowers, no sun. Only that broken-down fence and a few pieces of crumbling stone. It's a hell of a place.

—It doesn't matter, Sarah said. Her eyes were still red. For that matter, so were Billy's and mine.

Billy pulled slivers of bark off an oak twig he had found in the yard. The fragments disintegrated in his hands.

—I don't know. It's only an acre of dirt with some stones stuck into it. But I think about it. No, I don't think. I feel about it. I'll be sitting in the roadster at a drive-in or working out in the gym, and I see it. Close-up of C.W.'s stone. Dissolve to the rustic fence with weeds climbing it. Fade to view of the whole marble orchard. Death standing at attention; all that fierceness and strength reduced to crumbling stone. And the living working life away to hold onto a patch of death.

—They belong to us, I told him.

Billy grinned. —No, he said softly. —They don't belong to anyone. Dying is the end of belonging. That place is like some kind of private club. You've got to be dead to join, but even the living have to pay dues. I don't want it. I'll settle for Forest Park or some other place in town. In fact, if I had it to do, I'd settle for cremation. Quick and easy, and none of the pain of picking out a lot and all.

—We don't have to pick out a lot. Momma wants him out there, I said.

—Why? Billy flared. —Just give me one good reason.

—Momma wants him there, Sarah said.

Billy shrugged. —All right. She wants it, so we'll do it.

—Anyway, it's ours, Sarah said. —Grammère and Grampoppa are there. Everybody is there. I don't care, but everybody is there, and it won't cost anything. We have to think of that.

—Good Lord, Billy moaned, throwing up his hands. —I'd pay for the cremation. I got some money saved.

—Forget it, I said shortly. —That's out.

—Why? Just one good reason why?

—Because your father isn't garbage, I said. —He wasn't before. He isn't now.

Billy paled and started out of his chair. —You bastard, he began.

—Shut up, I said, but sorry for it already.

—It wouldn't matter to me, Sarah was saying. —I wouldn't care. Because it's over, and what they do with the rest . . .

—It's never over, I said. —Nothing is ever finished. It's only different.

—You gonna preach, Billy sneered, still hurt by what I had said.

—No, I told him. —I'm going to get hold of Mr. Morgan, so he can carry Father out. With the gas rationing, they might . . .

—They don't ration hearses, Sarah said.

V

Uncle Ellender was as small and brittle as a bird's bone picked clean and parched white in the sun.

—It's a nice place, he said. —On the far side of your poppa is C.W.'s boy, John Edgar Turner. He was in the war, too. Got hurt at Sharpsburg. Come home and went back and got hurt again at Cold Harbor. He didn't even bother to come home that time, and the last time he got hurt was out in front of the courthouse at Appomattox when some smart Yankee thought he'd get some southern buttons to take home. C.W.'s boy cracked his skull for him, and got some ribs stove in and a year in the Federal prison. He might have killed the last Union in that war.

—No, that happened out in New Mexico, I said. —Father said it happened on a ranch. We won that day.

—Sure, Uncle Ellender said. —Listen, look. This is my place. By my brother, your grampoppa. What do you think?

—It looks fine. A little close. Aren't those graves on the other side?

Uncle Ellender looked at the sunken mounds closely, frowning. —You're right. I'd be right pushed up against them, wouldn't I?

—It looks like it, I said. —Were they niggers that belonged to the family?

Uncle Ellender was still frowning. —No, he said. —No. They . . . wait a minute. I *know* who they were. Just wait a minute.

—It doesn't matter, I said. —I just came to see how Father's place had settled. I wanted to see if we could get the stone and have it set before Billy leaves.

—It *does* matter, Uncle Ellender said. —There aren't any strangers in here.

—They're sending him to Africa.

—Who? Billy?

—Yes.

Uncle Ellender rubbed his chin and scuffed one of the grass-covered mounds with his toe. —Sure, he said finally. —It's them. The Dark Corner. That's who they are.

—It's dark enough, I said. —But the whole graveyard is dark.

—No, he said. —This end of the parish. Where Caddo and Red River parishes and the Texas line meet. They used to call this whole section the Dark Corner.

—During the war, Uncle Ellender went on, —this part of the country was almost empty except they used to send Yankee scouts up from around Baton Rouge to feel us—them, I mean, the Confederates—out. So they put an outpost here. Most of the men were simple, and the sergeant was more than simple. He was ignorant and brutal, but he loved the country. You have to set it up that he loved the South. Unless you like horror stories without a point.

—So they stayed there, and the supplies came every so often, and then once in a while. Then not at all. But that was all right. Because in a year they had shot four men with Union papers on them, and a couple of others who were probably Yankees or if not at least were not Confederates when every man able to ride in this country should have been.

—What about the plantation? I asked. —It was here. It had been here since George Robert Winston. Where were our people?

—The men were fighting. Virginia, Vicksburg—one boy in Tennessee and Alabama with Joe Wheeler. Uncle Ellender paused, rubbing his chin. —We never got him back. His name was George William. They never heard anything. They looked and spent money they didn't have after the war looking so they could bring him back. When I was young, your grampoppa wrote a man we knew from Minden who was in Washington in a bureau. That was in 1887, but nothing came of it.

—Where did the women go? I asked him.

—Shreveport, he said. —It was no good out here and they needed women in the hospital. So they were alone out here. I mean the soldiers.

—What did they do about supplies?

—They made do. And the longer they stayed, the harder it got. A couple of them got killed. All the Yanks didn't go easy. A few of them killed one another. Loneliness or corn liquor, or maybe—probably—pure boredom. By the time it was over, there wasn't but the sergeant and two of the men.

—Where did they go?

—Oh, Uncle Ellender said, —they didn't. They never budged. Except one of them finally got shot by the sheriff in 1869.

—What . . .

—They stayed on out there. He pointed out into the woods that we had hunted, Billy and I, when we were young. The family had reserved that right when the land, all except the graveyard, was sold. —Deep in. Further than you ever went, my uncle said, as if he were reading my mind. —Maybe across the parish line. Nobody knows, because they never found the place.

—Why? I said. —What for?

—Good God Almighty, Uncle Ellender said, —how would I know? They just did it. I asked your grandfather, who was a young man then, and he only smiled and told your daddy and me they did it and nobody could even ask them why.

—Because if you went in there without a Confederate uniform, they shot you. If you wanted to know bad enough, and got you an old uniform, they'd ask you your regiment, and who commanded, and then, you failing or not convincing, they'd shoot you anyhow. Two men never came out, and then it got to where nobody cared enough to try it. It was backcountry, and they were like cougars. You stay away from them and they'd stay away from you. Except the one the sheriff shot.

—But they got here. The other two got here.

—Sure, Uncle Ellender said. —By the hardest. It was one fall and your grandfather and your great-grandfather had shooed a doe in here. They shot doe then, and even if they hadn't, they would have, because it wasn't gentleman hunting like before or since. It was hunt or go without, because there wasn't a hundred thousand dollars' gold in the parish. Not yet. The Republicans were still up in town.

—So they were out here camped, and it was evening, and they heard that doe or something, and when they came over by the fence, they saw him. The sergeant, with hair down his back, and a hide shirt, and no pants worth calling attention to. And he had the last of them, that last man in his arms. Dead, and his eyes staring up into the pine tops like he was looking for a star to reckon by. A fever. Remember that. Not hunger or exposure or general debility, but a fever. Maybe off a deer, most likely yellow jack or typhoid. But the man was dead, and what the sergeant had carried in weighed ninety pounds and was six feet two inches long.

It was growing late, and a long drive back. I had to put Billy on the train in a few hours. But I wanted the rest of it. Uncle Ellender had got around to picking his place in the graveyard. If I waited, I might never hear the rest. And Billy and I would have time when he came back from whatever he would have to do in Africa.

—So they put him here, I primed Uncle Ellender again.

—And the sergeant had fever, too, Uncle Ellender said, sitting, unconsciously, I guess on his father's headstone. —Fever that burned what meat was left off of him, twisted his mouth into an upside-down crescent, and pushed his eyes half out of his head. Fever takes a week. Your grandfather and his father only nursed that sergeant three days. When he was reasonable, he told them how it had been. He even came to believe they were Southerners. I reckon he had to, because of what he had to ask.

—The nursing, I said.

—Naw. Uncle Ellender waved his hand depreciatingly. —A Yank might have done that. But when his time was up, he turned to your great-grandfather. "You know what I want," he said. "You know." "That's right," your great-grandfather told him. "I know. It's all right. You lay back and rest easy. It's as good as done." So when it was over, they put him here alongside what was left of his man. They would have got a stone, but there wasn't any money then. Not for a while yet. That was in 1875.

—My God, I said. —How long . . .

—Thirteen years, Uncle Ellender said. —And sixty some odd

since then. So they're beside your poppa, and you'd have to jostle him or them to put us next to one another. So you better put me right down here below. It's a good place, and it digs easy as further up. That is, if youall was to do the job yourselves.

VI

There were no trees at the end of the road, and after we had walked a few hundred yards, even the soil played out. There was only rock: slabs, slides, broken chunks the size of a fist, the size of a barn. It was tan, almost colorless, and ran up to the solid face of cliff and mountain high above us. Between where we walked and the mountains there seemed to be, at first, nothing but that monotonous scrabble of rock and a few hopeless fragments of bush that pushed upward, seeking sunlight in place of water and soil they could not get. But then I saw what remained of the chapel.

It was the color of the rock—was the rock itself. What remained of it had been hewn out of the cliff and painstakingly piled up by hand. There was no way to tell how old it was. It might have been part of the original formation for all I could tell.

—Over here, the Italian said. He stepped beyond the blasted entrance to the chapel. —They holed up in here. There was an OP for their artillery. They were dropping stuff over the mountain onto the road. They had machine guns and a lot of antitank stuff. You couldn't get up here, and it was too tight for planes. What are you gonna do?

—I don't know, I said. —What do you do?

—You go in. The Italian shrugged. —You go in, and they kill you because they got to kill you, and while they kill you, some of your people get in close enough to kill them. Then what have you got?

—A lot of corpses.

—A clear road, the Italian said.

We stumbled over the broken rock at the side of the chapel. The Italian stooped and began tossing chunks of stone to one side. —It keeps falling off the chapel, he said. —We cleared it out of here three or four months ago. But it keeps falling. The shells they fired trying to get them out before those poor bas . . . sorry. It keeps falling off.

He pushed away a last handful of small fragments. Thick in dust, there was a slab of lighter rock. The Italian blew across it, his breath raising a tiny cloud that eddied upward, and dissolved. WILLIAM WINSTON TURNER, 2D LT., it said. There was a serial number and nothing else.

—Some of the stonemasons around here did it, the Italian said. —They cut these stones for the whole division. A job lot. I kind of let the contract. Nothing but the first-class stuff. It's nice.

I kept trying to connect Billy with the slab, with the cloudless sky and the ravaged colorless cliffs above us. I kept trying to see his face below the rim of an anonymous helmet as he looked up at this place dark with smoke, bright with countless bright threads and interstices of gunfire. My blood, my brother staring up at the place where he was about to die, knowing he was about to die. I wondered if he had known what the dying was about.

VII

—What for? Billy had said. —Because it's a war. Because when there's a war, you fight.

—That's no good, I told him. —Let them draft you. At least that makes sense. Then you can't help it. Then you have to go.

—Let's not argue, he said wearily. —I'm going, and that's it. When they come for you, you'll go.

—That's right, I said. —When they come for me. Because then it gets to be a question of whether I'm afraid to go. Which I'm not. But right now I don't hate any Germans and I don't love any Northerners. There's nothing I want to fight for.

—You've spent too damned much time with Uncle Ellender, he sneered. —Boys in gray.

I flushed and stood up. —Boy, you may be getting a soldier suit, but you badmouth me and I'll put you in a hospital before you even get out of the parish.

—All right, he said. —Let it drop.

It was the same when my mother talked to him. Not of duty or of her feelings, or even of his responsibility to finish the college Father's money had paid for. She only asked him to take his time, but his time was then, and Father's dying only slowed him by a week or so. Even Sarah was shaken by that.

—Running from death to death, she said. —Doesn't he care?

—I don't know, I told her. —Ask him.

—Ask him what? Ask him why?

—No, I said. —Let it drop.

At the station, we shook hands and Billy touched my arm. —You'll see, he said. —You'll understand.

—All right, I told him.

—No, he said, —listen. One thing. If something should happen, if it turns sour and I get it, do one thing. Don't let them put me in the graveyard. I don't want it. Let them burn me, or just leave me alone. I don't want to come back to there. Okay? You'll know what I'd want.

—All right, I said. —I'll try to do right.

—That's my big brother. He grinned as he climbed on the train.

For me, the rest was the Pacific, killing people I rarely saw and never learned to hate. I was a good killer and a lucky one until they shot a leg from under me, and then they let me stop killing and come home. Between the time I left a California hospital and got to Shreveport on the bus, they had got the telegram about Billy.

—You need plenty of rest, my mother said. —Your grandmother used to say a leg wound was always worse than it seemed. They keep opening up if you don't stay off the leg.

—Mother, tell me about . . .

—No, she said. —There's nothing to tell you. He went out and there it was, and he looked at it and took it. They say he did it very well, and that we should be proud of him.

She stopped for a moment, and her face, still almost unlined, tearless and controlled without the tense demeanor of control, was half-turned from me. —Are you proud of him? she asked.

—I don't know, I said. —Is it enough to do something well even if you don't know why you do it?

—All right, she said. —When this is over, when they finish with it, you'll have to go and decide what to do about him.

—That's your decision, I said.

—No, she told me. —I'm a woman. I don't know why he went or what he got killed for. How could I decide? You can't know any less than I do. When it's over, you'll have to decide.

VIII

—I'm from Jersey, the Italian said. —I was over here to see my old man and the lousy Fascists put me in the army. Right now I'm a prisoner or something. They kept talking about trying me for treason because I got stuck in the lousy Italian army, but they don't talk about trying the local guys who joined it. They're all free. They may not even let me go back to the States. I got nothing here. I never shot anybody. They had me hosing down mules and patching tires. I don't even know what it was all about.

—Don't feel by yourself, I said.

—These guys like your brother. I don't know. Sooner or later these Germans had to come out or starve. What's the rush you should get killed for a few days?

—He was probably afraid of that, I said.

—Huh?

—Afraid they'd come out. What can you do if they come out? Or the other way: what if they are Confederates, or what if it's over? What could you do then?

—Huh?

—Nothing, I said and sat down on a shoulder of rock near the grave.

—They can leave him here where he did it, the Italian said. —Except nobody comes up anymore. They don't figure to rebuild the chapel, and it keeps falling on him and the others. Or you can have him taken down to the big cemetery with all the others. Or you can have him shipped home.

—Can I have him cremated? I asked.

The Italian's eyebrows came up. He kicked at a chunk of the crumbling chapel. —Gee, he said. —I don't know. I mean, for what's left of him, it don't seem worth the effort. I mean, he's been here almost two years wrapped in a tent half.

—That's right, I said.

The Italian turned and walked a few paces away. Unhurriedly he opened his fly and pissed against the dusty foundation of the chapel. —I been needing to do that for an hour. It's almost dark. In the dark, without no light you pee all over yourself.

—We can go now, I told him. —Whenever you're ready.

IX

—You know what your father and his people wanted, my mother had said. —You know what I want. Maybe you even know what he would have wanted.

—He always told me . . . I began.

—No. Not what he said, not what he told you, she interrupted me gently. —What he would have wanted. He didn't see the end of it, and no one twenty years old should be bound or understood simply by what he says. Words are nothing. They dissolve in the wind. You'll have to go farther than words to know what he would have wanted.

—I think he wanted to be free. Even of us. Of the rest of them.

Those strangers in the graveyard that Uncle Ellender kept introducing us to.

—Strangers, my mother repeated quietly. —How do you expect me to understand either side of that? Your father worked eight-hour shifts after twelve-hour days to hold onto that land. After the rest was gone, all of them, Ellender, your father, their cousins over in Georgia, saved to clear it. I didn't understand that when we had to borrow furniture after we married. Now I don't understand what you say about Billy. Maybe all of you are crazy. Either they're your father's or they're strangers. Or maybe they're only dust. I don't know. But you do. You will.

—I'll have to know, I said.

X

Back in Paris I started for Lieutenant Murphy's office. But first I stopped at a bar, across the street, and what started to be one drink became an afternoon full of them.

It was dark when I stopped. I had not eaten since my plane left Rome, but I felt no hunger: only an overwhelming emptiness. There was still the decision to make, and neither the Pernod nor the strange lacy beauty of the Champs Élysées was making it easier. I heard a montage of voices playing across one another like so many gramophone records, cracked and faint, out of an immensely distant past. There was Uncle Ellender, my grandparents, my father, Sarah, Billy, and even my own voice repeating over and over again the pleasantries and inanities we had uttered when life seemed to be a single long pleasure excursion to be ended, if ever, by rising, Assumption-like, from the top of the Eiffel Tower in a cascade of champagne bubbles.

But there was no sudden rising for any of us. Only the measure of living from one day to the next—until we reached, one at a time, a road that needed to be cleared, a hill to be stormed. Or something less dramatic but just as lethal. And after that, for whoever of us was left, there would have to be one more decision.

—Mr. Turner, Lieutenant Murphy said. —May I sit down?

I was not even surprised to see him. —Surely, I said. —What are you drinking?

—Coffee, he said. —It's late. I have to be up early. How was your trip?

—I was coming by to see you about that, I said. —Tomorrow.

—You could tell me now. Or then. It doesn't matter.

—Yes, I said. —It does matter. If I tell you now, it might not be the same thing I'd tell you tomorrow.

—Maybe . . .

—Maybe tonight, I said. —Sober I'd make a mistake. When I'm sober, I think the way I'm supposed to think. I think the way everybody thinks, the way he thought.

—Your brother?

—My brother.

My brother who was dust and frail khaki cloth and a fold of rotting canvas now. Who had had no time between death and burial to feel the darkness, the awful chill of foreign soil closed about him. No time to realize what had to lie beyond that rutted hill, the broken church, if his storming it meant anything at all.

—He'll be peaceful there. The lieutenant breathed softly as if the sound of breathing might offend.

I smiled at him. He was thinking. I had the advantage of him. A waiter set down his coffee and a Pernod I had not ordered. I looked across and down the tree-lined street at the Arc de Triomphe. In the late evening mist, it seemed no more than a pile of organized stone. But inside were the names of a hundred fields spread half across the world, and at the front of it a single flame burned for all of them who should have been at home beneath the soil for the sake of which, willingly or not, they had been sacrificed to eternity.

—No, I said. —He might have thought he would. Even the fire wouldn't have consumed enough of him for that. He knows better now. If he doesn't know better, the whole thing is absurd.

Murphy shrugged. —It could be, he said. —The longer I work at it, the more I believe it.

—Send him home, I said. —If we're going to be absurd, we may as well do it this way. We've been doing it for a long time.

Murphy shrugged and rose from his seat. —All right, he said. —I'll have the papers for you in the morning. You could have done this in Rome, you know.

—No, I couldn't, I said. He walked out onto the boulevard, and I looked upward through the ashen bonelike limbs of a tree at the dark sky full of stars, each one its own monument and promise, caring nothing for all the rest that blinked into light or shattered into nova across the endless untraveled heavens. At the foot of the tree there was a circle of brown earth—not reddish clay like back home, but soil at least. My eyes needed it. I finished the drink and walked toward the Boulevard Hoche where I would find neither peace nor happiness amid those chipped and half-remembered gramophone phrases chortling scratchily through the alcohol again. And tomorrow there would be duty and judgment and propriety to balance and test again. But it was done, and there would be no changing it. In darkness there can be no understanding. Only trust.

The Arrangement
Shreveport: 1958

I

I met the Grosvenors when they first came to Shreveport from California. The night we met, at someone's barbecue, we talked and discovered that we had both worked for the old Chicago and Southern Airlines out of Memphis.

—I flew into Shreveport once and liked the looks of it. So when we got a chance, we came back from the Coast.

John Grosvenor flew for Mexicali Oil. He was on call twenty-four hours a day in case some executive wanted to fly to San Francisco or Kuwait. But it was an easy enough flying job, since he might be off four or five days running. He called himself a high-priced chauffeur. —Sometimes it's like piloting lunatics. They drink all the time. Once they played Russian roulette from Waco to Tulsa. I'd like to swap jobs with you.

No, he wouldn't. I fly my own biplane dusting crops all over the South. I've piled up four planes and walked away from all except the one that exploded. That one tossed me about fifty or sixty yards. It seems my father was right: you just can't get killed—can't even die—until, inside, you want to die. He believed it (my father) and when he was finished doing everything he wanted to do, he died. But what Grosvenor said interested me. Maybe he did want my job. Maybe he had flown washtubs and airborne nightclubs until he was ready to die.

Grosvenor's wife came over to be introduced. I especially remember that meeting, that first impression, because in light of what I knew afterward, of the way I was forced to share something of their lives, that first encounter was more than just an exchange of names.

She was, how shall I say, pretty? All right. But a certain kind of pretty I had not seen much—or perhaps any—of, and could not code it into my extrapolations of what to expect from people. I am, though no one knows it, the inventor and sole user of a psychic Bertillon system. I think a man's—and especially a woman's—character is on the surface, there to be read. If you have the instinctive tools to discern the runes of body and face, of eyes and mouth and hands and even clothing.

Sarah Grosvenor seemed thin and lively, constantly amused, almost beaming, as if every meeting were a possible doorway into some new hilarity. At first, when she offered her hand and I was a little slow to take it (Southern women tend not to shake hands, and when they do, look out), I thought her wide smile was founded in my cloddishness. But no. Sarah was, whatever else, sincere. Not honest, especially, but sincere. The difference being that there are few honest people around, and they can be dangerous, but are worth the risk; sincere people are not very scarce, because sincerity is easier than honesty. And sincere people, if they make much of it, are lethal. I expect Lenin was sincere. I'm sure Bismarck and Lincoln were.

She laughed when her husband told her about my crop-dusting. —John always wanted to try that. I told him not to. It would seem so absurd if he should get killed the one time he went up in one of those antiques.

—They're pretty safe, I said. —You almost have to try to get killed in one.

—Yes, she said, her smile less frenetic, almost fixed, as if it were the end result of a careful and adroit cosmetician. —Yes, she said again. —It must be tempting.

Which seemed an odd remark at the time. But the sort you pass off between beers and barbecued chicken, and for the rest of the evening I sat with friends across the room from the Grosvenors, occasionally watching them.

She was barely of middle height, and gave the impression of being almost emaciated, thin as a diet-conscious spinster. But the impression must have been my psychic Bertillon at work, because as I watched her, I noticed that her calves, her upper arms, her hips and thighs outlined against a pair of dark slacks were better than adequate; that her breasts were full and deep under a silk blouse, and I wondered if she were wearing a brassiere. *Of course,* I thought. *Women who smile and make peculiar fatalistic remarks always wear brassieres. Or is it that they always don't?* Her hands lay folded in her lap as she talked, but they seemed too much controlled, as if, time and again, independent of her wishes, they were about to loose themselves and begin to complement her words with gestures. Once, her right hand broke free and moved with odd and awful clumsiness before her until she glanced down at it, her brows contracting the least bit, and the hand, like a broken kite, drifted back into the certain grasp of its partner.

Her husband appeared not to pay much attention to conversation. He crossed and uncrossed his legs, dropped a phrase into the common stew of words, and for the rest studied a reproduction of some Mary Cassatt painting across the room over the fireplace. He was not ill at ease. Simply restless, as if he were waiting for a phone call to fly his drunken suicidal employers to Tierra del Fuego. I remember thinking he might find life a more toothsome item if his executive plane dropped an engine next time up.

Someone else in our circle noticed his restlessness. —Sure, Lambert Moseley said. —He just came back from his sabbatical.

—Sorry, I said. —What's that?

—He . . . no, they've got an arrangement. He was telling us the other day. Once a year he takes off for a week. Just vanishes. He don't tell her where he goes or what he does that week, and she don't ask.

The other men laughed. But Ella Moseley frowned. —Why don't you hush, Lam? That's nobody's business.

—Meaning everybody's business, someone said brightly.

—Sounds like a good deal. Formula for a perfect marriage, I said. —You could stand a lot during the year waiting for that week.

Ella still wasn't pleased. —You can hush, too, Edward. —You don't know anything about marriage. You're not supposed to grin and bear it waiting for a week's reprieve.

—Hell, her husband said, —marriage ain't much to grin about, but there's plenty to bear. Maybe if I could have me a week off every year . . .

—You'd make an ass of yourself in Biloxi or Grand Isle and get carried home drunk with your pockets picked and your head pushed in, Ella said, not quite good-humoredly.

—Now, honey, I don't fool with that kind of girl, Moseley said, grinning. —I just like a nice quiet . . .

—Oh, shut up, his wife said, clearly out of sorts.

—Maybe he doesn't even fool with women, I said. —Maybe he drinks the whole time. I had a friend in Liberia who took his two weeks off, flew down to Cape Town and stayed drunk in a hotel till he was due back on the job. Never even saw a woman.

—Some kind of degenerate, Moseley said, pointedly ignoring his wife. —Whoever heard of drinking alone? If you can't get twelve apostles to drink with you, you sure ought to manage a Magdalene. . . .

—That did it, Ella said, almost slamming her glass down, and rising to go.

II

I saw the Grosvenors a few more times that spring before I started dusting. Once we crossed paths down on Milam Street, and stopped in the Caddo Coffee Shop for a cup.

—Someone told me you fly for fun, Sarah Grosvenor said. —That you don't need the money.

I shrugged. —I can live without the money. But I need the flying.

—But not just flying. You could get a job like John's.

—I couldn't stay with it, I said.

—Too safe, John said in a tone of self-depreciation. —On your job you never need a vacation. Your job is your vacation.

Sarah was bright, crystalline again. Her voice was a little louder. —Live dangerously, she said, as if her smile, the edge of euphoria in her voice gave the tired remark new life, new meaning.

—Not really, I said. —Not dangerously. Just differently. I expect I'll get tired of it sooner or later. Finally, everything goes flat if you stay with it long enough.

Sarah Grosvenor looked not at me, but at her husband. He stirred his coffee aimlessly and stared at the paneling. Then, reaching in Sarah's purse for cigarettes, he filled the lengthening silence. —Sure, it's that way with everything. You can ruin your taste for a favorite food if you eat it too much or too often.

There was a kind of rhetorical, an almost pleading quality to his voice as if he were trying to convince me of an unlikely story or about to ask me for a loan on the strength of his sincerity. He did not look at his wife as he talked, did not, as almost anyone will normally do, move his head, the focus of his attention from one of us to the other. Sarah Grosvenor's lips compressed, and I could see suddenly, as if my Bertillon had turned prescient, how she would look in ten or fifteen years. The illusory thinness would become real, haggard. The cords of her neck and arms would stand out, veins begin to show through the skin at her wrists, the inside of her arms. Her eyes, blue and attractive now, would acquire that staring look so akin to the total and unremitting expression of horror one sees in those who are near death and know it. I almost turned away from her.

—You've got it made, her husband said, still attempting to fill the silence, the almost sidereal vacuum that had come to hover over the table and chill us all. As he said it, I thought of their arrangement and swallowed the rest of my coffee quickly.

III

I was in London the next year living in a basement flat in Burton Lane, only a ten-minute walk from Piccadilly and even closer to the bookshops around Berkeley Square and Grafton Street. It was a vacation and something of an education. Simply walking along Victoria Embankment, past the light poles graced with dolphins, watching barges and tugs move up and down the Thames, was almost as much kick as a power stall in my old Waco. I took a course at the University of London, and spent my evenings pub-crawling either over in Deptford or in Soho. Which is where I came across John and Sarah Grosvenor again. After a big thing about how strange to meet on a crowded London street (which is not quite as improbable as people like to make out: it has happened to me three or four times in Paris, and once in Hong Kong, where I met the doctor who delivered me coming out of a fan-tan parlor), we went to a bad cheap Greek restaurant and managed to gag down things claiming to be chicken pilaf and Thracian wine and went through the inevitable and monstrously dull motions of catching up on what we'd been doing since that peculiar coffee conversation in Shreveport.

—All over the damned globe, John Grosvenor told me. —You're here because you want to be. I have to follow those hole punchers to Siberia if they get the urge.

—*I* want to be here, Sarah said, her eyes moving over fly-specked and fraudulent Greek decorations on the greasy walls. —I think it's wonderful. We're going to Paris day after tomorrow. You have to tell us what to see. We have a week off. We want to see something besides the inside of planes and hotel rooms. Look, here are the tickets.

She held out a pair of reservations on the Dover channel boat, but I was looking at John. His face was that of a man before a firing squad. Or more to the point, of a pilot frozen to the wheel of a plane going in. Too low to jump, too much speed for the faintest chance of survival. He tried to speak, to say something, and my Bertillon cut in again. In his funk, he wanted to change the subject, tear up the inoffensive steamer tickets—anything. But that was absurd, no good at all. And he was thinking, turning in his mind the alternatives left. And I understood. He could not take her to Paris. Not *would not*. If he had simply meant to deny her the trip, he would not have been trapped in confusion: to deny her would have required forethought and an act of will. It was *could not*. He hadn't told her, and couldn't decide whether to cover awhile longer or to use me as a kind of damper, a mechanism to control the worst of her response when she found out that the trip—her trip—was off. I waited, despite myself, interested in whether he would play the man, swallow another mouthful of the execrable wine and wait until later. Or make an acquaintance do work hardly fair to ask of a friend. And I knew the answer to that even as I framed the question in my mind. I signaled the waiter and had the check in hand, was studying my watch with sudden and total interest, had set my speech and even got the first syllable or two out past the dry sour aftertaste of the wine (which had been as full of resin as a pitcher's palm) when John Grosvenor made his move.

—Honey, I'm afraid we'll have to . . .

Sarah stopped dead. She had been rattling on while I watched her husband. Something about the Louvre, something else, a rhetorical question, about the Tour l'Argent. But at his first word she stopped. Again, it was that indescribable and overpowering silence from outer space. Full of the raw stewing emotional implications of their life together. She on the offensive, projecting darts of anger and frustration; he turning them aside, trying to pretend that they were unjustified, irrelevant, childish. Even unnoticed. He with what looked like the fragments of half a smile on his lips. She with an expression of mingled pain and contempt and near hatred that even Perseus's shield would not have turned aside.

The silence was too full to be broken. I half-rose from my chair, ready to forget the change from a ten-pound note if I could just leave them with it, with the rotting nerve ends of their marriage which lay between them now like a carrion suddenly and awfully disinterred. But her first words dropped me back into the seat. The witness, who, on the edge of nausea, is told there will have to be another application of voltage, that the condemned is not yet done with his ordeal.

—Don't say it, she spat at him. —Don't say anything.

—Look, these people pay my salary. They want to fly up to Edinburgh and Glasgow about some North Sea properties. I can't help it.

She was staring at the clumsy murals on the restaurant wall: a ham-handed Greek shepherd dallying with a milkmaid whose ankles were as thick as young trees. Her eyes were wide, unfocused, as if she were in shock, her nostrils flared wide.

—No, you can't help it. You can't help anything, she said carefully, her voice barely controlled.

—We'll get some time later, her husband went on soothingly as if he were trying to calm a troubled and potentially dangerous child. —We'll have our week in . . .

—Our week? Our week, Sarah almost shrieked. —No. *My* week. She dropped one of the steamer tickets back into her purse and, while John watched, tore the other carefully to pieces and threw the bits on the table in front of him.

—My week, she said, anger and triumph blended in her voice. —*My* week. I'm going. You can chase your tail to hell if you want.

And she was gone. But only a few steps ahead of me since I did not want to paddle in the muddy backwater of John's apologies and explanations, lies and self-deceptions. I saw her step into a cab, her profile sharp and bright and angry under the blinking colored lights of Berwick Street.

IV

She had nothing to do with my flying to Paris a few days later. I had no wish to complicate my life by mixing in hers. It was peculiar, I remember thinking. She was an attractive vital woman: honey-blond hair, a fine body, a presence. And yet I had no desire for her. I wondered then what desire springs from. Sometimes the shape of an ankle, the musculature of a leg as its possessor crosses one over the other. A smile; the dark flow of a contralto voice. I thought that probably there are as many kinds of desire, as many triggers for it, as there are conceptions of woman in men's minds.

Which did little to answer the question of why Sarah Grosvenor did not interest me. I am not given much to introspection, and the whole business should have vanished from my mind. But there was a small mental fishhook in it: I was beginning to dislike her husband considerably. Being less than kind, more than ordinarily mean, I could have taken pleasure in deceiving him, in taking his wife for a night or a week for whatever intrinsic pleasure she might have in her, and then saying to myself: all right, John Grosvenor, we're quits for the use you made of me in Soho. Paid in full. I could— maybe even would—have done that or something like it with a woman far less interesting, much less abstractly desirable than Sarah. But not her. Not because I could not bring myself to do it, to initiate it, but because I could not, even creating scenes of tender and passionate adultery in my imagination, find the trigger, the imperceptible beginning, that moves our will from negation or dead center into the path of action.

Anyhow I was done with the dolphins and the Thames and ready for something else a little more chaotic. So I headed for Paris. I didn't spend much time in the small towns of Europe. I knew small towns well enough. Minden is pretty much the same, Germany or Louisiana. Paris is something else. Like flying, in a way, and almost as dangerous. Nobody has invented a parachute so you can bail out of Paris. I was completely sober only two days there, and the morning of my flight home I remember waking in a park off the Boulevard Haussmann with a gendarme kicking my foot and asking me what I was doing sprawled on the damp grass in a park that had been locked overnight.

V

It was the better part of two years before I got back to Shreveport. There had been a job for me in Tangier flying arms to Katanga in a Union Minière plane. But that secession went the way of my great-grandfather's, and in the late summer I was home and ready to do some dusting. Somehow I had become a minor celebrity because of the job, and there were parties I could not very well avoid. At one of them, I saw the Grosvenors.

John Grosvenor patted me on the shoulder and asked why I hadn't sent for him, that gunrunning was even better than crop-dusting. I tried to be polite, only pointing out that the shoulder he was massaging was tender since an African doctor had gouged a UN bullet out of it.

Then I saw Sarah. At first I was not sure. There was some peculiar and imprecise similarity, perhaps in the way she held her hands, using them only rarely, and then not well. But she did not look the same. Her hair, always richly, softly golden, was flat, dry—almost of no color at all. Her skin was no longer young: tendons and veins interrupted its flow, and that illusion of delicacy, thinness had altered into a reality of brittleness and emaciation. I thought for a moment she had been sick—or perhaps was. I thought of tuber-culosis, cancer. Then the Bertillon went on as her eyes met mine, smoldered into something like life for an instant, went out and turned away in a single movement. And I remembered those first two days in Paris, the sober ones.

VI

It was dark, hardly four in the morning when I arrived. But I had slept on the plane, drowsed in the bus, and was ready to begin

walking as soon as I gave my bags to a growling concierge at the
Orient Hotel in the Rue Constantinople. The streets were damp,
and a light misty rain was falling. As if I had ordered it. I walked
into the rue de Rome and on down toward the Opéra. It must have
been nine before I remembered breakfast. But by noon or so I was
ready for rest. Paris, someone said, is for sipping.

That night I turned up toward the Place Clichy. Not for the girls,
but for a bohemian restaurant where I had friends. No one was
bohemian anymore. The owner, Lemoins, was from Abbeville
(France, not Louisiana) and when we had met during the war, flying
fighter planes all day and drinking wine from a blue crockery
pitcher all night, he had sworn his grandmother was ravished by
Arthur Rimbaud, and that his bastard blood had told not in the
ability to write, but by making him, without effort or training, the
greatest, most sensitive chef in France. Which is to say, in the
world. After the war, he had proved it. At least to my satisfaction.

Nothing had changed. My friend waved as I came in, finished
talking to a redhead, and then took me to a booth in back. It always
irked me a little that after six or seven years he greeted me as if I had
been in last week.

—You want the chicken with truffles, he started. —Don't be
swayed. The rest is inedible.

—How have you been? I asked him.

—Fine. The tournedos are terrible. Someone broke a cork in the
Bordeaux and used it anyhow. Next, they'll put Roman cheese on
them. But I did the chicken myself.

—I like the escargots and the hare, I said.

—Rubber washers and scorched rat, he told me. —You stick with
me, baby. I got you through the war alive. I'll get you out of this restaurant alive. We'll go up to my place. I've got some waitresses. . . .

When the food came, it was spectacular as usual. In the middle of
the cloth, the redhead, smiling and in a waitress's short skirt and
frilly cap now, placed a big blue crockery pitcher of *vin ordinaire*.

I was almost finished when Sarah Grosvenor came in. She was
with a big shoddy-looking Frenchman with thin hair pasted to his
shapeless head, a suit without a tie, and two enormous sleepy eyes,
lids half-closed like an ugly owl's. He did not help with her chair, but
hunched in his own, staring out across the other tables, slouched on
his elbows, one finger jammed in his mouth exploring his teeth.
Sarah was talking to him. I could hear her voice, but no words. She
seemed animated, but almost apologetic as if it were necessary for
her to convince him that her intentions were good. She smiled,

coaxed. Her hand rested on his arm and he ignored it. He continued to rummage in his jaw and stare ahead, his heavy lids rising only a fraction as the redhead came past with my coffee. Otherwise, he acted as if he were alone. When another waitress came to their table, Sarah looked at the menu and began trying to order slowly, with exaggerated correctness in something not much like French she had probably learned and learned badly in high school. The man cut her off, waved the waitress away, demanding wine. —But the lady, the girl began. —Never mind the lady, the Frenchman replied, an ironic accent on "lady." —Just bring wine. The lady does all right on wine.

Sarah understood nothing but the word "wine." Her smile was faded but still there as she looked from one face to another, and when the girl was gone, she gave an affected little shrug, which would have drawn just the proper laughter in Shreveport among the other more or less young matrons, and put the menu aside.

Lemoins came to the booth. —When we close down, we'll take the girls to church. He grinned and winked. While we had been stationed in Normandy, he had debauched innumerable girls in the hedgerows after convincing their parents of his piety and suggesting that perhaps their lovely daughter would like to attend the novena.

I was still watching Sarah and her companion. —Mother of God, Lemoins said. —You don't want that one.

—No, I said. —The redhead will be fine.

—What do you keep watching that one for? You like American women better?

—No, I said. —I know her. She lives in my town.

—Louisiana? She doesn't talk like Louisiana. I thought she was a Yankee. He pronounced it "Yon-key." He had learned the distinction while we flew together and kept it in mind as a point of international sophistication.

—California, I said. —She came from California.

—She's a mess. You don't want to fool with her. I'd rather see you eat the tournedos.

—What's wrong with her? Don't you think she looks good? Maybe she's not religious enough for you.

—She looks all right. Tired inside, but all right. It's not her looks. She comes in every night. Four nights in a row now. With different men. Christ, she's trying. You know what? I bet you fifty francs against a phone token she's knifing her husband. Trying to.

—That's funny, I said.

—It's not so funny, Lemoins answered. —I know one of the men. He was in for a drink this afternoon. He said she picked him up in the rue d'Infer asking directions with a map of London in her hand, and then swallowed hard and asked him if he'd go to dinner—just dinner—with her. If she'd pay. So he comes here and manages to spend a hundred francs. New francs. I told him he was a pig.

—What happened? I mean afterward.

Lemoins grinned. —Her husband is your business rival. He owes you money. He has insulted you.

—No. I think he's a pig, too.

—Well, I can't please you. Nothing happened. The man couldn't take it.

—Take what? How do you mean?

Lemoins shrugged. —I don't know. He didn't say. I think she wanted it too much. She got him to take her to the hotel. He thought he'd go up and favor her and ask for a few hundred francs. I told you, he's a pig. But he backed out. She stood there taking off her clothes, making conversation, trembling, wanting and not wanting. As if she'd die if she didn't and kill herself if she did. I don't know. This man isn't complex. It bothered him. He just got a handful out of her purse and left. He felt sorry for her. Even a pig can feel.

—Sure, I said. —If you jam a butcher knife in his throat.

—All right, Lemoins answered. —Even a pig can understand. This woman is trouble. Am I right about the husband?

—Yes, I told him. —She has a score against him.

—Awful. It makes one sick to think of her trying so hard to shame him with her own body. Like killing an enemy by diving out of a plane and dragging him after you.

—It's pretty sure anyhow. Bullets miss. This way is sure.

—I don't know. It seems too much to sleep with one pig to shame another one. I don't know. Nothing is sure.

—Except death, I said, watching Sarah and the Frenchman again.

—Not even that, Lemoins said. —Ultimately, of course. But hardly ever when it would be useful. The miser always outlives his fawning nephew. You remember the day flying back from Karlsruhe-Durlach?

—Yes, I said. —The odds suffered a setback.

—Nothing is certain. Your woman over there is a mess.

The redhad brought coffee. She whispered something to Lemoins, her eyes on the expressionless Frenchman with Sarah. Lemoins's eyebrows raised.

—She says this one is famous, he told me.

—Famous.

—I don't know your word. He's the king of pigs. With a special attraction. Or curse, depending on how one looks at it. He has more bastards than Farouk. He is formidable. How would you say it?

—I don't know. Formidable sounds all right.

—If she takes him to bed, he'll give her a child.

—I hope it doesn't look like him.

—I can't tell you that. Lisa hasn't seen any of them. Maybe he hasn't seen any of them himself. He has no mercy, no friends.

As Lemoins talked, I saw Sarah's face tighten, her hands toying nervously with the wineglass sitting untasted before her. She still talked earnestly, but the Frenchman was beginning to shake his head, brows furrowed, eyes even more tightly lidded. He spoke in short incomplete sentences out of the corner of his mouth. Sarah's voice, monotonous, droning with the rote sound of hopelessness in it, rose. As Lemoins finished, Sarah's escort stood up, turned to face her for the first time.

—Not enough, he growled in heavy provincial accents. —Never mind the rest of it. Not enough.

Sarah was staring up at him, her face luminous in the dining room's soft yellow light. Her expression was awful. As if at that instant the long-corrupted sore of her life had burst, and she was faced with a vision of shame and degradation and damnation, perhaps with a sight of Satan himself. And him spurning her. The Frenchman dropped a coin on the table and turned away. He caught sight of Lemoins.

—For the wine, he said. —The wine is pretty good. And then he vanished through the front door just as Sarah lowered her eyes in the direction he had spoken, saw Lemoins, face averted from her. And saw me.

VII

As I watched her now at the party, she glanced away from the woman she was listening to. Her eyes met mine again, but only for a moment did they hold. She seemed like an automaton, and as she looked away, I could tell nothing. The Bertillon fed me only bland tapes marked INSUFFICIENT DATA, as if it were focused on the face of someone dead. It was as if she had not seen me, had not recognized me. But that was impossible. I had been too closely bound up with what I thought must have been the nadir of her life. I remembered how it had been after the Frenchman left Lemoins's, after Sarah, leaving even her purse behind, overturning her chair, had run blindly out into the rain.

—Ugh, Lemoins had said. —Does she go after him?

—No, I told him. —Anywhere except after him.

—Possibly she will end it.

—I don't expect. I don't think she'll do that.

—Why not? What can she do? Her plan is ruined.

—I don't know why not. Anyhow, she doesn't have a plan. You're the logician. Not even French women have plans. You ought to know that.

One of the waitresses came up and brought coffee. She whispered to Lemoins.

—Maybe it was you who brought me through the war, he said shaking his head. —You have beautiful intuitions. You know the redhead?

—You mean my date for church?

—She's gone. To meet the pig. She left word she is sorry. He moves her too much to resist.

Later, only a little drunk—not even drunk so much as warm inside and feeling very well—I headed for Sarah's hotel. Some small place inevitably down on the Left Bank. A firetrap which rivaled the George V in cost and had no grace beyond its location on what at the moment was the correct side of the Seine.

It was late, but the concierge was still behind his desk in a robe and slippers. When I asked for Sarah's room, he studied me.

—You are her husband?

—No. I am a friend from her town.

—Umm, he said. —She said her husband might come. She said that when she arrived. I wish he would come. Do you expect him?

—No, I told him. —I wouldn't count on it.

—I think the madame is ill. She seems distracted. Perhaps American women are usually distracted.

—Quite a bit, I said. —Has she asked for a doctor?

—No. No one has gone to her room. Except night before last. Another friend from her town, the concierge said slyly.

—It's a pretty big town.

—Full of Frenchmen.

—Louisiana is famous for its Frenchmen.

—They have excellent Parisian accents.

—Indubitably. Every one of them. Ville Platte is a little Paris. New Orleans is Paris itself. One never hears English except among the lower classes.

—*Voilà*, the concierge said, pointing me up the stairs. —What a country!

She was hunched on her bed in the dark. Only the ghastly light from a streetlamp broke the shadows. The door was partly open, and I stepped into the room. I could smell the whiskey. It was as if someone had used a perfume atomizer filled with bourbon on every curtain, the cushions of the chairs, the lampshade, the bed and Sarah herself. I had never thought of bourbon as the odor of defeat. Since then, I cannot think of it any other way.

—I brought your purse, I said. —Your money and your passport are in it.

She was squatting under a blanket on the bed, knees drawn up beneath her chin in the unconscious pose of a mental patient. Her face, turned toward the pale heartless light looked blue with cold, as if I were seeing her through the porthole of an interplanetary ship and she were floating in the deep and inexorable and lonely void between far distant stars that burned with icy brilliance. I put the purse down and moved back toward the door. There was a quart of Cadet back in my hotel room, and I needed it. The feeling of well-being I had brought from Lemoins's and smuggled past the concierge and up the dismal carpeted stairs was drained away. I am only a flier, not a spaceman.

—I have my dignity, she said, in a strange and distant voice, as chill and impersonal as that of the operator who connects us with Rome or Khartoum emotionlessly, caring nothing except that certain switches are properly depressed.

—Sure, I said. —Of course, you do.

—I was the weak link. Everything else resisted him. He had to break me.

—I see, I said. Not seeing at all, wondering if she were talking about the Frenchman or Grosvenor.

—So it had to be me. So I'm here. When someone pushes through you as if you're cellophane, you have to do something, Edward. You have to.

—Sarah, can you sleep?

—I can love, she said, turning to face me, letting the blanket fall from around her, revealing her bra and panties, her long and perfect legs. Her lips were moist, and her head thrown back. —I can do that. Do you believe I can do that?

—Good Lord, yes, I said, moved not by her so much as by her body. —Sure, I believe it.

—I can fill a man, she said in reverie, her arms suddenly thrown wide, her hands moving in the most graceful all-embracing gesture I had ever seen. —I can twist him inside until all he remembers is me. He'll taste my mouth, smell my hair, feel my breasts forever. Do you understand? Edward?

She was drawing me out of the ship. I could feel the heat, the arcane and indescribable heat of a star issuing from her as she drew me like metal to a lodestone. But beyond that flare of a sun's core, I sensed the cold vacuum of the universe. Behind her head was a wide expanse of window, and through it, playing on her disheveled hair, engulfing her, touching my legs and feet, the electric midnight blue of deep space or the sea's unsounded caverns.

I moved toward her, desirous and repelled, as if the specter of Helen so long dead had arisen before a man who was no necrophile.

Her arms, her shoulders were perfect. In the half-light, as she dropped the straps of her bra and slid her panties down her legs, I could not see a mole or a freckle. Her flesh was one unbroken, uninterrupted continuum, and her hands drew me down to her.

—Yes, she said. —You know what I can do. What I will do. Anything. What do you want?

But the voice. Her voice was querulous, pleading, a denial of what she had said, what she was. Her eyes were staring past me, large and unfocused into the dark as if behind me were another man, behind him yet another. Her hands fondled me mechanically, and the star, the nova, began dwindling into ashes, falling away like fragments of a broken planet. Only the cold remained, gut-freezing cold of an illimitable void that no word or act or feeling could possibly fire.

—Poor Sarah, I said unforgivably, without volition, without anything but compassion for her and for all the travelers without maps in other identical rooms. I tried to find her lips, but before my words died away, she had stiffened, pushed me back, moved across the bed.

For a long moment we faced each other across the immeasurable distance of a wrinkled sheet and two wrong words.

—No, she said at last, her voice controlled, low, like that of an elderly woman deciding against her usual afternoon walk. —No, I think not. You'd better go, Edward. You're so full, so unbelievably full.

—I don't want to go, my body made me say.

—Yes, you do, she answered, pulling the blanket over her and turning to face the streetlamp that burned beyond the window stained with mist.

VIII

The party was almost over then, and I still had my first drink in my hand. I had been leaning in a doorway staring at Sarah for God knows how long. But she paid no attention. A few men came up to ask about Katanga or something, and I tried to make sensible conversation. I mentioned Sarah.

—Looks like hell, Lew Burns said. —I was going to take my wife to Europe, but I reckon not.

—Has she been ill? I asked.

—No, Lambert Moseley said. —She looks the same way she looked when they got back. Something happened over there. I was talking to somebody who thought she'd gotten raped.

—Wow, Lew said. —He must have been one mean sonofabitch. What do you reckon he did?

—You want me to define rape?

—Listen, a tumble never left a woman looking like that.

John Grosvenor was drunk. Expansively, self-satisfiedly drunk. He came up to us, making a show of leaving my shoulder alone.

—You need . . . I'll tell you what you need, he said. —You need a little vacation.

—I just came from a two-year vacation, I told him.

—Naw, you ought to go west. Punch some cows. He leered.

—Say, Lew Burns asked. —What's wrong with Sarah? She's not looking so good.

Grosvenor spread his hands and let his shoulders bounce. —Years, I guess. Who's young? Some of us start breaking up before we're out of college good.

—Youall been doing a little private drinking? Moseley asked him.

—No, Grosvenor answered, making a wide gesture. —It's all in the open. I don't ever drink alone.

—Listen, Grosvenor went on, turning to me. —Why don't you come on with me next week? I'm going to fly west. We could fool around a little.

I tried to keep loathing out of my face, and my fists in my pockets. —I don't think so. I'm starting to dust next week.

—I'll be doing some dusting myself, he said, nudging Lew Burns.

—How long you be gone? Moseley asked him.

—I don't know, Grosvenor said, staggering slightly, weaving a little as he tried to focus his eyes out across the room where Sarah still sat, expressionless, hands drawn up in her lap. —I don't know. About a month probably.

The Night School
New Orleans: 1965

I

It was always dark at that hour, and the last block I walked to the night school was like a journey through some blind passage deep under the earth. There were trees to block off whatever twilight might be still fading from the sky, and the single streetlight, even when it was on, looked like the sun of our earth seen from the steppes of Pluto.

At the end of the block, I would see lighted windows, and sometimes the shadow of a man gesticulating against the light. As I came closer, there would be other forms drifting toward the light from many directions, like uncertain moths. Some of them were simply patches of motion along the concrete paths that led from one mock Gothic building to another like ghosts doomed to work out a term of punishment for whatever impudent crimes or ignorant misdeeds they might have committed in the light of day.

But some of the dark edgeless figures would resolve themselves into people I knew. I always met Major Marker. He was very precise and made it a point to reach our building just at seven forty-five. Then there would be fifteen minutes for a cup of coffee before the class began. That semester, we were in Advanced Management. It was taught by a large soft fat young man named Goslee who began each class speaking very loudly, then dropped almost to a whisper when he heard the shrill racket of his own voice. He did not know much, but we needed the credit. So we would sit impassive and try to listen. Sometimes we would read books for the next class.

—You're a minute and a half late, the major whispered as I reached the main entrance. —Shape up. At first you're late. Then you drop a course. It ends with your leaving school. Not resigning. Just vanishing. Remember Luckman.

I remembered. Luckman was a well-dressed quiet young man who had been working toward the Bachelor of Arts. He did well, and we were proud of him. Nothing of the night school about him. You couldn't tell he was night school, and we all thought the world

196

of him. Then he began missing classes. At last, we heard he had been dropped from the rolls. Months later Tarantella found out. Luckman had been promoted at his job. Tarantella had met him downtown. At first Luckman had tried to ignore him. But Tarantella was persistent. He found out. They had made Luckman head of the drafting division on the strength of his work and his ability to handle people. And they had told him it would be nice to finish college. But best take his remaining hours in summer school, or a few each semester. In the day school. And that was the end of Luckman.

—I'm not late often, I said, dropping my dime into the coffee machine. —Don't worry about me.

The major shrugged. —Casualties, he said, running his finger across his pencil-thin mustache. The major looked like Brian Donlevy in *Wake Island*. He had been in France and Germany, though. They had hurt him terribly, someone said. Now he lived alone out on Claiborne Avenue and kept a Doberman pinscher and walked him late at night after school on a chain leash. —You're going to have casualties.

Then Fernando materialized out of the darkness. Fernando was small and very black, and it seemed to me that he had a trace of British accent either from movies he watched on television or from his Bahamas mother, whom he spoke of often with much love.

—Gents, he said and grinned and found a dime in his striped pants and fed it to the machine as soon as my coffee had finished pouring. —Gents, how do I find you?

—In a dingy hall waiting for Management, I said. Somehow I was depressed this night.

—Crosses, Fernando said. —We all got crosses.

—When I'm finished . . . I began.

—How long have you been in the night school? the major asked me absently.

—Nine years, I said. —You know. You were here when I came.

—That's right, he said. —I was just testing your memory.

Fernando danced a step or two and gazed outside into the darkness. Far away, on the other side of the campus, the day students' dormitories gleamed, each lighted window like a bright particle in some distant galaxy. Some evenings you could hear laughter and music coming from the dormitories or the fraternity houses across the street.

—I got me an A on the last history test. Fernando laughed and showed his teeth. —All about Byzantium. Oh, don't I know the

Byzantines! Up at work, I'd take me a paperback and study Byzantium. The art, gents, and the politics. What would you like to know?

Fernando was a hairdresser during the day at a Negro beauty shop. We liked him despite the fact that he was in the cultural courses instead of the commercial. We found it a little hard to trust a cultural man after Luckman.

Tarantella blustered in, waving a shabby notebook. —Sonofabitch, he hissed, and threw the notebook down. He was not much taller than Fernando, and covered with hair. Sometimes he wore a sport shirt and the hair burst forth at his open collar like a fountain of fur. He took commercial courses with us. He worked for the Yellow Cab Company and had moved from driver to radio dispatcher and said he could become chief dispatcher if he could show them a Bachelor of Commercial Sciences degree. Even the general manager, who was his brother-in-law, didn't have a Bachelor of Commercial Sciences degree but only a diploma from Meadows-Draughn Business College, which warranted that he knew shorthand and typing and business arithmetic. Which is why his brother-in-law hated and possibly feared him, Tarantella told us.

—Son of a sobbin' bitch, Tarantella cried, and stomped on the notebook. It had the school seal on its cover, and the major stiffened when Tarantella kicked it across the hall into the coffee machine.

—I come up here at five-thirty today. Took off work. I wanted a cup of coffee in the union. I come up just to get a cup in the union. You know what? They closed it. At five they closed it just as I come in.

—They always close then, I said. —That's when they open the dormitory cafeteria. They always close the snack bar then. There's nobody to serve after that.

The major coughed and Fernando giggled. Tarantella gave me a spiteful look. —We're here, he said. —What do you think, we're ghosts or something? We're here. We get here, and there's nothing but this goddamned coffee machine.

—And Goslee, Fernando recited, numbering his dark fingers. —And Cross and Talbot and Jenkins. We got American History to McKinley. We got Survey of English Literature. We got Rise of Political Parties in U.S. We got . . .

—All right, the major said. —We know them all already.

—We got pig iron. Fernando roared with laughter.

But the major and Tarantella were morose. They both stared at me. —What's wrong with you, Turner? Tarantella asked me. —You just don't catch on. Don't it bother you that they close the place down just when we're getting here?

—It's the night school, I told him. What was he angry about? —It's a public service, they say in the catalogue. It offers working people a chance to improve themselves and complete . . .

—Pig iron, Fernando was singing. —Oh, the Rock Island Line, that Rock Island Line . . .

—Shut up, Tarantella spat at him, still staring at me. A couple of other people I knew had drifted up for coffee by then. They stood listening to us.

—Complete nothing, Tarantella cut in. —If this is a school, they ought to run it like a school. Leave the snack bar open. Have a little life in the place. There's nobody around but us. You never even see the day students. It's like they wanted to cut us off. And the teachers—did you know the people they got teaching us are people just like us? They work all day too, and then come to pick up a few bucks at night. They don't even use the good day people on the faculty. They got a man in banking and fiscal policy who won a prize last year. You reckon he ever teaches a night course? No. He teaches those kids in the day school, but we never see him. We're older. We could really understand him. But hell, no.

—And we got a man in modern European good as A. J. P. Taylor, Fernando said. —They say he looks like Toynbee and knows like Toynbee. A great man. Sometimes he even teaches a freshman course. But they never had him in the night school.

The major had been fidgeting. —A little social life, he put it. —It would be nice if we were invited to the dances they have. Meet sometime and exchange ideas with the day students.

—Ha, Tarantella spat. —What exchange ideas? You think those day kids would listen to you? They got the same courses you take. Only you got a broken-down clerk with a master's degree or some instructor padding out four thousand per. They got the Brandon Professor of Finance. They got a man who helped put the Jap banking system back together after the war. What are you going to exchange? It ain't exchange here; it's shortchange.

Some of the people nodded. I almost smiled, thinking after all it was just a cup of fresh coffee Tarantella missed.

Fernando put an index finger next to his temple. His carefully manicured fingernails shown like an opal against his dark skin. —One day, he said, I'm gonna go to the day school, don't you know? Sure I am. I'll get up with the sun and smile and say, time for class now. And I'll put on my slacks and a clean white shirt my momma pressed and a V-neck sweater and a pair of loafers and pick up a brand-new notebook and come walking up here when the bell rings. It'll be cool in there and everybody with sleep in his eyes but me, and the professor will ask the big question and I'll say, well, it's just like this: after the fall of Constantinople in 1453, still the influence of the Byzantine spread its strange charm . . .

The major shook his head irritably. —That's silly. It's all the same. The textbooks are the same. The rooms are the same. The desks are the same. It's the same courses. All I wish is that we could . . . exchange ideas sometime.

Then the bell rang, and we wadded up our empty coffee cups and moved away to our classes like things drawn down the shadowed halls at the end of invisible strings.

The major sat in front of me and I watched him taking notes. He would start writing when Goslee began in that loud high voice of his, and he would go on writing in large characters, turning up page after page of a yellow legal pad. He always carried an old-fashioned briefcase with him and it was full of such pads, each one covered with his great laborious scrawl. I wondered how he could write all through the class and still understand anything. He never looked up. Even when Goslee paused, suddenly terrified by the shrill ridiculous sound of his own voice and began again in a low prayerful tone, the major would go on writing. Everyone in the course thought of him as very studious. When the class was over, I stopped at Mr. Goslee's desk. He stared at me, mouth still quivering from his last whispered sentence, his ponderous face rilled with sweat. I had missed a class because of a headache the week before. I had such headaches sometimes, and in other courses I would borrow notes from someone and copy them. It was a common practice, but I had not had a class with Goslee before, and I felt I should ask his permission.

—I could ask the major for his notes, I said. —He takes very complete notes.

Goslee's eyebrows lifted, and he pursed his lips. —The major?

—Major Marker.

—Mr. Marker, Goslee said, like a saleslady correcting an erring customer. Someone claimed he had seen Goslee with a tired humdrum bespectacled woman and three thin bespectacled children in washer-faded shorts and Mickey Mouse T-shirts. Someone else had said: —It was his sister, then. Or he's trying to reach her husband.

—We call him major, I said.

—Humph, Goslee sniffed. —I wonder why.

—In the army, he was . . .

—A sergeant. They made him a major for a while, but it was only a temporary rank. His permanent grade was master sergeant. I saw it in his record. If you could call it a record . . .

—Anyhow, I cut in, trying to mask my surprise, —his notes . . .

Goslee heaved himself out of his chair and began filling his attaché case with papers and books. It looked like an expensive case, but it was only Samsonite, not real leather. —I don't care, he said. —Suit yourself. The man isn't even registered in the course, you know.

—No, I didn't . . .

—The man doesn't really *take* courses, you know. Goslee grinned at me, his large fleshy face seeming to shrink to a single point of malice. —I mean he pays to audit. They told me to let him take the tests. But he's never *passed* a test in any course. He doesn't take them for *credit*, you know.

My expression gave me away, and Goslee was seduced by my astonishment. He went on compulsively. —Marker has been registered in one course or another since 1945. You know how long that is? Twenty years. You know how many credit hours he has? None. Zero. Not a single one. He did one test for me, but it was some kind of rambling idiocy about something that happened to him at a bridge near someplace. Is there a place called Remagen?

—Yes . . . I think it's . . . a town.

—Anyhow, Goslee said, snapping his case closed and heading for the door, —anyhow, if you want to use his notes . . . he broke off and giggled, his fat pale hand switching off the classroom lights as I passed him and walked down the corridor back toward the coffee machine.

II

For a few days, I made sure to arrive just in time for class. I didn't want to see the major. If I saw him, he would read Goslee's revelation in my eyes. I cannot hide things well. When I lie, I am always caught. My mother claimed it was because I was a good boy and could not learn to lie well. I lie badly, but it has nothing to do with being good. Lying is only a facility like perfect pitch or sensitivity to color: one has the ability or not. To compensate, I try never to become involved in a situation where only liars can prosper.

I avoided Tarantella and Fernando, too. If they could not read my knowledge, at least they would disturb me with their talk about the day school. All I wanted was to be happy. Being happy is not to be unhappy. Not being unhappy is to avoid thinking that you might have whatever you want. If you become unhappy, you brood toward action, and action always gets twisted in the endless skein of its own dogged operations and comes to nothing. Only the very good and selfless or the exceptionally clever and ruthless can do anything with action, and finally, they too are caught in its tangle and get something very different from what they had allowed themselves to want. It is no use to start things.

But I saw other people during classes and afterward, and they all were talking about Tarantella and the major. It seemed that they had gone to see the director of the night school about facilities—one of the people laughed and said the major had used the word "amenities," and Tarantella and the director had both stared at him. The discussion had come to nothing, finally, and the night school people were disturbed now, and uneasy. Before, they all had thought of the day school as being a different dimension—something which occupied the same space-time continuum as their world, yet outside it, beyond experience or comment or understanding.

Now that was changed. Tarantella had begun it with his anger over the coffee shop's being closed. And kicking his notebook with the school seal across the hall into the coffee machine. People said that no one used the coffee machine in the day school because there was real coffee brewed in large urns, and you put exactly as much sugar and cream as you wanted in it when you filled your crockery cup. This seemed silly. The machine was handy and anyone could bring a thermos if he wanted his own blend. But still they talked as if coffee from an urn were some special thing beyond price.

And they said, too, the bookstore was always closed at night. One tall thin boy with dirty hair, a beard, and grease-blackened fingernails would stand for long moments, his face pressed against the plate-glass windows of the bookstore, squinting, trying to penetrate the gloom within.

—You can almost make out the titles, he told me, trembling with frustration. —But not quite. And they only stay open at the beginning of the term. The day school people can go in and browse as long as they want. They can pick up books and read a little of them to see if it's what they like. We have two nights to buy textbooks, and even then, the salespeople have been working all day, and if you ask for something they don't have, they'll snap at you.

It went on that way for a week. There had been thefts from cars. It didn't happen to the day school people. But at night the campus police were checking cars around the dormitories for day students making love in the shadows. They paid no attention to the cars of night school people parked around the classroom buildings. One evening a security guard stopped one of the night school people and demanded identification. He was rude, peremptory, everyone said. There was a scuffle, and they took away the night school student in handcuffs.

From that night onward, the muttering grew louder. People who had never even spoken to one another began congregating in the hallways, around water fountains, wherever there was a little light. Someone used pink lipstick and scrawled an obscenity across the glass front of the bookstore. Someone else jammed the coffee machine, and kept jamming it every time it was cleared. Even the cigarette machines and the candy-bar dispensers were jammed.

People began dropping out of classes. One evening there were only four people in Goslee's Advanced Management, and Goslee's voice rose to a new pitch before it fell away to an inaudible whisper. His eyes were large and white and darted toward the door constantly as if he expected someone to come in and denounce him to his tiny class. But those who did not come to classes were not absent from night school. They were there in the corridors and outside the Gothic buildings talking about the arrest and the thefts, about the coffee and the bookstore and the poor instruction and the shoddy hypocrisy of the catalogue, which claimed all classes were identical in day and night school.

Tarantella was with them, talking loudly. He wondered who had jammed the coffee and candy machines. Someone had said that a drunken day student from one of the dormitories or fraternity houses was doing it simply to inconvenience the night school people. And Tarantella told them, anyhow, do you know that no one in the night school was ever asked to join a fraternity or sorority? Nor the journalism club. Nor the Alliance Française.

—I checked. I checked everything. The catalogue says we got a right to all facilities and privileges as day students do. That's a lie. They know it's a lie. They think we're cattle. They think, okay we got these buildings to pay for. It's no good using them just from eight to five. So we can take the clods at night. We can open up to the dagos and niggers and use instructors who work cheap and part-time people and clerks who got a master's degree in something. And give 'em machine coffee and close the bookstore. . . .

Until one night there were stenciled signs on all the walls and

doors when I got to night school. There would be a meeting of all
night school people at eight o'clock. To voice grievances. Everybody
come.

It made me sad. Everything was changed. The night school wasn't
to blame. Nobody was to blame. What good was all this? Nothing
changes. Only people change. Luckmans leave, and somebody else
takes his place. Maybe they'd open the bookstore one night a week
and after the novelty wore off, nobody would go in, and some old
lady would doze behind the cash register waiting. Or they'd open
the coffee shop and all those tables, that vast space which was
always dark when we came at seven, would swallow the dozen or so
people who might walk all the way from the classroom buildings for
a cup of coffee. It would all be sad and come to nothing. I could see it
as if it had already happened.

But, I thought, *it shouldn't happen that way. It's an awful thing to
know what is going to happen and not act to change it.* I thought I should
act.

So all day while I was working, filing, checking invoices at the
Decatur Coffee Company, I thought. If anything could be done,
what could be done? What could I do? I was eating at the hotel coffee
shop next door when it came to me. Then I wasn't sad anymore, and
I ordered a piece of pie and coffee after my special. And got back to
work twelve minutes later.

All afternoon I thought about the day school and how Fernando
had imagined it. The girls lovely, their fresh complexions and long
scrubbed legs. Their laughter at a table over coffee. Their laughter,
the particular beauty which can only exist if you are without care,
master of your moments and your days. I thought of fraternity
meetings and pep rallies for the basketball team, of Christmas
dances at the American Legion camp on Lake Pontchartrain. I
thought of long quiet evenings studying in the dormitory lounge
with a blond girl who curled her smooth legs under her and smiled
and yawned as I read history or explained chemistry. I saw us
staring out a large picture window my imagination had constructed
at others walking under old twisted oaks, or at a tall Christmas tree
trimmed and lighted in the garden of the dormitory to cheer us all
before the holidays began. I did not think of the night school or its
problems at all. I took the afternoon for myself.

At seven-thirty I reached the hallway where the coffee machine
sat mute and choked with false money. Tarantella was surrounded
by others in jackets or sports clothes, all trying to talk at once. Next
to him, the major was deep in conversation with the bearded young

man who wore glasses and had long dirty hair and fingernails to match. The major would nod very seriously and note something down on one of his yellow legal tablets. Next to him, Fernando stood swinging a key chain in long intricate maneuvers. He grinned, waved, and started toward me.

—You never heard such business. He laughed. —More Byzantine every minute. They're putting together a list of grievances. Speeches, and then a grand march to the dean's house.

—You mean the night school director's office.

—Oh, no, you thinking small. To the college dean's house. Now he'll just be done with coffee after a fine meal. Sitting down in his study to contemplate truth. To browse among his books for words to say to people tomorrow. And then, Jesus leave the table, here's the whole night school with ole Tarantella leading 'em like the pie-eyed piper. Can you see it? Shut your eyes and lemme know. Baby, I mean the whole night school. And Mrs. Dean has fear. The baby Deans cry to see Daddy there on the porch facing all the whole night school. Makes you think of history, don't it?

—What's his name?

—Who?

—The dean of the college.

—Oh, that's funny. Nobody knows. The name in the catalogue is wrong. They got a new man. Nobody knows his name.

—Then how can they find his house?

—Somebody is on a committee to find out. They're going to the dorm to ask a day student. They'll get it.

I shook my head. It didn't remind me of history. It reminded me of someone sick and wanting waffles; nothing but waffles would do, rich and brown, swimming in butter and syrup, crisp and garnished with bacon. And when the waffles come, he cannot eat them. Cannot, but tries and vomits, lies back down sullenly again beneath his oxygen tent to suck on ice and try to breathe, remembering at last that he is an invalid and the world's best things are beyond his consumption and digestion.

—Come on, Fernando said, catching hold of my arm as the night school people moved outside. —While we walk, I'll tell you a story. You want to hear a story?

—What? I asked, distracted by the crowd which pushed us out into a dark quadrangle behind our classroom building.

—Tarantella . . . Fernando began.

But then the space around us became bright as day. Tarantella was up on a card table someone had dragged from the janitor's closet.

He was pointing at the lights, clusters of lights atop the Gothic buildings on all sides.

—See? Look! You see 'em?

The whole grassy quadrangle was lit completely. Trees stood out in dark olive contrast with the light grass. The concrete walks were blinding white. Flower beds were so crisply illuminated that the marks of rakes were visible in the finely turned earth.

—They've always been there, Tarantella cried out. —Those lights were always there. Have you ever seen 'em?

Nobody had seen the lights. Nobody knew there were lights.

—One of the school electricians is in the night school. He knew where the switches are. Now look.

All around us there was light. From one end of the campus to the other there was one rippling blaze of light. On every Gothic building, in the tops of trees, over the parking area, down from the dark tower above the chapel and from the peaks of the student union floodlights suddenly came on. And there was a loudspeaker system. Tarantella waved his hand, and there was music, loud at first and then suddenly soft so that we could hear Tarantella's voice again.

—They use it for graduations, and only somebody leaving the night school ever saw all these lights. And for the spring fete they turn on all the lights and play music all over the campus. But they don't have night school that week. It's spring vacation, and we're not here when they turn the lights on. You see? Now you see, don't you?

—The director told me, Fernando was trying to say, but I couldn't hear him for the shouts and uproar around us.

Then, without warning, the lights died, one at a time slowly. The music faded and we were suddenly blind, with only the shimmering ghost coronas of the quenched floodlights, a faint echo of music surrounding us. And Tarantella's voice telling everyone to march with him to the dean's house.

But Fernando and I stayed behind. In the empty quadrangle, we stood like paralyzed water birds aware of a threatening sound, unable to grasp its genesis or what it meant.

—He said this was ill-advised, Fernando faltered in the unlit silence. His voice was that of a child.

—Who said?

—The director. He thought I had something to do with the commotion. He said it was silly, that a simple request . . . Then he told me about Tarantella.

Told him that Tarantella was a provisional student in the night school at the order of the state parole board. And because the psychiatrist who was handling his case free was a member of the college board of regents.

Fernando touched my arm. —He stole a car in New Orleans and drove it to Minden and his sister's husband got him off. Then he did it again and they put him away at Angola and his wife took the kids. But his brother-in-law knew somebody on the pardon board and got him out and gave him a job. Now they make him stay in an approved rooming house and check in two times a week and they talk to his boss and tell all his teachers and they told him if he goes traveling again in somebody's car, they'll put him away for good.

—You made it up, I said.

—No, no, I didn't. The director said ain't that a nice representative, and I said I don't know. What is supposed to be nice about a representative? And if you let somebody in the night school, ain't we all the same? And he told me that was all.

We found a late-night place open and I went in and bought two Dixie Cups full of coffee. Fernando and I stood on Carrollton Avenue drinking it and only smiled when a police car slowed as it passed and the policemen inside stared at us like trained basilisks eyeing two ill-matched birds.

The next evening was Friday and we found out the march had come to nothing because when at last they had found the dean's house, he was out for the evening addressing a meeting of the Kappa Alpha alumni back on campus at the fraternity house. So I began talking to people, one at a time, a few together. And they liked my idea. The major ignored me, and said to the bearded boy who stayed with him constantly now that I was undependable, not to be trusted. That I had not marched. But no one else paid attention and by the end of classes, we had gotten a start. Action felt strange. Most strange because in the midst of it you feel as if it is inevitable and what you say and do is all you can say and do. And yet tentative, as if it is only a broad joke which could finally draw nothing more than laughs. But it went on, and a committee formed itself and voted against another grievance meeting. And Monday, we decided, we would have the money and make our choice.

III

When they gave me the money, each of the night school people handed me a slip of paper, too. With their choice of representative. Three of us counted the slips and Fernando won.

—You must have stuffed the ballot, a man named Gates said with a laugh.

—No, I said, —but I'm glad he won. He's just right. We couldn't do better.

—No, Gates said, studying the darkness at the end of the hall in which we were standing. —No, he's a good representative. Better than most of us.

It was seven forty-five or so when Fernando arrived. Everybody was there in the quadrangle waiting. Some of the women nudged one another and pointed out how small and neat Fernando was. The men grinned sheepishly for the most part, anticipating Fernando's surprise. Only Major Marker and Tarantella and the bearded boy stood apart. They watched us as if we were renegades, heresiarchs who had deserted a great cause.

But Gates brought Fernando over to the orange crate where I was standing. Someone had taken it along the night before so that Tarantella could use it at the dean's house. Then he had brought it back in case there was a use found for it.

So we all stood in the unlit quadrangle. I squinted out into the darkness, but it was impossible to see anyone. There were only a few shadowy forms just in front of me, and I couldn't tell who they were. I spoke to the patch of darkness nearby that seemed to be Fernando.

—Fernando . . . I began, trying to decide how loud I should speak, how large my audience might be. —Fernando, I have eight hundred dollars here. Almost everyone in the night school has contributed, and we all voted on who should get the money. We wanted somebody to enroll in the day school and go every day, and then come back and tell us about it. Some people say we don't get what we should in the night school, that the classes and the teachers and the uh . . .

I wanted some other word, but it wouldn't come. —The amenities are better there. But nobody knows, so we took up this money and picked you to go for us. We all hope you have a good time, and we know you'll come back and tell us everything.

I got down then, wondering if I'd spoken enough or too long. Then I heard the other people speaking out of the darkness. —Fernando, they called, and there seemed to be a lot of them. —Speech, Fernando. Speech.

A small gathering of shadow near me clambered up onto the orange crate. —I don't know, he started. His voice was soft and distant as a child's, both frightened and exultant to be out so late in the dark. —I don't know. Youall so kind to me. I mean, you could of sent a smart boy or a man who's been here a long time. You could of sent Charles Turner himself or Mrs. Griggs. I just can't say why you want to take a chance on me. But I'm gonna do it. I'm gonna go and see everything and talk to people, and come back to tell youall. I won't miss nothing, don't you worry. Come final time, I'll be back to thank you right.

Afterward, in the halls, as people went on to their nine o'clock classes, I saw the major and Tarantella. They said nothing, and even the bearded boy had left them and was arguing about social justice with a crippled elderly lady who had to use canes and who had given me twenty dollars for Fernando.

IV

Fernando worked in the beauty shop at night, and took his classes in the day school then. Once in a while, I would see someone who had heard that he was doing well. But no one said they had talked to him, and now and then I would feel a quick instant's chill, almost panic, and wonder if my idea had been a good one. In action, there are countless imponderables. To move a finger is to risk moving the axis of the earth. But most of the time I felt good. I would catch myself grinning at work as I checked invoices against deliveries, thinking that now, at this very moment, Fernando was in class showing how much he knew, or lounging in the snack bar with coffee, talking to professors and students. He would have a date on Saturday night when he was off work. Maybe a basketball game or a movie. It occurred to me that I had never seen him in daylight. I guessed that his smile, his neat clothes, his warm chocolate color, would seem even more pleasant with the sun streaming down on him and his friends from out of a cloudless sky.

It was almost the end of the term when Gates told me about Tarantella. They had picked him up breaking into a brand-new Coupe de Ville down at the Olds-Cadillac place. They found that he had not been coming to the night school for over a month, and had been living with a woman who was divorced with two young daughters. They were taking him back to Angola, Gates said. He was a menace to society. Which seemed true, but it made me sad anyhow.

Then it was finals week and I had no time to think of anything but Goslee's test and my other courses. The major didn't come to Goslee's test, and when the period was over, Goslee packed all the

papers in his attaché case and gave me a crooked feminine grin.
—Well, whose notes *did* you use?

—Nobody's, I told him. —I just let it go. It wasn't on the test.

—A good thing. He giggled. —I was thinking of you.

I almost said thank you, but he was gone then, and I turned off the light myself and walked out toward the quadrangle for a little air before my last test.

Someone took my arm. —There you are, a child's voice almost whispered. —Been waiting for you. Did you do good?

—I don't know, I told Fernando. —I can't ever tell. How about you and your . . .

—Oh, beautiful, he said aloud. —Just wonderful. Lord, if only I could . . .

His voice trailed off. The major had stepped up to stand beside us. He said nothing, so Fernando went on. —Oh, in the morning, I'd get up and dress and walk all the way. People would stop and offer me a ride, but I didn't want to miss any of it. So I'd walk all the way. And there would be these girls walking to their first class with sleep still in their eyes, and them all fresh from a shower with nice ironed blouses and their hair all combed nice—you ought to see the way they got their hair—and maybe one of them would wave to me and say, " 'Lo, Fernando," and I'd go on to class then.

—They were friendly? I asked.

—Oh, Lord, they were so kind. Everybody. In classes they'd say, "Fernando, have you got paper? Do you need a pencil?" And I'd say, "Oh, thank you, everything is fine."

—The teachers?

—Good. So good. I saw the man who won the prize, and he shook hands with me and asked me to come to his office and what course was I going to take. And he told me the night school teachers were very good, highly respected. He said he'd like to teach a night course soon as he could.

Gates and Mrs. Griggs and some of the others had come up then. Most of them looked worn-out from their test. They gathered around Fernando like children come to hear of a circus in a town far away.

—And the union. In the afternoon, we'd play cards or talk about the basketball or drink nice fresh coffee. They were all good and kind, them day students, and they laughed and told stories and said how glad they were to be in the school. They liked all their teachers and one day the boys said, "Fernando, we sure would like you to pick out a fraternity and join it. Which one you like?" But I said,

"No, thanks, I got to go back to the night school because of all my friends and . . ."

—What about us? someone asked excitedly. —Did you tell them about us?

—Oh, Lord, that's what we talked about most. They knew about youall, and they were so proud on account of how hard everybody works in the night school. They wished they could do as good. And they said they wished we could all come and be with them. You know, all of us come and be in the day school.

The major cleared his throat in the darkness. —I've got to be getting on, he said. —I wanted to tell youall good-bye.

—Where? somebody asked. The major had been in the night school longer than anybody. He could remember when the night school reopened after the war. —Where are you going?

—Well, they want me back in service. I can't talk about it. But they need me. I hate to leave, but if they need me . . . I know certain things . . . the intelligence . . .

Everyone shook hands with the major and offered to buy him coffee from the machine if he got a chance to come by and see us. Then he walked away and vanished in the shadows, and it was as if he had never been among us.

Fernando was talking again, breathless, telling us the same things he had already said. —And they wished we could all come and be with them. Said they wished we all could come to the day school. . . .

Then the people began to move off, talking to one another, and Gates and Mrs. Griggs congratulated Fernando and left so that we were standing alone in the quadrangle. A security patrolman passed by and paused to watch us. Then he began walking again.

—I'm glad about . . . I began, but I could see Fernando wasn't listening. I moved as close as I could and saw that his head was down and his hands hanging by his sides. I was tired, too. The finals were hard always, and this term's especially. Then the bell rang and it was time for my last one. —You did a fine job . . . I began.

—Leave me be, Fernando said softly, and started walking toward the trolley stop. I followed him for a step or two, but he paid no attention, and I watched him merge finally in the mottled light and darkness of the tree-lined passage under the weak illumination of the streetlights.

I went back into the building, but it was no use. I could not focus my eyes to read the examination, and I knew I had nothing to write anyhow. So for two hours I studied my empty test booklet dreaming of action, great surges of vengeful words and deeds that would shake down the stars and shatter the sun, merge daylight and dark and change the face of creation. But then the instructor called time, and we all filed out into the hall where janitors were sweeping, and behind me I heard one of them cough and turn out the light.

Baton Rouge, 1962
Covington, 1968

The Actes and Monuments
(1978)

As for myself, I am not sorry but I commit myself into God's hands, and I trust he will give me mouth and wisdom to answer according to the right.

—John Foxe's *Book of Martyrs,*
The Actes and Monuments

The Actes and Monuments

After the coronary, I quit. I could have slowed down, let things go easier, taken some of the jobs where little more than appearance was required. But I didn't do that. I like to believe that I cared too much for the law. No, I *do* believe that. Because if I had cared nothing for the law, I would have played at being an attorney—or else simply stopped being involved with law at all. But I did neither.

Rather, I let go my partnership and began looking for some way to use all I knew, all I was coming to know. It wasn't that I couldn't stand pressure; I could. I could stand quite a bit of pressure. What I could not stand was the tension that never lets up, the sort of thing generated by corporation cases that might go four or five years without resolution. Brief peaks followed by relaxation: those, the doctor said, would be all right.

So I was thirty-eight, a good lawyer by any standard—including the money I had let collect in stocks. A bachelor, and a one-time loser on the coronary circuit. What do you do? Maybe you settle down in Manhattan and have fun? Maybe you don't. There is no room in Manhattan for fun—not in the crowd I knew, anyhow. You are either in it or out of it; that was the rule, and everybody understood and accepted. Poor Harry wasn't in it. So Harry had to walk out of it. Who needs to be pushed?

But Harry is no loser. Not since Harry climbed out of Brooklyn Heights and into Yale Law School. No, Harry has to find himself a blast he can live with. Out of New York. So where? London? Not really. We don't function well in other places. Rio, Athens, Caracas, Tokyo? Any one of them is easy with my contacts. But they are imitations of what I am having to leave.

So Harry comes on very strong. Much stronger than anyone can credit, believe. Who knows where I caught the idiot virus that took me down there? Maybe it was *Absalom, Absalom,* which I once read, not understanding a word of it, but living in every crevice of time and space that the laureate of the Cracker World created.

It is no overstatement to say that my friends paled when they received postcards from Vicksburg. It was much too much. They were old postcards. Pictures in mezzotint of the Pennsylvania memorial, of the grass-covered earthworks outside the town. Post-

215

cards which must have been printed at the latest in the early 1920s, and which had been in the old flyblown rack waiting for my hand almost half a century. I cannot remember what I wrote on the cards, but it must have been wonderful. I can say it was wonderful, because except for one slightly drunken phone call from Manhattan late at night about a week after I arrived, I got no answers to those cards at all. Perhaps they never arrived. Perhaps they slipped back into the time warp from which I had plucked them at the little clapboard store outside town where there was a single gas pump with a glass container at the top, which the proprietor had to pump full before it would run down into the tank of my XKE.

Should I tell you about that man? Who sold me gas, counted out my change, made no move at my hood or windshield, and told me in guarded tones that he had seen a car like mine once long ago. A Mercer runabout, as he remembered. Never mind.

I rented a place—leased it. Almost bought it right off, but had not quite that kind of guts. It was old, enormous, with a yard of nearly an acre's expanse. I came that first day to recognize what an acre meant in actual extent. I stood in my yard near an arbor strung with veiny ropes of scuppernong, looked back at the house through the branches of pear trees, past the trunks of pecan and oak strung with heavy coils of that moss that makes every tree venerable which bears it. My house, on my property. Inside I had placed my books, my records, my liquor, what little furniture I had collected in the brownstone I had left behind.

My first conclusion was that the coronary had affected my mind. I could have committed myself to Bellevue with my doctor's blessing. Or, secondly, had I found in some deep of my psyche a degree of masochism unparalleled in the history of modern man? Is it true that Jewishness is simply a pathology, not a race or a religion? Perhaps I had, in the depths of my pain and the confusion attendant on my attack, weighed myself in the balance and found my life and its slender probings at purpose wanting utterly. Could it be that a man who, in the very embrace of probable death, can find no reason for his living except the sweating grab of life itself housed in a body, looks at all things and condemns himself to Mississippi?

Or finally, grossest of all, was there an insight in my delirium whereby I saw Mississippi not as exile, not as condemnation, but as a place of salvation? Must we somehow search out the very pits and crannies of our secret terrors in order to find what for us will be paradise? Consider as I did, in retrospect, that no man of normal responses raised in Manhattan is going to look for himself in the deep South. And yet how many of those men of normal responses are happy? How many die at the first thrust of coronary, dreaming as life ebbs of a handful of dusty dark-green grapes, a sprig of verbena, the soft weathered marble of an old Confederate monument within the shadow of which might have lain the meaning of their lives? I offer this possibility only because we are, most of us, so very miserable living out the lives that sense and opportunity provide. I wondered afterward, when I came to understand at least the meaning of my own choice, if we do not usually fail ourselves of happiness—of satisfaction, anyhow—by ignoring the possibilities of perversity. Not perversion. Those we invariably attempt in some form. No, perversity: how few of us walk into the darkness if that is what we fear. How few of us step into a situation which both terrifies and attracts us. If we fear water, we avoid it rather than forcing ourselves to swim. If we fear heights, we refuse to make that single skydive which might simultaneously free and captivate us. If we cannot abide cats, we push them away, settling for a world of dogs. You see how gross my insights had become.

In order to live, I thought, standing there, staring at the strange alien house which was now my legal residence and the place where I was determined to create, as in a crucible, the substance of my new life, it may be essential to force, to invade, to overwhelm those shadowed places we fear and, fearing, learn to ignore as real possibilities even when we know them to be real, to be standing erect against a hot sky windless and blind to their own beauties, realizable only to those of us who come from distant places.

A simpler explanation was offered me later by one of Vicksburg's most elegant anti-Semites, a dealer in cotton futures who, loathing my nation and my region, my presumed religion and my race, became a close friend. He suggested that Jews, for their perfidy, are condemned to have no place, to strike no roots.

—Don't you live always out of a moral and spiritual suitcase, he asked slyly. —Isn't it notable that there has never been any great architecture of the synagogue? How many of you speak the language of your great-grandfathers? Isn't placelessness a curse?

—Yes, I told him in answer to his last question. —Indisputably yes. But think of the hungers of a placeless man. Can you even begin to conceive the mind of a man who has suffered a failure of the heart once, who has fled all ordinary lives and come to Mississippi?

—No, he said, no longer joking or arch. —No, I can't conceive that mind. But I expect there must be riches in it. You'll be using

your talents, he half-asked, half-stated. —You'll be going to help
niggers with the law, won't you?

—Yes, I told him. That certainly. Not that it will mean a great deal.
Only the reflex of the retired gunfighter who no longer hopes either
to purge the world of good or evil but whose hand moves, claws at
his side when pressed, out of a nervous reaction so vast and profound that the very prohibition of God himself could not stop it.

—Good, he said. —Not about the niggers. Everybody in the
country wants a try at that sack of cats. But not your way. We've
never had a man who came loving, needing, down here to do that
kind of thing. I want a chance to see this. It has got to be rich.

—What, I asked. —What will be so rich?

—Why, seeing a Yankee Jew fighting in the South because he
needs her, because he loves her. Did you ever in your life hear the
like of that?

How could I help loving? Where else could I come across such a
man? But he was the least of it. There was, at the garage which saw
to my car, an avowed member of the Klan who asked me why I had
come so far to die. My answer satisfied him. —Because, if you have
got to die, it is stupid to die just anywhere and by an accident of
some valve in your heart. If it comes here, I will know why and
maybe even when.

He looked at me and scratched his head. —My Christ, he said. I
never heard nothing like that in all my life. You are a fucking nut.

—How do you like it, I asked him over the hood of my Jaguar, now
dusty and hot with April sun.

—Why, pretty well, he said, grinning, putting out his hand without volition or even, I suspect, the knowledge he had extended it. I
took it firmly, and he looked surprised. As if the last thing on earth
he had ever expected to do was shake hands with some skulking
Yankee kike determined to stir up his coloreds.

By this time you have dismissed me as a lunatic or a liar or both.
Very well. You only prove that the most profound impulses of your
spirit can find their fulfillment in Fairlawn, New Jersey. Good luck.

But if your possibilities are . . . what? More exotic, then I want to
tell you the proving of what I found here in Vicksburg, Mississippi. I
want to tell you about Mr. Grierson, and the cases we worked on
together—cases which, whatever else, have found me for myself. So
saying, I have to retreat to my first conclusion. The coronary affected my mind. This I'm sure of. Because, satisfied beyond any
hope I brought from Manhattan with me, I am still enough of a
rationalist to see that my satisfaction, my new life, and what Mr.

Grierson and I do—have done—is beyond even the most liberally construed limits of ordinary sanity. I am not a mystic, thus able to excuse any deviation in myself, blessing the lunacy as a certain portent. I am a sensible man who, so cast, must admit that he has found sense nonsense and empty, and that a tract of lunacy laid out before him has bloomed like the distant desert glimmering before Moses as he lay down at last, his final massive coronary denying him the power to cross over Jordan and dwell some last loving days or months or years amidst the plenty that his lip-chewing endurance had reared up out of the sands.

I was handling now and again the smallest of cases for certain black people who had heard that an eccentric Yankee lawyer had come to town and would do a workmanlike job of defending chicken thieves, wife-beaters, small-time hustlers, whores, and even pigeon-droppers. This alone would have drawn me little enough custom, but it was said, further, and experience proved it true, that the Yankee did his work for free, a very ancient mariner of Yankee lawyers doomed to work out his penance for bird mangling or beast thumping by giving away his services to whatever Negro showed up with a likely story. It was said that if you had no likely story, he would help you make one up—not inciting to perjury, you realize. Only fooling with the facts in such a way as to produce a story diverting enough to keep the judge from adding a month or so to your sentence for the boredom you caused him in addition to the inconvenience of having to keep court for the likes of you. All that aside, I seduced by asking no fee. It was at first amazing to me how a Negro was willing often to take a chance of six months or a year in jail to avoid a fifty-dollar fee, even when he had it. For some reason I could not at first grasp, my own logic had no purchase with them. Think: suppose a man offered you free legal service. Wouldn't you, like me, presume that the service would be about worth the price? Yes, you would. But how do you suppose the blacks reasoned? One of my chicken—actually, a pig—thieves explained why he trusted me. You got a nice house, ain't you? Yes, I said. You out of jail yourself, ain't you? Yes. You look like you eats pretty good. I do, I eat very well. Except no pork. No saturated fats. Huh? Never mind. Oh, religion, huh? All right. Anyhow, if you got a good house, if you look like eating regular, and if the judge let you stand up there, you got as much going for you as any jakeleg courthouse chaser I seen.

It was that very pig-robber who carried me down to town one day in search of a law book. Something to do with statute of limitations on pig thievery. It seems that my man was charged with having stolen a pig in 1959, the loss or proof of it having come to light only in the last few days. I wanted to make absolutely sure that there was not some awful exception to ordinary prescription in Mississippi law when the subject was pigs. There are some oddities in Texas law having to do with horses. I had never had much practice connected with livestock in Manhattan. I thought I had better make sure.

So I was directed by a deputy, who was everlastingly amused by the nature and style of my practice, to the offices of Mr. Grierson.

They were on a side street just beyond the business district. Among some run-down houses that must have been neat and even prime in the 1920s but which had lost paint and heft and hope in the 1950s at the latest, there was a huddle of small stores. A place that sold seed and fertilizer and cast-iron pots and glazed clay crocks that they used to make pickles in. Just past the pots and crocks, there was a flat-roofed place with whitewashed doors and one large window, heavy curtains behind it, across which was painted

FREE CHURCH OF THE OPEN BIBLE

There was a hasp on the door with a large combination lock hanging through it. I wondered what might be the combination to the Open Bible.

Just past the church, there was another storefront building standing a little to itself. There was a runway of tall weeds and grass between it and the church and it was set back a little from the sidewalk with a patch of tree-lawn in front. On either side of the door was a huge fig tree, green and leafy and beginning to bear. Through the heavy foliage, I could see that there were windows behind the trees. They seemed to have been painted over crudely, so that they looked like giant blinkered eyes which had no wish to see out into the street. Above the door itself was a sign made of natural wood hanging from a wrought-iron support. On it was graved in faded gold letters cut down into the wood

W. C. GRIERSON
Atty at Law

The door itself was recessed fairly deeply and I got the notion that it was not the original door, that it had nothing really to do with the building, which was, like those nearby, simply a long frame affair— what they—we—call a shotgun building, although much wider and longer. I stood there in the early summer sun looking at that door as if it were the entrance to another place. Why? I rubbed my chin and thought, and then I found, back in the fine debris of my old life, back behind the sword-edge of my coronary, the recollection of another summer afternoon spent with a lovely woman at some gallery, some wealthy home—somewhere. We had gone to see paintings, and there had been one among all the others that I could not put out of mind. It had been by the Albrights, those strange brothers. Of a door massive and ancient, buffed and scarred, the very deepest symbol both of life and of the passage through which life itself must pass. On its weather-beaten panels hung a black wreath, each dark leaf pointed as a spike, shimmering in the mist of its own surreality. My God, I remembered thinking, is death like that? Is it finally a door with a wreath standing isolated from air and grass— even from the materials which are supposed to surround the fabric of a door? And then I thought, the lovely woman beside me talking still about a Fragonard she had spotted nearby, of Rilke's words: "Der grosse Tod. . . . —The great Death each has in himself, that is the fruit round which all revolves. . . ." But the title of the painting was *That Which I Should Have Done I Did Not Do*, and I could find neither sweetness nor rest in that.

Later, when I had done with the lovely woman, I remember somehow managing to go back and see the painting again. It was evening then, winter I think, and whether in a museum or a private home (I could remember such things with perfect clarity before my heart failed me) I was alone, standing before it with the light soft and nothing but loneliness stalking the roofless windowless doorless wall-less room there with me.

I had gone back looking for some release from it, I think now. I had gone back not for appreciation—any more than one goes back to see Grünewald's Isenheim altarpiece for reasons of art. I wanted to find the key to that door—the flaw, the crack in its reality. To be free of the Albrights and their loathsome portal, I had to find, somewhere in the canvas, a false note, a tiny piece of sentimentality or stupidity. But there was nothing. The weather of the painting was unfathomable. It did not change. Even with the summer brightness purged from the room, it was the same—as if the door, the wreath, the very canvas had the power to absorb or reject exterior light so as to keep the painting always within that awful twilight which flowed like sidereal influence out of the door's dead center—the wreath which lay hanging against it like a demonic target or some emblem of absolutism linked with the imperturbable power of death itself.

Yes, I am still standing in front of that frame building in my town of Vicksburg, and yes, looking inward past the great fig trees at the shadowed door which now after all looks only the least bit like that other one, the weather, the light, the substantiality of all things being so much less dense. Reality spares us; we do not have to know what else there is very frequently, do we? A colored boy, no more than twelve, walked by in a polo shirt and worn corduroy pants. He exchanged a quick glance with me and stepped on past, a transistor radio hanging from his neck, a tiny tinny thing which crooned:

> . . . *looks like the end, my friend,*
> *got to get in the wind, my friend,*
> *These are not my people, no, no,*
> *these are not my people* . . .

Surely he had his radio aimed at me. How could he tell? And was the announcer a friend of his? He an agent of the station which had discovered me, an alien, waxing in their midst. All of this I thought in jest, putting sudden flash-cuts of the Isenheim crucifixion out of mind, reaching for the doorknob, and stepping inside.

I do not know why I was not prepared. I should have been. No reason for me to suppose that a lawyer's office here, in an old frame building, would have the sort of Byzantine formality I remembered from New York. Receptionist, secretary, inner office—with possibly a young clerk interposed somewhere between. But the mind is stamped inalterably with such impressions when we have done business a certain way for a very long time.

So I was not prepared when Mr. Grierson turned in his chair and smiled at me and said, —Well, this is nice. Mighty nice. I don't know as I expected it.

—I beg . . . I began. Then I tried again. Best not beg. —I'm sorry. Have we met? Is it better to be sorry than to beg, I thought instantly. Too late.

—You'd be the lawyer just come down. Got you a house and everything.

My God, I thought, even a B-movie would tell you that things travel like lightning here. He probably knows what you paid for the lease, what you owe on the house if you pick up the option. Knows your last address, your last place of employ. Knows about your little chicken-thief cases, your car . . . I almost thought, about your coronary.

—Yes, I said, putting out my hand as he rose and offered his. —I'm Harry Cohen.

He motioned me to a chair near his desk and I sat down, trying as

I did to begin the task of seeing him, of seeing this place in which he worked. Trying at the same time to put out of mind the impressions I had created, had begun to suppose from the moment the deputy had told me where to come. If we could only stay free of our own guesses, what would ever make us wrong in advance?

He walked over to a large safe against the wall to the left of the door. It was taller than he was, and the door opened slowly as he turned the handle. He stood reaching into its dark recesses, his back to me. I wondered what he was looking for as his voice came to me, small talk like a magician's patter, over his shoulder.

—Yes, Mr. Cohen. It's kind of you to pay a courtesy call. A custom languishing. Not dead, but in a bad way. A fine custom. Men who stand to the law shouldn't meet for the first time arguing a motion before Basil Plimsoll or one of the other boys on the circuit here. . . .

I scanned the room as he spoke. I would deal with him later. It was a bright room—almost the opposite of what the door suggested. Or was it only the opposite of what the Albrights' door suggested?

On the wall over his flat desk, the shape and design of which had vanished long ago, I suspected, beneath a welter of papers and books, there were three old tintype portraits. Only they were not tintypes. They were fresh modern reproductions of tintypes. In the center, in a military uniform I almost recognized, was that stern beautiful face one recognizes without ever even having seen it. It was Lee. To his right, left profile toward me, hung that other one, that crafty rebel whose religion had almost severed the continent, Jackson. I did not know the third. He had a Tartar's face, long, bony, richly harsh—as if only in that uniform, only involved in that calling of arms, had his life meant anything to him at all. His eyes were straightforward and overpowering even at a hundred years' remove. And yet they were somehow at ease, their intensity more a matter of something evoked in the viewer than something essential to the eyes themselves. He had a high forehead, hair long, black, brushed back. His beard was a careless Vandyke, and the effect was that of seeing the man who had last closed the Albrights' door, nailed the wreath on it, and walked away, hands in uniform pockets. Whistling.

The rest of the room was austere and predictable. Near a long window there was a rocking chair done in some kind of chintz. Another table covered with papers. A third table in a corner with a coffeepot on it, a wine bottle or two, half a loaf of bread, and a plate upon which rested, glowing faintly, a large wedge of cheese. It

looked like cheddar from where I sat. It was a room without quality—except for the portraits, which were, I thought, a ritual obser-
vance no more meaningful to this man whose life had been lived in
another country than washing his face in the morning, spitting at
noon, closing his eyes at night.

Mr. Grierson turned from the safe, hands filled with two tumblers and a dark brown bottle without a label. It had no cap. There
seemed to be a cork stuck in it. He set all of it down on the edge of
his desk and pulled the bottle's stopper with his teeth. The liquor
was the lightest possible amber, a cataract of white gold as it twin-
kled into the glasses.

He smiled up at me. —You'll like it, he said. —Maybe not this
time. But you let me send you a couple bottles. You'll come to like it.

—Corn, I said.

—Surely. Comes from upstate. Costs more than it used to. Bribes
are just like the cost of living.

I sat back and sipped a little. It was peculiar, nothing like store
whiskey, really. It was a shock in the mouth, vanished as you swallowed. Then it hit the pit of your stomach and paralyzed you for the
briefest moment. Then great warmth, a happiness that spoke of
cells receiving gifts, of veins moving to a new rhythm, muscles
swaying like grain in a breeze-swept field. It was lovely. Nothing
like whiskey. More like sipping the past, something intangible that
could yet make you feel glad that it had been there.

Mr. Grierson sat watching me now. As I took another swallow,
deeper this time, I watched him back. A man of middle height, aged
now but hale. Steel-rimmed glasses revealing large innocent blue
eyes that seemed never to have encountered guile. He had that
almost cherubic look that one associates with country doctors—or,
in certain cases, with Southern politicians. He wore an old suede
coat cut for hunting. I had never seen anything like it. It was a soft
umber and fit as if it had been his own pelt originally.

—Your jacket, I couldn't help saying, feeling the whiskey lift me
and waft me toward him, toward his smile. —Could I get one . . .

—At Lilywhite's, he said.

—Here?

—London, he said apologetically. —And even there back in 1949. I
wouldn't reckon they make 'em like this anymore.

He wasn't putting me on, I could tell. But I could tell too that he
enjoyed that level of conversation. It pleased him to please with
pleasantries. One moves from one series of set exchanges to another. An infinite series. And when the last series is exhausted, it is

either time to go, or you have lived out your life and death clears its throat, almost loath to interrupt, and says that it is time. I thought I would not want to go on like that.

Did I tell you that, on the far side of the coronary (Oh God, how that word has come to press me with its softness, its multiple implications. Corona. Carnal. Coronary. A place, a name, the vaguest warm exhalation glimmering from an eclipsed sun. Shivering golden and eternal around the glyph of a saint. Called then a Glory. I lay for weeks thinking Coronary, wondering when it would reach into my chest once more and squeeze ever so gently and bring out with its tenderness my soul, toss that gauzy essence upward like a freed dove to fly outward, past morning, past evening, past the blue sky into the glistening midnight blue of deep space, and past that even to the place where souls fly, shaking great flakes of its own hoarded meaning outward, downward on all suns and the worlds thereunder.) I had had a certain gift with exceptionally sharp teeth. Yes, I had been cruel. I had enjoyed finding certain lawyers in the opposition, men I had known who were blessed with a kind of unwillingness to go for blood. They worked within the confines of their dignity, their gentleness, their inadequacy. But I worked elsewhere and won invariably. But such work tightens the viscera. One cannot play bloodster without gradually coming to possess the metabolism of a jaguar, a predator. Was it imagination, or did I come to see better in the dark as I aged in my profession? Was I a little mad, or did I move more smoothly? Did my walk take on a certain ease, a bit of stealth? Did I smile with that humorless lynx-eyed expression that flows from the second sight of the killer? If it had not been for my success, I would have gone to a psychiatrist saying, Doctor, there is in me a germ and I fear it grows. Watch your throat, Doctor. What? Yes, I invent metaphors for killing. I am not psychopathic. Never that, not at all. No, I must kill without killing. I am a child of the century. Do you understand?

But Coronary came upon me, slackened the knotted nerves, the plaited muscles. I cannot say if I look younger or older now, but I am much different. I do not—no, will not—want to pursue and strike and rend. I am more peaceful. I want to do my part. And what is my portion will come to me. It is chess after professional football. But, even so, not Mr. Grierson's gambit, not at his tempo. Though even as I looked at his pink uncreased face and considered the folds and inlets of the world behind him, I wondered if his pleasantries, his kindliness were not analogous to mine. What if one has, in passion or confusion, or as habit, taken men of another hue out and strung

them to a near tree? What if that is how, for a small age, we have
shaken from ourselves that rage that can tear a whole society to
pieces? Suppose, from outside, something like Coronary should
come? What might we do in the shadow of knowing that we cannot
ever lynch again on pain of dying? Chess, after all, is a pleasantry
profoundly complicated, Byzantine in its intricacies. Is there something in this?

—Another little drink, Mr. Grierson suggested. —I believe you've
already found something in it.

—I was thinking . . . of martinis.

—No comparison. Next step from corn would be . . . perhaps a
pipe of opium.

I did not even wonder if he spoke from experience or from some
book by Sax Rohmer. I wanted to go on.

—Mr. Grierson, I wonder if you have the *Southwest Reporter*
from . . .

He poured each of us another glass. —I have it all, he said. —I
think my . . . library will fill your . . .

I looked around. There was a single bookcase across the room,
and only a handful of books in it. I must have looked doubtful. He
gave me the oddest of small glances, and I took refuge in my
whiskey.

—Maybe we should go on into the library, he said, rising and
walking toward a door at the back of the room which I had not even
noticed until now. It was painted the same dull color as the rest of
the office. There was a hook nailed badly to the door with coats and
jackets and what looked like an old fishing hat hanging from it.

I followed him and stepped ahead of him as he opened the door.

What shall I say? I have to tell you that Coronary fluttered not far
away, and I stepped in and turned in the new room slowly, slowly,
taking it in, feeling, thinking in a simultaneity resembling that first
moment of the attack.

So this is what lies behind them, Southerners. There is always
that front room, the epitome of the ordinary, a haven for bumpkins.
And behind, in one way, one sense or another, there is always this.
No wonder even the most ignorant of them is more complex, more
intricate than I have ever been. They stand upon this. This is behind
them, within them. My God, what does that make . . . us?

Because it was, properly speaking, not a room. No, many rooms.
It went on, back at least four more rooms and perhaps side rooms
off each of the main rooms toward the back. And I knew without

even entering the others that they were all more or less like this one I was standing in.

Filled from floor to roof with books. Thousands upon thousands of books. Books in leather and buckram, old, new, burnished bindings and drab old cloth. Behind and around the shelves the walls were paneled in deepest cherry wood. Before me was a beautiful nineteenth-century library table surrounded by chairs. It was like the rare book room of a great private library. I moved spellbound toward the nearest shelf. It was . . . religion. What was not there? Josephus. The Fathers in hundreds of volumes. The Paris edition of Aquinas. Was this a first of the Complutensian Polyglot? Scrolls in ivory cases. Swedenborg, Charles Fort. A dissolving Latin text from the early seventeenth century. The *Exercises* of Ignatius. Marcion, Tertullian. And I could see that the rest of the room was of a kind with those I was looking at.

—I had a house once, Mr. Grierson was saying. —But even then it didn't seem fitting to have all this stuff out where my clients could see it. Folks here can abide a lot of peculiarity, but you ought not to flaunt it. You want to keep your appetites kind of to yourself.

This in a deprecating voice, as if possession of books, especially in great number, was somehow a vice—no, not a vice, distinctly not a vice, but an eccentricity that must disturb the chicken thief or the roughneck with a ruptured disk. Was it a kindness to spare them this?

—I think you'll find most anything you'll need here, Mr. Grierson said softly. —Except for science. Not much science. Darwin, Huxley, Newton—all the giants. I kind of gave up when they went to the journals. They stopped doing books, you know.

—Yes, I said. Still thinking, this is where the Southerners have stored it all. You ask, how could Faulkner . . . how could Dickey . . . down here, in this . . . place . . . ? This is how.

I knew that this was madness. I did not question that. This time, had there been a psychiatrist close by, I would have gone to him at once without a doubt. Because, after all, this was not what I thought, but worse: what I felt. I *knew* it was not so, and still I *believed* it.

—This is where I do . . . my work, Mr. Grierson was saying.

—Work, I repeated as we entered another room filled with literature. All of it. My hand fell on a shelf filled with French. Huysmans, Daudet, de Musset, Mérimée—and a large set of portfolios. They were labeled simply Proust. I took one out. It was bound in a gray cloth patterned in diamond-shaped wreaths, each filled with star-like snowflakes, smaller wreaths, featherlike bursts gathered at the bottom, nine sprays flaring at the top.

—It was the wallpaper, Mr. Grierson was saying. —That pattern . . .

I opened the portfolio. In it were printed sheets covered with scrawling script, almost every line of print scratched out or added to.

—Proofs. Of *Du côté de chez Swann.* I was in Paris . . . in 1922. Gide . . . anyhow, I came across . . .

—Of course. You've studied them?

—Oh yes. The Pleiade text isn't . . . quite right.

We went on for a long time, shelf by shelf. But we did not finish. We never finished. It could have taken weeks, months, so rich was his treasure.

I left at dusk with Grierson seeing me to the door, inviting me back soon, offering me the freedom of his library. I was back home sitting under my arbor with whiskey and a carafe of water on a small table beside me before I recalled that I had never gotten around to checking in the Mississippi code as to its position on pigs and those who made off with them.

The pig had prescribed, sure enough. But on the way out of court, I found myself involved in another case dealing, if you will, with similar matters.

They were bringing in a young man in blue jeans, wearing a peculiar shirt made of fragments, rags—like a patchwork quilt. He had very long hair like Prince Valiant, except not so neat. He was cuffed between two deputies. One, large with a face the color of a rare steak, kept his club between the young man's wrists, twisting it from time to time. There seemed somehow to be an understanding between them: the deputy would twist his club viciously; the young man would shriek briefly. Neither changed his expression during this operation.

—What did he do, I asked the other deputy who looked much like a young Barry Fitzgerald.

—That sonofabitch *cussed* us, he told me with that crinkly simian smile I had seen in *Going My Way.* —We should of killed him.

—Local boy, I asked.

—You got to be shitting me, he answered, watching his partner doing the twist once more. —He's some goddamned Yankee. Michigan or New York, I don't know. We should of killed him.

—Did you find anything in his car?

—Car your ass. He was hitching out on U.S. 80. We better not of found anything on him. I know I'd of killed him for sure. I can't stand it, nobody smoking dope.

—What's the charge?

—Reviling, he said, eyes almost vanishing in that attenuated annealed Mississippi version of an Irish grin. —Two counts.

—Two?

—We was both there. He was vile to Bobby Ralph and me both.

—What did he say?

—Wow, Barry Fitzgerald's nephew crinkled at me. —We should of killed him and dumped him in Crawfish Creek.

—What?

—Pigs.

—Sorry?

—You heard. Called us—Bobby Ralph and me—pigs. My God, how do you reckon we kept off of killing him?

I think it was a question of free association. Pigs. I had had luck with pigs so far. Maybe this Yankee sonofabitch—pardon me—was sent for my special care. God knows the care he would get otherwise. Just then Barry's partner gave the young man a final supreme wrench. He came up off the floor of the courthouse hallway at least three feet. He squealed and looked at me with profound disgust.

—You old bastard, he drawled, hunching his shoulders, —would you let 'em book me so I can get these things off?

—I'm a lawyer, I said.

—You're fucking bad news, the young man said wearily.

—See, Barry said, as his partner shoved the young man down the hall toward the booking room. —Reckon we ought to take him back out and lose him?

—No, I said. —You don't want to do that.

—No, Barry said, walking after his partner and their day's bag. —No, you lose him and the feds shake all the feathers out of your pallet looking for him. Christ, all you have to do to make him important is lose him. Or paint him black.

—You leave the ninety-nine lambs and seek the one that's lost, I said, striving for his idiom.

—Anyone does that is a goddamned fool, Barry said over his shoulder. —And he's going to be out of the sheep business before he knows it. Lost is lost.

Later—you guessed it—he sent for me. On the theory that I seemed to be the only one in the town able to speak English as he knew it, as opposed to lower Mississippian. We talked in a corner of his cell. There was a sad Mexican and a local drunk in the cell with him. The three had reached a kind of standoff between them. None could understand the others. Each seemed weird to the others. Since they had no weapons and were roughly the same size, an accommodation had been arranged. No one would begin a fight which could not be handicapped.

His name was Rand McNally. He might have been a nice-looking young man if he had wanted to be. But he was not. His eyes were circled, his skin dry and flaked. I could not tell precisely what color his hair was. He had a small transistor radio the size of a cigarette pack stuck in the pocket of his shirt. It was tuned to a local rock music station:

> She's got everything she needs,
> She's an artist,
> She don't look back . . .

—The Spic stinks and the redneck keeps puking over there in the corner, Rand McNally told me. —But that's all right. I've got it coming. I deserve it. Jesus, I wish I'd kept my mouth shut.

—Or stayed out of Mississippi.

—It was an accident, Mississippi.

—Some say that, I told him.

—Oh shit. I mean being here. I was running away from a . . . girl. It came up Mississippi.

—Where are you from?

He sat back and fingered his essay at a beard. It was long and a kind of dark red. I supposed his hair was probably the same color if it was washed. The beard was sparse, oriental. Above it, he had large green eyes which somehow gave me a start each time I looked squarely into them. I am not used to being put off by a physical characteristic, but those eyes, deeply circled, seemed to demand a concentration and attention I had no wish to muster. They seemed, too, to require the truth. Not knowing the truth, I evaded such demands whenever possible. I wished I had let him pass on with Barry Fitzgerald's kinsman and his partner. No, I didn't.

—I don't know, Rand McNally said. —From one place after another. I just remember serial motels and rooming houses. The old man was an automobile mechanic. I never had the idea it started anywhere. I mean, it had to start somewhere. I got born, didn't I? But I remember it being one dump after another forever. Al's Garage, Bo-Peep Motel; Fixit Tire Company, Millard's Auto Court; Willie's Car Repair, Big Town Motor Hotel. Somewhere the old man had a woman and she had me—told him I was his—and then on to the next place. She dropped off somewhere. I think he whipped up on her. I seem to remember something. About money? Sure, probably. I don't remember her.

I saw his father, a great tall harried man with grease worked permanently into the skin of his knuckles, under his fingernails, with the soul of Alice's white rabbit, an ancient Elgin running fast in his pocket, and a notebook listing all the small towns, garages, and motels he was obliged to move through before it was done. One entry said: *Get Son.* Another said: *Son Grown. Leaves.* There were faded, smeared pencil checks beside each entry. Life lived between Marvin Gardens and Reading Railroad.

—How do you want to plead? I asked him.

He shrugged. —Make it easy on yourself. I've got a couple of months to do here. Price of pork.

I had not thought him intelligent enough to have a sense of humor. We smiled at each other then. The transistor was quacking another of its vast repertoire of current tunes:

> *These are not my people,*
> *No, no, these are not my people.*
> *Looks like the end, my friend,*
> *Got to get in the wind, my friend . . .*

—I'm going to plead you innocent. No malice.

He tossed his hair back and smiled up at me. His green eyes seemed to hang on mine for a long while. It surprised me that someone so worn, so ground off by the endless procession of new people in his life could reach across to the latest in that anonymous parade with even the appearance of interest.

—No malice, he said. —That's true.

It was late that evening when the phone rang. At the other end was Billy Phipps, one of the county attorney's assistants. His voice was lazy with an undertone of something like amusement or exultation. I did not like him. He was provincial as a Bronx delivery man and took pleasure in the webbing of paltry law as it snared those who had not the slightest idea of its working. His own ignorance made him delight in that of others.

—Well, what do you think of your boy Rand McNally? he asked.

—Not a lot, I said, wondering why he would bother with a call on such a matter. —It seems silly to put him on the county for a little mild name-calling. Hadn't you ought to leave room for rape-murderers?

At the other end of the line, I could hear Phipps draw in his breath.

I pause only to say that I neither believe nor disbelieve in magic, precognition, spiritualism, and so on. I am not prejudiced. But I come to feel that all we do in the four dimensions of our world is like the action of water beetles skating on the surface of a still lake, turning our tricks between water and air, resident truly, fully, in neither, committed vaguely to both. Are we material—or other? I receive hints from varied sources. If you have loitered at the gates of Coronary, you must wonder. Is a massive heart seizure only a statistically predictable failure of meat-mechanism? Could it be counted a spiritual experience? Who, what seizes the heart? Who, what attacks the heart? Could it be an entrance into the indices of those currents which play above and below the beetle, in the great eternal world where there are neither serials, sequences nor statistics? Where forever, possibly, dear God and his precious Adversary choose to disagree as to the purpose of their copulation? At my worst—or best?—moments, I seem to hear, like a radio signal from the most remote reaches of time and space, the voices of the Entities making their cases over and over, yet never the same, because each permutation is a case unto itself. Is it the voice of God one hears, arguing point by point, A to B to C, coolly, without rancor or regret—like Herman Kahn? Is it Satan who sobs and exults, demands, entreats, laughs, chides, tears a passion, and mutters sullenly? Or are those voices reversed? Maybe I am gulled, believing in polarities. Why not? Could not God howl and sob the Natural Order of Normal Occasions, while Satan urges quietly the Stewing Urgencies of Madness? Why not? And why should we not in one way or another receive darts and splinters from those age-long and intricate arguments?

So much to explain my mind as I heard Phipps draw in his breath. *Jesus,* I thought, *a message.*

—What did he tell you? Phipps asked quietly, his normal sneering country manner gone altogether.

—Nothing, I said. —What do you mean?

—Counselor, we got a telegram from Shreveport. They want to talk to Pig-Boy. About a rape-murder.

—Ah, I said, and felt those faintest stirrings in my chest. Not even a warning, only the dimmest—can I say, sweetest—touch of recollection, of terrible nostalgia, from the distant geographies of Coronary. Like the negative of a photograph of a memory, saying: This twinge, this whisper, is what you felt without noticing before you came that day for the first time upon the passage to Coronary. Be warned and decide. Is it a landscape you wish to visit again? Is it, pulsing once more, a place where gain outmeasured loss? Stroke the contingencies and wonder your way to a decision. You have been once across the bourn from which few travelers return. Do you have it for another trip? And will that trip too be round?

—Ah, I said again to Phipps. —Let me get back to you, all right?

It was all right. Spatially, Rand McNally was fixed. This allowed certain latitude with time. Tomorrow would be just fine. Since the rape-murder, evocation of a nameless victim cooling after life's fitful fever 350 miles away in North Louisiana, was fixed irrevocably in time and there could be, for those to whom its being was announced, no moving from it even as it receded backward and away now, one more permutation in the patterns spoken of in that bower where God and His Son ramble on to no probable conclusion.

Is it strange to say that, after the call from Phipps, I found myself thinking less of the long-haired boy than before? Before, I had been searching for a way to free him from, at most, a three-month term in jail. Now, when he might stand within the shadow of death or a lifetime in prison, he seemed somehow less a point of urgency. Perhaps because I believed not only that he had committed that rape-murder in another place and time, but that he had, in passage from one serial point called Shreveport to another called Vicksburg—both noted as mandatory in a book like his father had been slave to—placed upon that act, called rape-murder by authorities who have the legal right to give comings-together names and sanctions, his own ineradicable mark: a fingerprint, a lost cap, one unforgettable smile caught by a barmaid in a cafe as he passed toward or from the fusion with another—presumably female—in that timetable inherited from his father, and for all either I or he could say, from the very Adam of his blood. However that might be, there was no hurry now. Ninety days in the county jail, so implacable only a little while before, no longer mattered. Which called to my mind, making me laugh inordinately, that on the day of Coronary I had developed a painful hangnail, had given it much thought. Until it vanished in the wilderness of my new world. Had it healed in the hospital? One presumed. I could not recall it after I had stepped out of that world in which one nags for the sake of a hangnail. It is a question of magnitude. When Coronary came, I was transformed into one who, having disliked mosquito bites, now used the Washington

Monument for a toothpick. Mosquitoes, landing, would fall to their deaths in the vastness of a single pore. And later, drinking off my bourbon and water and sugar, I slept without dreams. Or, as I am told, dreaming constantly, but remembering none when it came time to awaken.

—I hear you reached in for a kitty and caught yourself a puma, my telephone was saying.

It was Mr. Grierson calling. He wanted to know if he could be of assistance.

—Seeing you hadn't figured on anything quite like this, he said blandly.

—Yes, I told him. Hell yes. Only small boys and large fools stand alone when they might have allies. Anyhow, I thought, McNally will barely have representation anyhow: a heart patient obsessed with the exotica of his complaint; an old man gone bibliophile from sheer loneliness. We would see.

We did. It was noon when we got in. Rand McNally stared out at the jailer in whose eyes he had obviously gained status. When he opened the cell, he loosened the strap on his ancient pistol. *This here bastard is a killer,* I could almost hear him thinking.

Mr. Grierson hitched up his pants, passed his hand over his thin hair, and sat down on a chair the jailer had provided for him. I made do with the seat of the toilet. Mr. Grierson studied the boy for a moment, then looked at me expectantly, as if protocol required that I begin. I nodded, returning the compliment to my elder. I had divined already how such things would move in Mississippi. Mr. Grierson returned my nod and cleared his throat.

—Well, sir, it appears that clandestine hog-calling is the least of your problems.

Rand McNally stared at him in astonishment. Then he laughed, looked at me, saw me smile despite myself. He went on laughing while Mr. Grierson sat quietly, an expression bemused and pleasant on his face.

—I'm glad you got such a fine spirit, son. You're gonna need it.

Rand McNally took the earplug of his transistor out and hung it through the spring of the empty bunk above his. The Mexican and the farmer were gone now. Perhaps released to the terrors and punishment of sobriety; perhaps simply transferred to other cells in honor of Rand McNally's new status.

—Huh? McNally said to Mr. Grierson.

—If you did to that lady in Shreveport what they say you did, you're gonna have a chance to stand pat whilst they strap you in the electric chair. Shave your head, I believe, before you go.

Rand McNally shuddered. Whether it was the standing pat, the chair, or the head shaving I could not tell.

—Well, Mr. Grierson asked him. —What about it?

Yes. Well, he told us. He was glad it was over; was tired of running. (—Sonofabitch only did what he did three days ago, Mr. Grierson observed later. —What do you reckon? Think he's been reading *Crime and Punishment?*) He had gone to work for an elderly widow in Shreveport, cut the yard for a meal, hung a shelf for a dollar, and come back the next day to whitewash a fence for two dollars. Had whitewashed most of the day with her looking on from her kitchen window past the blooming wisteria and lazy bees. Near sundown, covered with sweat and whitewash, he had gone inside to get a glass of ice water and his two dollars. As he drank, the woman squinted out at the fence, saying, —It'll take another coat. —Huh? Rand McNally said. —Another coat. Then I'll pay you, she said softly, smirking at him, some last wilted, pressed, and dried whisp of her ancient femininity peeking through. At the very worst time.

She said something else that he could not remember and he picked up a knife with which she had been dicing peaches and pushed it into her throat. Then he pushed her over on the kitchen table, pulled off her clothes and down his pants, made with that agonized and astonished crone the beast with two backs, blood, coughing, and great silence between them. In retrospect, he was mildly surprised by it all. It was not, he told us, a planned happening. He was curious that, following the knife, he had discovered himself erect. Why he pressed on with it, distasteful and grotesque as it was, he could not say. But when he was done—he did get done, by the way—he found that she was still very much alive, admonishing him with one long bony liver-spotted finger.

So he got the remainder of the whitewash, dragged it back into the house in a huge wallpaper-paste bucket while he held up his pants with one hand. While she lay there mute, violated, bleeding, he whitewashed the kitchen: the walls, floor, cabinets, stove, icebox, calendar, and four-color lithograph of Jesus suffering the little children. Chairs, hangers, spice rack, coffee, tea, sugar and flour bins, breadbox, and cookie jar. All white. At last he rolled her off onto the floor, whitewashed the table, and put her back in the middle of it. After studying it all for a moment, he decided, and whitewashed her too. Which, so far as he could remember, was all he could remember.

—Ummm, Mr. Grierson said. —So she was alive when you were done with your fooling?

—Alive and kicking, Rand McNally said without smiling. —You see I got to die, don't you?

—Well, Mr. Grierson said, looking at me, —you ain't done much by way of making a case against that. Do you want to die?

—Everybody wants to die, Rand McNally said. He was picking his toes, disengaged now, considering certain vastnesses he had talked himself to the edge of.

—Right. At the proper place and time. How do you like the Chair?

—Ride the lightning? What a gas, Rand McNally almost smiled. —Anybody'd do that to an old lady has got to pay the price. You know that's so. The price is lightning in this state.

—Well, Mr. Grierson said, getting up stiffly. —Let me study on it, son. I'll see you.

As we left, Rand McNally was screwing the transistor's plug into his ear. —Christ, he said, —a sonofabitch would do that has *got* to die.

Outside, we passed Billy Phipps talking to a couple of police we didn't know. Phipps nodded to us. I supposed they were from Shreveport.

—Do you smell Rand McNally . . .

— . . . sneaking up on an insanity plea, Mr. Grierson finished my sentence. —Indeed I do.

—It looks good. From slimy start to filthy finish, doesn't it?

—Ummmm, Mr. Grierson hummed, smiling. —All he's got to do is convince a jury he's Tom Sawyer . . .

— . . . and she was Becky Sharp . . . ?

He looked at me sorrowfully and shook his head as if only a Yankee would have pressed it that awful extra inch. —Thatcher, he said. —But there is a question still . . .

— . . . ?

—If he *is* trying to get himself decked out with an insanity plea, the question is, why *did* he kill the old lady, and then do that to her? If he hadn't, he wouldn't need any kind of plea at all, would he?

That afternoon under the scuppernongs I felt as if I were waiting for some final word, some conclusive disposition of my own case. There was a dread in me, an anxiety without an object. I thought ceaselessly of Rand McNally and his insane erection in the midst of an act of violence. I thought of his surprise at it. I thought of my own prophecy over the phone to Phipps. What had brought him to this place, this conclusion? He had stepped from life into process: extradition, arraignment, indictment, trial, sentencing. I came to feel that he had ceased to exist, to be a human being owed and owing. He was no longer a proper object of feeling. Now one only *thought* about him. One took him into account along with Dr. Crippen, Charles Starkweather, Bruno Hauptmann, Richard Speck, and the others of that terrible brotherhood whose reality is at once absolute and yet moldering day by month by year in antique police archives or grinning dustily in the tensionless shadows of wax museums.

It was just after supper when Mr. Grierson appeared. He pulled into the drive in a 1941 Ford Super DeLuxe coupe. It was jet black and looked as if it had been minted—not built, minted—an hour or so before. He wore a white linen suit and a peculiar tie: simply two struts of black mohair which lay beneath and outlined the white points of his narrow shirt collar. It was not that his car and clothes were old-fashioned; it was that while they were dated, they were not quaint or superannuated or amusing. As if by some shift Mr. Grierson had managed the trick of avoiding the lapse of time, of nullifying it so that what had been remained, continued unchanged. Could one pile up the past densely enough around himself so as to forbid its dwindling? And what would happen if the rest of us shared that fierce subterranean determination to drag down the velocity at which today became yesterday? It would fail, of course. You cannot disintegrate the fabric of physics. But what would happen?

We spoke of the weather, hot and dry, the bane of planters hereabouts. No sweet June rain. Only scorching sun, the river lying like a brown serpent between us and those like us in Louisiana. It was the mention of Louisiana that Mr. Grierson chose as his pathway past the amenities.

—He's crossing the big river tomorrow. Waived extradition.

—Oh? Did you . . . ?

—Talk to him again? Oh yes. Surely.

He smiled at me, knowing what thoughts had crossed my mind and instantly been dropped as I asked my question.

—He was forcefully apprised of his rights. Not once, but several times. And he repudiated every one of them in obscene terms.

—What? I don't . . .

—He said it was a goddamned piss-poor legal system that gave all these rights to a . . . fucking pervert.

Mr. Grierson looked embarrassed for the sake of the quotation.

—Jesus, I said, almost dropping the bottle of sour mash from which I was pouring our drinks. —Christ, he *is* crazy. He *must* have been reading Dostoevski.

—I don't know, Mr. Grierson said. —He gave me this. Said it was your fee.

He handed me a greasy fragment of oiled paper—the kind they wrap hamburgers in. There was what looked like a quatrain scrawled on it in No. 1 pencil:

> *It's bitter knowledge one learns from travel,*
> *The world so small from day to day,*
> *The horror of our image will unravel,*
> *A pool of dread in deserts of dismay.*

—What's that? I asked Mr. Grierson. He smiled and sipped his whiskey.

—You can come over to my place and look it up, he said. —The idea is interesting. Wine don't travel well.

— . . . the horror of our image . . .

—Seems what broke him up was that business after he stabbed the old lady. He didn't seem much concerned about the stabbing, you know. It was . . . the other.

—And the finale . . . ?

—The whitewashing? Oh no, he liked that fine. You can't make up for it, he told me. But you do the best you can. That boy is a caution . . .

We sat drinking for a while. I shook my head and said, not so much to Mr. Grierson as to myself, —It's . . . as if Rand McNally were a . . . historical figure.

—Well, yes. That's so. But then, we all are.

—Yes . . .

—But history ain't like grace, is it? It has different rules. Which is to say, no rules at all.

I stared at him. Grace? What might that be? Luck? Fortune? I had heard the word. I simply attached no meaning to it. Now this old man set it before me as an alternative to history. I felt that dread again, some low order of clairvoyance wherein I imagined that Coronary might open once more: at first like the tiny entrance to Alice's garden—then like the colossal gates of ancient Babylon. It struck me at that instant with ghastly irrationality that grace was the emanation of vaginal purpose and womb's rest. Is grace death?

—Is grace death? I heard myself asking aloud.

—It could be, Mr. Grierson answered. —I can imagine in a few years I might ask for that grace. But not altogether. History is the law. Grace is the prophets. History comes upon us. I reckon we have to find grace for ourselves. The law works wrath rather than grace, Luther said.

—That line . . . the horror of our image . . .

—Yes. Well, that's what brought grace to my mind. I think that boy has just broke into and out of history.

— . . . ?

—Something else I remember from Luther: certain it is that man must completely despair of himself in order to become fit to receive the grace of Christ. . . .

—I didn't know you were a Lutheran.

—Hell, I'm not. Never could be. Most often, I quote Calvin. But you always go for water out of the sweetest well, don't you?

—You mean Rand McNally doesn't care anymore? He's done with the motels, the garages?

—No and yes. He cares all right. He wants to get on with it, don't you see? He's sick of problems. But no, there won't be any more motor courts and repair shops for old Rand McNally.

—Problems . . .

—What happened to him that evening in that old woman's kitchen? Do you know? How is it that killing moved to something like what they call an act of love? Neither fit the hour's need. What happened? That's the problem.

I felt very warm, my face flushed, my hands wet as if I had just climbed out of the river. Believe me, I was afraid. I thought it was another attack. They call the coming of Coronary an attack. Tryst might be better. Liaison, assignation.

—You feeling bad? Mr. Grierson asked, pouring us both a little more whiskey.

—No, I lied. —I'm fine. Just thinking. Was it grace that came on Rand McNally? Is that what you want to say?

—Lord no, Mr. Grierson smiled deprecatingly. —That'd be crazy. Grace to kill and rape an old woman? Naw, I never said that. I wasn't speaking *for* grace, you know.

—He's insane. They'll find him insane.

—Sure. So was Joan of Arc. So was Raymond of Toulouse . . .

—Raymond . . . ?

—A hobby of mine, he spread his hands. —I take on old cases sometimes. Not Joan. She's all right, taken care of. But Raymond . . .

Who was an Albigensian—or at least no less than their defender in his province. Tormented by orthodox authorities most of his life, he died outside that grace which Rome claimed to purvey exclusively, and lay unburied in the charterhouse of the Hospitalers for 400 years. Mr. Grierson told me much more—told me that he had written a 300-page brief in Latin defending the acts and character of Raymond of Toulouse as those of a most Christian prince. But that was, he said, with a perfectly straight face, ancient history. He was working now on the defense of Anne Albright, a young girl burned during the Marian persecutions at Smithfield in 1556. It was to be a class action, aimed at overturning the convictions of all those Protestants burned under Mary Tudor.

—What about the Catholics? I asked sardonically, draining my whiskey.

—Fisher, Southwell, Campion? No need. The world's good opinion justifies them. As well waste time on More or Beckett. No, I go for those lost to history, done to death with no posthumous justification.

—That's a mad hobby, I told him. Somehow his pastime made me angry. At first I supposed my anger came from the waste of legal talent that so many people needed—like Rand McNally. But no, it was deeper than that. Could it be that I, a child of history, descendant of those whom history had dragged to America, resented Grierson's tampering with the past? How many of yesterday's innocents, perjured to their graves, can we bear to have thrust before us? Isn't the evil in our midst sufficient unto the day?

—The past is past, I said almost shortly.

Mr. Grierson looked disgusted. —My Christ, he said. I had never heard him speak profanely before. —You sit under an arbor in Vicksburg, Mississippi, and say that? You better get hold of history before you go to probing grace.

We were quiet for a long while then, Grierson's breach of manners resting on us both. At last he left, walking slowly, stiffly out to that bright ancient automobile that came alive with the first press of the starter. I stood in the yard and watched him go, and found when I went into the house again that it was much later than I had thought.

I found myself gripped by a strange malaise the next day, and for weeks following I did no work. I walked amid the grassy parkland of the old battlefields. I touched stone markers and tried to reach through the granite and marble to touch the flesh of that pain, to find what those thousands of deaths had said and meant. It was not the Northern soldiers I sought: history had trapped them in their statement. It had to do with the Union, one and indivisible, with equality and an end to chattel slavery. That was what they had said, whether they said it or not. But the Southerners, those aliens, outsiders, dying for slavery, owning no slaves; dying for the rights of states that had no great care for their rights. In the name of Death, which had engulfed them all, why?

But I could find nothing there. It was history, certainly: the moments, acts frozen in monuments, but it told me nothing. I could find nothing in it at all. One evening as the last light faded, I sat on a slope near the Temple of Illinois and wept. What did I lack? What sacred capacity for imagining had been denied me? Could I ever come to understand the meaning of law, of life itself, if all history were closed to me?

Or was it not a lack but a possession which kept me from grasping the past as it presented itself, history as it laid down skein after skein of consuming time about us all? I imagined then that it was Coronary. That I had been drawn out of history, out of an intimacy with it by that assault. What was time or space to an anchorite who stared forever into forever? How could sequence matter to one who had touched All at Once? When I tried to concern myself with practical matters, I would remember Coronary and smile and withdraw into myself, forget to pay the net electric bill on time, suffering afterward the gross. Surely, I thought, I cannot care or be known within history because I am beyond it, a vestal of Coronary, graced with a large probable knowledge of how I will die. Knowing, too, that superflux of certain action can even hasten the day of that dying. I know too much, have been too deeply touched to succumb to history. I have no past, no particulars, no accidents. I am substance of flesh tenderly holding for an instant essence of spirit. I am escaping even as I think of it. Surely, I thought, a vision of one's dying must be grace. Yes, I am in grace, whatever that means.

Toward the end of some months of such odd consideration, I saw a small notice in a New Orleans paper that announced, purported to announce, the judgment of Louisiana on Rand McNally. He had been found incompetent to stand trial. Yes. The People had adjudged him insane. Not culpable. Simply a biological misstep within history. To be confined until the end of biology corrected the error of its beginning.

I found that I was sweating. As if in the presence of something immutable, and preternaturally awful. It had no name, and I could give it no shape. I began to reduce the feeling to an idea. Was I sorry? How is that possible? Capital punishment is a ghastly relic from past barbarism. To place a man in such a state that he knows almost to the moment the time of his death is . . .

Is what? The blessing of Coronary? My God, is it punishment or grace? I sat with my face in my hands, feeling my own doomed flesh between my fingers, trying to plumb this thing and yet trying not to let the juices of my body rise stormlike within, carrying me toward that dark port once more.

One evening a few weeks later, I drove downtown and bought two dozen tamales from a cart on a street corner. It was an indulgence, the smallest of sneers behind the back of Coronary. It was possible to go on with bland food and a rare glass of wine so long as the notion dangled there ahead that one day I would buy tamales and beer and risk all for a mouthful of pretended health.

I carried home my tamales, opened a beer, and began to eat with my fingers. The grease, the spices, the rough cornmeal, the harsh surface of the cheap beer. Before the attack, in New York, I would never have dreamed of eating such stuff, but to live in grace is to dare all things. Then I looked down at the faded stained palimpsest of the old newspaper. Above Captain Easy, next to the crossword puzzle, was a short article. It told of a suicide, that of a mad rapist-killer about to be sent to the State Hospital, how he had managed to fashion a noose of guitar strings and elevate himself by a steel support in the skylight.

It was Rand McNally, of course. No doubt enraged by a system so blind and feckless as to suffer his kind to live, a self-created lynch mob determined to do justice to himself. My hand trembled, spilling beer. A rapist-murderer will lead them, I think I thought. A little later that evening, my second cardiac arrest took place.

Dr. Freud, with the most fulsome humility, I say you should have been in there. You would have forgotten physiology: it was not the smooth agonized tissue of my heart which sent tearful chemicals upward to trek the barren steppes of my brain. No, in there, within the futureless glow of Coronary, I was constructing my soul. What, precisely, transpired there? Why should I not smile like Lazarus and suggest that the price of such knowledge is the sedulous management and encouragement of your own coronary involvement? Because I need to tell it. That is why we do things always, isn't it? Because we must. Not because we should. Which is what Rand McNally came to know, isn't it? And why he came to want death, demand punishment for himself, because he was no longer able to count on himself: what he did was outside any notion of *should*, was wholly given to *must*. Isn't that the way it is with animals?

But never mind. I am not guessing. That is part of what I have to tell you. I saw Rand McNally in there, and Joan of Lorraine, Raymond of Toulouse, and Anne Albright. All in Coronary, yes, Dr. Freud. Being a man dead, there is no reason one must honor time or space, chronology or sequence, in his hallucinations.

It was the Happy Isles, where I was, looking much like the country around Sausalito. There was worship and diversion, of course, and the smoky odor of terror. Two Mississippi deputies dragged Raymond before the Inquisition. Anne Albright was condemned once more for having denied the doctrine of Transubsegregation. They claimed that Joan had stolen something: Cauchon, pig? A Smithfield ham? Mary Tudor curtsied to Lester Maddox as they sat in high mahogany bleachers in Rouen's town square. Agnew preached against the foul heresies of all spiritual mediums while shrouded Klansmen tied Rand McNally to a stake, doused him with whitewash, and set him afire.

I think I saw Jesus, now only an elderly Jew, in a side street weeping, blowing his nose, shaking his head as the Grand Inquisitor passed in triumphant procession, giving us both a piercing stare, blowing us kisses. Behind him in chains marched Giordano Bruno and John Huss, Mac Parker and Emmett Till. Savonarola was handcuffed to Malcolm X and Michael Servetus walked painfully, side by side with Bobby Hutton. The line went on forever, I thought, filled with faces I did not know: those who had blessed us with their pain, those suffering now, those yet to come. I wondered why I was not among them, but old Jesus, who was kind, and whom they ignored, said that there were those who must act and those who must see. It was given, God help me, that I should see.

There were other visions which I have forgotten or which I must not reveal. I saw, in the ecstasy of Coronary, the end of all things and was satisfied. It was only important that nothing be lost on my account. What does that mean?

—What does that mean? I asked Mr. Grierson when he came to the hospital to visit me, as soon as they allowed anyone to come at all.

—Ah, he said, his pink scalp glistening in the weak light above my bed. —Economy. You got to note all transmutations. Correct all falsehoods. Don't you see that? Lies, falsehoods, perversions of reality—those are man's sovereign capabilities. Only man can rend the fabric of things as they are. Nothing else in the universe is confused, uncertain, able to lie, except man. And through those lies, those rifts in reality, is where all things are wasted. But . . .

—But what . . . ?

—Well, Mr. Grierson smiled. —That's what my hobby is about.

—Your . . . cases . . . Anne Albright . . . ?

—Sure. No lie survives so long as the truth is stated. Those are the terms of the game.

—I don't see . . . what if people *believe* the lie . . . ?

—It doesn't matter. Tell the truth. Sooner or later that mere un-provable undefended assertion of the truth will prevail.

—How can you believe . . . ?

Mr. Grierson shrugged. —How not? We got all the time in the world. When the profit goes out of a lie, nobody wants to bother defending it any longer. That's where grace joins history, you see?

I did. I *did* see. He was right. A lie *couldn't* stand forever. Because there is no history so old, so impervious to revision that the simple truth doesn't establish itself sooner or later. Like gravity, the conse-quences of truth can be avoided for a while. Sometimes a little while; sometimes a great while. But in the end, that which is false crumbles, falls away, and only the truth is left. So long as that truth has been once stated, no matter how feebly, under whatever pain.

—Yes, Mr. Grierson said quietly, taking a sheaf of yellowed pa-pers out of his briefcase. —What with all the time you've got on your hands just now, I reckoned you just as well get started.

—Started . . . ?

He handed me the file. —In southern Texas, summer of 1892, there was this Mexican woman . . . they gave her something like a trial, then they went ahead and lynched her, which was what they had in mind all along. It was the late summer of 1892. There was a panic that year, a depression, some trouble in Pullman Town . . .

I lay back, eyes closed, veteran of trances. Why not tell you of one part of my final vision? Why not? Yes, I saw, larger than the sky, what they call the Sacred Heart, burning with love for all the uni-verse. I saw its veins and arteries, how we every one moved through it and away again, the sludge of lies and torture and deceit choking its flow like cholesterol. I saw that heart shudder, pulse erratically. I saw the fibrillation of God's own motive center, and I cried out that I should share his pain, and rise to the dignity of sacrifice.

Yes, I came then to realize why Rand McNally had gone out of himself. In order to find himself. To tell the truth. Time matters only to liars, and they are, at last, worse than murderers, even rapists of old ladies. Because, caught in the grid of His truth, they yet try to evade, even as they see time vanishing before them. Grace is his-tory transcendent, made true at last. And faith is the act of embracing all time, assured of renewing it, making the heart whole once more.

—It's an easy one, Mr. Grierson told me. —They did Rosa Gonzales wrong. You won't have any trouble . . .

I smiled and reached for the file.

—I don't think I'll ever have any real trouble again, I told him.

Old Men Dream Dreams,
Young Men See Visions

I tried to remember if I had ever felt better. No, I had not ever felt better. And I could remember. I was only fifteen. And I was driving alone in my father's 1941 Ford to pick up Helena.

It was the first time I had ever had the car alone. That was a victory. My mother had fenced, thrust, and parried with my father, who said I was too young, too wild, too inexperienced to take a girl out in the car. —Later, he said. —How much later? my mother asked. —Be reasonable, my father said. —That's right, my mother answered. —Be reasonable. The girl expects him. In the car. Do you want to shame him? —He can be degraded, humiliated, and dishonored as far as I'm concerned, my father told her. My mother gave him a distant wintry smile, one of her specialties. Like an advocate cross-examining an unacknowledged embezzler or black marketeer. —Be reasonable, she said with smooth earth-scouring irony.

—All right, my father shouted, turning to me at last, admitting that I was party to the contest—indeed, the plaintiff vindicated. —Take it. Take the goddamned thing. Go out. Wreck it. Cost me my job. Kill yourself.

And then he tossed me the keys.

I parked in front of Helena's. She lived off Creswell Avenue in a nice part of town with solid houses and large pleasant lawns. We had met at one of those teenage dances sponsored by parents who took great stock in supervised activities. They were awful, except that you could meet girls. The day after, I had walked from Jesuit High over to the girls' school to catch her as classes finished in the afternoon. It was a long walk—no, it was a run, because she got out at the same time I did and they would expect her home within an hour. Her parents were very strict, she had told me at the dance.

So when she came upon me as she walked up Kings Highway, she smiled with delight, and wordlessly we walked past Fairfield, past Line Avenue and down the shallow hill that ran alongside Byrd High School where the Protestants went, where eventually I would go when the Jesuits determined that I was bound to end badly, indeed, already bore a bad name. We reached Creswell and slowed down. I took her hand. We stopped at the little bayou where the street dipped, where water stood several feet deep in the road after a heavy rain. We looked down at the brown water and she asked me what kind of fish might live in there. Before I could answer, she realized that we had walked a block past her house. She grinned and lowered her eyes as if admitting to an indiscretion. I shrugged and did not admit knowing all the time that we had passed that fatal street, ransoming ten precious minutes more by my pretense.

We met and walked so almost every day unless the weather was very bad and her mother drove to the school to pick her up. At last, one day Helena asked me to come home with her to meet her mother. It was a beautifully furnished house, done in what I know now to have been good unobtrusive taste, though strongly feminine. Today I would put such a furnished house down as the work of a moderately talented interior decorator. But in 1949, I doubt that it was. People in Shreveport then had more substantial vices. They had not yet come to the contrafaction of sophistication.

As I waited for Helena to find her mother back in the unknown regions of the house, I stood caught up in a net of feelings that I had never experienced before. I saw Helena's round bright unremarkable face, her quick excited smile. I conjured her body, her slender legs and ankles. Sexuality was the least of it. That part was good and without complications because it was no more than an imagining, a vague aura that played around the person of every girl I met without settling into a realizable conception. Because then it seemed that an actual expression of unconcealed desire would surely smash itself and me against an invisible but real obstacle as unsettling as the sound barrier. No, it was something else that made me raise my arms and spread them as I smiled into a gold-framed mirror there in the foyer. I loved someone. It was a feeling composed and balanced between heights and depths that flared through me, leaving me exultant and ready for new things in the midst of a profound and indeterminate sadness. I looked at myself quizzically, arms akimbo, hair badly finger-combed. Was it the one or the other? Neither my own emotional history nor the mind Jesuits had already forged in me had warned of ambivalence. It was disquieting and thrilling, somehow better than certainty. It was a victory taken from the flood of moments I lived but could not order. But even as I studied the physical shape of love in my face, I saw in the mirror, watching me from the parlor, a small face, serious, almost suffering, the face of a tiny Cassandra, mute and miserable. For just an instant I thought insanely that it was Helena creeping up behind me on her knees. I was hot with embarrassment, chilled by something less personal, more sinister, as if a shard of some tomorrow had fallen inexplicably into the present. But the tiny disturbed copy of Helena's face vanished and I stood alone again, fumbling with a dog-eared Latin reader filled with the doings of Caesar.

Helena's mother was neat, attractive, the very picture of an efficient mother and housewife. Her eyes were dark, her face unlined in that metastatic poise of a woman who has passed forty by chronology but remains for a month or a year as she must have been at thirty. She met me graciously, prepared Cokes for the three of us and introduced me to Helena's small sister. I recognized the wraith in the foyer mirror. She did indeed look like Helena. Only without the smile, without the capacity to be excited and filled by a moment. I tousled her hair patronizingly, seeing in her eyes even as I did so a look that might have meant either *I know what you're really like.* Or *Help.*

It was a few days later that I asked Helena for a date. I had had a few dates before: humiliating affairs where my father drove me to the girl's house, took us to a movie, then came back and took us home afterward. But this would be different. This would be my first real date. And with someone I loved.

When I reached her house it was already dark. The air was chill. It was November, and the wind swept across my face as I opened the old car's door. Her porch light burned beyond the trees like an altar candle and I moved from the car toward it, key in my hand like power, into the circle of weak light close to Helena. When I rang, it was her mother who opened the door. Even tranced by the current of my triumphs and the size of coming pleasure, I noticed that her smile was forced. Had she had a tiring day? Or had she heard ill of me somewhere? That was possible. I had already the first stirrings of a bad name in certain Shreveport circles. But I forgot her expression as she introduced me to her husband, Helena's father.

He stood up heavily, a short red-faced man without charm or presence. He had reddish hair and that odd parti-colored complexion of certain redheaded farmers I knew who were most sensitive to the sun and yet obliged by their calling to work under it always. He looked at me as if I had come to clean the drains and was for some reason he could not fathom intruding into his parlor.

He shook hands with me perfunctorily and began at once to give me instructions as to where Helena and I might go, where we couldn't go. He brushed aside an attempt by his wife to make conversation and continued, making certain that I knew the time

Helena was to be home. Eleven o'clock. He asked me to repeat the time back to him. I did so automatically, paying little attention because as he spoke I could make out the rank smell of whiskey on his breath. Every word he uttered seemed propelled up from his spreading shirt front by the borrowed force of alcohol. As he went on talking, he looked not at me but past me toward the door as if the effort of actually seeing me was more than he could bear. I stood silent, glancing at his wife. She was gnawing at the corner of her lip and looking down the hall toward the back of the house. At the edge of the dark hall I thought I could see, dim and distant, the face of Helena's little sister.

Then Helena came. She was dressed in a pale red woolen suit, high heels, a piece of gold jewelry like a bird of paradise on her shoulder. Her father turned from me, studied her, and said nothing. There was a flurry of last words and we were outside walking toward the car. As soon as the door closed, our hands met and clasped. We said nothing because both of us were back in the foyer of her house, the tension, her father, and mother vanished, annulled, decomposed by the look that had passed between us as we saw one another. We had sensed the whole garden of possibilities into which we were about to step. She came from her room assuming a schoolboy awaited her, only to find a slightly nervous young man in a sports jacket standing before her father armed with the key to an ancient car. I had been waiting for a girl, but a young woman came to meet me. What joined us then, a current of our spirits, was all the stronger because neither of us had ever felt it flow forth to meet its counterpart before.

We reached the car. As I slid under the wheel, I turned to Helena. She was looking at me and her hand moved to meet mine again. We sat for a long moment until, embarrassed by the weight of our feeling, we drew apart and I started the car. Helena noticed that the inner doorhandle on her side was missing.

—That's to keep you in, I tried to joke, suddenly ashamed of my father's old car, seeing for the first time its shabbiness, the dusty dashboard, the stained headlining.

—I don't want to get out. Except with you, Helena said, her eyes large, the beginning of a smile on her lips.

For a while we drove. I headed in toward the city driving up Highland Avenue past Causey's Music Shop where I had learned the wherewithal of my bad name. I played trumpet every so often in a roadhouse across the Red River in Bossier Parish. It was called the Skyway Club and had bad name enough to splotch any number of fifteen-year-olds who could talk Earl Blessey, the band leader, into letting them limp through a chorus of "Blue Prelude" or "Georgia on My Mind." Before the Skyway Club and I were done with one another, I would have lost and gained enough things there to be worth any number of bad names.

We drove into downtown and looked at the marquees of the Don and Strand theaters.

—What would you like to see? I asked Helena.

—I don't think I want to go to the movies, she said.

—What would you like to do?

—Could we . . . just go somewhere. And talk?

—Sure, I said. —We could go to the Ming Tree over in Bossier . . . No, your father . . .

—Why don't we just go out to the lake?

As I turned the car, I reached for her shoulder and drew her close to me. The lake was where people went when they had no reason to waste time with football games or movies. They went there to be alone, to construct within their cars apartments, palaces, to be solitary and share one another for a few hours.

Cross Lake was cold and motionless, a bright sheet under the autumn stars. Around us, trees rustled in the light breeze. But we were warm and I lit a cigarette and listened to Helena talk. She told me that she was sorry about her father. I said it was nothing. He was only thinking of her. He didn't know me. No, she said, he was thinking of himself. He drank at night. He sat drinking in the parlor talking to himself, cursing his wife and the children sometimes. Sometimes it was worse than that. She said she wanted me to know. Because if I were to think less of her . . .

—That's crazy, I said, turning her to face me. And we kissed.

It would not surprise me to find that moment, that kiss, the final indelible sensation last to fade from my mind as I lay dying. Not because I am sentimental. I have used and misused kisses and promises, truths and lies, honor and fraud and violence as the years moved on. That world where I knew Helena recedes from me more rapidly each day, each year, shifting red with the sting of its velocity, but never vanishing, its mass increasing in my soul toward infinity as, one who has managed the world as it is better than well, I am subtle enough to recover those fragments from the past which at the moment of their transaction were free from plan or prophecy or the well-deep cynicism of one who recognizes the piquancy of an apparently innocent moment precisely because he knows not only that it will not, cannot last, but because he has long before taken that fragility, that ephemeral certainty into account in order to enjoy his instant all the more.

And so I remember that kiss. It was well done. Our lips fused, moving together as if contained in them was the sum of our bodies. Without the conscious thought of sex we achieved a degree of sensuality unmatched in all the embraces I had still to seek or to endure.

—I love you, I told her.

—You can't mean it, she said.

We kissed again and then sat looking at the water, each of us touched beyond speech. We held ourselves close and sent our happiness, our exultation out to move among the pines, over the water, toward the cold observant stars keeping a time of their own. We sat that way for a long while.

In retrospect the appearances of banality are simple to determine. But the fact of it was not present between us that night. Banality presumes a certain self-consciousness, a kind of *déjà vu*, a realization explicit or implied that what one is doing has values other than those which seem. Or that certain values are missing. There must be a sly knowledge that the game in hand is not only not worth the candle, but hardly worth striking the match.

But Helena and I knew nothing then but one another and the shape of our victory. We were not repeating for the tenth or even the second time a ritual tarnished in its parts and lethally sure in its conclusion. We had for this moment conquered chance and youth, our fathers, the traps and distances laid for us. We were alone beside Cross Lake and no one on earth knew where we were. We belonged to ourselves, to one another. We did not know that neither of us, together or apart, would ever find this time and place, find each other like this again. It will always be exactly like this, we would have thought. Had we thought. It was not banal. The rest of our lives might be so, but not tonight.

Tonight we told one another of our troubles and our hopes. We said, each in a different way, that our fathers made us unhappy. That one day we would leave Shreveport, journey to London and Paris, to the farthest places we could imagine. Only now, after tonight, we would go together. We talked about much more, words cascading over each other as we exchanged all that we had been and done apart, all we planned and wished for together. Until, amid a moment of silence, a pause for breath, Helena looked at her watch.

—Oh God, she gasped, her face stricken.

—What?

—It's . . .

—We're going to be late . . . ?

—It's . . . almost four o'clock. In the morning.

We stared at one another. I lit a match and looked at her watch. It was eight minutes to four. I closed my eyes. We were supposed to be home by eleven. Even my father would be aroused, knowing that I wasn't at the Skyway Club with Earl. I tried not to think about Helena's father, but his squat body, his nearly angry face, rose in my mind again and again like a looped strip of film.

—Oh God, I do love you, Helena said.

We kissed again, touched, embraced. Her nylon-covered legs rose and touched my body. My hand found her breasts. None of which we had intended. The fruit of the tree in that garden we entered was the knowledge of time, of duration: time past, time lost. Even then, in those hysterical seconds, we were trying not so much to hasten passage from recognition to fulfillment as to claim what we might before it was too late, before we were separated and everything died.

But we stopped. We were not brave enough. We were too wise. We could not bring ourselves to wager what we had found against the sullen covenant of all our fathers. We kissed one last time hastily and I started the car, the beginning of an anguish inside me even as my heart beat insanely from her touch.

I cut the engine and coasted up in front of Helena's house. It seemed as if I had not seen it in centuries. Inside, many lights were on and I could see that the front door was a little ajar. Helena turned to me and touched my arm. I could see that there were tears on her cheeks, and the anguish grew.

—Go on, she said. —Don't come up to the house with me. He'll be awful, really . . .

—No, I said without thought. —I'm going to take you to the door.

I was not frightened, only apprehensive. I had been in too many hassles to spook before the event. There was always time to flush, sometimes only a second or two but always time. Anyhow, I had that fifty-foot walk to make, I knew. My bad name did not include cowardice, at least not of the overt and measurable kind. More important, there would be nothing left if I drove away, left the field and Helena upon it to her father. Our triumph would dwindle to an absurdity. I was not yet old enough to weigh those things against reality. What we had found in one another was real, I thought. And I was not a boy any longer. What you do not defend, you cannot keep: the oldest of all rules.

We walked toward the lights. Out of our world back into theirs. We did not walk hand in hand and later I would wonder how much of the future had been bent around that smallest of omissions. As we reached the door we could hear Helena's father. He was now very drunk and he was cursing and bullying her mother.

— . . . nice. Oh yes, Jesus son of God what do you reckon he's done . . . my baby. That little bastard. Telling her it's all right, taking off her . . . clothes . . .

I closed my eyes and blushed as if I were guilty of it all and more. Helena looked down at the concrete steps. Then she pushed open the door and stepped into the foyer to forestall any more of his raving.

—Hello, everybody, she said loudly, almost brightly, in that tone she used to greet me when we met after school each day.

Her father whirled about, his face red, thick, inarticulate with anger. Standing just behind Helena, I could not quite see the look that passed between them but it seemed to me that she nearly smiled, pale and upset as she was.

—Get to your room, her father spat out, swaying from side to side as he moved toward us. Toward me. —No, don't say anything. I'll see to you later.

Helena's mother shook her head and signaled Helena to go, to leave it alone. But Helena wasn't ready.

—No, I want to say . . .

But her father pushed her out of the way roughly in order to face me. Her mother stepped forward behind him and took her from the foyer. She was beginning to cry.

—What did you do? he rasped. —Where did you take her? What kind of dirt . . .

He clenched his fists in front of my face. I thought coldly that he could smash me to pieces easily. But for some reason the realization meant nothing.

—We talked, I said. —I'm sorry we . . .

—Talked? You liar . . . you . . .

Helena's mother, her face anxious, truly frightened, came back into the foyer. She touched her husband's arm. He shook her off. Now he was swaying, blinking.

—Nothing happened, I said, considering the immensity of that lie.

—I think you'd better go now, Bill, Helena's mother said, motioning me toward the door with her anxious eyes.

I started to say something more, but I could think of nothing more to say. Then I backed toward the door, too old by far in the ways of Caddo and Bossier parishes to show my back to a drunk who held a score against me, a blood score. The occasions of my bad name had made me cautious. Before I reached the door, there in the gloom of the dark hallway I saw, dressed in a long nightgown, the figure of Helena's little sister. Her face was pinched and no larger than an orange it seemed. Her eyes were wide with excitement and certainty.

As I stepped outside, Helena's father, who had followed me with his inflamed eyes, began to weep. He twisted his fists into his eyes, his shoulders quaking. He turned to his wife, who looked after me one last time and then gave her attention to her husband. He leaned against her like a child swallowed in the skirts of his mother. Behind, the little girl stood alone, one hand pressed against that duplicate of Helena's face.

—My little girl, her father sobbed as if he knew Helena to be dead. —My baby . . .

I turned then and breathed deeply, walking slowly toward the black mass of my father's sequestered Ford. I stopped at the car door and looked back at Helena's house under two cedar trees, dwarfed by a sweep of sky pricked with distant stars. I breathed again, taking in the chill early morning air like one who stares down from some great height at the place where his lover sleeps or the field where his enemy lies broken. Then, full of some large uncertain joy, I sat down in the old car and jammed the ignition key home.

Pleadings

I

Dinner was on the table when the phone rang, and Joan just stared at me.

—Go ahead, answer it. Maybe they need you in Washington.

—I don't want to get disbarred, I said. —More likely they need me at the parish prison.

I was closer than she was. It was Bertram Bijou, a deputy out in Jefferson Parish. He had a friend. With troubles. Being a lawyer, you find out that nobody has trouble, really. It's always a friend.

—Naw, on the level, Bert said. —You know Howard Bedlow?

No, I didn't know Howard Bedlow, but I would pretty soon.

They came to the house after supper. As a rule, I put people off when they want to come to the house. They've got eight hours a day to find out how to incorporate, write a will, pull their taxes down or whatever. In the evening I like to sit quietly with Joan. We read and listen to Haydn or Boccherini and watch the light fade over uptown New Orleans. Sometimes, though I do not tell her, I like to imagine we are a late Roman couple sitting in our atrium in the countryside of England, not far from Londinium. It is always summer, and Septimius Severus has not yet begun to tax Britain out of existence. Still, it is twilight now, and there is nothing before us. We are young, but the world is old, and that is all right because the drive and the hysteria of destiny is past now, and we can sit and enjoy our garden, the twisted ivy, the huge calladiums, and, if it is April, the daffodils that plunder our weak sun and sparkle across the land. It is always cool in my fantasy, and Joan crochets something for the center of our table, and I refuse to think of the burdens of administration that I will have to lift again tomorrow. They will wait, and Rome will never even know. It is always a hushed single moment, ageless and serene, and I am with her, and only the hopeless are still ambitious. Everything we will do has been done, and for the moment there is peace.

It is a silly fantasy, dreamed here in the heart of booming America, but it makes me happy, and so I was likely showing my mild irritation when Bert and his friend Howard Bedlow turned up. I tried to be kind. For several reasons. Bert is a nice man. An honest deputy, a politician in a small way, and perhaps what the Civil Law likes to call "un bon pere du famille"—though I think at Common Law Bert would be "an officious intermeddler." He seems prone to get involved with people. Partly because he would like very much to be on the Kenner city council one day, but, I like to imagine, as much because there lingers in the Bijou blood some tincture of piety brought here and nurtured by his French sires and his Sicilian and Spanish maternal ascendants. New Orleans has people like that. A certain kindness, a certain sympathy left over from the days when one person's anguish or that of a family was the business of all their neighbors. Perhaps that fine and profound Catholic certainty of death and judgment which makes us all one.

And beyond approving Bert as a type, I have found that most people who come for law are in one way or another distressed: the distress of loss or fear, of humiliation or sudden realization. Or the more terrible distress of greed, appetite gone wild, the very biggest of deals in the offing, and Oh my God, don't let me muff it.

Howard Bedlow was in his late forties. He might have been the Celtic gardener in my imaginary Roman garden. Taller than average, hair a peculiar reddish gold more suited to a surfing king than to an unsuccessful car salesman, he had that appearance of a man scarce half made up that I had always associated with European workmen and small tradesmen. His cuffs were frayed and too short. His collar seemed wrong; it fit neither his neck nor the thin stringy tie he wore knotted more or less under it. Once, some years ago, I found, he had tried to make a go of his own Rambler franchise, only to see it go down like a gutshot animal, month by month, week by week, until at last no one, not even the manager of the taco place next door, would cash his checks or give him a nickel for a local phone call.

Now he worked, mostly on commission, for one used car lot or another, as Bert told it. He had not gone bankrupt in the collapse of the Rambler business, but had sold his small house on the west bank and had paid off his debts, almost all of them dollar for dollar, fifty here, ten there. When I heard that, I decided against offering them coffee. I got out whiskey. You serve a man what he's worth, even if he invades your fantasies.

As Bert talked on, only pausing to sip his bourbon, Bedlow sat staring into his glass, his large hands cupping it, his fingers moving restlessly around its rim, listening to Bert as if he himself had no stake in all that was passing. I had once known a musician who had sat that way when people caught him in a situation where talk was inevitable. Like Bedlow, he was not resentful, only elsewhere, and his hands, trained to a mystical perfection, worked over and over certain passages in some silent score.

Bedlow looked up as Bert told about the house trailer he, Bedlow, lived in now—or had lived in until a week or so before. Bedlow frowned almost sympathetically, as if he could find some measure of compassion for a poor man who had come down so far.

—Now I got to be honest, Bert said at last, drawing a deep breath. —Howard, he didn't want to come. Bad times with lawyers.

—I can see that, I said.

—He can't put all that car franchise mess out of mind. Bitter, you know. Gone down hard. Lawyers like vultures, all over the place.

Bedlow nodded, frowning. Not in agreement with Bert on his own behalf, but as if he, indifferent to all this, could appreciate a man being bitter, untrusting after so much. I almost wondered if the trouble wasn't Bert's, so distant from it Bedlow seemed.

—I got to be honest, Bert said again. Then he paused, looking down at his whiskey. Howard studied his drink, too.

—I told Howard he could come along with me to see you, or I had to take him up to Judge Talley. DWI, property damage, foul and abusive, resisting, public obscenity. You could pave the river with charges. I mean it.

All right. You could. And sometimes did. Some wise-ass tries to take apart Millie's Bar, the only place for four blocks where a workingman can sit back and sip one without a lot of hassle. You let him consider the adamantine justice of Jefferson Parish for thirty days or six months before you turn him loose at the Causeway and let him drag back to St. Tammany Parish with what's left of his tail tucked between his legs. Discretion of the Officer. That's the way it is, the way it's always been, the way it'll be until the whole human race learns how to handle itself in Millie's Bar.

But you don't do that with a friend. Makes no sense. You don't cart him off to Judge Elmer Talley, who is the scourge of the working class if the working class indulges in what others call the curse of the working class. No, Bert was clubbing his buddy. To get him to an Officer of the Court. All right.

—He says he wants a divorce, Bert said. —Drinks like a three-legged hog and goes to low-rating his wife in public and so on. Ain't that fine?

Bedlow frowned, shaking his head. It was *not* fine. He agreed with Bert, you could tell. It was sorry, too damned bad.

—I'm not going to tell you what he called his wife over to Sammie's Lounge last night. Sammie almost hit him. You know what I mean?

Yes I did. Maybe, here and there, the fire is not entirely out. I have known a man to beat another very nearly to death because the first spoke slightingly of his own mother. One does not talk that way about womenfolk, not even one's own. The lowly, the ignored, and the abused remember what the high-born and the wealthy have forgotten.

—Are you separated? I asked Bedlow.

—I ain't livin' with the woman, he said laconically. It was the first time he had spoken since he came into my house.

—What's the trouble?

He told me. Told me in detail. It seemed that there had been adultery. A clear and flagrant act of faithlessness resulting in a child. A child that was not his, not a Bedlow. He had been away, in the wash of his financial troubles, watching the Rambler franchise expire, trying hard to do right. And she did it, swore to Christ and the Virgin she never did it, and went to confinement carrying another man's child.

—When? I asked. —How old is . . . ?

—Nine, Bedlow said firmly. —He's . . . it's nine . . .

I stared at Bert. He shrugged. It seemed to be no surprise to him. Oh hell, I thought. Maybe what this draggle-assed country needs is an emperor. Even if he taxes us to death and declares war on Guatemala. This is absurd.

—Mr. Bedlow, I said. —You can't get a divorce for adultery with a situation like that.

—How come?

—You've been living with her all that . . . nine years?

—Yeah.

—They . . . call it reconciliation. No way. If you stay on, you are presumed . . . what the hell. How long have you lived apart?

—Two weeks and two days, he answered. I suspected he could have told me the hours and minutes.

—I couldn't take it any more. Knowing what I know . . .

Bedlow began to cry. Bert looked away, and I suppose I did. I have not seen many grown men cry cold sober. I have seen them mangled past any hope of life, twisting, screaming, cursing. I have seen them standing by a wrecked car while police and firemen tried to saw loose the bodies of their wives and children. I have seen men, told of the death of their one son, stand hard-jawed with tears running down their slabby sunburned cheeks, but that was not crying. Bedlow was crying, and he did not seem the kind of man who cries.

I motioned Bert back into the kitchen. —What the hell . . . ?

—This man, Bert said, spreading his hands, —is in trouble.

—All right, I said, hearing Bedlow out in the parlor, still sobbing as if something more than his life might be lost. —All right. But I don't think it's a lawyer he needs.

Bert frowned, outraged. —Well, he sure don't need one of . . . them.

I could not be sure whether he was referring to priests or psychiatrists. Or both. Bert trusted the law. Even working with it, knowing better than I its open sores and ugly fissures, he believed in it, and for some reason saw me as one of its dependable functionaries. I guess I was pleased by that.

—Fill me in on this whole business, will you?

Yes he would, and would have earlier over the phone, but he had been busy mollifying Sammie and some of his customers who wanted to lay charges that Bert could not have sidestepped.

It was short and ugly, and I was hooked. Bedlow's wife was a good woman. The child was a hopeless defective. It was kept up at Pineville, at the Louisiana hospital for the feebleminded, or whatever the social scientists are calling imbeciles this year. A vegetating thing that its mother had named Albert Sidney Bedlow before they had taken it away, hooked it up for a lifetime of intravenous feeding, and added it to the schedule for cleaning up filth and washing, and all the things they do for human beings who can do nothing whatever for themselves. But Irma Bedlow couldn't let it go at that. The state is equipped, albeit poorly, for this kind of thing. It happens. You let the thing go, and they see to it, and one day, usually not long hence, it dies of pneumonia or a virus, or one of the myriad diseases that float and sift through the air of a place like that. This is the way these things are done, and all of us at the law have drawn up papers for things called "Baby So-and-so," sometimes, mercifully, without their parents' having laid eyes on them.

Irma Bedlow saw it otherwise. During that first year, while the Rambler franchise was bleeding to death, while Bedlow was going half-crazy, she had spent most of her time up in Alexandria, a few miles from the hospital, at her sister's. So that she could visit Albert Sidney every day.

She would go there, Bert told me as Bedlow had told him, and sit in the drafty ward on a hard chair next to Albert Sidney's chipped institutional crib, with her rosary, praying to Jesus Christ that He would send down His grace on her baby, make him whole, and let her suffer in his place. She would kneel in the twilight beside the bed stiff with urine and stinking of such excrement as a child might produce who has never tasted food, amid the bedlam of chattering and choking and animal sounds from bedridden idiots, cretins, declining mongoloids, microcephalics, and assorted other exiles from the great altarpiece of Hieronymus Bosch. Somehow, the chief psychologist had told Howard, her praying upset the other inmates of the ward, and at last he had to forbid Irma's coming more than once a month. He told her that the praying was out altogether.

After trying to change the chief psychologist's mind, and failing, Irma had come home. The franchise was gone by then, and they had a secondhand trailer parked in a run-down court where they got water, electricity, and gas from pipes in the ground and a sullen old man in a pre-war De Soto station wagon picked up garbage once a week. She said the rosary there, and talked about Albert Sidney to her husband who, cursed now with freedom by the ruin of his affairs, doggedly looking for some kind of a job, had nothing much to do or think about but his wife's abstracted words and the son he had almost had. Indeed, did have, but had in such a way that the having was more terrible than the lack.

It had taken no time to get into liquor, which his wife never touched, she fasting and praying, determined that no small imperfection in herself should stay His hand who could set things right with Albert Sidney in the flash of a moment's passing.

—And in that line, Bert said, —she ain't . . . they . . . never been man and wife since then. You know what I mean?

—Ummm.

—And she runs off on him. Couple or three times a year. They always find her at the sister's. At least till last year. Her sister won't have her around any more. Seems Irma wanted her to fast for Albert Sidney, too. Wanted the sister's whole family to do it, and there was words, and now she just takes a room at a tourist court by the hospital and tries to get in as often as that chief psychologist will let her. But no praying, he holds to that.

—What does Bedlow believe?

—Claims he believes she got Albert Sidney with some other man.

—No, I mean . . . does he believe in praying?

—Naw. Too honest, I guess. Says he don't hold with beads and saying the same thing over and over. Says God stands on His own feet, and expects the same of us. Says we ain't here to shit around. What's done is done.

—Do you think he wants a divorce?

—Could he get one?

—Yes.

—Well, how do I know?

—You brought him here. He's not shopping for religious relics, is he?

Bert looked hurt. As if I were blaming him unfairly for some situation beyond his control or prevention.

—You want him in jail?

—No, I said. —I just don't know what to do about him. Where's he living?

—Got a cabin at the Bo-Peep Motel. Over off Veterans Highway. He puts in his time at the car lot and then goes to drinking and telling people his wife has done bastardized him.

—Why did he wait so long to come up with that line?

—It just come on him, what she must of done, he told me.

—That's right, Bedlow said, his voice raspy, aggressive. —I ain't educated or anything. I studied on it and after so long it come to me. I saw it wasn't *mine*, that . . . thing of hers. Look, how come she can't just get done mourning and say, well, that's how it falls out sometimes and I'm sorry as all hell, but you got to keep going. That's what your ordinary woman would say, ain't it?

He had come into the kitchen where Bert and I were standing, his face still wet with tears. He came in talking, and the flow went on as if he were as compulsive with his tongue as he was with a bottle. The words tumbled out so fast that you felt he must have practiced, this country man, to speak so rapidly, to say so much.

—But no. I tell you what: she's mourning for what she done to that . . . thing's real father, that's what she's been doing. He likely lives in Alec, and she can't get over what she done him when she got that . . . thing. And I tell you this, I said, look, honey, don't give it no name, 'cause if you give it a name, you're gonna think that name over and over and make like it was the name of a person and it ain't, and it'll ruin us just as sure as creaking hell. And she went and named it my father's name, who got it after Albert Sidney Johnston at Shiloh. . . . Look, I ain't laid a hand on that woman in God knows how many years, I tell you that. So you see, that's what these trips is about. She goes up and begs his pardon for not giving him a fine boy like he wanted, and she goes to see . . . the thing, and mourns . . . and goddamnit to hell, I got to get shut of this . . . whole *thing*.

It came in a rush, as if, even talking, saying more words in the space of a moment than he had ever said before, Bedlow was enlarging, perfecting his suspicions—no, his certainty—of what had been done to him.

We were silent for a moment.

—Well, it's hard, Bert said at last.

—Hard, Bedlow glared at him as if Bert had insulted him. —You don't even know hard. . . .

—All right, I said. —We'll go down to the office in the morning and draw up and file.

—Huh?

—We'll file for legal separation. Will your wife contest it?

—Huh?

—I'm going to get you what you want. Will your wife go along?

—Well, I don't know. She don't . . . think about . . . things. If you was to tell her, I don't know.

Bert looked at him, his large dark face settled and serious. —That woman's a . . . Catholic, he said at last, and Bedlow stared back at him as if he had named a new name, and things needed thinking again.

A little while later, they left, with Bedlow promising me and promising Bertram Bijou that he'd be in my office the next morning. For a long time after I closed the door behind them, I sat looking at the empty whiskey glasses and considered the course of living in the material world. Then I went and fixed me a shaker of martinis, and became quickly wiser. I considered that it was time to take Zeno seriously, give over the illusion of motion, of sequence. There are only a few moments in any life and when they arrive, they are fixed forever and we play through them, pretending to go on, but coming back to them over and over, again and again. If it is true that we can only approach any place but never reach it as the philosopher claims, it must be corollary that we may almost leave a moment, but never quite. And so as Dr. Freud so clearly saw, one moment, one vision, one thing come upon us becomes the whole time and single theme of all we will ever do or know. We are invaded by our own one thing, and going on is a dream we have while lying still.

I thought, too, mixing one last shaker, that of the little wisdom in this failing age, Alcholics Anonymous must possess more than its share. I am an alcoholic, they say. I have not had a drink in nine years, but I am an alcoholic, and the shadow, the motif, of my living is liquor bubbling into a glass over and over, again and again. That is all I really want, and I will never have it again because I will not take it, and I know that I will never really know why not.

—It's bedtime, Joan said, taking my drink and sipping it. —What did they want?

—A man wants a divorce because nine years ago his wife had a feebleminded baby. He says it's not his. Wants me to claim adultery and unclaim the child.

—Nice man.

—Actually, I began. Then no. Bedlow did not seem a nice man or not a nice man. He seemed a driven man, outside whatever might be his element. So I said that.

—Who isn't, Joan sniffed. She is not the soul of charity at two-thirty in the morning.

—What? Isn't what?

—Driven. Out of her . . . his . . . element?

I looked at her. Is it the commonest of things for men in their forties to consider whether their women are satisfied? Is it a sign of the spirit's collapse when you wonder how and with whom she spends her days? What is the term for less than suspicion: a tiny circlet of thought that touches your mind at lunch with clients or on the way to the office, almost enough to make you turn back home, and then disappears like smoke when you try to fix it, search for a word or an act that might have stirred it to life?

—Are you . . . driven? I asked, much too casually.

—Me? No, she sighed kissing me. —I'm different, she said. Was she too casual, too?

—Bedlow isn't different. I think he wants it all never to have happened. He had a little car franchise and a pregnant wife ten years ago. Clover. He had it made. Then it all went away.

Joan lit a cigarette, crossed her legs and sat down on the floor with my drink. Her wrapper fell open, and I saw the shadow of her breasts. —It always goes away. If you know anything, you know that. Hang on as long as you can. 'Cause it's going away. If you know anything . . .

I looked at her as she talked. She was as beautiful as the first time I had seen her. It was an article of faith: nothing had changed. Her body was still as soft and warm in my arms, and I wait for summer to see her in a bathing suit, and to see her take it off, water running out of her blond hair, between her breasts that I love better than whatever it is that I love next best.

—Sometimes it doesn't go away, I said. Ponderously, I'm sure.

She cocked her head, almost said something, and sipped the drink instead.

What made me think then of the pictures there in the parlor? I went over them in the silence, the flush of gin, remembering where and when we had bought each one. That one in San Francisco, in a Japanese gallery, I thinking that I would not like it long, but thinking too that it didn't matter, since we were at the end of a long difficult case with a fee to match. So if I didn't like it later, well . . .

And the Danish ship, painted on wood in the seventeenth century. I still liked it very much. But why did I think of these things? Was it that they stood on the walls, amid our lives, adding some measure of substance and solidity to them, making it seem that the convention of living together, holding lovely things in common, added reality to the lives themselves. Then, or was it later, I saw us sitting not in a Roman garden in Britain, but in a battered house trailer in imperial America, the walls overspread with invisible pictures of the image of a baby's twisted unfinished face. And how would that be? How would we do then?

Joan smiled, lightly sardonic. —Ignore it, and it'll go away.

—Was there . . . something I was supposed to do? I asked.

The smile deepened, then faded. —Not a thing, she said.

II

The next morning, a will was made, two houses changed hands, a corporation, closely held, was born, seven suits were filed, and a deposition was taken from a whore who claimed that her right of privacy was invaded when the vice squad caught her performing an act against nature on one of their members in a French Quarter alley. Howard Bedlow did not turn up. Joan called just after lunch.

—I think I'll go over to the beach house for a day or two, she said, her voice flat and uncommunicative as only a woman's can be.

I guess there was a long pause. It crossed my mind that once I had wanted to be a musician, perhaps even learn to compose. —I can't get off till the day after tomorrow, I said, knowing that my words were inapposite to anything she might have in mind. —I could come Friday.

—That would be nice.

—Are you . . . taking the children?

—Louise will take care of them.

—You'll be . . . by yourself?

A pause on her side this time. —Yes. Sometimes . . . things get out of hand.

—Anything you want to talk about?

She laughed. —You're the talker in the family.

—And you're what? The actor. Or the thinker?

—That's it. I don't know.

My voice went cold then. I couldn't help it. —Let me know if you figure it out. Then I hung up. And thought at once that I shouldn't have, and yet glad of the minuscule gesture because, however puny, it was an act, and acts in law are almost always merely words. I live in a storm of words: words substituting for actions, words to evade actions, words hinting at actions, words pretending actions. I looked down at the deposition on my desk and wondered it they had caught the whore *talking* to the vice-squad man in the alley. Give her ten years: the utterance of words is an act against nature, an authentic act against nature. I had read somewhere that in Chicago they have opened establishments wherein neither massage nor sex is offered: only a woman, who, for a sum certain in money, will talk to you. She will say anything you want her to say: filth, word pictures of every possible abomination, fantasies of domination and degradation, sadistic orgies strewn out in detail, oaths, descriptions of rape and castration. For a few dollars you can be told how you molested a small child, how you have murdered your parents and covered the carcasses with excrement, assisted in the gang rape of your second-grade teacher. All words.

The authentic crime against nature has finally arrived. It is available somewhere in Chicago. There is no penalty, for after all, it is protected by the First Amendment. Scoff on, Voltaire, Rousseau, scoff on.

My secretary, who would like to speak filth to me, buzzed.

—Mr. Bijou.

—Good. Send him in.

—On the phone.

Bert sounded far away. —You ain't seen Howard, have you?

—No, I said. —Have you?

—Drunk somewhere. Called coughing and moaning something about a plot to shame him. Talking like last night. I think you ought to see Irma. You're supposed to seek reconciliation, ain't you?

—I think you're ripe for law school, Bert. Yes, that's what they say to do.

—Well, he said. —Lemme see what I can do.

I was afraid of that. When I got home the house was deserted, and I liked that. Not really. I wondered what a fast trip to the Gulf Coast would turn up, or a call to a friend of mine in Biloxi who specializes in that kind of thing. But worse, I wasn't sure I cared. Was it that I didn't love Joan anymore, that somewhere along the way I had become insulated against her acts? Could it be that the practice of law had slowly made me responsive only to words? Did I need to go to Chicago to feel real again?

I was restless and drank too many martinis and was involved so much in my own musings that time passed quickly. I played some Beethoven, God knows why. I am almost never so distraught that I enjoy spiritual posturing. Usually, his music makes me grin.

I tried very hard to reckon where I was and what I should do. I was in the twentieth century after Christ, and it felt all of that long since anything on earth had mattered. I was in a democratic empire called America, an officer of its courts, and surely a day in those courts is as a thousand years. I was an artisan in words, shaping destinies, allocating money and blame by my work. I was past the midpoint of my life and could not make out what it had meant so far.

Now, amid this time and place, I could do almost as I chose. Should it be the islands of the Pacific with a box of paints? To the Colorado mountains with a pack, beans, a guitar, pencils, and much paper? Or, like an anchorite, declare the longest of nonterminal hunger strikes, this one against God Almighty, hoping that public opinion would force him to reveal that for which I was made and put in this place and time.

Or why not throw over these ambiguities, this wife doing whatever she might be doing on the coast of the Gulf, these anonymous children content with Louise up the country, contemplating chickens, ducks, and guiney fowl. Begin again. Say every word you have ever said, to new people: hello, new woman, I love you. I have good teeth and most of my mind. I can do well on a good night in a happy bed. Hello, new colleagues, what do we do this time? Is this a trucking firm or a telephone exchange? What is the desiderata? Profit or prophecy?

Bert shook my arm. —Are you okay? You didn't answer the door.

I studied him for a moment, my head soft and uncentered. I was nicely drunk, but coming back. —Yeah, I said. —I'm fine. What have you got going?

—Huh? Listen, can I turn down that music?

—Sure.

He doused the Second Symphony, and I found I was relieved, could breathe more deeply. —I brought her, he said. —She's kinda spaced out, like the kids say.

He frowned, watched me. —You sure you're all right?

I smiled. —All I needed was some company, Bert.

He smiled back. —All right, fine. You're probably in the best kind of shape for Irma.

—Huh?

He looked at the empty martini pitcher. —Nothing. She's just . . .

His voice trailed off and I watched him drift out of my line of sight. In the foyer, I could hear his voice, soft and distant, as if he were talking to a child.

I sobered up. Yes, I have that power. I discovered it in law school. However drunk, I can gather back in the purposely loosed strands of personality or whatever of us liquor casts apart. It is as if one were never truly sober, and hence one could claim back from liquor what it had never truly loosed. Either drunkenness or sobriety is an illusion.

Irma Bedlow was a surprise. I had reckoned on a woman well gone from womanhood. One of those shapeless bun-haired middle-aged creatures wearing bifocals, smiling out from behind the secrecy of knowing that they are at last safe from any but the most psychotic menaces from imbalanced males. But it was not that way. If I had been dead drunk on the one hand, or shuffling up to the communion rail on the other, she would have turned me around.

She was vivid. Dark hair and eyes, a complexion almost pale, a lovely body made more so by the thoughtless pride with which she inhabited it. She sat down opposite me, and our eyes held for a long moment.

I am used to a certain deference from people who come to me in legal situations. God knows we have worked long and hard enough to establish the mandarin tradition of the law, that circle of mysteries that swallows up laymen and all they possess like a vast desert or a hidden sea. People come to the law on tiptoe, watching, wishing they could know which words, what expressions and turns of phrase are *the ones* which bear their fate. I have smiled remembering that those who claim or avoid the law with such awe have themselves in their collectivity created it. But they are so far apart from one another in the sleep of their present lives that they cannot remember what they did together when they were awake.

But Irma Bedlow looked at me as if she were the counselor, her dark eyes fixed on mine to hold me to whatever I might say. Would I lie, and put both our cases in jeopardy? Would I say the best I knew, or had I wandered so long amid the stunted shrubs of language, making unnatural acts in the name of my law, that words had turned from stones with which to build into ropy clinging undergrowth in which to become enmeshed?

I asked her if she would have a drink. I was surprised when she said yes. Fasts for the sake of an idiot child, trying to get others to do it, praying on her knees to Jesus beside the bed of Albert Sidney who did not know about the prayers, and who could know about Jesus only through infused knowledge there within the mansions of his imbecility. But she said yes, and I went to fix it.

Of course Bert followed me over to the bar. —I don't know. I think maybe I ought to take care of Howard and let *her* be your client.

—Don't do that, I said, and wondered why I'd said it.

—She's fine, Bert was saying, and I knew he meant nothing to do with her looks. He was not a carnal man, Bert. He was a social man. Once he had told me he wanted either to be mayor of Kenner or else a comedian. He did not mean it humorously and I did not take it so. He was the least funny of men. Rather he understood with his nerves the pathos of living and would have liked to divert us from it with comedy. But it would not be so, and Bert would end up mayor trying to come to grips with our common anguish instead of belittling it.

—I never talked to anyone like her. You'll see.

I think then I envisioned the most beautiful and desirable Jehovah's Witness in the world. Would we try conclusions over Isaiah? I warn you, Irma, I know the Book and other books beyond number. I am a prince in the kingdom of words, and I have seen raw respect flushed up unwillingly in the eyes of other lawmongers, and have had my work mentioned favorably in appellate decisions which in their small way rule all this land.

—Here you are, I said.

She smiled at me, as if I were a child who had brought his mother a cool drink unasked.

—Howard came to see you, she said, sipping the martini as if gin bruised with vermouth were her common fare. —Can you help me . . . help him?

—He wants a divorce, I said, confused, trying to get things in focus.

—No, she said. Not aggressively, only firmly. Her information was better than mine. I have used the same tone of voice with other attorneys many times. When you know, you know.

—He only wants it over with, done with. That's what he wants.

Bert nodded. He had heard this before. There goes Bert's value as a checkpoint with reality. He believes her. Lordy.

—You mean . . . the marriage?

—No, not that. He knows what I know. If it *was* a marriage, you can't make it be over. You can only desert it. He wouldn't do that.

I shrugged, noticing that she had made no use of her beauty at all so far. She did not disguise it or deny it. She allowed it to exist and simply ignored it. Her femininity washed over me, and yet I knew that it was not directed toward me. It had some other focus, and she saw me as a moment, a crossing in her life, an occasion to stop and turn back for an instant before going on. I wondered what I would be doing for her.

—He *says* he wants a divorce.

She looked down at her drink. Her lashes were incredibly long, though it was obvious she used no makeup at all. Her lips were deep red, a color not used in lipsticks since the 1940s. I understood why Bedlow drank. Nine years with a beautiful woman you love, and cannot touch.

He told you . . . I'd been unfaithful.

Bert was shaking his head, blushing. Not negating what Howard had said, or deprecating it.

—He said that, I told her.

—And that our baby . . . that Albert Sidney wasn't . . . his?

—Yes, I said. Bert looked as if he would cry from shame.

She had not looked up while we talked. Her eyes stayed down, and while I waited, I heard the Beethoven tape, turned down but not off, running out at the end of the "Appassionata." It was a good moment to get up and change to something decent. I found a Vivaldi chamber mass, and the singers were very happy. The music was for God in the first instance, not for the spirit of fraternity or Napoleon or some other rubbish.

—What else? she asked across the room. I flipped the tape on, and eighteenth-century Venice came at us from four sides. I cut back the volume.

—He said you . . . hadn't been man and wife for nine years.

—All right.

I walked back and sat down again. I felt peculiar, neither drunk nor sober, so I poured another one. The first I'd had since they came. —Howard didn't seem to think so. He said . . . you wouldn't let him touch you.

She raised her eyes then. Not angrily, only that same firmness again. —That's not true, she said, —no. Bert nodded as though he had been an abiding presence in the marriage chamber for all those nine long years. He could contain himself no more. He fumbled in his coat pocket and handed me a crumpled and folded sheet of paper. It was a notice from American Motors cancelling Howard Bedlow's franchise. Much boilerplate saying he hadn't delivered and so on. Enclosed find copy of agency contract with relevant revocation clauses underlined. Arrangements will be made for stock on hand, etc.

It was dated 9 May 1966. Bert was watching me. I nodded. —Eight years ago, I said.

—Not ten, Bert was going on. —You see . . .

—He lost the business . . . six months after . . . the . . . Albert Sidney . . .

We sat looking at the paper.

—I never denied him, Irma was saying. —After the baby . . . he couldn't. At first, we didn't think of it, of anything. I . . . we were lost inside ourselves. We didn't talk about it. What had we done? What had gone wrong? What were we . . . supposed to do? Was there something we were supposed to do?

—Genes went wrong . . . hormones, who knows, I said.

Irma smiled at me. Her eyes were black, not brown. —Do you believe that?

—Sure, I said, startled as one must be when he has uttered what passes for a common truth and it is questioned. —What else?

—Nothing, she said. —It's only . . .

She and Bert were both staring at me as if I had missed something. Then Irma leaned forward. —Will you go somewhere with me?

I was thinking of the Gulf Coast, staring down at the face of my watch. It was almost one-thirty. There was a moon and the tide was in, and the moon would be rolling through soft beds of cloud.

—Yes, I said. —Yes I will. Yes.

III

It was early in the morning when we reached Alexandria. The bus trip had been long and strange. We had talked about east Texas where Irma had grown up. Her mother had been from Evangeline Parish, her father a tool-pusher in the Kilgore fields until he lost both hands to a wild length of chain. She had been keeping things together working as a waitress when she met Howard.

On the bus, as if planted there, had been a huge black woman with a little boy whose head was tiny and pointed. It was so distorted that his eyes were pulled almost vertical. He made inarticulate noises and rooted about on the floor of the bus. The other passengers tried to ignore him, but the stench was very bad, and his mother took him to an empty seat in back and changed him several times. Irma helped her once. The woman had been loud, aggressive, unfriendly when Irma approached her, but Irma whispered something, and the woman began to cry, her sobs loud and terrible. When they had gotten the child cleaned up, the black woman put her arms around Irma and kissed her.

—I tried hard as I could, miss, but I can't manage . . . Oh sweet Jesus knows I wisht I was dead first. But I can't manage the other four . . . I *got* to . . .

The two of them sat together on the rear seat for a long time, holding hands, talking so softly that I couldn't hear. Once, the boy crawled up and stopped at my seat. He looked up at me like some invertebrate given the power to be quizzical. I wondered which of us was in hell. He must have been about twelve years old.

In the station, Irma made a phone call while I had coffee. People moved through the twilit terminal, meeting, parting. One elderly woman in a thin print dress thirty years out of date even among country people kissed a young man in an army uniform goodbye. Her lips trembled as he shouldered his duffel bag and moved away. —Stop, she cried out, and then realized that he could not stop, because the dispatcher was calling the Houston bus. —Have you . . . forgotten anything? The soldier paused, smiled, and shook his head. Then he vanished behind some people trying to gather up clothes which had fallen from a cardboard suitcase with a broken clasp. Somewhere a small child cried as if it had awakened to find itself suddenly, utterly lost.

Irma came back and drank her coffee, and when we walked outside it was daylight in Alexandria, even as on the Gulf Coast. An old station wagon with a broken muffler pulled up, and a thin man wearing glasses got out and kissed Irma as if it were a ritual and shook hands with me in that peculiar limp diffident way of country people meeting someone from the city who might represent threat or advantage.

We drove for twenty minutes or so, and slowed down in front of a small white frame place on a blacktop road not quite in or out of town. The yard was large and littered with wrecked and cannibalized autos. The metal bones of an old Hudson canted into the rubble of a '42 Ford convertible. Super Deluxe. There was a shed which must have been an enlarged garage. Inside I could see tools, a lathe, work benches. A young man in overalls without a shirt looked out at us and waved casually. He had a piece of drive shaft in his hand. Chickens ambled stupidly in the grassless yard, pecking at oil patches and clumps of rust.

We had eggs and sausage and biscuits and talked quietly. They were not curious about me. They had seen a great deal during the years and there was nothing to be had from curiosity. You come to learn that things have to be taken as they come and it is no use to probe the gestations of tomorrows before they come. There is very little you can do to prepare.

It turned out there had been no quarrel between Irma and her sister's family. Her sister, plain as Irma was beautiful, who wore thick glasses and walked slowly because of her varicose veins, talked almost without expression, but with some lingering touch of her mother's French accent. She talked on as if she had saved everything she had seen and come to know, saved it all in exhaustive detail, knowing that someone would one day come for her report.

—It wasn't never any quarrel, and Howard had got to know better. Oh, we fussed, sure. My daddy always favored Irma and so I used to take after her over anything, you know. Jesus spare me, I guess I hated my own little sister. Till the baby come, and the Lord lifted the scales from my eyes. I dreamed He come down just for me. He looked like Mr. Denver, the station agent down to the L&N depot, and He said, "Elenor, I had enough stuff out of you, you hear? You see Albert Sidney? You satisfied now? Huh? Is that enough for you? You tell me that, 'cause I got to be getting on. I don't make nobody more beautiful or more smart or anything in this world, but I do sometimes take away their looks or ruin their minds or put blindness on 'em, or send 'em a trouble to break their hearts. Don't ask why 'cause it's not for you to know, but that's what I do. Now what else you want for Irma, huh?"

Tears were flowing down Elenor's face now, but her expression didn't change. —So I saw it was my doing, and I begged Him to set it right, told Him to strike me dead and set it right with that helpless baby. But He just shook His head and pushed up His sleeves like He could hear a through-freight coming. "It's not how it's done. It ain't like changing your mind about a hat or a new dress. You see that?"

—Well, I didn't, but what could I say? I said yes, and He started off and the place where we was began getting kind of fuzzy, then He turned and looked back at me and smiled. "How you know it ain't all right with Albert Sidney?" he asked. And I saw then that He loved me after all. Then, when I could hardly see Him I heard Him say, "Anything you forgot, Elly?" but I never said nothing at all, only crossed myself the way Momma used to do.

Elenor touched her sister's shoulder shyly. Irma was watching me, something close to a smile on her lips. —Well, Elenor said, —we've prayed together since then, ain't we, hon? Irma took her sister's hand and pressed it against her cheek.

—We been close since then, Charlie, Elenor's husband, said. —Done us all good. Except for poor Howard.

It seemed Howard had hardened his heart from the first. Charlie had worked for him in the Rambler franchise, manager of the service department. One day they had had words and Charlie quit, left New Orleans which was a plague to him anyway, and set up this little backyard place in Alec.

—Why the fight? I asked Charlie. He was getting up to go out to work.

—Never mind that, he said. —It . . . didn't have nothing to do with . . . this.

Elenor watched him go. —Yes it did, she began.

—Elenor, Irma stopped her. —Maybe you ought not . . . Charlie's . . .

Elenor was wiping her cheeks with her apron. —This man's a lawyer, ain't he? He knows what's right and wrong.

I winced and felt tired all at once, but you cannot ask for a pitcher of martinis at seven-thirty in the morning in a Louisiana country house. That was the extent of my knowledge of right and wrong.

—A couple of months after Albert Sidney was born, I was at their place, Elenor went on. —Trying to help out. I was making the beds when Howard come in. It was early, but Howard was drunk and he talked funny, and before I knew, he pulled me down on the bed, and . . . I couldn't scream, I couldn't. Irma had the baby in the kitchen . . . and he couldn't. He tried to . . . make me . . . help him, but he couldn't anyhow. And I told Charlie, because a man ought to know. And they had words, and after that Charlie whipped him, and moved up here. . . .

Elenor sat looking out of the window where the sun was beginning to show over the trees. —And we come on up here.

Irma looked at her sister tenderly. —Elly, we got to go on over to the hospital now.

As we reached the door, Elenor called out. —Irma . . .

—Yes . . . ?

—Honey, you know how much I love you, don't you?

—I always did know, silly. You were the one didn't know.

We took the old station wagon and huffed slowly out of the yard. Charlie waved at us and his eyes followed us out of sight down the blacktop.

IV

Irma was smiling at me as we coughed along the road. —I feel kind of good, she said.

—I'm glad. Why?

—Like some kind of washday. It's long and hard, but comes the end, and you've got everything hanging out in the fresh air. Clean.

—It'll be dirty again, I said, and wished I could swallow the words almost before they were out.

Her hand touched my arm, and I almost lost control of the car. I kept my eyes on the road to Pineville. I was here to help her, not the other way around. There was too much contact between us already, too much emptiness in me, and what the hell I was doing halfway up the state with the wife of a man who could make out a showing that he was my client was more than I could figure out. Something to do with the Gulf. —There's another washday coming, she whispered, her lips close to my ear.

Will I be ready for washday, I wondered. Lord, how is it that we get ready for washday?

The Louisiana state hospital is divided into several parts. There is one section for the criminally insane, and another for the feeble-minded. This second section is, in turn, divided into what are called "tidy" and "untidy" wards. The difference is vast in terms of logistics and care. The difference in the moral realm is simply that between the seventh and the first circles. Hell is where we are.

Dr. Tumulty met us outside his office. He was a small man with a large nose and glasses which looked rather like those you can buy in a novelty shop, outsize nose attached. Behind the glasses, his eyes were weak and watery. His mouth was very small, and his hair thin, the color of cornshucks. I remember wondering then, at the start of our visit, whether one of the inmates had been promoted. It was a very bad idea, but only one of many.

—Hello, Irma, he said. He did not seem unhappy to see her.

—Hello, Monte, she said.

—He had a little respiratory trouble last week. It seems cleared up now.

Irma introduced us and Dr. Tumulty studied me quizzically. —A lawyer . . . ?

—Counselor, she said. —A good listener. Do you have time to show him around?

He looked at me, Charon sizing up a strange passenger, one who it seemed would be making a round trip. —Sure, all right. You coming?

—No, Irma said softly. —You can bring him to me afterward.

So Dr. Tumulty took me through the wards alone. I will not say everything I saw. There were mysteries in that initiation that will not go down into words. It is all the soul is worth and more to say less than all when you have come back from that place where, if only they knew, what men live and do asleep is done waking and in truth each endless day.

Yes, there were extreme cases of mongolism, cretins and imbeciles, dwarfs, and things with enormous heads and bulging eyes, ears like tubes, mouths placed on the sides of their heads. There was an albino without nose or eyes or lips, and it sat in a chair, teeth exposed in a grin that could not be erased, its hands making a series of extremely complicated gestures over and over again, each lengthy sequence a perfect reproduction of the preceding one. The gestures were wholly symmetrical, and the repetition exact and made without pause, a formalism of mindlessness worthy of a Balinese dancer, or a penance, performance of a secret prayer, played out before the catatonic admiration of three small blacks who sat on the floor before the albino, watching its art with a concentration unknown among those who imagine themselves without defect.

This was the tidy ward, and all these inventions of a Bosch whose medium is flesh wore coveralls of dark gray cloth with a name patch on the left breast. This was Paul, whose tongue, abnormally long and almost black and dry, hung down his chin, and that, the hairless one with the enormous head and tiny face, who coughed and petted a filthy toy elephant, that was Larry. The dead-white one, the maker of rituals, was Anthony. Watching him were Edward and Joseph and Michael, microcephalics all, looking almost identical in their shared malady.

—Does . . . Anthony . . . I began.

—All day. Every day, Dr. Tumulty said. —And the others watch. We give him tranquilizers at night. It used to be . . . all night, too.

In another ward, they kept the females. It was much the same there, except that, wandering from one chair to another, watching the others, was a young girl, perhaps sixteen. She would have been pretty—no, she was pretty, despite the gray coverall and the pallor of her skin. —Hello, doctor, she said. Her voice sounded as if it had been recorded, cracked and scratchy. But her body seemed sound, her face normal except for small patches of what looked like eczema on her face. That, and her eyes were a little out of focus. She was carrying a small book covered with imitation red leather. *My Diary,* it said on the cover.

—Does she belong here? I asked Tumulty.

He nodded. —She's been here over a year.

The girl cuddled against him, and I could see that she was trying to press her breasts against him. Her hand wandered down toward his leg. He took her hand gently and stroked her hair. —Hello, Doctor, she croaked again. —Hi, Nancy, he answered. —Are you keeping up your diary?

She smiled. —For home. Hello, Doctor.

—For home, sure, he said, and sat her down in a chair opposite an ancient television locked in a wire cage and tuned, I remember, to *Underdog.* She seemed to lose interest in us, to find her way quickly into the role of Sweet Polly, awaiting the inevitable rescue. Around her on the floor were scattered others of the less desperate cases. They watched the animated comedy on the snow-flecked, badly focused screen with absolute concentration. As we moved on, I heard Nancy whisper, —There's no need to fear . . .

—Congenital syphilis, Tumulty said. —It incubates for years, sometimes. She was in high school. Now she's here. It's easier for her now than at first. Most of her mind is gone. In a year she'll be dead.

He paused by a barred window, and looked out on the rolling Louisiana countryside beyond the distant fence. —About graduation time.

—There's no treatment . . . ?

—The cure is dying.

What I can remember of the untidy wards is fragmentary. The stench was very bad, the sounds were nonhuman, and the inmates, divided by sex, were naked in large concrete rooms, sitting on the damp floors, unable to control their bodily functions, obese mostly, and utterly asexual with tiny misshapen heads. There were benches along the sides of the concrete rooms, and the floors sloped down to a central caged drain in the center. One of the things—I mean inmates—was trying slowly, in a fashion almost reptilian, to lick up filthy moisture from the drain. Another was chewing on a plastic bracelet by which it was identified. Most of the rest, young and older, sat on the benches or the floor staring at nothing, blubbering once in a while, scratching occasionally.

—Once, Dr. Tumulty said thoughtfully, —a legislator came. A budgetary inspection. We didn't get any more money. But he complained that we identified the untidy patients by number. He came and saw everything, and that's . . . what bothered him.

By then we were outside again, walking in the cool Louisiana summer morning. We had been inside less than an hour. I had thought it was much longer.

—It's the same everywhere. Massachusetts, Wyoming, Texas. Don't think badly of us. There's no money, no personnel, and even if there were . . .

—Then you could only . . . cover it.

—Cosmetics, yes. I've been in this work for eighteen years. I've never forgotten anything I saw. Not anything. You know what I think? What I really *know*?

— . . . ?

Tumulty paused and rubbed his hands together. He shivered a little, that sudden inexplicable thrill of cold inside that has no relationship to the temperature in the world, that represents, according to the old story, someone walking across the ground where your grave will one day be. A mockingbird flashed past us, a dark blur of gray, touched with the white of its wings. Tumulty started to say something, then shrugged and pointed at a small building a little way off.

—They're over there. One of the attendants will show you.

He looked from one building to another, shaking his head. —There's so much to do. So many of them . . .

—Yes, I said. —Thank you. Then I began walking toward the building he had indicated.

—Do . . . whatever you can . . . for her, Dr. Tumulty called after me. —I wish . . .

I turned back toward him. We stood perhaps thirty yards apart then. —Was there . . . something else you wanted to say? I asked.

He looked at me for a long moment, then away. —No, he said. —Nothing.

I stood there as he walked back into the clutter of central buildings, and finally vanished into one of them. Then, before I walked back to join Irma, I found a bench under an old magnolia and sat down for a few minutes. It was on the way to becoming warm now, and the sun's softness and the morning breeze were both going rapidly. The sky was absolutely clear, and by noon it would be very hot indeed. A few people were moving across the grounds. A nurse carrying something on a tray, two attendants talking animatedly to each other, one gesturing madly. Another attendant was herding a patient toward the medical building. It was a black inmate, male or female I could not say, since all the patients' heads were close-cropped for hygienic purposes, and the coverall obscured any other sign of sex. It staggered from one side of the cinder path to the other, swaying as if it were negotiating the deck of a ship in heavy weather out on the Gulf. Its arms flailed, seeking a balance it could never attain, and its eyes seemed to be seeking some point of reference in a world awash. But there was no point, the trees whirling and the buildings losing their way, and so the thing looked skyward, squint-ed terribly at the sun, pointed upward toward that brazen glory, and almost fell down, its contorted black face now fixed undeviat-ingly toward that burning place in the sky which did not shift and whirl. But the attendant took its shoulder and urged it along, since it could not make its way on earth staring into the sun.

As it passed by my bench, it saw me, gestured at me, leaned in my direction amid its stumblings, its dark face twinkling with sweat.

—No, Hollis, I heard the attendant say as the thing and I ex-changed a long glance amid the swirling trees, the spinning build-ings, out there on the stormy Gulf. Then it grinned, its white teeth sparkling, its eyes almost pulled shut from the effort of grimace, its twisted fingers spieling a language both of us could grasp.

—Come on, Hollis, the attendant said impatiently, and the thing reared its head and turned away. No more time for me. It took a step or two, fell, and rolled in the grass, grunting, making sounds like I had never heard. —Hollis, I swear to God, the attendant said mild-ly, and helped the messenger to its feet once more.

The nurse in the building Tumulty had pointed out looked at me questioningly. —I'm looking for . . . Mrs. Bedlow.

—You'll have to wait . . . she began, and then her expression changed. —Oh, you must be the one. I knew I'd forgotten some-thing. All right, straight back and to the left. Ward 3.

I walked down a long corridor with lights on the ceiling, each behind its wire cover. I wondered if Hollis might have been the reason for the precaution. Had he or she or it once leaped upward at the light, clawing, grasping, attempting to touch the sun? The walls were covered with an ugly pale yellow enamel which had begun peeling long ago, and the smell of cheap pine-scented deodorizer did not cover the deep ingrained stench of urine, much older than the blistered paint. Ward 3 was a narrow dormitory filled with small beds. My eyes scanned the beds and I almost turned back, ready for the untidy wards again. Because here were the small children, what had been intended as children.

Down almost at the end of the ward, I saw Irma. She was seated in a visitor's chair, and in her arms was a child with a head larger than hers. It was gesticulating frantically, and I could hear its sounds the length of the ward. She held it close and whispered to it, kissed it, and as she drew it to her, the sounds became almost frantic. They were not human sounds. They were Hollis's sounds, and as I walked the length of the ward, I thought I knew what Tumulty had been about to say before he had thought better of it.

—Hello, Irma said. The child in her arms paused in its snufflings and looked up at me from huge unfocused eyes. Its tongue stood out, and it appeared that its lower jaw was congenitally dislocated. Saliva ran down the flap of flesh where you and I have lips, and Irma paid no mind as it dripped on her dress. It would have been pointless to wipe the child's mouth, because the flow did not stop, nor did the discharge from its bulging unblinking eyes. I looked at Irma. Her smile was genuine.

—This is . . . I began.

—Albert Sidney, she finished. —Oh no. I wish it was. This is Barry. Say hello.

The child grunted and buried its head in her lap, sliding down to the floor and crawling behind her chair.

—You . . . wish . . . ?

—This is Albert Sidney, she said, turning to the bed next to her chair.

He lay there motionless, the sheet drawn up to what might have been the region of his chin. His head was very large, and bulged out to one side in a way that I would never have supposed could support life. Where his eyes should have been, two blank white surfaces of solid cataract seemed to float lidless and intent. He had no nose, only a small hole surgically created, I think, and ringed with discharge. His mouth was a slash in the right side of his cheek, at least two inches over and up from where mouths belong. Irma stepped over beside him, and as she reached down and kissed him, rearranged the sheets, I saw one of his hands. It was a fingerless club of flesh dotted almost randomly with bits of fingernail.

I closed my eyes and then looked once more. I saw again what I must have seen at first and ignored, the thing I had come to see. On Albert Sidney's deformed and earless head, almost covering the awful disarray of his humanity, he had a wealth of reddish golden hair, rich and curly, proper aureole of a Celtic deity. Or a surfing king.

V

We had dinner at some anonymous restaurant in Alexandria, and then found a room at a motel not far from Pineville. I had bought a bottle of whiskey. Inside, I filled a glass after peeling away its sticky plastic cover that pretended to guard it from the world for my better health.

—Should I have brought you? Irma asked, sitting down on the bed.

—Yes, I said. —Sure. Nobody should . . . nobody ought to be shielded from this.

—But it . . . hasn't got anything to do with . . . us. What Howard wants to do, does it?

—No, I said. —I don't think so.

—Howard was all right. If things had gone . . . the way they do mostly. He wasn't . . . isn't . . . a weak man. He's brave, and he used to work . . . sometimes sixteen hours a day. He was very . . . steady. Do you know, I loved him. . . .

I poured her a drink. —Sometimes, I said, and heard that my voice was unsteady. —None of us know . . . what we can . . . stand.

—If Howard had had just any kind of belief . . . but . . .

—He just had himself . . . ?

—Just that. He . . . his two hands and a strong back, and he was quick with figures. He always . . . came out . . .

— . . . ahead.

She breathed deeply, and sipped the whiskey. —Every time. He . . . liked hard times. To work his way through. You couldn't stop him. And very honest. An honest man.

I finished the glass and poured another one. I couldn't get rid of the smells and the images. The whiskey was doing no good. It would only dull my senses prospectively. The smells and the images were inside for keeps.

—He's not honest about . . .

—Albert Sidney? No, but I . . . it doesn't matter. I release him of that. Which is why . . .

—You want me to go ahead with the divorce?

—I think. We can't help each other, don't you see?

—I see that. But . . . what will you do?

Irma laughed and slipped off her shoes, curled her feet under her.

Somewhere back in the mechanical reaches of my mind, where I was listening to Vivaldi and watching a thin British rain fall into my garden, neither happy nor sad, preserved by my indifference from the Gulf, I saw that she was very beautiful and that she cared for me, had brought me to Alexandria as much for myself as for her sake, though she did not know it.

— . . . do what needs to be done for the baby, she was saying.
—I've asked for strength to do the best . . . thing.
—What do you want me to do?
—About the divorce? I don't know about . . . the legal stuff. I want to . . . how do you say it . . . ? Not to contest it?
—There's a way. When the other person makes life insupportable . . .

Irma looked at me strangely, as if I were not understanding.
—No, no. The other . . . what he says.
—Adultery?
—And the rest. About Albert Sidney . . .
—No. You can't . . .
—Why can't I? I told you, Howard is all right. I mean, he could be all right. I want to let him go. Can't I say some way or other that what he claims is true?

I set my glass down. —In the pleadings. You can always accept what he says in your . . . answer.
—Pleadings?
—That's what they call . . . what we file in a suit. But I can't state an outright . . . lie. . . .
—But you're his counsel. You have to say what he wants you to say.
—No, only in good faith. The Code of Civil Practice . . . If I pleaded a lie . . . Anyhow, Jesus, after all this . . . I couldn't . . . Plead adultery . . . ? No way.
—Yes, Irma said firmly, lovingly. She rose from the bed and came to me.
—Yes, she whispered. —You'll be able to.

VI

The next evening, the plane was late getting into New Orleans. There was a storm line along the Gulf, a series of separate systems, then monotonous driving rain that fell all over the city and the southern part of the state. The house was cool and humid when I got home, and my head hurt. The house was empty, and that was all right. I had a bowl of soup and turned on something very beautiful. *La Stravaganza.* As I listened, I thought of that strange medieval custom of putting the mad and the demented on a boat, and keeping it moving from one port to another. A ship full of lunacy and witlessness and rage and subhumanity with no destination in view. *Furiosi,* the mad were called. What did they call those who came into this world like Irma's baby, scarce half made up? Those driven beyond the human by the world were given names and a status. But what of those who came damaged from the first? Did even the wisdom of the Church have no name for those who did not scream or curse or style themselves Emperor Frederic II or Gregory come again? What of those with bulbous heads and protruding tongues and those who stared all day at the blazing sun, all night at the cool distant moon? I listened and drank, and opened the door onto the patio, so that the music was leavened with the sound of the falling rain.

It was early the next morning when Bert called me at home. He did not bother apologizing. I think he knew that we were both too much in it now. The amenities are for before. Or afterward.

—Listen, you're back.

—Yes.

—I got Howard straightened up. You want to talk to him?

—What's he saying?

—Well, he's cleared up, you see? I got him to shower and drink a pot of coffee. It ain't what he says is different, but he *is* himself and he wants to get them papers started. You know? You want to drop by the Bo-Peep for a minute?

—No, I said, —but I will. I want to talk to that stupid bastard.

—Ah, Bert said slowly. —Uh-huh. Well, fine, counselor. It's Cabin 10. On the street to the right as you come in. Can't miss it.

I thought somebody ought to take a baseball bat and use it on Howard Bedlow until he came to understand. I was very tight about this thing now, no distance at all. I had thought about other things only once since I had been back. When a little phrase of Vivaldi's had shimmered like a waterfall, and, still drunk, I had followed that billow down to the Gulf in my mind.

They were fantasies, of course. In one, I took Irma away. We left New Orleans and headed across America toward California, and she was quickly pregnant. The child was whole and healthy and strong, and what had befallen each of us back in Louisiana faded and receded faster and faster, became of smaller and smaller concern until we found ourselves in a place near the Russian River, above the glut and spew of people down below.

Acres apart and miles away, we had a tiny place carved from the natural wood of the hills. We labored under the sun and scarcely talked, and what there was, was ours. She would stand near a forest pool, nude, our child in her arms, and the rest was all forgotten as I watched them there, glistening, with beads of fresh water standing on their skin, the way things ought to be, under the sun.

Then I was driving toward Metairie amid the dust and squalor of Airline Highway. Filling stations, hamburger joints, cut-rate liquor, tacos, wholesale carpeting, rent-a-car, people driving a little above the speed limit sealed in air-conditioned cars, others standing at bus stops staring vacantly, some gesticulating in repetitive patterns, trying to be understood. No sign of life anywhere.

The sign above the Bo-Peep Motel pictured a girl in a bonnet with a shepherd's crook and a vast crinoline skirt. In her lap she held what looked from a distance like a child. Closer, you could see that it was intended to be a lamb, curled in her arms, eyes closed, hoofs tucked into its fleece, peacefully asleep. Bo-Peep's face, outlined in neon tubing, had been painted once, but most of the paint had chipped away, and now, during the day, she wore a faded leer of unparalleled perversity, red lips and china blue eyes flawed by missing chips of color.

Bert sat in a chair outside the door. He was in uniform. His car was parked in front of number 10. The door was open, and just inside, Howard Bedlow sat in an identical chair staring out like a prisoner who knows there must be bars even though he cannot see them. He leaned forward, hands hanging down before him, and even from a distance he looked much older than I had remembered him.

Bert walked out as I parked. —How was the trip?

We stared at each other. —A revelation, I said. —He's sober?

—Oh yeah. He had a little trouble last night down at the Kit-Kat Klub. Bert pointed down the road to a huddled cinder-block building beside a trailer court.

—They sent for somebody to see to him, and luck had it be me.

Howard looked like an old man up close. His eyes were crusted, squinting up at the weak morning sun, still misted at that hour. His hands hung down between his legs, almost touching the floor, and his forefingers moved involuntarily as if they were tracing a precise and repetitious pattern on the dust of the floor. He looked up at me, licking his lips. He had not shaved in a couple of days, and the light beard had the same tawny reddish color as his hair. He did not seem to recognize me for a moment. Then his expression came together. He looked almost frightened.

—You seen her, huh?

—That's right.

—What'd she say?

—It's all right with her.

—What's all right?

—The divorce. Just the way you want it.

—You mean . . . like everything I said . . . all that . . . ?

—She says maybe she owes you that much. For what she did.

—What she did?

—You know . . .

—What I said, told you?

—Wonder what the hell that is, Bert put in. He walked out into the driveway and stared down the street.

Bedlow shook his head slowly. —She owned up, told you everything?

—There was . . . a confirmation. Look, I said. —Bert will line you up a lawyer. I'm going to represent Ir . . . your wife.

—Oh? I was the one come to you. . . .

I took a piece of motel stationery out of my pocket. There was a five-dollar bill held to it with a dark bobby pin. I remembered her hair cascading down, flowing about her face. —You never gave me a retainer. I did not act on your behalf.

I held out the paper and the bill. —This is my retainer. From her. It doesn't matter. She won't contest. I'll talk to your lawyer. It'll be easy.

—I never asked for nothing to be easy, Bedlow murmured.

—If you want to back off the adultery thing, which is silly, which even if it is true you cannot prove, you can go for rendering life insupportable. . . .

—Life insupportable . . . ? I never asked things be easy. . . .

—Yes you did, I said brutally. —You just didn't know you were.

I wanted to tell him there was something rotten and weak and collapsed in him. His heart, his guts, his genes. That he had taken a woman better than he had any right to, and that Albert Sidney . . . but how could I? Who was I to . . . and then Bert stepped back toward us, his face grim.

—Shit, he was saying, —I think they've got a fire down to the trailer court. Youall reckon we ought to . . .

—If it's mine, let it burn. Ain't nothing there I care about. I need a drink.

But Bert was looking at me, his face twisted with some pointless apprehension that made so little sense that both of us piled into his car, revved the siren, and fishtailed out into Airline Highway, almost smashing into traffic coming from both directions as he humped across the neutral ground and laid thirty yards of rubber getting to the trailer court.

The trailer was in flames from one end to the other. Of course it was Bedlow's. Bert's face was working, and he tried to edge the car close to the end of it where there were the least flames.

—She's back in Alec, I yelled at him. —She's staying in a motel back in Alec. There's nothing in there.

But my eyes snapped from the burning trailer to the stunted and dusty cottonwood tree behind it. Which was where the old station wagon was parked. I could see the tail pipe hanging down behind as I vaulted out of the car and pulled the flimsy screen door off the searing skin of the trailer with my bare hands. I was working on the inside door, kicking it, screaming at the pliant aluminum to give way, to let me pass, when Bert pulled me back. —You goddamned fool, you can't . . .

But I had smashed the door open by then and would have been into the gulf of flame and smoke inside if Bert had not clipped me alongside the head with the barrel of his .38.

Which was just the moment when Bedlow passed him. Bert had hold of me, my eyes watching the trees, the nearby trailers whirling, spinning furiously. Bert yelled at Bedlow to stop, that there was no one inside, an inspired and desperate lie—or was it a final testing.

—She is, I know she is, Bedlow screamed back at Bert.

I was down on the ground now, dazed, passing in and out of consciousness not simply from Bert's blow, but from exhaustion, too long on the line beyond the boundaries of good sense. But I looked up as Bedlow shouted, and I saw him standing for a split second where I had been, his hair the color of the flames behind. He looked very young and strong, and I remember musing in my semiconsciousness, maybe he can do it. Maybe he can.

— . . . And she's got my boy in there, we heard him yell as he vanished into the smoke. Bert let me fall all the way then, and I passed out for good.

VII

It was late afternoon when I got home. It dawned on me that I hadn't slept in over twenty-four hours. Huge white thunderheads stood over the city, white and pure as cotton. The sun was diminished, and the heat had fallen away. It seemed that everything was very quiet, that a waiting had set in. The evening news said there was a probability of rain, even small-craft warnings on the Gulf. Then, as if there were an electronic connection between the station and the clouds, rain began to fall just as I pulled into the drive. It fell softly at first, as if it feared to come too quickly on the scorched town below. Around me, as I cut off the engine, there rose that indescribable odor that comes from the coincidence of fresh rain with parched earth and concrete. I sat in the car for a long time, pressing Bert's handkerchief full of crushed ice against the lump on the side of my head. The ice kept trying to fall out because I was clumsy. I had not gotten used to the thick bandages on my hands, and each time I tried to adjust the handkerchief, the pain in my hands made me lose fine control. My head did not hurt so badly, but I felt weak, and so I stayed there through all the news, not wanting to pass out for the second time in one day, or to lie unconscious in an empty house.

—Are you just going to sit out here? Joan asked me softly.

I opened my eyes and looked up at her. She looked very different. As if I had not seen her in years, as if we had lived separate lives, heights and depths in each that we could never tell the other. —No, I said. —I was just tired.

She frowned when I got out of the car. —What's the lump? And the hands? Can't I go away for a few days?

—Sure you can, I said a little too loudly, forcefully. —Anytime at all. I ran into a hot door.

She was looking at my suit. One knee was torn, and an elbow was out. She sniffed. —Been to a fire sale? she asked as we reached the door.

—That's not funny, I said.

—Sorry, she answered.

The children were there, and I tried very hard for the grace to see them anew, but it was just old Bart and tiny Nan trying to tell me about their holiday. Bart was still sifting sand on everything he touched, and Nan's fair skin was lightly burned. Beyond their prattle, I was trying to focus on something just outside my reach.

Their mother came in with a pitcher of martinis and ran the kids back to the television room. She was a very beautiful woman, deep, in her thirties, who seemed to have hold of something—besides the martinis. I thought that if I were not married and she happened by, I would likely start a conversation with her.

—I ended up taking the kids with me, she said, sighing and dropping into her chair.

—Huh?

—They cried and said they'd rather come with me than stay with Louise. Even considering the ducks and chickens and things.

Hence the sand and sunburn. I poured two drinks as the phone rang. —That's quite a compliment, I said, getting up for it.

—You bet. We waited for you. We thought you'd be coming.

No, I thought as I picked up the phone. I had a gulf of my own. It was Bert. His voice was low, subdued.

—You know what, he was saying, —he made it. So help me Christ, he made it all the way to the back where . . . they were. Can you believe that?

—Did they find . . . ?

Bert's voice broke a little. —Yeah. He was right. You know how bad the fire was . . . but they called down from the state hospital and said she'd taken the baby, child . . . out. Said must have had somebody help . . .

—No, I said, —I didn't, and as I said it I could see Dr. Tumulty rubbing his hands over eighteen years of a certain hell.

—Never mind, listen . . . When the fire boys got back there, it was . . . everything fused. They all formed this one thing. Said she was in a metal chair, and he was like kneeling in front, his arms . . . and they . . . You couldn't tell, but it had got to be . . .

I waited while he got himself back together. —It had got to be the baby she was holding, with Howard reaching out, his arms around . . . both . . .

—Bert, I started to say, tears running down my face. —Bert . . .

—It's all right, he said at least, clearing his throat. There was an empty silence on the line for a long moment, and I could hear the resonance of the line itself, that tiny lilting bleep of distant signals that you sometimes hear. It sounded like waves along the coast. —It really is. All right, he said. —It was like . . . they had, they was . . .

—Reconciled, I said.

Another silence. —Oh shit, he said. —I'll be talking to you sometimes.

Then the line was empty, and after a moment I hung up.

Joan stared at me, at the moisture on my face, glanced at my hands, the lump on my head, the ruined suit. —What happened while I was gone? Did I miss anything?

—No, I smiled at her. —Not a thing.

I walked out onto the patio with my drink. There was still a small rain falling, but even as I stood there, it faded and the clouds began to break. Up there, the moon rode serenely from one cloud to the next, and far down the sky in the direction of the coast, I could see pulses of heat lightning above the Rigolets, where the lake flows into the Gulf.

Keep Them Cards
and Letters Comin' In

—Here's an old-timer, neighbors. It's Ernest Tubb's great hit, "Rainbow at Midnight." All right, Ernie . . .

It was a million miles to the ground and still I could see the sides and bottom of every furrow, each red clod of hardpan—even the brown bugs clambering up their own high hills. I was five and dressed in pants sewn from a Purina sack. My shirt was courtesy of an old muslin pillowcase. It was a million miles to the ground and my father, a country mile away, called to me softly, —Use your heels, boy. Just prod him easy. Just easy, and hold the reins so he has a little slack. He'll go for you. He don't know it's your first . . .

—Christ, Billy Dee was muttering. —I was down at Archangel's last night. Those billies drink like fish. Had some girls out from Fort Worth tryin' to screw their way to the Opry. One little old blond swore to Billy Graham it was her first . . .

My toys were tiny cans, little metal cans just the right size for my hands. Momma taught me how to read them: Garretts Scotch Snuff, Garretts Sweet Snuff. Miz Moseley dipped and even with things close and money tight as a tick, she had to have her snuff. She said there was double pleasure in it for an old widow-woman: the snuff itself and seeing me 'range the brightly labeled little cans like soldiers one time, or like neat cheerful houses in a prosperous town the next. Sometimes I would dig a trench in the bare grassless dust between our shotgun house and Miz Moseley's, and Momma would pour a coffee can full of water into it. Then I could float my snuff cans and sit back chunking pebbles or pieces of rock-hard dirt at them. Above, the sun sat like a high sheriff, his gleaming eye on the little world I had made, called into being. Below, Miz Moseley would sit on her dusty porch and watch absently, wiping reddish sweat from her neck with a bandanna handkerchief, chuckling at everything I did.

—You can't beat the old ones, neighbors. They just don't hardly make 'em like that no more. Now here's Hank. No need to tell you, but I will anyhow. It's "Half as Much."

—Man, you got to be the king of hoke, Billy Dee said to me. His face was gray and pasty-looking. I saw that his hand shook when he tried to light one of his Players Navy Cuts. —What you can't beat is that Fort Worth stuff, he grinned bleakly. He didn't look happy. He looked tired and cross and strung out, and he kept staring out the window of the control room into the dark outer reception room as if he was expecting somebody to turn up. But he didn't. He didn't know anybody more in Los Angeles than I did, and the few people we knew were people we worked with. Not folks.

. . . you only build me up to let me down . . .

When Miz Moseley died, they washed and dressed her and laid her out in her own parlor. All around her coffin there were flowers grown in folks' own yards and everybody who came brought food, and they sat with Bubber Moseley who came over from his job in Birmingham, where he sold shoes in a Baker's store, and T-Tommy, his younger brother, who had worked the place after their daddy died and looked after Miz Moseley and their sister Ruth Ann. Except Ruthie got to running with a bad crowd at the Consolidated School and finally run off with some man she met at a roadhouse up to Bessemer. And about that time T-Tommy got drunk and cursed his brother over their momma's coffin, cursed him and cursed his lost sister and took to cursing everybody and was about to go for some blasphemy when somebody took him off to the bedroom. And Bubber, left behind at the casket with his big, well-manicured hands that fooled with women's ankles all day and smelling of some kind of toilet water, stood looking like a floorwalker in a big city store trying to sell that coffin with his dead mother inside. I remember my mother saying Bubber was embarrassed by all of it. Said he had gone to Birmingham and now he was ashamed of his own people. Said he had got T-Tommy drinking in the first place by saying they should let a funeral home take care of Miz Moseley. —What's a funeral home? I asked, thinking maybe it was like a house where dead people went on living some terrible kind of life. —It's a place where people send dead folks they don't care anything about and let strangers take care of them and make up their faces and pretend to be sad and all. —I wouldn't go to no funeral home, I told her. —You bet your stuffin' you wouldn't, she answered, clasping me to her side and squeezing me hard.

—I still get requests for this one, believe it or not folks. Seems like a new generation's found out about old Tex Williams and "Smoke, Smoke, Smoke."

—That sonofabitch must of made a million off that, Billy Dee said when I had closed the mike. —It don't pay like it used to. Eddy

Arnold, Red Foley, sure. Even Lefty Frizzell and Webb Pierce. But not for a ordinary stiff. Hell, in the old days if you didn't make it to the Opry you could get along on the Hayride. Why they used to nearly throw money at you down in Shreveport. They had this big hot old hole-in-the-wall of a municipal auditorium, but it paid all right. And them girls in Bossier City, why Lord. I remember old Bobby Lynch bought him a piece of Lytton Industries after a run on the Hayride and a year on the road. Just lays back and squints one eye at the ticker tape now, thanking all them crackers in Kentucky and West Virginia, all them Georgia wool-hats and Louisiana coon-asses for setting him up. But it don't pay like that now. Agents, arrangers, union dues, sidemen. Every time you open your mouth to sing, some bastard tries to get his finger in there and feel around for loose gold.

I cued up something by Patsy Cline and shook a Parliament out of the pack. My head still hurt. It felt like it was going to hurt for a long time, and I still had two hours to do.

—Jesus, Billy Dee said, —you never seen anything like the road nowadays. I had me a gig in Texarkana last month and afterward they said they was going to feed me up. They brought in cornbread and sorghum and greens and a big stinking piece of sowbelly. Shit, I liked to of choked to death just looking at it. All those old bastards wearing $50 shirts and $250 suits and string ties and they get together to eat that crap and make like the 1930s was the best time ever. It was some kind of a damn ceremony. I never ate none of that crap since I was sharp enough to come in out of the woods. You ever eat that stuff?

It was bright cold so that your fingers stuck to the iron of the plowshare if you licked them and pressed them against the chill steel and the pasture shone with a million bright diamond chips in that early morning and Poppa said the winter was done, broken, no matter how cold and that it was time and so he had been out three hours already when the sun was full up, leaning into the fresh furrows between Chief and Bolivar, his stringy arms tight, knotted, and the earth breaking open slowly, grudgingly, heaving up and falling back in great chunks before the blade of the plow, the singletree dancing as if it was happy to be on the move again and I could smell the sharp masculine tang of burning hickory coming from the stove back at the house and despite the cold I could see strings of sweat coursing down Poppa's face and when he came back to me at the end of a row he would smile and pause with the reins around his neck and ruffle my hair and I would shiver not only with the cold but with some special kind of love that was mixed with him and the earth and those dumb mules and the sun small and pastel and distant and the million jewels it had strewn across our land. Then Momma would beat on the barrel hoop with her cooking spoon and he would drop the reins and lift me up high as if he was going to throw me at the sun, set me on his shoulder, and I could feel the huge warmth of his body through my thighs as we moved in long strides toward the house, and I could feel the new strength he drew from the freshly turned earth and the sun and the springtime. —No eggs, Momma would say. —But biscuits and side meat. Nice lean meat. —Fine, Poppa would tell her. —Only I wisht you'd git with Miz Robbins and see if'n she wouldn't like to swap off eggs when her hens was a'layin and yours ain't. Why don't you do that? But Momma would act like she didn't hear because she felt somehow it was marked against her if her hens were scarce while Miz Robbins's laid. So we ate and I watched my father's Adam's apple working, his jaws mincing the food, his lips moving as he drew in the grits and wiped his plate with half a biscuit. And I remember thinking that he, my father, was immortal. That he would never sicken and die like Miz Moseley, but go on forever because the land and the sun and those dumb mules needed him. I needed him. I thought that there was a cycle, a web of circumstance between him and the land, a covenant like that between Abraham and the great God, one that would never be ended. I would break out in a silly smile and study my own plate, looking for some sign of my own deathlessness—my own plate with a crowing rooster crude and beautiful painted on it but almost worn away by washing. As if to say that nothing is immortal except the dream of immortality and that passes from generation to generation.

And the biscuits that never rose and the slab of pale meat streaked with reddish brown, running fat which congealed on the rooster, covered him, and over the meat and grits the heavy syrup somebody said came in tank cars all the way from Louisiana and it was all so good and filled me up full and felt inside like the bright spangles of dew all across the sparse grass of the pasture. It was good and even then I knew it was good and there was nothing to do but sing about it, open my child's mouth and make up words to tell myself how lucky I was to be in Sprotts County, Alabama, the son of Tink Miller, but I was seven and had no voice yet and knew no words. But I thought even then God's grace one day I would.

—Yes, I said. —I've eaten it.

—Ain't it the worst?

I felt my soul going and I said nothing. Then I noticed over my own smoke the pungent sweet funky smell of Billy Dee's cigarette. It was not a Players.

—How long you been on that stuff? I asked him.

. . . I go out walkin' after midnight . . .

—I ain't *on* nothin'. It just beefs up the day when you're low. You don't get *on* it. Just helps the world sit up and smile.

I didn't want to argue with him. I didn't have any business arguing with him. What was the difference between his cigarettes and my bottle? My father had not been a drinking man. In a county of hard drinkers and compulsive patent medicine takers, he would not even use aspirin, but would lay down under a tree or on the porch if a headache got past bearing. The body has what the body needs, he would tell us. Just feed it proper, work it regular.

He lived long: outlived all his sons but me. Had pictures in an old cookie tin of those faraway graves: Saipan. Tinian. Le Shima. And with those, other dog-eared pictures of blurred smiling anonymous young men standing at ease, arms akimbo under some vanished alien sun. One with an old-fashioned round helmet on, his eyes lost forever in its shadow, his mouth curled at the corners, one hand almost raised as if, but for the impatient photographer, he would have waived to us. Two other photos almost identical to one another: boys thin and long of shank and forearm, large of hand, dressed in badly fitting khaki, standing almost at attention in front of a large sign, upon which, faded and archaic in its sign painter's detail, there was an eagle, globe, and anchor, and the word QUANTICO. *On the back of one of the pictures was scrawled simply* July 1938. *On the other,* HI FOKES. *Jan 1942. Brothers all I cannot remember as separate people because they had grown up and gone away before as afterthought, as coda, my father and mother got me. They, my brothers, only tall presences who would come from time to time and share a week's meals at long intervals and we—they, usually one at a time, and I—would stare at each other in mute and invincible astonishment, wondering aside from human custom what relationship lay between us. Russell. Pickett. Joseph. They would hold me clumsily on their knees, unsure of what to do, how to entertain a small tow-headed boy whose claim to their affection was flawless, whose presence in this family that had been theirs was some kind of mystery.*

But Russell, who watched and listened and came to understand not only change but probably even growth before he bled and drowned at nineteen in the surf on the beach at Saipan, found me one day in the grove of scratch pine at the top of our piece of land where I was trying to sing about the blue jay who stopped there each noon to jeer and curse at me for a minute's time before he flew off to some greener place. And they all chipped in with Russell and bought me a cheap shiny unutterably beautiful guitar and Pickett, forever distracted, easing his crotch with the side of his hand and

*dreaming of the next bar, the next bus station or truck stop, the next
bleached blond with thirty minutes of heaven between her skinny thighs,
taught me how to tune it, to chord, to play five simple cadences in C and G,
in B-flat and F, paying no mind to my frowns or bitten tongue or clumsy
fingers, staring out over the scarred acres that had fed him, that he would
never work on account of his restlessness and some strange hunger caught
like a sickness from the exhaust of a passing truck and small-town pool-hall
beer—even if he had not been even then on collision course with a destiny
beyond all our worst dreams on an island halfway around the world. But
then paying only an ear's attention to my struggles and cuffing me lightly
when a chord I should have mastered went wrong. —Un-un. G-seventh.
Goddamnit boy, G-seventh.*

—Here, Billy Dee said, offering me one of his smokes out of the
Players box. —Take you to the West Indies and back in ten minutes.
Give you something to tell them pone-eaters who listen to you.

—No thanks, I told him, reaching under the turntable for my
pint.

—Oh, he grinned. —The milk train. Don't you like the express?

—Sure, I lied. —Only when I'm working I got to stay on the local.

Billy Dee was reading some of yesterday's mail. It was always
pretty sad. Letters from retired railroad men, widowers, or old
bachelors who had thought to leave the cold of Kentucky or Missouri or Tennessee when they had done their thirty years, who had
heard always of California, the golden land. Letters from old ladies
whose sons had brought them from Fort Payne, Alabama, to Oak-
land, from Forbing, Louisiana, to San Jose. Lord God, the distances. From Andromeda to the edge of the Milky Way. But I read
every one and sometimes I would feel a passing chill as it seemed I
was reading a letter from Momma or Poppa. Or Miz Moseley.

—Chee-rist, Billy Dee guffawed. —How can you stand it? Listen:

> . . . come from nice people to this place were no body knos the
> Bible and Jesus Name is taken I dont kno a thing to say or do
> every thing is upside down my boy says you go to church they
> get the rong idea if it wasnt for yore music I belive I would just
> go down in my bed and not rise agin God bless you I remember
> when you made Victrola record of have a little talk with Jesus it
> done every body home so much good . . .

—Ain't that a shame? You just can't turn 'em on, Billy Dee said.
—Every goddamned one of 'em misses the pea patch. They all half-
starved and fretted over the spades votin' and how the highways

was cuttin' up farms, and now somebody hands it all to 'em and they . . .

—Cut it out, I snapped, and opened the mike. —Yes, neighbors, it's a nice cool Sunday mornin'. Why you could hoe an acre and not raise a sweat back home. Time to patch that harness before church meetin' time, I bet. Keep you reminded, here's Red Foley and "Just a Closer Walk with Thee."

I flipped off the mike and skewed the record on its way, feeling some sudden wash of fever pour through my mind from a corner of memory I could not even discover, flush out into the open field of consciousness.

—Man, Billy Dee said, —you're something else. How do you keep it up? Go out and put away a lobster thermidor and then come in here and lay that country shit on them. I just don't see how you can do it.

I closed my eyes and wondered not so much how I did it, which did not matter since the doing was not even conscious any longer, but something like chording an old tune. I wondered why I did it and why, even doing it, I did not break free from between these turntables, knock him down and stomp him, hurt him bad with his pasty face and his funny cigarettes and his loud hurtful mouth. Then I remembered that my last record was six years old and had done no better than the two before, and that for the distance of a thousand miles—no, two thousand—Billy Dee was the only living creature who would walk half a block to see me, and that even two thousand miles away there was nothing much but a slow spreading stain of cheap subdivision houses on what had been my father's land and a used car lot plumb in the middle of the vanished pines where once a blue jay had warned me.

—Here's another jewel, Billy Dee giggled:

> . . . never knew what it was to cry a tear but last spring my dear wife passed on to glory and that doctor in Bakersfield said well you got to take it like a man. But it was almost ten years ago I was last what you could call a man and I can't take it so good. I go down to the cemetery and fool with a few flowers and remember back in El Dorado listening to your little string band down out of Memphis. I wish to sweet Jesus I could take hold of that day again, maybe live just one tune . . .

—Wants you to play one of your old ones, Billy Dee finished. —Man, what a case.

—They're all dying, I said finally. —You get to feeling like a

hospital orderly up here. Make the patient's last hours bearable.
Why the hell do you sing?

—Hell, a song is a song. I mean it ain't anything hokey about
singing how I lost my girl.

—Last girl you lost was because you wouldn't pay for her abortion, I told him. He grinned, sucked on his cigarette and held the
smoke in his lungs for a long moment, then exhaled it slowly.

—Gonna make a song out of that, too. Be another couple of years
and they'll let you play a song about that.

—I shrugged. —Probably right. Maybe sooner than that.

—Well, live and let live, he smiled, dumb with narcotic pleasure.
—You got a bag to fill, just like me. We all got to make it. You hear
about Slim Cupples?

—What?

—In hard at Bakersfield. Seems they found him with some little
kid. Son of the International Harvester representative. How about
that? Floppin' your sponsor's kid. It ain't no end to it, is there? Poor
old Slim.

*My father lay on the pallet near the front door because it was cooler there
of an evening and I would sit beside him and strum a tune, sometimes sing,
mostly old gospel songs: "There Will Be Peace in the Valley," "What a Friend
We Have in Jesus." His eyes were enormous now and his body wasted away
until his legs looked like fleshless branches, like the legs on one of those
prison-camp inmates they had just found in Dachau or Ravensbruck. He
was feverish always now and since he would not take the medicine, the
narcotic which the doctor prescribed, which my Nashville money could
buy, sometimes he would break for a moment and scream, curse his pain and
the dry red soil and the stunted trees and the penurious cotton going to weed
in our fields for lack of his hands. Curse the Lord God for the uselessness of
it and then, remembering another harvest gone wrong, he would burst into
tears for Russell and Pickett and Joseph, for all our weedy flesh and for his
pain. I would try to ignore him then because it was not a thing to be noticed
between us, but I could feel a great void opening inside me, a gigantic and
immeasurable chasm bridged only by his breath, by the sharp bitter sound
of his hurting, and I imagined that when he was done dying I would turn
slowly to stone—not die myself, but turn into granite, my own soul neither
damned nor saved but simply drained of the moisture, the sun, the soil of its
living, its moving replaced with some adamantine composition, asphalt or
concrete, until at last, like the Sphinx, I would stare mute and mindless out
of stone eyes over the ages with nothing inside but the barest fading memory
of his huge agony, my unknown brothers' baroque sacrifices, the plaintive*

piddling sound of some talentless hand searching the chords of a song about Jesus and his love. All that and two white mules.

In the back room, my mother lay in stupor. She had borne a great deal, but Poppa's slow dying was too much and I had come home not only to see to him but to cook and keep things decent as she would have had them had there been anything left in her able to resist time and loss and the simple unnamed destructive operations of the world. She lay in their old bed, eyes almost as wide as his, listening, ears tuned not simply to his occasional cries but to the most hidden cracked music of his breathing. As if when it ended, so would her vigil and her life—which had been no more—no less—than a vigil anyhow.

But it was not that way. Because when he died, she rose from her bed to see to him, to help me close his eyes and wash him and ease his thin bunched limbs. And what killed her like a bolt of Jehovah's wrath was not his dying, but the decision of the county coroner's office that my father could not be buried on our place, could not be laid to rest in the earth he had farmed, from which he had drawn the stuff of all our lives, from whence he had sent three boys to die defending after all not some mythical United States that none of us cared about, but that very piece of land now denied him. They said he would have to be buried in a cemetery called Souls Rest on the outskirts of town where a machine dug his grave and a man with studied woe in his face pushed a lever to lower the coffin into the alien earth, soil paid for with that worthless Nashville money and sanctified with Souls Rest Inc.'s promise of perpetual care. Between a lawyer who had built supermarkets all over Alabama and a woman from New Jersey whose husband had left her there when he was transferred to Chicago.

—You ever hear from Hazel? Billy Dee asked, trying to seem casual.

—No, I told him. —No, I never hear a thing.

—Somebody saw her in Houston, he began.

—That right?

—Said she was talking marriage with some guy worked for Al Parker Buick. Top salesman in the Southwest last year . . . said he.

I can stand the drinkin' and I can even stand the girls once in a while but I can't stand the people you drag in here and I ain't even goin' to try. It's one thing puttin' up with you stoned and its one thing hearin' from someone that you crawled in and out of every bed in Little Rock and Tulsa. But I be goddamned if I'm goin' to put Willard Jenkins to bed with him throwin' up all over me or feelin' me up, and I be double-goddamned to hell if I'll get up and cook breakfast for Bill Slater's sluts when I know his wife and kept the kids for her last week.

It was that way with Hazel and me almost from the first. I had met her and married her in Savannah playing at some county fair or other and her idea of the good life was to pull together a few dollars and crawl up in the red-dirt Georgia hills somewhere and drag the road in after her. Wanted chickens and a hog. Wore cotton drawers and dresses off the rack of whatever general store we passed by. Liked to buy quilts along the road and stop and drink apple cider in southern Virginia at those run-down stands. She had the body of some Hollywood starlet, but there was no way of telling her that the old days were over and that good or bad a man—or a woman either—has got to stay up with things. Not because he wants to but because there just isn't any kind of place back in the hills where they can't reach in and lay the arm on you, tax you or draft you or talk you into buying a new Pontiac or at least offer you twenty-six weeks between Cincinnati and Columbia. I told her I was a musician, not a dirt farmer. What else could I be? They had laid a tar cover over my father's land and it was no use planting a crop somewhere else. And she said —That's nice. I like music just fine. And she probably did. But what she didn't like, couldn't even come to stand, was the life that goes with music, the whiskey and the hours and the traveling and the kind of easy way that goes with the music or maybe even makes it possible for a man to sing the same song a thousand times as if he meant the words and was discovering again every turn and deep in the music itself. I loved her and I loved those hills, but there wasn't anything back in the country but rusting trucks up on blocks and a handful of old shriveled-up croppers, black and white, who worked cheaper than machines, collapsing cotton houses and zany copper-turreted churches like the one I had buried Poppa and Momma out of. I didn't like the way things were any more than her, but you can't go back. There is no way on God's earth to go back. You got to go on, and on was Nashville and Chicago and the West Coast. Country music wasn't some kind of religious society. It had got to be big business and business people have got their own ways. If you want to be in business, you got to go along. So I forget what night at which party Hazel just walked out. I can't remember. I just remember that I woke up the next morning with this girl from Pensacola who wanted to audition for a show out of Corpus Christi and I told her, trying to figure where Hazel had got to, that I would see what I could do.

—Hey, folks, have you tried the chili that's *all* beef? Till you've tried Longhorn chili, you've been getting shortchanged on the meat side. Unless youall are vegetarians, don't let 'em sell you beans when you pay for beef. Make sure next time it's Longhorn chili—the *all*-meat chili. And talking about getting what you pay for, here's a dish bound to be to your taste. Eddy Arnold and a golden record. It's "Anytime."

—My God, Billy Dee croaked, shaking his head and staring out into the empty reception room again. Then he looked at me and I returned his stare, swallowing a little whiskey. My head was still hot and getting a little fuzzy. The whiskey felt fine going down though, so I was all right. I was just fine.

—I just don't see how you do it, he began again.

—I do it, you dumb bastard, because I want to eat and don't want to heft a spade. 'Cause I'm not still on the gravy train like you. 'Cause the rubes like an old hand at the mike even when there ain't enough of them paying 98 cents a record to keep him singing. On account of I got nowhere to go and nothing to do but this.

—Listen, he began angrily, putting out his cigarette.

—Listen your ass. I got to listen to this damned country music. I got to read those letters so I can acknowledge some of them on the air and be sure of one or two listeners listening to me listening. I got to hear myself romancing about that swill they call chili. But I don't have to listen to you.

He was on his feet swaying, looking sicker, even more pallid than before. Then he got hold of himself. He remembered the distance between us. He remembered the edge he had and he tried to grin. But the pot had gone bad on him and my whiskey had only given me what passed for a spine. He had one kind of edge. I had another, and no poor sonofabitch that ever spent him a weekend in hell would have swapped places with either one of us.

—Why do you reckon I come by? he asked slowly, as if I might not understand his words.

—'Cause you just got to shoot the shit with somebody, and no-body not trapped behind a couple of turntables is going to sit still and listen to you.

He raised his head and shook it slowly. —I come by 'cause I thought it might be nice to play like you was still alive, like you still mattered. It was a kindness made me come by.

I stared dead in his eyes. He still had that sick diseased grin like what you might see on a calf or a wolf dead six or eight days. I thought probably considering the shape he was in I could take him easy, throw him down the steps, and make that do in place of living for a week or two. Then I thought, even now I'm not gone that far. Not quite. Pretty soon, but not just yet.

—I won't bother you no more, he was saying stiffly, trying for a dignity that neither of us could muster. —I won't . . .

He managed to get to the door then and, turning, holding tightly to the jamb, he studied me as the record on the turntable played out.

—It's a shame about you and Hazel, he said. —Real shame. She was one fine piece of ass.

He was gone before I could stumble out into the dark reception room, and I thought, you ought to have let him have it while you could. It was stupid to hold back. But then I almost fell down, managed to get back to the console and segued into another record without opening the mike. I laid my head against the cold metal of the engineering panel. In front of my eyes the volume needle danced mindlessly to music I could not hear and I watched as it ticked off space and time, Alabama and Nashville, Hazel and a handful of brown-edged photos. When at last it subsided and I opened the mike, I felt better because I could feel no worse. The next sip of whiskey would go down like blessed velvet.

—Yes folks, it's a long way home but your smilin' country boy brings it a little closer every cotton-pickin' morning. Just stay tuned for that old-time music. And whatever you do, you got to keep them cards and letters comin' in.

Every Act Whatever of Man

I

It was his habit to come to the courthouse early when he had business there. He would nod to the janitor as the large ancient doors opened, and then, the rising sun behind him, he would walk up and down the silent shadowed corridor, a dog run with offices, chambers, and courtrooms off to either side.

When he had a trial, he would do the last-minute acts of mental construction at this time, search out the questions to be asked that he had not discovered yet. On those days, he would pace rapidly through the shadows, hardly noticing the dark obscure portraits of long-dead judges that adorned the walls along the corridor or even noticing later the growing number of lawyers and functionaries as they came in to begin their day. Not until his opponent, or the clerk of the court where he was to try, came up to him would he cease his pacing and look up, distracted, to see that the sun was high and it was time to work.

Other times, when there was no trial, he would go to five o'clock mass in the tiny Church of the Holy Redeemer, and then, Christ upon him, would pace the courthouse corridor, rosary in hand, his thoughts not religious in the common sense, but pieced together out of almost seventy-five years of life, fifty at the law. His study was Christendom, that long wave of meaning which had reached from Jerusalem to Byzantium, from Aachen to St. Stephanie, Louisiana. He would remember his father, a sorrowful mystery, blurred by forty years gone. He would remember the town when vegetable carts and a butcher shop had done his family and friends for a supermarket. There had been a time when young people stayed in St. Stephanie, or, leaving, spent a year or two or three in New Orleans, came back to marry and begin a family, telling no one anything of that Carthage to the east where, in the Quarter, souls were lost and sin lapped at the steps of St. Louis Cathedral, like water from the Mississippi, against levees which often did not hold.

He would consider what it meant to serve the law, to bring a poor man's suit, and walk away afterward, some small piece of justice done. He would think of what he had seen on the late news: terror, assassination, acts of vengeance, things so foul that their like had never been seen in this courthouse and, God willing, never would be.

It was as if he were forging a new rosary, one other than that handed to St. Dominic. One no less mysterious or laden with grace, but one in which the great hierophantic events in the life of the Savior were replaced with the happenings of the day. He would consider the little girl raped, killed, her body dismembered and thrown into the river there at New Orleans. And as he considered, he would recite a decade of the rosary for the repose of that small soul, but even more for her family and loved ones who even then must be suffering an agony which the child in her innocence was far beyond.

Or he would reflect on the priests who deserted their calls—a decade to bring them faith and return of grace again. Or he would remember his very special intention: those children destroyed by abortion, whose half-formed bodies and slumbering souls had been, by the millions, given over to a holocaust as violent, vicious—and legal—as that of the Nazis against God's Chosen Ones.

Sometimes a groan would escape him as he paced.

—Sir, the janitor might say. —Mr. Journe, is something wrong?

He would come to himself then, smile, shake his head, slip his rosary into his pocket, still keeping hold of the bead he was telling, and go on pacing as the sun rose on another day in the courts.

That morning, as he paced, a young clerk came up to him quietly. —Mr. Journe, Judge Soniat would like to see you. . . .

He looked up. Michael Soniat here at this hour? He glanced at his watch. It was barely seven-thirty, two and a half hours before court. He walked behind the young clerk, whose name he did not know— there were so many nowadays, they came and went so quickly. It was just before he reached the oaken door of the judge's chamber that he lost count of his beads.

II

Miss Lefebre put down her copy of *Screen Stars* with the picture of Jack Nicholson on the cover. The old man had moved—or was it that the rhythm of his breathing had changed perceptibly? Or was it simply that they had the monitor set absurdly high again. Anyhow, that shrill high keening hurt her head, and she reached over and pushed the button that silenced it. Then she looked at the old man.

He was large. Not fat, but wide and fleshy. Even lying there, he gave the illusion of strength, each of his hands as large as both of hers put together. His face was flushed with that appearance of bogus health you come to recognize, even expect, in the terminally ill. His eyes were open. Not staring, as is so often the case with patients in coma, but simply looking out at the far wall where some pious old lady had insisted they hang a crucifix. It was as if he were giving minute and indefatigable scrutiny to that image of wood and plaster, seeking its meaning, trying to penetrate its accidents, that he might discover the essence within or beyond, wherever essences reside.

Miss Lefebre smoothed the bedclothes out of habit, though the old man, paralyzed and motionless, had not disturbed them. There was, beyond the facade of professionalism which the LSU nursing school had given her, some feeling for old people like him. Alone, dying inch by inch, kept alive by the virtuoso mechanics and electronics of the doctors. It was, she thought, following the old man's eyes, always the young doctors who ordered the machine hookups in cases like this. And she thought she knew why. The old doctors had made their peace with death. They had seen worse than death. Perhaps, beyond that, they believed that death was, for all its horror, a gateway, an ending in which a new beginning was implicit. The young doctors believed in nothing whatever but their own skill and their capacity to develop new machines, new techniques to press death back farther and farther.

The old man's lips moved, and Miss Lefebre was mildly surprised. Then she heard a deep grating sound so harsh and elemental that it seemed to be coming from the very walls of the hospital room. It took her several seconds to realize that it was a human voice. —Ah, Mrs. Baxter, the voice said, —must not hate, and surely must not study on revenge. Time is short, and the Lord . . . put that girl out of your mind . . . make a good act of contrition. . . .

III

George Slack was sitting on the back porch eating a cantaloupe. It was chilled, tangy, and sweet. He looked out over the yard past the swimming pool, down toward the somnolent river where his power boat was moored. He was in a state of unthinkingness, simply appreciating what there was, and what he had of it. He tried not to think of Amy, because he would not see her until Wednesday. He could never see her on weekends, of course, and even during the week it wasn't smart to simply plan meeting at a bar—much less a local motel.

Now he was thinking of her, thinking of her eyes, her casual laughter. The way she responded to him. She was the girl he should have met thirty years before. If he had stayed in New Orleans, taken the job with the wholesale coffee distributors there on Decatur Street . . . by now . . .

For some reason, as he set down his spoon, he looked at his hands. They were the hands of a man moving deep into the wrong end of middle age, liver-spotted, the flesh drying, showing veins and tendons clearly, as if the skin were becoming transparent, a palimpsest upon which each year etched additional lines.

My God, George Slack thought with a sudden shock. I'm dying inch by inch. Pieces of me are sloughing off, veins clouding up. It's really true. He closed his eyes, because it was embarrassing even to think silently that way. As if he had not been taught always that life was a passing shadow pointed toward eternity, toward that other life which would never end.

Even now, he could remember Father O'Malley hearing cate-chism in the parochial school, and he remembered, too, that of all his classmates he was most attentive, most anxious to know his whole duty and to hear the promises of God. Because, in those days, he had feared death very much. He had lost his father and mother in an automobile wreck, had been raised by his mother's sister, and he had believed somehow, for no certain reason, that the death which had claimed his parents that rain-swept evening in 1936 was await-ing him, too, a curse not to be put off, but to be completed at last by his own death.

So he had been devout for several years. Perhaps it had been the beginning of the Second War that had convinced him of the com-monness of death, that he had no special rendezvous with it, and that in fact the mystifications of the Church had little or nothing to do with a natural phenomenon which came in time to all things born on the earth.

He had tried to talk about it to Father O'Malley. The war was on then, and the regular baseball coach for the high school team had enlisted in the Marines. (He would not be back. He would vanish like smoke while on a patrol deep into the jungles of Guadalcanal with the Second Marine Division, only to arise once more as a gold star and a blue, white, and red diamond-shaped patch dotted with stars in the trophy case of the St. Stephanie high school, that and a slightly blurred photo from years before, when he had been young and lean—his first year coaching—before the beer and crawfish, fried chicken and andouille had gotten to him.) So Father O'Malley knocked out flies and grounders, squinted at the infield play, and explained to the boys how baseball was a figure of life itself, and that to win at either called for discipline, strength, skill, and faith.

—Yeah, one of the older boys nodded cynically, —but in life, if they catch you far enough off base, they kill you.

Father O'Malley had fixed the boy with his large beautiful brown eyes, started to say something, and then let it go. It was the spring of 1943, and kids were talking differently. Especially if they were reaching draft age about graduation time.

After practice, he had walked back to the rectory of the church with the priest. It was that strange moment between daylight and twilight he had always called "the yellow moment," when, for perhaps five minutes, all things—trees, houses, cars, even people—are touched by a tone of rich deep yellow, a tone from the pallet of some Flemish master.

When he had told Father O'Malley of his doubts, the priest had laughed. Not in a casual way to indicate unconcern, but a rich deep laughter as old and wise and affectionate as the priesthood itself. He had put his arm around George Slack's shoulders.

—How old are you now, boy?

—Seventeen, Father.

—Well, that's old enough. Old enough to be fighting for your country in a few months.

—Yes, Father.

—There's something I meant to tell you one day. Later, I thought. But the Lord picks his time for these things. How much do you recall about the accident?

—The . . . accident. I remember I was at home, waiting. It got late. A state trooper brought Aunt Grace . . . then I went to stay with . . .

—Ah, and you never saw them again?

—They . . . closed the coffins. I never . . .

—I was at the hospital that night. When they brought your mother and father from Madisonville. . . .

—You saw . . . ?

Father O'Malley hunched his shoulders and they walked on. It was twilight now, and the edges of things had started to blur and run. Ahead, he could see the bulk of the church and the small rectory beside it. The cross on top of the church was outlined against the pink and gray clouds, the crimson and gold streaks of last light even then fading from the sky.

—Your mother was . . . They . . . She was gone. But your father . . .

—He was . . . alive . . . ? They always told me they were . . . both . . . instantly . . .

—Ah, well, what do you say to a ten-year-old boy, Georgie? Do you give an exact report on the terrible thing that . . .

—No. No. I guess you . . . make it easy. . . .

—With no way to make it easy. But you don't add weight to the cross he has to bear. . . .

They had reached the rectory. Old Mrs. Wise, long dead now, had fixed hot chocolate while they moved into Father O'Malley's study. It was dark and quiet there, only a single small lamp on the battered old desk. The walls were solid with bookcases filled with crumbling leather volumes whose titles were undecipherable. A window was open, and the chill spring breeze blew in, adding sharpness to the scent of old leather and incense that seemed part of the structure of the room. The chocolate came, and George Slack had put his fielder's glove down between his feet and sipped the hot brew, waiting for what Father O'Malley would say, dreading when he should begin.

Father O'Malley picked up a blackened pipe, which was almost invisible in the soft light from the study lamp.

—Ah, he had only a few minutes. He was in much pain. He spoke of you, of your dear mother. Then, because we both knew he had somewhere to be, he made his confession. And I had hardly done with absolution, but he was gone. That easily, Georgie. It was a fine noble man's kind of death, you know?

The tears had come, but they did not flow, and he had hardly heard the homily the priest addressed to him on a Christian death, using as text that of his own father. After a while, he had risen, thanked Father O'Malley, and left. Only weeks later he had graduated, joined the Army Air Corps, and spent a year of horror in the skies over Germany and central Europe.

George Slack came to himself, the emptied cantaloupe before him, his hands gripping the edge of the table. Something had called him back. It was a sound in the kitchen. Elizabeth came into the breakfast room, her arms loaded with flowers. It's spring again, he thought. Thirty-three years on. His wife smiled at him. She still possessed that dark almost Latin prettiness—what they used to call a "languishing" quality—that had drawn him to her long ago. But now it required effort on her part. She worked at it, and still the patching showed. There were no liver spots on her hands. Her waist was still small, but her eyes seemed to have grown smaller, more deeply seated. There was a look of wornness, wisdom, about her. She looked . . . kindly, now. As one who would, whatever the circumstances, do her duty. Christ, he thought, it's happening to her, too. And I don't care. I don't give a goddamn. I just . . . want to see Amy.

—For Father O'Malley, Elizabeth said, almost brightly.

—He won't see them, George said, and felt a flush come to his cheeks. He wasn't that kind of person. He didn't *want* to be that kind of person. He wanted to be decent—with Elizabeth, with the old priest he had not spoken to in almost thirty years, with his daughter, Jill—with everyone but Amy. With her, he wanted to be indecent. Constantly.

Elizabeth looked away, and went on arranging the flowers. —It would be nice if you . . . wanted to visit. . . .

—It would be pointless. I haven't seen him . . . I don't go to his church. . . .

—He is . . . part of St. Stephanie. If he had tended your car for fifty years . . . if he were a gardener who had seen to your yard for fifty years . . .

Her eyes were wide now, and he wondered if the anger was simply a response to his impiety, his lack of decorum. He wondered if she could possibly know anything, feel anything. The waning of his emotion had not snapped the bond between them. She *could* know—without knowing that she knew.

—You'll have to appear decent, whether you want to or not. Jill took my car. She had some errands to run for Dr. Aronson. Then she's going to pick up Amy and bring her back for the weekend. Some young men are taking them to Baton Rouge . . . an auto race or . . .

He got up from the table, dropping his napkin.

—You'll have to drop me by the hospital . . . at least that.

He turned toward her, his face filled with an unfelt and unintended irony. —I can do . . . at least that, he said.

IV

—Morning, Walter, Judge Soniat said, looking up from his desk.

—Mike, I never knew you to be an early riser, Walter Journe said, sitting down, looking about for Miss Althea, who always presided at pretrials and other meetings, presenting the lawyers with steaming mugs of the thickest, blackest coffee in south Louisiana.

—She's not here, Walt. She came real early, brewed it, and left. Fix your own. First time in thirty years. Won't kill you.

—Want a little freshening? he asked the judge, who nodded.

He poured the coffee, leaving Judge Soniat's black, considering some cream for his own.

From behind him, he could hear Soniat rustling through papers.

—You heard about the old man, Walt?

—What? Ah, Father O'Malley, of course.

—Like someone discovering the timbers they built this town on, and chopping one down.

—Yes. My God, do you know he's been here, has been seeing to people . . . how long?

—Nineteen-twenty-seven. In the spring. You aren't that much older than I am, son.

—Served in the Great War, didn't he?

— . . . from the Irish Channel. Told me once he came home with the stink of men's blood on him, and never got free of it or slept a night through until he . . .

— . . . entered the seminary. Said he'd lie or cheat, steal or blaspheme before he'd hurt another of God's creatures again.

They sat, the rising sun cutting a golden path between them on the judge's desk. The steam from their coffee rose in the sunlight, twisting, flattening as the breeze moved it here and there.

Judge Soniat pushed a blue and yellow box of cigars toward him. Journe reached in, took out a long slender stogie. Marsh-Wheeling. Since 1840. One of those things you come to expect. Part of the weather—like great Gulf clouds, magnolias and jasmine and gardenias in the spring. Things you count on.

—He's got no people, Walt. Nobody. His only heir will be the diocese.

—You have his will?

—Drew it up in 1940. Never wanted anything changed. Church gave him everything. Wants to give it back.

—Is there . . . any . . . chance?

—Not a goddamned one. Spoke to old Aronson last evening. Says the sooner the better. Stroke destroyed his brain. The cognitive and operative sections are gone. Just like an explosion in there. . . .

—How long . . . ?

The judge shrugged. —Can't say. When he came in, one of the young residents put him on the machines, you know. Worked like a beaver to keep him breathing. Damned kids. They're so bright. Smart as hell. . . .

Journe smiled. —But, you're thinking, maybe they could use some judgment?

—I don't know. What am I supposed to say? I'm just a country judge, Walt. Father O'Malley is . . . what?

—Eighty. Maybe a year or so more. . . .

Soniat got up from his desk, scratched his uncombed gray hair. He laughed without humor. —You know, goddamnit, he married Mary Ann and me. And he was there when . . .

—I remember . . .

—Used to go up to the . . . house every two weeks with us until Michael Junior died.

Journe remembered the small boy he had seen only twice, once as a newborn, once in his coffin. He had been an extreme mongoloid. He had died in the East Louisiana Hospital of an infection. It was not uncommon.

Soniat's voice was blurred. —He didn't have to go up there. . . . Said Mike was one of his parishioners, too. Said God never, never gave us a burden we couldn't bear. Proved it. Showed it to us. Made his own teaching flesh.

The judge sat down again. He was silent for a long time. Then he passed a legal-sized sheet of paper over to Journe.

—It's an order ready for my signature. I want you to take over as curator. I don't want to give this one to some kid out of LSU or Tulane. . . .

Journe nodded. You give these small jobs to the youngsters, ordinarily. It gets them before the court, and they pick up seventy-five dollars here, a hundred there. It is what lawyers do. But sometimes even a simple task has overtones, becomes a ceremony. Judge Soniat would not hand over Father O'Malley to some young man who did not know him, had perhaps never seen his face.

—I called the chancery in New Orleans, told them what the situation was. Said they'd send someone over . . . his confession, if he can. Last rites, anyhow. . . .

—And the church . . . ?

—Oh, they'll have visiting priests for a while. . . . Do you remember . . . ?

—Barely. It seems like he was always here.

—No, before him was an old German priest . . . had served with the Union army in the Confederate War . . . used to preach the evils of rebellion . . . old bastard. . . .

—You can't remember that. . . .

—Oh, I remember him. I most especially remember my father telling him one Sunday after mass that good Southern people didn't require political education from . . . a Hun. . . .

They both laughed.

—My God, in those days . . .

—My mother knew we were all in for excommunication . . . but they sent Father O'Malley instead. His first sermon . . .

—That I do remember, somehow. How he was the son of rebellious people himself, and understood those deep passions. . . .

— . . . spoke of the Easter Rising, compared it with the War . . . people, rightly or wrongly, put upon too long. . . .

—And then saying that, at last, only resurrection, not insurrection, could cure the anguish of proud people—a rising against sin, weakness, the flesh. . . .

They were still again.

—I'll be goddamned if I can figure remembering a sermon from . . . what . . . ?

—Almost fifty years ago, Journe said smiling.

Soniat smiled, too, as he signed the order. —And they say old men can't remember.

—Oh, Michael, Journe said, rising slowly. —We remember just fine. What we want to remember.

V

Dr. Amadeus Aronson had finished his breakfast in the hospital cafeteria. Now he would walk out on the grounds for fifteen minutes or so. Then it would be time for rounds. Sometimes he was tired, already irritable before any silly ass on the staff gave him reason. It had to do with certain pains he could not be rid of, and which would not kill him. Minor arthritic changes. Where they hurt.

He took one step onto the porch, surveyed the old oaks and magnolias that surrounded the hospital. He was proud of them. Twenty years ago, when the hospital board had obtained this plantation land from the Callais estate, the architects had wanted to clear out all the old trees—"a solidly modern appearance" was what was wanted. Dr. Aronson had pointed out that it was much easier to replace insensitive architects than hundred-year-old trees. He had made his point, and now there was hardly a window in the complex from which patients could not see trees which had been planted long before they were born, and which would outlive them. Perhaps that was the essence of what he had wanted to say through his practice: the continuity of generations. Birth eases death as death heals birth. If a man sees himself in perspective, life should be a joy. He is a partner in the festival of being, an invited guest along with his fellows, society, the cosmos. Under God.

It was then that Miss Lefebre found him.

—Doctor, the old . . . Father O'Malley . . .

Dr. Aronson turned quickly. —Is he . . . changed?

—He's . . . Doctor, he's talking.

Dr. Aronson snorted. The help you get nowadays. —That, Miss . . . what's your name?

—Lefebre, Doctor. Amy Lefebre.

—That, Miss Lefebre, is impossible. His speech centers were destroyed by the cardiovascular accident. He cannot move. He cannot talk. He is not conscious, despite his eyes remaining open. You heard someone in the hall.

The young nurse was very pretty. She was, in fact, exceptional. Dr. Aronson found it hard to believe he had not noticed her. But what was she saying?

— . . . made my report. I invite the doctor to come examine his patient who is not only talking, but who will not shut up, and who is even imitating other people's voices. . . .

Dr. Aronson reached out for Miss Lefebre's arm, pulled her close, sniffed her breath—which was very sweet—glanced at her arms, stared into her eyes, and thumped her gingerly on the elbow with his finger. She jumped. He studied for a further moment. —I'll come, he said.

VI

Miss Casey Lacour was president of the Ladies Altar Society of Holy Redeemer Church. As such, she was the acknowledged liaison between Father O'Malley and the ladies of the congregation. It was her task to carry back to the others his wishes regarding the decoration of the church and such other ancillary matters as were the responsibilities of the Altar Society.

She had served for almost twenty years. Not so much because she was beloved as that she had the time and the willingness to see to details, while the other ladies simply offered an afternoon here or some money there. Miss Lacour took her work seriously. She had virtually memorized the liturgical year, and as years drew on, she came to know what the priest wished on Easter, on Christmas, at Pentecost. She knew which feasts he regarded as significant, and which of less importance.

Miss Lacour had spent numberless afternoons with Father O'Malley. Indeed, she had made the nine First Fridays each and every time they had been offered, so that the treasury of graces she had stored up was inestimable. She had been the solid center of support for every novena and vigil at Holy Redeemer for thirty years, and no morning mass had been celebrated without her presence in almost that long.

Now she was desolate. Since Monday, she had divided her waking hours between the silent empty church and the waiting room of the hospital. She had tried by prayer to maintain her closeness to Father O'Malley, who wandered now in a limbo between life and death, and to blot out from her memory the awful events that had suddenly torn asunder the fabric of her life. Somehow, she had not expected this. She had supposed that one day her life would end amid the physical and spiritual furniture she had so carefully collected and lovingly arranged. At such cost. For so long.

She had envisioned the end of her life in many ways: as she placed, so early on Easter morning, a last perfect lily in a vase before the statue of Christ risen, there would be a moment of hazy forgetfulness, and she would find herself standing in fact before the Holy Redeemer she had so long served. All the sacrifice and grace that had been hers on earth now compacted into that symbolic lily she held out to Him. He would smile and receive it, and her eternity would begin.

Or it would be during confession. There in the darkness, she would be reciting to Father O'Malley the threshold sins of pride, anger, covetousness that were the curse of involvement with the Altar Society ladies who, individually, sowed so little and yet wished to reap all. Then she would reach the Great Sin once more. She would recite what had happened that spring day in 1944 still again, whispering it breathlessly from yet another vantage point, trying to explain to the distant and momentarily impersonal spirit of love and understanding on the other side of the grate that forgiveness was not, could not be perfected until the discovery was complete, until the confessing was done.

And Father O'Malley would say to her, sighing, —Casey, Casey, it is all done when the will moves forever away from its sinful object. When the heart turns around, it is forgiven. Now you must learn to give up that afternoon, all the wrongful ecstasy and the awful guilt of it. It will never be April 21st of 1944 again. Not in all eternity. The young man is dead; the child is dead, never lived, indeed. It is forgiven. . . .

And she would die then, feel her soul drift out from her old unrealized indifferent body, feel the chill of time and space evaporating, the essence of herself, which was ageless and eyeless, longing for eternity and light. Then she would reach the downs, a field in Sussex in April while the invasion was preparing, and he would be there, and it would happen again, only untainted by flesh and the curse of earth, and she would be ashamed of nothing because sin, *that* sin, is of the flesh only, and whatever else, there would be no windblown dark November following, no sudden letter announcing the end of April dreams turned to blood and death in the hedgerows. But most of all, beyond all else, no rush of terror, no trip to London to the small hospital in Wigmore Street. No, not in death. Nor the boat trip home, the time in New York and New Jersey, where in her desperation . . .

Miss Lacour opened her eyes. She had not been sure whether she would find herself in the small pew before the side altar of Holy Redeemer or sitting in the quiet waiting room of the hospital. It was the hospital, and she saw Dr. Aronson moving rapidly down the hall toward Father O'Malley's room, his face dark and concerned. She rose and followed him quickly. She tried to speak to him, but he didn't even hear her soft voice. He entered the room and, almost without thought, she followed him. A young nurse was with him, and as Miss Lacour stood in the shadows at the back of the room, the doctor and the young nurse moved close to the bed where Father O'Malley lay. The doctor examined him closely, shining a small flashlight into his open eyes. He checked the vital signs, then read the chart quickly. For a moment, there was no sound in the room at all. Then Dr. Aronson spoke, his voice low, incredibly vicious.

—I want you to erase . . . this last entry. Do it now and initial it.

The young nurse stared back at him coldly. —I will not falsify that chart . . . not for . . .

—Ah, Casey, what in God's name can I say to you . . . ?

The voice was that of Father O'Malley. Or, it was almost his voice. But not quite. Not the tired gentle voice she had known during the last years. It was rather that voice rejuvenated, made stronger, younger.

—You can . . . tell me . . . it's all right, Father. . . . Tell me that . . .

Miss Lacour's eyes widened. It was her own voice that she heard now. Only not quite. Rather her voice as it had been. In 1955, perhaps. In 1960. But hers, down to the tremulous undertone, the inaudible gasp, holding back those hysterical tears that remained everpresent even now. Then it was Father O'Malley's voice again.

—It *isn't* all right, girl. Not in this world or the next. It *is* forgiven, has been since I pronounced the words of absolution over you thirteen years ago . . . but . . . all right? My God, how can a thing that happened in the world, a thing done, ever be erased, made not to have occurred . . . ? Can you unring the bells of Holy Redeemer, Casey Lacour . . . ?

It had been 1958. Now she remembered. That very tone, those very words. In the confessional, in the secret August heat. He had told her that a thing done was eternal, because by its very happening in God's imperfect world, it subsisted in eternity, in His perfect mind. She felt herself falling back against the wall as Dr. Aronson leaned down over the old priest, his face a mask of astonishment and something akin to fear. The young nurse stood close by, her eyes flaming with triumph, a cold smile on her lips.

—Oh, girl, I know your shame, your desperation, the loss of your young man . . . but in God's mercy, you could have spared the child . . . what kind of demon took you to that English hell where they . . .

And her voice cut in, almost strangled with sobs—even as it had eighteen years before. —Not without him. He swore he'd come back. That we'd be one. . . .

—And, damnit, Casey, so you were. You sinned with him, but don't you see? That new life, the one you threw away in London . . . it was his and yours. . . . He tried to keep his promise. . . .

Miss Lacour was sitting on the floor now. She was not unconscious, only transported, and her eyes were fixed on a lithograph of the Holy Family that hung above his bed. Where she had placed it the day after his attack. Father O'Malley's eyes still probed the room's shadows far above her head where Jesus Christ in plaster simulacrum lay against varnished wood.

Dr. Aronson stood by the bed, shaking his head as the old priest talked on. Miss Lefebre was checking the connections on the bank of glistening machines on the far side of the bed. Her eyes crossed those of Dr. Aronson time and again.

—I'm sorry, Miss . . . Lefebre. These things don't . . . happen. Never in the literature, never in my experience . . .

—Don't bother, Doctor. It's just that I'm . . . a good nurse. I don't . . . hear things.

—Of course not.

His hand touched hers on the bed sheet where she was smoothing it. —You're . . . a splendid nurse.

Neither of them saw Miss Lacour struggle to her feet, and open the door and leave. Later, if asked, they could say with utter certainty that she had not been to see Father O'Malley that day.

VII

It was early evening now, and the sun was beginning to lose itself in the clouds that were coming up from the Gulf. A tall thunderhead stood over the town, and the TV weatherman over in Houma had said there was a 50 percent chance of evening showers that night.

Walter Journe sat in his office which was, in fact, one of the two parlors of his home. He had finished writing up some small matters, and at the bottom of the papers he had come across the order signed by Judge Soniat by which he was made curator for Father O'Malley. He picked it up and stared at it as if he had never seen it. What a curious thing, he thought, and laughed silently at the pun. The curator had once stood for ancient Roman soldiers, to protect their interests when they fought outside Italy. It was the Republic's way of protecting those absent in her service. And later, for those who, though at home, yet were absent—the *furiosi*, the mad, whose spirits sojourned elsewhere though their bodies lay within the jurisdiction of the state.

Mr. Journe loved the Civil Law because there came to it no problem that men had not struggled with before. And not simply Englishmen whose Common Law was as rough and recent as their ways, but Spaniards, Frenchmen, Germans—even Russians and Arabs. All had their civil codes. To be a civilian lawyer was like standing for a moment at the end of the law's long intricate web. This strand, two millennia old, still grew, was vital, and no man who served within it was left alone with his problem. If the code of Louisiana had no answer, then the Code Napoleon. If not that, then Justinian or Gaius, the *Corpus Juris Civilis*. What work could man undertake that had not been done before, by those of every tongue and hue who had preceded, those brothers in the law?

He set the order out on his desk, clear now of the week's matters. How was it, he wondered, that he should be seeing to a man who had always seen to him? Father O'Malley was the only priest he had known as a grown man. When he had come back from law school in New Orleans, they had become friends. They would go fishing.

Sometimes, on a long weekend at a fishing camp Journe owned near Ville Platte, they would pass the evenings, after cleaning up the dishes, with a mason jar of good local liquor. Father O'Malley had always claimed that Prohibition was against the law of nature, and that no man was obliged to obey a law aimed at altering the very nature of man itself.

One night, after many drinks, he had told Journe about Ypres, the second battle, when the Germans had used poison gas for the first time. How incredible it was to see men drowning in their own fluids, how many of his friends farther toward the sea had perished.

He spoke of the Great War, of men drowning in mud, of trench rats as big as dogs, of men killing German prisoners, no more than boys, shooting them in retaliation for the ugliness and hatred of it all, while the boys cried, —*Bitte, bitte.*

They sat in the dusk there, watching the individual shadows of the cypresses melt and blend into blocks of shadow. Father O'Malley drank another glassful of the whiskey. His voice was getting thick now, and Journe knew he was approaching his limit even though he could no longer make out his face.

—Years later, the curse of it on me, when I entered the seminary in Cork, can you guess how I disposed of it? Can you? Hell no, Walter Journe, you decent man, you. I said, "Bless me, Father, for I have sinned. In the war, I killed. . . ." "Ah," but my confessor said back, "in a just war, killing is no sin." "Aha," I answered him back, "if that's so, how is it I'm as sure to be damned for it as the sun will rise, and our Jesus died to save?" After a while when I saw there'd be no reply, I left the good old man who would see me through to ordination with his own best thoughts, and I went outside, and I cried . . . bitter, bitter the tears . . . and all that twenty-five years ago, and more. . . .

Later, Journe had helped him to bed, and the next day they had driven in Walter's 1935 Ford V-8 back to St. Stephanie. They had always been friends thereafter, but they did not fish or drink together any more, and Journe came to understand what the seal of the confessional meant. The ultimate privilege of the ultimate advocate with his ultimate client.

Journe put the paper aside. It was twilight now, and sure enough, rain had begun to fall. He walked out onto the front porch just in time to see a car pulling into his oyster-shell driveway and to squint at the darts of rain falling through the headlights.

VIII

Jill Slack sat in the car until Amy Lefebre came out. It had started to rain, and she just didn't feel gracious. She was tired. Tired of her family. It seemed strange that all the time she had been growing up her family had been wonderful. Or, at the least, covert. Now it was like a snake pit. Her father hardly ever spoke to her mother, and her mother seemed to have an inexhaustible catalog of petty slights and annoyances that she wanted to work through with Jill. Over and over again. Second childhood, she considered. Both of them. Or what was that other thing? *Games People Play?* Mother's adult to father's child? Or the other way around? She had read a review. Or had she read the book? Anyhow, she felt dragged out. Which was a shame. Clay Moore was coming from Lafayette where he worked at Exxon. Clay was fun. They'd always made it real good together. She didn't know the other boy. Somebody from New Orleans, somebody Amy had known at school. Sometimes Jill wished she had finished school. Not that she wanted to nurse, but it was something. Something to tell people you were, something you did. Doing something was important. No, it wasn't—to her—but people seemed to *think* it was important. Nowadays, you had to *do* something. No one ever asked what her mother did. She was a mother, a housewife. That took care of that. But someone always wanted to know. . . .

Amy pulled open the door, and almost fell into the car. Her hair was glistening with rain, and against the distant lights of the hospital, her profile was perfect. Jill loved Amy, really loved her. But you get tired of perfection. Thank God she had a simply miserable disposition to go with those looks.

—Christ, what a day, Amy said. She was looking in her purse for her cigarettes. She found one loose, and cursed when her wet hands soaked it through. She had not even looked at Jill yet.

—This one you'd never believe. Everything that could happen did. Miracles, encounters, goofs, confrontations, sudden reversals, attempted seductions, general screw-ups . . .

—Sounds like an ordinary day at City General, Jill said as she started up the car.

—No, really. I almost got fired for writing the truth on a chart, and an hour later he . . .

—Who?

—Oh, you know. Aronson. King of the Jungle. An hour after he wanted to fire me, he was trying to put the make on me.

—Really? Dr. Aronson? God, I didn't know he even had one, much less gave it any consideration.

—Ummm . . . I'm not sure. I sort of think it . . . was my mind.

Jill laughed out loud. The rain was still hard, and the headlights of passing cars refracted into thousands of needles of light. It was hard to steer straight. —Come on, big lady. You've got a perfectly fine mind . . . but I never saw anyone pay it the slightest attention. Your . . . other things keep getting in the way.

Amy nibbled her lip and tried to comb her hair in the dark. It fell like thick burnished silk to lie along her shoulders as if there were no rain at all. —No, really. It was . . . what happened with Father O'Malley. . . .

—How is he? He baptized me, gave me First Communion. . . .

—Ummm . . . he's different.

—Better . . . ? Worse . . . ?

—Different. I mean, he's supposed to be a vegetable, you know. Terrible hemorrhage in the brain. Some kind of aneurysm. Blew his brains out, according to Aronson. Just a matter of a few days . . . but today, this morning, he began to talk. . . .

—That's a hopeful sign, Jill said, concentrating on the road.

—Dummy, you didn't *hear* what I said. His brain is gone. I mean, gone. Deep coma . . . you remember the lecture from second year. . . .

—But you said . . .

Amy blew a fat smoke ring. It broke up on the windshield, and turned to mist on the glass.

—He's talking, but not consciously. You won't *believe* what he's doing.

— . . . ?

—He's . . . he's repeating confessions. . . .

—Oh, Amy, my God. That's gross. Really . . .

—Hon, I'm not being . . . blasphemous or whatever you call it. . . . He's doing it. He started this morning. Something about a Mrs. . . . Baxter. Something about Mrs. Baxter wanted revenge against some girl. . . .

—I never heard of a Mrs. Baxter. Not ever. And I know everybody in town. . . .

—That was just the start. And anyhow, it's not the *weirdest*. . . . He does *both sides*. . . .

—What?

—I mean, he does the voice of the other person, too. He says what he said. But he says what they said, too. God, it's . . . it's weird.

—Amy, you're putting me on. . . .

—No, there was a Mrs. Tohler . . . she lost a son in some war. She
. . . couldn't stand to have her husband touch her. Something, it
wasn't clear. Anyhow, he died at Le Shima . . . somewhere in Viet
Nam, I guess. She hated her husband . . . because he was alive, and
her son Eddie was dead . . . so Father O'Malley told her he couldn't
give her absolution until she worked it out. He was . . . really hard.
Said she was a corrupt woman, loved her son too much, unnaturally, and then she broke down and told him what she had done
when the boy was small. . . .

Amy stopped as the car pulled down the shell-and-gravel drive
under the portico. She'd been at the house often, had visited since
the days she'd been Jill's roommate in New Orleans. But she was not
used to it. George T. Slack, oil and gas properties. This was what
you could get with oil and gas properties. Twenty-six rooms, swimming pool, tennis courts, a cathedral ceiling in the living room, and
a step-down nook near a walk-in fireplace. Hell, why didn't it
snow? Or why hadn't she met George T. Slack when he was hus-
tling his first well? Of course, that was probably before she was
born. But it sounded like an exciting time. He'd been in the Air
Corps. Bombing Germany. He'd been hit with flak, had lain in the
waist of the ship near his gun watching his blood flow, then slowly
freeze. Which saved him, he said. Over Frankfurt, the bloody cold
had frozen his blood. And, he had gone on, staring at the small
pitted scars in his legs and stomach, nothing unthawed me—until
you. It had been very good, really. Elizabeth and Jill had been in
Dallas for a week of shopping, and when her shift was over, she'd
go to the house, sleep, swim, fix a salad, and choose a wine. Then
he'd come and, like a college boy, couldn't wait for it. Beside the
pool, in bed, in the living room. Once, in the kitchen, she'd astonished him with her own favorite kind of loving. Something Elizabeth couldn't even have imagined. —Not with a blueprint and a
book of instructions, he'd gasped.

As they got out of the car, Amy picked up her overnight case and
started up the steps, thinking of the aftermath. Wednesday evenings. In a tiny place he rented outside Boutte. They'd have dinner
at a small Cajun restaurant and then go play house for a few hours.
It was a dingy place, but he was very good. She liked the feel of his
body. Not just a good-looking carcass, but the body of a man who
had flown three miles above the earth, sending down judgment.

Once she had grown glum about it. It could go nowhere. He'd
never walk away, and Elizabeth would live to be eighty. Once, on a

weekend, when he'd been in Kuwait or some impossible place, she'd gone . . . to confession.

The implication of that struck her just as she came into the kitchen where Elizabeth was pouring coffee. Elizabeth looked up and saw the expression on Amy's face. She smiled warmly. She had always liked Amy. Surely the most intelligent and sensible of Jill's friends.

—You look as if you'd seen a ghost, Amy.

For a moment, Amy was speechless. She was trying to recall what she had said, whether Father O'Malley had called her by name. Even if he hadn't, would it matter? Maybe he hadn't called Mrs. Baxter by name, either, the first time. How could anybody know, or be sure?

—Oh, no ma'am. It's just the rain, the storm, and I'm . . . I guess I'm beat.

Elizabeth Slack handed her a cup of coffee. —Then it won't break your heart that your young man and Jill's both called. Said the storm was awful north and east of us. Some of the roads are out. . . .

—Oh, really? No, I'd rather sleep. It's a good night for sleeping.

She and Jill and Elizabeth drank their coffee and chatted awhile. Oddly, Jill never mentioned what Amy had told her about the priest. Somehow, to Jill, it was not a central matter. She was still very young, and changes go almost unnoticed.

IX

In his hospital room, Father O'Malley was breathing steadily. It was late now, and only the night lamp gave soft illumination to the room. His eyes were still open, but there was an expression almost of hilarity on his face. His lips were moving, but no sound came forth. The night nurse glanced in. When she had no other duties, she ordinarily sat with the old man. She was one of his parishioners, and it pleased her to attend this impromptu vigil. But earlier he had been talking, some of it peculiar, something about damned filthy fuckers, strafing the trenches. . . . There they go, those damned fuckers. . . . She would say nothing to anyone, of course, but she was astonished. Even in delirium, a priest . . . It tested her faith. She looked at the rank of glowing instrument faces in the large bank beside his bed. The insane thought came to her that it was the machines that made him talk so. She shook her head, and went to check the other intensive care rooms. But all the same, what kind of sense did it make to hook up an eighty-year-old man with his brain gone to that bank of super-expensive gadgets. Father

O'Malley was gone, and had left behind the merely human remnant with its insufferable dirty mouth.

X

The young priest smiled, and Walter Journe smiled back at him. Father Veulon was from New Orleans. He was assigned to the archdiocese. He went where there was trouble, where decisions had to be made. He was of the new clergy. He had had a course in decision-making at Harvard Business School while he was taking his Master of Sacred Theology at the seminary. He really felt more comfortable with professionals, he told Mr. Journe. There is an apostolate of lawyers, doctors, and businessmen. Mr. Journe said he had no doubt of it. Father Veulon asked if he anticipated any legal difficulties, such as with Father O'Malley's will being probated. Mr. Journe raised his eyebrows slightly, and allowed that, at least in the country parishes, there was one formality before probate would be possible.

—And what is that? Father Veulon asked.

—The testator must be dead, Mr. Journe told him.

XI

It was almost midnight, and the rain had softened. It fell gently, barely making a sound against the trees, the roof of George Slack's house. It had not stopped, but the thunder was distant now, moving eastward. She could hear it, sullen and inchoate, toward New Orleans. The rain fell quietly, its sound muffled against the leaves in the gutters of George Slack's house. She came to herself, awake suddenly, and eyes open, looking out into the yard where certain lights illuminated the distant pool, where oaks and magnolias stood in sharp relief against the bulk of shadows behind.

She had tried to sleep, but it was impossible. In her half-consciousness, she heard Father O'Malley telling again the sins of his people, assigning to them penances, arguing the meaning of what had happened to them and because of them in a world they had not made, nor he accepted. She thought how small, condensed it all sounded. Had the world actually become larger?

Was it possible that Father O'Malley's world had been determined in its size by his consciousness? Or was her world an illusion, not nearly so large as she would like to imagine? Everything depended on this. She had to know. But there was no way to know. She was left on her own.

It was then that she heard the door open. She did not grow tense, because she knew who it must be. She heard his breathing. Then she heard his voice.

—Amy . . . ?

—Yes.

—Oh my God, how I love you, he said, his voice as distant, hollow, and uncertain as a boy's.

—Oh Georgie, she said, and what she had been thinking vanished from her mind.

XII

The rain was hardly more than a soft tattoo on the leaves of the trees and plants now. Even though the sky was still clouded over, one could walk without being soaked, and that was what Miss Casey Lacour was doing. She had put on her best suit, and now she was walking through the bare shower toward Holy Redeemer Church. She was smiling a smile no one had seen in thirty years. Her face, just for then, was that of a woman half her age.

Because, she thought, I am walking somewhere for the first time since I got off that train at Kings Cross Station, heading toward a rendezvous with death. Now I am walking toward . . . Ah, God, please love me. He—or she—would be thirty-two years old today, and walking in this small rain. Wouldn't he? Oh Christ, forgive me for waiting so long. And in your heavenly mercy, touch that good priest who so long ago gave me absolution and tried to give me understanding, and please Jesus, let them be waiting for me, my husband and my son . . . or my daughter, if it was so in your eternity. . . .

The rain became heavier then, and Miss Lacour increased her pace almost to a run to reach the cover of Holy Redeemer Church before it became a downpour again.

XIII

It was almost morning, but Judge Soniat had had a restless night. He rose, the usual pain in his lower back, the usual bad taste in his mouth. He slipped into his robe, and walked slowly through the darkened house which his ability and labor had purchased. Even his bare feet sounded hollowly in this house of no children. Oh

Jesus, he thought, I should have left years ago. Why stay in a place where seeds cannot . . .

The morning paper awaited him there on the front steps. As if a surgeon had laid it there. Precisely where it should have been. A blind man could have found it. He picked it up, threw away the rubber band, and glanced at the headlines as he walked back toward the kitchen.

HUNDREDS DIE IN BEIRUT

the newspaper told him. He closed his eyes and walked the last few yards to the coffee pot without even seeing where he was going.

XIV

Early Monday morning, George Slack was awake. He called his lawyer and headed for his office. He was waiting for a phone call. All his nerves were alive, ready, prepared for action. Even beyond his horror, he had not felt so alive in thirty years. It was strange to be challenged at all. Much less from such a strange quarter. But George understood the way things are: a challenge is a challenge. Where it comes from is secondary. Isn't it?

XV

Mr. Journe strode back and forth in the hall of the courthouse. He had a trial this morning. At ten o'clock. He had read the depositions, reread all the evidence. His lady had been injured by the act of another. This morning would see the truth told. As he paced, he reconstituted the testimony of the opposition in his mind. There was no doubt. He would win.

But down the hall, at Mike Soniat's door, he saw the young clerk beckoning to him. He frowned. Even the hall of the courthouse at six-thirty in the morning has no privacy. People will be . . . everywhere. With demands, with needs. Lord God.

Mike Soniat had already poured the coffee. He looked very tired.

—We've got a problem, he said.

—I reckoned that, Walter Journe said. —But I've already talked to the young man. The insurance company has decided to make a last stand here. Lord, they all remind me of Custer.

—No, Soniat said. —Father O'Malley.

—What?

—A petition for an injunction . . . to . . . end heroic measures. . . .

Walter Journe squinted at his friend. He had never had any problem in understanding Mike Soniat before. He might disagree with his decisions. But he understood him. —I don't think I'm . . .

Soniat's face was expressionless. He held a paper in his hand.

—I have here a petition which asks that I order all extraordinary measures ceased in the matter of Father Cornelius O'Malley, that I direct the hospital and its staff to allow him death with dignity, to end his suffering. . . .

—I . . . don't understand, Mike. What the hell . . . ?

Mike Soniat leaned back in his chair, his face still revealing nothing. —Walt, haven't you heard? Where the hell do you live? In a vacuum-sealed box?

Journe took that as an insult. He put his coffee down. —I live, goddamnit, in my house. Where I have lived for fifty and more years. What's going on here, Mike . . . ?

But even before he answered, Walter Journe knew that the case was altered, that it was a lawyer talking to a judge. Not Walt talking to Mike.

—He's at the point of death, Judge Soniat said. —But somehow he's . . . talking. About people. About everything that ever happened in this town. . . .

Journe was not sure he grasped what the judge was saying. —Talking, he said.

—It's something . . . that happens. He's repeating . . . all his confessions, everything. From God knows when . . . until now. . . .

—My God, Journe said. —How is that possible . . . ?

The judge shrugged. —They found Miss Lacour this morning . . . in the church . . .

—What . . . ?

—Dead. She had gone there . . . when? Saturday night or Sunday morning. She had cut her wrists. There was this note. . . .

The judge handed a piece of paper to Mr. Journe. He took it gingerly, read it slowly, thinking of Casey Lacour, such a fine lady. Oh Lord, the cost of being a survivor.

> I go to meet those who have awaited me for thirty years. I go gladly, because Father O'Malley, even in his last days, has made me see that I should have paid long ago the small price of life for the great gift of love. God, his illness is my health. Thank you, God, and forgive my hurrying. Please. Please.

—Dr. Aronson called. Said the old man had been talking about what Miss Lacour had told him years ago. About a boy she met while she was in England. About a baby she . . . didn't have. Maybe a nurse's aide told her. It doesn't matter. . . .

Mr. Journe stared at the judge. —That's right. It doesn't matter.

There was silence between them for a moment. That silence that comes between rivals in the law. After a moment, Journe came to himself.

—Who filed the petition . . . ?

—John Doe, Judge Soniat said.

—What the goddamned hell are you talking about?

—It's valid. We have an attorney of record from Baton Rouge. . . .

—Who the hell's the plaintiff . . . ?

—He alleges irreparable damage, a proper interest . . . and that he cannot make himself known . . . because to do so would . . . amount to the same damage. . . . He alleges the old man can't recover, can't even live more than a few days . . . but that many people will be hurt if he goes on. . . .

Journe felt his face flush with anger. —That's not a petition . . . that's a bad joke. . . .

Judge Soniat returned his glare. —We're going to have a hearing at eleven o'clock. Is that convenient for you, Mr. Journe?

—I don't believe this. . . .

—There's law on it. You've read that New Jersey case. . . .

—This isn't sonofabitching New Jersey, your honor. . . . This is Louisiana. . . . Who's a plaintiff that has any proper relationship to Father . . .

—Father Veulon . . . from the archdiocese . . . he . . . joined with the John Doe plaintiff . . . to end Father O'Malley's . . . suffering. . . .

—My God, Mr. Journe gasped. —Mike, is this a . . . setup?

Judge Soniat's eyes did not waver. —I'll see you at eleven o'clock, counselor, he said.

XVI

Elizabeth Slack was carrying her flowers into the hospital when Dr. Aronson met her.

—For Father O'Malley . . . ?

—Yes. How is he?

—He's terminal. A matter of hours or days.

—He can't . . . recover?

—No, Liz. I'm sorry. . . .

She went onward, toward the corner room, pushed the door

open, smiling, and before Miss Lefebre could say anything, Elizabeth had placed the vase full of daffodils on the table beside the bed.

—That much, at least, Amy, she said triumphantly.

Amy returned her stare without emotion. —Mrs. Slack, no one is admitted . . .

—And why not? Elizabeth asked, her voice rising. Dr. Aronson said . . . he said there was . . . no hope. How can we hurt one with no . . . hope?

Amy was about to answer, but she was too late. And she, like Elizabeth, was transfixed by that deep, strong distant voice that brought back a past neither of them had known.

—Ah, my sweet Christ, Father O'Malley said. —What have you done, George? Do you know what you've done? In that car? It was an accident, wasn't it . . . ?

And another voice answered, a voice neither Elizabeth nor Amy had ever heard.

—Ye . . . yes, Father . . . killed . . . killed the whore, didn't I . . . didn't . . . I?

—You killed a woman you swore to love and honor till death, you damned fool. . . .

—She . . . they . . . everybody . . . knew . . . everybody but . . . me.

—What of the boy, George? What about your son?

—No. No . . . her . . . *his* son. Not mine. Blood tests. In Baton Rouge. I . . . that . . . bastard . . . not mine, you understand . . . not mine . . . It's certain . . . not mine. . . .

Father O'Malley was silent for a moment, his dry lips working. His eyes closed, and it seemed that there were tears on his cheeks, but it was impossible to be sure, because Miss Lefebre moved so quickly, her small cloth mopping his expressionless face.

—Really, Mrs. Slack . . . Dr. Aronson . . .

—Shut up, Elizabeth said, her eyes wide, her ears perked. —Just shut up, Amy. . . .

—George, you're dying, do you know it? You're dying with her blood on your hands . . . in the name of Jesus, make a good act of contrition. . . .

—My ass . . . I'd kill her a hundred times, do you hear? Do you . . . do you . . .

—George, in God's name, think of the boy . . . think of your immortal soul. . . .

— . . . Ga . . . Goddamn the bastard, and my soul . . . is . . . is . . .

Father O'Malley fell silent, his eyes fixed on the distant crucifix. Elizabeth watched him, hardly believing what she had heard.

—Mrs. . . . Slack . . . you've *got* to leave, do you understand . . . ?

Elizabeth shook her head, closed her eyes for a moment, then turned to Amy. Her voice was soft, composed, her smile serene. —Of course, Amy, I don't know what . . . I was thinking of. . . .

XVII

Dr. Aronson was meeting the press. He had hardly gotten to the hospital before the newspaper and television people began demanding, on behalf of the public's right to know, that he clarify certain stories which had already traveled as far as New Orleans and Baton Rouge. It was said that a priest in St. Stephanie had gone mad and begun blackmailing those who had gone to him for the sacrament of penance. There had been one death, possibly as many as three. Someone questioned whether, at the insistence of certain church officials, the priest was being confined there at the hospital under deep sedation. Dr. Aronson shook his head and said, —No comment. But it was not as simple as that.

—Is it true, a young woman from Channel 6 in New Orleans asked, —that there is . . . something . . . abnormal about . . . Father O'Neill's ailment . . . something . . . beyond . . . medicine. . . .

My God, Aronson thought. Demonism. Voodoo.

—No, he said. —Father O'Neill . . . I mean Father O'Malley suffered a severe cardiovascular accident last Wednesday. His brain was . . . virtually destroyed. . . .

—Then how can he be doing these things, a reporter from *The Advocate* demanded.

—He isn't doing anything, Dr. Aronson shot back, angrily. —Except dying.

—Look, doctor, some of us saw that note. The one the old lady wrote. One of the deputies at the sheriff's office . . .

— . . . nothing to do with Father O'Malley. She was elderly, lonely. . . .

—Some of your staff says the old man is talking, telling things that happened in the 1920s . . . that he was talking in foreign languages. . . .

—A volunteer nurse's aide said she heard the living voice of her

mother who died in 1941, making a confession . . . heard her mother confess an act against nature with her father. . . . She says she's
considering suit . . . ruined her memory of her family. . . .

XVIII

—George, Amy was saying. —George, is that you? Listen, honey
. . . what? She is? Oh, my God. Don't pay any attention to anything
she tells you . . . really, she's making it all up, she's a spiteful bitch.
No? Believe me . . . she . . . what? I'm not. I never asked you for . . .
Oh, goddamn you. . . . Go ahead. And every single word she says
is true. . . .

XIX

Mr. Journe had just put the finishing touches on an act of sale that
would be passed the next day when Father Veulon strode into his
office with that ubiquitous confident smile of his. It was as if he had
an arsenal of expressions, each stamped out to grace an occasion,
but none which was not rehearsed, the result of considerable market research. He was not much like Father O'Malley.

—Yes, Father, what can I do for you? Father Veulon sat down
unasked, raised the crease in his black trousers, glanced at his
digital wristwatch and smiled.

—At . . . eleven, I think . . . the hearing . . .

—Yes?

—Judge Soniat tells me that . . . your representation in a case . . .
like this is . . . pro forma.

Mr. Journe bristled. —About as pro forma as your consecration of
the host, Father. . . .

—But . . . you're court appointed . . . for legal purposes . . .

—Father, the nature of my representation is a legal matter. What's
your interest . . . ?

—I . . . I've spoken with His Excellency. . . .

—And who would that be . . . ?

—I mean the Archbishop, of course . . . He feels that any pro-
longation of Father O'Malley's life . . . under the circumstances . . .
given the hopelessness of it . . . He would prefer . . . death with
dignity. . . .

Mr. Journe's eyes locked on those of the priest. —I never saw that
kind, he said. —Ordinarily they puke and bleed and gasp. They give

up very slowly, unwillingly . . . perhaps, though, you have a charm . . .

Father Veulon tried to look scandalized. —I thought . . . you were . . . a Catholic, Mr. Journe. . . .

—So did I. But then Judas was a Catholic, wasn't he?

—So you mean to . . .

—Right to the Supreme Court, Mr. Journe said. —Good day, Father.

XX

He had gone now, and Elizabeth was relieved. Truly, there is an ecstasy in being free from a burden you can no longer justify. She giggled aloud as she poured herself a cup of freshly brewed coffee. —Bastard, she shouted into the empty house. —Bastard . . .

It was not freedom from him, from the Bastard. That was nothing. It didn't matter. One Bastard or another, or none at all. No, that didn't matter. It was the other thing. About what she had heard, she could feel compassion. He was a person who could not do well with that truth suddenly jutting out of the earth after forty years as if it had never been buried in those two graves that he never visited on that rainy January day so long ago. As if, rather, it had only been placed in a time machine, sent off to return with full vigor and potency a little later.

Her face lost its hilarity. She was thinking of Father O'Malley. For some reason, she was remembering an afternoon in 1946. It was his last year with the baseball team. The young men were coming home now, somebody had said. It was possible to obtain the services of someone more suitable. The boys had resented it, but in 1946, boys did not strike or sit in. They only played their hearts out and somehow made the Class A semifinals. She had gone on the trip to Baton Rouge on the bus, with George. One of their first dates. The team had lost in the semifinals. But they had lifted Father O'Malley high on their shoulders, carrying him back to the bus when the game was over. She remembered him there, up high, flustered, tears in his eyes, a man of fifty who had never really learned to take love and admiration in stride, his hands touching the hands, the caps, the shoulders and faces of his boys.

—Ah, God, she had heard him almost shout, —how the Lord loves good fighters, boys. . . .

The tintype of that moment stayed fixed in her mind for a moment, and then began to fade, the background first, then the boys and the tumult, even the warmth of the June day until at last, like the smile of Alice's cat, there remained in frozen frame only the flushed face of Father O'Malley, a lock of gray hair over his eyes, unfading, sharp-edged, as if his presence had been the only truth of that day so long ago.

She closed her eyes and opened them, and he was gone. He had not blurred and then slowly disappeared like the rest, like George, like that distant weather encircling the ephemeral game. He had only vanished.

I wonder, Elizabeth thought, if he is so sharply etched because I knew somehow what he bore, what everyone of us put upon him, and what he could not put away, give over, share with anyone else. We had our births and deaths and agonies. He had his own, and all of ours. My God, how can all that die? How can he?

She drank down her coffee, and started for the car. Somehow it was changed now, changed utterly. She could hardly remember the pain or the hatred she had felt Saturday night when she had awakened to find the bed beside her empty. What she had come to know, she knew. But it no longer had meaning. It was changed. She saw that they were all Bastards, teasing, hurting, because they were alone. She had heard those last terrible moments of his father's life, and she had thought she was running from the room with her awful new weapon to scourge him, to twist away his pride and self-respect, to punish him. But she hadn't. She had fled, fearing another revelation, one meant for her from that dying oracle created by fifty years of silence amid them and their ways.

She climbed into her car, started it quickly, and did not hear the uncharacteristic squeal of tires as she pulled out of the driveway.

—Ah, God, she said aloud over the music of the easy-listening station, —how the Lord loves a fighter.

XXI

—I'll see you in chambers, gentlemen, Judge Soniat told Walter Journe and the attorney from Baton Rouge. —You come along, too, Father Veulon. I'll recognize you as a friend of the court. . . .

—Where's the principal? Mr. Journe asked harshly. —I want to see the plaintiff. . . .

—He's represented, the judge said shortly. —This is Mr. Amacker from Price, Moses, and Amacker in Baton Rouge.

They shook hands as they walked toward the judge's chambers.

The courtroom was almost full now with newspaper people, TV reporters, and a gaggle of townspeople.

Mr. Journe stepped before Judge Soniat's desk. —I want the plaintiff, Mike. He's alleging irreparable harm, and I have the right to examine him on that allegation . . . under the act . . .

—This isn't a criminal trial.

—In Louisiana, the rules of evidence are identical . . . and there's a death involved. . . .

Judge Soniat brushed him off. —Now, gentlemen, I mean to settle this in chambers. Then we will go out there, I will read my decision in about two minutes, and these nasty sons of bitches from the city—sorry, Mr. Amacker, Father, I mean the newsmen—can go crawl back into the walls and under the rocks where they came from. . . .

—I'm filing for supervisory writs just as soon as you get done, Mike, Mr. Journe said. —Unless they all go home with no story at all.

Judge Soniat looked across at Miss Althea, his secretary. She was crying, and the tears were dropping onto her stenographer's pad.

—Now, gentlemen, Mr. Journe is here to show cause why I should not grant a permanent injunction ordering the hospital to cease and desist from taking any extraordinary measures to preserve the life of Cornelius O'Malley, lately pastor of Holy Redeemer Church, now in the parish hospital, under the care of Dr. Amadeus Aronson. It is alleged that Father O'Malley is, in fact, clinically dead, but that he is being kept alive by mechanical means which are cruel and unnatural, although he has no hope of recovery or of leading a meaningful life. It is alleged further that in his terminal condition, without his volition, he is, and has been for several days, revealing the secrets of the confessional and things told him by hundreds of people in the most strict and holy confidence, and that these revelations have already caused pain, suffering, and death, and will cause much more, including to the John Doe who institutes this suit because of the irreparable damage that will be done him if certain things told by him to said Father O'Malley should be revealed. . . .

The voice of Judge Soniat droned on. It appeared that there was no end to the petition. Mr. Journe almost smiled, imagining the terror of John Doe, one who confessed and assumed that that was the end of it—not only in the next world, but in this one as well. Now, suddenly, he was faced with the horror which had plagued even Guido da Montefeltro, burning in hell: that his sins should be revealed on earth. Mr. Journe considered what might be the value of a confession when one was prepared to end a life rather than have his sins revealed. Surely the good Southern Baptists had found a better solution: open confession before the congregation; or none at all. Perhaps a secret confession was no confession, simply a deal. I will set my wickedness out before God, with the understanding that it shall never be known to man. But who had been most injured by the wickedness? Was the right of man to know and to forgive less than that of God?

— . . . be removed from any and all mechanical devices or support systems of whatever kind, and allowed to die a natural death with dignity.

Judge Soniat was done. He took off his glasses.

—This appears to be a case of first impression in Louisiana. Once the ways of death were . . . beyond our tampering. Now . . .

He stared out the window. They could hear the soft sound of Miss Althea's sobbing. The sun was high and hot, and through open windows the sweet, incredibly pure fragrance of magnolia and gardenia came.

The judge's head snapped back around. —Damnit, Althea, stop that sniveling. . . .

The sound stopped abruptly, then began again, perhaps a little louder. —I'm going to get me a tape recorder in a minute or two . . . I mean it.

Miss Althea was quiet. —Mr. Amacker, did you want to add anything to your petition?

The young lawyer cleared his throat. He was not ill at ease. Not civilized enough to be nervous, Mr. Journe considered. Another technician.

—Your honor, the situation we have here is unique. We have a wonderful old man who passed most of his life in this town, whose contribution . . . but now, in the closing hours of his life, he . . . he's jeopardizing the very community and people he served for fifty years. He is, according to Dr. Aronson, clinically unable to support his own life without the marvelous instruments and mechanisms at the hospital. . . .

There was much more praise of the hospital, of the town, of the court, and especially of Father O'Malley. Mr. Journe considered it sounded more like a testimonial dinner speech than a demand for capital punishment. But Amacker was good. He knew how to go about it. He knew better than to play the prosecutor, knew that the judge had nerved himself up to consider this petition, was obviously nerved enough to issue the order. It would not take much to wreck that readiness. No, Journe, he's a smart young bastard. Not going to do my work for me.

Amacker was finishing. —Heavy with years, loaded down with memories of his people's anguish. If he could, he'd say, "This shouldn't go on. I'm hurting people in my final delirium that I'd rather die for than hurt. . . . Better death with dignity. Now. Once and for all . . . ."

Amacker smiled kindly at Mr. Journe. —After all, what does Father O'Malley have to fear from death? His whole life has been . . . a preparation for it. . . . After this death, there is no other. . . .

Amacker's voice almost broke as he concluded. Mr. Journe shook his head. This little bastard would be governor or senator in a couple of years. He was a lot better than good. He'd covered almost all the ground.

Judge Soniat looked over at Mr. Journe. —Well, Walter?

Mr. Journe looked around the room. —Does Father Veulon plan to have a say . . . ?

Soniat looked at him. —Father . . . ?

Father Veulon gave the judge one of his most organized smiles. —I had thought . . . after Mr. Journe was done . . .

—Oh, no, Father, Mr. Journe said. —If you're speaking for the writ, you can do it right now. . . .

—But I . . . I have only Father O'Malley's interests . . .

—Crap, Mr. Journe heard himself say. —I'm his curator . . . you're his hangman. . . .

—All right, Walter, Judge Soniat said. —Watch your mouth. If you want to talk, Father, it'll have to be now. . . . I want this thing done right.

Father Veulon shrugged. Mr. Journe smiled almost imperceptibly. Their orchestration was thrown off. Not an important thing, but something.

Father Veulon spoke of the sanctity of the confessional, the price in human suffering that had been paid through two millennia in order to assure the silence that Father O'Malley was now breaking, through no fault of his own. He pointed out how the priest's affliction was causing him to break his most sacred vows and, by doing so, to injure his people, his priesthood, and the church itself.

—Nothing in church doctrine demanded this extraordinary treatment, Father Veulon said. —Death is not the great terror, after all. When there could be no meaningful life, then wasn't it time to cease the almost demonic determination to keep the body alive at all costs . . . ?

—Death is the common end, Father Veulon said. —Why should it be resisted when such resistance is of no help to the dying, and a positive injury to those who must go on living . . . ?

The room was quiet for a moment. Then Mr. Journe got up, stretched, and walked around the capacious chambers.

—I guess I must be missing something, he said, —because you all make killing seem so right, so inevitable. You make it sound like ending a life is the greatest favor you can render. What youall are setting forth for the judge to consider is that a lawyer and a priest say that justice and truth can best be served by getting this old priest underground as fast as it can be done. . . . What can I say to that? I feel like somebody picked me up and took me back forty years and 3,000 miles away. I feel like some poor devil of an advocate before a Nazi court arguing that you shouldn't kill or maim a feebleminded woman, and that maybe even killing Jews for the sake of the state misses what the state is about. . . .

Mr. Journe argued for a long time, but he couldn't break out of the Alice-in-Wonderland feeling, as if Judge Soniat and Amacker and Father Veulon were no more than a pack of cards, and that this whole business was like Moot Court back in school, that, when it was done, everyone would laugh, and say "April fool," and go home, and Father O'Malley would either recover despite the diagnosis, or he would die in his own time, surrounded by people who loved him. Mr. Journe knew better, but that feeling still clung. So he decided to end it. How do you argue with a pack of cards?

—If it weren't for his talking, no one would be here. It's not death with dignity you want. It's silence and secrecy. If I could guarantee that, you'd all go home. But you and your miserable John Doe, you want him quiet, and it happens that the only way you see to manage that is by seeing him dead. . . . It won't be the first time some guilty conspirators remembered that dead men tell no tales.

That last seemed to bother Father Veulon, but Mr. Amacker just continued to look concerned.

Then Mr. Journe's eyes narrowed. He looked at Judge Soniat for a long moment. —It's as if, seeing that it was a burden on society, a priest should refuse to baptize or give care to a helpless feeble-minded child. . . .

Mr. Journe heard his own voice, but he could not believe the words. He would have supposed that he had never spoken them, that they had been no more than phantasmagoria of an old man lonely too long, words thought but never spoken. But Judge Soniat's face gave proof that he had spoken his thoughts. Michael Soniat stared at him, his face bleached by sudden emotion.

I shouldn't have done that, Mr. Journe thought in the pendulous silence which swung above them, both men speechless, but with the very burden of soundlessness passing from one to the other with the fierce urgency of terminal conversation. I shouldn't because the old man wouldn't have, not to save his life.

He said more, remembering none of it, able later only to conjure the recollection of a fabric of skewed language fluttering like torn curtains in the window of an empty house. He would remember feeling abstracted, removed from the small circle whose shadows, pinned to a distant book-lined wall, grew perceptibly shorter as he argued. He would be amazed that he could have gone on until one o'clock, Amacker and Veulon at first passive as funeral mutes, then restless, eyes wandering out to the sun-flamed street where the town's blood flowed, cell by cell, in the people passing, incredibly unaware of the loss being compounded so near their ordinary ways, and finally paying no attention at all, looking at Judge Soniat with pleading expressions, almost as if they had decided to join with Journe in his struggle against death with dignity.

But it isn't compassion or understanding or the power of words that drives them, Mr. Journe remembered thinking. There's no turning around in the bastards. They're just hungry. And they need to piss.

He paused, tried to remember what he had said, what he might have left unsaid. It was late. Finish it. Never just stop. Unworthy of the craft. There must always be a coda. To let them know you could go on all day.

—I didn't know that you demanded a man's death because he spoke the truth, because, as a matter of fact, you're dead certain he is speaking the truth, the whole truth, and nothing but the truth. . . . What we demand of a man in court can get him killed nowadays. . . . No, I didn't know that. . . . It took a big-town lawyer and a hotshot priest to let me know. . . .

He stopped then. It was way past one o'clock and he was tired. He was trying to think ahead, to the Court of Appeal, to the Supreme Court, to what he would say there. There was talk between Mr. Amacker and the judge, and then, almost before Mr. Journe could grasp what he was saying, Judge Soniat was giving them his decision.

— . . . of opinion that this writ should issue, since no medical purpose can be served by the mere extension of bodily functions where all sentient and meaningful life has ended irreversibly. . . .

Mr. Journe's shoulders slumped. The pack of cards had assumed the status of reality.

—I'll be filing for an appeal, Mr. Journe said slowly, not comprehending the look of pity in Judge Soniat's eyes. The judge turned to his secretary.

—Miss Althea, you dial up Justice Walker. . . . He said he'd be standing by. . . .

The judge turned to Mr. Journe. —We'll step out, Walter, so you can speak to Justice Walker. . . . I talked to him this morning. . . . The Supreme Court is ready to take this case directly as *res nova*. . . .

Mr. Journe could tell that Amacker and the priest had known. It came across his mind that he had lived too long, much too long. God knows what the world would be like in another twenty years. But, surely, he had lived too long.

Mr. Journe watched Miss Althea slowly dial the long distance number of the Louisiana Supreme Court. He remembered her telling him not so long ago that it seemed unnatural, long distance with no operator. Then, suddenly, as he watched her head bent over the push-button telephone, he saw her for just a moment as she had been thirty-five years before. He had known her mother and father, her brother who sold used cars in Slidell and died in a fishing accident in Lake Borgne. Lord, how he knew the details of the lives he had lived out his own among. But not the inside, not the portion that Father O'Malley knew.

Could there be such a thing as a spiritual delict, Mr. Journe wondered. *Every act whatever of man that causes injury to another obliges him by whose fault it occurs to repair it.* That lovely convoluted prose of the code. *Every* act. Of course, not that of a child of tender years, not that of a *furiosus*, one gone in his own visions, out beyond the reach of common reason. But Father O'Malley was neither a child nor a madman. Could his stroke absolve him? No, nothing could. Every act whatever. And what act had the old man not known? His act had been to reveal those other acts; his tort to bring up to light the shame and pain and evil of a whole community. Ah Lord, today we do not send the scapegoat forth. If he names the sins put upon his head, we simply pull him off the machine.

—I've got Justice Walker . . .

Miss Althea was starting to cry again. She put down the phone and followed the others out of chambers.

Mr. Journe stared at the phone and picked it up. The voice at the other end was one he recognized. Leave it to Michael Soniat. He had chosen the one Supreme Court judge they both knew: Harold Walker. Short, jovial, a Santa Claus of a man. From their district. A fine legal scholar, an activist who used the code like a canvas to sketch out his own ideas of the meaning of the law, and who always required that whatever formula you used, you got down to the rights and wrongs of a case. Mr. Journe's heart sunk within him. Harold Walker was a pragmatist.

He remembered arguing a case before the Circuit Court of Appeal before Harold went to the high court. Mr. Journe had had a fine case. He had had the law, the code, even the precedents, for whatever they might matter. But Harold had interrupted his argument, and fixed him with that affectionate jovial smile of his, and asked, —Well, well, Mr. Journe, you've laid it all out for us, and I see what you're saying. But is it right?

Lord God, is it right? What kind of a maniac judge asks that of a lawyer? The judge is supposed to answer that question, not the advocate. No, the lawyer, having taken a case, is supposed to have only one view, and to argue that view until a final decision cuts him short. No one has the right to ask the advocate to judge. He cannot. It is not his function.

—Hello, Harold, Mr. Journe said, and then he listened.

When he hung up, he sat down, drew out a white handkerchief, and wiped his forehead. Justice Walker had not asked him what was right this time.

XXII

It was late afternoon now, and Miss Lefebre was on duty next to Father O'Malley. He had been quiet for a long time. She had wet his lips with water. She was very high. Was it Percodan, Darvon? She couldn't remember. Something. Oh, Christ, she should have had courage, should have left her enameled pillbox alone. Now her head was full of peculiar things raised up from her childhood. Was she moistening the lips of Christ, or was what seemed to be cotton really coals, and were those the lips of the prophet Isaiah, or was she out on the edge of something she couldn't handle? Christ, why don't people just lie down and die?

But if that was what she really felt, then why was she touching the old man's lips again so quickly? Why were her lips touching his dry pink forehead where the silver hair had been combed back so immaculately?

XXIII

George Slack was drunk and walking toward the hospital. He was not clear on his purpose. Perhaps he wanted to hear his father's voice through the lips of the old man. He could not remember his father's voice, and amid the liquor it had come to him that he would be willing to hear that voice say anything, admit to any crime, profess any horror. Just to be able to hear that voice again.

He stumbled once, and fell into some shrubbery, but after a few minutes he got to his feet and started again. It began to rain. It was a soft rain, and he hardly noticed it, only the gradual wetting of his suit which grew heavier and heavier, until at last he threw away his jacket, pulled off his tie. But he kept walking.

XXIV

The raindrops fell on Elizabeth Slack's windshield and they made her feel very old. Make the small rain to fall, she thought, wondering where those words had come from, suddenly, into her mind. Her anger had passed. Even the pain had begun to ebb. It was her pride, after all, wasn't it? The notion that she could be all things to him, and no one, truly, is all things to anyone. Not even to themselves. People reach for what they need, most especially when they feel the slow inexorable pain of age, terminal and irreversible, coming upon them. They do not suppose that it can be altered. They only imagine that it can be put off, held at bay for an hour, a day, a week. I think they are probably older afterward, she thought. They use up something of themselves in trying to hold off what is coming to be themselves.

She wondered where he was now. The rain fell harder. The radio, between easy-listening tunes, said that the rain was general all over south Louisiana, from Lafayette up as far as McComb. It ran down her windshield like tears, and Elizabeth shivered, re-creating in her mind that winter rain long ago, in 1936, and a car out of control like the man within it, hurtling toward a concrete bridge abutment so recently completed by workers for the WPA. To end his agony, to defeat the woman who had hurt him already beyond defeat, thinking not at all of the child who was waiting, who would wait for forty years for word of what had befallen them.

—Oh, my God, can you forgive me? Elizabeth said aloud, unsure of whether the forgiveness she asked was God's. Or his. Wherever he was. Now, tonight. In the rain.

XXV

Dr. Aronson was driving. In the seat beside him Judge Soniat and Mr. Journe sat silent. In the rear seat Father Veulon watched his breath fog the side window. He would try to get back to New Orleans tonight, rain or no rain. Even if he had to rent a car.

The car pulled up in front of the hospital. There were a number of cars there with the call letters of TV stations in New Orleans and Baton Rouge.

—Goddamn, Dr. Aronson said. —Excuse me, Father. Oh, the hell with excusing me. Those stinking vultures . . .

They sat wordless for a moment. —Vultures follow killers, Mr. Journe said.

—That's uncalled for, Judge Soniat said roughly.

—Don't push me, Michael, Mr. Journe said. —This isn't your courtroom. . . .

Dr. Aronson shrugged. There was nothing to be done. He could see another clump of reporters around the side of the emergency entrance. —As well here as there, he said, and opened his door.

The rain was coming in gusts now, and the men ran clumsily under the portico of the hospital, pushing past reporters who shouted questions at them and followed them into the reception area and down the corridor until two sheriff's deputies sent ahead by the judge pushed them back roughly and kept them there in the reception area, where visitors and families of patients looked at them with astonishment.

They brushed the rain from their garments as they walked, still silent, saying nothing to one another.

The room was dark after the brightly lit corridor, and for a moment they could not penetrate the darkness with nothing but the night-light above the bed and the glow of the instruments for illumination. Then they came to themselves, and saw Amy Lefebre kneeling beside the bed, her hand intertwined with the unresisting hand of Father O'Malley, whose eyes remained fixed on the crucifix, which must have seemed as distant as the moon, if, indeed, he could see it at all.

Father Veulon hurried to assist Miss Lefebre to her feet. It was obvious that she was not herself. Somehow she had hurt her hands, and they were bleeding. A nurse's aide took her outside, and even within the room, it was possible to hear her voice, and the muted sounds of the reporters down the corridor.

— . . . killing a saint . . . God forgive . . . bless me, Father. . . .

Judge Soniat exchanged a glance with Dr. Aronson. —Did you want me to read the order, doctor . . . ?

Dr. Aronson stared back at him. —I really think we can . . . do without that, Judge.

Father Veulon went to the bed and began to give Father O'Malley the sacrament of extreme unction. He placed the holy oil on his head, his hands, his feet. Father O'Malley stirred, his lips moved, as if they were searching for a voice to give them meaning. His eyes seemed to follow Father Veulon. . . .

—Ah, son, Father O'Malley said, his voice hoarse, coming from a vast distance. —No, no, you must give that up. What worse crime is there . . . ?

Another voice came from him. —But . . . it's . . . it's what I *am*, Father. Isn't it . . . isn't love what . . . we're supposed to have?

—Not love . . . a thing that kills the spirit . . . the ruin of all fleshly ruins. My God, better you be with a poor innocent girl. . . .

—No, I don't *want* that. . . .

Father Veulon reddened, did his work quickly.

—I'm . . . through now, he said, making a final unconvincing sign of the cross over Father O'Malley, who had fallen silent again.

—All right, Doctor, Judge Soniat said, and the doctor moved toward the machines.

Mr. Journe moved toward the bed. He took the old man's hand in his, some of the chrism rubbing onto his fingers. —Go in peace, Cornelius, Mr. Journe said, tears running down his face. —I tried to . . . never mind. I'll be along in no time at all. . . .

Father O'Malley roused again, his eyes turning toward Mr. Journe for sure. He looked at him for a long moment.

—For your penance, he said, —say ten Our Fathers, ten Hail Marys . . . and a good act of contrition . . . now . . .

While Dr. Aronson snapped switches, Mr. Journe knelt beside the bed. Behind him, Judge Soniat found himself kneeling, too, saying —Oh, my God. . . .

XXVI

When they came out, the reporters had been pushed outside by the deputies, and some had left rather than stand in the rain. There was one car with the call letters of a TV station in New Orleans owned by the Jesuits, and Father Veulon, after making cursory farewells, hastened to it, spoke with the driver briefly, and got in as it drove away.

Just beyond the portico, George Slack lay in the rain, coatless, a rill of blood running down his mouth where a deputy had struck him, mistaking him for an exceptionally obstreperous reporter. Beside him, Elizabeth knelt, wiping away the blood, telling him, in a voice so soft that it could hardly be heard above the rustle of the rain, that not a word she had told him earlier was true, and that he had to try to get up now, try to get to the car. They had to go home.

Then there were only Judge Soniat and Mr. Journe left standing under the portico. The rain had let up, but it had not stopped. They stood speechless beside one another, hearing, above the soft sound of the rain yet falling, the louder sound of it dripping from the eaves of the hospital, from the trees all around, scuttling downward to earth through the drains. In the distance, a pair of headlights lanced through the darkness for a moment and then were lost again in the gloom.

Judge Soniat cleared his throat and started to walk down the driveway. He paused for a moment, and without quite turning, looked backward at Mr. Journe.

—See you in court, Counselor, he said, and then walked on.

The Southern Reporter
(1981)

The Man Who
Slept with Women

I

—You know how to handle women? my uncle Shad used to say down at the Glass Hat. —Shit on 'em. Don't ask 'em nothing, don't answer no questions, don't smile at 'em. If you talk, lie. If you buy 'em something, make sure you can hock it. Don't put no initials on anything. So you can give it to the next one when the one you got goes flat.

—Or starts swelling, somebody would put in.

Uncle Shad should know. In a triangle formed by Kilgore, Texas, and Texarkana and Bossier City, Louisiana, Uncle Shad was known universally as a Mean Ass. With the exception of Bad Son of a Bitch, that was the most honorific title a man could hold. It signified that he was solitary, vicious, incapable of truth or charity, except within a limited circle of friends and kin, dedicated to every form of hedonism this side of sadism, not necessarily excepting certain forms of violence known only to a people who had passed from hogs and cotton and whiskey-making to drilling, dusting, and bartending in less than a generation. Uncle Shad was my mother's brother, and he was celebrated wherever drinking, whoring, stomping, and wholesale outrage was the bill of fare. Which covered the greater part of Bossier City, especially Highway 80 toward Minden and Vicksburg east and Dallas west. Up and down that strip he stalked, strutted, slouched, and staggered. Drinking, kicking, biting, or swamping whatever rose (or fell) before him. And if there was one thing on God's misshapen earth he did dearly love, it was to drag me, his nephew, out of a night with him.

—Treat a whore like a lady . . . Uncle Shad would bawl.

—And a lady like a whore, all the roughnecks and tool pushers in the Tower Bar and Grill would yell back.

—And the world's rare snatch is gonna fall open for you like a sailor's satchel.

Because Uncle Shad despised my mother. He didn't hate her—no, he loved her. He truly did. But he despised her. He could not bear to

345

touch her, and ten minutes was the outer limit of his ability to converse with her. She made him shudder.

Because she was very good. Good and most men thought beautiful, well married, thoroughly cultured and deeply religious.

—And she grew up in a cornfield five miles out of Tyler, Texas, Uncle Shad once told me, —without a pot to piss in or a window to throw it from. Daddy ran a pair of mules and later a tractor and worked up to croppin' shares whilst I learned the oil business and got sand in my ass from swallowing drilling mud. And your mother she went to work at the Woolworth's five and dime, and then at a restaurant called the Jumbo Grill and met your paw who was two years further on gargling mud than me. Who got lucky on account he had a head of naturally pure silver hair when he was nineteen, and the boss on that lease, Mr. Arch Riley, took twenty a week out of your paw's check for ole Whitey, and when he was twenty-one, called him down off a rig and handed him twenty-one thousand dollars in cash money and a sixty-fourth piece of forty-four thousand dollars a year. And said, "Get your funny-looking ass over to SMU and take a college degree in geology." And on the way, he picked up your momma 'cause she had to have the reddest red hair he ever seen, and said to her, "We can make it, sugar. You get you a degree in French literature, 'cause Jesus and Judas knows it ain't a thing from here to Brownsville as cultured as a degree in French literature." And in a couple of years, that's what happened.

—How come I got brown hair? I asked Uncle Shad.

—Say, he said, eyes widening. —You sure do. Ain't that the shits?

Uncle Shad weighed two hundred and forty except when he went to fat. Then it was two-eighty, but you couldn't tell. He was six foot three and very meaty around the face with chops for jaws and a wide, heavy-lipped mouth that looked all right because of his size. And small brown almost kindly intelligent eyes that were pressed far back on either side of a nose so often broken that you only speculate on what it had originally looked like.

When he smiled, there was no guile in it, and people wanted to love him. My father loved him. Possibly more than he loved mother. He would have spent most of his time drinking with Uncle Shad except he was usually in Beirut or Lisbon, Cairo or Kuwait, and Uncle Shad would not leave the Texas-Louisiana border for any amount of money my father had yet thought to offer. The last figure Shad had turned down was thirty thousand a year as honcho in what he called one of those chickenshit heathen kingdoms down in the Persian Gulf's steaming crotch.

—Maybe it was the French literature, Uncle Shad said at last, cracking another can of Schlitz.

—Huh?

—Huh what, you skinny little bastard?

—I mean, sir.

—You bet your scrawny ass you mean, sir. Maybe the French literature made you have brown hair.

I didn't see that. —How, Uncle Shad?

—How do I know? It sure turned your momma inside out. Last time I come to the house, she says, "*Entre nous*, Shadrach . . . *vis-à-vis* Tommy." Listen, she wanted to talk about your milieu and your something or other. Said I was bad for all of 'em.

—What did daddy say?

—Didn't say shit. He was in Mexico City. You know, if I'd been born with a head full of silver hair, they'd of reamed out a mare's ass with me and then claimed I was too old for the workmen's compensation act. Your poppa . . .

We drove down to Blue's Red Devil. We always kept moving because after Uncle Shad picked me up at Byrd High School and I didn't show for dinner, Momma would start phoning. By now she would have got hold of the Bossier Parish sheriff and started some song and dance about them letting a fifteen-year-old minor do the joints in company of a dangerous madman, blood kin and local custom aside. And seeing the kind of money my father's company spread in Bossier Parish, they would come looking. But they knew the whole story, and they would start at the nearest bar to the Red River, the Hurricane, and work out. By the time they hit the Ming Tree, we would be at the Wooden Shoe. By the time they had a drink and try at the Shoe, we would have bypassed the Skyway Club, which had fallen to ruin anyhow with Early Blessey's band cut out, and would be at the Tower Bar and Grill. They always came across us at the Mistletoe, a deadly wretched place with barmaids who were too far gone in age, vice, or disease even for the Tower.

—Thanks to Jesus for canned beer, Uncle Shad would mutter, studying the girl who brought five cans through the gloom and a Seven-Up for me.

Then Deputy Pritchard would arrive. He was short, bald, mild-eyed, and faintly ridiculous in his Stetson and boots, with one khaki pants leg in and one out. There was no way on earth to see Deputy Pritchard as dangerous. Which was odd, considering he had killed six or eight men over the years in single combat, and had won the National Pistol Championship in 1948.

—Pritch, Uncle Shad would say, —you can have this here beer or kiss my ass.

Deputy Pritchard would shake his head and lift his belly as he slid into the booth beside me. —It ain't no choice, he would answer. —Why don't you hand me that beer.

And they would talk. It was a ritual and almost without variance. Uncle Shad would ask questions, and Deputy Pritchard would answer. Then Deputy Pritchard would ask and my uncle answer. There was virtually no exchange of information at all. Which was just fine because they were not talking to exchange information, but to touch one another with words, reassure each other of continuing amity and respect. They had grown up on the rigs together, and one had saved the other's life or something, which I never was able to make out and had no chance to ask about and the straight of which even they may not have recalled. Then when the beers and the doings were satisfactorily done, Deputy Pritchard would turn to me as if he had only then noticed that I occupied the corner of his booth.

—Son, he would say gravely, —your momma give us a call. She seemed to think you had gone off with some crazy man.

—His momma can fuck a bull baboon, Uncle Shad would mutter.

Deputy Pritchard was always amazed. —I'll overlook that kind of talk, seeing it's your own blood kin. But I never heard such talk about a lady. . . .

—You'll overlook it 'cause I'll pull off your arm and stuff it up your dying ass, Uncle Shad would grin dangerously.

Deputy Pritchard would purse his lips and shake his head. —I believe your momma was right, boy. This here man is a dangerous lunatic.

—No, I would answer, making one of my first entries into the rough stylized banter of men, —he's my uncle.

—You mean, Deputy Pritchard's eye widened, —this here is the widely known bad man Shadrach Courtney?

—The same, Uncle Shad would say, smiling.

—The one without no balls, no brains, no guts? The one they call the living miracle?

Then Uncle Shad would reach under the table and dig his fingers into Deputy Pritchard's thigh just above the knee or lean across and put a neck lock on him. People sitting at the tables or dancing to the jukebox would pause and move aside, not knowing for sure whether it was funning or serious. Knowing only that both or either of them there in the booth with a skinny fifteen-year-old could clean out the place single-handed, and that anything serious between them was likely to work harm for a wide circle all around.

Then they would break it off and grin at one another, finish the last of their last beers, and we would leave.

It would be late by then, and cool, and we would stand outside in the gravel of the parking lot and they would swap stories of sexual heroism or reports of new degeneracy. They would talk about women they had both known and the legends of endurance and cruelty from those days. Shootings and cuttings, accidents and assassinations. Deputy Pritchard would chronicle the newest wave of whores reputed to be working the town, and oftener than not, Uncle Shad would evaluate them one by one and list them according to his own arcane system.

—It ain't no use with the blond at Kim's. I bought her three drinks. But she's waiting for love.

—Reckon if you told her you had ten thousand dollars . . . ?

—That's love.

—Maybe you could send her to college, Deputy Pritchard began.

—Lay off that shit, Uncle Shad answered. —College could of ruined the pussy of the Queen of Sheba.

—That boy goin' to college?

—I'd as soon put him out on the grass.

Then we would climb into Uncle Shad's jeep and wave to Deputy Pritchard and head back toward Caddo Parish and my mother's cold, inarticulate, exceptionally well-bred anger.

All my life I had heard about hard rows to hoe. By the time I came along—which is to say by the time Mother decided to have me—the rows and the hoes were pretty much all gone. We had three gardeners and a tree surgeon from Lambert's nursery on retainer. But there are other rows and other hoes. Me? I had Mother. Who, once she decided to have me, having me, decided to have me all the way. I was sixteen the summer in question, and, sure as God lost a boy, I was still sleeping with Mother. Whenever my father was out of town. Which was mostly. I didn't like it. It gave me the creeps. But what are you going to do? I kind of wanted to tell my father, but there never seemed to be time, and anyhow, I could hear the conversation as it might well go, and it seemed creepier than the fact. So I told Uncle Shad.

—My God, it's unnatural. Does she . . . Lord, I knew she'd gone all to hell, but that French stuff.

It seems he'd mentioned my mother's college major to one of his pub-crawling pals, who in turn introduced him to de Sade and

Restif de la Bretonne. —Lord, he said again, rubbing his chops. —We got to do something about this. We got to . . .

He didn't enlarge on the something. But instead of us just crossing paths at the Glenwood Drug Store every once in a while, Uncle Shad started picking me up after school before Cromwell, Momma's Jamaican chauffeur, showed up. Then we'd eat and maybe catch an early movie, go by the tame joints in downtown Shreveport, and fall in on Bossier City like a ton of fists and pimples. And, after a month or two of this, I was beginning to catch on. I saw a lot, and I never was stupid. By the time we started for home each time, things were getting clearer and clearer. Home was just a place, not a permanent illness.

II

Only this particular night we never made it. Just below the new bridge we were doing maybe fifty-five, splitting the difference between Bossier City's speed limit of thirty-five and Uncle Shad's normal cruising speed of seventy-five. Uncle Shad was drinking out of a bottle he kept in a brown paper sack under the front seat. Between sips, he was talking to me.

—Next time out, we'll go down to Mississippi. I got a friend runs a blind tiger and has him two hundred acres. When the revenuers get close, he goes to shooting deer out of season, and when the game wardens get the wind, he fires up that still again. Something going on year around. Two years ago, one of them revenue men shot the kneecap off a game warden. While Eddy and some friends laid out in the brush watching, drinking popskull and eating venison.

Just then, out of the corner of my eye, I saw a blur pull out of a side street as fast as a doe downwind. Then nothing. I didn't feel or hear anything. It was like being a television set and somebody got tired, yawned, and turned me off. I hope to Christ dying is like that.

Next thing I knew, I came back on, and it felt like I was in the middle of some crazy commercial. I couldn't make out where I was, and colors and shapes ran into one another something fierce. I could hear Uncle Shad. He was talking close by. Not loud, but very earnest.

—I tell you what. If this little old boy dies, I'm gonna start off making you fuck a furnace. . . .

There was water all over the place. Maybe we had hit a space-warp like in *Amazing Wonder Tales* and I had got thrown into a fountain in the Place de la Concorde. Anyhow, it was coming down all over me, and I was spread-eagled out on my belly. But I couldn't feel my legs much, and I seemed to be jackknifed around the middle somewhere. Breathing was a bad go. I realized I was grabbing one mouthful of air at a time like a fish on the bank. It scared me a little, but I was still half off, and it seemed I had been breathing that way for a long time.

—And then I'm gonna make his momma a necklace out of your roasted nuts. . . .

There were red lights flashing, and white and black things moving around, and way off I could hear what sounded like the whole Shreveport police department coming on with their sirens high. Somebody started lifting me up.

—On the other hand, if he's all right, I'm just gonna give him a baseball bat and a bad bulldog and let him see to you himself.

Then Uncle Shad was leaning over me. —Looks like somebody run you through a screen door. How does it feel?

—What feel? I got out.

—Your face, you dumb bastard.

—Face?

He shrugged and let whoever it was unwind me from whatever it was I had gotten wrapped around. But he looked worried, and that pleased me. Maybe my mother's blood was inside after all. If it was, a good deal was leaking out. Anyhow, as they pulled me up, I could see that the top half of me had gone through the jeep's windshield. They had sprayed it and the old wreck we'd hit to keep off fire before they untangled me. Then I could see the little colored man Uncle Shad still had by his collar, talking to him in that even, conversational tone. He looked like I felt, and drunk to boot. A couple of Bossier City police were standing beside them, trying halfheartedly to pry Uncle Shad's fingers out of the little fellow's shirt. They lowered me onto the stretcher about then, and I felt like I was dropping to the bottom of a very expensive dry hole. Which is when that same cosmic viewer got bored once more, and I got turned off again.

III

For my next exploit, they had rigged me out in a white robe that covered my front and tied in back, leaving me bare-assed as a heifer at a hayride. And everything but my eyes was bandaged from my neck to the top of my head. I felt like some king's twin brother or a package left over from Christmas. There were people fooling around

on the other side of the room, and of course one of those jugs full of
water up over the bed with a length of rubber hose running down to
my arm. And folding up sheets just at the edge of my vision, a
blond who had almost made redhead with a twat that would pull up
the blood pressure on a mummy. I felt awful, but that girl whose
face I hadn't even seen, had me ready to eat. I wouldn't have
minded dinner, either.

Then came the deluge. I could hear her all the way down the
corridor outside:

—Don't lie to me. He's dead.

—No, somebody said, not sounding especially happy about it.

—He's crippled for life. Say it. I can take it. Don't lie to me. I can't
stand a sonofabitch lies to women.

—No, actually . . .

—Actually, when you went in for exploratory, you found out his
spine . . .

—No . . .

—Something worse? His little genitals . . . ?

I reached down before he could answer, and whispered along
with him:

—No . . .

—My son, my only son is in there, and you won't tell me . . .
what . . . if you have pity for a mother's . . .

—He has contusions, multiple lacerations, and possible internal . . .

—Internal. *Injuries.* She said, sounding like a pathologist on *Young
Doctor Malone.*

—Possible.

All this time, I wasn't just dead positive it was her. At first her
voice was high and harsh, something stringy and mean in it. Then,
when she got to asking about my little parts, it dropped back to that
fine Pierremont contralto I was used to. It was Mother, all right.

—Possible, she repeated, her voice moving into the upper reaches
of baritone. —Will he . . .

—Ma'am?

—Will he . . . be all right?

—Oh, yes ma'am . . .

—You're lying like a dog, she told him smoothly. —I can see it in
your eyes. Shad's run him into a wall and made a vegetable out of
him, right?

—Oh no . . .

—How much is that drunken son of a bitch paying you? Don't you
know I can tell? Don't you know you can't hide it from a mother?

Don't you know I'll sue the ass off this place for false pretenses, pain and suffering, misrepresentation . . .

—Ma'am, would you like to go in?

She came through the door with this tall young doctor who looked like he could use some of my jug himself. She was dressed like it was show time at the Stork Supper Club, complete with that damn silly-looking silver fox thing and platinum earrings I had tried to steal once or twice. —He's probably got no more mind left than a horsefly. Sonny, she said, staring down into my bandages. —Sonny darling, speak to me. Speak to your mother.

—Glaaah, I said. —Gro-gro-gro. Whaag.

The doctor slumped against the wall, and for the smallest split second Mother's eyes opened wide. Then she started to swing at me and caught herself. —Thank God, she sighed, her fingertips touching the snood of gauze that kept me from biting them. —Your mind's not gone.

She pulled up a chair and sat down beside the bed while the doctor, scarce recovered, busied himself around my bed. When he reached to take my pulse, I pulled my wrist loose and went to scratching my crotch. Like the Red Cross nurse on the poster, he wanted to serve. But what kind of guy tries to get to a good-looking woman through her injured child?

—All he's done is destroy your face. Nothing much, Mother went on, her voice now controlled and cosmopolitan again, that touch of unidentifiable accent, that sweet contralto moving like syrup in the room's small echoless extent. As she ended each sentence, that eternal note of sadness managed to creep in. It almost broke, that succulent voice: Madonna, Livia, Medea. Something like a song, like a sob.

—He's evened the score. By turning my baby into a monster.

—Grr, I said. Even without bandages, on my feet and moving, I used gutterals, monosyllables, grunts, and certain vague shiftings of the shoulders when it was necessary to converse with Mother. What the hell, was Jesus a big talker when Mom was on the scene? Does the ice cube know what puts the cold on it? Then the Young Malone gave up. Short of an enema or something strange, there was nothing else he could even fake doing for me. I guess he thought of it and passed on the enema. The other he had in mind for Mom. If only he knew.

—You worthless reproduction of your old man, she whispered to me as the door closed behind the white knight. —You creepy little bastard. No, don't gargle at me. One lousy croak or cough and I'll pour this pitcher of water in your mouth and nose holes.

She'd do it. She really would. She was like an artist whose canvas won't hold still when it came to me. She had this vision of a handsome prep-school student, football and maybe even polo player, wearing a crimson blazer and doing the Rhodes-scholar bit and all. What she gets is atavism. Back to the khakis and axle grease. 30.06 Springfields in the fall and a growing determination to squirm into the very bowels of Caddo and Bossier Parish lowlife. With Uncle Shad playing Virgil in a jeep. This is rough on a little old East Texas girl who parlayed sweet legs, a wild backside, generous superstructure, and a random grab at a silver-haired Energy Source into maybe ten or twelve million dollars with trimmings. The trouble with big money is, you feel obligated to do something with it. When you run through cars, pools, houses, clothes, and maybe a couple of jaunts while the Energy Source is out supplying the world, you cast about. And discover you've got a kid. Ahah. *Now what do you reckon he might do, become, think, be, if I was to . . .* Off to the races. Except Shad is all over the dark hours with a passkey to the underground. Oho. And those late-night occasional phone calls I've been getting long-distance from my father for almost a year. Coming with scary regularity just when I need them. As if Uncle Shad was keeping him plugged in. A hundred and fifty dollars will get you ten or fifteen minutes on Southern Bell from almost anywhere to might near every place.

—I'd just as soon leave it go, I said finally, one hand in my crotch and the other hovering under the sheet to guard my mouth and nose holes.

She slapped the arms of the chair. —Well I ain't. Not near. She was getting mad again and that far-off wild-assed Davy Crockett twang was coming on, along with some home-style grammar. Right there, between the cultivated and the vicious, you could love her. If you had a soul made for loving and fast as a blacksnake.

—I'm gonna camp here till I can get a look at what that godforsaken drunkard has left me.

—You? How come you? It's my crummy face.

—Your face your ass. Who do you reckon will have to pay for the surgery to get rid of the scars?

Ahah. I hadn't thought of that. Maybe one long livid white scar down the side of my jaw like the son of a bitching Desert Fox or something. Then I thought: with my luck, fate has randomly distributed across my face a grid of nine squares filled with smaller scars in the shape of noughts and crosses.

—What do you bet daddy pays for it, I snickered.

—For all your father knows, she answered, getting control again, —I buried you a week and a half ago out at Forest Park Cemetery. I tried to get hold of him all evening. Nobody in Paris or Rome knows where he is. Somebody said, try Indonesia. Which is not a city, but some heathen backwoods country full of Reds and Chinamen.

—The Chinamen are Reds, I told her, not sure of that, but wanting a cheap point.

—Never mind. Your father is out of it.

Oho. True. Has been out of it for a long time. Meets me once in a while coming in as I'm going out to school. Or vice versa. Once we played tennis and he strained his back letting me win and trying to make it look straight. He is the living image of the Man from Glad. So help me God, the first time I saw that commercial, I thought I'd faint. Then I saw it was Union Carbide, which he doesn't own yet, and laughed through a pair of cheese sandwiches and a beer some-body left in the upstairs refrigerator. Oh Dad, poor Dad. Hell, poor me. I didn't not love him. I loved him like a picture of Roy and Trigger I got when I was four. But you get so tired of throwing out all those rays of gee and wow, and getting back a big emptiness. Sooner or later the signals weaken, and love is something you remember and approve. But it's in the inactive file. Man from Glad, how would you like a boy about sixteen who doesn't know his ass from Buck Rogers and is badly mauled about the head and ears? That's what I thought.

—Listen, I'm going to get the nurse to stay with you, my mother said. —While I go find out if you can go home. You'd rest better at home.

—No, I said, listen . . .

But she didn't listen, and I was talking to the door. For a minute. Then it opened, and that blond groin-grabber came into the room. At flank speed. I thought maybe they had me wired, and the board lights were saying I had gone critical on them. But then, right behind her came Uncle Shad, one hand about four inches away from her twat. The four-inch gap was explained by the fact that his other arm was filled with boxes.

—Honey, you move like you was mounted on twenty-one jewels, Uncle Shad whispered hoarsely. —Now you just stay put there for a little bit.

Then he turned to me. —Boy, you asleep?

—Mother's here.

—So you ain't asleep. Or likely to be. Listen, I brung you some stuff.

One of the boxes was Chicken Delight. Ten assorted backs and wings. I think I like backs and wings best. Mother swore it was because my father and Uncle Shad ate nothing else. More likely it was because she always made me eat the breast when I was little. Uncle Shad said he didn't even know a chicken had a breast until he was twenty, away from home and buying his own. —Which was six years after I found out girls had 'em. Ain't that odd?

Another box was full of Budweiser. —If you're old enough to get broke up, you're old enough to get boozed up, he said, placing the last box, the biggest one, on my sheeted legs. The box was leaking a yellow liquid. —Pickles and stuff? I asked.

—No, he said, pulling it open and lifting out some wriggling something. —It's a bulldog puppy.

—Mr. Shad, the nurse said, —I don't think . . .

—Sugar, do I know you? Uncle Shad turned and moved toward her. —I just feel I know you.

She was a good nurse and a hard case. Didn't stir an inch. Stood her ground smiling. —No sir, you don't. But you knew my momma. She . . .

—Your momma. Why sure, Uncle Shad said, getting an arm around her shoulders in friendly fashion as he dropped the puppy back on my legs, —And your momma used to work . . .

—At Schumpert Hospital, the nurse said, still not backing and filling like a sensible girl.

—She wasn't no nun, was she? he asked, letting his arm drop around her waist.

—Oh Mr. Shad, no. She did the night emergency desk and one night . . .

—My God, when Larry Milby tore loose my ear, and there was this angel right straight out of heaven . . .

—Yessir, and she . . .

—She sure did, and we . . .

—Yessir, youall did, and she never apologized nor anything, my momma didn't, and anyhow she . . .

Meanwhile the puppy and I were staring at each other. He was either in shock or bilious, because he didn't pay the Chicken Delight any mind. He was pug-faced and irritable looking, and seemed mature for his size. But I could feel him trembling against my legs.

—Would you like a little Chicken Delight, Uncle Shad asked the nurse. —Or a Bud? Your momma was partial to rye whiskey. Drunk nearly a quart sitting up with me to see that ear didn't fall off and get swept away.

—Yessir, no, I mean I don't want any chicken and I can't have a Bud on duty, but momma . . .

Uncle Shad was kissing her neck and backing her over toward the bathroom door. She was holding her own, but not doing much to settle him down. Caught in the flush of maidenhood by a legend, I thought, as the puppy stalked up my legs and sniffed his way onto my chest. Her mother ought to have kept her mouth shut. Also I was hoping that bulldog puppy had pretty much done his duty before Uncle Shad unboxed him. Just then the phone beside my bed rang, and the blond nurse tried to go for it. But Uncle Shad had her pretty well, as you would say, in hand.

—Honey, what do they call you? Uncle Shad asked, getting her just inside the bathroom door and his hand just inside her uniform. Where the RN badge was pinned. —Catch that goddamned phone, he called back over his shoulder as the door closed.

—They call me Teenie, the nurse was telling him.

—I sure don't know why, Uncle Shad cooed, and that was the last I heard. For a while.

With all those bandages, the phone was beyond my line of sight, so I had to fumble for it. As I finally got hold of it, Mother came booming back through the door.

—Hello, I said into the phone, pressing it against the gauze over my ears.

—Hello yourself, Mother answered. Then she stopped cold, staring at the Chicken Delight and the beer. The puppy had lost his control and was throwing up down at the foot of the bed. I didn't blame him.

—Hello?

—Mr. Thomas Thompson, plu-eeze, some mechanical operator petitioned.

—You got him.

—Go ahead, plu-eeze.

—Hello?

And from a distance so vast that the call must have been placed light-years ago, I could hear him. The voice was tiny and twiny, but it was his, and I could see him in a white suit, his face tanned and carefully honed by providence for Great and Remembered poker games.

— . . . Remember Princip . . .?

—Sir?

— . . . in Serajevo . . . Herzegovina. Remember your history? They . . . Ferdinand . . .

—Sure, yessir, I remember.

— . . . Said you got banged up. You all right?

—Yessir, I'm fine, just a couple of cuts and . . .

— . . . Coming home soon as . . . You never saw such . . . mountains. Like Spain or Tennessee . . . want?

—Nothing. I'm just fine.

—Who *is* that, my mother wanted to know. —Is that . . . ?

—Tell Shad it's all fine. Salvation everywhere. . . . Tell him to hold Caddo and Bossier and East Texas together.

—Yessir. What should I tell . . . Mother?

—What? she asked, reaching for the phone. —Let me talk.

—Nothing, I heard from that enormous distance. —I'll be home . . . just get some rest . . . you hear?

—Yessir, and then she wrenched the phone from my hand and clapped it to her ear. —Tommy, she started. —Tommy? Then she put the phone down on the bed, a peculiar expression on her face. Like when she had first seen the bulldog puppy: mingled distaste and disbelief, each struggling to oust the other.

—It's a dial tone. There's nobody on that phone. I believe you *have* lost your reason.

—Oho, I told her. —It's a magic phone. There's never anybody on it unless you believe there is. If you don't believe, all you get is the dial tone.

—Anyway, she said, pursing her lips, ignoring my lunacy, —anyway, how could he find out less than two hours . . . where the hell did that . . . The bull puppy had taken his life in his paws and jumped to the floor. He was lurching about, trying to find something.

—And this beer . . . Jesus Christ, all you need is a six-piece band and some floozies.

She stopped dead, a can of beer in her hand. You never saw such a look. Orphan Annie eyes. Mouth like a tragic mask. —Oh, that wretched sonofabitch. Where is he? You tell him to take that goddamn beer and that goddamn puking bulldog, and . . . if he shows up again in this . . .

Just then the bulldog puppy sniffed what he was after and lumbered into the bathroom door. It opened easily, and there was blondie, her dress down and up, too, and Uncle Shad with something down and something up.

—*Mon dieu,* mother gasped, and I was proud of her. It showed real self-breeding. Meanwhile the bulldog pup was up on his hind legs lapping water out the commode, and Uncle Shad was trying to lever the door closed again with his elbow or his foot or anything he had free to operate with. But I was proud of him, too. He never even considered calling it a night. Finally, mother went over and pushed the door to. Then she came back and sat beside the bed, stunned.

—They said you could go home in the morning.

—No, I said. —I need rest.

—At home . . .

— . . . is where I can't rest. Maybe a glorious month in Herzego-vina . . .

—Where?

— . . . or Bossier. I don't know.

—Tom . . .

She never had called me anything but honey or baby. Tom sound-ed all right.

—We could take a trip . . .

—No, I said. —Maybe next time.

She was angry and puzzled, but that fine feeling for how things were, that power of atmosphere analysis that had carried her from cotton patch to crystal palace never missed a vibration. She knew just how it was. And what to do.

—Well, she said. —You tell Shad I'm surprised at him.

—Sure, I said. —Sure you are. I'll tell him.

She still had a beer in her hand. —You mind if I take this?

—Drink it in good health, I told her.

—Your daddy says that.

—I know.

She was at the door. Not wanting to leave. Dead certain she'd better. —Was that . . . phone call . . . ?

—Why, Momma, I said, —it was the Bossier Brothel, Incorpo-rated. Wanting to know how that nurse was working out.

The door shut quietly, and I eased back. Sometime back they had given me a shot or a pill so I'd sleep. So I thought I'd cooperate. Just as I was taking off for Bosnia, or Bossier, I heard Uncle Shad's voice. He was talking to the nurse. —You got to be kiddin'. And she's sixteen? Looks like your twin sister? Wants to be a nurse? Lissen sweetheart, you tell your momma me and my nephew are gonna come by and . . .

Then he was over my bed, looking at me, the nurse under one arm and that sullen bull pup under the other. —Lissen, I got news for you, he was saying.

As best I could, I turned back on for a minute. —And I got some news for you, I said.

Nothing Succeeds

I

Mr. Landry came to himself sitting on the terrace of the Forum, a Turkish restaurant. On Telegragh Avenue. In Berkeley, California.

In front of him, past a plate of lamb pilaf and a glass of retsina, out beyond the ornamental metal fence which divided the premises from the street, a young man without shirt, shoes, or socks was on his knees in front of a young woman who appeared to be wearing only a poncho. The young man's hands were under the lower draping of the poncho, and he was caressing the young woman in a manner not to be described. And this in the soft chill twilight, just before dusk, in that city across from the city by the bay.

—My God, young Fourier gasped. —This place . . . Sodom by the sea . . .

Mr. Landry said nothing. He had already committed his indiscretion for this trip. Flying from New Orleans, he had had three martinis, three glasses of wine, and three Courvoisiers. His head hurt and his sentiments were vague. He could not quite believe in the reality of what was passing before him. He remembered now why men drank. To spare themselves reality. Considering what lay out there, he could not blame them. He had not drunk so much since those days in the Kappa Sigma house. At Tulane. In 1926, in the fall.

—I see it, but I don't believe it, young Fourier was saying. —It's like a show. Like some crazy sonofabitch putting all his dreams on a stage, one after another.

Young Fourier half rose to his feet. He had found another tableau now. A street band of incredibly dirty and hairy men, some young, some not so young, standing on the sidewalk half a block down, playing, singing. They would whip their guitars and pass from hand to hand a single cigarette. The music was not unpleasant. The words were unclear and distant. Something about John's Band. At one point, the guitar accompaniment fell away, and Mr. Landry was almost shocked by the wonderful purity of the few bars of *a capella* that followed. He shook his head. The young man and the young woman still stood in front of the Forum, still engaged in their rite.

The only difference was that now the young woman had begun to move sinuously in time to the distant music. The young man began to nibble the young woman's thigh.

—Maybe he's broke, young Fourier snickered. —Maybe he can't afford anything . . . to eat. Young Fourier coughed, appalled at his own words. He had had six martinis, nine glasses of wine, and Courvoisiers beyond his counting on the way out from New Orleans. The curse and the temptation of first-class air travel. He was LSU School of Law, 1963, well aware that Mr. Landry suspected him of bestial tendencies. Tulane peopled the law offices of New Orleans, as a rule. The country parishes were left to LSU. It was supposed that Tulane produced gentlemen. Still, young Fourier had been at the top of his class. Mr. Landry had taken a chance. Now young Fourier glanced at Mr. Landry, who was squinting down at the band.

—I think it's the Grateful Dead, young Fourier volunteered.

—God rest their souls, Mr. Landry said, and sipped his retsina.

They had come to California to find Lancelot St. Croix Boudreaux III. He had been gone some five years now, gone, as the Civil Code had it, from his domicile, his ordinary place of habitation. No one in Breauxville had heard from him. No one on the Island had the slightest idea where he might be. The last word from him had been a large dog-eared postcard mailed from Sausalito. It had had a picture of Sather Gate on the front, and on the other side, a line of barely intelligible scrawl in Greek. The Old Man had sent for Mr. Landry, who had translated it for him. Mr. Landry well remembered Colonel Lance Boudreaux, body twisted with age and arthritis, sitting propped in an ancient rattan chair on the sun porch of the Mansion.

—Well, the Old Man had asked, —what the hell does it say?

—It says, "Rejoice with me, for I have conquered the Kosmos."

The Old Man had stared at him malevolently. —René, I don't need a goddamned joke. What's that supposed to mean?

Mr. Landry had shaken his head. —It . . . I don't know. Christ said it . . . somewhere.

—If I could get hold of that crazy young sonofabitch . . .

But he couldn't. Mr. Landry knew how much money the Old Man had spent trying. Detectives. Special investigators. A Louisiana state trooper placed on detached service as a favor to the man who dominated agriculture in South Louisiana. One report had come back from the trooper and then silence. It was generally thought that he had defected and might be found somewhere in San Francisco with a flower between his teeth, mind and body rotted by dangerous drugs and controlled substances, more easily obtained there than good licorice down home. Anyhow, no one in Breauxville or on the Island had any idea what Sather Gate was, and no one, including Mr. Landry, who at least had the advantage of having lived in New Orleans since his college days, could say what Lance might mean about conquering the Kosmos. That year, the rice and hot-pepper farmers on the Island and around the town were worried about the weather. There had been a novena for rain at the Immaculate Conception Church. The rain had come, and there was a big thanksgiving festival. Colonel Boudreaux, volatile as the pepper sauce which had made his family fortune almost a century before, had built and dedicated an altar to Mary Queen of Heaven. Even he had no illusions about how to deal with the Kosmos.

Mr. Landry shivered. It had turned chilly now, and the lights along Telegraph Avenue had come on. The parade of the peculiar had not ceased. The band was playing something about a dire wolf, and youths in leather jackets and Kit Carson rawhides, girls with Indian feathers and Betty Boop makeup stood about listening, smoking. One boy with a Mohawk haircut, wearing only a loincloth, was stretched out on the sidewalk insensible. He had not moved for quite a spell. But no one paid him any mind, and Mr. Landry supposed people knew whether he was all right or not. He drank more wine, and thought that he should have brought winter clothes. It was summer here, and almost as cold as a New Orleans winter day. Hate California, it's cold and it's damp, Mr. Landry thought randomly. My God, that warning from so long ago. Tommy Dorsey and His Clambake Seven. It was not the weather of Louisiana. Nothing about California was like Louisiana.

— . . . the list, young Fourier was saying. —We go up to the university tomorrow. A professor in Eastern religion. Some physicist . . . the police . . .

They had come to find Lance Boudreaux, to take him home. At least to tell him that he was universal legatee to his grandfather's estate, that he was heir not only to the Island and to 6,000 acres of prime farm land on the mainland growing peppers and rice and cane, but to the factory and the business itself, which turned a yearly profit of millions sending the Island's torrid pepper sauce to countries everywhere, most of which had not even existed in 1869 when the first Boudreaux had managed to scrape together enough money to purchase the Island from a carpetbagger who had been shot up on four separate occasions, whose cabin had been burned down with fearsome regularity every time he had left it to go into Breauxville to purchase supplies. Altogether the estate was estimated to be worth some seventeen million for tax purposes. In fact, thirty-five million was more like it.

Eight days before, L. St. Croix Boudreaux I had died on the Island. Mr. Landry had been there. As he had been present at every important event in the chronicles of the Boudreaux family since 1927, the year he had taken over from his father a law practice begun in 1880, when the first Breauxville Landry had come home from Rome, Georgia, after fifteen years of wandering beyond that day he had been cast loose from Forrest's cavalry after his nation died. Mr. Landry had continued to take care of the Boudreaux business even after he had moved to New Orleans and established a staid and careful banking and real estate practice there. He kept a home near the Gulf and a tiny office in Breauxville chiefly for the Old Man, who would trust no one but him. Not because the Colonel had any great opinion of his legal talents, but because the Old Man never changed anything. He could abide sin, but the very idea of change seemed demonic to him; hence Mr. Landry, who was perhaps less rigorous on the point, but felt guilty because of his willingness to meet the times as they came, had never even attempted to suggest that another lawyer, closer to home, would be more immediately available to the Island and its master's needs. And the years had gone by. Mr. Landry could remember when he was a boy fresh out of law school, and the Old Man was no more than forty. He had seemed immortal, as if the Island would sink and the land turn to granite before he would be stirred, moved to leave this place where his people had been so long. But, Mr. Landry thought, looking out and up at the cold dark green shadows of alien hills, nothing endures. Things change. There is a succession of all things. We rise into light, stare into the sun, and then pay the penalty to time for our existence. Nothing succeeds but succession, he thought wryly. What was that phrase they always used in law school? *Le mort saisit le vif.* The dead enseize the living. The living have nothing not willed them by the dead. Not even life itself.

The Old Man had died hard. It had been a lonely death in the Mansion there on the Island. Covered with gingerbread, the legacy of the first Boudreaux who had come to the Island a hero for no other reason than taking it from some Yankee scum hated for his Anglo name by whites and blacks alike, the house had grown as each new generation had come along, until in the time of the Old Man, the family had begun to shrink. Colonel Boudreaux had come back from the Great War a hero like his ancestor, crossed with sashes and decorations from Belgium and France, each almost mad with pleasure at the notion of decorating an American who spoke French and bore a recognizable surname. But he had had a single son, no more, to raise as carefully as another man might have collected Limoges porcelain—only to see him take to the sky in the 1930s and make an independent living dusting crops through the southwest parishes, hurling his patched biplane over cotton fields from dawn to dusk as if he were determined to destroy the Colonel's pleasure. But it appeared the Old Man's will had sustained him, and Lance Boudreaux II had survived three crashes in order to enter the Army Air Corps in 1940 and rise to the rank of colonel himself before, at last, amid a conflagration too vast even to be managed by his father, Lance II had gone down in the winter of 1944 over the oil fields of Romania.

Dying, the Old Man had called for Lance. Servants, some of them the children of West African blacks who had been brought to the Island before the turn of the century, speaking nothing but their own brand of French, swore the Old Man was calling for his son. Some, less traditionalist, had claimed he was calling for his grandson. But it made no difference. Neither could be produced. The grandson had vanished amid the turmoil of California as surely and as finally as the son had vanished over Ploesti. So that Mr. Landry had sat there during the final hours, being spoken to as if, at almost seventy, he were son and grandson alike, hearing what had been and what was to be, how the Island would sustain them all until the very ramparts of infinity itself were breached, and the Truth should come to relieve them of their burden.

Mr. Landry had drifted into sleep once or twice, only to be awakened by one of the blacks bringing the narcotic required by the Old Man, and a glass of fine Napoleon brandy for this lawyer, this man whose sole duty it was to remain awake, to hold to his duty until the end. The cool stare of the servant reproved him, and he had thrown down the brandy and sat straight in his chair.

He had remembered the boy. Not well, for he had been hardly more than a cipher, a presence in a distant room somewhere when the Old Man and Mr. Landry did their business. Lance III had been a curly-headed shadow, the sole remnant of his father's life, purchased, as it happened, from his mother for a price. His mother, found by Lance Boudreaux somewhere between Orange, Texas, and Lafayette, Louisiana, on one of his airborne careers across the bottom of the state. In a diner, in an auto court, in a dime store, or to put aside euphemism, in a whorehouse. His mother, who had come into Mr. Landry's New Orleans office one autumn afternoon in 1954 at the invitation of Lance I, whose mansion she had left almost before Lance II had gotten across the sea, and who, for reasons buried in her heart and possibly in the soil of Romania, had, in return for a cashier's check for $250,000, signed an authentic act by which she gave over permanent custody of her son to his grandfather, agreeing that the Old Man should adopt him and treat him in all particulars as if the boy were his own son, as if, in fact, there had been no generation intervening. She had smoked and read, smoked and signed. It was done, and the young Italianate man with her, most recent in a long succession—her chauffeur, someone had snickered, 'cause he rides her—rose, offered his arm, and guided her back to the dusty Cadillac parked downstairs.

—Did you want to see him . . . before . . . ? Mr. Landry had asked her. —You see, there are no visiting rights . . . not ever. . . .

She had paused for a moment, as if she did not understand what he was saying, what he was asking her. —See him? He's dead . . . isn't he?

—No . . . I mean his . . . your son.

—Oh. No. I saw him. Last Christmas. He looks like Lance. Exactly like Lance. He'll die, too. You watch. You can't depend on them. They act like gods, nothing can hurt them. Then, when they get you to believing it, they go and die. No, I don't want to see the sonofabitch. . . .

She had gone to Houston then, had lived in a suite at the Shamrock Hotel for four years in what Mr. Landry had been given to understand was a state of sybaritic luxury and perpetual unrelieved drunkenness, hiring and discharging chauffeurs one after another, having, on occasion, more than one at a time, buying extra cars to justify them if not to anyone else, at least to herself, not because morality was at issue, but because of the extravagance so shameful to a girl from a South Louisiana diner, auto court, or even whorehouse. Until one evening, full of Black Jack and Nembutals, she had fallen or leapt ten stories onto a lower roof and bounced, broken and bloody, into the swimming pool to bob there, a shambles of ruined meat, amid hysterical guests of the hotel, who, no soberer than she, could not fathom this thing in the water which had invaded their evening's pleasure and floated there before them, draining red fluid into the scented water, semblance and prophecy of last things. Her most recent chauffeur had left her, it seemed, and her money had run out. But Mr. Landry, who had a long recall, was never sure it had not been an older and deeper wound that had sent her spiraling down out of the sky into the oil-rich of Houston even as Lance II had gone down into the oil of Romania.

Fourier had finished his stuffed grape leaves, downed the last of the wine, and begun on his list again.

—You know, he quit Tulane, but he seems to have finished med school at UCLA. If he wanted a new life, why do you reckon he went back to medical school all the hell and gone out here?

Mr. Landry gestured to the moustached waiter for more wine. It was absurd. He was mildly drunk, but he did so anyhow, and saw a grin of anticipation appear on the face of the Turk or Greek or whatever he was. As the wine flowed, the tip mounted. Mr. Landry smiled back at him. It was the only normal, calculable response he had seen since landing at the San Francisco International Airport. —*La vita nuova*, Mr. Landry heard himself mutter.

—How's that, sir? young Fourier asked.

—Everybody wants a new life, Mr. Landry said. —Only what they really want is the old life. Once more. To do better.

Young Fourier's face was flushed. He was beginning to feel his liquor. —Shit, you know, that's true. . . .

Mr. Landry did not smile. He stared at Fourier. Even a man taken in drink should control his language better. An attorney in New Orleans, at least one connected with a good firm, did not use such speech. Not even in his sleep. Conclusions might be drawn.

The wine came, and it was cold and tart, the resin adding a fresh element to the old flavor of decent, not excellent, white wine. That was why they added it to the wine, the ancients. Not to preserve, but to enhance.

Mr. Landry remembered Lance's room—no, rooms, really, in his grandfather's mansion on the Island. Like a pawnshop, Mr. Landry had thought. Rooms filled with books; records; equipment; laboratory supplies; musical instruments; film projectors; a heap of cameras, including Rolleis, a Speed Graphic, a Leica; rakes; spades; oyster knives; rifles; shotguns of every gauge; a rack of pistols, including black powder weapons, Colt's Navy, Remington Army; reproductions of paintings from every conceivable period nailed to the wall in and out of frames, including a Rousseau which might well not have been a reproduction; three-dimensional chess sets; television monitors; uniforms of armies current and long disbanded; flags from nations no longer in existence; bundles of periodicals ranging from the *Yellow Book* to *Acta Chemica*, journals representing every imaginable profession and interest; tents; and uninflated life rafts; cracked wooden Buddhas; archaeological rubbish from the pre-Columbian period of the Americas and from Sumer and Akkad; canteens; axes; magnifying glasses; retorts; microscopes; and a great chart of the zodiac which almost covered one wall, its corners pinned down by enlarged photos of Proust and Rommel, an Indian swami of uncertain identity, and Artie Shaw—all this and so much more. There was a coin collection, including U.S. gold pattern coins which had never been issued. There were stamp albums and envelopes full of bank notes from failed countries, bottles filled with formalin in which there floated and bobbed the decayed ruins of two-headed kingsnakes, large worms from the Amazon, and an embryo of something like a pig or an ape, which, heedless of gravity, hovered like a tiny dancer, its something like a mouth caught in a permanent leer, its unfinished limbs swaying in the cloudy fluid, filled with a faint golden dust composed, it seemed, of cells from the thing itself.

But Mr. Landry could not, for the life of him, place amid this recollected clutter the face of Lance Boudreaux III. He could, in memory, see there sprawled between a large crate of clay pigeons and a lithography stone, the figure of a small boy sitting cross-legged above a board of some kind, a shiny instrument in his hand, and to one side a large leather-bound book obviously older than the Boudreaux holdings themselves, in some strange language, its print large, some passages in red. Mr. Landry remembered looking down, his eyes still sharp in those days, seeing just these words: *O Diabolus, Dominus Mundi, ad Servus Tuum, Veniat. . . .*

He had thought little of it. The Latin, after all, was not strange to him. He had served mass from his tenth to his seventeenth year and could recite the ordinary of the mass, his part and the priest's, without a falter. As it happened, he did not know what all the words meant, and Father Briscoe had suggested that he not bother to learn, as it might confuse him.

Still he had known what those words meant. What he could not bring to mind was the board, and whether anything was on it. Nor could he remember the boy's face. All he could conjure up were a pair of green eyes and a strange distant sound in the background, something over a local radio station with the improbable title "Thermopylae."

—By God, it's . . . Jerry Garcia, young Fourier said. —Look.

The street band had come closer now, and the one Fourier had noticed looked much like all the rest, bearded, a little rotund, long unkempt hair, work clothes, a guitar clutched to his belly. He paused in front of The Forum, smiled a beatific smile. The young people around clapped. —This is for Lance, he grated, —wherever, whenever. The One Who Stands. . . . Then he began to sing, and the others, hirsute, pallid, grasping a variety of instruments, joined in.

The Turk brought baklava, and young Fourier whispered that they could use one more bottle of the retsina. The waiter looked at Fourier and then at Mr. Landry. Could they manage yet another? No, Mr. Landry thought, but goddamn the Turks. He nodded soberly. One more. As he walked away, Mr. Landry tried to make out the lyrics of the song. Something about out of the earth, out of the earth, the soul of the earth, the soul of the earth, the soul of forever. The wine came then. They ate the dessert, paid the bill and left tip enough so that the waiter paid no mind when they rose carrying not only the bottle of wine with its cheap paper label, but the two glasses as well.

They walked back to the Carleton Hotel then, Mr. Landry taking care, walking slowly, a little unsteady, looking into the windows of the bookshops, headshops, small restaurants specializing in natural food where he could buy a bowl of brown rice for twenty-five cents, complete with a pair of chopsticks which broke in two when you drew them from their cheap paper wrappers. There was Robbie's Chinese walk-in, and a place that specialized in hot dogs of various kinds. There was a newsstand on the corner near the campus with copies of *Rolling Stone, Crawdaddy,* and other papers dedicated to music and nature and how to build a cabin in the Sierras or the Rockies without help and without nails.

The hotel was quiet, its lobby dark. Only the desk area was lighted, and as they passed to go to the tiny elevator, Mr. Landry thought he saw figures reclining in the lobby, on sofas, chairs, and even on the floor. There was only the night clerk awake, his eyes wide and fixed on a telephone switchboard without lights, a cigarette caught between his teeth, and the sweet distant stench of smoke, which young Fourier identified as that of extremely fine dope.

When he reached his room, Mr. Landry expected that he would fall asleep quickly that night. But it was not so.

Instead, as he lay down, he found himself standing in subdued sunlight, under a live oak tree. Before him, in the cool morning glow, between rows of blooming gardenias, were a terrace with a small fountain and open French doors. Mr. Landry could hear music coming from beyond the doors. A Mozart sonata.

He stood for a long moment, breathing deeply. By God, Mr. Landry thought, not here. Even dreaming. Even drinking too much for the first time in forty years. I don't want to be here, because even now, so old that the very memory of love seems an embarrassment, I can't stand it. I would rather dream of hell, Milton's flames and Dante's ice, than remember what I have not thought of in almost thirty years.

But nothing changed. He was still there, in the courtyard of the house where they had lived when they were first married. The music stopped, and he heard her voice continuing the melody, low, crystalline, close by. He had wanted to think the sonata came from a phonograph, but he realized that then they had had no phonograph. There had only been the piano brought from Mandeville, from her father's summer place across the lake. Later there would be a phonograph, and music from it in the morning before the sun broke through the trees. He would put on Albinoni or one of the Marcellos, or perhaps Vivaldi before she woke. He would brew the strong rich coffee and chicory which they ground and mixed themselves, and set two cups on the linen cloth draped fresh each morning on the metal and glass table at the shaded end of the terrace. And when the sun's first light touched the peak of the fountain, he would go into the bedroom, lean down and kiss her, waking her gently, bringing her back into this pendant world they shared, knowing that nothing in it mattered so much as her presence, her smile, her love.

Then they would sit on the terrace and talk until the sun touched the edge of the cloth and he rose to gather up his papers and walk down to St. Charles Avenue where the trolley ran. Only in the depths of winter was that ritual broken, or on those mornings when rain drove them into the breakfast room.

He was still standing, it seemed, in the back of the yard near the old brick wall covered with English ivy. He walked toward the terrace then, toward that melody he had not heard in so many years, knowing that he would not get through the open doors because, even dreaming, that was too much to hope for, and that never before in the years intervening, since that last morning they had spent on the terrace, had he found her image again as he slept. He thought, because if I could walk through those doors, there is nothing in the universe, given that I could see her face, which could draw me out again. I would die there, go to hell there, and laugh at the cost, saying how can you scare off a man who has not cared whether he lived or died in thirty years, who has had nothing to wake up for but the bitter law in thirty years? As if, God forbid, death were something other than an end to life, indeed rather the terminus of all things, beyond which nothing lay at all. By then, it seemed, he was on the terrace, that previous voice so close that he knew she must be sitting just within the shadow of the doors, on the piano bench sorting through her music, searching for something to follow the Mozart, most likely one of Bach's inventions. He remembered then, not the day but the epoch. It was 1938, the spring. He was doing well. Not as well as he would do later, but well. She was not pregnant then, would not be for months yet. But she would be in the fall of 1939, and that pregnancy for which she had hoped and prayed would silence the music for all time, leaving not even a child behind. Nothing but pain. He stepped hopelessly into the dark doorway, turned.

And found himself blinking into pale sunlight falling through the blinds of the room. He looked around the faded walls covered with cracking wallpaper. The woodwork, varnished many times, was dark with age and scarred by the transient blows of generations of baggage and bellmen. Strange what the sun does to whatever it touches, searing away the blur of the commonplace, individuating each scar and crease, setting apart that thing as standing forth in itself alone.

Mr. Landry rose slowly from his bed and walked over to the washbowl beside the windows. The mirror was in shadow so he switched on the weak naked bulb above. He saw his face then, and a spear of shock thrilled him. Awakening from the terrace, from the mild New Orleans spring morning long ago, he had almost forgotten. I am nearly seventy now, he thought, looking at the spare controlled wizened face that had not belonged to him on such a morning long ago, which had only lurked then in the well of possibility, presuming the practice did not kill him, in case he survived the loss, the winter afternoons and interminable evenings alone. In case he was unfortunate enough to extend his life across time, missing each likely chance to die until he came at last to stand behind this ancient alien face that she had never seen, would, by the grace of God, never know.

I'm even older than that, he thought, shaving slowly, carefully, with a straight razor she had given him that last anniversary they had been together. It shone in the pallid sunlight, its edge honed deep into the heavy body of the steel. He had used it for over thirty years and more, as if to do other might be to deny the meaning, the magnitude of his loss. I'm so old that I can't hold it off any more. Only a little while to go, and it's catching up with me. As if dying were no more than the sum of things you love rushing up from behind, overcoming you, rescuing you from time.

He began to dress. He had control of himself now, and he did not think how many times he would be willing to die in order to enter those French doors two thousand miles and thirty years away, to turn and find her there, three, five years into their marriage, leafing through her music, suddenly looking up surprised, saying, —René, do you know the time?

Yes. He knew. The summer of 1938. On State Street and sometime past eight in the morning. Almost time for him to be downtown in those oak-lined, book-filled caverns where the minor keys of his life were scored and played out.

Down on Telegraph Avenue, he could already hear music and see people moving though the sun had barely risen high enough to touch the street. They looked as if they were dressed in rags. Women wearing loose ugly dresses and shawls over their heads. Men wearing cloth caps and cheap coats and ragged pants. He remembered Prague just after the war, but he could not remember that the sun ever shone. The people there had dressed like these, had moved like ghosts or sleepwalkers amid the tumbled ruins of their city and their lives. But they had had no choice. Something alien had invaded their lives. *Das Dritte Reich,* a demonic vision separated entirely from reality. It had come upon them, and when finally it had dissipated, there was another vicious dream to take its place.

He shook his head, staring downward. But why do these children pretend? Why do they act as if they were the remnant left over, the human particles somehow not claimed by the holocaust? Jesus, he thought, it doesn't take artillery, does it? It doesn't take the Nazis. It takes no more than the destruction of the soul. In Prague there had been music, too. Street music. A blind violinist sitting on a box next to the broken wall of the gutted railway station. Before him on the shattered pavement lay his cap with a few coins in it and on his chest, on the lapel of a frayed suit coat which did not match his pants was a beautiful ribbon with a military decoration hanging from it. He played only two or three songs, but Mr. Landry remembered how strange it seemed that one of them was "I'll See You Again," as if out of his darkness the violinist chose to mock the visible world and all that it purported to contain by mocking himself.

II

Young Fourier knocked. He was casually dressed, without a tie, his hair fluffed up as if he had not combed it. He noticed Mr. Landry's long inquisitory look. He smiled what Mr. Landry supposed he considered an ingratiating smile.

—When in California, young Fourier laughed. Mr. Landry walked to the elevator. On the way down, he studied the list of faculty members they were scheduled to meet with while Fourier studied a map of the campus. The lobby was empty now, and a new clerk was behind the desk.

Just outside, there was a newspaper rack, and the headline of the *San Francisco Tribune* howled BAY HORROR KILLINGS. It seemed that in a nearby suburb south of the peninsula, in a place called Daly City, police had discovered the bodies of a number of people hideously murdered, as if according to some ritual. The body of one young woman had been cut almost in two. There was evidence that she had been in an advanced stage of pregnancy, but no fetus had been found.

Mr. Landry almost dropped the paper. He wondered sometimes if these things actually happened, or if there was a stable of demented journalists somewhere paid California-size salaries to conceive of the most incredible degeneracies that diseased and fevered minds could invent. But he knew better. In the firm there was one young attorney whose lot it was to handle such criminal litigation as could not in conscience and good business be avoided. He had casually told Mr. Landry enough of his own experiences to convince. The story in the paper was doubtless true. For a fleeting moment, Mr. Landry wondered which of his sins might be the specific one for which he had been condemned to live into this generation.

He threw the paper into a receptacle as they began to walk toward Sather Gate. Along the way, students seemed to be everywhere, handing out leaflets of one kind or another. Some supported, some attacked, but all were written in a dialect only approximating English, and each one howled a Great Outrage, a Crowning Act too Loathsome to be Borne.

—They really get steamed up, young Fourier observed, steering Mr. Landry toward the cafeteria.

—But it's all the same, Mr. Landry said, peering through the handful of urgent messages that had been pressed upon him.
—Support the Farm Workers' Union, don't buy table grapes, free

Huey Newton, open admissions and no tests for minorities, abortion at state expense, or we will bring down the social order. What is anyone supposed to make of that?

—It's all nonnegotiable, Fourier allowed, his eyes crinkling as the first shafts of sunlight reached the broad cool plaza.

—Ummm, Mr. Landry smiled approvingly. —Nothing is nonnegotiable . . . except . . .

—They don't have that out here, Fourier said quickly. —Everyone is too young to . . .

Mr. Landry nodded. He looked around as they entered the cafeteria line. Fourier was right. It wasn't surprising to see so many young people on a campus, but he could not remember seeing anyone much over thirty since the plane had set down across the bay. Toyland. An adolescent fantasy.

As they ate their eggs, Mr. Landry mused. —I wonder why young Boudreaux would have come . . .

—Here? Didn't you say he was . . . weird?

—Ummm. He wasn't . . . I never said . . . weird. Out of the ordinary.

—Sir, every spook and freak and stranger in the country is tuned in here. It's the music and the politics and . . . everything. It's where it's at.

—You mean, where it is.

—Whatever. But if Mr. Boudreaux's grandson was . . . out of the ordinary, he'd . . . This is weirdsville, sir. There's not a normal person within ten miles of us right now. Skin-freaks, dope-freaks, bomb-freaks . . . these people do anything they want.

Fourier looked around. At the next table, two blond girls in shorts and halters were eating and talking rapidly. Mr. Landry had the notion that both were attractive by the standard of the time, allowing for the fact that they were barefoot, hair uncombed, breasts almost exposed in the loose halters, and the shorts so closely cut that one of the girls, when she moved her legs, exposed a portion of pubic hair. Mr. Landry was not shocked. He had visited zoos before. However worthy animals might be, they did not clothe themselves, and some of their personal habits were coarse.

As he regarded them, one of the girls was saying to the other, —. . . told me, you want an ace in Math 390, you got to give head. That's it, honey. You know any chick with an ace in there, you know she's been down . . .

Young Fourier blushed. Mr. Landry turned away, understanding only the syntax and grammar. The words meant nothing at all.

—This is the heart of the beast, Fourier was saying, as he threw down the last of his bad coffee quickly and picked up his tray.

They walked through Sather Gate into the academic campus, and on toward a low building done in some style only to be described as a California view of Spanish colonial. Inside it was cool and subdued. At a desk a young woman with olive skin, burning dark eyes, and a peculiar accent spoke softly into a phone and told them that Professor Khaldoun would see them.

The office door was deep scarlet color, and on it Mr. Landry and Fourier saw the lovely swirls and rises of Arabic script. Underneath, in small roman letters it was declared that here stayed Professor Khaldoun, professor of Middle Eastern thought. Below that was pasted a crudely mimeographed broadsheet which declared the unyielding determination of the Palestinian people to recapture their homeland. And, incidentally, to scourge from the face of the earth those who had usurped it.

They knocked and entered, in time to see Professor Khaldoun face down on a small carpet, a shaft of sunlight embracing him. He completed some formula in which he was involved, and rose quickly, smiling, to greet them.

—You will pardon me, he said in excellent English. —It must be done. You are the lawyer Landry from New Orleans?

Mr. Landry bowed, offered his card, and pumped hands with Professor Khaldoun in that peculiar fashion he had learned from distant French kin, which was the style almost everywhere but in America.

—You come about Lancelot, Professor Khaldoun said musingly, as he moved to a small table behind a cluttered desk and began to prepare cups of strong dark coffee.

—Yes, Mr. Landry began, staring along with Fourier at the process, almost unable to wait for the thick aromatic brew after the nasty stuff they had had in the cafeteria.

—Your letter said his grandfather . . . was no more?

—Passed on, Mr. Landry answered in a similar hushed tone. It is of the essence of advocates that they be able to take on at once the color of the place where they must work. It is not a conscious thing, or it would be useless. It is an inherent capacity by which he who would preserve or alter the status of a situation in which he is alien shifts his cognitions into the key dominant among the contenders with whom he deals.

—Allah, may His name be praised, is just. So be it.

—Amen, Fourier said almost mechanically. Mr. Landry did not

look at him. It fitted nicely and was to be expected. Fourier's family, originally from Breauxville, was Baptist and of a peculiarly demonstrative sect given to baptisms in the bayou and penitential utterances on Wednesday evenings so loud that passing Catholics were chilled at the sound of booming declarations of the most intimate personal failings, as if someone had put their own whispered confessions on an amplified loudspeaker.

—And by that passage of his ancestor, Lancelot has become rich?

Mr. Landry's expression did not alter. He was used to greed by proxy. —He has become universal legatee to a considerable estate. . . .

The professor placed steaming coffee before each of them and sat down. He smiled indulgently.

—A considerable estate. By the standards of your South, I am sure.

Mr. Landry's eyes narrowed. —A considerable estate. By Saudi Arabian standards, I should think.

The professor's eyes widened. —Land?

—An island, and perhaps 6,000 acres of the richest farmland in Louisiana. There is also a lagoon, and a number of servitudes on adjacent estates.

Professor Khaldoun spread his hands. —What can I tell you?

He told them a great deal. He told them of a tall, bearded, green-eyed young man with a silver star emblazoned on his forehead, whether by tattooing or some other means he could not say. He said that this Lancelot, who never used any other name, had appeared before him at the end of a quarter, had demanded, under university regulations, to take the final examination in a graduate seminar on late medieval Islamic thought, and had, before the professor's eyes, completed the nine-part examination in less than an hour.

—When he handed me the papers, he said I was wise, and it was good to contend with me before Allah, may His blessings embrace us. And when I looked at the papers, he had written the examination in Arabic.

Moreover, because of this wonder, the professor had followed Lancelot's doings thereafter, had even gone to hear the opening of his band at the Hungry i, a club in San Francisco reserved for only the most immediately popular rock bands. There he had heard the peculiar rhythms and Eastern melodies of Lance's group—but most strange, the lyrics.

—I cannot remember to quote, he told them. —But names like "I talk to the sword," "Doom at the bottom of your cup." That one, it was about poisoning. It said he had come from a violent place, a place where men were connoisseurs of guns and knives, a barbarous place. But that he sought a place without violence, where all contention was settled without the shedding of blood. Where those who could not exist together would vie with poison—poisoned food and drink, poisoned garments, poison in flowers, in rings, poisoned letter-paper, vials of poison gas in autos. And there was this terrible refrain,

> Belladonna, deadly nightshade,
> make again music that once was made,
> Angel of death, dark as the sea,
> prey upon those who pray not for me.

—Is this what is taught in New Orleans? Professor Khaldoun asked.

—No, Mr. Landry said. —No. I think not.

—The juju, young Fourier began.

—Jews, the professor mused. —It is not surprising. The Kabbalah. They are a venomous people. Their ways . . . but of course you know. . . .

Mr. Landry rose abruptly, thanked the professor, telling him that there were others that must be seen. They held each other's eyes for a long moment. Then the professor shrugged. —He last came here after obtaining his doctor of medicine degree. He had already degrees in physics and philosophy. That time he was clean-shaven, indeed, his head was shaven, and the star was gone. He wore a caste mark where it had been. We talked. He said that he embraced the cause of all those who had lost what nothing else could be subsituted for . . . that he would be the physician of the world.

—You understood. . . .

The professor's eyes flashed. —Of course, I understood. . . .

Mr. Landry was astonished to see tears in the professor's eye.

—He will give back to the bereaved their lost homeland. . . .

Fourier and Mr. Landry exchanged glances as they walked back into the outer office where the sultry secretary fixed them both with her dark eyes.

— . . . and so you had better not to seek him, because . . .

Mr. Landry was astonished to find himself turning, looking at the professor as if from a great distance. —If I forget thee, O Zion . . .

—Selah, Fourier said hoarsely, and the young secretary said some-

thing in a harsh vicious whisper in no language either of them understood.

—Deny him his inheritance, they heard the professor cry after
them, his voice muffled by the partitions and the distance down the
dimly lit hallway, —keep it from him, or perish with your kind. He is
Lancelot, a true Christian, a hater of those whom all Christians hate
. . . a true . . .

III

Professor Hellstrom awaited them in his office. Mr. Landry approved of him at once. The office looked like a monk's cell. There
was no desk, only a table, three chairs, and a blackboard covered
with that peculiar arcana of the physicist which had shaken the
world more profoundly than all the pother of Hegel, the ranting of
Marx. Young Fourier was amazingly subdued as they entered the
office. He held Professor Hellstrom's hand for a long moment.

—I . . . never thought . . . to meet you, sir . . .

Hellstrom was a man of middle height, deeply tanned, his eyes
almost hidden by thick glasses. He smiled broadly. —You do physics, son?

—I did . . . in college. Enough to know that . . . nothing is like it
was before you . . .

—I ain't Einstein, son. Just an old East Texas boy who got through
Sam Houston State in math . . .

— . . . and shared a Nobel prize for tensor analysis of photon
vectors.

—I should have been a metaphysician, the professor laughed.

—You are, Fourier said, and subsided.

Mr. Landry felt uncomfortable. He did not grudge Fourier his
knowledge, his capacity to evaluate, however crudely, the work of
another. He only wished he had done as much. He said nothing.
Only watched the two of them as the professor lit a long slim cigar
and offered one to Fourier.

—You got one hell of a young lawyer here, Mr. Landry, Hellstrom
said. —You know that?

—I didn't know it, Mr. Landry said honestly. —I'm beginning to.

—Don't a lawyer have to be able to see into things? He's got to take
on as many roles as there are, don't he?

—I think he does. All things to all men.

—He knows all you need to know about what I do, Hellstrom

said, leaning his ladderback chair against the wall. —I wish my goddamn genius graduate students knew as much. Hell, Lance knew it. That's how he walked in here, did himself a Ph.D. in S-matrix theory in a year and half and walked away. Shit, he raped the goddamned department, you know?

—Sir?

—Tunneling theory. He did some equations that would make God cry for the sheer beauty of them. Take a look at this.

Professor Hellstrom slammed his chair to the floor, grabbed up a piece of chalk and a rag, and began to scrawl equations across the chalkboard with one hand as he erased with the other. —This is what he did. Described how the proton world-line has to be calculated outside any dimensional structure, how virtual particle exchange is no sort of exchange at all. Look.

More equations. Fourier leaned forward. Mr. Landry sat back. Professor Hellstrom wrote faster and faster. —Sonofabitch, take a look at this.

—No time coordinates, Fourier said.

—That's because exchange doesn't happen in time. All determinable dimensions are consistent. Do you understand?

—Then, there is no pion exchange in I-space. . . .

—Wrong. There is. The nucleon is defined variously as proton or neutron depending upon the positionality of the pion. But not dimensionally. The exchange is not a physical event. It's a mental event, and that goddamned Louisiana coonass figured how to set it out. . . .

—That's . . . Nobody . . . Fourier began.

—Right. It's all a crock, Hellstrom said. —Except for one little old thing. The sonofabitch set out equations that fit the data. Nobody believes they mean anything. Shit, when I back off, neither do I. But now and then, just once in a while . . .

—He joined physical and mental events. In a unified mathematical field.

—Yeah, that's what I think he did. But the bastards in this department . . . bunch of goddamned positivists. Proof doesn't mean a damned thing to them. Logical rigor, beauty, that damned perfection of something that works straight out, upside down, or sideways—they don't give a damn. Listen, if I hadn't had that damned piece of gold from Stockholm, they'd of told Lance to go take him a degree in astrology. . . . The finest mind since Niels Bohr . . . and these dumb bastards . . . They're looking for the next transuranic element. As if Glenn Seabourg hasn't given us enough of those damned phantoms.

—Do you know where he is? Mr. Landry put in. —We have to find him.

—Ain't that the damnedest thing? Hellstrom winked at Fourier. —All this and a bundle of money, too. Naw, I don't know. All I know is this damned school had the best mind in thirty years, and all these cretins in physics wanted to do was burn him at the stake. Listen, there's people in this department would like to put out a contract on Feinmann. . . . You don't know what it's like. Some of these guys come to colloquiums and quote Einstein: "God doesn't play dice with the universe."

—That's nonsense, Mr. Landry said. —Of course He does. It's His universe, isn't it?

Professor Hellstrom sat down at his table. From somewhere he pulled forth a bottle of Jack Daniels. —Youall don't know what a relief it is to sit down with sensible men. You bet your sweet ass He does. Lance said this cosmos, the choirs of heaven and the furniture of earth, is His entertainment. He whiles away eons in loving play, and this pendant universe shall sum zero, ending like a great prelude and fugue, everything coming out.

—Right, Mr. Landry said. —Praise be His name.

—Right, Professor Hellstrom repeated. —I tell you this: Lance *knew.* Physics ain't just experiment and reasoning any more, you know. It's . . . something else. Lance used to say go listen to Bach. Put on the Second French Suite for harpischord. Number is all. You remember what Paul Dirac did? Pure mind. Pure insight. Let the goddamned experimentalists fool around in the mud. Kids like to make mud pies. But it's mind. Pure mind. If I can set out the positron in my mind, if it's rigorously correct, if it's beautiful . . . then it's true. Because . . .

—What we do in the mind is more than just . . . Fourier began excitedly.

—Right, Hellstrom cut him off. —It's the only truth. The world is a place we have in the mind . . . the only world there is. Lance knew. The last time he came by, he told me. He said, I have put down the darkness. I mean to bring the light. I am the one who stands. . . .

—Is there somewhere we might look for him? Mr. Landry asked.

—Sure, Professor Hellstrom grinned. —Somewhere in the dimensional structure of our world. He hasn't figured out yet how to be free of it. In his mind he knows . . . but . . .

—Yes?

—He's still made of meat. But if anyone can break free, he's the one. Lance is . . . he understands . . .

IV

They walked back the way they had come then. It was close to noon. Students poured out of the classroom buildings, and they saw workmen putting up audio equipment near the stairs of the administration building. Blacks with absurd hairdos, intense young men with thick glasses, women with broad shoulders, all were gathered watching grimly as the loudspeakers were set in place. Down toward the end of the walk, where Telegraph Avenue struck the purlieus of the campus, half a dozen pushcarts had drawn up, and students were buying hot dogs, burritos, or brown rice with sambals from hairy proprietors. Mr. Landry and Fourier chose the brown rice, a health food, according to the placard on the side of the cart. It was nice and strong and they put soy sauce on it and ate it with chopsticks, squatting there at the mouth of Telegraph, looking down its length in the glare of sun from a cloudless sky, able to see almost a mile, utterly unlike the humid Louisiana noontime when clouds were building toward thunderheads and the moisture spread a haze over everything not immediate and close at hand.

As they ate, a man came out and placed a box on the pavement close to them. He was the epitome of rednecks. Fourier shook his head and Mr. Landry watched him closely. They wondered if he could be from California with that red hair, that face like a side of aged beef covered with freckles. As they watched, students began to gather around, laughing, speaking to him in good humor.

—Hey, Hubert, where you at? What's the good news, Hubert?

The man smiled back at them, drew some of them close and spoke to them earnestly. From under his nylon jacket he drew a tattered book, struck it with his hand, driving home some point he deemed important.

—Must have stolen it from the Gideons, young Fourier observed. —See?

—He looks like someone from Shreveport, Mr. Landry said. —Or Plain Dealing. Or Oil City.

—He's fixing to preach, Mr. Landry, young Fourier said.

Mr. Landry rose to his feet, aware for the first time that he had been sitting on the grass in his business suit. With his Dobbs hat on. Something in the air, he thought. Maybe if we could just get all these poor devils to Texas, they'd be all right. Maybe they ought to declare California unfit for human habitation.

He was dusting pollen and grass off his pants when he heard, over Hubert's breathless, excited nasal drone, another round of applause. He looked up to see another box being placed on the pavement some ten or fifteen feet from where Hubert was preaching. But the young man setting up the box was astonishing. He was tall, hair long and twisted in contorted bundles like the locks of a gorgon. His face bore an unchanging expression somehow both sneer and triumphant smile at once. He wore a set of evening dress clothes, complete with white tie and tails, so old as to have lost its smooth blackness and turned a dark green, the color of patina on an ancient coin. He wore a top hat and a long cloak of a hue not quite matching the suit. His formal shirt was filthy, and in place of cuff links Mr. Landry saw he had twisted paperclips to hold his cuffs together.

He worked with feverish speed. When the box was set up, he draped it with a piece of seedy scarlet velvet. Then, down on his hands and knees, he scratched out a pentagram with a piece of charcoal, placing indecipherable initials in the five points of the star.

—I don't believe it, young Fourier was saying. —Do you believe it?

—I'm looking at it, Mr. Landry said. —I guess I *have* to believe it.

By then, Hubert had noticed the new arrival. He stopped in midsentence and watched the young man jump to the top of the box, lift his arms above his head, and scream out in a voice of amazing volume and power, —*Satanas diabolus*, here in the blaze of noonday, here at the end of the Western world, come to us, bless us, send us your power and confusion, grant us chaos, and slaughter us all—dead, dead, dead. . . .

Cheers from some of the students who had been listening to Hubert, and who now moved to encircle the tall boy. He swirled his cape, twisted his body, and uttered short, piercing squeals like those of a trapped bat.

—Some prayer, Fourier observed. —How the hell can you get an audience with stuff like that? Who wants to die?

—O God of Israel, God of Abraham and David, cast down the infidel, the unbeliever, Hubert intoned as if it was a formula he had used often before.

The young man turned on him, laughing exultantly.

—That's him, he howled. —You invoke him, too. The one you call God is Satanas, creator of the world, enemy of the pleroma, hater of the uncreated . . .

—O God of Moses . . . , Hubert began.

—God of Moses, the young man echoed, —send us the doom reserved for the gentiles. Let us know of you by way of your judgment on us. O God of the festivals and lights, God of the popes and emperors, God whose madness and cruelty is the model for all mankind, God whose whores and pathics are everywhere, God who crucified him who came, the New Anthropos—bless the tongue of this prophet, and let his mouth run with blood. Teach him blasphemy, and show him how to kill. . . .

Fourier had been speaking to a long-haired girl standing nearby. —She says it goes on like this almost every day. She says last Good Friday was something else. . . . The nut in the tuxedo was crying out for the death of Anthropos, whoever the hell that is, and Hubert was crying for the blessing of innocence in the blood of the lamb. Said it started to rain, and Hubert called it grace. The other nut called it blood.

Hubert paused until his antagonist at last ran out of breath.

—I tell you this, he said. —I hope the Lord burns your rotten ass for a thousand years, that's what I hope . . . you goddamn commanist. . . .

The students booed. Fair play for the devil. The Satanist crowed triumphantly. —You see, brothers, he curses his own God. . . .

—Jesus and the Holy Spirit, put him down, Hubert howled. —Send him down to suffer with youall's enemies . . . enemies . . .

—Jesus is a joke, the young man shouted back.

—Hey, young Fourier said, turning toward Mr. Landry just in time to see him move toward the box the cloaked young man was standing on and, with a single hard kick, upend him, sending him sprawling into the rice cart, overturning it too and causing confusion among the scattered long-haired students. —Go it, Hubert yelled. —See, the Lord answers; the Lord provides; now don't he?

Young Fourier pushed two haltered sunbleached blonds aside, grabbed Mr. Landry, and began walking rapidly across the street, down Telegraph, toward Dwight Way. —I want one of them big hot dogs down the street, he said in a controlled conversational tone.

—That miserable bastard, Mr. Landry said, to the astonishment of Fourier, —taking our Lord's name in vain.

—Well, Fourier said, his pace increasing, —I know what you mean, sir. Bunch of perverts . . . whole state full of 'em.

The perverts, at last having gathered themselves together, headed out behind the young man. His cloak was befouled with rice, and behind him, looming like an omen, was Hubert singing out praise for him who had brought the godless low and walked in grace before his God.

—Listen, we could let that hot dog go. I mean, we got a lot of places to go. . . .

—Go with God, Hubert cried after them, eyes and arms aimed heavenward. The young man in the cloak and those who followed had stopped now, as if the love of evil caused short-windedness.

V

It was a hovel. She lay inside on what Mr. Landry called a pallet. Fourier squinted, his eyes watered from incense.

—Yes, when he came out of the swamp, when he came here, he was just wanting everything, wanting to get shut of whatever it was back there. He said that in July all over the island when the peppers bloomed you could smell the heat, smell the mud, the rot in the swamps. It was a paradise of heat and moisture, no matter what way you turned. Birds, egrets—what he called water turkeys, gulls. The sky full if you shouted across the water. Listen, I don't know. All I know is what he told me. What do I know about all that swamp crap? He told me that in the evening he would go down to the water and watch the bugs rising, the fish hitting at them, the moonflowers opening for their single night of blooming, the birds calling out of sleep, as if even having wings was no caution against bad dreams. And the nutria and the muskrats and the snakes. Oh Christ, the whole island was alive. The soil, the water, the trees, the plants in the bayous—there wasn't anything at rest. And he was alone in the middle of that, his father had gone down, his mother too, and that old man not caring about anything but sending the message on. What message? Oh, God only knows. Some kind of crazy Southern thing. How can I tell you? You ought to know. You're from it, both of you, aren't you? Anyhow, we met at Gillie's the first night. Gillie the head. From Charleston or Atlanta. Working in physics till they caught him standing on line in front of the accelerator. No hair after that. Eyes almost gone. Had gone into the rad lab on an acid trip, looking for the substrate, the Boundless from which all arises and to which all returns. His fingers and toes started to go later. Something was wrong with the blood, so he couldn't even play lead anymore, only slap out rhythm. Nothing but nubs, see. But Gillie told him it was worth it, that he'd seen the God of Dirac and all his works. Jesus, I should have known right then, you know? But we stayed, listening to Gillie and that funny spade broad who read him *I Ching* and *The Journal of Physical Letters* everyday. She was juju. Came from some godforsaken island, Haiti, Martinique. Someplace where they do magic, you know. When the pain started making Gillie scream and even smack didn't help, she'd whisper to him and he'd laugh and they'd go into some dance. She called it smoke trance. Said she could bring back the dead with it, that they'd be zombies, but that was all right because all the whites she knew were already zombies, though she couldn't figure out how since nobody but her knew the smoke trance. Said she could keep Gillie alive, even with all those pieces of forever lodged in him. What? Yeah, the radiation. It was tomorrow that came out of the accelerator. Said it was wrong to rush things up like that, make them come before their time, and that's why they hurt us when we conjured them. Gillie used to argue with her, said we needed to get on. She'd say, all in good time, fool. They know about good time all over this prison, man. So when we left Gillie's, it was almost dawn. You want to go to my place, I said, till you find a place. Naw, he said. Here's what I want you to do. Take me to the ocean. I want to see it when the first light comes. It's not much, I said. The sun comes up on the other side. You can only see sunset on this ocean. He laughed, and we got in his Land Rover, this big thing like a jeep full of every kind of crap you can imagine. Books, microfilms and a reader, clothes, bottles of stuff, tools, cooking gear, a guitar, but mainly books. Gillie said he would be a great physicist, only why bother, there was shorter ways. But we drove across the Golden Gate into Marin County and found this place, so when the sun rose, and the fog started burning off, he could see it spreading out, mile after mile, to the horizon. I never seen a ocean before, he said. Then he kind of looked all around. It ain't much, he said. I expected . . . something. It's only the biggest ocean in the world, I said. Yeah, I know, he told me. Ain't that a goddamn shame. I don't know; it pissed me off. I come from Sacramento, and this is the best ocean there is. This cracker was putting it down. Why don't you just go on back where you come from, I asked him. I will later, he said. My end is my beginning. Not now. Want to screw? Yes, I said. Afterward, we got this place and he went to school. You know, he signed up at Cal, and he signed up at the med school. He was taking his M.D. and this Ph.D. in physics and this degree in music theory. He started at five in the morning and kept going till one or two. Maybe four hours sleep. On the weekends he played lead with guys over at the Fillmore unless he was playing viola with the crowd of creeps in the quartet at Grace

Church. And there was the poetry he wrote in class, and the music while he was eating lunch. Had this notebook with lined paper and music paper. Carried it to the toilet, kept it beside the water bed, woke up even in that four hours and scrawled things down. Like that for four years. He finished the physics and the music, but they kept giving him trouble in medicine. The residency, when he gave each patient a mantra and told the ones dying that they were and that it was good, that they had been tarrying too long, that it was time to go home. They tried to get rid of him, and he cursed the chief physician, and the next night the big shot smothered in a motel with some nurse, and they found both of them dead and naked with him on top, and they never let Lance forget. Anyhow, you know, we stayed together for four years. Everybody said, Christ, how can you stay with this guy? How can you stay with anyone so long anyhow? Gee, you know, I told them, you never screwed this guy, you never had him. Listen, you know, it was worth it. All we did was drink a lot when he was off, and take the Rover out into the country with Inglenook Cabernet and watch the sun rise and watch it set. I mean, you know, I wanted everything from him. I told him I wanted his baby. You know what? He hit me. He said anybody who wanted a baby was evil, slave of the demiurge, wanting to trap perfection in flesh, to lessen the God, to drive sparks of divinity into the darkness of life. He knocked me down, and he asked me if I was pregnant, and I said yes, and he said, you stinking whore, you're not even married. How can you be pregnant, you slut, tell me that? I said, what; he said, no. I said, don't; he said, yes. And he kicked me in the stomach and hit me with a wine bottle and somewhere along the line I zonked out, and later when I woke up, we were at Gillie's, and his woman was leaning over me and I wasn't pregnant anymore. She said, you were sick, but now you're well. Praise Lancelot, because he knows. Praise the Great Lord who hates all ills and cures us from the sickness of life. You know what? He took me to this real cool apartment, this place near the bay, and he left this envelope and kissed me and said he couldn't take any more chances, that I had bad ways, and anyhow, he was movin' on. I said, no, you know. What will I do? You're weak, he said, you'll do just fine. Bye-bye. I cried for a long time, and I bled a lot, but later, when I got sober or whatever you get, I looked in the envelope and there was ten thousand dollars and a year's lease for the apartment in it. So I said, oh shit, it's all over anyhow, you know, and I called Kip Mendosa, and I said, hey Kippy, listen, you always dug me, you wanted me, huh? Come on to this groovy place and listen, get me a couple of bags huh? No, I know I never did. But now I want to, okay? Yeah, yeah, I can learn anything you know. Living is so bad, really, huh? Really. And I only saw him once. Saw him with some woman at the concert down in the canyon. In Strawberry Canyon. Mechanix Illustrated Celestial Dragon Dong, you know? His hair was real long, tied back. He had all these people with him, and the chick, you know, it made me want to hurt him real bad. Because she was pregnant, real pregnant, and hanging on him, you know, and he liked it. Even across half the canyon, I could tell, really. You know?

VI

It was evening again and Fourier was watching a waitress in Japanese costume as she walked quickly and gracefully toward the table, a huge tray balanced on her shoulder. It was dark now, and they sat, the three of them, in a restaurant on Fisherman's Wharf.

— . . . the first time, it was something about drugs. I've got it here.

Lieutenant Raphael riffled through pages in a file he had brought with him. —We had a snitch lay out a little trip ol' Lance had in mind. Down to Mexico in the Rover, and back with ten or fifteen kilos of hash. He was going the back way, the snitch said, across the desert, up through the Superstitions till just above the border.

—Did you . . . ? Mr. Landry let the rest of his question hang, as if he didn't want the answer.

Fourier's attention wandered. The Japanese waitress set out raw fish and sauce before him. He began to eat, his eyes holding hers. She was very beautiful, her expression smooth and cheerful, enameled in place like her hair. Fourier wondered what it would be like to make love to a woman so perfect, so complete. Nothing was perfect or complete where he came from. It was wild and half made up, mad with growth, unkempt. As she finished, smiled, and turned away, he wondered if she was what civilization meant.

—Oh, we went after him. The whole business. Men everywhere, choppers, close cooperation with the Mexicans. You name it. . . .

— . . . ?

—The sonofabitch drove right through us. We never saw the Rover, and the next night they found the snitch next to the fence at the San Diego naval base with his throat cut and a tarot card tucked into his pocket, the hanged man. The word was, hash dropped nine dollars a cut that day.

—The snitch, Mr. Landry began. —Did you ever . . . ?

—Very seriously dead; not a clue. The hanged man, Raphael said. —Seemed unnecessary. Editorial comment.

Raphael pitched into his fish. —The next time was that business at the Four Square Gospel Tabernacle. I saw him that time. Hell, I heard him. They broke up, you know.

—The woman he was with . . . ?

—Huh. There wasn't a woman then. Naw, she turned up later. It was the tabernacle that broke up. It seems he came in one Sunday, and the preacher asked for a witness. So your boy witnessed. Held forth from nine in the morning till four in the afternoon. By seven o'clock, they had a new church. Church of the Living Fire. When the preacher locked up that night, all he had left was the building, and a few old Four Squares who couldn't hear a different drum if you pounded it with a barge pole. There was some trouble about the building, and that's how we got involved.

—You heard him . . . preach?

—I guess that's what you call it. He talked and they listened.

—What'd he preach about? Fourier asked, his attention drifting back. —I mean, I thought he was . . . some kind of hippy.

—Not that night. Naw, he had on a suit, and his hair was cut short. Preached on the last things.

—Last things, Mr. Landry repeated, thinking for no reason of a terrace cool and pure in the rain.

—Last things, Raphael repeated, and fell silent. The waitress brought their main courses, fluffy shrimp tempura, sukiyaki. —He said what had been, and what would be. He told us from whence we were flung and where we're going, what we were and what we're going to be. He . . . started to . . .

He paused, chopsticks suspended, eyes distant. —He said a lot of crap, Raphael finished shortly. —Impressed the peasants, that was all.

At the end of the meal, the waitress brought green tea. They sipped it slowly, as if it were a ceremony of their own. —The last time, it was just an accident. The emergency room of the university hospital. We had a cop with a magnum slug through his lungs. He was spitting blood, and somebody called his wife down in Richmond, and I was holding his hand, and the doctor in the emergency room was working over him, and I heard him say, he's going to make it. The slug was AP, not a wadcutter. Nobody knows how to do anything anymore. And I looked up and it was Lance, and I damned near passed out, because you get used to seeing certain people in certain places, and this bastard you see everywhere. He looked at me and said, "Not to worry, cher; this one ain't ready to leave yet." I started to say something, but they came to take Alec to surgery, and I had to go, and I saw your boy kind of dancing down the corridor with his stethoscope waving, singing something like, *Goodbye, Joe, me gotta go, me-o, my-o* . . .

Outside, they could hear thunder over in the county. The windows of the restaurant began to mist with rain. —Did the cop . . . Fourier began.

—Oh yeah, Raphael said. —Fine as wine. Got well, left the force. Works at City Lights Books. Reads poetry. Laid down his sword. Police shrink called it posttraumatic stress neurosis. Wow. Goodbye, Joe . . .

Mr. Landry gaped at the check, pushed it toward Fourier, who set his gold American Express card on top of it. The waitress's smile enlarged, as she moved away.

—Is Lance . . . I mean, do they want him . . . now? Mr. Landry asked Raphael.

Raphael studied Mr. Landry for a moment. —I don't know, he said. —I don't. Even if I did, I don't know how hard I'd look. Alec and I . . . were tight. But, down in Daly City . . . aw hell, it doesn't mean anything. There are so many spooks in this town that anything that gets done is gonna get done twice.

—What? Fourier asked. —It might be a . . . lead.

Raphael shrugged. —Down there, they had a bad killing. Bunch of heads. One girl cut up. They found it in her hand. . . .

—What? Fourier asked again.

—Tarot, Raphael said. —The hanged man.

VII

—If they had a cathedral, like Notre Dame or something like that, I'd look for him there, Fourier was saying.

It was the next day, cool and clearing. The radio claimed there would be rain later. They sat on the terrace of the student union, looking out over the campus, wondering where to go next. —Or an opera house, Fourier finished.

—I think it's time we went home, Mr. Landry said. In fact, it was not the failure to find Lance Boudreaux III that depressed him. It was California. In its beauty, its almost theatrical perfection, it made him sad. It is finished, he thought. There isn't anything to be done here. California is the reward for having trekked across America, across Texas and Arizona, or from Missouri and Kansas, through

Colorado. All the anguish, the loneliness, the dry-blazing days and chill nights sprawled out across the continent. Came here, from New England in the 1840s, from Tennessee and Alabama in the late 1860s, from Oklahoma and Nebraska in the 1930s. The weather was never extreme. The people smiled. The vegetation was never wild, not like the kudzu and wisteria in Louisiana that grew everywhere, on houses, fences, weighing down young trees and clogging storm drains. Lance Boudreaux had left the Island and had found his way here, where the sun was pale, and the breeze cold and damp from the Pacific. Let him stay here and freeze, Mr. Landry thought. I should go home. Maybe he belongs here now. Maybe this is his country.

—Christ, Fourier said. Mr. Landry looked up to see a long-haired girl, slim and lovely, walking across the terrace, a big German shepherd on a leash behind her. She was naked above the waist except for an unbuttoned leather vest. She paused, looked around, and saw Fourier and Mr. Landry staring at her. She walked over to the table and smiled. —Are you the lawyers looking for Lance?

Mr. Landry stood up, almost bowing. —Boudreaux . . . ?

—Ummm. Somebody said . . . you've got something for him.

—We represent the estate of his grandfather who . . .

— . . . kicked . . . ?

—Ummm. Yes. Gone now. Leaving only . . .

—Lance. How much?

Fourier grinned at her. —Don't ask, honey. You wouldn't believe it.

Mr. Landry frowned. —A substantial sum, he said. —Do you know . . . ?

—Ummm. Might. But I don't know you.

—What's the difference? Fourier asked.

—Narrow-minded people, the girl said. Her smile was lovely. She had a flower over her ear, tucked in her pale hair. —There are people, you know, *people* who don't like Lance. Who want to hurt us . . . him.

—We have certain papers, Mr. Landry began again. —Authentic acts . . .

—Wow, the girl said, leaning forward, shoulders back. Time stopped for Mr. Landry. Her breasts opened that same cool garden in his heart. Twilight came, and he felt a catch in his throat. He had not seen such things in so long. —Wow, authentic . . . that's what Lance just loves. . . . He says you've got to feel it and then *do* it. . . .

—Do what? Fourier asked, his eyes fixed not on hers, but down below.

—Anything, she said. —Any old thing at all. I'm Miz Minerva. You can call me Min. . . .

—Can you take us . . . ? Mr. Landry asked, coming back from another place.

—Ummm. Gimme your name, and I'll let you know. I got to tell Lance who it is. . . . Does he know you? I mean, really *know* you?

—No, Mr. Landry said. —No, I don't think so. But I knew his father and his mother. I knew his grandfather.

—Gee, Min said. —I never knew my father. I don't know if I even *had* a grandfather.

—Everybody has a grandfather, Fourier told her.

—Not *authentically,* Min said. —Not so they notice it. I don't even know where my father came from. I mean, he could have been from *Tanzania.* . . .

—I doubt it, Fourier said dryly, moving his chair closer to Min's, his eyes scuttling about her like small animals.

—Christ, I don't even know anybody who ever *knew* their grandfather. In California . . . I mean, *nobody* in California . . .

—Yes, Mr. Landry said gently, —California . . .

—Okay, listen, Min said, seeming to lose interest in the talk. —I got to go now. I'll get back to you, huh?

—The Carleton Hotel, Fourier said. —You know?

—Oh yeah. See you . . .

She rose, one last movement of her shoulders leaving silence in her wake. Mr. Landry and Fourier stared at her as she left, the shepherd padding behind her. Mr. Landry finished his coffee. Fourier forgot his.

Min turned as she reached the broad walk that led to Telegraph Avenue. —See you . . .

VIII

They waited for two days, going no farther from the hotel than it took to eat, and even then leaving word and money with the clerk to pay street people to find them if a call should come from Min.

On the third evening, they were eating at Robbie's. A dollar and a quarter for all the chop suey and fried rice you could eat. Cafeteria style. Mr. Landry used his silverware. Fourier had managed to learn his chopsticks in the time he had been there. Someone on the street was singing "Roll Over, Beethoven" at the top of his lungs. A police car passed, lights blinking, but no siren. Silent running. Fourier looked up. Satan's messenger was there. He held his top hat in his hand, turning the rim rapidly in his dirt-encrusted hands. He stared down at Mr. Landry, who paid him no mind, eating his chop suey slowly, turning the bean sprouts around the fork, as if it were spaghetti. His eyes were light, a peculiar green, and he paid no mind to Fourier.

—You are the one, he said portentously, flicking his cloak about him. —You are the *one*. . . .

Mr. Landry looked up from his meal. —I doubt it, he said. —Get thee behind me, beast. And let Him who saved the world send thee down to darkness . . . forever. . . .

The Satanist backed away. —Forever . . . ?

Mr. Landry gave him a wintry smile. —For as long as there is. . . .

—He sent me for you. He says you're supposed to come with me.

—Shit, Fourier blurted out. —Who sent you?

—The One Who Stands. He says for you to come. . . .

Fourier looked at Mr. Landry. —I think I ought to whip up on this bastard, he said. Mr. Landry shook his head.

—You mean Lance Boudreaux? he asked.

—That is one of his manifestations, the Satanist said. —Now is the time. He could pass on at any moment.

—Oh, bullshit, Fourier said, pushing his chair back, his brow furrowed. Mr. Landry saw him for the first time as a country man, unhappy in the presence of evil, dejected in the presence of sin. Beyond his education, Fourier hated baseness for its own sake, and for the first time, Mr. Landry was reconciled to him. He reached out and touched Fourier's arm. —Louis, let it alone. We have to finish this.

They started to rise together, Fourier's eyes wide, having heard for the first time his own Christian name in Mr. Landry's mouth. —Sure, yes sir. Right.

In the street, there was a Volkswagen van parked. It was covered with symbols: pentagrams, peculiar Latin quotations, a dragon with its tail in its mouth, an incredible creature possessing sexual organs both male and female, signs of the zodiac, the names of forgotten gods, Babylonian, Sumerian, Egyptian, and across the front, something with wings, terrible claws, and a great gaping scarlet emptiness where otherwise a face might be. Fourier looked at Mr. Landry as the side door slid open. Mr. Landry was about to nod when a boy dressed in work clothes with a necklace of seashells and a gold stud through his nostril twitched his sleeve. —From the hotel, he said, and Mr. Landry, forgetting he had left money with the clerk, handed him two dollars as he passed the paper over. On it was written in a small neat hand the words, "Raphael has something you need to know."

—The perfect master is waiting, the Satanist said.

—Hey, Fourier asked him, —you reckon Minerva is gonna be . . . wherever it is we're going?

—She is Helena, the Satanist whispered, —the great mother. She follows the Lance. . . .

—She is one great mother, Fourier said. Then he looked at Mr. Landry. —A message from Min?

—No, Mr. Landry said, thinking whether to take time for a call or wait until later, until he had seen Lance Boudreaux III and gotten his business done.

—The time is now, the Satanist rasped, prodding Mr. Landry in the ribs. —Will you, won't you, will you, won't you, won't you . . .

Mr. Landry followed Fourier into the van. As the Satanist reached out to slide the door shut, Mr. Landry stared out into the darkness at him. —I won't, he said. —And when this business is properly done, I mean to whip your evil ass.

As the door slid shut, the last two things Mr. Landry noticed were the leer of the Adversary, and the look of utter astonishment on the face of young Fourier.

IX

It was somewhere in the mountains behind the university near Strawberry Canyon as far as they could tell. The inside of the van was even more bizarre than the outside. In there, painted in some luminiscent pigment on plastic was a three-panel mural of a Black Mass. The scene was set in the dark center of a forest, like the Schwartzwald or the Ardennes. There was a crescent moon standing high above the trees, luminous clouds bathed in moon rays giving the appearance of motion. Down below, in a clearing and among the gnarled leafless trees, figures of strange shapes moved toward a central place where there stood a circle of stone, and in its midst, an altar upon which lay a beautiful blond woman who looked astonishingly like Minerva, her body nude, full breasts pointed toward the dark skies, her eyes open, fearless, staring upward at a presence poised above, with a body formless as shadow and the lurid bearded face of a man. The thing poised there held in a claw a piece of flint or granite aimed not at her heart, but at her belly, full, as if with child. There was an understanding between them, the demon above, the demon below. Mr. Landry saw Fourier shiver, his mouth twisted in disgust. Fourier had come to California curious. He was beyond that now.

They drove. The van turned this way and that, moved up into the hills past silent houses dark in the night. As they rose higher, the fog began, that same fog that Mr. Landry had seen before, coming in from the Pacific slowly in the late afternoon before the sun faded behind it, inundating the Golden Gate bridge, filling the bay. It seemed to cloak the van now, to swathe it and remove it from the town below or the mountains around. The Satanist sat in the front passenger seat. The driver beside him was hairless, his head and neck thick and bare. As he drove, Mr. Landry heard him breathe. It sounded as if he were snorting, as if he were angry or disgusted. He shifted gears violently, making the van jump as it slewed around the tight curves. The Satanist's hair was matted, as it lay in long greasy coils on the threadbare, filthy collar of his cloak. Mr. Landry noticed that his own jaw was tight, so tight that he could not swallow. He had never been so close, staring ahead at someone he wanted to kill. It had grown on him slowly. At the campus, watching the dark cloak whirl, at the Chinese cafeteria, staring, claiming. To be a lawyer was to know that evil comes no harder than words or a turning away. The Satanist was a comic figure—no, rather he would be in the South. In Breauxville or New Orleans, his garb, his words would draw a crowd of puzzled yokels, black and white, perhaps a Baptist or a Witness who would frown and listen, and after a few amazed moments, swing, lash out and knock him down in front of the loungers and weekend shoppers while the laughter welled up all around. But here, somehow he had become real. As if the worship of death, sickness, disease of the soul, the Great Refusal, was the other face of a coin that stood on edge across the continent, Januslike, transposing realities. What was real in the South was fantasy here; what was real in California was a joke down South. To cross a desert is to pass through a door. Mr. Landry closed his eyes. He was there again, and his jaw lost its tension. The music was a fantasy, he thought. How right. He could not tell whether he was thinking or remembering. Something of Telemann. Quick, mercurial, terse. He felt a trace of cool wind across his face.

—Time to go in, he said aloud.

—What? Fourier said, a little too loudly, his voice piercing in the confines of the van. The Satanist twisted his head around. The driver snorted.

—Nothing, Mr. Landry said quickly, realizing that the breeze he had felt was not off the Mississippi or Lake Pontchartrain. The Satanist had opened his window and was lighting a thick cigarette wrapped in brown paper.

—You all right? Fourier asked Mr. Landry in a whisper. —Is it getting to you?

Mr. Landry smiled. —Fine, he said.

One of the results of aging in the law is that you are not easily gotten to. By the time you have been at it thirty or forty years, you have done so many things no one should have to do that something has drained out of you, to be replaced with the law, like a creature trapped in mud which is hard pressed for a long, long time, leaching away the soft parts, making everything over. In stone.

He remembered going to Houston to identify that woman who had been Lance Boudreaux III's mother. She lay nude on a chrome shelf that slid out of a wall. He did not recognize her face. It was distant, cool, wholly at peace. He had never known her that way. It was the wedding ring, bitten deep into the flesh of her finger, that he knew. He wondered why she had not had it cut off, sold it, or thrown it away. What had she loved, what hated? He took her back to be buried on the Island. The Old Man had little ceremony. One evening the coffin arrived, the next morning it was buried next to the gravestone with Lance Boudreaux II carved upon it, underneath which there was nothing. Because nothing had been sent home. Because there had been nothing to send.

That had not mattered to the Old Man. Because almost nothing mattered to him. Except that he had a fine sense of symmetry, and there in less than an acre were all those who had gone before, or at least a stone to note their having been. And a stone for a dead son disintegrated over Romania. And the body of a woman who would rather have been dumped in the landfill of East New Orleans than be laid to eternal rest in that soil just offshore, under the eyes of that old man.

—Where, Mr. Landry had asked, —is Lance?

—In school, the old man had said, drawing his pipe, striking it on a stone named for some anonymous Didier who had died in this place, whose relation to it was not even known to those whose forebears had lived here a hundred years. —Nothing. No need . . .

Mr. Landry frowned, trying to remember what his fee had been for bringing her home. It had been high. He charged the Old Man not simply on the difficulty or importance of the matter, but on whether he wanted to do it or not. He had not wanted to. Had not wanted to look upon her dead face, nor see to it that she was

brought in death to the place she had fled in life. Not because he
honored her unspoken wish, or even felt he should. She was Lance
II's chief mistake, compared to which crashing his fighter was no
more than a minor slip. But it seemed cowardly to bring one dead to
a place she would not have willingly come to in life. It had not been
the first time he had done such a thing—indisputably from cowardice that other time—and so he charged a great deal for his bad
conscience. It had not helped at all.

The van skidded to a stop, the motor died, and in the silence
following, all he could hear was the snorting of the bald driver
whose face he had not even seen. No one moved for a long moment.
Outside, the fog was so thick that Mr. Landry could see nothing.
There was only the weird glow from the black lights which illuminated the murals. Then, almost without motion, the Satanist
opened the door and stepped outside. He disappeared into the fog,
but they could hear him breaking underbrush, crushing leaves,
then his footsteps sounded crisply, as if on brick or flagstone.

—Come on, he called from the fog. —Come on.

Fourier reached over and opened the sliding door of the van.
Tendrils of fog and the chill night air invaded, making the inside like
the outside, the outside like the inside. Mr. Landry stepped out
gingerly and waited for Fourier whose arm he took. Not because
Fourier could see any better than he, but because Fourier could
stand a broken leg better. Young legs mend. They should shoot old
men with broken legs. They mended no better than horses.

—Why won't you come on? the Satanist's voice came from the
darkness. —He waits.

Fourier cursed under his breath. —He can goddamn well wait.

Mr. Landry clucked at him. —You sound like you belong here.

He could hear Fourier's breath catch. —No sir, no way. These are
not my people.

They turned a corner or topped a hill. Even later, trying to reconstruct that moment, they could remember only that one moment
they were in darkness, the next in light. There were eucalyptus
trees and Pacific cypress all around, a fountain in the center of a
Spanish patio illuminated softly by hidden lights. To their left there
was a glass table, beyond French doors soft light, and piano music
from within.

It was Mr. Landry's turn to gasp. He almost staggered, reached
out to steady himself against a tree trunk. He closed his eyes and
listened. The second French suite. She had played it when she was
very happy, very sure of herself. The stone in him began to melt.

There were still soft parts. He began to move toward the open French doors. The fog was thicker now, and he felt its moisture condensing on his face.

—Whoa, Fourier said, catching his arm. —Wait for me.

As they reached the door, the music stopped, and he could hear the rustle of pages turning. He stepped through the door and brought himself to look to the left, where the piano was, where it should be. There was nothing but a large chair, an ottoman, and a low table where a pipe smoked in a marble ashtray. He turned back, confused. Across the room, there was music again. Something from Haydn, a sonata.

—Hi, Minerva said, her fingers moving quickly across the keyboard. She wore a long sari of some peculiar shade between blue and green.

—Uh, hi, Fourier began, but the volume of the music suddenly rose, and its character changed. It was the "March of the Meister-singer." Fourier turned, and across the room, he saw Lance Boudreaux III.

Mr. Landry shook his head to rid it of the pain of remembering. The man coming into the room had long hair, a beard, and a long sarape. He was tall, broad, his belly beginning to sag. There was a long scar that began on his temple and vanished into the beard. He was smiling, and he swept across the bare wooden floor toward Fourier. —The lawyer, he said. —You're the lawyer from down there.

His voice was low and smooth, and it filled the room, covering the piano's last notes, the snuffling of the driver who stood now at the French doors with the Satanist. Mr. Landry saw his face for the first time. It was sallow and wrinkled. The driver looked as old as Mr. Landry at first glance. His eyes were round and large and deep. His nose was like a beak. He and the Satanist seemed to be waiting for something.

Fourier's eyes were almost as wide as the driver's.

—That's him, over there, he managed to get out, pointing at Mr. Landry. Lance turned slowly, and Mr. Landry could see him in three-quarter and profile before they stood face to face. He tried to see in any view some semblance, some resonance from the past that would recall the room in the old house on the Island, and the small hunched figure leaning, chin in hands, over a large shabby book. There was nothing. Not a hint.

—Uncle René, Lance Boudreaux said. His smile was a light source. —You came all the way here . . . to see me. All the way out . . . here.

—Lance, Mr. Landry answered, automatically extending his hand.

Lance Boudreaux took it in both of his. His fleshy face, hand-some, deepset dark eyes, was aglow with unfeigned pleasure. —So long, Lance said. —What? Almost fifteen years now.

—Nearer twenty.

Lance Boudreaux's smile broadened. He took Mr. Landry's arm and steered him toward a rough Mexican-style staircase. —No, he said softly, as they began to climb the stairs. —That last time . . . you didn't see me . . . behind the house, in the graveyard.

Mr. Landry found himself breathing heavily as they reached the landing. From down below, he could hear Minerva's playing. Some-thing dark, dominant. A Rachmaninov prelude, he thought. —That day . . . the cemetery . . . but your grandfather said . . . you were in school.

They climbed higher, past the second floor, into a small room with heavily timbered, time-darkened stucco walls, but with large high windows that opened the walls to the night. Down below, the lights of the bay area curved like a necklace from Richmond down to San Jose, with San Francisco a shining pendant obscured and concealed by waves of fog. They paused there, silently watching the festival of lights.

Lance Bourdreaux poured brandy into two large snifters. He and Mr. Landry drank. Then he poured again.

—No. In the magnolia, the great big one. Not thirty feet away. I could hear . . . Lance Boudreaux fell silent, his eyes clouding. —Nothing. No need. He didn't even want me to see her then.

Mr. Landry threw down his brandy and poured another. The music from below, like the distant lights, was faint, shuddering over the distance from its source. This place, the very state itself, was cold as a tomb when darkness came. Brandy was what was wanted.

—But I did . . .

—Did what?

—I saw her. When youall were gone. When it was dark. Then she was mine. I had my tools, the archaeological tools. The ones he bought me when I said I wanted to go with her and he said, no, you can't do that, but you can go anywhere else, and I said all right, the Yucatan, thinking that will do it, he'll let me go with her, and if I do, she'll come to love me. But he sent me down there. Honest to God. Bought all the stuff, hired guides, a campsite, maps from the Center for Mesoamerican Studies. That was when I realized that you could do anything, or even stop anything, if you had the money and laid it on the barrelhead. You remember Hamilton, the big nigger? The one who ran the sheds and killed that little Frenchman Espagnol who tried to burn the place when he was fired? Sure, you remember. You defended him. You got him off. He took me down there, Hamilton did. We went down and dug and dug. For months. Snakes, spiders the size of your hand, tropical storms. Your skin got to mildewing. But we got down . . . Mixtec, Olmec . . . I have pieces in the National Museum. Where the screen of water falls in the courtyard. . . .

Lance turned away, still talking. In the semidarkness, lit only by an enormous menorah, tapers almost as large as paschal candles, each of a different height, Mr. Landry could hardly make him out, could see only his outline against the stars and lights. His voice was no longer the splendid captivating bass it had been below. It was soft, reedy, almost preadolescent, and the hurt in it was as palpable as the quick sear of the brandy as it speared the throat. There is a kind of speech that passes between men which seeks to tell, and another kind which aims only to evoke, to establish a thing in another mind free of judgment or consideration. Lance's speech was of that second kind. Mr. Landry was not a listener. He was a hearer now. He was a familiar singularity from the past, a point in the field of Lance Boudreaux's recollection, something like a milepost long passed, something to fix those old days amid the flux of these.

— . . . when it was dark, I dug down with my tools. The dirt was soft. Down to my own beginning, to my denial. I opened the coffin, and she was still there. I didn't even recognize her. She was a stranger I might once have walked past in the French Quarter, a face I might have seen in a car passing along Highway 61. Sleeping in Christ, the priest had said just a few hours before. But empirical observation proved that false. She was dead in there. She'd never sleep again. The undertaker's paste was shrinking, and I could see where . . . the fall. She had fallen a very long way. . . .

Mr. Landry stared at Lance's back as he reached for the bottle. He was beginning to listen now. —My God, why . . . ?

Lance turned back, but he was paying Mr. Landry no mind even as he took the bottle from Mr. Landry's hand and poured the large snifter full again. He was not telling Mr. Landry anything. He was living it again. Mr. Landry happened to be present. That was good, because it would not do for just anyone to be present. No, not quite that. More than present: a cause, a reason for the reliving, though not an efficient cause, not a sufficient reason.

—Looking very prim. Like she'd never taken a drink, never hired her a dago lover, never done a wrong thing. Like being dead was a cure and answer to everything, like it made everything all right. . . .

Mr. Landry poured the last of the brandy into his glass. Even before he could raise it to his lips, Lance Boudreaux drew out another from some hidden trove, breached it, and filled his own glass again, then topped up Mr. Landry's. On the Island, in the Mansion, Mr. Landry suddenly remembered, brandy had been all the hard liquor there was. No bourbon, no scotch, no gin. Courvoisier V.S.O.P., or one had to dip into a bewildering array of vintage wines from France, some dating back to the 1880s. I think I'm getting to be an alcoholic, Mr. Landry thought. I forgot how much I could handle . . . even after she . . . I held together. But this one trip. In the long run, he tried to remember what Keynes had said. In the long run, we succeed . . . at nothing.

— . . . said goodbye. Not to her. The hell with her. I just had to see the actual physical source for what I was saying good-bye to. It was the loneliness, the waiting for her at least to come see me between studs, even if she couldn't do her plain duty, what even a lousy white-trash family like hers must have raised her to do, or there wouldn't have been any children from them. . . .

The brandy had reached Mr. Landry by then. He was distanced from what he saw and heard. The room took on the character of a stage turning slowly above the distant city lights, the faded music below, the wheeling stars.

— . . . then I poured in the kerosene and set it off. . . .

Mr. Landry heard him, but it didn't matter. He was noticing how the stars looked like reflections of the lights of San Francisco in a profound and darkened pool.

— . . . nothing but carbon. How could carbon, a little calcium, and some trace elements have hurt me so much? That's when I decided to do physics, to do religions, too. Medicine wasn't going to be enough. Later, years later, each time I practiced medicine, I thought, this is only carbon, some mess of elements you're patching or adjusting. It will fall again. There's no truth here. Not at this magnitude. . . .

Mr. Landry heard, but he was not listening. He lifted his full glass in a silent toast to the half circle of lights down there, to the strains of a muffled Scarlatti sonata which shivered on the crisp California air. The brandy, the music, and the stars were real. The rest was a delusion. Old men suffer those when they have been alone a very long time.

— . . . then I put her back. I was done with her. Like those three dago chauffeurs who walked away when they had got whatever it was they wanted from her. More than that. I pushed the archaeological tools in, too. Because I was done with digging, rooting in the earth, the past. Once, when I was small, I had thought to go to Romania, to pay whatever they'd charge to let me dig until I found him. . . . So I could look, even if at nothing more than broken bones and bits of khaki cloth. If only that, then that at least. She cured me that night, translated me to physics, to magic. . . .

Squinting, Mr. Landry had noticed movement in the grove of trees below, out behind the main house. A man, tiny as an ant, with long hair, came to the side of a large swimming pool. He led a child by the hand. He began to bathe the child in the water. A thin cloud of vapor rose from the pool. Beyond the pool, Mr. Landry saw others. A fire or two outside small tents or shacks apparently thrown together out of plywood and tar paper. The more closely he focused his eyes, the more he could see.

Mr. Landry pointed down there. —What . . . ?

—Niggers, Lance Boudreaux said quickly. —They're my niggers.

Mr. Landry shook his head. The man and child at the pool were, even at this distance, obviously not black.

—But . . .

—No, they're niggers. I scooped 'em up and brought 'em here. Off the roads, out of the alleys. Got some of 'em at the hospital while I worked there. Fair number from jail. Listen, I got a Louisiana state trooper down there youall sent out to find me. But it don't matter. What you got is just pieces of people. Hands, hearts, brains, guts, all the other things. But not a goddamned one with all of it together. They see me saving 'em. If I say, work, and bring it all back home to me, they do it.

He smiled crookedly. —Now, if I was to say, go kill, 'cause that's what has to be . . . why, they would. Look at 'em down there. They live like niggers, they think like niggers. They're my people. They need me . . . and they go out and dance and shuffle and beg in the streets and bring me whatever they get. Nothing held back. I make a nice crop. . . .

Mr. Landry sat down. Lance Boudreaux opened one of the large windows and stepped out onto a balcony beyond.

—See, Uncle René, these people are fellahin. Racked up, burned out. They were clerks or waitresses. They managed filling stations or ran a minigolf. One of 'em was a computer programmer. Some of 'em were at the university. There's a few come back from Viet Nam with their heads on upside down. Lots of musicians and artists. Writers. I think there's even a lawyer out there. Couple of doctors. One did five big ones for controlled substances. The other one got ruined with a malpractice suit. Wouldn't let him operate on a dead goat. But they're all laid back now. They hang around and take groceries from me and smoke grass I pick up across the bay. Nobody asks 'em anything. Nobody breaks their hearts. They do what I say, and the rest is okay. . . .

—The one downstairs . . . they're insane. The one in the dirty cloak thinks you're God . . . or . . .

—Satanas. Yeah, well, they're probably right. What the hell . . . they never came across anything like me before. . . .

Lance Boudreaux turned around unsteadily. He had put aside the snifter and was drinking from the bottle now. His grin was visible through the mass of beard. —Hell, you've seen 'em in the streets. Any sonofabitch who can drink a quart of whiskey and still walk, anybody who can make a decision and stick to it. Anybody who can handle that little madonna downstairs—that's a god. Or a devil. They're wreckage, Uncle René, zombies. To a zombie, a living man's a god. To a woman surrounded by freaks, a man who stands is a god. Don't you take it too serious. People always construct what they need. It don't have anything to do with you or the people back home. Anyhow, everything is full of gods, remember?

Mr. Landry shook his head. He did not remember. Everything is full of pain. Whatever you love is certain to die. Nothing gets better with age. What does it mean for a man to claim he is a god? Is it a way of saying he can't be hurt any more?

—It's just the Island again, Lance Boudreaux said abstractedly. —Only bigger. The Old Man would love it. He could have taken over California. Nobody leaves me. I'm . . . their life. That's what he had, isn't it? He didn't just live his own life. He lived the Island and every sonofabitch on it. Now he's dead, and you come for me. He had everything but *droit du seigneur,* and if he'd wanted those hairy-legged slatterns, he'd of had that too.

Mr. Landry found that he had carried his thin briefcase up the stairs with him. He put it down on a dark slate table covered with cunningly wrought symbols, and fanned out a large bundle of legal-sized sheets.

—I have the papers, he said, as if he had heard nothing that had gone before. —You must accept the succession. No need for benefit of inventory . . . there were no debts to speak of. . . .

Lance Boudreaux paid no mind. He went on drinking, talking, staring alternately up at the stars and down at the lights. He paid no mind to the man and child beside the pool who had somehow heard his distant voice and now knelt side by side, arms extended upward toward him. Others around the fires and in the tents and shacks had heard, too, and slowly came through the fog to gather around the pool.

—It bothers you, Uncle René, those . . . things I got down there. . . .

Mr. Landry paused. In court or out, he always paused when what he would say had not been long considered. Words have consequences.

—Lancelot, he said at last, and softly, —I am very old and tired, too. This trip, this place—I mean the state—these people cause me great discomfort. I only want to do my duty and go home. . . .

—Ah, Lance Boudreaux said as softly. He came back into the room and squatted beside Mr. Landry. —Duty . . . the most sublime word in the English language. . . .

Mr. Landry looked at him in astonishment, but Lance Boudreaux's expression behind the dense beard bore no sign, not the slightest, of irony or sardonic intention.

—Look out there, Uncle René . . . see 'em coming? They want a look at me. See? It's my duty . . . they want to see their god. . . .

Lance stood up, swayed a moment, belched, and stepped back onto the balcony, falling against the rail, recovering. A chill shard of breeze carried back to Mr. Landry the smell of brandy and a strange carnal odor, that which one comes upon in a zoo. By the wolves, by the great cats.

He threw up his arms as if to bless them, and the nearly empty bottle of brandy looped upward from his hand and then spiraled down to fall into the pool, troubling the motionless waters. Immediately those below began jumping into the pool to recover the mystery vouchsafed them.

—See, Lance Boudreaux said, his voice beginning to blur. —Even if they're wrong, they won't be the first . . . Baal, Astarte, Mazda . . . we bring the poor bastards comfort. Just by standing. Look at 'em. . . .

Mr. Landry arose only a little steadier than Lance. He stepped carefully to the opening where he could see. Down there, the tiny people, garbed in rags and outrageous costumes, were drinking from the bottle, passing it from hand to hand, touching their naked children with the liquor. From behind and below, he could hear the unutterably distant sound of the piano: "Pavane pour une infante defunte," slow, solemn, each note a threnody.

Lance Boudreaux turned, leaned precariously against the rail now, outlined by stars above, lights below. —He . . . left it all . . . to me . . . ?

Mr. Landry was still looking down at the pool. It made him sad. Nothing changes. Only appearances. The beast remains what he always was. —What? Yes. There was no one else . . . yes. All of it. Some was always yours under Louisiana law. By representation . . .
      — . . . ?
      — . . . your father's legitim . . . his forced portion . . .
      —My father? But he . . .
      —It doesn't matter. Our law chains the generations together. Through property if nothing else . . . if you should have a child . . .
      —Ah, Lance Boudreaux muttered, coming inside, almost slamming the door. —You see, they worship wholeness . . . the deaf sob for music, the blind for color and form, the soulless for a movement within that tells them they're alive, tells them what to do. The Island hurt me. But it took nothing away. . . . You're a god, too. . . .
      Mr. Landry almost smiled. This time he paused only for an instant. —No. Not me. . . .
      —You're from down there, from home. You're still whole. You could . . .
      Mr. Landry did smile, a wretched smile not fit to see.
      —Become vice-regent of California? No, only the young are gods. And they get cured. One way or the other.
      He quickly folded up the papers as Lance Boudreaux found still another bottle of brandy. No one would be signing anything tonight. He could not imagine why he had even taken the papers out. It was his opinion that Lancelot Boudreaux III was not of sound mind. If he was to succeed to his grandfather's estate without a curator, there would be a hearing first. And in Louisiana, not here. God knows not here. No place west of Texas. Perhaps no place west of the Sabine River.
      Lance Boudreaux did not notice Mr. Landry putting the papers away. He was drinking, talking. Not to Mr. Landry. Not even to himself.
      — . . . take the sonsofbitches to the Island. Solitude. Isolation. Carbon and a little calcium . . . traces . . . It doesn't matter so long as you don't let 'em hurt . . . don't let 'em hope. No, hurt . . .
      Mr. Landry began the long treacherous descent down the unlighted stairs, tottering now and again, hearing the heavy tread of Lance Boudreaux close behind him. It crossed his mind to wonder if Lance was homicidal or simply dotty, taken with the kind of mania, the mild will to one thing so common along St. Charles Avenue and in the quiet old uptown streets where families had lived well over a century, ruminating on the whirlwind which had enwrapped them

when Mr. Jefferson bought them from the bourgeois emperor of the French. Quietists who had never heard of Port Royale; Jansenists who supposed they had invented self-denial and punishment; exorcists who used Jack Daniels to put away the business that stalks at noon; ancient feckless magicians living on dividends, who had been taking moderate doses of cocaine since the time it was legally used as an ingredient of Coca Cola.

They reached the bottom floor. Mr. Landry saw Fourier seated next to Minerva on the narrow piano bench. The top of her sari was loose and when she leaned forward over the keyboard, Fourier would lean with her. At the French doors, the Satanist and the driver had not moved. Their eyes caught Lance Boudreaux as if they expected instruction or revelation. Minerva was playing one of the Brahms piano sonatas now—no, it was the theme from the Second Piano Quartet.

Lance Boudreaux stumbled behind the long ornate bar. Back there, it was dark mirrored panels. The bar top was of black marble with chrome accents. Art deco, they had called it, Mr. Landry remembered. It had gotten nowhere in New Orleans. Only the WPA had made use of it here and there in parks and public buildings. It belonged in California.

— . . . forced portion, Lance muttered to himself. —I get that. No matter what. From my father. Listen, he said louder, so that the Satanist and the driver could hear. So that Minerva, Fourier, and Mr. Landry could hear him. —Listen, down South, where the old gods were, where the new gods will arise, they have these laws. Families are big. This is my Uncle René, because when I was too small even to know what an uncle was, that's what they told me to say. And it's real, because he never went away. He is an old bastard who brings the law down, who hasn't got the smoke of life left in him, but he was always there. Like the goddamned statue of the Confederate dead. He never bought a trailer and moved away or had a divorce . . . and now he's brought me . . .

Lance fell forward against the polished black marble bar. —He's brought me to my . . . kingdom. . . .

Mr. Landry felt his face turn red. But why should it? This was no court. It was not even Louisiana, and as for whatever it might be that Lance Boudreaux called the smoke of life, he was most surely right. It had drifted away one morning light-years ago on a silent patio in a town across the universe. When the music stopped.

—You can't keep things . . . from the kids, Lance Boudreaux gasped, laughing into his water tumbler of brandy.

The Satanist and the driver stared at Lance Boudreaux. Then they stared at Mr. Landry. Then they began to snicker. Quietly at first, then more loudly. The eyes of the driver were wide, insane. He had come close to Mr. Landry now, and there was a rank, sickening stench about him. He was not an old man as he appeared from a distance. He was quite young. But his skin was incredibly wrinkled, his features pinched as if his face had been squeezed in a vise.

As they laughed, Lance Boudreaux rose up from his elbows behind the bar. He paused there as if posed against the back bar for photographs to be taken, a wide smile spreading across his bearded face. He nodded his head toward the mirrored shelves behind, raised his eyebrows. The Satanist pointed gleefully, the driver slapped him on the back. Mr. Landry followed their eyes, past the bar, past Lance Boudreaux III, to a shelf of the back bar where, amid bottles of gin and crème de menthe, was a jar containing a thing something like a pig, curled members inward, and which, heedless of gravity, hovered like a tiny dancer, its something like a mouth caught in a permanent leer, unfinished limbs swaying in the cloudy fluid, filled with a faint golden dust composed it seemed of cells of the thing itself. And at the base of the jar there was an irregularly trimmed paper tab posted upon which was written in a neat hand, LANCE ST. C. BOUDREAUX IV.

It was then, just as Mr. Landry's eyes registered the jar, its contents, and its label, that the flat distant emotionless voice seemed to sound within the room itself.

—This is the police. You in the house. Throw down your arms. Come out with your hands on your heads. This is the police. You in the house . . .

Throw down your arms, Mr. Landry frowned. What is that supposed to mean? Then he saw the guns. . . .

The driver and the Satanist had M-16s. They had gotten them from behind the bar and were moving toward the French doors. Lance Boudreaux came up from behind the bar with something that looked like a sten gun, except that it had a large round barrel, and an enormous clip below. —This is the appointed time, dogs, Lance Boudreaux shouted. —The beast is here. . . .

Mr. Landry looked across the room. Minerva was standing beside the piano with a Kalasnikov assault rifle. Fourier was moving back from the piano as Minerva turned to a window, broke it with the barrel of her gun, and fired a burst out across the patio, into the fog. But before the echoes of her fire had died away, the room was annihilated. Mr. Landry dropped from his barstool to the floor.

Falling, he heard and saw the striated mirrors behind the bar shatter, the shards of glass flying like shot across the room, as the lamp near the piano exploded into pieces. He could not see Fourier, but even in the darkness he could hear him. —Sonofabitch, gimme a goddamned gun. . . .

—No, Mr. Landry called out. —Let it be, Fourier . . . let it be.

Everything was fine down there for Mr. Landry. The clatter of gunfire did not disturb him. He had closed his eyes, thinking this was God's will, he would go on here in California. Why not? Why shouldn't a man die in a foreign place? He was surely justified, being in this artificial hell by way of doing his duty, wasn't he? Afterward, someone would surely send him home.

Above, he heard that rich deep voice so alien that he felt even now he should recognize it. —I am the one who stands. . . . They cannot end this thing we have begun. . . .

But by then the fire from outside had become incredible. It was as if someone out there were throwing masses of metal into the room. Bullets hit the piano, and Mr. Landry could hear the strange harmony of strings plucked randomly. Another burst raked the bar just above his head, and he heard bottles and glasses breaking. It crossed his mind to wonder if, among the bottles of bourbon, scotch, and gin, that jar had been shattered, its contents poured out on the shelves of the back bar.

At the French doors, he could see the driver and the Satanist. The Satanist was standing, firing at random into the fog. The driver knelt, firing too. Suddenly, there was light, and following it, another shattering blast of fire. Mr. Landry saw the Satanist fall, a mist of blood and flesh spraying from him. The cloak flew up, and Mr. Landry could see the dirty starched shirt shatter, pieces of it flying away as the Satanist stumbled backward, his voice suddenly louder than the gunshots. —*Diabolus . . . Dominus . . .* Then it was quiet again, and the Satanist lay sprawled backward, part of his head gone, his body riddled. Thank God, Mr. Landry thought. So far, so good.

—Fourier, Mr. Landry called out.

—Sir, Mr. Landry heard from across the room.

—Stay down, you hear?

—Yes sir, I do. But Minerva . . .

—Hit her one up side her head, Fourier. That's best. . . .

—Yes sir. . . .

Then there was another burst of fire, and in the midst of it, Mr. Landry saw shadows out on the patio. The driver rose up from the floor, and as he did, there was a brilliant interlock of lights from outside. They fell across the driver, and at that moment there was a stab of flame from outside which quenched itself in the body of the driver who, in the very instant of dying, shouted, —Oh Unknown Lord. . . .

As some of the shadows from the patio entered the room, materializing into men in black uniforms with what looked to Mr. Landry like baseball caps and dark short guns, there was suddenly a strange whispering sound from just above, from behind the bar. The figures coming through the French doors spun backward, one falling into the piano, another into an end table, spilling a lamp and ashtrays across the floor. Mr. Landry craned his neck and saw Lance Boudreaux III leaning forward over the bar, a long thick-barreled gun pointing out toward the darkness.

—Who's next? he roared in a harsh country accent. —Come on, boys. My ass is a cabbage patch. There's enough here for all you sonsofbitches. . . .

Later Mr. Landry would remember his own astonishment, thinking of that language, those words, welling up amid death and disorder, in the wake of death befuddled by mystery. He never left home, Mr. Landry remembered thinking. Never even left.

Then he looked up, and once more the shadows were invading, only this time their guns were firing. As they moved across the room, Mr. Landry saw a blur behind the piano. For a fraction of a second, he thought it was Fourier, and he almost rose himself to shout him down, out of the path of what he knew would be coming even before he could shout. But it wasn't Fourier, and as he focused on the girl, Minerva rose from behind the piano, her sari pulled down, her long blond hair hanging down, veiling her golden breasts.

—Hey, she cried at the shadows, —hey . . .

For the smallest of instants, the shadows turned, they and their weapons tranced, as if they were substantial, of flesh instead of mist. Then, as Mr. Landry watched in horror, Minerva raised from the shattered keyboard of the piano the assault rifle, aiming it at the shadows. But there were others coming from behind who had seen nothing but the motion itself, as if it were disembodied. The bullets stitched across her breasts, planting ghastly scarlet flowers there, slapping her backward like the blow of a callous lover. —Oh wow, she whispered from the darkness down there.

The shadows turned then, and Mr. Landry thought they were about to fire at him. They strode into the light and he could see that they were men, young men, whose faces were darkened with burnt cork. Their guns were not pointing at him, though, and he saw their eyes shining out above their smudged cheeks, aimed behind the bar. . . .

—Praise the Lord, Mr. Landry heard Lance Boudreaux yell. —You godless scumbags. . . .

He heard that peculiar whispering sound again, and then the deafening clatter of the guns before him. One of the shadows fell, his baseball cap coming off, showing his light hair, his white forehead, clearly dead. Behind the bar, something was struggling, thrashing in the broken glass back there, snuffling, sounding like some kind of animal. —Ah, ah, ah, it croaked. I am ready, Mr. Landry thought. Lord God, I am surely ready now. But the sounds went on, and after another moment, there were arms lifting Mr. Landry from the floor, assisting him across the rubble scattered over the floor, past the bleeding bodies of the Satanist and the driver. The last thing he could remember later concerning that night was Fourier, dirty, confused, covered with blood not his own, half stumbling, half supported by a pair of shadows like those who were carrying Mr. Landry. Somehow, they were brought close together, the two of them.

—Aw shit, René, aw Jesus, you know what's happened. . . . young Fourier blurted.

For a small moment Mr. Landry didn't answer him. He was trying to gather himself back together. Fourier was an associate. It was important to give good example. Always. Even then.

—Yes, Mr. Landry managed to cough out. —I know. Everything. It . . . it's all right. . . .

He lost consciousness then. He had never lied to an associate before.

X

Mr. Landry came to himself aboard Flight 671. He had recollections of what had passed in between. He remembered being carried out on an ambulance stretcher. He remembered Lieutenant Raphael poised there above him, his face red, suffused with anger.

—You crazy old bastard, Raphael was saying, —why didn't you . . . The boy said you got my note. . . . The people in Daly City . . . It was Lance . . .

—Because, Mr. Landry remembered saying, —because it wasn't right. . . .

—Right?

—Never mind, Mr. Landry remembered telling him. —You couldn't understand. It's . . .

—Couldn't understand . . . what was . . . right . . .?

Mr. Landry remembered feeling a certain triumph then, a certain fulfillment. —Right . . . not what was . . . right.

They were in the sky now, above Las Vegas according to the pilot. Heading back to New Orleans. At least that is what the pilot said, taking into account his accent, translating what the pilot was telling the passengers. Back to New Orleans.

Mr. Landry looked to his left. He was seated on the aisle. At the window was Fourier, his head bandaged, his eyes downcast. Mr. Landry studied him, considering what he had been to begin with, what he was now. He was pleased, Mr. Landry was. Not simply with this boy, this Louis Fourier, but with himself as well. The very essence of life, he considered, was to have something set before you, something that had to be done. And to achieve it, to do what needed to be done.

He shook his head slowly, trying to clear it of the shadows, the uncertainties. He was not quite right just yet. There were still blank spots in his memory—as there had been when he had been called upon to appear before the Superior Court in and for Marin County, the State of California.

He looked up, and the stewardess was before him. She was tall and tanned, her body luxurious, her smile certain and assured. She bent down over him. —I'm Kim, she said. —Is there anything I can get you?

Mr. Landry smiled up at her, his eyes meeting hers and holding them. —I would like a . . . double martini and some writing paper, he said softly.

Kim's eyes swept past him, holding for a moment on the unmoving figure between him and Fourier.

Then her eyes moved onward. —Excuse me, sir, she said to Fourier. —What would you like to drink?

Fourier made no response at first. He was staring out of the window, down into the Grand Canyon. Kim spoke again, and his eyes moved from the depths 35,000 feet below. —Honey, he said, —lemme have a double martini right now, and keep 'em coming every ten minutes till we get home . . . I mean New Orleans, you dig?

Kim stared at him, then at the bandaged burden between him and Mr. Landry. —Yes, of course, sir, she said, moving away a little faster than she might have, had it not been for the certain tension she felt there.

No one spoke for a long moment after she moved down the aisle. Mr. Landry heard the smooth insistent roar of the jet engines behind them.

—Lord God, Fourier breathed, —you know, I . . . I think I really . . . loved her. . . .

For a long moment Mr. Landry said nothing. His eyes were pressed shut. Yes, he knew that. Yes, he knew. That for the rest of his life, Fourier would remember that. —Louis, he said, —you got to get used to . . . losing. You know what I mean.

—Yes sir, young Fourier said. —I mean, I really do understand. . . .

Mr. Landry saw Fourier's eyes fixed on the seat between them. The seat where Lance Boudreaux III sat, his head bandaged, his eyes fixed on the front of the first-class compartment, unmoving, steady as the rock and sand below over which the plane was passing. The bandage on his head was not as large as the one Fourier wore, and his close-shaven face was free of emotion. He looked like a slightly pudgy boy of twenty or so. Depending on how you looked, and from what angle, there appeared to be a slight smile on his lips.

The stewardess returned with the drinks and some paper. —Thank you, Kim, Mr. Landry said, smiling up at her. He took the paper she handed him, and as he sipped his drink, took out a pen, and began to sketch out the terms of an order of interdiction he would file with the court when they reached home. Fourier watched him glumly. —They should of killed the sonofabitch, he said softly, —instead of giving him to you. I'd never of given him to you . . . He'd never of gotten out of my jurisdiction alive. . . .

Mr. Landry went on writing. —He's a dead man to the law, he said slowly. —You heard the doctors. The bullets blasted away everything. Everything. We're taking home a carcass. There's nothing there . . . It eats and sleeps. . . .

Fourier was silent for a moment. — . . . killed all them people, he said. — . . . ought to push him out of this plane.

—Louis, Louis, Mr. Landry said, shaking his head, sipping his drink.

It was then, as Fourier turned away and leaned his head against the window, eyes closed, that Mr. Landry felt his sleeve being twitched. He felt cold for a moment, but when he turned, it was only the clawed hand of Lance Boudreaux III aimlessly scratching. As Mr. Landry looked, Lance's face remained what it had been since that night when the police ambulance had come to take him away from the shambles of the house in the canyon, a sea of tranquility, depthless, imperturbable, purposeless. But as he reached over to free his sleeve, the hand plucked his pen away. Before he could even attempt to retrieve it, the hand, moving as if it had a life of its own, settled on the paper on Mr. Landry's tray. In large childish letters the hand quickly traced out something almost unintelligible, yet obviously more than random scrawl. Then the hand was done, the pen lying beside his martini glass.

Mr. Landry squinted to read. Yet . . . still. I am the . . . One Who. Stands.

Mr. Landry picked up the paper, stared at it, then crumpled it into a ball before he could bring himself to look at Lance Boudreaux.

When at last he did, nothing had changed. Except that the impression of a smile on Lance Boudreaux's lips was much stronger. A virtual certainty.

Mr. Landry threw down his martini and lay back in his seat. They were hardly half an hour into their trip, and they had still a long way to go.

A Day in Thy Court

For a day in thy court is better than a thousand.
                                            —*Psalms 84:10*

I

When the bass struck, it was like nothing else he had ever experienced. He could not count the fish he had caught in his life. But the way it happened with bass had never gotten old. Each time was a beginning. Even now, he could look forward to rising early, walking down to the old boat dock, moving almost soundlessly out across the mirror-smooth lake to the river. If there was a single thing he would remember from this long-dwindling botch men were pleased to call life, it would be this time, those times that were a single time as the Indians had known, a single fish, a single fisherman in the twilight beyond the death of the last day and before the rising of the next. He did not remember her. Nor did he remember not remembering.

He had lapped his fly line into a pocket of shadow so deep that he had only known the popper was placed because he heard it fall clean and saw the merest reflection of the ripples that fanned out from it. He had let it lie, then drawn back a foot or so of the line. It was as if someone had taken a motion picture of the small yellow fly lying twitching on the dark water until the bass hit, and then had edited it, cutting out those frames that showed the fish striking. So that there was only film before and after, but no picture at all of the instant when the fly vanished below the surface in a blur of foamy water.

The line ran a few feet, and he slowed it with the edge of his left hand, not grasping it, only letting the weight of his hand serve as a drag, keeping the fish from going out as rapidly as he might, holding against its downward rush, tiring it, making it spend itself to reach the deep of the river. He watched the line slash the water, away from a patch of hyacinths, then back toward it again. He wants to go for the roots, but he can't find the right place. They're too thick for him. He needs a passage. The fish darted downward, and he towed back on the line, easing it as he felt the pressure slide off to one side and the line move in a broad circle toward the open water.

Once there, it was easy. No gift greater than patience was required. The fish must be a young one. It had gone out into the open water halfway across the river where no maneuvering was possible. It had not headed directly toward the boat in order to slacken the line. Now he could feel the time between surges like the space that measures labor pains. Her first had been her last. Down there, with a small fire in its mouth, the fish was tiring. She had tired. Then, almost as suddenly as the bait had disappeared, the pull on the line fell off and he drew the slack in as quickly as he could, touching the automatic reel so that line would not pile up on the gunwale or in the bottom of the bateau. Maybe he's older than I thought. Or a fast learner. Here he comes.

The boat still lay in shadow a dozen yards from the shore. But the first rays of sunlight had begun to cut through the thin cover of trees to the east, to play on the thread of the river. So that when the bass broke water twenty yards from the boat, it leapt into a glory of first light. It twisted and shook its large head, the sun glinting and shimmering on the green-gold scales of its back and sides. As it fell back, he heard that sound as of a distant pistol shot, invisible concomitant of a bass leaping, whether at the end of a line or at an insect or small bird almost escaped. He could not remember when he had first heard it. He did not remember the sound of her sobbing, unable to speak. He did not remember that.

As the bass vanished again, he drew the line in quickly, feeling only last tentative darts this way and that, without plan or direction. He saw the long leader break the water then and pulled the line up beside the boat and reached into the water. He caught the bass by the lower part of its large mouth and lifted it carefully into the air. Once he had hold of the lower jaw and bent it down with the fish's weight, it was paralyzed temporarily. Water drained off it, and its dark, beautiful eyes glinted in the sun. He remembered like a gnomic prayer his father's admonition never to touch a bass with dry hands. It would cause a fungus that would kill the fish if you released it afterward. He did not remember the carmine moisture on her lips, dry final coughing. He lay the fly rod down lengthwise in the boat, and began to work the fly loose. It was caught in the muscle and bone in the upper part of the mouth, and the barb had to be backed out the tear through which it had entered. The muscle had been torn by the fight, and it was easy to inch the hook out. When it was clear, he held the bass up against the distant pattern of sun on the river, its life full and rich in his hands. Then, slowly, as if regretting, he lowered it back into the water and released it.

For a moment, the bass lay still, as if it had no memory of the water. Then, almost as quickly as it had taken the fly, it vanished back down there.

He paused and shook a cigarette out of the crumpled *Picayune* pack. He had been smoking for fifty years now. They had become hard to find, even in Louisiana, by the 1960s. He had ordered them since then from a shop on the corner of Royal and Canal in New Orleans. Crashaw swore the Thing had arisen as a result of them. He had paid him no mind. There was another source for that. He had considered time itself, the anguish of watching the world sloughed away around him. Friends, customs, buildings, institutions lost. Other things. He did not remember the first time he had seen her. The wonder of. The cigarette smoke was burning his eyes, and he stroked the wine-colored water with his paddle, the slight motion carrying smoke away to dissolve in the shadows.

It was almost full light by then, and far down the river, around the bend toward Madisonville, he could hear a motor. At first it stuttered and choked off. Then it caught on, its pitch changing as it did so. He pushed the bateau a few yards on, skirting a fallen log which had been sinking slowly into the river for years. For some reason, he had always associated the fallen tree with Laocoon, caught in the toils and folds of a serpent, perhaps named time. And, in recent years, with himself as well. He could remember when the tree had fallen, when he had had to draw in his line and set the rod aside in order to paddle around it. No, he thought. I go back before that. I remember before it fell. I can remember when it stood on the bank. It was before the war. Lightning. One night, and then it was dead, and it stayed that way for years. He did not remember telling her they called such a tree a widow-maker, her frown and sharply inhaled breath. When I came back from France, it was down. I asked Dexter. He said it was the late summer of 1943 while I was drinking Watneys bitter and waiting for what was coming.

As the log fell away behind, he thought of Judge Robert Edward L. Blakely, and his last trial. —Fish or cut bait, boys, the old man told them when they paused too long between questions. —You know what I got in here isn't going to wait on you. Anyhow, it's getting on to fishing time, and I be damned if I'm going to be here when the heat breaks. Call your next witness, counselor.

He blew smoke up into the cool air as the bateau drifted into shadow again. So many courtrooms, so many trials. So many compromises. He checked the long plastic leader of his line. It was still clear of nicks and solidly embedded in the main line. There was a good stretch of water ahead. He had caught many fish there over the years. The river did not curve, but it had cut deeply into the bank, stranding cypresses, which stood alone in the shallow water, providing places for the fish to nest or feed. But the wide lagoonlike place had to be fished carefully. He had to cast long, staying well away from the bank because the water was no more than two or three feet deep across the whole area, and he had learned as a youngster that a boat moving closer than the drop into deep water would clear the place of bass in a moment. It was a challenge to fish it well.

He remembered that they would gather in the judge's office at noon, the lawyers who had practiced with him and before him over half a century. They would bring their lunches and eat with him, some who had not carried a brown paper bag since they were children with a sack or a round tobacco can full of cold fried chicken and stale biscuits. They had simply begun to drop in one day, unplanned, undiscussed among one another. To pass the time.

Because the word had gotten out from Dr. Ishmael at the parish hospital. Terminal. Inoperable. Painful. Weeks. At the most, a few months. And their coming to lunch was more than tribute. It was that they wanted to be with him for as long as they could, and being lawyers, doubting all, out of an abundance of caution, they reckoned on no more time than each day provided. They would eat and laugh and drink illegal whiskey, sometimes the very evidence of a moonshiner's recent trial. It would be poured ceremoniously out of mason jars into water tumblers, while someone noted the incredible rate at which cases for the making of illegal whiskey tended to be dismissed in Judge Blakely's court. For lack of evidence.

—Well, Ed, the judge would say, —we got to enforce the law. But sometimes we need to retard it a little. If anybody on this sorry wheezing globe should know you can have too much damned law, we should.

They would laugh and tell stories on one another, implying every sin, recalling feverishly the old times, times the young lawyers would never see the like of: when the Old Regulars ran New Orleans as if it were a great lottery set up for their benefit, when Huey was governor, when he threatened to expropriate Standard Oil—which they knew and he knew he could not do, and yet . . . And when the courthouse clock struck one, they would rise without being bidden. The old man would rise last among them, and lift his tumbler filled to the brim for the third time in an hour. He would hold it aloft and say softly,

—Gentlemen, I give you Robert E. Lee.

—To Lee, the others would respond, and then, downing the balance of their drinks, file out into the cool, dark halls of the courthouse.

He could see them all now, the old and the young, standing in the musty chambers against the backdrop of buckram-bound lawbooks: *St. Martins Reports*, the *Louisiana Annual*, the *Southern Reporter*, *Orleans Appeals*, the *Annotated Civil Code*, copies of Planiol and the *Code Napoléon*, of Pothier and Laurent, and all the other written instruments by which they lived together. He could see them in his mind's eye, thirty-eight years gone now, the old long dead, the young old, standing as if in one of the engravings of the Mermaid Tavern, the *Signing of the Declaration*, or the *Solvay Conference of 1913*. His friends and brothers, the root and branch of his life. Yet not the flower because he would not see her, head thrown back, laughing, rain falling through sun, scintillating against the windowpane in that shotgun cottage where.

He had heaved up the motor and was paddling with his left hand, sometimes cross-paddling to hold the bateau close enough but not too close. Now he was casting the line in long graceful whorls that arched across the sky from the thread of the river behind into the lagoon ahead, barely missing the outstretched branches of the cypresses, falling soundlessly in the water, placing the yellow bug with its white rubber legs little more than six or eight inches from his target fifty or sixty feet away.

The sun was high now, almost midway above the river. The windless surface of the river was scattered with darts of light. Even so, there were shadowed places, bunched groves of cypress, oak, and gum growing in the water or thickly clustered along the bank, where the water ran dark even at noon. By now, the big fish had gone down, but there was always that odd one who swam his own way, kept his own hours. Ordinarily, fishermen went in about now, ate and lounged and waited for the heat to break, for the fish to rise and feed again.

I don't have that kind of time, he thought. What with the Thing working around the clock. Anyhow, I never *did* go in. I never did want that statistical fish. I wanted my own fish, and that crazy bastard just might sleep all night, get up at noon, work until three, and go down again. That's the one I wanted to see.

He smiled, thinking that he had probably put almost as many fish back into this river as he had taken from it. He took only what he could eat. He never gave fish away, and he never stored them in a freezer. When he ate them, they were caught to order. He did not remember her, arms wet with cooking oil, yellow with cornmeal, saying.

The end of the lagoon lay ahead, where the bank came back out, and the shallows measured no more than three or four yards. He had really not expected anything of it today. The sun was too high, and the water was too shallow. But sometimes, the younger bass, less affected by the heat, would move in there to feed, safe from jackfish and gar. They would hit the bait like giants. He loved to see them shake and twist, dancing on the sunny water. It occurred to him that these green-golden fishes had meant as much to his life as the course of the law. But even as he thought it, he laughed aloud. Because bass were as much a part of the law as he was, as were the courts in which he had passed his life, the attorneys with whom he had lived it out. The law is *lex*. The bass is *logos*. She was. He remembered a passage from one of the old Greeks, something about how deep lies the logos, so deep that no dive could reach it. You could not, deep-diving, find the depth of the soul, though you traveled the whole way down, so profound is its logos. That was it. And I'll know soon enough about that. There's so little way left to go now.

The insects were mostly in now. Mosquito hawks, june bugs—all the mites that drew the fishes upward toward the light. They vanished under leaves, even into cracks in the bark of trees as the sun reached its height. They waited for that strong light to break and then, at dusk, they would begin to sound and feed and flit across the water once more in that cycle that bracketed late March to November.

At the end of the lagoon there was a space where raw soil had broken into the water, rootless, without grass or weeds. When there was a heavy rain, the wash-off flowed there. Then the bass would stand off a little to strike at the food carried to them by the flood. At any other time, there were no fish there, and so he drew in his line in order to move past, back into a clump of trees and marsh grass where frogs bred and the bass stalked like tigers. But the pain hit him then. As if someone had opened a door or raised a window shade, and agony looked in. It was not such a pain as to make a man moan. Rather to make him scream. Except that it had come so often lately that he only bent double in the boat, making it slosh from side to side in the water.

—Ahhh, he sobbed, holding to the gunwales. It was a sob because he knew always that the door, the shade was there, knew what lay behind it. He was accustomed to it. He was not used to it. You do not get used to pain that drives directly to what you had once taken for the center of your being and resonates there, thick with death, bright, awful chord steeped in the timbre of ageless loss. Each time it comes, it must unman you. Or take you away. As she lay dying, he had held.

He came to himself and raised up from the bottom of the boat. He took a bottle from his worn denim jacket. He threw down three of the small yellow tablets inside, washing them down with a handful of river water. The plastic bottle had a paper label curled up inside. It said, "For Pain. One Tablet Every Four Hours." But even Howard had admitted the absurdity of that. They had sat one evening in his office.

—Nothing, Dr. Howard Crashaw had told him. —Not a god-damned thing to be done. Oat-cell carcinoma. God couldn't cure it. . . . No, that's wrong. That's a stupid medical technician's claim. *We* can't do anything. It's too fast. By the time there's enough to biopsy, it's off and running. Maybe it's the cost of what we do, what we are. . . .

—All right, he remembered saying. —How do we handle it? This is the age of dope, isn't it? Should I just take some kind of con-sciousness-expanding thing and go out till it happens . . . ?

Howard had been astonished by the question. As if he had not been supposed to know about such things. Howard was a good doctor, and he shrank from what he did not know. He understood Howard's feelings. He was going to die, and soon. But Howard would live after. And what was now a mystery would, one day before long, become elementary. And Howard would think of him, and the vast parade of others who had gone before because he, Howard, could not then grasp what any intern could explain now.

He sat back in the boat smiling. The drug took effect almost at once. When he took three of them together, they did very well. You tended to wonder what trivial pain might be dealt with by one of them. There was a peculiar side effect he had hated at first that was still the prime reason he did not simply keep enough of the stuff in his system to stave off the pain altogether. It seemed to him that when he had taken enough of the pills, he could feel the Thing in him, working, moving from cell to cell, breaking loose in bits and flowing in the pressured stream of his blood to some new location to commence working again. Under the spell of the narcotic, it seemed he had an occupant rather than a disease, something dredging, probing inside him, seeking some sort of truth, which it could not find because he would not remember, destroying, rejecting the rest.

It was absurd, and he had come to look at the whole thing as a metaphysical conceit fostered by the drug. Still, to sense the Thing working eased nothing. He closed his eyes and breathed deeply then. He smelled the rich deepness of the water, amalgam of decay and generation, death and birth, fallen leaves and rotten logs. He picked up his rod and pulled in the rest of his line and paddled a little further, past the bald place on the bank.

As he did so, he touched the monofilament leader again, running his finger along it. If there were as much as a tiny nick in the line, it would part under pressure at far less than its test weight. You could not see the nicks the line picked up from rubbing over a sunken log or a slight projection of rock or riprap. Sight was useless. You had to touch, to test with your hands. As they had touched. The line was sound, and he let it trail over the side as he stroked farther on.

Past the wash-off, the bank hooked in again. Only here the water was deep because this place was at the bottom of a long slow curve in the river, and took the force of the current when the water was high. The current would try to flow straight, would burrow into this cul-de-sac, and then straighten out and move on down toward the town, farther on toward Pontchartrain. The place was a grove of tall trees that had once been on the bank before the erosion had taken it away and pushed it back. Most of the oaks and gums had died. The willows had retreated to the bank to wave softly above palmettos and scrub. But the cypresses still stood, closed in together, their branches forming a canopy over the whole area. There were even a few quaking, oozy little islands supported by intricate tangles of roots, composed of a little earth, decades' deposits of rotten leaves and water plants. But, except for shafts of sunlight, which pierced through where the trees were more widely spaced, the whole grove lay in perpetual shadow. Even at high noon, the fish could be seen swirling, striking toward the back where the darkness faded into the bank itself.

He called this place Venus's arbor. He could not. Did not remember. Why? Because this was the hardest place to work on the river. It required great patience. It required knowledge of the water. Because if you moved too quickly, or without knowledge, you might go aground. To get off again, you would have to make noise, and the sound would carry all through the grove. The swirls and strikes would vanish at once, as if nothing had ever been there. She had.

With. Him. He had to stifle a laugh of exultation. He did not remember why. The pain was down for a little while, and this was the good place. Where they had come. Away from. Down in the bottom of the boat was a bottle. He picked it up. It was wet from the tiny leakage that covered the bottom of the bateau with perhaps a half-inch of water. A famous first, he thought, studying the dripping label. Old Overholt. Good solid rye whiskey. The best. Never mind the young lawyers with their light Scotch, their Black Jack and Wild Turkey. No, this was of old. He remembered how they had customarily gone over to the little restaurant across from the Gretna Courthouse after a trial, the winner buying the loser as much whiskey as he could drink, then paying for the cab home, or taking him there yourself. Takes nothing from winning, Judge Blakely had used to say, and makes a man consider losing as no worse than second place. They always drank rye, chasing it with Jax beer. During one bone-wracking murder trial, a terrible case that stretched out over the better part of a month, he and an assistant district attorney, despising the trial and everything related to it, preempted the usual custom and spent one long afternoon recess drinking together, handicapping the jury, betting on who would be foreman. Afterward, they had gone back to court plain drunk, spared lasting ignominy only by the fact that Judge Blakely had come looking for them to discuss a motion, and had stayed to have a few himself.

—Counsel will approach the bench, Judge Blakely had directed when they had gotten back into court, weaving, hardly able to find counsel's table.

The judge had leaned forward, waving away the reporter. —Boys, I'd entertain a motion for recess until tomorrow, he said without a trace of expression. —I don't know about you, but I can't count the damned jury.

—What jury? the assistant district attorney asked, squinting.

Then the three of them—bone-tired, sick of the trial, seeing no possibility of justice in it where killer and victim had together, over the years, constructed the bloody denouement—had gone back and drunk some more. And she had. Waiting afterward. So tired, but.

Now he was looking at the bottle again, paused beside a huge cypress. He had never taken a drink of hard liquor before when he was fishing. A little beer, perhaps. But not whiskey. No one who knew what he was about drank out on the water. The river was as beautiful as anything God had placed on the earth. But its *logos* was hard. It allowed no errors. A hand in the wrong place meant a cottonmouth bite. To reach up into a tree for a snagged bait without parting the branches first meant a hornet's nest would empty itself on you. Men died on the river every season because they were foolish or headstrong. Or because they drank. Drinking cost you the edge, and nobody could afford to lose the edge. Because no one knew the river. They only guessed. They surmised. Once he had run full tilt into a massive floating log and ripped out the bottom of his boat where no log had been ten minutes before. They knew this much: a barometer below thirty, an east wind, a recent bad rain, and there would be no luck. Most especially the east wind. God knew why. But why the Thing? God knows.

He opened the quart of whiskey, thinking: the first time in fifty years that he had ever so much as carried a bottle in his boat. His father had been death on it. He himself had lost an uncle to it. The river has rules, like the rules of court. Only more rigorous. And the people who live in such a water-riven state all know the rules. His housekeeper had looked at him strangely this morning when he put the bottle into the tackle box. —Well, what about that, Mr. Sentell? I never seen you . . . If she was here . . .

He could not remember the rest of that sentence, and he opened the bottle quickly and drank deep. At this age it was good to break the rules. Because the rules were for the young. To preserve them for something else. He was beyond that. Time makes poets of us all. He grinned broadly. Now he could write his name in water. Or good rye whiskey. Deep-diving into time itself. Half a century is enough to hold to the rules. Most of his friends who had held to the rules until the last day were nonetheless dead. He thought, if I had a billion dollars, I couldn't reconstruct that scene, that picture with us all drinking in Judge Blakely's chambers. Lord, he thought, we're all commorientes. Every dying is contemporaneous with every other. Tulane Law. Class of 1929. How many were left? He could see them all, strong, arrogant, assured, with an old city, a state awaiting their coming to the bar. But wait, he remembered thinking even then, his father and mother smiling, proud, blessing him for realizing in his own success the continuation of their hopes.

But wait. What about twenty, thirty, fifty years on? Her eyes sparkling, her kiss. Which he did not. Remember?

He took another drink and turned the boat ever so slightly so that it would point into the grove. Then he quickly back-paddled. No, he thought. Not now. I don't feel like it. There was a dry place, a place raised at the back of the grove, and there they had promised. No, I'll come back here later. When the sun is down. That's the best.

He moved on toward the mouth of a cut that led to the country club marina. It was wide and deep, cut back into the bank on a perpendicular. There was little growth down at the edge of the water, but there was a myriad of broken stumps and half-sunken logs. The fish there were mostly small, but the feed was good, and sometimes the large bass would move in there, eating small bream and goggle-eye. He knew of a corner where the white bass tended to swim and feed. They were no good for a fight, but they made better eating than anything besides the bream.

He felt the Thing rising again, that feeling of probing, as if pain were a conscious entity looking for a place to break through, to reduce him to a moaning cringing body full of tubes on a hospital bed. Howard had said: —When it gets bad enough, you'll have to give in. Nobody can take the last of it. We can make you comfortable. We can goddamned sure do that. . . .

Howard had turned away, and he had thought there were tears in his eyes. He was touched. He had not thought that the young doctor had liked him so much. Come on, Howard, you know better than that. I've been an uncomfortable man all my life. I'll just keep coming back for more and more dope, and you'll give it to me, pusher for superannuated lawyers. . . .

They had laughed and had some drinks. And when they had drunk enough, Howard told him he should find another doctor, that he was no good. Howard said that he had tried, but he was no damned good because he couldn't even master the very first thing about being a physician, which is to see your patients as problems to be solved, equations to be rebalanced. Howard had cried outright then, saying that he had never lost a patient without losing some of himself, that the worst was children, but that it was all terrible, and that he was going to give it up and take what money he had and buy a fishing camp somewhere or go back to divinity school and become an Episcopalian minister. Then, drunk as a barroom cricket, Howard had mentioned another patient. They both had known. He had spoken of her with love, had said how. Her last.

He could not remember that. He took another pull on the bottle and remembered his freshman year in law school. He had done the Civil Law, but that year he had been reading poetry. Oh my God, I haven't thought of poetry in forty years. There had been a girl, he could not. Remember her name? He had written a poem for. Someone. The silliest possible thing. Writing. A poem. Suddenly he could even remember the name of one. He had written. Someone. Several poems. One had been *Viajera*. Voyager. That same time, he

had worked on a law review article. "The Civilian Law of Lease."
Not poetry at all.

He found himself almost past the cut then and had to paddle
backward to keep the current from driving him so far that he might
have to lower the motor to get back. He could no longer paddle
against the current in the river. That had bemused him. He could
remember paddling six or seven miles against the current years
ago. It had been easy. But not now.

With a few good strokes he left the river and entered the smooth
water of the cut, past the roots and dead branches that lined the
entrance. Perhaps twenty yards in, another cut went to the left. The
cuts made a box, one branch, the one he was on, running back to
the country-club docks, the other, the one to the left, turning back
upon itself. In the middle was a raised section of land with a ten-foot
levee around it. In there was a sludge pool which served as a giant
septic tank for the tract of houses around the country club. Without
plan, fish eggs had gotten into the ten- or twelve-acre pond, and the
catfish especially had grown immense on the influx of human
waste. None of the inhabitants, mostly Yankees, would fish there.
Local people, unconcerned about the fishes' diet, came frequently
to catch enormous catfish, fat and tasty.

He leaned back against the canvas seat he had bought. It was the
first support he had ever had. A compromise with the Thing. The
boat rode now, tideless, almost unmoving, its only momentum that
of his last thrust with the paddle. He sipped some rye and studied
the place. The sun had just barely started down, and the air, warm
before, had almost imperceptibly begun to cool. He had forgotten
his watch, but it must be close to two. Things hurried in November.
They had met. In November, the warmth faded, and twilight was
brief. But it didn't matter. The whiskey provided all the warmth he
could need. The pain was still seeking a way up, but it had not found
it, not yet. In a little while, he would take some more pills.

—Now be careful. This is a morphine counterfeit, Howard had
told him. —Only it's at least a factor of five more potent. I mean, this
stuff is terrific. No matter how bad . . . it gets, no more than two
every two hours. Even that's dangerous. And nothing to drink. I
mean, *nothing*. You could . . .

—Die? he had finished the sentence. —Hell, that would be a loss.
Cut off in his prime . . . Shit, Howard . . .

Now he had to choose. Up ahead, along the way to the docks and
slips, there was good fishing on both sides. Once, during a light

spring shower, he had had seventeen strikes in twenty casts and had boated fifteen bass and bream just right for frying. It happened like that sometimes. But that was the straight way. It was where the smart fisherman went when things were right. To the left, the cut was narrower, closer, with willows and even a few cedars growing out over the water, and the better part of thirty years' rubble accumulated along the banks and in the water. It was very nearly impossible to use a fly rod in there because there was no back room, no space in which to let the line arch before you sent it forward toward its target. Almost no one fished that cut. It wasn't worth the trouble. The few who tried it always used a spinning rig. He let the bateau coast for an instant more. Then, with an almost demonic thrust, he dragged it into the left cut.

Things were even more quiet there. The slight wind that had cooled him during high sun died, deflected by the shield of trees that rose suddenly and solidly along the bank there. And he remembered the poem.

> Voyager, we have caught a maze of
>   dainty starlings spearing sun
>   from out eyes' corners as we marched
>   heads down and hearts askew.
>
> And voyager, we have marked each feathered
>   renascence, bold matter skipping mad
>   through quaint informal jays, secret
>   journeys deadly swift performed by
>   marble hawks.
>
> No wonder, earthbound, each of us must
>   fret and string the long hot silent
>   busy afternoon into fluttering dusk,
>   a hope for music.
>
>> Our souls have made
>> poor matches; we are
>> darkling,
>> and the hollow of our
>> bones is filled with
>> dust.
>
> Shall the shape of morning, voyager, be
>   that of delectable sparrows spangling
>   your ears, dancing crystal figures
>   ·in the shrill delightful air,

or will you hasten with us into profitable
day

and limp by noon?

His eyes were closed as he remembered. Jesus Christ. Did I do
that? Did I really? I guess I. Saw the love. When she had finished.
Reading the shoreline, he began to reel out a short length of line. If
you could handle a fly rod properly, you could do without the back
space. All you needed was room enough to roll the line. You laid out
a length, and kept your rod low, forcing the line into a circle, so that
as it moved, the end would land almost as accurately as if you had
cast in the ordinary manner.

Then he saw on the bank, among cypress, willow, and gum, a
single camphor tree. He gave the bateau a push and let it come into
the bank. He reached up and drew down a handful of the leaves and
pulled them off, crushing them in his hand as he did so. He closed
his eyes and breathed deep, the pungent sharp odor of camphor
filling his nostrils, almost a call back to the world. He felt tears
spring up in his eyes. Nothing to do with anything. What? The
hidden unconscious anguish of the body about to be parted from
those things that moved it. Yes, only that. What he had wanted to
say in the poem almost forty years ago. To Someone. That there was
a part of him not bound to the law, or a child of rules and procedure.
A part bound only by the bright sky and the deep water, the spring
grass and the acrid odor of leaves burning in the fall. What she had
found and loved as much as. He hated the interruption, but the pain
had found its way through, patiently, with a wealth of time in which
to search. He shrugged, reached for the plastic bottle of pills, threw
down another three—or was it four—and then washed them down
with a shot of rye.

He held the bottle in his right hand and paddled with his left. He
moved quickly into the overcast of the cut and began rolling his line.
Almost immediately, he felt a touch on the yellow bait he could
barely see in the shadows. He drew back and cast again. Nothing.
And again. This time, the initial tug sustained itself, and he drew
the rod upward, dodging the overhanging branches, pulling in line
with his left, touching the automatic reel with the small finger of his
right hand as he did so. The bottle was getting in his way. He was
about to gather rod and line into his left hand in order to cap the
bottle when the pressure on the line suddenly faded.

A goggle-eye, he thought. That's the way they always act. You get
a solid hit, a short run. Then they fall off. They've got no fight in

them. There was no reason to worry about the bottle. He could handle the goggle-eye still holding the bottle in his hand. You simply had to reel them in quickly, because if they managed to get some slack on the line, they might slip away. As he drew the line short, he saw the fish. Perhaps ten or twelve inches long, fat. A goggle-eye. He boated the fish which hardly struggled as he freed it from the hook. Then he pushed off with his paddle, and began to coast slowly down the slip again. He rolled the line up under the low-hanging branches. Suddenly, up ahead, in the thread of the stream, there was a roiling in the water. Perhaps fifty or sixty yards away. He smiled as he saw the shovel-head of an alligator moving toward the far bank. Even as his boat moved toward it, it paid him no mind. When it had reached the shore, it crawled from the water slowly, moving up the bank foot by foot. He watched it move. Water streamed down its sides. From where he sat, he could see the alligator's head in profile. The corner of its mouth seemed curled upward, as if it were grinning. As if to recall old mortality and the long dying fall of those who, long ago, had crawled up onto the shore never to return.

It was then that the pain surprised him, breaking through without the least warning. For the smallest portion of a second, he lost himself and thought. Of her. He concentrated on the pain, the richness, the texture of it as it moved across his chest, into his abdomen. Metastasis. Movement. The Thing was like a concerto within him, moving, surging, finding its own path from one place to another. He could not stand its rhythm, strumming across his wasted ribs, up into his throat. Almost remembering. Something more powerful, more awful than the pain threatened to break through. Dark hair, dark eyes. Dark water splashed as he shivered in the boat. He took two more pills, wondering if, on account of them, he might pass out. He had learned, to his surprise, that he had an incredible resistance to narcotics. Even Howard had admitted it one day when they had gone out for a few drinks. He had taken six pills in an hour. While he drank.

—An ordinary man would be . . . out. I mean, what the hell is with you, Bob?

He had smiled, leaned across the table, one eyebrow raised. —You are not dealing with an ordinary man, doctor. You are dealing with . . . Cancer Man. . . .

The words had hardly been out before he realized that they were wrong. He did not need to see Howard's stricken face. He knew. There are things you cannot play with, even if they belong to you. He and Howard had never gone drinking again. It seemed ironic to discover when you are nearly seventy years old that you have not yet learned all the rules.

He cast again quickly, and another goggle-eye took the bait. He brought the fish in slowly, detached it from the hook, and stored it with the other in the bait well. He was casting rapidly now, hardly concerned where the bait might fall. That night. In Houston back from Austin, where they had spent their first night. Together with the descending sun, there was a rising breeze. Now he began to feel that it was deep autumn. The bug lighted beside a great sodden stump. He could not remember how long the stump had been there. He thought perhaps before his time. Because the broken tree that had once stood above it had surely vanished before he could remember. The memory of man runneth not to the contrary. Then, almost as quickly as the bug hit the water, it vanished. For a second, he wondered if possibly it had broken off the line. But then he felt a sudden and powerful downward tug and jerked back on the line quickly to set the hook. This could be the one. Every time he had walked into the courtroom and set down his briefcase he had thought, *This could be the one.* But none had been. That Great Case had never materialized. There had been many that brought him wealth. There had been some that had even become benchmarks in jurisprudence. But not that one, the one that carried to the horizon, that changed what was to what would be. No, in his life, only she.

He frowned and held the line close. Not tight. Close. The distinction was elementary. It was the difference between a trust that something large and worthwhile was on the line, and the certainty that a small fish had hit that was worth no more time than might be required to draw him up and free him from the hook. Almost any fish might punch the line in that initial burst. Especially goggle-eye. They would hit hard and run well, and then suddenly collapse. But if the pressure of that first surge should continue, even grow stronger, what then? If you had not taken the first drive seriously, most often you lost the fish that pushed onward. Because the hook was not set. Because you had doubted, had assumed wrongly. But if you held closely at the first, you could manage things. To hold tightly was to lose the line to that fish that you had doubted.

The line cut sharply out from his left, from under the trees across the bow of the boat. He had to lean forward quickly with his body to make up for the slowness of his response with the line and the rod, to keep the line from fouling under the boat. This isn't a goggle-eye. It isn't a small bass, he thought. This is something else like. Their first kiss. The Cotton Bowl. Oh dearest, I think I'm in love with. You come to sense the extraordinary when your hands and mind have spent enough time at a craft. He remembered that time. It boiled down to the final argument to the jury. His plaintiff crippled horribly. A cruel defense. The assumption of risk. Ladies and gentlemen. You are Art Clifford. And this is what you did. Did you assume that risk? Given that life, that experience, did you suppose things would go that way? Because if Art assumed the risk, we all do. Is this one of those risks we assume? It was dark and late. He was utterly alone in his victory, opposing counsel youthful, angry at his loss, refusing to go for drinks. He had had a few by himself. She had come, her face expectant. Yes, my love. One of the Great Days. Oh, sweetheart, let's go and try. Try to think about this moment. This fish. Love? You can't mean it.

He could not tell yet what he had on the line. Maybe he had foul-hooked a good two-pound bass. A fish hooked in the gills or along the back as it plunged at the bait seemed much larger than one fair-hooked. He let the line run through his fingers as slowly as he might. Every pound of resistance tired the fish a little more. You resist as much as you can. Once a federal judge had thrown a pencil at him in anger. He had been very young, uncertain of what he was about. Oh Lord, instruct thy servant. The line ran through his fingers, and he began to feel the friction. Oh, my dearest, it doesn't end. It is always there like an anthem. Did Beethoven do a tenth symphony, *Ode to Pain?* The weight on the line became greater and greater. It pulled on his matchstick arms and began to pull the bow of the bateau slowly back in the direction from which it had come. He let line run, heard it stripping from the fly reel. The line was twenty-pound test. It should hold.

The slow turning of the boat, the whiskey and the drugs made him dizzy. He stroked the water with his sawed-off paddle, holding for a moment rod and line in one hand. It was a risky maneuver, but at the stern of the boat was a nest of roots and broken branches. If the boat became snagged there, the fish could use the weight of the boat to break away. The boat broke clear, and he dropped the paddle into the bottom of the boat, quickly reaching for the loose line with his freed hand. Even as he did so, he could feel the strength of the fish down there. Then, in an instant, the line went dead. Not simply limp, loosing its tautness. Dead. He dragged it in with his left hand and the automatic reel pulled it in even more quickly than he could reel, but no matter how much line he could draw in, there was no feeling in it. Dead.

He leaned back in the boat, his back against the canvas seat.

Gone. It had to be a good one. Gone. What the hell. That's what it means to come out here, he thought. Then, even as he relaxed, the line went taut again, and more than that, almost burned his hand as it ran out.

Christ, it's still on, he thought. It's fixing to come up now. It's a monster. It might even be a gar. Too much for a bass. It had never been his house, it was what she had wanted. Uptown. He had wanted a place on water. Where he could keep in mind the movements of the moon, the pulling of the tide. He had watched her instead.

Then almost fifty yards out, nearly on the other side of the cut, the fish broke water. It did not spring into the air like the two- and three-pounders. It was much too large. Rather it rolled, tossing its enormous head to rid itself of the tiny fly hook which had become embedded in its jaw. It was dark green above, and as it rolled out beyond the shadowy trees, he could see the off-white glint of its belly. It had to weigh over fifteen pounds. He had seen ten- and twelve-pound bass over the years, though he had never caught one even that size. This one was bigger. It rushed at the shore like a torpedo. It actually leaves a wake, he thought. My God, what a fish.

It struck the bank blindly, twisted almost back upon itself, and went down again, headed this time up the cut toward the dogleg to the right, which led to a dead end clogged with brush, fallen logs, and dead branches. The fish couldn't know about that rubble. It was almost a quarter of a mile away, he thought. Then he thought again. Unless it lives in there, under the rubbish. They like that kind of cover. Especially the big ones, the old ones who have lived forever.

The boat moved slowly as the fish dragged against the line. I never knew a fish to fight like this. He's moving an eighty-pound boat with a two-hundred-pound—no, a hundred-and-thirty-pound—man in it. His eyes clouded, and the pain burned up and through like a tiny sun in nova. He almost dropped the rod, but habit made him grip it and the line in one hand. He reached once more for the pills and washed two down with whiskey. Then he sat waiting for the Thing to be pressed down again, the flame of pain quenched for a little while.

Now the bateau was at rest. He was tired. His head was swimming a little from the drugs and liquor. For the smallest fraction of a moment he wondered if he should try to horse the fish in. Or cut the line. He was very tired. But that was no way to leave things. Her lips had been. Rich and warm, the sun was settling toward the horizon. There would be no more than another hour of light. Probably a good deal less. He would catch the fish. There was no reason now to preserve his strength. He looked down at his wasted arms where the sleeves of the jacket had been pulled back as he worked the rod. He could see the outline of his thigh bones sharp against the cloth of his work pants.

Then the line rose and the boat began to move again, taking his mind off what was happening to him. The boat had almost reached the dogleg by now, and he tried to draw in a little line. A cloud passed across the sun, and he noticed for the first time that rain clouds were moving in from the north.

Now maybe I really should cut the line, he thought. As he pulled on the line, there was an answering opposite tug from below. War with a submarine. And maybe the fish was stronger now. He could feel the trembling in his arms and legs, in his hands. But the pain had subsided and he was all right now. There was plenty of whiskey left, and he possessed a wilderness of pills.

As the boat turned into the right angle at the dogleg, he heard the first drops of rain begin to fall on the water. It sounded as if someone were dropping kernels of rice onto paper. Rice in her hair, the veil. He raised the canvas seat a little and pulled out his poncho. He pulled it over his head before the rain reached his boat. Down the length of the cut, he could see the pile of broken timber, limbs, branches, and brush that marked the end of the water. If you left your boat and walked overland perhaps ten yards, you found yourself close to the boat docks and slips at the head of the main cut.

The fish did not relax its pressure, and he knew that if it was headed for the brush pile, and if it could reach it, there would be no chance of landing it. It was time to do some horsing. He shook a cigarette out of the crumpled pack, and struck a kitchen match against the side of the boat. He took a long pull on it and began putting more pressure on the line. He was surprised to feel the boat slow. Another pull, and some of the line came in. He touched the automatic retrieve and wound in the excess line before it could get tangled in the boat. The trembling in his arms had stopped, and he leaned forward. The rain was falling softly, regularly, and the clouds had all but effaced the sun. It was going to be dark soon now.

Old brother, he thought as he continued to draw in the line, you don't want to be drawn into the element above, no matter that you're heavy with years and feeling the change of water temperature more all the time. I'm hooked, too. They're fishing for me. I have to go. We all do. We can't stay in our element. We're not meant to stay here. They draw us up.

The line eased still more, and he found that he was pulling it in almost as fast as the retrieve could handle it. He felt a tentative probe from the pain, but it was only a distant landscape, uninteresting; present, but of no moment. Then he saw the fish.

At first he thought it was dead. For a bass it was immense. He had never seen one so large. As he drew it toward the bateau, loglike, twisting and twisting, he wondered if he could pull it aboard even if there was no fight left in it. When he got it alongside, he could tell that it was still alive. The eyes were dark, beautiful and dark as the water. The eyes of a dead bass turn quickly to a bright incongruous gold. It was at least six or eight inches across the back and as he peered down on it, he saw its gills moving slowly, fanlike, sweeping the dark water. It wasn't dead. It was simply tired. The bass was very old and had fought itself out. Against great odds. For a long time. In the room with her. Wasted and tired. An old woman now, and. He came to himself still staring at the fish. He could not get his net around it. It looked to weigh close to thirty pounds. But bass don't reach thirty pounds. He did not remember those last hours. She.

He reached down into the water with both hands and caught the big fish by the lower jaw. In a single motion, he lifted it into the air. He held it sparkling aloft, the dying light making of it a great shadow-fish against the darkening clouds. Then, of a sudden, its weight was oppressive and his arms too weak to support it longer.

He lowered the fish back into the water. Quickly, he leaned over the side of the boat and worked the bait loose. It was easy to do, and he enjoyed the quickness and clarity of his work. You can still do something right, you heap of old diseased rubble, he thought.

Now he fumbled for the rye whiskey without looking for it and took a long drink. Down in the water, the bass lay unmoving. Oh darling let me go. Let me. I only hate to leave. You. Could see the fish revive. Its tail moved suddenly, and it dived deep, its bulk vanishing from his sight in the broken surface of the water where the rain fell.

Then it was dark, and when he came out of the cut, he felt the full force of the wind that always blew along the river, whatever the season. He edged the bateau against the shore at the mouth of the cut, in the cover of a magnolia tree so tall and full that the rain did not penetrate it. Among the leaves at its base, he found some twigs and brush and branches still dry. He piled them up and made a fire. Then he cleaned the goggle-eyes and cooked them in a skillet with cornmeal and grease he had brought.

When he was done, the rain had stopped, the clouds broken, and the sky was clear. The moon was beginning to rise, and it had never looked so large and yellow. He had trouble balancing when he stood up. Hours in the boat makes you lose a sense of the land, he thought. For a little while its very solidity is alien, and the perpetual movement of the water is in your veins. He was very tired now, and the pain had begun to come back, waves against a collapsing shore. Still, when he had cleaned up, he stood awkwardly and pissed into the fire, watching with boyish pleasure as the flames died under his water.

He took up what was left of the fifth of rye and studied it against the rising moon. Then he took a few more of the pills and drank down the rest of the whiskey. The bottle of rye was empty. So was the bottle of pills. Things had come out even. He tossed the bottle toward the sky, watching childlike as it arched across the stars and fell with a soft sound into the river. For a moment, as he climbed back into the boat, he felt young and strong again. He left his rod and tackle and the rest of his equipment behind, taking only his paddle. The boat moved out onto the broad plane of the river.

Then he was looking for that certain place again, the grove where he had not fished this afternoon. Where he had not fished for almost nine years. He did not. Would not. Remember why? He saw the inlet canopied by tall cypresses out there ahead of him. Above, the Milky Way arched over him, a path of stars that seemed to plunge to earth within the grove ahead. It was a place where. He paddled slowly, paying no attention to the darkness, seeing Venus glowing in the sky, constant, asking him to remember.

Now the grove arose from the darkness, separated itself from the undifferentiated bulk of the shore's darkness, a configuration of trees and floating plants like no other. At the back, far back from the open water, there was a place. Where the land rose inexplicably and became solid, more than a mass of roots and rotting leaves. Where even on a dark night, the air crisp and chill, one could find. Her eyes had been closed. —I know, she told him, setting sun touching her uncovered breast, —why this is your favorite place.

He could feel the tears coursing down his cheeks. —The fishing is good, he said aloud, hearing his words flow in the darkness like the river.

—I know, he heard her laugh from beyond the shadows.

He remembered then, and the weight of loss was nothing compared to the memories.

Crushing out the anguish of losing her had distorted everything else. He felt tears on his cheeks, mourning not so much the losing as the time wasted not remembering.

In the chill night he stood up as the boat left the current and drifted into the utter darkness of the grove. Mist was rising there, whirling across the shattered stumps, skipping between the tranced and silent trees. He was amazed to find that the moon's light penetrated even there and made the still water glisten like a ballroom floor. He stretched out his arms and she was in them, his arms strong and full once more. Out there above the moon, he could see the plane of the galaxy itself, path of heaven, as the boat skewed and turned slowly to the music of night birds and crickets. The Pleiades, a starry court, snared his eyes, whirling, turning, and she, judges, advocates, all the suppliants found at last their *logos* and their meaning.

So that when the boat struck a cypress knee there in the quiet pool, he could not quite judge the motion of the distant stars or the touch of the autumn night from that of the dancing tree-crowns, that of the cool beloved water that sustained his fall, summation of yearning and pain. A court adjourned, another opening.

The Great Pumpkin

Mr. and Mrs. Twitty were retired. That is, Mr. Twitty was retired. Mrs. Twitty had nothing to retire from.

They had come to Belle Isle to enjoy life. They had that coming. So many years really *not* enjoying life, only looking forward to enjoying it. They had lived in Pittsburgh, Pennsylvania, and no one enjoyed living there.

Mr. Twitty had traveled in rainwear for forty years. He sold raincoats and galoshes in Ohio, New Jersey, Pennsylvania, Indiana, and a small piece of Illinois. Whenever anyone asked him what he did for a living, Mr. Twitty had a naughty thing he told them. Mrs. Twitty always blushed if she were there, no matter how many times he said it. People would always laugh and nudge each other, but Mr. Twitty would only smile.

They had a little cottage at the end of Humming Bird Lane in Paradise Villa. It was a nice little house with ivy and some honeysuckle growing around the door. It had belonged to an old maiden lady who had died of cancer without any relatives and it had sold cheap. Mr. and Mrs. Twitty had been lucky to get it, and they knew it.

During the day, Mr. Twitty would putter around the house or walk down to the artificial lake and go fishing. When he did, he always caught something because it was a well-stocked lake kept exclusively for Paradise Villa residents. But he never kept anything that he caught, because as a matter of fact he didn't like fish. They never had fish. He didn't know if Mrs. Twitty liked fish or not, but he supposed she didn't.

While he puttered or fished, Mrs. Twitty would spend her time in the kitchen or cleaning up. They had a very strict schedule of meals, with the same dishes at lunch and dinner each day of the week. The menu was made up of dishes Mr. Twitty liked, and every Monday's lunch and dinner was like every other Monday's. It was the same every other day, except that sometimes on Sunday, Mrs. Twitty would fix up a surprise. There was really nothing to clean up at all, but Mrs. Twitty tried anyhow, looking in the most remote and out-of-the-way places for dirt. When, as would occasionally happen, she came across a pocket of dust or grit, she would smile and attack it with Top Job or Mr. Clean and enjoy herself immensely.

They had never had any children, the Twittys. Not that they hadn't wanted them. They had. But one doctor spoke of a deformed uterus and another of low sperm-count, but all their expectations and talk didn't make babies and none had ever come. They were sorry, the Twittys. It was just too bad.

Because they loved children. One of the nicest things about Belle Isle was that there were lots of families with children. At Christmas, the smaller ones would go from house to house singing carols, carefully herded along the cold winding streets of Paradise Villa by a mother who had volunteered to do so the previous year in the glow of the children's sweet innocent chirping. They would ring the bell and warble "God Rest Ye Merry Gentlemen," in a loose, quavering, off-key way all their own. It was nice to see them, and it gave a special meaning to the Holy Season. Mr. Twitty would smile, almost embarrassed as the children sang. Mrs. Twitty would sigh. They did not talk about the children afterward. Mr. Twitty would turn on the television and they would watch a movie or a comedy show, sitting in their chairs close beside one another.

The older children were rougher, noisier, and not very polite. Some of them had motorbikes or cars and would roar up and down the streets in the evening, wrecking the silence and the peace of Paradise Villa. The local newspaper frequently editorialized about the lack of firm discipline and steady goals among American youth, but it never mentioned much by way of specifics, and the children of Belle Isle were never pointed out as examples.

Now it was October. There was a crisp pleasant chill in the air, and folks like the Twittys were looking forward to Thanksgiving and the holidays. But first there was that holiday especially for children—the spooky exciting time of Halloween. The Twittys especially liked Halloween because it gave them a chance to plan and prepare surprises for the kids. And they liked to watch the Charlie Brown television special about the Great Pumpkin.

The Great Pumpkin, Mr. Twitty said, was that wild exciting event that everybody always looks forward to, waits for, hopes for in his life. Something different and wild and maybe even dangerous. But something special. Mrs. Twitty's eyes got large as she listened to him, because Mr. Twitty never talked that way. It put her in mind of a time, long ago, when Mr. Twitty was gone to Philadelphia and she had met a man at the May Company department store, and they had talked, and he bought her lunch and asked her to go with him to his hotel. He was a traveling salesman like Mr. Twitty and was only in town for a day or two. The strangest part was that she could not actually remember either what she had said or done. She was confused, because often, especially when lonely and blue, she would fantasize that she had smiled, touched his hand, said yes, and gone, and that they had sinned together, wildly, madly. But she suspected that this was not memory, really, but just fantasy. Anyhow, she smiled inwardly, *that* had been her Great Pumpkin.

So they waited until the 30th of October and then Mr. Twitty candied apples while Mrs. Twitty baked brownies and they cooked up some lovely chocolate candy together. It was a clear sunny day, and while the brownies baked, Mr. and Mrs. Twitty walked down to the store. Mr. Twitty was still talking about the Great Pumpkin. He said that, traveling on the road, he had often pretended that, at one stop or another, someone in authority would say, —Well, Twitty, you're a real goer. I like your style. Now we've got a little deal set up, and . . . But it had never happened. Only once, someone he could not even remember had sold him a $200 interest in an oil well they were drilling near Amarillo, Texas. He had never even heard what came of it. Maybe they never drilled it, or maybe they did and hit water. Or maybe they gushed all over west Texas, made 10 million dollars, and just never let him know. But the Great Pumpkin had never come along, and probably, Mr. Twitty smiled wisely, even if it had, it would have surely turned into a giant rutabaga.

Mrs. Twitty smiled and tried to remember the name and face of *her* Great Pumpkin, but she couldn't, and when Mr. Twitty made his joke about the rutabaga, she laughed right out loud right there in the supermarket. Not so much about the rutabaga, as for not being able to remember what her Great Pumpkin had been like.

When they got home from the store, it was evening. They took cellophane of various colors, ribbons, and a number of small toys made in Hong Kong and began to make up little parcels for the children. Mr. Twitty paused and tacked up skeletons and black cats and witches and bats made out of pasteboard in the foyer and on the front door. By bedtime, everything was ready, and Mr. and Mrs. Twitty fell asleep talking softly of how much fun it would be next evening when the little ghosts and goblins came trick-or-treating.

The next day seemed very long. It was downright strange. Almost as if there were some indescribable tension between Mr. and Mrs. Twitty, although of course there wasn't. And they didn't talk all morning, and at lunch—it was Tuesday, and so Campbell's Golden Mushroom soup—they just ate quickly and nibbled their Dutch Rusk and then went off again: Mrs. Twitty to dust furniture she had dusted the day before; Mr. Twitty for a walk he really didn't feel like taking. The sun was already low and no one was on the streets. The trees were mottled gold and red, leaves beginning to fall like so many lovely coins scattered down the cold dismal streets. Once Mr. Twitty saw something dark flit through a stand of pine trees in a vacant lot he was passing. He laughed aloud at his instant's fright. Never too old, he thought, almost taking pleasure at the vestige of childishness still stored inside his aging body.

Mrs. Twitty was sitting alone in the parlor in front of the vacant television screen when he got home. The house was very warm, and Mr. Twitty almost felt faint. His nose itched. Somebody coming, he thought. Mrs. Twitty's whatnot, each shelf covered with tiny glass animals he had sent her over the years from so many dull towns, caught the last sunbeams, broke them into colors, and broadcast feeble tendrils against the mirror over the fireplace. Like a light show, Mr. Twitty thought. He was up on things, and had seen something on the television. Then the swirl of colors faded and vanished, and Mr. Twitty sighed as he took off his heavy sweater.

Mrs. Twitty's hands were folded in that certain way she had when she was nervous or tense. Sometimes she would begin talking when she felt that way, talking almost at random, saying nothing, really, just going on. But not this time. She just sat while Mr. Twitty hung up his sweater and turned on the evening news.

It was awful, of course. It always was. War and hunger, pride and bigotry. Morals going, customs already gone. Crime up, prices up. As if the end of the world Billy Graham preached was coming inevitably closer and closer with nobody and nothing able or willing to hold it back. Mr. Twitty wondered if maybe Jesus come again was going to be everybody's Great Pumpkin, and then wondered at his own crazy thought.

—Almost time for the Great Pumpkin, Mr. Twitty heard himself say aloud.

Mrs. Twitty felt a chill travel up her spine as he said it, and couldn't imagine why, thinking at the same time that it was odd, what with all their talk, neither of them had thought to buy a pumpkin and carve a jack-o'-lantern out of it.

—Yes, Mrs. Twitty said after a while. —They'll be coming anytime now.

And they did. They came in threes and fours and half dozens and once in a group of at least fifteen. They would ring the doorbell and shriek in loud tiny piping voices, —Trick-or-treat, trick-or-treat, whreee . . . !

Each time they did, Mr. and Mrs. Twitty would exchange a smile, get up from the television, turn down the volume, and go to the door. Just inside, in the foyer, there was a nice little table Mr. Twitty had bought at an exclusive antique shop in Sandusky, Ohio, and had sent to Mrs. Twitty after he had done something really awful at a buyers' convention in Youngstown. On the table they had placed the little parcels, and when Mrs. Twitty opened the door, Mr. Twitty would quickly count the number of youngsters and pick up enough parcels for them. He would hold them while Mrs. Twitty took one at a time and handed them to each costumed child with a smile and a kind word.

All kinds of twilight and midnight folks turned up in miniature form: devils and caterpillars, spidermen and catwomen, tiny pigs and lank clowns, outlaws and ruffians, galley slaves and hottentots, mad scientists and magicians. There was an anthology from zoos, graveyards, alchemists' garrets, abandoned castles, sewers and bell towers, opium dens and witches' hovels. It was as if all the forgotten and ignored of the earth, from the past, the present, the future, beasts, men, myths and nightmares, all had risen to go abroad on this one night to remind the ordinary world and the sleepwalkers in their homes of what they would most like to forget.

It went on for three or four hours, and then only a few came, and finally there was a long lull. The late news came on, repeating the stories told earlier, or at least telling stories just like them. Then it was bedtime. Mr. Twitty rose, stretched, turned off the television and the floor lamp and started toward the foyer. The table was almost empty. Only five or six of the little parcels were left. Just as he touched the light switch, there was a roar outside, as if all the motorbikes in Belle Isle had come blasting to a stop right in front of Mr. and Mrs. Twitty's house. Almost at once, there was a hammering on the door, and as Mrs. Twitty came into the foyer, both of them heard a flurry of voices outside howling, —Trick-or-treat, trick-or-treat.

Mrs. Twitty was tired, but she put her smile in place, and Mr. Twitty picked up the remaining parcels, and Mrs. Twitty opened the door.

Out there they saw a gorilla, a skeleton, a cowboy, and a spaceman.

The Gorilla was large and hulking and threatening. Mrs. Twitty drew her breath in sharply when she saw him. He was covered with dark, moth-eaten fur, and his face was frozen in an expression of insane and insensate fury or lust or hatred or anguish, or a mixture of them all. His eyes were so deep-set that they were almost invisible, simple pits in which something like madness burned.

The Skeleton was very convincing. It looked like the very spirit of death itself, each bone articulated against the blackness of some fabric behind, and shimmering with what appeared to be some kind of phosphorescent paint. The Gorilla grunted and chuffed evilly; the Skeleton made no sound at all.

The Cowboy wore purple jeans, a shirt covered with fancy silver scrollwork, a bandana around his neck, a Stetson, and a mask. All but the jeans and the scrollwork were black, and Mr. Twitty wondered if western outlaws had looked like that when they went out to work. You could see only a little of his face beneath the mask, but what you *could* see looked rough and mean, and gave the Twittys no reason to want to see the rest.

Behind the others, the Spaceman wore white uniform-like coveralls, only they were very tight and molded to his body. Around his head was a plastic helmet that looked for all the world like a fishbowl. The face inside was unmemorable, even-featured, characterless, the face of no man and every man—as if it had been issued by some government agency that would hold him responsible for its condition when it was returned. On his right shoulder, the Spaceman wore an emblem, and it confused Mr. Twitty, because right where Neil Armstrong had worn the American flag, this Spaceman wore an iron cross.

As the Twittys watched them, they all watched the Twittys.

—Took you long enough to answer, the Cowboy drawled. —You hard of hearing, pops?

Mr. Twitty didn't know what to say. He half-offered one of the parcels to the Cowboy, realizing even as he did how absurd the gesture was. The Spaceman saw this motion and his discomfiture, and laughed. It was a strange distant sound, hollowed and muffled by the plastic helmet. As the Spaceman laughed, the Gorilla pushed forward, past Mrs. Twitty, and into the foyer. The others followed behind him.

—Listen, Mr. Twitty was saying, still off-balance, uncertain of what to say or do.

—We're listening, we're listening, the Spaceman assured Mr. Twitty from a long way off as the Gorilla eyed Mrs. Twitty closely and then moved on into the parlor. —We just got to use your phone, he said.

The Skeleton closed the door and put its blank white skull close to

Mr. Twitty's face. It tried to grin; the supple mask warped into a terrible leer.

By the time Mr. Twitty had gotten himself together and realized how outrageous all this was, the Cowboy was on the phone dialing. As he waited for an answer, he took out a cigarette and lit it. It was thin and brown and fat in the middle, and looked a good bit like the roll-your-owns Mr. Twitty had smoked as a young man. After a long drag, the Cowboy passed the cigarette to the Gorilla who did the same and held the smoke in his terrific lungs and rolled his eyes and he handed the cigarette on to the Skeleton.

—Whew, the Skeleton coughed.

—Hello, Annie, the Cowboy barked, exhaling the smoke at last. —It's The Kid. What you got on? I got three studs over here, and we're all so horny we honk. Can youall handle us? Huh? Lord yes we got dope. We got stuff you can smoke, drop, shoot, sniff, line. Hell, honey, I got some new stuff you can just look at and go . . .

Mrs. Twitty's smile wasn't gone yet—only fading, but it was in poor repair. She wasn't sure what the Cowboy was talking about, but somehow she felt it had to do with the world that kept coming toward hers in the evening news.

—All right, Annie. Sure. Okay.

The Cowboy read off the Twittys' phone number, and said he would wait for her call. He told Annie it was a matter of life and death that she clear out a little space, because it was gash or go down tonight.

The Gorilla and the Skeleton had seated themselves in Mr. and Mrs. Twitty's chairs and turned on the television. The Spaceman stood near the sofa with an odd sneer on his face. He had had his turn with the cigarette and now you could hardly see his unexceptional face for the mist of smoke swirling in his helmet.

—You boys have got to . . . Mr. Twitty began, but the Gorilla roared at him, waving its hairy arms and looking horrid. Mr. Twitty held his chin firm, but didn't finish what he wanted to say. It was the first time he had really felt old, too old to face things like this blasted gorilla—although, in fact, he had never faced much of anything even in the army, where he had worked in supply. The Cowboy sucked on his smoke again and sauntered over to Mr. Twitty, walking as if they were both in an old western bar.

—Pops, the Cowboy said, his mouth almost unmoving below the mask. —Whyn't youall just sit down and do your evening Bible-reading or whatever you do to pretend you're still groovin'? We got to wait for this call, okay?

Mr. Twitty was about to say, no, it wasn't okay at all, but he felt the pressure of Mrs. Twitty's hand on his arm, and he said nothing. He felt a sudden surge of love for his wife course through him, something positive and real, more than habit, that he had not felt for years. She was concerned about him, and somehow knowing that made the nasty deep taste of fear in his throat much easier to bear. He could stand on his dignity now; she had released him from the necessity of acting.

—All right, Mr. Twitty said, almost easily. —Just for the call.

The Spaceman laughed distantly, a nasty laugh. —Thanks, he said from a long way off. —Thanks a lot.

The Gorilla was laughing at one of Johnny Carson's more inane double entendres. Maybe the Skeleton was, too. How could you tell?

—Hey, mumsy, the Cowboy suddenly asked Mrs. Twitty. —You got any Southern Comfort?

Mrs. Twitty didn't know what to say. But her ravaged smile brightened ever so slightly.

—We've always loved the South, she began hesitantly. —That's why we moved here from Pittsburgh, Pennsylvania, and we never . . .

—Aw, you stupid cunt, I mean whiskey, the Cowboy cut her off. —Where the fuck are you people at?

Mrs. Twitty's lower lip trembled. —We . . . don't have any whiskey, she began again. But they were ignoring her now.

Mr. Twitty felt his ears and scalp growing hot. He had never heard that kind of talk before a lady, least of all Verna, Mrs. Twitty.

—Now listen, I want you to watch yourselves, he began, but before he could say anything else, the Gorilla had swung around in his chair and hit him with something large and heavy. The blow sent Mr. Twitty sprawling across the room, and when he managed to clear his head of what at first he thought was a ringing in his ears, but which was actually Mrs. Twitty screaming and screaming, he saw that the Gorilla had some kind of gun and that the Skeleton was hitting Mrs. Twitty with his fists over and over again, that her face was cut, and that the Skeleton was making some kind of strange high sound in its throat.

Mr. Twitty tried to climb to his feet to help Mrs. Twitty, but as he did, the Cowboy kicked him right in his privates, and Mr. Twitty went down again with a blinding, gut-ripping pain he had not felt in forty years. He must have passed out, because when he came to himself again, everything had changed. The Gorilla was still watching television all right, but the Cowboy was handing him another cigarette and was sitting in Mr. Twitty's chair. The Spaceman was just resetting his helmet and passing a bottle of Jack Daniels to the Skeleton, who now sat on the sofa next to Mrs. Twitty and had stopped beating her. When the Skeleton had slugged down a half-pint or so, it handed the bottle to Mrs. Twitty, who took a long pull on it almost matter-of-factly, as if she had been doing it for a long time.

Mr. Twitty wondered how long he had been unconscious, but as he tried to move, another blitz of pain shot through him and he moaned out loud for a pain that no man his age should have to suffer. When he looked again out of the mirage of his pain, the Cowboy was handing Mrs. Twitty one of those cigarettes. And she was taking it.

—Goddamn, Mr. Twitty heard himself say, but nobody paid any attention. The Skeleton was smoking and the Cowboy was with the Gorilla again, and they were watching the late movie, something about things from another planet. The Spaceman was out there laughing.

—Hey, old honey, the Cowboy called over his shoulder, —that old goof ever ball you any more?

Mr. Twitty tried to turn back to see Mrs. Twitty's face again, but even turning his head was pure agony.

—Ball . . . ? Mrs. Twitty said in a voice soft and filmy as if she were wearing a space-helmet, too.

—Screw, honey. You know. Intercourse?

—Oh, intercourse.

The Gorilla threw up his paws and coughed and roared. As he did so, Mr. Twitty could see the gun in his lap. It was a sawed-off automatic shotgun. Mr. Twitty could tell, because it was just like an old Remington he had had when he was younger, except without much barrel, and hardly any stock at all.

It went on like that, the smoking and drinking for what seemed a long time from where Mr. Twitty was lying. Once he wondered where they had gotten the whiskey, and what the cigarette made them do, but this drifted out of his mind again as did the picture of Mrs. Twitty drinking and smoking with them. What would they do if she refused? The Cowboy was talking about the James Gang, and the Spaceman said something about Moondog. The Gorilla growled about the Animals, and even the Skeleton whispered a name that sounded like the Grateful Dead. Mr. Twitty heard all this pass in and out of his mind, and he thought he must be going crazy, but he was beginning to come out of it a little, and found that he could, if he was careful, move again. Then the Cowboy was smoking and saying things about sex and none of it made any sense at all.

The telephone rang. The Spaceman caught it, listening for a moment with the receiver up against his helmet. Then he hung up.

—No dice, the Spaceman said hollowly.

—Shit, the Skeleton croaked, almost aloud.

—Ain't that just too goddamned bad, the Cowboy muttered. —No way?

—What she said, the Spaceman answered.

The Gorilla kicked in the television screen, and the room went dark, sparks flying everywhere. The Skeleton threw the almost-empty bottle of Jack Daniels at the mirror over the fireplace. The Spaceman turned over the whatnot, and all of Mrs. Twitty's little glass animals crashed and tinkled to the floor. The Cowboy unzipped his jeans, went over to the sofa, ripped off Mrs. Twitty's skirt and underthings and began raping her. She squealed, but it was a funny sound, and the horror that flooded Mr. Twitty wasn't just the kind of horror he might have expected only a few hours ago.

And he could hear the Cowboy:

—Yipee, the Cowboy was yelling. —Aw-haw. Round 'em up, head 'em out . . .

And he could hear when the Cowboy was finished, and then the Skeleton. And the Spaceman.

The Gorilla got up from Mrs. Twitty's chair where he had been sitting staring at the shattered television screen. The gun in his lap slid down his furry thighs and landed on the floor as his huge paws fumbled with his hairy crotch, revealing parts just like those of a human being.

Mr. Twitty turned his head. He couldn't help it. There was no more deadly pain to use as an excuse for not seeing. He had to. He heard the Skeleton whispering how great it was to be dead, and the Spaceman said he was spaced out. The Cowboy told them it was all Dodge City, and no shit. The Gorilla was mounting Mrs. Twitty, pawing her, burying his huge head in her naked breasts and grunting and growling. Mr. Twitty saw this, and saw Mrs. Twitty's small pale hands caught in the Gorilla's thick roan fur.

He turned away. His eyes moved over the shadowy alien landscape of the parlor lighted only by the distant light in the foyer. He saw the blasted television screen, Mrs. Twitty's chair turned over, the parcels of candy and brownies and toys lying where he had dropped them.

And he saw the shotgun where it had fallen from the Gorilla's lap as he got up to go to Mrs. Twitty.

It took a long time to crawl that far. More than all his sixty years and more still. It was as if he had been crawling all his life, trying to cross that cold parlor floor, trying to reach that sawed-off shotgun. Could it be that those thousands upon thousands of miles he had driven in sun and rain, twilight and dawn, determined to get the job done, the sales quota filled and then some, had all been some kind of silly rehearsal for this? Well, why not? What else had those miles meant? Because in all his labor, he had never really felt right before, not selling those goddamned rubbers and raincoats. But if he could cross this five yards. Could that be it? So late. So near the end with nothing at all, years lost as were those thousands of miles.

He could still hear the Gorilla grunting, rocking, rolling, as he reached the gun at last, checked the safety instinctively, as when he had gone shooting long ago, and slowly turned over.

The Gorilla was still at it, Mrs. Twitty's fingers caught spasmodically in the fur of his neck. The Cowboy was playing with himself, telling the Gorilla to hurry up, that he wanted another go. The Spaceman's helmet was foggy again, and the Skeleton had a fresh cigarette, trying to light it from the glowing butt of the last.

Mr. Twitty's first shot took off the Skeleton's skull. What Mr. Twitty remembered in his brief afterwards was not the blood and bone fragments and tissue splashed against his parlor wall, but the tiny sparks, like a flurry of fireflies, which spiraled away and upward into the darkness as the two cigarettes were blasted to one side.

But he saw all that in much less than a fraction of a second, because he was already pulling the trigger again, his second shot catching the Cowboy right in the groin he was playing with. The Cowboy was knocked backward and down, but he fell, back against the wall in such a way that his hands, relatively unhurt, went on playing, rummaging in the cavern of red slush for a second or two.

The Spaceman saw it coming and had just time enough to try to choose something to throw at Mr. Twitty. But he was still trying to pick between a vase with a picture of Cape Kennedy on it and an ashtray made of nose-cone ceramic when the charge hit him squarely in the chest. He sat down immediately, and as Mr. Twitty watched, praying in another part of his mind that there was no plug in the gun, that it held either four or five shots instead of the legal three, the Spaceman's helmet began to fill with blood which coursed from his mouth as if it would never stop flowing. It bubbled over his mouth, over his nose, but as he fell over backward, Mr. Twitty was already up on his feet aiming at the Gorilla.

The Gorilla was finished now. He was on his feet too, backing up toward the door, all the hatred and fury and lust gone from his face, his manlike crotch wilted, small and flabby now. Have you ever seen a terrified Gorilla?

—Please, the Gorilla was saying in a high cracked voice almost like that of a young boy. —Please, mister, for God's sake . . .

—Whoever heard of a Gorilla saying please, Mr. Twitty said as he pulled the trigger.

The Gorilla vanished in a tornado of fur and pieces of what appeared to be gorilla-meat. Mr. Twitty frowned, because he knew he had not hit him cleanly, and he could hear the thing flopping on the floor of the foyer. Flopping and howling just like the animal he was. But Mr. Twitty felt fine. Really fine. Later, he thought, I'll feel real bad, but shit I do feel fine just now.

—His name was George, Mrs. Twitty was saying from the sofa. —George Grotz. He traveled in cosmetics, and I *did* go, Sweet Jesus, I *did* go. . . .

Mr. Twitty walked over to her, the sawed-off shotgun still fine and full in his hands. He looked down at her where she lay, naked, bleeding, exhausted, something like a lunatic smile on her bruised lips, kissed by so many things.

—Went where? Mr. Twitty asked her.

Mrs. Twitty opened her eyes and smiled up at him. — . . . me to know and you to find out, she whispered, and then drifted off.

Mr. Twitty could still hear that thing flopping in the foyer, and he intended to do something more, use that shotgun just once more, but he couldn't get it together, and before he could sort out some very strange impulses, the blood-high he was on faded and he passed out. The last thing he heard was Mrs. Twitty flopping and that dying ape cooing, — . . . George, George . . .

When the police came, they took one look and beat Mr. Twitty back into consciousness. One of them went around taking off masks, identifying the things Mr. Twitty had disposed of. He kept giving them the names of human beings, and sobbing as if his heart would break. While they waited for ambulances, they checked the brownies for hash. They sniffed the candied apples for lysergic acid. They examined the candy for signs of broken razor-blades or ground glass. They broke up several of the toys to find out if they contained explosives. One young detective who could not control himself kept cuffing Mr. Twitty every time he tried to tell what had happened, until an old detective told him to watch it, that the shriveled-up old scumbug was supposed to have some civil rights.

They paid no attention to Mrs. Twitty at all until one of the detectives noted that the soft-cushions weren't really red, and that possibly she was too mutilated to just be out on whiskey or dope after all.

A newspaper reporter came in, saw everything and vomited in the corner all over the rubble of Mrs. Twitty's glass animals. Then he pulled himself together and looked through the personal effects of the Cowboy and the Skeleton, the Spaceman and the Gorilla. It turned out that they had all belonged to prominent Belle Isle families, although Mr. Twitty, still fuddled, couldn't understand that at all.

They booked Mr. Twitty for what the junior assistant district attorney called Murder One, and tossed him into the county jail's bullpen with drunks, dope fiends, car thieves, draft-dodgers, muggers, lily-shakers and other perverts. When word got around that Mr. Twitty had butchered four young boys in cold blood, the drunks and muggers turned on him and beat him senseless. One of the perverts scratched him with its long fingernails, and a dope fiend, still riding speed or strung out after acid, climbed up the iron bars of the bullpen and screamed insane things at him even after he couldn't hear any more.

Mrs. Twitty died in the hospital from internal injuries and hemorrhaging that night, but Mr. Twitty never heard about that, either, because he was in a coma when the guard came next morning to take him to his arraignment, and by late afternoon he died without making a statement. Death was attributed to his having fallen down in the bullpen, and it was hinted by a spokesman for the district attorney's office that perhaps narcotics were involved.

So Mr. and Mrs. Twitty never saw the newspaper articles about their bestiality or about the vast outpouring of public sentiment at the funerals of the Gorilla and the Cowboy and the Skeleton and the Spaceman. They had all gone to the same high school, and an editorial said that rarely had an American community been so tragically bereaved. The editorial also pointed up a moral in it all: something about how the jealousy of the past blighted the chances of the future. Some people wrote in, agreeing with that editorial, and one old maiden lady wrote saying things were not quite so simple. But nobody bothered to answer her, and that was the end of that.

The Southern Reporter

I

It was late in the afternoon when Judge Lambert took a break. It was after a particularly bad clash between Caswell, the prosecutor, and Tony Vallee, the defense attorney. Judge Lambert, an old-timer who had sat on the First Judicial District Court in Shreveport since 1936, who had grown old and even mild on the bench, told Caswell and Vallee that one more such encounter would interrupt the trial— while both counsel served a day or two in the Caddo Parish Courthouse jail.

—With time enough to contemplate the monument down below, dedicated to the memory of the Confederate Soldier, who did his duty and held his tongue.

Dewey Domingue shook his head, spun his stenotype around, and walked out of the courtroom, down the length of the long antiseptic courthouse hall toward the coffee machine. He put his quarter in and watched while the plastic cup filled. A long time ago, Mrs. Mitchell, the deputy clerk, had kept a pot of dark brew cut with chicory on a hot plate in the clerk's office. The coffee had been good then, the way it should be. The way Louisiana coffee always was. But she had died in 1951, and her replacement had moved out the coffeepot and had a machine put in.

Dewey stood drinking the thin, tasteless stuff, watching witnesses, attorneys, parties to suits walking up and down the hall. He had seen it all already. Seen them and their antecedents walking up and down, stopping to talk in twos or threes, standing alone, smoking, leaning against the wall, staring into the late afternoon sun blankly, as if the stench of cigar smoke and snuff which no deodorant could purge from the hall had tranced them all.

In the First Judicial Court in Shreveport, both civil and criminal matters were heard. A reporter never knew what he might draw. One day, it was a suit on an open account. The next day it might be an ax murder or a mother who had decided to toss her children down an incinerator. Sometimes Dewey couldn't believe the words that flowed out from under his hands onto the tape. There were times when, staring down at the testimony, he could not believe those words had passed through his fingers. Sometimes, especially lately, he got the words wrong because he didn't even know what they meant.

> Q. What did you do then?
> A. Well uh you know like it was. Me or him so, you know, I cut him. I had this here sticker an he run at me an I uh stuck him on along his . . . gulley. He dropped an uh I tried to catch the Horse an an uh it was maybe fifty sixty bags uncut and uh uh he come up again an he tried to off me an uh you uh know uh . . .

Gibberish. And yet every time, no matter what they had done, there was always an appeal. Always the translation of those cryptic tapes into human language. Murray did that. He was Dewey's typist. Had been since 1949. Before that, he had been in the army. Murray couldn't remember how he had learned to type, or so he had once told Dewey. Only that he had learned when he found out in 1941 that if you could use a typing machine, they didn't put you in a rifle company. It had been a natural response for Murray. Yet now he was ashamed of it. When he drank a lot, he would tell Dewey that by rights he ought to be lying dead in the surf of some stinking Pacific atoll or long mouldering under the soil of France or Germany.

—One day I hadn't never seen no damned typewriter. The next week I was doing sixty words a minute. Now that's a natural-born coward for you. And if it had took a hundred and twenty, I'm mortally sure I could of done it. Ain't that a shame? Can't hardly spell his name till the hard rain starts to falling. Then all of a sudden he's a miracle worker, huh?

—I never knew anybody worked to get himself in a situation where he was bound to die, Dewey had told Murray early on.

—Hell, I would have got to be a great cook, but I couldn't boil me an egg without I messed up the yolk. Don't fret about them days. Man can't spend his life looking backward, can he?

—Well, but I do, Murray said, and drank some more, and then went home out to Dixie Gardens where he had some kind of run-down old home and a wife. He had never asked Dewey out to his house, not in almost thirty years of working together, and Dewey never pried into anything, never asked any questions. You didn't go to prying when you worked with a man and he did his job. Dewey had learned that a long time ago. You take Murray. All he was was a typist, but he always came to court. Said he could do a better job of transcribing when he'd heard it all for himself. Dewey reckoned he was still down there in the courtroom waiting for it all to begin again. Murray never drank coffee. He drank beer and an awful amount of hard liquor. But he never missed an assignment, was never late. What else can you ask?

Dewey finished his coffee, crushed the flimsy cup contemptuously in his hand, and tossed it into a wastebasket lined with a plastic sack of some kind. Let me tell you what you can do with your damned machine coffee and your plastic garbage sacks, Dewey was thinking when Hilda came by.

Hilda was old. She was older than the present courthouse. She had worked for the First Judicial Court since when nobody could remember. She cleaned up the courthouse, the clerks' and judges' offices. She was old and black and angry and everybody made room for her and nobody gave her any trouble. Hilda paid no attention to you until you had been around the courts for twenty years or so. She was not about to clutter up her memory with names and faces and particulars of fly-by-night people. Enough trouble to keep straight the ones who mattered, the ones who were there all the time. She remembered as if it were yesterday the stir when Huey Long was elected governor. Caddo Parish had gone against him, but Hilda swore she had paid her poll tax and voted for Huey. He was a North Louisiana boy, a Protestant, and had no use for New Orleans. What more could you ask? They said he was a socialist. But what would he do about a parish in his own stomping ground that went against him?

—Didn't do a damned thing, Hilda would recount, her black face seamed with a repetition of laughter fifty years from its first expression. —Didn't do nothing bad. Didn't do nothing. No road repairs, no hep for the schools. Lissen, Old Huey lef 'em alone . . . Strickly alone. Never did 'em nothing. And they jus' couldn't get up to faultin' him. Them was quiet years, don't you know?

—What you say? Hilda asked Dewey.

—Can't say it, Momee, he answered. If you were an old-timer, you called Hilda Momee. Nobody new had ever tried it. —How about you?

—I hear youall got a rape trial in there, she said.

—Not yet, Dewey smiled. —All the criminal assault I heard about so far is what them lawyers has been doing to each other.

Hilda didn't smile back. She stuck her mop in the wheeled bucket and took out her pack of Camels.

—It's a bad one, she said. —Girl name of Miranda Ferriday come up from Coushatta and got her a job over to Jumbo's Bar in Bossier City. Nice girl. Lookin' to go to Meadows-Draughn Business. Had some typin' and shorthand from Coushatta High. Fella name of Santidy started comin' in, sniffin' round her. She cute, an' Jumbo make 'em wear them cut-off dresses, see? One night he took her out. Hardly got clear of the bar when he went after her. Poor thing never had a chance. Santidy a big man. Come from out west somewhere, I don't know. He did it, though. He did it, and that's sure.

The essence of a courthouse is the play of stories that moves within it. In the clerk's office, the civil sheriff's office, between the judges' clerks, between lawyers, between the women who clean up the courtrooms and the blind man who sells sandwiches and magazines in the lobby, there is a constant current of telling and hearing, of guessing and supposing as to the cases that are being acted out before the bench. The stories have no necessary connection with what will enter the records of each case. The rules of evidence do not constrain clerks and custodians, deliverymen and lawyers outside the purlieus of the court. What passes in the hallways of the courthouse may be strange, inaccurate, tainted with the passions of the storyteller. Still it may be nearer the truth than those pages that will be read by the court of appeal.

—That's sure, Hilda said again. —Santidy done it, and that poor girl fit him, see? She done tried to keep him off her, keep him away, but he wasn't havin' none of that. He meant to git what he went for, see? An' he did. Yes, he got it. I say jus' lucky they cotch him.

—Who got him? Dewey asked, now for the first time interested in the case, intrigued. He put much faith in Hilda's version of things. Over the years, had there been a morning line on the result of trials, and had he bet Hilda's insights, he would have been a wealthy man. She knew.

—Well, the police got him. What you think? Happens that poor girl's brother a police. Come up out of Coushatta a while back. What? Maybe two years. Got him a job with the Benton Sheriff's Office. Little girl live with him, see? An' this Santidy goin' to rape her out in front of the house, not even knowin' her brother a police an' him in the very house right then. Ain't that a shame?

—Well, if that's so, I reckon it is, Dewey said.

—What you mean if that's so?

—I reckon I mean, a lot of women claim . . .

Hilda looked disgusted. —You bet. Lots do. An' a good number be lyin'. But not this one, see?

Hilda drew on her Camel cigarette, leaned back against the wall.

Her eyes, old and filmed, seemed softer than Dewey could remember. He paid a great deal of attention to the old woman. They were friends, contemporaries. They knew what few others knew.

—You know, Hilda said almost nostalgically. —I can remember when a man did that to a woman was as good as dead . . . Never got to trial. . . .

—But . . . wasn't it mostly . . . ?

—Nigger men? Sure enough. When they took 'em out, I used to say, shame. That's an awful thing. . . .

Hilda mashed out her cigarette on the sole of her shoe.

—Sure, that's what I used to say. But now is now. An' I know what's goin' down jus' as well as anybody. An' I tell you this: was they to go to lynchin' again, an' be fair . . . Take 'em all out that did what that damn Santidy did, never mind no color . . . you know what?

—What?

—I wouldn't say shame. I wouldn't say one damn thing but good enough for 'em.

Dewey was surprised. —That's hard, he said. —Now, Momee . . .

—Don't Momee me, boy. I'm an old woman, an' I see what we got goin' nowadays. You know what we come to? No Jesus. That's what we got. You turn away from Jesus, what you expect?

—Not much, Dewey said. —No, I wouldn't expect too much.

—You ain't got no Jesus, your ass in a sling, see?

—I believe so, Dewey said soberly. And he did. That was what he believed. He had believed it for a long time.

Dewey Domingue had come up from the Florida Parishes to Shreveport in 1939. He had worked in Hammond on the railroad and out of Madisonville crabbing and had, before he was twenty, gone into New Orleans against the advice of all his people, hoping to better himself. He had a strong clean handwriting taught him by his mother, and he had come to spell English words tolerably on his own. He was not ashamed of his French, but he wanted to go forward in the world, and you didn't go forward using Cajun French. No, what you did was learn that English that the big people, the important people used. So he had gotten himself a job in the New Orleans Civil District Courts. He had learned shorthand after awhile. They paid good money. But God knows he had not bettered himself. It was just as his people had said. New Orleans was a terrible town, and no decent young man could sustain himself there. Not for long. He had lost his faith in New Orleans. He had consorted with whores and men who lived off them. He had taken to the night life. Lord, the things he had seen. Women shameless and forlorn, stripping off their clothes, offering themselves on table tops and long oaken bars. Drunkenness and gambling. Even sodomy. If there was a filth in the world that had not found its way to New Orleans, Dewey did not know its name. Except for one drunken Sunday afternoon when he had accidentally stumbled into Saint Louis Cathedral behind a pack of gawking tourists, he had not been to mass since he left the parishes. Was that bettering himself?

Looking backward, Dewey could remember those days as if they were disconnected scenes from an old movie. He remembered working the courts during the day, his mind already on sundown, on the Quarter. He remembered the heat that would rise within him, the fantasies that played across the ragged unfinished stage of his mind as he sat writing, amanuensis with the panoply and color and tension of Saint Anthony's temptations firing his hopes for evening.

At last, more to assure himself those evenings than for any other reason, he had set up housekeeping with a girl from Baton Rouge no wiser than he. It had been the strangest game: the two of them putting aside whatever they had been before they came to New Orleans, wordlessly pretending that this was their place, this the form of their lives.

Each night they would go from one steamy club to the next. The one run by a woman, gross and overweight, who nestled an enormous ruby between her vast breasts and smiled off questions, saying that the blood-red stone was the price her virtue had brought so long before when things were really good, before the Navy had put everyone out on the street. Or the one run by a man from New York who had once piloted the China Clipper until the liquor took him, and he found himself in the bowels of Shanghai when it was the sewer of the world. They would drink and sing and dance until they were exhausted with the world. Then they would go back to their tiny one-room apartment on Royal Street, turn on the oscillating fan and make what passed for love between them until dawn. Time for him to go to court. Time for her to go to the oyster bar and wash and clean until opening time.

He had known something was wrong. Not the sin or the shame of it, not simply the commonness, the trashiness of living that way. It had gone deeper.

It would be years later before he would find the words to say, even to himself, what had really been wrong with it. It was that, growing up in the parishes, somewhere, somehow, he had come to expect more. Was what he felt for the girl (named Viola, for all it mattered then or later; from Clinton, not Baton Rouge, for all anyone cared at the time or afterward) all there was to feel? Was it some flaw in him or in her? In both of them or in the world? They had met and hungered and said it was fine to eat when you are hungry, isn't it? Who makes promises to gumbo or fried trout? Being free is doing what you want to do, isn't it? Sure, Dewey had told her, a little less certainly than the question had been asked—but just as sure he wanted to be free.

Freedom wasn't a place or a thing, but what it seemed to be was a golden glow suffusing whatever else the idea of it touched. They were free. New Orleans was free. This life was what it was to be free. Wasn't it? Sure, Dewey told himself. I can say what I want, do what I want. Can't I?

Still there existed the shadow he could hardly trace through the days and nights, some faintest sour residuum that only forced its way into consciousness when he was exhausted during a trial recess or very early in the morning as he strode out under the faded parchment of the sky in the dark streets before dawn.

Then there had been that afternoon in August when it had been too hot to go on, when the judge had recessed court on account of the ungodly heat, saying they would reconvene at seven in the evening and go forward in that way until the heat wave broke. Dewey had been upset, irritated that he would have to lose a night on the town, walking and talking, drinking and dancing with his woman, sitting with the sports and musicians in the clubs, listening to the pulse of real life as it drummed in the streets after dark.

When he reached the apartment, he heard sounds inside. The heat was awful, enough to make his head swim. Maybe the sounds were from next door. Maybe he ought to go down to the A & P and pick up a dozen bottles of beer. Maybe he should go by the oyster bar. He shut his eyes, key in hand, defeated, broken already, with nothing fine and free to do or say, nothing at all left but to practice the tiny heroism of turning the key in his own door and walking into the future he already knew lay spread in the stark heat of midday there.

All she had said, almost dreamily, was —Oh, shit, Dewey, what are you doing home so early?

Later, sitting with his fifth double bourbon in hand, he would remember it as if it had been etched in the contours of his brain so that another angle, another view would confront him no matter what direction he might choose to push his thought. The fact was not so awful as the encounter, the reality of it being stamped in his memory past remove, past casting out or burying or even attempting to forget.

Later, sitting there, he thought he had not loved her, could never have loved her. But if that was so, than where did the pain come from? Was it just the instantaneous sight of that pale, naked, hairy body he had glimpsed for less than a moment moving rhythmically, absurdly, over her? Was it some diminution of his own manhood that had called inexorably for violence he had not even thought of at that moment?

No. He had not loved her. But she had been what he had voluntarily put in the place of love. He had made himself a life full of substitutions, hadn't he? Surely he had. He had burned himself out so thoroughly that whatever there might have been in life beyond was now barred to him forever. Not by law or creed or opinion, but by his own loss of feeling, that horror and cynicism now as much a part of him as his eyes, his ears—his memories.

He had drunk then. For a brief while, he had managed to hold on to his job at the Civil District Courts, but finally that had gone, the judicial administrator angrily firing him when it was found that the stenographic transcript for a whole trial was a hopeless muddle, which even Dewey himself could not interpret.

After that, he had taken to drinking cheap wine and sitting in Lafayette Park in the afternoons as autumn came on. He talked to the men who came there, and they told him that life made no sense at all, that it was good to watch dogs seeking lampposts or fire hydrants, and to listen to music when one could. But that life made no sense at all.

He did odd jobs for people who had known him in better days. When there were no jobs, there was the Salvation Army with good rich soup, a dry corner in a deserted warehouse where amid the cooling nights he could hear the distant, hopeless foghorns of ships entering and leaving the port, sounding as if they were mourning a home they would never reach, perhaps one they could not even recall.

It was deep winter when his string played out. He awoke to find himself lying on the grass at the base of the Lee Monument, his eyes suddenly open, staring up toward the chill sky, and finding there the image of Robert E. Lee, arms crossed, hat pulled over his eyes, staring north where the enemy lay, where it had always been. The next thing he remembered was a young resident at Charity Hospital telling him that the Huey P. Long Bridge was a better and easier way to go than what he was doing to himself.

And after that, he remembered being on the street outside the hospital, walking along Tulane Avenue back toward downtown, where everything had happened to him. The Huey P. Long Bridge lay behind him. Perhaps there was an inch or two left to his string. As he walked, he found he had no feelings at all—but still there was an awful thirst.

Then, almost to Canal Street, at the verge of the Quarter, he had seen an ancient truck from which men were selling produce: oranges, strawberries, tomatoes, cushaws. There were two of them, and they were speaking French. Yes, of course they would share their lunch with him. How had he come to live in this place? No, of course they didn't. No, they came here only to sell what they grew. This was no place for a decent man to live. Hadn't his priest told him about this place? Yes, Dewey lied. Of course he had. One more question: Would there be a little work for a man who wanted to . . . walk away?

Afterward, when he was himself again, or at least some self that could work and sleep and leave the liquor alone, he had considered going home. Bastien and Robert, his truck-farming friends, said that was the thing to do. Home. Or west to Evangeline Parish where even now people lived life the way it was meant to be lived.

No, Dewey thought. At least not yet. There has got to be something else that has to be done. Maybe feelings can be rescued, found again, but not home. Not with a family or normal people watching, wondering what has gone wrong inside their kinsman. Better another place. Surely better a place where one is . . . What? Free?

Then he had found himself a map of Louisiana one Sunday afternoon, and looked it over. After considering for the length of that long dreary Sunday afternoon, he had packed his things, gone to the bus depot, and bought a ticket for Shreveport, the farthest place he had any knowledge of. He had heard of Texas and Mississippi. He knew there were such places as Arkansas, New York, and France, but those places had no more real existence for Dewey than did Samarkand or Tycho or the Asteroid Belt. Not in 1939.

So he had gone to Shreveport and found himself a job there in the courts. Lord knows he had tried hard to live a good life. And it had turned out to be easy. There was no Bourbon Street there, no steady, inescapable invitation to sin, no depravity so general and sustained that a man could not avoid it if he walked out into the open streets. All a man had to do was mind his business. There was Bossier City, surely. But that was across the river, and he did not go there. Had no call to go there. He did his work and went home and listened to the radio and read the *Shreveport Times*. On weekends, he would ride out to Ford Park and walk under the tall pines, or go to the public pier on Cross Lake and hire a boat and fish. He would bring a box of worms and fish from before daylight until after dark, often taking home a mess of bream and small cat. Since he had no place to keep them, he always gave them to Murray. Years earlier, he had hoped— perhaps even expected—that Murray would ask him out to Dixie Gardens to share the fish, fried in cornmeal with hush puppies, french fries, and a little salad. But that had not happened, and after a few years, Dewey had stopped expecting that it might. Still he went on handing the fish he caught over to Murray as if they were in some way an established tribute in kind, something he owed.

He snapped out of his remembering in time to see Hilda limping off, pushing her mop and bucket before her. She turned back, fixed Dewey with her eyes. —You gonna see. That Santidy guilty as sin, you hear?

—Well, Dewey said, and Hilda disappeared around a corner. But now Dewey was interested. All there had been so far was Vallee, the defense, against Caswell, the prosecutor. Rhetoric against rhetoric. But if Hilda was right, as she usually was, then maybe he should pay attention. Usually he didn't. Nothing was at issue but somebody's time, somebody's money. It was funny how everything got reduced to that in court. Somebody was going to serve time or he wasn't. Somebody was going to have to pay money or he wasn't. But Hilda didn't care about that. She never had anything to say about a case unless there was more at issue. Dewey would pay attention now.

Murray came out of the courtroom, wiping his forehead. He almost always came to the trials. He would joke and say he had to be at the trials to make out Dewey's transcript, but they both knew better. Dewey was the best they had at the stenotype in the First Judicial Court. No, Murray came whenever he didn't have a tran- script to type up because he loved the courts. Dewey understood that. Murray had been hurt in the war. He had lost a leg sitting in a headquarters company office. A shell had come in and killed almost everyone in the office. Somehow, Murray had survived. He should have been proud, Dewey reasoned. How many clerk-typists had been awarded the Purple Heart? But somehow that shell had made Murray ashamed. Now, even though bereft of his leg, he seemed to live in a world of his own, wishing that leg had been lost in some better venture. He had once told Dewey that lesser men had been injured in the Battle of Bulge or the crossing of the Remagen Bridge. Others had lost much less lying amid the ruin of their own flesh, staring across the Rhine toward the smoking distant bank, like Moses at Pisgah, seeing with sadness and relief a shore they would never reach. To lose so much sitting behind a typewriter, typing the company sick list was a terrible thing, Murray would say.

—Judge is ready, Murray said.

They began again. Vallee's objections served as punctuations to the testimony. Police officer who had been called. Her brother, her boss at Jumbo's. Then Caswell, the assistant district attorney, called Miranda to the stand. Dewey watched her walk toward the witness stand. She was small, with dark eyes and long jet-black hair and smooth olive skin. Dewey watched her, his eyes following as she walked to the stand, eyes down, and seated herself in a silence drawn around her like a shawl.

Miranda Ferriday did not look like a North Louisiana girl to Dewey. He remembered such girls in the bayou country, in Hammond, in New Orleans. He was drawn to her. Dewey did not care for the washed-out blonds and dull brown-haired girls with freckles and pale skin who peopled the upper parishes. But then he had not much thought of girls since he had left New Orleans for the shame of those days. This girl was different. As she was sworn, Dewey could see the two of them, him and her, together. Lord, how long had it been since he had had such feelings? Twenty years? No, more nearly thirty. It didn't matter. As Miranda sat waiting for Caswell to begin his questions, Dewey's fingers poised above the stenotype. From somewhere inside him there arose that power and horror that he almost forgot he possessed merely by being a man. He was astonished at himself. The old Adam might lie silent for twenty years or more and yet not be slain. But then Caswell began, and Dewey's fingers followed him.

Caswell was gentle, considerate. He was a large man, coarse and overweight, his shirt collar pressing into his neck. But it seemed that he knew how awful Miranda's experience had been, how difficult it was for her to recall it, to testify about it before the court and the jury. Still, in order that justice be done, and that others might not suffer as she had, she realized the importance of her testimony. —Isn't that so? Caswell asked. Miranda looked up at him and nodded slowly, her expression suddenly intense, her eyes watchful.

She told of her home down in Coushatta. Her father had owned a filling station until he came down with consumption and had been sent to the Pines TB Sanatorium. Her mother had died in a house fire, and she had come to Shreveport to be with her brother, a deputy sheriff in Benton, Louisiana, Bossier Parish.

Miranda admitted that she did not like the work at Jumbo's. But Mr. Jumbo was nice to her. He was himself a retired policeman, a friend of her brother's. Anyhow, you had to have work. Nobody in her family didn't work. Everyone was supposed to work, weren't they?

Yes, she had met one Santidy there. He had come from the west. He said California. Is there a Bakersville? Bakersfield? All right, yes, I reckon. And he would come in most especially on Monday and Friday evenings, usually late. He liked funny drinks. Sidecars, grasshoppers, screwdrivers, Manhattans. He was tall and dark and always laughing. He noticed her. He talked to her. He took to leaving her five-dollar tips. He liked to buy drinks for everybody in the place and to have people notice him. He worked up at Oil City, sometimes in East Texas: Kilgore, Longview, Tyler, Gladewater, Marshall. It was his job to strip old wells. He was one who knew how to get the last drop out of wells nearly empty. There was good money in it. He used to laugh and ask Miranda if she was a stripper, too. She would blush and ignore him then.

As Miranda went on, interrupted by Caswell's questions, Dewey let her voice carry him back to the long cuts and bayous around Lake Ferdinand, south of New Orleans. He remembered trips with his father to those places, austere, the banks and shores covered with harsh brush and palmetto. His hands worked automatically, putting down the words she said. He could close his eyes remembering and go on typing, listening and recording without hearing or caring. Still, he did care, and he could not tell just why. He wished he could take a break now. He needed to go outside.

On a certain night, Miranda said, Santidy had come in. He was flush with money, buying round after round of drinks, people applauding when someone behind the bar would, for a moment, cut off the jukebox and tell who had bought the drinks for the house. The people at the tables, along the bar had come to know Santidy and appreciate him. He drank and she served. It came near closing time. He asked if she had a way home. She said, No, no she didn't. He laughed and touched her, saying, Let me take you home, honey. You know it's dark and a long, long night. At first she ignored him. But after all he was very popular. Somehow she supposed that someone so well known, so much thought of in the place, would be trustworthy. At the very least for the distance between Jumbo's bar and her brother's home.

But it had not turned out that way. No, rather he had taken her in his car, driven away from Jumbo's, gone this way and that, twisting up one street and down another until her head had begun to spin. Then, somewhere along the levee, he had stopped the car, turned to her and told her in the most obscene terms what he expected, demanded of her. She had almost fainted, but before she could, he was upon her.

The rest of it was difficult to follow, the outpouring of one who could hardly remember coherently what she had to tell. What had happened to her? Dewey listened to it all. His fingers moved, independent of what went on, but still he heard.

Santidy had brought her home, sure enough. He had stopped his car out in front of her brother's house, where he had said terrible things to her, where he had taken her again, done what he wanted to do with her. She had fought against him, had cried out, had wept and pled with him. But none of it had mattered.

And when he had done with her, he had laughed once more, opened the car door, and pushed her into the street. Like garbage. And driven away.

Caswell patted his brow with a folded handkerchief and sat down. —Thank you, Miss Ferriday, he said. —That's all I have.

There was a moment's pause then. Dewey relaxed, thinking, Hilda was right. Now that's the way it was. Then Vallee stood up for cross. Dewey hoped Judge Lambert might call for a recess. But the judge looked at Vallee and said nothing. Dewey spaced his tape and waited.

At first Vallee was as quiet, as gentle as Caswell had been. He asked Miranda about her past down in the country, asked about her home life, about her religious education, asked if she had had boyfriends back then. Miranda answered openly, like one without guilt. But then the questioning closed in, became more personal. Vallee began stalking her like a wolf, moving question by question from counsel's table toward the witness stand until he enclosed it, his arms almost around it as he pressed one question after another. Dewey didn't like his method. It was almost as if he were embracing her, drawing her close, as if his questions were intimate rather than public. He wanted to know about her sexual experience as a young girl. He wanted to know about her lovers, and he was so close to her, it was as if he deemed himself her next friend rather than an attorney doing what was expected, demanded of him. Vallee wanted to know why she had chosen Jumbo's as a place to work. Surely she had known that Jumbo's was a swinging place, a place where the live crowd came. Hadn't she picked Jumbo's for that very reason? Hadn't she come up from the parishes looking for action? Wanting excitement? Wasn't that the way it was?

Dewey made a record, listening and typing. Yet still he heard. Surely no one saw him shudder as Vallee pressed on, his voice soft and insinuating. He had heard so many of them, Dewey had. Lawyers who could somehow alter reality to suit their cause. It was like listening to the serpent arguing with Eve. Only Eve hadn't been to law school as the serpent surely had.

> Q. Now Miss Ferriday, you're a grown woman, aren't you?
> A. Yes. Sure. I guess so.
> Q. Well then, if a man approaches you . . .
> A. . . . Approaches me . . . What do you mean . . . approaches?
> Q. Come now, Miss Ferriday. I mean a man who approaches a woman . . . as a man . . . approaches a woman.
> Mr. Caswell. Objection, Your Honor.
> The Court. Yes, Mr. Caswell . . . ?
> Mr. Caswell. I suggest, even in these times, a man may approach a woman with something other than rape in mind. . . .
> Mr. Vallee. May it please the Court, I'm sure I haven't suggested anything like that in my questioning. . . . May counsel approach the bench?
> Mr. Caswell. Indeed, Your Honor. Since approaching seems to be the essence of counsel's questioning. . . .

The lawyers went up to the bench before Judge Lambert, and Dewey relaxed for a moment. There was a nice irony in the fact that when the lawyers reached the very peak of their concern, moving to the bench to argue a point of law, the reporter could relax, because their argument, however intense, was not recorded. Dewey closed his eyes and let all his faculties ease off. Part of being a court reporter was responding to the court, knowing when to catch every word, and knowing when to relax.

Over his shoulder, he heard the cut and slash of argumentation passing between Caswell and Vallee. But he also knew who would prevail. In a close matter, the defense always prevailed. Judge Lambert would have it otherwise, but he did not want to be reversed. That would most likely call for another trial. Judge Lambert did not want another trial. He was old now and tired. If he could, he would mete out the death sentence for rape on a *prima facie* case. But that was not possible. Not with the weight of federal courts above seemingly committed to the proposition that every criminal defendant was a prince, about to be victimized by the prosecution. So Dewey rested, knowing that when they went back on the record, it would be Vallee's question. That was how the game played.

Sure enough, when the conference at the bench was done, Vallee asked his question again.

> Q. Miss Ferriday, let me ask you again, when Mr. Santidy asked you out . . . asked you to leave Jumbo's with him . . .
> A. Yes . . .
> Q. I mean . . . You knew what he had in mind, now didn't you?
> A. . . . In mind . . . I don't . . . what . . .
> Q. Come now. You're not a child . . .
> A. No . . . that's . . .
> Q. You knew where it was leading, now didn't you?

There was a sudden silence, and Dewey's head turned around to see her. She sat in the witness box helpless, trying to find words to tell the truth.

> A. No. I mean, I never thought . . .
> Q. Come now, Miss Ferriday, you've worked at Jumbo's quite a while, haven't you? When a man asks you out . . .
> A. No, listen . . . I try to be . . .
> Q. When you go out, it's just for a drink and a quick trip home, right?
> A. Yes. Listen, I never . . .
> Q. Right. You never. That's why you choose to work at one of the roughest lounges in Bossier City. . . .
> Mr. Caswell. Objection. I ask that counsel's last remarks be stricken. No foundation has been laid to suggest that . . .

It was almost dark now. They had broken for dinner. Dewey had picked up a chicken salad sandwich down in the lobby before the blind man shut up for the day. He had gotten a half-pint of milk, too. Now he sat in the back bench of the courtroom, eating slowly. Murray limped up and sat beside him.

—Shit, I'm tired. Ain't you?

—You know it, Dewey said.

—It's a goddamned shame, Murray said. —I mean having to go through this crap.

—Huh?

—I mean, you know that lousy bastard did it. He raped her. . . .

—Well . . . Yes, I reckon . . . I mean . . .

—Aw, come on, Dewey. You better believe it. I mean, that little girl thought she had a ride home, and he pulled her down. . . .

Dewey chewed for a long time. Then he swallowed and washed it down with some milk. —I just can't hardly believe a man would do that to a young girl. I mean . . . even today . . .

Murray snorted, and a rill of coffee ran down his chin. —I be goddamned if I ever will understand you, Dewey. I mean you live in the same world with the rest of us. You read about that whore in Chicago who wanted to go to a party and couldn't find no baby-sitter for her six-months-old baby girl? Huh? Yeah, well, it was in the *Journal*. What she did? Well, she threw the baby down a trash incinerator. From the sixth floor. Yeah, well, that's today for you. This world is a shit heap. I mean, that greasy-looking bastard Santidy, he done just what Caswell makes out that he did. I wisht they'd just let me have him. Boy, you just give me five minutes alone with him . . . Us veterans know how to handle 'em. . . .

Then Murray stood up slowly and limped back and forth in front of the judge's bench saying what he would do to Santidy if they let him have the motherless sonofabitch. It was bad, what he said, and Dewey almost gagged on his sandwich. While Murray limped and fulminated, Caswell, the prosecutor, came in. He stood back and listened for a minute or two. Then he told Murray he wished to hell he had him on the jury.

—That greaseball is going to walk, Caswell said, staring at his fingernails.

—You think so? Dewey asked, surprised.

—Sure, Caswell said. —Easiest thing in the world. I don't know why we even try these things. Ought to take rape off the books. Maybe put it under assault with a deadly weapon.

Murray and Caswell laughed bitterly together. For a moment Dewey didn't understand.

—Everybody's a whore—except your own wife or mother or sister. That's the way these goddamn juries see it. I bet I've lost twenty cases like this if I've lost one.

—That's . . . terrible, Dewey said.

—Sure it's terrible, Caswell told him. —But that's the system, ol' buddy. Can't diddle with the system, right?

Caswell was tired, Dewey could see that. He let his bulk settle into one of the chairs back of counsel's table. He was not an old man, rather a man of indecipherable age, probably in his forties. But his face was heavy, lined, wise—like the countenance of an elephant, full of scars and wrinkles. Dewey seemed to remember that Caswell had been local commander of the American Legion. —I've won a lot of 'em and lost a lot of 'em, you understand?

Caswell closed his eyes and leaned back in the chair he had chosen. —Lord God, I been every way you can be. We used to be able to put some of 'em in the chair. All you had to do was spring that girl on him. Let her tell folks what had happened.

Caswell opened his eyes, grinned slowly. —But that was when your old ordinary juror still believed there was such a thing as a nice girl. Seems like a long time ago.

—Makes you wonder, Murray said. —Maybe the system don't work. I mean, what did we fight for? So some nasty bastard could come in here and do whatever the hell he wants. I mean, a girl like that . . . She *had* to work, and them places . . .

Caswell stared at the polished limestone behind the judge's bench. —Nothing in this shit-eating society works any more. The whole damned thing's coming unglued. You think this is a bad case? Hell, at least the girl's alive. He didn't push her eyes out. He didn't cut off her tits. I try capital cases. Murders like you wouldn't believe if I was to tell you. Absolute proof, and the goddamned jury hands 'em five years. Just time to get ready for the next one.

Caswell told them the circumstances and details of a recent case. Dewey and Murray looked at each other, sickened. Caswell laughed sardonically. —That's what you can do to a nine-year-old girl in Louisiana. And get twenty years. Parole maybe in seven.

—My God, Dewey said, numbed by what he had heard.

—Evidentiary rules, Caswell snorted. —That dirty piece of filth had three assaults on minors on his record. He'd been a time bomb waiting to go off. Could I show that? Hell, no. He hadn't been convicted. One thing and another, and they'd dropped the charges or let him plead to a lesser offense. They *knew* that bastard was gonna kill a child. . . . And when he did, I couldn't tell the jury what he'd been pulled in for three times before. . . .

—Maybe we're trying the wrong people, Murray said ominously.

—You want things to change? Caswell asked rhetorically. —I can give you a formula. Let every last family in this country have a rape or a murder in it—not a robbery. That won't get it. It's got to be one of the big ones. Better it happen all on the same night. . . .

—Like to Pharaoh and the Egyptians, Dewey put in.

—From the White House to the cropper's shack down on the river. Then these damned beasts of burden would start handing out death sentences like prizes in Cracker Jack. Give me five, six hundred executions a year for ten or fifteen years. You'd be downright amazed how quiet things would get.

—Them as do wrong has got to pay the price, Murray said. —Everybody knows that.

—Bullshit, Caswell said easily. —Nobody knows no such damned thing. I tell you what. People kinda like to see a smooth operator get by with something. You look at that girl, Miranda. Putting law and decency aside, who wouldn't like to get her in a car, talk to her. Kiss her. So then she decides she's gone far enough, but your imagination is already a long way past a little kiss, so you kind of manhandle her a little. You pull off her blouse. None of that old high school fooling with buttons. This is the big time. You just grab it by the front and . . . Ah, look there. Big fine boobs almost busting out of her brassiere. But that can wait, cause when you see what she's got, you go for the skirt. Get in between her legs with one hand, cover her mouth with the other. Lay on top of her. Don't let her get loose . . . Oh, them long luscious legs . . .

Dewey and Murray looked at one another, then back at Caswell, whose eyes glinted as he went on in more and more bald and intimate detail, describing what it must have been like to rape Miranda Ferriday, rape her right down into the ground. Dewey couldn't help being drawn along, reenacting in his own mind what Caswell was saying. It was awful, but in the recesses of his mind, Dewey could feel that old Adam pulling, clawing at the structure of his own control.

When Caswell finished, he was breathing rapidly, smiling, looking from Murray to Dewey and back again. —Now when you come right down to it, saving the law and decency, all that's worth a little risk, ain't it? I mean, just reckon you didn't know any better, or even knowing, didn't give a damn? Say you'd been raised in California. Hell of a way to pass an hour, huh?

Murray was blushing. Dewey stared at the floor.

—Shit, Murray said in an injured tone. —I thought you was against that kind of thing.

Caswell's expression of visionary pleasure vanished as if someone had shut a door in his heavy red face.

—I am, he said. —I sure as hell am. But I know what sin is. A man's got to know what sin is if he's gonna fight it. You see that, don't you?

—He hadn't ought to lust after the sin he's fighting, Dewey said quietly. —He ought not to know it all that well. . . .

Caswell shrugged, heaved his bulk out of the chair, glanced at his watch. —You boys are nice. But you're shit-kickers. You got it in for

Santidy 'cause he cut that little girl. I got it in for him 'cause he broke the law. Reckon if he had spent a little time, talked her into a good screw right out in the car, telling her about love and the stars and how happiness was just a pant and a promise away? You'd still have it in for him. I wouldn't. That's good stuff, and a man needs it. But the law says you got to be polite. Mustn't grab. Got to ask. You got to have it *given* to you. Now a shit-kicker sees sin as corruption and damnation. A lawyer sees it as disorder. It don't make a damn what's done, so long as it's done orderly. And orderly means law. Hell, I'd slap a child away from his own table for grabbing at the chicken on a platter. Same way with Santidy. I'd like to see him slapped right out of this world.

Caswell made a broad gesture. —Why, I don't give a damn if they legalize murder—so long as they set out rules, so everybody can know 'em.

Murray stared at him. —What if some woman was to throw her six-months-old baby down an incinerator chute? How about that?

Caswell narrowed his eyes. —We got a law against that.

Dewey hardly dared ask. —What if we didn't?

Caswell laughed, the sound rich and fluid, coming from deep within him. —Well, you couldn't get her for littering, could you?

—Jesus, Murray said and moved off.

Dewey licked his lips. There was something he wanted to say, but he wasn't sure he had the right. After all, he had sinned, had done terrible things even though a long time ago. Still, it seemed something had to be said.

—I . . . think . . .

Caswell smiled at him. —I bet you do, Dewey. You're always mighty quiet, but there's something going on with you, ain't there?

—I think it's got to be more . . . than just law.

Caswell frowned. —Now coming from an old-time court reporter, that's goddamned near treason. Hell, Dewey, if we ain't convinced you, I think we got trouble . . . Right here in River City. . . .

He laughed, but Dewey didn't join in. Something was hurting him. As if there had been something lost, something he could not name or put into words. Something Caswell purposely slighted in his buffoon's performance about law and order. Dewey thought as hard as he could, his eyes squinted almost closed.

—It don't change a thing because you say it's legal. Even if you pass a law . . .

Caswell leaned down over Dewey, his large eyes shining with an almost maniacal certainty.

—I don't blame you. I honest to God don't. When I come up to Shreveport from down at Jena, I felt the same way. Hell, even before that, before I went to LSU Law School, I knew right from wrong better than any circuit judge in this chicken-shit state. My folks learned me good and evil. Reverend Trotter set 'em out clear as good water in a running stream. But . . . things don't go that way.

Caswell stood up, and moved away, his back to Dewey. Suddenly he turned, pointing his finger at Dewey as if court were in session, and Dewey the witness being examined.

—*You* know what's good and evil. *I* know what's right and wrong. But the courts don't. People don't. Lord God, the mind of man can conjure up wickedness that decent folks never even thought to prohibit. And that don't even take into consideration the mind of woman. Do justice, folks say . . . but not to me. Whatever I do is okay. Abortion, sodomy, adultery, rape . . . Whatever we learned was wrong as kids is just all right today. You got to put good and evil out of your mind, Dewey. You got to. Because they won't let us keep those words. They don't mean anything. What I can't figure is how you've held on to 'em so long. Don't you see what I mean? Forget good and evil. Think legal and illegal. Maybe we can make a stand there. . . .

His voice trailed off, and Dewey could hear in it for the first time Caswell's pain, the sense of loss that was barely papered over by his cynicism. He walked back to the prosecutor's table and picked up a file. Dewey thought he could see tears in Caswell's eyes.

—You got to take the law and grab hold of it, and say: Law, be thou my good . . . Nonlaw, be thou my evil. Now you *got* to do that. . . .

—No, Dewey heard himself say, his voice louder than he realized until he heard it. —Because law is supposed to come out of what's good. You can't make no kind of good out of law. . . .

Caswell sat down again at the distant table, and Dewey could see now, sure enough, that tears were coursing down his cheeks, down that face that looked like a side of fresh-slaughtered beef. Caswell shook his head like an old bull pestered by a myriad of flies.

—Well, goddamn it, you got to. You ain't got any choice. Because if you don't, it'll kill you. It'll break your heart. You know what I mean?

—No.

—Hell, Dewey . . .

—I can't help it, Dewey said. Things don't get to be . . . other things 'cause you put another name on 'em. You could make laws all year. If they was wrong, they'd be wrong. And a jury can't make wrong right.

—It'll break your heart thinking that way, Caswell told him.

—Look, I'm gonna be district attorney one day soon. People like me, you know? After that, I could go to the legislature . . . Hell, I could be governor. I could do that. I got a lot of support out in the parishes.

—Well, Dewey said softly, —I reckon you could do all that. But it wouldn't change nothing. Wouldn't make a good man bad, or a bad man good. . . .

Caswell rubbed his eyes, threw up his hands.

—I'm wasting my time, he said. —You ain't heard a goddamned thing I've said. Can't you see all that good/evil stuff has gone by the board?

Dewey said nothing, and Caswell was quiet for a long moment.

—But I wish it hadn't. I wish, after this no-nut jury lets Santidy go, I wish you and me and that crippled feller . . . What's his name?

—Murray, Dewey said. —He ain't crippled. He's a war veteran.

—Who ain't? I'd like to see the three of us go find that greasy bastard and give him a little justice. Not law. Justice.

—That seems what folks ought to do, Dewey began.

—But we can't. Those old fools on the Supreme Court says we can't, and all those New York Jew liberals. Mustn't do. Naughty. Man who does that is *not* going to the legislature, right? Right. No, he's gonna pick up a few years for violating that ugly bastard's civil rights. So all right. I understand. No justice. No damned justice. What we're doing here folks is the law. We're gonna smile if we win and smile if we lose. 'Cause that's how we all get along, ain't it, Dewey?

—That's what you tell me.

—And it's gospel, ol' buddy. You just sit there and do your job, and see how this case comes out. See what happens.

Judge Lambert opened the door of his chambers and signaled to his minute clerk who was almost asleep on the last bench in the courtroom. He got up slowly to round up Vallee and Santidy, and whatever witnesses might be left. When he had them all lined up, he would bring out the jury. Then it would all get started again. Dewey went back to his stenotype and got ready. He did not look at Caswell. It was hard to think about all he'd said.

The rest of the prosecution's case wasn't much. Yes, the coroner said, there was evidence of recent sexual intercourse when he examined Miranda. Yes, there were bruises and minor abrasions. Yes, they were consistent with an assault. No, they did not prove assault. And so on. Yes, the investigating officer said, when Santidy was arrested, there were scratches. Small ones on his hands and face. But . . . yes? Vallee asked, Weren't there others? Large ones, the officer said. Down his back.

Vallee spun toward the jury, his eyes gleaming as if he and they shared knowledge of a certain filthy joke between them.

—Where?

—Down his back, around his shoulders.

—That's all, Vallee smiled, pleased, already opening another witness folder.

When the State's case had finally wound down to its conclusion, Vallee smiled again, and called his only witness. It was Santidy.

Santidy had been sitting, almost slouching in his chair throughout the trial, like some somnolent animal, sleepy and well fed, only marginally aware of what was passing around him, unconcerned that somehow it all had to do with him. Dewey had watched him off and on, especially while Miranda was testifying. As she answered Caswell's questions, he would turn and shake his head, grin at Vallee, who would smile back and shake his head as if the two of them, firm in the truth of Santidy's innocence, could only look with bemused indulgence on Miranda's pathetic, hysterical lies.

Santidy rose then, seemed to stretch a little as he walked to the witness stand with measured insouciance. Dewey glanced around and saw Murray's jaw tighten as Santidy was sworn.

Then Santidy sat down in the witness chair, a mild, benevolent smile on his lips. He was tall, well built, with broad shoulders and narrow hips, much like one of those male models who show off expensive clothes for department stores and clothiers. He seemed composed, uninvolved, as if he were at most a witness rather than a defendant. He had a thick bush of silky hair with enormous sideburns, a gold diamond ring on his left little finger, and he wore a tight, close-fitting body shirt open at the collar, with some kind of Indian piece of silver and turquoise on a chain around his neck. His slacks were deep crimson and his loafers were brightly shined.

What he said was simple enough, and if he hadn't been lying, Dewey would have believed him. But you could look at him and see what he was. He thought he was above the law, above anybody's justice. He was here in the courtroom to oblige, not to be tried.

As his fingers raced along, Dewey remembered the old days in Bourbon Street. It had been an outskirt of hell. Women debased, enjoying their shame; men worse than animals, their very senses deranged by whiskey, their minds dissolved in lust and an appetite for disarray. He could barely remember a sequence of bawdy nights there, and the great overarching sense of freedom he had felt. Anything was possible. All was permitted. The deadly sins were a catalogue from which you could pick whatever you chose. Pederasty, violence, gambling, robbery, filthy pictures, whoredom— what was there that the mind of man might contemplate that could not be accomplished on Bourbon Street? So long as it was indecent, destructive of the soul? And then that hot August day.

Dewey shuddered as his fingers did their work. He wondered if his years in Shreveport had made up for his sojourn in that place. Who knows? He would wait and shudder until Judgment. What had he done but put the evil aside? Had he ever, even once, struck out against it? Was it enough, to be justified, to flee evil? Or must it be confronted, struggled with, vanquished? Was it sufficient to carry on that struggle within one's own soul—or must it be carried dauntlessly into the world?

Then Vallee began his questioning. What had happened that night? Had there been . . . sex?

Santidy was smiling as the questioning began, but his expression became progressively more serious as Vallee pressed on. At the mention of sex, Santidy hung his head like a chastened peacock. As if, on the instant, his flaunting manner faltered, and he suddenly shed years, became younger, more innocent. Dewey watched and could hardly believe.

—Yes, Santidy whispered. —Yes, there had been sex. God help him.

Vallee was silent for a long moment. As if ritual words had been spoken. Then, most quietly: —Tell us about it. We want to know, to understand.

He had gone often to Jumbo's after work. He was a stranger here, but the promise of good honest work had brought him east from California. He had worked in Texas, then in northwest Louisiana. He would come down to Shreveport to break the monotony, to see people enjoy themselves. To find enjoyment of his own. A lot of oil men came to Shreveport, to Jumbo's. It was a friendly place. One could enjoy himself there in a decent manner: a few beers, a few laughs with friends.

Yes, he knew Miranda. Everyone knew Miranda. Of all the girls at Jumbo's, she was the loveliest, the most interesting. She was very friendly, and she made him feel less lonely. Bakersfield, California, is a long way from Shreveport. But Miranda's smile made the distance less awful, less depressing. Jumbo's was a real nice place, and Miranda was part of the reason.

Dewey frowned. Only a little while ago, Vallee had been talking about what a bad place it was, how a girl who worked in such a place should know what men who frequented it really wanted. Now Santidy was making it out to be a home away from home. The jury will notice that, Dewey thought. They'll have to notice that.

Vallee asked Santidy if he had offered Miranda a ride home that night. Santidy smiled, looking a little confused. He didn't understand. Vallee reminded him that Miranda had made that claim. Santidy shook his head slowly.

—No, she must have forgot. It was the other way around. She . . . asked me.

And he had been perhaps the least bit hesitant to give her a ride. Yes, he liked her, but he had heard remarks—nothing specific, more often a single word from one of the boys, accompanied by a quick smile. Words and expressions that might make one wonder.

Vallee paused, acting as if he were surprised to hear such a thing. —What kind of words? Santidy shook his head. He had sisters at home. He would never smear a young woman's reputation. His people never tolerated such a thing.

Vallee glanced at the jury, as much as to say, see how much all this unpleasant business pains this boy? —We've got to know, Alberto. You've got to tell us. You understand that, don't you?

Santidy nodded sadly, cleared his throat. They had said that Miranda was a punch, a tramp, that she went from man to man, that she was insatiable, and no one man—or two or three, for that matter—could satisfy her. Of course, Santidy had not believed that for a moment.

Caswell was on his feet, objecting, demanding that the testimony cease until he could lodge a continuing objection to this blatant hearsay. Vallee grinned, claiming that the testimony led toward framing the defendant's state of mind at the time of the alleged incident, hence was admissible. Judge Lambert pursed his lips, ruled sustaining the objection. Vallee shrugged, smiled reassuringly at Santidy, and began again.

Dewey found himself sitting at the stenotype, fingers motionless. Testimony was over, final arguments closed, and he could hardly remember a word of it all. Judge Lambert was charging the jury, giving them the law upon which they were to judge the facts presented to them in testimony and by document. Dewey watched dully as the jurors listened, their faces revealing nothing. Finally the instructions were done, and the judge sent the jury to deliberate. The courtroom emptied slowly. Miranda's brother came up to assist her, casting a venomous look at Santidy and Vallee. Murray came up and sat at counsel's table near Dewey as Caswell wiped his face with a large pocket-handkerchief.

—That sonofabitch *is* gonna walk, Murray said. —He's not gonna serve a day or an hour. He's got it made.

Caswell nodded. —You got that right. Vallee's got the formula down, and old Santidy is a superstar. Why, that boy could bring Miranda's brother around if he had a little time.

—I believe that greaser could rape every woman in Caddo Parish, one at a time, and still walk. He'd only have to spare twelve of 'em, Caswell said.

—How's that, Dewey asked.

—Why, he ought to leave enough to make up a jury to acquit him.

—Hell, Murray said angrily. —Maybe a couple he stuck it to would vote for him. You never know. Not nowadays. You can't know. How could you?

Caswell shrugged. —Youall want some coffee? We can walk down Milam Street to the Grill. They're not coming back for an hour or so. Take 'em that long to argue themselves out of following their old-time instincts.

Murray and Caswell and Dewey walked downstairs and outside. The air was cool and crystalline. Only a few cars moved down Texas Street, mostly in the direction of the bridge to Bossier City. Caswell and Murray moved ahead of him, and Dewey paused in the deep shadow beside the Confederate Memorial. It was large and graceful, a spire reaching up into the leaves of the ancient live oaks, pointed toward the cold and distant stars. At the four corners were granite busts of Lee, Jackson, Beauregard, and Allen. High above, looming under the canopy of oak leaves that circled like a garland, was the figure of an anonymous Confederate soldier. He stood, rifle between his broken shoes, staring north out of stone eyes, as if tonight, this very night, it all might begin again, and he was ready for it. Dewey stared upward, feeling for the first time in all his years in town, in the courthouse, that this place was a shrine. He could not say just what it meant, but there was something. Something ravished, taken by force, something lost and gone now. And these generals had fought and spent years of their lives to protect that something, to save it. That nameless soldier had died time and time again for its sake. Dewey felt himself blush with shame for some omission he couldn't even bring to mind, much less name. He averted his eyes from the monument, as if in darkness it still shown too bright for him.

—Hey, Dewey, you comin'? Murray called back to him.

—Yes, Dewey said, and walked on after them.

II

The jury filed in, and it was over in minutes. Not guilty. One of the women on the jury was sobbing, but another had something close to a smile on her lips as Santidy came forward to shake hands with them, thank them for their vindication. Dewey watched as if he were viewing a movie, as if what he was seeing had little relation to reality at all, and none whatever to him. He turned slowly, as Judge Lambert discharged the jury, obviously displeased, but not enough so to speak his mind as on occasion he did. Caswell sat sweating, a smile not unlike that of the woman juror's on his lips. Behind him, Dewey caught only a fleeting glimpse of Miranda, her brother helping her on with her coat, and speaking loudly words Dewey couldn't make out for the commotion. But Miranda was paying no attention to her brother. She was looking across to the defense counsel's table, not at Santidy, but at Vallee, and her expression was one of horror so profound, so all-encompassing that it shocked Dewey, making him recall the face of a dead man whose body he had once come across in an alley off Ursulines Street in the French Quarter. While he was a beast. That was how Miranda looked: as if she were about to die, enthralled by the last and most brutal indignity we all must surely suffer. As she turned away—no, was turned away by her brother, who was still talking, something made Dewey turn back toward the defense table where Vallee sat withdrawn into a pool of silence, insulated from Santidy who stood next to him laughing with some of his friends from Oil City. On his face, Vallee wore an expression of cynical and analytical certainty almost as absolute and embracing as had been Miranda's mask of horror.

He's happy now, Dewey thought. He's just planning to do it again. He's just waiting for the next one to come knocking on his door. He's a rapist, too. Just like Santidy.

—It's no use living in a country where this kind of shit can go on, Murray was saying. —I mean, it wasn't a sign of justice . . . Not a sign.

They were at Murrell's Grill on Kings Highway. Caswell was eating eggs and grits and sausage. He had stuffed his mouth with biscuit, and thus was forced to listen to Murray's tirade. Finally he finished chewing, shook his head.

—Goddamn it, Murray, what is all this justice crap? You been around the court as long as I've been lawyering. Why does this one stick in your craw. Hell, you and I seen a lot worse. Remember the Culpepper case?

Murray turned pale, put down his fork. For a moment, his expression was very still, very distant, as if he were having trouble keeping his food down.

—I don't remember no Culpepper case, Dewey said, trying to remember some case, some situation so monstrous that it would gag Murray.

—You wasn't up here yet, Caswell said, his eyes fixed on Murray. —This was way back before the war. I was in law school. Old man lived in Dixie Gardens—near Murray, matter of fact . . . Caswell laughed as Murray, still speechless, motioned him to shut up.

Caswell grinned. —It was a tough case. Ask Murray about it some time. . . .

No one said anything for a long time. They ate, Murray still shivering. Caswell finished his last biscuit, and Dewey sat thinking.

—He did do it, didn't he? Dewey asked at last.

—Huh? Caswell replied.

—Santidy. He did it to that girl, didn't he?

Caswell's eyebrows rose as he chewed. He swallowed and grinned. —What do you want, Dewey? You want me to give it to you in writing? I wouldn't have prosecuted the sonofabitch if it didn't look like he did. Beyond a reasonable doubt. But *did* he? I wasn't there. Maybe he asked nicely, and she changed her mind right in the middle . . . Maybe he forgot to ask. . . .

Caswell picked up the check, took a few dollar bills out of the pocket of his vest.

—I really need to know, Dewey said quietly. —I do.

Caswell looked at him with amused weariness. —You've changed, Dewey. Hell, I remember when you used to do a hell of a job reporting and kept quiet. Maybe it's age. Maybe we all done our jobs and kept quiet too long.

Caswell stared out the window behind Dewey into the dusty empty street beyond.

—You know what, Dewey? I don't know whether that lousy California greaser done it or not. And I'll tell you something else. If I'd been there that night, if I'd been in the car watching, I still might not know. Things have their own way of happening, and sometimes you can't say who did what. Maybe it wasn't no crime at all. Maybe it was just . . . bad manners.

Caswell swung his bulk up out of the booth, and started toward the cash register. —I can't spend the night joshin' with you boys. I got me an armed robbery over in Division G in the morning, and I flat *know* what happened there. . . .

Caswell paid and left, and Dewey looked at Murray, who was still shook up a little. —He didn't have to mention Culpepper, Murray said. —I mean it's been a long day. He didn't have to bring that back. . . .

Dewey stared at Murray. —What the hell was the Culpepper . . .?

Murray shivered. —Forget it, he said, and rose from his seat. —Just forget it. It was a long time ago, and you don't want to know.

They left then, climbed into Murray's car. Murray was shot, worn out, shaken. He didn't want to drive. Dewey barely knew how since he had never owned a car of his own. But he got behind the wheel and started out, driving stiffly, carefully down Kings Highway toward Murray's home, which he had never seen, never been invited to. When they reached the house, Murray asked him to spend the night on the back porch. There was a daybed there for friends who might stay over. Dewey thanked him, and they went into the kitchen for a nightcap.

Murray brought out an unopened bottle of Old Overholt and cracked the seal. It was harsh and rich, and Dewey felt as if he'd been in that kitchen every evening for years. Murray had control of himself now, and threw down two drinks for every one of Dewey's.

—I get drunk every night, Murray said, his tongue going loose, his eyes angry. —You didn't know that. Well, it's so. I come home from typing up them goddamned transcripts, and I get drunk. Ever since the war. Almost every night. I may have got to live in this shit-eating world, but it ain't nobody said I got to do it cold sober. No, I don't have to do that.

Murray got more excited as he drank the rye whiskey. He got up, opened a cupboard above the gas stove and brought out a Colt automatic and laid it on the oilcloth of the table.

—It's a .38 special on a .45 frame. Customized. Best automatic pistol in the world. Take a look. No, pull the clip and push back the receiver.

Dewey picked up the gun. It was lighter than it looked and felt smooth and reassuring in his hand. As if he had held it many times before.

Murray was mumbling now, to himself, drunk, nearly to the

point of collapse. —If I could just get that lousy, filthy bastard in the sights of that . . .

—Santidy?

—Yeah. Him or . . . Culpepper. . . .

—What did Culpepper . . . ?

—Forget it. If I could get that spic in my sights . . . Oh, Lord . . . I never did get no Jap or German in my sights. . . . You know what I mean?

—I guess so.

Murray was close to passing out. —It ain't no justice left in this . . . world. You know that?

Dewey finished his third drink. He had not put the automatic down. —Yes, he said after a moment. —I guess I do. . . .

Murray shook his head, drunken tears flowing down his cheeks. —It ain't no justice, I can see that now.

He staggered to his feet and picked up the bottle of rye whiskey. —I'm going to bed. I can finish this in my bed. You know something, Dewey? I throwed away a leg. It wasn't no use. I never killed one of them sonsofbitches, but even if I had, it wasn't no use . . . wouldn't have helped anything at all.

Murray vanished into a dark hallway, and Dewey could hear him fall against something. Murray cursed, and then there was silence. Dewey looked at the whiskey in his glass for a long moment, remembering that Murray had been a typist. He hadn't killed anybody. Then Dewey drank his whiskey down.

He lay on the daybed with a pillow under his head. It was deep night now, and he could see the stars through the screen of the porch. Millions of them standing in the sky unmoving. There were insects strumming against the screen, and he could hear the naïve chatter of tree frogs just beyond the porch. From the distant bayou, he heard the deeper, more assured drone of bullfrogs.

Dewey lay quiet for a long time, thinking, trying to make his mind focus, but it was no use. There were only images passing across his mind like the motes that pass across the surface of the eye, which can never be seen clearly because they are part of the eye and move as the eye moves. He could not remember anything very clearly. It seemed as if the trial had been a long time ago, perhaps the day after he had come to himself in the French Quarter. Or the day he had arrived in Shreveport.

Dewey could not remember clearly when he had not been a reporter. Reporters were pledged to put down the truth in the cause of justice. That was hard to do in the midst of a trial, but he had always managed. And that had been enough. Other people had other things to do, but that was what a reporter did, and no one could expect any more.

It was then that he noticed he still had the pistol in his hand.

III

His knuckles were white, his fingers drained of blood, as he held onto the steering wheel crossing the Texas Avenue bridge into Bossier City. It was very late now, and there was little traffic, but the lights of Bossier City were still on. At the foot of the bridge on the left, he could see the Hurricane Lounge, a sign out front that said, WITH MAJOR AT THE PIANO. Down on the right, the Ming Tree, farther on, the K-9, and the Kickapoo Lounge and Motor Courts. Then the lights began to fall away, and the signs said U.S. Highway 80—the highway to Mississippi, to Monroe and Vicksburg. He drove another mile or two, until he saw the stark white-plastered building that said TOWER LOUNGE AND MOTEL and on the right, smaller, lit not by neon piping, but by old-fashioned bulbs, JUMBO'S LOUNGE, LIVE MUSIC NITELY.

Dewey pulled into the large parking lot and turned off the key. He took off his glasses and wiped them. He was sweating, and they had fogged up. Now that he was here, he could not quite determine what he should do. No, that wasn't right. He knew what he should do, but he couldn't figure out exactly how to do it. He had never planned such a thing before, had never even imagined himself involved in such a thing. That was a bad handicap, because you couldn't practice this as you practiced shorthand or stenotype.

He could go inside, find him, and do it. Whether he was caught made no difference. But there was always the irreducible possibility that someone might stop him, deflect his aim. Then it would all be silly and useless, like the trial, like his life—and justice would lose again, be raped by his incompetence.

It would be easier to wait. Outside no one could stop him. Out here it would work. Then it occurred to him for the first time that Santidy might not be there, that already he might be with some other young woman, willing or not, in one of the greasy motor courts he had already driven past. Dewey had no idea what kind of car Santidy drove, and suddenly he felt his own determination draining away. It was silly. Murray was right. There is no justice any longer, and only its withered institutionalized wraith keeps things from flying apart.

Well, all right, Dewey thought. Maybe that's so. But we got to do our best. The Lord never asked a man for better than his best, did he?

He got out of Murray's Dodge and stood under the stark blue lights that rendered the parking lot almost as bright as day. He pushed his glasses close to his eyes and stared at the door of the place. Out of the corner of his eye, he saw on his right a sudden glitter, as if someone had turned on a light and quickly extinguished it again. He looked over there, and could see no more than a blur. I ought to check that out, he thought to himself. If I'm going to do this right, I ought to check out everything, hadn't I?

He walked behind Murray's car, and along the rank of cars parked on his right, squinting at each one in turn, inwardly embarrassed at the idea of playing at detective, a grown-soft old man who knew nothing of rough trades, but who had a thing that needed to be done, nonetheless.

He had gone perhaps twenty yards, past a dozen or so cars when he stopped. He frowned for a moment, forcing his eyes to focus on a long dull line of metal along the fender of an old Ford that was parked pointed directly at the door of Jumbo's. He squinted and stared until he could make out, behind the barrel of the rifle, the low-lying silhouette of a man. He was on his knees, propping the rifle on the car fender. He looked tired, and the barrel of the rifle wavered, catching the parking lot lights, then losing them. Dewey watched the man, studied him. He was not a stranger. Dewey had seen him before, and even not able to identify him, somehow his presence inspired Dewey.

That means he's here, Dewey thought. Somebody else wants him. That means he's got to be here.

Dewey stood behind the line of cars, silent, his eyes on the man with the rifle. It never crossed his mind that the man might be waiting for someone else, someone besides Santidy. That never occurred to him. No, the question was, should he speak to the man—or wait and see what happened.

It's important, Dewey thought. I really got to decide. Would it be just as good if some stranger done it? Or is it something I got to do myself? That's what I got to decide. What counts? That it gets done? Or that I do it?

It was then that for some reason he remembered the Confederate Memorial in the court square. Not so much the great men at the four corners, but most especially that single anonymous infantryman at the top of the column, that Confederate soldier without a name who stood, almost a hundred years later, still faithful in memory to his people and his duty. Then, remembering, Dewey began to move toward the rifleman, his own decision made. There was something that had to be done, and he had to do it.

But before he had taken more than half a dozen steps, before he could make himself known to that distant anonymous rifleman, the door of Jumbo's opened, and amid a burst of laughter, five or six men came out. They were all drunk, having a good time. The first one out almost stumbled down the three steps. The others seemed almost like an escort for this first.

He steadied himself, then came down the steps smiling, his arms around his fellows. Dewey squinted across at the rifleman, trying to be sure. The man at the foot of the steps was surely Santidy. Dewey couldn't make out his words, but he could hear the boasting, self-important tone. He was the center of attention, and the others listened to him, hardly trying to put in their own remarks. Of course. Why not? He was the hero tonight, wasn't he?

Dewey stared down the length of the car toward the knot of men. As he did so, he realized that the man kneeling in front of him had hunched forward, his right elbow up, and was leveling his rifle at the group. Oh Christ, Dewey thought, he's going to do it.

—No, Dewey heard himself whisper harshly. —No, Mister. Don't do it.

The rifleman turned, his face pale, distant, as Dewey came abreast of him and moved just as quickly past him.

—Wait, the rifleman said, his expression one of astonishment and recognition. —Ain't you the . . . ?

Then Dewey recognized him. It was the brother. The girl's brother. Miranda's brother.

—Wait, he called after Dewey. —You got no business . . .

His voice fell away as Dewey came out from between the cars and moved more quickly toward the men standing, talking, laughing at the foot of the steps of Jumbo's place.

Dewey pushed his glasses back again with his left hand as he came near them. They paid him no mind, and he could see Santidy up close now. It was easy to recognize him. He wore white slacks and a red shirt with a white vest over it. His hips moved as he swapped words with his friends. He made an expansive gesture with his hands, as if in some way he encompassed the world with his actions. It was a good night, a wonderful night. Maybe the best night of his life. Wasn't that what he was thinking?

Dewey pulled the .38 out of his belt as he came close to the men, and one of them saw him coming. The man was short and had sandy hair that looked as if he used grease on it. He called out shrilly, but Dewey paid him no mind. As he closed with them, now only yards away, he saw that all their faces seemed a strange, sickly blue as if they were not human at all but some species of degenerate creature that spent its life in moist caverns where the light of day never reached. It was the hue of the lights above the parking area, of course, but Dewey did not make that connection then. He was in motion.

—Christ, the sandy-haired one said, and Dewey remembered later how preposterous the name of Our Lord sounded in the mouth of a beast.

—Hey, what is it? another called out when he suddenly saw Dewey. As if he expected an answer, an explanation.

What Dewey saw was the tight slacks that Santidy wore. He had no consciousness of aiming and firing. All he thought about was Santidy's skin-tight pants.

The first explosion surprised him as if he had somehow not expected the gun to make such a noise. He paused for the smallest part of a second, shaken by the sound and its immediate echo off the front of the building. Those around Santidy melted away as if they had been no more than mist, projections of his own ego, or as if this strange show were not happening in the physical universe, but on some theological stage, and they had received their cue to exit. But the surprise, the instant of hesitation did not really even slow Dewey down. Now he was facing Santidy who stood alone. They were alone in the sterile blue of the dusty parking lot. Time had stopped, Dewey remembered thinking. It was not happening in the world. Not this.

—Aw, Christ, Santidy moaned, staring down at the crotch of his white slacks, ruined by Dewey's first shot. —Aw, Jesus, Santidy sobbed, staring at the bleeding ruin between his legs.

Dewey stepped still closer then, until he could have reached out and touched Santidy with his hand. But he didn't touch him. He raised the pistol just as Santidy looked up, his eyes hollow and distant and almost objective, as if somehow, even in his hour of triumph, he had been aware in his blood that judgment was on the way, that retribution was no less sure than physics, and that between his acquittal and that doom there might just be time enough for a few drinks, a few laughs.

—Aw Christ, Santidy moaned again. —Mister, he crooned, —Mister, for Christ's sake . . .

The sound of the second shot did not surprise Dewey. What was amazing was how Santidy seemed suddenly to rise from the asphalt of the parking lot and hurtle upward into the door of the roadhouse.

—Mister, Santidy whispered, the front of his white vest suddenly as red as his shirt, the shirt itself glistening with a hue it had not had before. —Mister. Then he slid down against the door and sat quite still, his eyes locked on Dewey's.

—All right, Dewey heard himself say. —All right.

He turned and moved back then toward Murray's car. He looked from side to side, the pistol up and ready, but the lot was empty. He knew that Santidy's friends were somewhere, behind the cars, across the highway calling the police. But they were not coming for him. He had expected they would be armed, but even that might not matter. As he neared the old Dodge, he realized that he had never expected to get this far. But he had, and he was still alive.

He had gotten the car door open when a figure materialized beside him so suddenly that he almost fired before he recognized the brother, Miranda's brother.

—Don't try to stop me, Dewey said. —I ain't done. I know you're an officer of the law, but it had to be done. It should of been done by the court. . . . That's where it should of been done. . . .

The brother moved back as Dewey climbed into the car and started it up. He began to back out, the motor roaring because of Dewey's unfamiliarity with motorcars and his rising nervousness. It was hard to control his hands and feet. As he fought the car into first gear, he could hear over the motor's roar the voice of the brother.

—Mister, thank God for you, you hear? Mister, thank God . . .

Dewey straightened out the car and pointed it toward the highway, taking his foot off the gas for only a moment.

—You're a good man, Mister. . . .

Dewey looked at the harried young man still holding his unfired rifle, his face covered with tears either of tension or thanksgiving, and then awkwardly aimed the car out into the highway as he pushed hard on the gas.

IV

After he had gone a mile or two, he slowed down. He had said something to the brother that he himself hadn't understood. What was it? He frowned and wished he had drunk more of Murray's Old

Overholt. There was something else that needed doing. But perhaps it could not be done tonight. He had done a good thing. His fingers eased around the steering wheel, and of a sudden he began to notice and enjoy the cool breeze blowing in the driver's window of the car. As he passed between the lights of Bossier City, he thought that perhaps he should have bought a car. For drives on the weekends. He could have gone to Texas to see the sights in Marshall or Gladewater. He felt relieved, fresh, buoyant. He had not felt so good in a very long time. Since he had fled New Orleans so long ago? If not, since when?

When he reached the Shreveport side of the bridge, he slowed down still more. He began to consider what would come next. There was a building, two or three stories tall, at the corner of Milam and Spring streets. But it was so late. Perhaps he should go back home, or to Murray's, and see to the end of his business tomorrow. He realized that despite the freshness, he was very tired. Couldn't it be done tomorrow, the rest of it?

No. If nobody had recognized him except maybe the brother, still people had seen the car. They must have. It wouldn't work tomorrow. No matter how tired he was, this was the time. They had been tired at Mine Run and Mechanicsville. For no reason, an old song popped into his mind. Now is the hour. That's right.

He twisted the wheel and turned left, almost coasting down Milam Street. When the light changed, he took another left. He inched down Milam block by block, until he reached Spring Street. Then he pulled to the left curb and parked. For the first time, he realized that he was a little drunk. Not dog-drunk, but drunk nonetheless. Outside, the single streetlight seemed to expand and contract as he watched it. That was how he knew he was drunk. Then there was a sinking feeling in the pit of his stomach as he noticed that the streetlight was the same awful stark blue as those at Jumbo's parking lot.

He shouldn't have drunk so much, he thought. This is important. It's the only important thing you ever did in your whole life, and you had to get drunk to do it. And you'd like some more. You'd like one more drink before you finish up. If you can finish up, which is doubtful at this hour.

Dewey leaned forward, his head on the steering wheel. He felt sick, drained. He called to mind the scene in the parking lot, Santidy staring down at his ruined groin. It had been like a dance, with Dewey leading. Santidy for the first time in his life playing the unwilling maiden, moving away, declining, praying, falling backward, bereft of his weapon, knowing at last what it meant to be raped. Terminally.

Dewey's head rose and he laughed, the sound more shocking than the reports of the pistol at Jumbo's. Not from the remembrance, or even from the drink. No, it was that he suddenly recalled what Father Ruiz used to say back home at the parochial school when some wayward boy required discipline: Knowledge maketh a bloody entrance. —Sure enough, Dewey heard himself say. —That's so, Father. Like opening a door and seeing something awful.

The remembrance and the laughter sobered him a little. He got out of the car and walked up to the front of the office building. The building was brick, painted white. The door was locked, and Dewey stared at it stupidly for a moment. Maybe Vallee wasn't there in his offices. In fact, it was silly to think he would be. After a long trial, after a big victory. But no. He *knew* Vallee was inside. He *knew* it, had known it ever since the moment in front of the Confederate Memorial when he decided what he had to do. Vallee would be in there.

Dewey looked around, then wrapped the .38 in his handkerchief and hit the glass of the door. There was no alarm, and a section of the glass fell away, crashed with little sound on the inside. He reached through and opened the door quietly. As he stepped in, he squinted at the shabby building directory barely illuminated by the blue light from the street. Then he moved quietly down the dark hallway. As he did so, he could see no light from any of the doors on either side of the passage. If Vallee were in there, wouldn't there be some light from under his door? But the number had been a large one. One-thirty-three. Maybe it was so far in the back that the light was invisible from here.

As he walked on, he almost tripped and fell as he reached a flight of steps that went up a landing, then down again. At the top of the landing off to the left were the stairs to the second floor. He looked down toward the back of the first floor. There was light coming from under a door. Not much light. Hardly enough to be coming from a desk lamp. Maybe Vallee had come here alone, celebrated with a few drinks, and fallen asleep; it would be necessary to awaken him. Maybe he was just taking care of last details regarding a case he thought he'd won, but which Dewey had reversed only a little while ago.

Dewey reached the door, listened. It seemed he could hear something inside, something hardly louder than heavy breathing, but he could not be sure. He turned the doorknob very slowly. To his surprise, it yielded, and the door swung inward silently.

For a moment Dewey hesitated, then moved into an unlit, cramped reception office. No wonder the light had been faint. It was coming from under another inside door marked PRIVATE. The sound Dewey had heard was louder now, and it sounded not so much like breathing as moaning. For a moment it crossed Dewey's mind that perhaps someone had been here before him. Miranda's brother, the young policeman? Could he have come here before he went to Jumbo's? Or maybe some outraged spectator in the court? God knows there was cause enough. What if it was so? What if Vallee was already lying in there dying? What if her brother had done for him? Should Dewey just turn and walk away? Was that sufficient? He thought not. Let every man put his own mark upon wickedness. Perhaps, before morning, there would be a veritable parade of just men who would make this pilgrimage. In fact, Dewey thought, I better get done what needs doing before somebody else shows up. He reached for the knob of the door marked PRIVATE realizing with a strange feeling that he had never in his life gone through a door so marked without permission—much less to murder the inhabitant. He heard the moaning more animated than before. The sound puzzled him. Then he heard the sirens. They seemed to come from Texas Street down near the bridge. That would be the Bossier City police. By now, the confusion surrounding Santidy would have been worked through. They would have tracked the car to the bridge. They would find it soon with the help of the Shreveport police. Only minutes to go. He turned the knob and pushed the door open, still quietly, the sound no louder than the moans within, which had turned now to snufflings, gruntings, choked syllables almost like human words. As the door opened, the sounds broke off with a sharp intake of breath.

Vallee sat in a large chair facing Dewey, his eyes almost closed, his face contorted as if in excruciating pain.

—Ahhhh, he sighed.

And Dewey saw in the weak light of a desk lamp turned away the head of a woman between Vallee's legs. When he realized what he was seeing, he staggered back a step in astonishment. The woman was kneeling in front of Vallee, and he was pulling her into his groin, masses of dark silken hair in his fingers.

As Dewey stepped back, Vallee must have heard him because his eyes opened and he stared, with an absurd smile on his lips, into the gloom where Dewey stood. The smile remained plastered on his swarthy face even after the first bullet had knocked him backward almost out of the chair when it plowed into his chest. Dewey fired again, lower, to erase what he was seeing, but not fast enough, because even as he fired, fired again and again until the hammer snapped futilely, he could still see the face of the woman as she turned out of passion into death. He could see her face even after the bullets had obliterated it, and he knew that he would go on seeing it until his last breath.

When he closed the door, he was still controlled. It had not fixed itself on him yet. He looked at his hands. There was a trembling, but not much. Only when he heard, from beyond the door that now said PRIVATE again, a heavy breathing, a snuffling and moaning certainly sounding of death, did he begin to run. He tripped up the stairs and down the far side, almost fell as he ran down the hall toward the blue light, and out into the sudden chill silence of Milam Street. He kept running until he reached Market Street. Then, winded, he slowed down. Walking a little farther, he stepped into the doorway among the display windows of Selber Brothers and stood silent, listening.

Sure enough, there were sirens, and down behind him, near the Pioneer Bank, toward the river, he could see police cars. But that was all right now. He crossed the street against a red signal that stopped nothing in the empty street.

Under the oaks in the courthouse square, it seemed cooler still as Dewey walked down toward Texas Street, cutting across the corner of the square, already seeing looming before him the shadowed mass of the Confederate Memorial. Dewey paused before it. Down to the right, at the edge of his vision, he could see the stark shining cross atop the First Methodist Church. To his left, the lights on the bridge. The sirens were still at that end of town. They might have found the car by now. They might have found more than that.

Lee, Allen, Beauregard, Jackson, Miranda. Dewey's hands reloaded the exhausted clip of the .38 as if somehow they were independent of his mind. Jackson. Miranda. He could not protect her. No one could. No one could be protected. Not Lee or Allen could protect anyone. It was. A lost cause. He thought, they don't build monuments to them any more. Because they don't want to be protected. They hate the ones that fight against the very nature within us. Santidy. Vallee. And someone.

Then Dewey felt the tears running down his cheeks and the enormous weight of the gun in his hand. He was immediately very tired. Tired as he had been that hot afternoon in the French Quarter in New Orleans long ago, before he came to himself. There was just no sense in being this tired. Nobody ought to put up with it. His eyes tracked up the monument until, in a light now gray, not blue, he could make out the distant face of that other anonymous soldier there. Now the secret was revealed. He had escaped. In the heat of battle, he had found the stone.

The sirens began again, and under their shrieking, Dewey could hear the waking murmur of the courthouse pigeons. It was almost dawn, and an empty Broadmoor trolley passed down Texas Street on its first trip out to the edge of town, and Dewey drew a deep breath of relief as he realized he had only one thing left to do. And then he would be free.

Previously Uncollected
"Heroic Measures / Vital Signs"
(1986)

Heroic Measures / Vital Signs

When the call from the state police came, Rawls had just handed over the keys of a new Buick Electra to Mr. and Mrs. Miley, who had come down from Plain Dealing to pick it up. He stood out on the hot concrete smiling and waving as they drove away, the old man veering a little as he moved the car slowly out onto Highway 80, trying to get used to the steering while his wife leaned toward him, surely telling him to be careful, to watch where he was going, as she had for over forty years, no matter what car they had owned.

Rawls was still watching them as they turned west and seemed to vanish into the white glaring path of the afternoon sun as surely as if they had suddenly run into a snowfield. Then he stood there watching nothing at all until Mildred called him on the loudspeaker, telling him he should pick up line four.

He shivered as he passed from the moist heat outside into the air-conditioning that was always set too high in the showroom and the tiny offices. Then he picked up the phone. For some reason, he paused before he spoke. There was that odd hollow sound that one ordinarily hears only when the call comes from some far place. Rawls rarely got long-distance calls, and none had done him any good.

This one was worse than all the others. Trooper Peterson from Minden was calling. Was he the father of Doreen Rawls? Rawls paused for a split second as if he had been asked to admit to an offense, as if his answer might involve him in something he wanted no part of. He had felt that way about Doreen for a long time. He was sorry and he wished he felt differently, but that was how he felt and it was useless to try to feel some other way. —Yes, he said when the fraction of a second had passed. —Yes, I am. What's happened?

What happened was that there had been an accident. A number of young people had been driving at high speed on the highway just west of Minden. The van had left the road and plunged into one of the abandoned gravel pits filled with water near the city. Passersby had tried to rescue them, but only Doreen had been pulled out. Trooper Peterson had six other calls to make, and as bad as this one might seem the others were worse. As for Doreen, she had been under the water quite a while before someone had managed to break open the rear door with a pry bar and pull her out. She had received emergency treatment in Minden, but the Parish Hospital was not equipped for medical problems of her sort, and an ambulance was taking her back to Shreveport. Did Mr. Rawls know where the Physicians and Surgeons Hospital was located? At the corner of Line Avenue and Jordan Street. They should be arriving in less than an hour. If there were other close kin, Mr. Rawls should notify them. The doctors in Minden seemed unwilling to hazard a prognosis regarding Doreen Rawls. Was there anything else, the trooper wanted to know. Anything he could do?

—No, Rawls told him. Nothing he could think of.

Rawls put down the phone then, taking care to set it right in its cradle. No one on the floor appreciated a line sounding busy during the summer selling season. The sales manager liked to point out that sometimes that first contact over the phone brought them in, and if they didn't come in, you sure as hell couldn't sell them, could you?

He walked slowly over to the salesmen's lounge and drew a cup of coffee out of the urn. But when he touched it to his lips, he didn't want it. It was black and bitter and cold. It tasted like dying. He stood with the plastic cup in his hand as if he couldn't decide what to do next. He was still standing there when Malik, the sales manager, came up to him.

—It's terrible, Malik said, fishing out one of his most somber expressions and fitting it to his dark face. Malik was a Lebanese or a Syrian or something. He was a master of internal disguise, able on an instant's notice to rummage in the grab bag of feelings and moods he had brought with him in his blood from that hot archaic distant land, to find the one most suitable to the moment, to the American situation he found himself in.

—Listen, you go on, he was saying. —Nobody can work with something like that hanging over him. —If the Lawsons come in for the LeSabre, I'll take care of them. It'll be your sale.

Rawls nodded, realizing that Mildred had been listening in on the line while he was talking to Trooper Peterson. It was not that she was a snitch for the company or passing on private conversations to Malik. No, it was that Mildred had no life of her own. She listened in on calls when they sounded tense or spicy or important. Just to take a silent part in them. She rarely told anyone what she had heard. So far as Rawls could recall, only once before had she told Malik what she had heard. One of the salesmen, Crawford, had gotten a call from his wife who told him she had taken an overdose of sleeping pills. Good, Crawford had told her. That's the best news I've had in years. Go lie down. Don't call anybody else. Mildred had told Malik, who had donned a ferocious expression, something from the old days in the mountains in whatever Middle Eastern country he had come from. He had told Crawford to phone the emergency squad, then go home and see to his wife. Not on your life, Crawford had said. She wants to go, she can go. What do you think? Dying's a big deal? It's not. It's not anything at all. If she doesn't kill herself, she's going to kill me. Christ, if she could, she'd kill all of us. Rawls remembered Malik standing there, Mildred, like a wraith, almost out of sight back near her desk. Both of them had looked at Crawford without speaking, and after a while the silence seemed to work upon him what Malik's words had not. He had shrugged and turned and left. He had never come back. Not even to pick up his last small commission check and his expenses. Someone said Crawford and his wife had moved to Gladewater, that he had gotten out of cars and was assistant manager in a hardware store. As far as anyone knew, the wife was all right. But then, Rawls remembered thinking, maybe she had been all right all along. Maybe she hadn't even taken the pills. Maybe it was some kind of a thing that Crawford and his wife did from time to time. Maybe it happened whenever she wanted to move on.

—They're good customers, Malik was saying. Rawls tried to pay attention to him. —They'll understand. A family emergency. I'll check them out in the car. It's your sale. Everybody knows. They all understand. You go on over to P & S.

Rawls looked around. The other salesmen, the ones who were not working a customer, were watching Malik and him. Over there, standing by her desk, Mildred was watching, no determinate expression on her face. As if she were waiting for something more to happen. As if, perhaps, she were expecting Rawls to break down and cry, leaning forward on Malik's shoulder, sobbing about his only child, his little girl.

Malik licked his lips, his eyes still on Rawls. He was waiting for Rawls to say something. It seemed something needed to be said, but Rawls stood in silence.

—I mean it, Malik said again, as if to fill the void or prompt Rawls into speech. —I mean it. We all understand.

Rawls took Malik's word for that. Still, it seemed amazing if it was true. If Malik understood, and the Lawsons were going to understand, and Mildred and all the other salesmen understood, why couldn't he understand? It was not that he doubted they understood. People seemed to understand a great deal that Rawls could not understand. Or perhaps what he did not understand was what they meant when they said they understood. Probably it was some kind of convention. It didn't mean that anyone actually grasped a situation, could place themselves within it, live it for a little while on their own. It must mean that they knew such a situation existed, and that it conformed in some fashion to circumstances not so out of the ordinary as to require lengthy explanation.

Something resembling panic seemed to crouch in Malik's eyes. He could not look away from Rawls. As if he suspected that in his silence Rawls was kneading the loss, the desolation of his daughter's condition, and might, at any moment, launch himself in blind and purposeless vengeance against any fixture of the world standing nearby.

—You go on now, Malik said, and Rawls found himself turning, walking through the electric eye controlling the main door that led outside into the August heat.

Out there, the sun stood halfway down the sky, but the concrete pavement seemed to waver, and the roofs and hoods of the ranks of parked cars waiting to be sold shimmered and eddied as if their blazing metal were melting, subliming away under the sun.

Rawls looked up to the sky. There were no clouds at all. No hope of an afternoon shower to break the heat and soften the evening. The sky was a delicate azure with a great bronze ball standing in its center. As he looked across the concrete toward his own car, the heat rising from the pavement bent the very space between, making it seem that the car was moving away from him even as he walked toward it. As if in strange evocation of Zeno's hapless arrow, Rawls was walking toward a vehicle poised at the horizon a distance to which would never lessen, never close, no matter how rapidly he moved, how earnestly he sought to reach his goal.

Of course it was only a trick of the light, but when he stopped beside his auto and reached out to open the door, the shock of the hot metal on his hand brought him back to what other people understood as reality. He opened the windows quickly, gingerly, and then stood outside a while longer to let the heat inside come down to a temperature he could bear.

As he cranked the engine and started off, the air-conditioning unit on his demonstrator began blasting at him. At first the air was warm and humid, but the fan was on high and in a moment or two Rawls found himself chilled by the jets of cold air playing across his cotton jacket and soaked shirt.

Rawls did not find it necessary to think as he drove across the Texas Street Bridge toward the P & S Hospital. He was not given to thinking in a discursive mode. What happened in his mind, aside from those moments when he had to calculate the price of an automobile or the difference between a new car and a trade-in, had nothing to do with thinking. What went on within him was a play of images. Just now he was remembering a garden he had seen somewhere long ago. Incredible flowers, large and colorful, carefully tended. Someone had gone to great pains with the garden, spent much time with it. Perhaps hundreds of people over hundreds of years had tended to it. Standing in the midst of that garden, it was impossible to see the end of it. He had not the least idea when or where he had seen the garden. Perhaps he had never seen it at all. Sometimes he imagined things. Not thoughts or ideas. Simply images.

The garden seemed to eddy and swirl like the air above the hot concrete back at the dealership, and then it dissolved and he could not remember it any longer. There remained no more in his mind than the abstract category of Garden. As if, moment to moment, there were no permanent Rawls, only that one who remembered a thing and then another who remembered something else. The Rawls who recalled the garden had gone on now.

What he should be thinking of was Doreen. He had not seen his daughter in almost two years. She was going to college, when last he had heard, at LSU-Shreveport. Even though they lived in the same town, they never saw one another. There was no reason that they should. No reason to pretend that the tenuous bond of blood somehow stapled them together. Each month when he paid his other bills, his utilities and his rent, he made out a check to Doreen and mailed it to the last address he had for her. Some post office box number at the university. He was sure she received the checks. Each month they would return to him endorsed in a wide thin spidery hand he did not recognize but assumed belonged to his daughter. Those checks going out, returning with her name scrawled on the back, were the sole nexus between them.

It had been that way since the divorce. Since Rawls and her mother had parted and gone their own ways almost two and a half years ago. Not because Doreen loved her mother and despised him for deserting her or causing her great pain, neither of which was true. More nearly because the parting gave her something like an excuse to be rid of them both.

The truth was, Rawls and his daughter had not gotten on. Sometime during her adolescence, whatever binds father and daughter together had failed them. There had been no argument, no ugly scene. No confrontation at all. They had just gone away from one another. He could remember when Doreen was very small and ran around the house like a small bright puppy, poking here and there, propelling herself into his lap at inopportune moments. He had pretended to be a pony for her, and a dog and a camel. Rawls smiled then, recalling the menagerie of creatures he had found within himself for her sake, into which his tiny daughter had transformed him.

Just then he realized that he was very hot again. The air-conditioner was blowing, but it seemed to do no good. It was as if he were in the depths of a jungle. Sweat poured down through his thin hair, down his face, especially from his eyes. Then he realized that it was because he was sitting in his car with the windows up and the motor turned off. He was parked in front of a run-down bar on Louisiana Avenue. He could not remember pulling in or cutting off his motor. He could not even remember wanting a drink. But he got out of the car and started toward the scarred wooden door as if behind it lay the end of a pilgrimage. He knew that above him, were he but to lift his eyes, the tall hospital building reared like an outsized tombstone behind the jumble of buildings that housed a gift shop, a convenience store, a karate training institute, and the bar.

It occurred to Rawls that he disliked hospitals. Nothing good happened in them. No, that was wrong. He knew better. People got born in them. People who would otherwise die were saved in them. Why would he have thought to think that nothing good happened in hospitals? New life and life saved was good. Everyone understood that.

He stepped inside the door thinking that perhaps everyone's understanding about hospitals was like their understanding of his present situation. Another convention, another attitude. No, he kept being wrong. Perhaps it was the phone call from the trooper. The good is a situation everyone has agreed to evaluate that way. The birth of a child *is* good; the death of a murderer or rapist *is* good. It is the same with the bad. No one goes around inventing goods and bads for himself. You can't live that way. Situations become imponderable if you don't take them as they are given.

The bar was dark and quiet. There was a blur behind it which, as his eyes became accustomed to the subdued light, took on the form of a tall lengthy mirror framed on every side by dozens of bottles. The stools in front of the imitation mahogany bar were all empty. One woman was sitting in a booth. He squinted and found himself in the distant mirror. Tall, thin, reddish hair, shoulders sloping and with no reasonable hope of ever straightening up again. He considered that his own presence seemed of no account to him. He did not dispise himself or walk about weighed down with some unspecified subterranean guilt. He was simply indifferent to himself. He would not miss himself if he were to find one morning that he was not there. Which thought he recognized obscurely as being absurd. He sat down on a stool too small for him and asked the bartender, who had materialized out of the gloom, for a double shot of sour mash. Rawls almost laughed aloud as it occurred to him that he did indeed value his presence when there was good whiskey to be drunk. He spoke to the bartender again and asked for a beer with his whiskey. A draft would be fine. Brand names meant nothing to him, especially now. He was drinking to quell the tightness he had felt inside since the call from Trooper Peterson, since Malik had come up to him and used him to show the depth and quality of his fellow-feeling. He thought he would have another couple of drinks and then find the pay phone and call his former wife, Delphine. Any way it went, he had that to do. He would as soon not do it. He didn't want to do it, because he did not like talking to Delphine any more now than when they were married. But it was no big thing, not some kind of dread that clutched him. Two more fast shots of whatever kind of sour mash this was would make the call inconsequential. Still, he wondered if he was obliged to go to the hospital first and find out what he could about Doreen before he made the call. Maybe he had ought to do it that way. After all, you don't just call a woman and tell her her little girl is in the hospital after being under water for a long time, and that, no, you don't know a thing more because it was hot on the way to the hospital and you stopped off for a drink or two. Delphine would not understand that. She understood almost nothing, and she would not understand that. Which struck Rawls as strange, since he *did* understand it. He tossed down the whiskey, chased it with beer, and gestured for another round. It was no convention this time. He would do better with a couple of drinks. He would not say something strange to the doctor or start in to tell how he had been a llama once for Doreen. With a pillow for a saddle. He would simply stand there wearing a pleasant expression and listen to whatever the doctor had to say and respond as appropriately as he could. He would likely even be able to avoid the questions that were flooding across the surface of his mind in a thin depthless stream, too attenuated to fix themselves in words just yet.

He finished the second whiskey and curled a finger at the bartender for a third. This would do it. He was cooler now and feeling
better than all right. Whatever they told him, he would just listen
and say nothing. He would not mention the old scruffy stuffed
animals that lay in a heap on the daybed on the back porch of the
house he still occupied, where Doreen had grown up, where he had
once been married. The puppy was named Jiggs, the snake Olaf,
the frog Feed. Don't ask why. Doreen named them and loved them
and played with them and then one day went on, leaving them
behind. He should have thrown them away. He had not gotten
around to it. Not in several years. Situations drift, he considered.
One day you feel strongly about something, another day the feeling
is barely perceptible. But you average. You can always average.
More or less, one thing taken with another, you love your wife and
your child more than you don't. Moreover, there is the relationship
itself to take into account. If it is your father or your son, your wife or
your daughter, ordinarily you will not want that connection broken.
You do not lose a relationship if you can avoid it. Someone had said,
You Are What You Eat. No, most of what we eat turns to shit. We are
our connections, our relationships. Whether we like them or not.
Rawls had learned that long ago.

He had never enjoyed selling cars. But he seemed to be very good
at it. People coming to the dealership liked him and trusted him.
They believed for some reason that he would be honest with them,
that he wished them well. Mildred, who handled the switchboard,
thought she understood. It's the way you smile, she had told him.
That little smile that says: Look, this is the Great American Game.
But I don't take it seriously. I leave that to the rest of them who think
that one day they'll own a place like this and smoke big cigars
smuggled in from Cuba. Me? I'm just like you. Making a living,
trying to have a good day. Make me an offer. I might take it.

Rawls had smiled at that. The truth was that he was honest. Not
out of some moralistic vision taught or discovered, but because it
was difficult and demanding to lie and misrepresent what he sold,
and because he did not have enough imagination to create alternative realities. He was not clever and it did not bother him that he
was not. He had become a master of the soft sell, simply standing
with a customer and looking over the auto that he had examined a
thousand times before, without praise or condemnation. Rawls
could answer all their questions, quote facts and figures, compare
costs. But for the rest it seemed to him that he served like that mirror
behind the bar. He reflected the customer's appetites, his dubieties,

his desires, his concerns. When he was talking to Rawls, the customer might as well be talking to himself. But that was what customers wanted. They did not want to be pushed or discouraged. You sold cars by becoming part of the customer's situation, by standing in the customer and becoming part of his interior monologue. That is what a relation means, Rawls thought. That is how you sell things. If the buyer and the seller cease to be two, become one, then the transaction is with oneself. A transaction with oneself is usually a safe transaction. One sells what one wishes to buy; one buys what the seller fancies.

—What do you think? a customer would ask quietly, intensely.

—I don't know, Rawls would answer with equal seriousness. He couldn't know. The customer didn't know yet. —I think . . .

—Yes, the customer would say, and continue looking, thinking, shopping, selling one car or another to Rawls and to himself. When the customer was done, Rawls would let him know.

—Don't you reckon . . .

—Uh-huh. That damn tan one with the white top.

—I believe so.

He was on his third double when he noticed the illuminated beer sign hung before the mirror back of the bar. It was an old sign. Busch Bavarian. Rawls did not know whether that brand was being brewed any longer. Once it had been popular throughout the South, but it seemed that no one ordered it anymore. The sign was brilliantly colored. Almost abstract mountain peaks stood gleaming in sunlight with a clear stream sluicing down through a deep gorge between the mountains. The thin rill of water was actually clear plastic tubing behind which some kind of oil roiled and turned slowly, poor imitation of bright water, filled with bubbles. The oil did not flow as water does. It probably never had even when the sign was new. The effect was as if, amid the sketchy clefts and shadowed slabs of granite, the water was falling down from high above in slow motion. Because the chill stream appeared to flow, to tumble laboriously over the crudely colored rocks and boulders and down to some green plain of reality out of sight beneath the bottom of the sign. Down there, the mirror took up where the sluggish stream of fraudulent water ceased.

In the mirror, he could see his face reflected. His eyes looked dark, ringed. It looked as if he had forgotten to shave this morning. He was without expression, a mirror reflecting a mirror. Doreen, in a fit of spite and anger, had once told him that he wasn't in it, that you couldn't watch and listen all your life and still be in it. She had said he was out of it, and somehow when she said it, he had understood what she meant beyond the silly argot phrases cribbed from her young crowd.

He looked back to the slowly racing, somnolent stream of plastic water tumbling in endless cycle through the beer sign. He watched it then for a long time and it seemed after a while that the water took on some character of reality, that he could almost hear it buffeting the rocks, feel that cold distant wind that must surely blow down from the mist-muffled slopes above. The wind coursed through his body like a god no one had told him of. The water flowed in his veins and his head, worn and craggy, jutted up into the clouds where the pale sun gave weak pastel light but no warmth at all. Up there, the clouds moved slowly with great measure across the azure canopy of the sky, and the meaning of their staid configurations was to stand in the stead of that which was not to be seen, conditionless, which did not change at all. As a mirror remains unchanged despite the endless nervous play of shadows across its face.

Rawls tore his eyes from the sign and found that his brief concentration on it had once more made the bar seem even darker than it was. No, that was not right. The bar was as dark as it was. The change was in himself. Except that mirrors do not change. They tell the truth unless they are warped or broken. He could see the blur of the bartender far down the length of the bar. He seemed to be talking to someone who had come in and was sitting on a stool. He could see nothing beyond. He took out a bill, squinted at it, decided that it was sufficient, and set it down beside his empty glass. He felt much better now. He felt better than he had in a long time. But as he turned on the stool to step down, vertigo seemed to flow over him like that gelatinous oil pretending to be water in the sign, almost carrying him off the stool. He reached behind him and took hold of the edge of the bar. His fingers pressed into the bland plastic as if they were caught in the minute crevices of a mountain ledge, holding him from the abyss below. He was all right after a moment. Not all right enough to stand and stride though the door, outside into the heat. But drawn back from that sickening moment in which the liquor's pleasure seemed to melt into dread. Then he realized that it was not the whiskey. It was that now he would have to go to the hospital. It was time he went there. By any measure of time, the ambulance must have arrived long ago. It was like a summons to jury duty or a parking ticket. It was a situation. You could not choose what you would do because if you did not do what people do, what everyone does, the situation would only thicken, change from a general situation of the kind in which everyone finds himself from time to time into one specific to you. To be safely out of things, you are obliged to do what everyone does, whatever is conventionally done. Ordinarily, you are called on to do no more, and then you are, in one way or another, sooner or later, relieved of the situation.

Rawls wondered if that was what Doreen had meant. Was it because he always did what was required so that he would have to do no more that made her say he was not in it? He recalled that before she became involved with people in saffron robes, she had belonged to some youth group at the college. She had talked a great deal about commitment then. At the very first, he had supposed for some reason that she was referring to the legal process by which people bereft of their senses or out of control might be placed in mental institutions by their relations. She had spoken of the need for commitment and he had agreed, saying it seemed many people might be better off in an asylum than on the streets. Doreen had stared at him in anger when she realized what he was saying. That was not what she had meant, and he knew it.

He had been surprised by her vehemence. No, he had not known it. If he had, he would have responded otherwise. When he realized that by commitment Doreen meant the investment of all one's emotion in some cause or task or idea, Rawls was still not sure what the fuss was about. Such an investment itself seemed evidence of derangement. Thus to be committed suggested the need for commitment.

Delphine, his wife, had shaken her head with an ugly laugh. Not because she had any belief in what Doreen was committed to at the moment—something faintly comic like pouring pig blood into government records of some kind—but because by then she missed no chance to sneer at Rawls. No ally was so base, no notion so grotesque that Delphine would not rally to it to take sides against him.

It did not bother him. By then, he could hardly remember a time when he had cared what Delphine thought, or whether she was even there with her puling and complaints about the money he brought home. Thus it had not bothered him when she moved out, either. She had gone to stay in an apartment with Doreen, mixed with her friends, and listened to their latest commitments without comprehension, without interest, happy simply to be included in something intense and strongly felt—whether it meant anything or not.

Before she left, Delphine had told him, in a moment of subdued rancor, that life had not turned out at all as she had hoped. It had all gone utterly wrong somehow. She had intimated that, in some way she could not quite grasp, the failure of her hopes had to do with him. Rawls had not taken what she said to heart. He had found over the years that there was no real relation between the words Delphine spoke and any object or activity in the world. The words were more in the way of a report on the weather in her soul: dry, bleak, a permanent harsh fetid wind blowing over lifeless sexual soil, broken spiritual slate, fractured emotional gravel. The last thing Delphine had said before she left was that she had come to see that she required some kind of commitment in her life. Rawls had said nothing, thinking that Delphine seemed likely to have her requirement fulfilled. One way or another.

He felt better then. The vertigo had passed. He could see again in the vast gloom of the bar and made his way to the door. Outside, the heat was still there in its imponderability, its stark presence. He strode through it to his car as if he were pressing against waves in a shallow inland sea. When he started to get into the car, an eddy of superheated air flowed around him like a whisper from Delphine's mind, its current making him pause. He reached over, started the engine, and turned on the air conditioner. After a moment, he climbed inside and shut the door as the heat fell away and he found himself in the mountains again. It did not matter that he could not see them as he had in that chipped beer sign in the bar. They were there, and he stood among the juts and dips of dark rock, looking down to the streambed filled with coarse gravel. Just above, the snowfield began, its edges frayed and melted like old lace, tiny streams of chill blue water dripping and spilling down to stone worn smooth that had not been dry in a thousand millennia.

The field rose on a steep incline upward into thick clouds. There was a faint drizzle, and the misty rain fell, pocking the stream that flowed by carrying away the melt from the edge of the snow. The clouds above were low and thick, almost of a piece with the dense mist that seemed to be gathering around him there, swirling over the boulders, soothing the broken heavy spears of granite where ice rested slim and transparent in cracks and breaks. It seemed to be twilight there, but he was certain it was not, because now and then the clouds and mist seemed to thin, and he could see a slash of lighter sky above, against which the rocks stood in silent frozen definition.

Rawls came to himself then, put the car in gear and eased out into the street. Traffic was light, and in a few minutes he pulled into the multi-storied structure where visitors to the Physicians and Surgeons Hospital parked. The walls and pillars of the garage were of cast concrete. Those rough surfaces, that irregular stoic density fascinated Rawls. His car turned and turned, circling upward, passing row after row of parked empty cars. He did not need to watch the shadowed path before him. It was enough to keep his eyes on those pillars, which seemed to march out ahead of him, appearing and disappearing. At last he reached the roof level of the garage where the pillars fell away and the tall azure sky appeared again, faded by the bronze sun. He sat there for a moment, his eyes becoming once more accustomed to light as they had become accustomed to the dark. It was as if he had trekked through a deep forest of dead barkless pale trees up into the tendentious light to see that razor-sharp line of demarcation between enduring concrete below, which measured its life in ages, and the distant sky arrayed with clouds that were never—even for a moment—quite the same. He was not thinking of his daughter then, but of the wandering fish in his aquarium at home as they passed through the column of air bubbles rising from the vent in the helmet of a tiny toy diver down below. Insouciant, incurious, rapt in their sinuous filmy cosmos, they swam indifferent to the surface of the water above, whence dwelled That One who sent food, whose electricity maintained the weather and light of their world.

The elevator from the roof of the garage was cool and almost dark, one of the lights in the ceiling broken. The elevator car was not air-conditioned, but the journey seemed breezy, chilled, as if on its way downward it passed through the heart of an icy mountain. Of course, he thought, the way down and the way up were one and the same. Rawls could hear a small fan humming above the dented dirty translucent plastic grille. The sound pulsed louder, softer. He found himself betrayed into its rhythm. Then he realized that he had reached the ground, the elevator had stopped, and the door was open. A woman out in the corridor stood facing him. When he became conscious of her, it seemed that she had been watching for him, waiting for a long time. He smiled and stepped past her, hearing the sound of the fan's single syllable fading in the distance.

There was a sign indicating the route to follow to the emergency room. He did not expect Doreen to be there, but someone could tell him something. If you were patient and in no hurry to find out, there was always, sooner or later, someone who knew something. He turned a corner and almost ran into a gurney being propelled along the corridor with an old man on it. A tall black orderly was pushing, and a thin Asian girl held aloft a bottle of fluid that flowed down into the old man's arm through a clear plastic tube that reminded Rawls of the sign in the bar. Perhaps they were sending chill mountain water into the old man's veins. Maybe he was being prepared rather than healed. Nothing wrong with that. Death should not be a surprise, it should be a reward. Rawls frowned. Why would he think that? Did that make any sense? Surely he would not say it to anyone. It sounded like something Crawford might have said. No one would understand. Rawls didn't understand it himself.

The girl at the emergency desk was perspiring, her hair in her eyes behind thick glasses, and it seemed to take her some while to understand what Rawls was asking her. Then, after fumbling with some papers that appeared to have nothing to do with his question, she nodded.

—One-thirty-seven, she said.

—One-thirty-seven?

—Yeah . . . One, three, seven.

He moved along a corridor so brightly lit that Rawls squinted as he walked, glancing at each room number posted on a dark plastic plaque on the wall beside the door even though he knew the room he sought must still be yards away. He looked down the hallway and saw a small knot of people outside a door. He increased his stride, supposing that it might be the room where they had put Doreen. Maybe the state trooper was still there. Maybe a number of doctors. It could be Delphine. He should have phoned Delphine. As he neared the group of people, he realized that he was smiling, approaching them as if they were all looking at a new station wagon. He tried to erase the smile because he was sure it did not suit the situation, but it was no use. The harder he tried to pull his face into a decent sobriety, the wider the smile became. It was as if the smile were some sort of visitation from which there was no escape. It was then that he realized he was drunk. Not to the point of illness or even disequilibrium, but distinctly, notably drunk. His feelings, his attitudes were not his. They belonged to some other, some inhabitant of the distillation. That one would guide him, speak for him. Rawls need say nothing. That other would defend him. It was a great release—no, relief.

—Would you be Mr. Rawls? someone said.

—Uh . . .

The man was bald in front with hair down to his collar in back. He wore a white coat and stood just inside a door on the far side of the corridor from the group toward which Rawls had been moving.

—Yes . . . I'm . . .

—Sanbourne, Basil Sanbourne. Your daughter . . .

—They called . . . the trooper said . . .

—It's bad, Mr. Rawls. Very very bad. . . .

—That's what the . . .

—I've been waiting because someone who has legal authority . . .

— . . . grown girl . . .

—In cases like this . . .

— . . . mother . . . ?

—Not yet. It seems she went to Dallas for the weekend. The people at her ashram . . .

— . . . ?

—The lady on the phone told me it was a communal . . .

—All right, yes. . . .

—So it seems you . . .

—Well . . .

—We're using heroic measures, Mr. Rawls. Dora's vital signs . . .

—Doreen. That's good. Whatever you can . . .

—Yes, well . . . There's no easy pleasant way to put it. The EEG is flat, utterly flat. . . .

—Uh . . .

—She was under water too long. If it had been an icy stream, a cold mountain river . . .

Rawls shook his head. His eyes had passed Dr. Sanbourne's glistening head and fixed on the room beyond. He could see only the foot of the bed, but there seemed to come from within a thin steady stream of chill air, as if they were preserving great blocks of ice inside.

— . . . brain-dead is what the journalists call it. You see . . .

—How long will she stay that way? Rawls asked, astonished at his own words. —You see, she failed the ninth grade. She was never any good at . . .

Dr. Sanbourne was staring at him in abject astonishment. Rawls could feel that unnatural smile creeping back over his face. He turned half away. He didn't want to prejudice Doreen's case, whatever that might mean.

—I'm afraid I haven't made myself . . .

—Yes, you have. Can I see her?

—Of course, but it might be better if you gave me permission to have an authorization typed up. These things are still terribly troublesome. The courts are medieval about . . .

—I'd like to see her.

Dr. Sanbourne shrugged his narrow shoulders, moved aside, and gestured Rawls into the room. If he had been ashamed of stopping for the liquor before, he was not then.

A brief glance revealed her lying under a blue light in what seemed an inordinately small bed. The rest of the room appeared to be filled with machines of a kind Rawls could not hope to understand. Some looked like stereo receivers, covered with controls and small indicators. Bells and whistles, one of the salesmen at the Sound City franchise called them. They could sell a stereo to a hi-fi addict even though they made little difference to the music. Others had the appearance of the instruments used back in the service department to check out electrical systems, timing, fuel efficiency. He saw what had to be some kind of oscilloscope on which the heartbeat and other vital signs were displayed. He recognized the device because he had seen it on one of the soap operas the salesmen tended to watch on dead afternoons. It, in turn, reminded him of the display of an electronic game in an arcade when it was not in use, the tiny signal bouncing aimlessly from one side of the screen to the other as if bodiless contenders funded with infinite patience were engaged in endless play. That smile tugged at the lower half of Rawls's face and he made no effort to erase it. He contemplated the ambit of the electric signal that represented Doreen's heartbeat for a long time.

Then he turned back toward his daughter. Her arms lay on the sheet, and they were covered, rather entwined in coils of plastic tubing, clear and flexible, and curls of insulated wire. Her eyes were open, and her forehead was covered with small plastic cups or patches with wires running over to one of the machines. An oxygen tube was taped to her nose, and her mouth stood slightly open. The blue light seemed somehow to heighten the emptiness of her stare, the isolation of her situation—the situation which Malik had told him everyone understood.

Rawls stepped closer to the bed, but nothing changed with the shortening of perspective. The light above the bed made it seem that her face was blue with cold, as if the chill of the room might be emanating from her rather than from the necessity of keeping the room temperature low because of the sensitivity of the equipment. He started to touch her, but something stopped him. At first, he thought it was that primordial horror of the dead or dying, of those who have ceased to be actors, subjects in the texture of the world, and have been reduced to the status of objects. Then he realized it arose more surely from his memory of Doreen's contempt, hatred, for him. Whatever she had felt, it had not invited his touch, and somehow, even in her present situation, he did not want to violate her feelings.

—You're a real idiot, she had said. —You just stand there with that goddamned silly smile and let the world roll past, no—roll over you.

—I don't manage the world. I'm just . . . here.

—Bet your ass you don't. It's bad enough as it is. God, what would a world you put together be like?

—I don't know. I never thought about it. It doesn't matter. Maybe there wouldn't be any people in it.

—Right on. Empty, cold, vacant. Nothing in it at all.

—Dogs . . .

—What?

—Dogs. And frogs. Birds, flowers, rivers, mountains, ponies, camels . . .

He remembered going on and on enumerating the items his world would contain, speaking faster and faster, louder to be heard over Doreen's contemptuous reply—compulsively, as if establishing in final and ultimate defense of himself a world constructed of words that reverberated and vanished as quickly as they were enunciated.

She had left then, with some caustic remark he did not hear because even as she walked out of the house with what she wanted to take along stuffed in a Pan Am travel bag, he was still talking, still naming entities.

— . . . rocks, clouds, baboons, vines, llamas, every kind of tree there is, and some new kinds I'd invent.

He had stopped then, his eyes on the door as he heard her climb into the Chevrolet demo he had bought her the previous year and drive away. The fish were swimming in the tank, fluttering up toward the surface as they sensed his presence. — . . . and fish, he remembered saying, almost shouting after her.

He found himself sitting in a metal chair beside the bed then, his hand reaching out gingerly, almost touching hers. There was a smear of dried mud on her wrist. It must have come from the accident, he thought, and the rill of cold water at his feet, flowing through broken stone and earth, shimmered under the pale sun, its light sifted blue haze through the branches of larch trees above. Someone in a white woolen poncho or cloak squatted near a tiny fire.

But Rawls's eyes refocused, and the fire was only one of the lights on the control panel of a machine pulsing and humming involved in some portion of the heroic measures Dr. Sanbourne had mentioned.

When Doreen had left that night, when she had been gone a few minutes, he remembered, he had found himself close to tears. There was no explanation for it. What would happen if people burst into tears every time another person went away? Was this a situation that other people could easily understand? He had doubted it, but how was he to know?

Now his eyes found the spirals of transparent tubing circling her arms. A clear liquid slowly rolled down from a suspended bottle above. A needle carried it into Doreen's arm. Rawls wondered if it was chill, pure, if it usurped the heart's useless warmth and freed one of the clinging infestations of flesh and blood that never proved true, never outlasted a season or two.

He shivered at the thought and closed his eyes. There, on the inside of his lids, the scene arose again. It must be early morning and the air was chill, vacant. He almost expected to see a camel or a llama. The wind sounded from high above, and the water running downward barely rustled in its rocky channels. The fire was small, and the one robed or cloaked seemed to be staring into it from within a hood that obscured the face. Rawls tried to call out, but found he had no voice; tried to move toward the fire, but found he was not in that place at all, simply an observer, out of it, watching with his eyes closed, able to see not only that single one, outlined vaguely in the mist against the dark cramped piled rock, but the sweep of the snowfield as it reared itself painfully above the tree line into the distant sky. Up there, snow was falling, softly at first, then furiously farther up until such puny landmarks as might distinguish one sector from another were obscured by its endless effortless falling.

He must have remained that way for a long time, because when he opened his eyes again, he found that his neck and shoulders were tight and painful, as if he had slept the night through in the cold room, in that unpadded upright chair. Doreen had not changed in any way. It was as if she had become part of an environment, her changes marked with the geological torpor that lifted mountain ranges, scooped out the deepest ocean, then wore them down and filled it up again. He wondered if there were time for her, in that place where she was. Was she, brain-dead as Dr. Sanbourne had said, already in some paradise of hippies and freaks, tripping on whatever equivalent of drugs and random thought we discover upon putting this life aside? Or was she trapped in some limbo beyond this living, yet not far enough?

Not that Rawls believed in anything. He neither did nor did not. If you asked him if he believed in an afterlife, he would have smiled and said nothing. If you had asked him if he did not believe, he would have said nothing. If you asked him if he did and did not believe, he would have maintained that smile which might signify wisdom or foolery. And said nothing.

He stood up and stretched, his glance passing over the machines without interest. There could be no question about it. The room was cold. Now and again, he could feel a breeze, stirred up somehow, pass over him. That explained the stiffness in his neck and shoulder.

When he had worked the stiffness out, he realized that he had no idea what he should do next. The whiskey had begun to wear off, and there was an emptiness in the pit of his stomach. If he was hungry, he couldn't tell it. But he felt something ought to be done, that he should change the situation. Not by some great act or decision. Not that at all. Rather he should move or go out into the hall or perhaps leave the place altogether, come back later.

He had thought that by sitting with her for a while, he would somehow be able to find Doreen amid the shambles left there in the bed by the accident. But that was no good. He would have done as well to sit by a stone and ask it for its provenance. Sooner or later, the doctor was going to come and ask again, go through his explanation once more. Rawls had no idea what to say. It would be easy to tell him to do what he thought best, but Dr. Sanbourne did not inspire such confidence, and Doreen, always one to speak up for herself, was going to give him no help at all.

—Harry . . .

He did not turn at first. His eyes were fixed on the blue light or the white light or whatever color it was that shone down on Doreen's face, and he had almost slipped back once more to that cleft in the rocks at the foot of the bed. But the voice broke him away, and finally, with something like a touch of sadness, he wheeled around. It was Delphine.

Not that he would have known by looking at her. He had recognized the voice when it broke into his thinking. She was dressed in what appeared to be cast-offs from a dance team that might have prospered in the 1920s. There was some kind of fillet around her hair, and the folds of the ocher robe fell all the way to the floor. Now that he thought of it, no one could have ever danced in such a thing. She looked more like a myopic fortune-teller: Madame Lasagna

Knows All Tells All. Actually, she knew very little, Rawls thought, his smile reawakening, but whatever she did know she had told over and over again.

—That's our little girl there, Delphine mumbled. It seemed there were tears on her plump cheeks. She looked healthy enough. Perhaps she had even lost a few pounds at the ashram.

—Yes, Rawls said, not looking back at Doreen, since he was sure she had not changed.

—Oh, God, how did it happen?

Rawls started to tell her what Trooper Peterson had told him, then he realized that the question was rhetorical. Either she had already been told or she didn't care.

—What are we going to do?

Rawls did not even think to answer that, since whatever was to be done would go forward without advice from him. He frowned then as he noticed for the first time that the hallway outside the room seemed filled with new people, all of them looking strange in much the same way as Delphine. One of them, a small man in a saffron toga who seemed either unaware or unconcerned that he looked like a damned fool, stepped forward. He had a small scraggly moustache and a goatee that contained no more than a dozen loose hairs. Rawls got the impression that he was the leader of the pack.

—There's no one in there, Delphine. You know that.

—What? Delphine asked, her expression at once becoming studious. As if the man in the toga was calling her to an overpowering effort of thought.

—That bed is vacant. Your little girl is gone.

Delphine stood frowning, caught in the midst of some great effort for a moment.

—Right, she said at last. —I see that.

—There's no one there, the small man said. —I think we should go and do japa.

The others behind him heard, and began repeating, —Japa, Japa, Japa.

For a moment it seemed to Rawls that Delphine had something other in mind, but at last she nodded.

—All right, she said.

The small man glanced at Rawls. He smiled broadly. Rawls didn't smile back. The small man looked like a faggot. Perhaps one could be a faggot and still prosper in an ashram.

—The doctors say they need the bed, the small man in the toga said. —They want to take Doreen's earthly sheath away.

—What? Delphine said. —I don't understand that.

The small man looked at the others behind him with an expression that suggested he had endured much from Delphine. Rawls thought he could understand that. But it didn't matter.

—They want you to sign something. Come sign it.

—All right, Delphine said. —If you say so. Will it be all right for her?

—It will be just fine, the small man told her.

Rawls felt his head pulled back just then. He turned away from the others and stepped back into the room where the snow was falling fast now, covering the bed, covering the chairs and the scarred linoleum floor, building up so rapidly that he was amazed that no one had noticed. It was deathly cold there, and the walls had fallen away and he could see in their place jutting ribs of dark stone fading as the snow fell.

The figure in the hood was beginning to climb, reaching out thin arms and clawed hands to take hold of the rock, to pull itself upward onto the base of the snowfield. The angle of ascent was steep and Rawls found himself flooded with vertigo, unable to understand how he managed to remain there above the field, disembodied, watching the other begin to press upward into the darkness, into the falling snow.

—Delphine, are you coming? She's gone. She's not there.

Rawls frowned, brushed the snow away from his hair, his cheeks.

—Yes, she is, he said. —She's not gone yet.

The small bald man stared at him.

—Who is this, Delphine?

—Harry, my . . . He's Doreen's daddy.

The man fluttered his hands and gave Rawls the kind of smile one reserves for children. —You see, he said, half to Delphine, half to Rawls, —the bodily existence has ceased. Your little girl is carrying out her struggle . . . on a higher plane.

Rawls squinted. The cloaked figure lost its grip on a ledge of iced basalt and rolled down the snowy incline until another outcropping of rock brought it up short. The figure rose to its knees, its covered head bent forward. Rawls felt an unutterable sadness, a distant chill compassion for it. The time and space lost would have to be regained.

—She's still here, Rawls said.

The small man raised his eyebrows. Obviously Rawls either wasn't listening, or he was simply too stupid to understand.

—The doctor told me that . . .

—The doctor doesn't know anything. She's still here.

The small man shrugged. —Let's go, Delphine. We should get this over with. If you sign the form, they can ignore him and . . .

Rawls felt his smile returning and saw his hands reaching out, grabbing the neck of the small man's saffron robe, throwing him out into the hall. He staggered across into the door opposite and sat down on the floor looking bewildered.

—Shit, Delphine said. —You know who that is?

—No.

—Sri Lingananda . . . Spiritual Director of the Dammapuka ashrama. . . .

Rawls ignored her and was about to push her out of the room too so that he could close the door, when Dr. Sanbourne and a security guard shoved past her into the room.

—I'm going to have to ask you to leave, Mr. Rawls, Dr. Sanbourne bleated. —We can't have this kind of . . .

Rawls moved back from him, and Dr. Sanbourne nodded to the security guard. The guard, no more than twenty or twenty-one, with a thin strengthless moustache and a look of something close to terror in his eyes, reached for Rawls's arm. Just then, the small man, Sri Lingananda, pressed forward.

—I want him arrested. I'll lodge charges. . . .

Rawls caught the security guard off balance, spun him around, and lifted his gun from its holster. He hit the guard behind his right ear and was surprised and pleased to see him wilt and fall to the floor much as Rawls had seen it happen time after time on television. Then he aimed the gun carefully at Sri Lingananda and pulled the trigger once.

The bullet caught the small man squarely in the right eye. Even as the impact lifted him up and backwards into the hall once more, tissue and bone spraying the others waiting there, Rawls noted the terminal expression of utter and unrelieved astonishment on Sri Lingananda's ruined face.

Dr. Sanbourne and Delphine pushed their way into the shrieking mob in the corridor, and almost before Rawls could grasp it, the hallway was vacant, silent.

Rawls took the security guard and set him in one of the chairs beside the array of machinery near Doreen's bed. He could not tell for certain whether the guard was still alive or not. One last glance in the corridor assured him as to Sri Lingananda's condition. The small bald man lay in a creeping enlarging pool of dark blood, his robe in disarray, one sandal off, his feet looking dusty and incongruous caught up in the twisted saffron fabric.

He heard people running, the squawk of a portable police radio down the hall, so he pushed the room door closed and began to pile things in front of it. There was a large piece of equipment that looked like a generator on a pushcart that he moved first. Then another cart with an array of small boxes that seemed not to be functioning at all. Probably they were there so that they could be charged for, despite the fact that they were unnecessary. Mildred had told him and the other salesmen that a hospital in Louisville, Kentucky, had done that when her sister had had a stroke. Finally, he moved the security guard, chair and all, to support the two carts, and knelt down to tie the guard tightly to his chair with the power cords of the unused machinery.

Then it was done, and Rawls shivered in the chill half-light, the snow beginning to settle on the shoulders of his sports jacket, in his hair, his eyebrows. He drew his chair up beside Doreen's bed again and sat down. He could hear the water flowing, the wind sobbing across the icy rocks and flat planes of the snowfield above. Something had changed with her. She did not have the look of one dead, brain-dead or otherwise. Her cheeks were flushed with life as if she had been—or was even now—undergoing some great exertion. Rawls heard her breathe deeply of the pure chill oxygen being pumped into her lungs. Now the snow had covered the blanket on her bed, fallen lightly on her dark hair. Somehow the stream had diverted itself and ran clear and cold over the brown scuffed shoes of the unconscious security guard, up around his ankles, his white athletic socks.

Behind Doreen's bed, Rawls could see the snowfield canted upward into the thick obscuring mist. Wind was catching the mist, creating eddies in it, breaking it up, whirling it back together ceaselessly in one new form after another. Rawls turned slowly in a full circle, realizing that nothing was as it had been before. The room, the machines, the distant sounds of police planning some desperate sally to capture the madman—all were fading. He sensed that he had never been so cold before, the sharp angular wind blowing from every point of the compass, cutting through his thin cotton jacket as if he were naked. Yet in some way he could not understand, the cold did not trouble him. He found himself preferring this comforting bone-deep chill to the fetid heat outside—or inside, or wherever it had been as he drove into the parking garage past ranks

of ancient pillars which as it turned out were the trunks of immense
larch trees, their branches bent under the weight of falling snow,
growing out of cold moist soil that had been worn by the ages off the
obtuse angles of dark granite beside the stream that now ran out
into the hall, where the wind ruffled its swift surface, where the
snow fell and melted and became nothing more than more water in
the stream.

The figure in the white cloak had regained its position on the dark
rocks at the edge of the snowfield. Now it stepped carefully, avoiding the slick sheaths of crumbling ice wedded here and there to the
stone. One step into the clotted snow, then another. Then one more.
Perhaps the cloak was a bed sheet, Rawls thought. Close to where
the bed had been, there was only the small shimmering fire. When
he extended hands that were not there, he could feel no heat. It must
be some other kind of fire.

As he watched, the mist, the low clouds began to waver and
dissipate. The cloaked figure was moving upward now, slowly but
confidently. It was as if the very passage of the figure divided and
dissolved the thick vapor, and in another moment or two Rawls
began to see light up there ahead of the stooped straining climber.
Down below, in the shadow of the boulders where the edge of the
field melted and melted forever, the fire flickered, faded, unfueled.

When the sun first broke through, it was sudden, overpowering.
One moment the mist was still swirling. The next it was gone, the
immense stretch of the snowfield exposed as it towered up into the
pale yellow light. Then the thick clouds began to go, to fade under
the strict unqualified glare. Rawls moved up through the thick
branches of the larches, their shabby textured perduring trunks,
then the delicate architecture of their needles, finally the trees themselves melding, amalgamating into the depthless dark granite below. The sound of the water, the final flicker of the fire whispered
away and all that remained of his vision focused on that distant
cloaked or sheeted figure moving up the incline of the snowfield,
which revealed itself to stretch up the slope of a mountain or glacier
so enormous that no end could be seen of it in any direction at all.

The sky above, midnight blue, joined the expanse of the snow at
each point of the horizon so that the world itself was fractured into a
field of darkness and one of light, soundless, motionless—except
for that tiny figure still barely distinguishable upon the bright sparkling surface of the snow against which Rawls had to squint. Just
then it seemed the figure turned and looked backward for a moment, but he could not be sure and at that great distance it hardly

mattered. Whoever it was, if it was anyone, was unrecognizable and even as Rawls watched, with something like tears forced out of his eyes by the glaring flared reflections from the receding field, the figure seemed to melt, merge with the undifferentiated white of the snow and was visible no longer.

—I understand, Rawls whispered as he heard the security guard moan, returning to what he probably thought was consciousness.

ORIGINAL PUBLICATION INFORMATION

"Reunion," in *Southwest Review,* vol. 48, no. 3, Summer 1963.

"First Blood," in *Georgia Review,* vol. 19, no. 1, Spring 1965.

"A Time to Embrace," in *Denver Quarterly,* vol. 2, no. 4, Winter 1968.

"The Lonesome Traveler," in *Arlington Quarterly,* vol. 1, no. 2, Winter 1968.

"The Retrievers," in *Arlington Quarterly,* vol. 1, no. 3, Spring 1968.

"The Night School," in *Massachusetts Review,* vol. 9, no. 3, summer 1968.

"Keep Them Cards and Letters Comin' In," in *Sewanee Review,* vol. 78, no. 1, Winter 1970.

"Old Men Dream Dreams, Young Men See Visions," in *Sewanee Review,* vol. 80, no. 1, Winter 1972.

"The Actes and Monuments," in *Sewanee Review,* vol. 83, no. 1, Winter 1975.

"Pleadings," in *Southern Review,* vol. 12, no. 1, Winter 1976.

"Every Act Whatever of Man," in *Southern Review,* vol. 14, no. 3, Summer 1978.

"Nothing Succeeds," in *Southern Review,* vol. 16, no. 1, Winter 1980.

"Heroic Measures / Vital Signs," in *Southern Review,* vol. 22, no. 4, Fall 1986.